Books by Jonathan Kellerman

FICTION

ALEX DELAWARE NOVELS

Guilt (2013)

Victims (2012)

Mystery (2011)

Deception (2010)

Evidence (2009)

Bones (2008)

Compulsion (2008)

Obsession (2007)

Gone (2006)

Rage (2005)

Therapy (2004)

A Cold Heart (2003)

The Murder Book (2002)

Flesh and Blood (2001)

Dr. Death (2000)

Monster (1999)

Survival of the Fittest (1997)

The Clinic (1997)

The Web (1996)

Self-Defense (1995)

Bad Love (1994)

Devil's Waltz (1993)

Private Eyes (1992)

Time Bomb (1990)

Silent Partner (1989)

Over the Edge (1987)

Blood Test (1986)

When the Bough Breaks (1985)

OTHER NOVELS

True Detectives (2009)

Capital Crimes (with Faye Kellerman, 2006)

Twisted (2004)

Double Homicide (with Faye Kellerman, 2004)

The Conspiracy Club (2003)

Billy Straight (1998)

The Butcher's Theater (1988)

GRAPHIC NOVELS

Silent Partner (2012)   *The Web* (2013)

NONFICTION

With Strings Attached: The Art and Beauty of Vintage Guitars (2008)

Savage Spawn: Reflections on Violent Children (1999)

Helping the Fearful Child (1981)

Psychological Aspects of Childhood Cancer (1980)

FOR CHILDREN, WRITTEN AND ILLUSTRATED

Jonathan Kellerman's ABC of Weird Creatures (1995)

Daddy, Daddy, Can You Touch the Sky? (1994)

GUILT

JONATHAN KELLERMAN

GUILT

AN ALEX DELAWARE NOVEL

BALLANTINE BOOKS

NEW YORK

Copyright © 2013 by Jonathan Kellerman

Published in the United States by Ballantine Books, an imprint of
The Random House Publishing Group,
a division of Random House, Inc., New York.

BALLANTINE and colophon are registered trademarks
of Random House, Inc.

ISBN 978-0-345-50573-6

eBook ISBN 978-0-345-53881-9

Printed in the United States of America on acid-free paper

www.ballantinebooks.com

2 4 6 8 9 7 5 3 1

First Edition

To Eva

Special thanks to Clea Koff, Terri Porras,
Miguel Porras, and Randy Ema

GUILT

All mine!

The house, the life growing inside her.

The husband.

Holly finished her fifth circuit of the back room that looked out to the yard. She paused for breath. The baby—Aimee—had started pushing against her diaphragm.

Since escrow had closed, Holly had done a hundred circuits, imagining. Loving every inch of the place despite the odors embedded in ninety-year-old plaster: cat pee, mildew, overripe vegetable soup. Old person.

In a few days the painting would begin and the aroma of fresh latex would bury all that, and cheerful colors would mask the discouraging gray-beige of Holly's ten-room dream. Not counting bathrooms.

The house was a brick-faced Tudor on a quarter-acre lot at the southern edge of Cheviot Hills, built when construction was meant to last and adorned by moldings, wainscoting, arched mahogany doors, quarter-sawn oak floors. Parquet in the cute little study that would be Matt's home office when he needed to bring work home.

Holly could close the door and not have to hear Matt's grumbling about moron clients incapable of keeping decent records. Meanwhile she'd be on a comfy couch, snuggling with Aimee.

She'd learned the sex of the baby at the four-month anatomical ultrasound, decided on the name right then and there. Matt didn't know yet. He was still adjusting to the whole fatherhood thing.

Sometimes she wondered if Matt dreamed in numbers.

Resting her hands on a mahogany sill, Holly squinted to blank out the weeds and dead grass, struggling to conjure a green, flower-laden Eden.

Hard to visualize, with a mountain of tree trunk taking up all that space.

The five-story sycamore had been one of the house's selling points, with its trunk as thick as an oil drum and dense foliage that created a moody, almost spooky ambience. Holly's creative powers had immediately kicked into gear, visualizing a swing attached to that swooping lower branch.

Aimee giggling as she swooped up and shouted that Holly was the best mommy.

Two weeks into escrow, during a massive, unseasonal rainstorm, the sycamore's roots had given way. Thank God the monster had teetered but hadn't fallen. The trajectory would've landed it right on the house.

An agreement was drawn up: The sellers—the old woman's son and daughter—would pay to have the monstrous thing chopped down and hauled away, the stump ground to dust, the soil leveled. Instead, they'd cheaped out, paying a tree company only to cut down the sycamore, leaving behind a massive horror of deadwood that took up the entire rear half of the yard.

Matt had gone bananas, threatened to kill the deal.

Abrogate. What an ugly word.

Holly had cooled him off by promising to handle the situation, she'd make sure they got duly compensated, he wouldn't have to deal with it.

Fine. As long as you actually do it.

Now Holly stared at the mountain of wood, feeling discouraged and a bit helpless. Some of the sycamore, she supposed, could be reduced to firewood. Fragments and leaves and loose pieces of bark she could rake up herself, maybe create a compost pile. But those massive columns . . .

Whatever; she'd figure it out. Meanwhile, there was cat-pee/overripe-soup/mildew/old-lady stink to deal with.

Mrs. Hannah had lived in the house for fifty-two years. Still, how did a person's smell permeate lath and plaster? Not that Holly had anything against old people. Though she didn't know too many.

There had to be something you could do to freshen yourself—a special deodorant—when you reached a certain age.

One way or the other, Matt would settle down. He'd come around, he always did.

Like with the house, itself. He'd never expressed any interest in design, all of a sudden he was into *contemporary*. Holly had toured a ton of boring white boxes, knowing Matt would always find a reason to say no because that was Matt's thing.

By the time Holly's dream house materialized, he didn't care about style, just a good price.

The deal had been one of those warp-speed magical things, like when the stars are all aligned and your karma's perfectly positioned: Old lady dies, greedy kids want quick cash and contact Coldwell and randomly get hooked up with Vanessa, and Vanessa calls Holly before the house goes on the market because she owes Holly big-time, all those nights talking Vanessa down from bad highs, listening to Vanessa's nonstop litany of personal issues.

Toss in the biggest real estate slump in decades and the fact that Holly had been a little Ms. Scroogette working twelve-hour days as a P.R. drone since graduating college nine years ago and Matt was even tighter plus he'd gotten that raise plus that IPO they got to invest in from one of Matt's tech buddies had paid off, and they had just enough for the down payment and to qualify for financing.

Mine!

Including the tree.

Holly struggled with a balky old brass handle—original hardware!—shoved a warped French door open, and stepped out into the yard. Making her way through the obstacle course of felled branches, death-browned leaves, and ragged pieces of bark, she reached the fence that separated her property from the neighbors.

This was her first serious look at the mess, and it was even worse than she'd thought: The tree company had sawed away with abandon, allowing the chunks to fall on unprotected ground. The result was a whole bunch of holes—craters, a real disaster.

Maybe she could use that to threaten a big-time lawsuit unless they carted everything away and cleaned up properly.

She'd need a lawyer. One who'd take it on contingency . . . God, those holes were ugly, sprouting thick, wormy masses of roots and a nasty-looking giant splinter.

She kneeled at the rim of the grossest crater, tugged at the roots. No give. Moving to a smaller pit, she dislodged only dust.

At the third hole, as she managed to tug loose a thatch of smaller roots, her fingers brushed against something cold. Metallic.

Buried treasure, aye aye, pirate booty! Wouldn't that be justice!

Laughing, Holly brushed away soil and rocks, revealed a patch of pale blue. Then a red cross. A few more strokes and the entire top of the metal thing came into view.

A box, like a safe-deposit box but larger. Blue except for the red cross at the center.

Something medical? Or just kids burying who-knew-what in an abandoned receptacle?

Holly tried to budge the box. It shimmied but held fast. She rocked it back and forth, made some progress but was unable to free the darn thing.

Then she remembered and went to the garage and retrieved the ancient spade from the stack of rusty tools left behind by the sellers. Another broken promise, they'd pledged to clean up completely, gave the excuse that the tools were still usable, they were just trying to be nice.

Like Matt would ever use hedge clippers or a rake or a hand edger.

Returning to the hole, she wedged the spade's flat mouth between metal and dirt and put a little weight into the pry. A creak sounded but the box only budged a tiny bit, stubborn devil. Maybe she could pop the lid to see what was inside . . . nope, the clasp was held tight by soil. She worked the spade some more, same lack of progress.

Back in the old days she would've borne down hard. Back when she did Zumba twice a week and yoga once a week and ran 10Ks and didn't have to avoid sushi or carpaccio or latte or Chardonnay.

All for you, Aimee.

Now every week brought increasing fatigue, everything she'd taken for granted was an ordeal. She stood there, catching her breath. Okay, time for an alternative plan: Inserting the spade along every inch of the box's edges, she let loose a series of tiny, sharp tugs, working methodically, careful not to strain.

After two go-rounds, she began again, had barely pushed down on the spade when the box's left side popped up and it flew out of the hole and Holly staggered back, caught off-balance.

The spade fell from her hands as she used both arms to fight for stability.

She felt herself going down, willed herself not to, managed to stay on her feet.

Close call. She was wheezing like an asthmatic couch potato. Finally, she recovered enough to drag the blue box onto the dirt.

No lock on the latch, just a hasp and loop, rusted through. But the rest of the box had turned green from oxidation, and a patch worn through the blue paint explained that: bronze. From the weight, solid. That had to be worth something by itself.

Sucking in a lungful of air, Holly jiggled with the hasp until she freed it.

"Presto-gizmo," she said, lifting the lid.

The bottom and sides of the box were lined with browned newspaper. Resting in the nest of clippings was something wrapped in fuzzy cloth—a satin-edged blanket, once blue, now faded mostly to tan and pale green. Purplish splotches on the satin borders.

Something worth wrapping. Burying. Excited, Holly lifted the blanket out of the box.

Feeling disappointed immediately because whatever was inside had no serious weight to it, scratch doubloons or gold bars or rose-cut diamonds.

Laying the blanket on the ground, Holly took hold of a seam and unfurled.

The thing that had been inside the blanket grinned up at her.

Then it shape-shifted, oh God, and she cried out and it fell apart in front of her eyes because all that had held it together was the tension of the blanket-wrap.

Tiny skeleton, now a scatter of loose bones.

The skull had landed right in front of her. Smiling. Black eyeholes insanely *piercing.*

Two minuscule tooth-thingies on the bottom jaw looked ready to bite.

Holly sat there, unable to move or breathe or think.

A bird peeped.

Silence bore down on Holly.

A leg bone rolled to one side as if by its own power and she let out a wordless retch of fear and revulsion.

That did nothing to discourage the skull. It kept *staring.* Like it knew something.

Holly mustered all of her strength and screamed.

Kept screaming.

CHAPTER

2

The woman was blond, pretty, white-faced, pregnant.

Her name was Holly Ruche and she sat hunched atop a tree stump, one of a dozen or so massive, chain-sawed segments taking up a good portion of the run-down backyard. Breathing hard and clutching her belly, she clenched her eyes shut. One of Milo's cards rested between her right thumb and forefinger, crumpled beyond recognition. For the second time since I'd arrived, she waved off help from the paramedics.

They hung around anyway, paying scant attention to the uniforms and the coroner's crew. Everyone standing around looking superfluous; it would take an anthropologist to make sense of this.

Milo had phoned the EMTs first. "Priorities. It's not like there's any emergency to the rest of it."

The rest of it was an assortment of brown bones that had once been a baby's skeleton, scattered on an old blanket. Not a random toss, the general shape was of a tiny, disarticulated human body.

Open sutures in the skull and a couple of dental eruptions in the mandible made my guess four to six months, but my Ph.D.'s in the wrong science for that kind of prophecy. The smallest bones—fingers, toes—weren't much thicker than toothpicks.

Looking at the poor little thing made my eyes hurt. I shifted my attention to details.

Beneath the blanket was a wad of newspaper clippings from 1951 lining a blue metal box around two feet long. The paper was the L.A. *Daily News,* defunct since 1954. A sticker on the side of the box read *Property Swedish Benevolent Hospital and Infirmary, 232 Central Avenue, Los Angeles, Ca.*—an institution just confirmed by Milo to have shut down in '52.

The homely, squat Tudor house fronting the yard looked to be older than that, probably from the twenties when so much of L.A. had taken shape.

Holly Ruche began crying.

A paramedic approached again. "Ma'am?"

"I'm fine . . ." Swollen-eyed, hair cut in an off-kilter bob mussed by nervous hands, she focused on Milo, as if for the first time, shifted to me, shook her head, stood.

Folding her arms across her occupied abdomen, she said, "When can I have my house back, Detective?"

"Soon as we finish processing, Ms. Ruche."

She regarded me again.

Milo said, "This is Dr. Delaware, our consulting psychologist—"

"Psychologist? Is someone worried about my mental health?"

"No, ma'am. We sometimes call Dr. Delaware in when—"

"Thanks but I'm fine." Shuddering, she glanced back to where she'd found the bones. "So horrible."

Milo said, "How deeply was the box buried?"

"I don't know—not deep, I was able to pull it up, wasn't I? You don't really think this is a real crime, do you? I mean a new one. It's historical, not for the police, right? The house was constructed in 1927 but it could've even been there way before, the land used to be bean fields and grapevines, if you dug up the neighborhood—any neighborhood—who knows what you'd find."

She placed a hand on her chest. Seemed to be fighting for oxygen.

Milo said, "Maybe you should sit down, ma'am."

"Don't worry, I promise I'm okay."

"How about we let the paramedics take a look at you—"

"I've already been looked at," she said. "By a real doctor, yesterday, my ob-gyn, everything's perfect."

"How far along are you?"

"Five months." Her smile was frigid. "What could possibly not be okay? I own a gorgeous house. Even though you're *processing* it." She hmmphed. "It's *their* fault, all I wanted to do was have them get rid of the tree, if they hadn't done it sloppy, this would never have happened."

"The previous owners?"

"The Hannahs, Mark and Brenda, it was their mother's, she died, they couldn't wait to cash out . . . hey, here's something for you, Detective . . . I'm sorry, what'd you say your name was?"

"Lieutenant Sturgis."

"Here's something, Lieutenant Sturgis: The old woman was ninety-three when she died, she lived here for a long time, the house still smells of her. So she could easily have . . . done that."

"We'll look into it, Ms. Ruche."

"What exactly does *processing* mean?"

"Depends on what else we find."

She reached into a jean pocket and drew out a phone that she jabbed angrily. "C'mon, answer already—oh, I got you. Finally. Listen, I need you to come over . . . to the house. You won't believe what happened . . . what? No, I can't—okay, soon as the meeting's finished . . . no, don't call, just come over."

She hung up.

Milo said, "Your husband?"

"He's an accountant." As if that explained it. "So what's *processing?*"

"Our first step will be bringing some dogs in to sniff around, depending upon what they come up with, maybe a below-ground sonar to see if anything else is buried down there."

"Else?" said Holly Ruche. "Why would there be anything else?"

"No reason, but we need to be thorough."

"You're saying my home is a graveyard? That's disgusting. All you've got is some old bones, there's no reason to think there's more."

"I'm sure you're right—"

"Of course I'm right, I own this place. The house *and* the land."

A hand fluttered to her abdomen. She massaged. "*My* baby's developing perfectly."

"That's great, Ms. Ruche."

She stared at Milo, gave out a tiny squeak. Her eyes rolled back, her mouth went slack, she pitched backward.

Milo and I both caught her. Her skin was dank, clammy. As she went limp, the paramedics rushed over, looking oddly satisfied.

I-told-you-so nods. One of them said, "It's always the stubborn ones. We'll take it from here, Lieutenant."

Milo said, "You sure as hell will," and went to call the anthropologist.

3

Liz Wilkinson had just finished a lecture at the U., would be over in twenty. Milo went to make more calls and I sat with Holly Ruche.

All vital signs fine per the EMTs, but she needed to rest and get down some fluids. They gave me custody of the Gatorade squeeze bottle, packed up and left for an emergency call near the 405 freeway.

The first time I offered the bottle to Holly she clamped her mouth and shook her head. The second time, her lips parted. Several sips later, she smiled and lowered her right hand until it rested atop my left. Her skin had warmed. She said, "I feel much better . . . you're a psychologist for victim aid?"

"I do what's needed, there's no set routine."

"I guess I am a victim. Of sorts."

"It had to be rough."

"It was horrible. Do you think he's going to dig up my entire yard?"

"He won't do anything unnecessary."

"That sounds like you're covering for him."

"I'm judging from experience."

"So you work with him a lot."

"I do."

"Must be . . . ooh." She winced, touched her belly. The black jersey of her top puffed. "She's moving like crazy—it's a girl."

"Congratulations."

"Girls rule." She grinned. "I'm looking forward to having a little BFF." Another grimace. "Wow, she's being really hyper . . . oh, my . . . that one smarted a bit, she's kicking me in the ribs."

I said, "First baby?"

"You can tell?" she said. "I'm coming across like an amateur?"

"Not at all. You're young."

"Not that young," she said. "I'm thirty-one."

"That's young."

"My mother had me when she was eighteen."

"That's younger."

She laughed, grew serious. "I didn't want that."

"Starting so young."

Her eyes shifted upward. "The way she did it . . . but I always knew I wanted it."

"Motherhood."

"Motherhood, house, yard, the whole domestic-goddess thing . . . it's going to be great." Looking past me, she took in the crime scene techs studying the tree segments. They'd arrived fifteen minutes ago, were waiting for Liz Wilkinson, had placed a white cloth over the blue box. The fabric had settled into an oblong; a deflated ghost costume.

Holly Ruche said, "I can't have them turning my property into a disaster zone or something. I know it's not much right now but I have plans."

Not a word about the tiny bones. I wondered why a married woman would avoid the plural form.

"It was all coming together," she said. "Then that crazy tree had to—"

Movement from the driveway caused us both to turn. A man around Holly's age, skinny-but-soft, bald and bearded, studied the felled tree before heading over. He wore a long-sleeved blue shirt, gray slacks, brown shoes. Beeper on his belt, iPhone in his hand, aviator sunglasses perched atop his clean head.

"Hey," she said.

"Hey," he said.

His wedding ring matched hers. Neither of them took the greeting beyond that. He had one of those faces that's allergic to smiling, kept several feet between himself and Holly, looked put-upon.

She said, "Matt?"

His attention shifted to the hand she'd continued to drape over mine.

I stood, introduced myself.

He said, "A doctor? There's a problem, health-wise?"

"She's doing well, considering."

"Good. Matt Ruche. She's my wife."

Holly said, "Doctor as in psychologist. He's been giving me support."

Matt Ruche's eyes narrowed. "Okay."

His wife flashed him a broad, flat smile. "I'm feeling much better now. It was crazy. Finding it."

"Had to be . . . so when can we clean up?"

"Don't know, they'll tell us."

"That sucks."

"They have to do their job, Matt."

He touched his beeper. "What a hassle."

"The stupid tree fell down," said Holly. "No way could anyone—"

"Whatever." He glanced at his phone.

I turned to leave.

Holly Ruche said, "Hold on, one sec."

She got to her feet. "Do you have a card, Dr. Delaware?"

I found one. Matt Ruche reached to take it. She beat him to it. He flushed clear up to his scalp. Shrugging, he began texting.

Holly gripped my hand with both of hers. "Thanks."

I wished her good luck just as Liz Wilkinson strode into the yard, carrying two hard-shell cases. She had on a pantsuit the color of bittersweet chocolate; same hue as her skin, a couple of tones lighter. A white coat was draped over one arm. Her hair had been straightened recently and she wore it loose and long. She saw me, waved, kept going.

Someone must've prepped her because she headed straight for the tarp, put on the coat, tied her hair back, gloved up, stooped, and drew the cloth back deftly.

"Oh, look at this poor little thing."

The bones seemed even smaller, the color of browned butter in places, nearly black in others. Fragile as lace. I could see tiny nubs running along the chewing surfaces of both jaws. Un-erupted tooth buds.

Liz's lower lip extended. "Buried under the tree?"

I pointed out the hole. Liz examined the blue box.

"Swedish Hospital? Never heard of it."

"Closed down in '52. What do you think the box was originally used for?"

"Maybe exactly this," she said.

"A morgue receptacle?"

"I was thinking something used to transfer remains."

"The baby died a natural death in the hospital and someone took the body?"

"Bodies don't stay in hospitals, they go to mortuaries, Alex. After that, who knows? Regulations were looser back then."

I said, "The box is solid brass. Maybe it was intended to transfer lab specimens and someone thought iron or steel increased the risk of oxidation."

She returned to the skeleton, put on magnifying eyeglasses, got an inch from the bones. "No wires or drill holes, probably no bleach or chemical treatment, so it doesn't appear to be a teaching specimen." She touched the tooth buds. "Not a newborn, not with those mandibular incisors about to come through, best guess is four to seven months, which fits the overall size of the skeleton. Though if the baby was neglected or abused, it could be older . . . no fractures or stress marks . . . I'm not seeing any obvious tool marks—no wounds of any sort . . .

the neck bones appear to be intact, so cross out strangulation . . . no obvious bone malformations, either, like from rickets or some other deficiency . . . in terms of sex, it's too young for sexual dimorphism. But if we can get some DNA, we can determine gender and possibly a degree of racial origin. Unfortunately, the backlog's pretty bad and something this old and cold isn't going to be prioritized. In terms of time since death, I can do some carbon dating but my gut tells me this isn't some ancient artifact."

I said, "The box was out of active use in '52, those newspaper clippings are from '51, and the house was built in '27. I know that doesn't determine the time frame—"

"But it's a good place to start, I agree. So rather than go all super-tech from the get-go, Milo should pull up real estate records, find out who's lived here, and work backward. He identifies a suspect, we can prioritize DNA. Unless the suspect's deceased, which is quite possible if we're talking a sixty-, seventy-year-old crime. That's the case, maybe some relative will cooperate and we can get a partial."

A deep voice behind and above us grumbled, "Milo has begun pulling up real estate records. Afternoon, Elizabeth."

Liz looked up. "Hi, didn't see you when I came in."

Milo said, "In the house making calls."

And taking the detective walk through the empty space. His expression said that nothing obvious had come up. "So what do you think, kid?"

Liz repeated her initial impressions. "Not that you need me for any of that."

He said, "Young Moses needs you, I appreciate your input."

Detective I Moe Reed was her true love. They'd met at a swamp full of corpses.

She laughed. "Moses appreciates me, too. Say hi when you see him, which is probably before I will."

She stood. "So what else can I do for you?"

"Take custody of the bones and do your wizard thing. If you need the box, you can have it, otherwise it's going to the crime lab."

"Don't need the box," she said. "But I'm not really sure I can tell you much more."

"How about age of victim?"

"I'll get it as close as I can," she said. "We can also x-ray to see if some sort of damage comes up within the bones, though that's unlikely. There's certainly nothing overt to indicate assault or worse. So we could be talking a natural death."

"Natural but someone buried it under a tree?" He frowned. "I hate that—*it*." His shirt had come loose over his paunch. He tucked it in, hitched his trousers.

Liz said, "Maybe covert burial does imply some sort of guilt. And no visible marks doesn't eliminate murder, asphyxiating a baby is way too easy. And it's not rare in infanticides."

"Soft kill," he said.

She blinked. "Never heard that before."

"I'm a master of terrible irony."

4

Milo and I returned to Holly Ruche. Her husband was gone. She said, "He had a meeting."

Milo said, "Accountant stuff."

"Not too exciting, huh?"

Milo said, "Most jobs are a lot of routine."

She scanned the yard. "I'd still like to know why a psychologist was called in. Are you saying whoever lived here was a maniac?"

"Not at all." He turned to me: "You're fired, Doc."

I said, "Finally."

Holly Ruche smiled for half a second.

Milo said, "That woman in the white coat is a forensic anthropologist."

"The black woman? Interesting . . ." Her hands clenched. "I really hope this doesn't turn out to be one of those mad-dog serial killer things, bodies all over the place. If that's what happens, I could never live here. We'd be tied up in court, that would be a disaster."

"I'm sure everything will turn out fine."

"Just one little teensy skeleton?" she snapped. "That's fine?"

She looked down at her abdomen. "Sorry, Lieutenant, it's just—I just can't stand seeing my place overrun with strangers."

"I understand. No reason to stick around, Holly."

"This is my home, my apartment's just a way station."

He said, "We're gonna need the area clear for the dogs."

"The dogs," she said. "They find something, you'll bring in machinery and tear up everything."

"We prefer noninvasive methods like ground-penetrating radar, air and soil analysis."

"How do you analyze air?"

"We insert thin flexible tubing into air pockets, but with something this old, decomposition smells are unlikely."

"And if you find something suspicious, you bring in machines and start ripping and shredding. Okay, I will leave but please make sure if you turned on any lights you turn them off. We just got the utilities registered in our name and the last thing I need is paying the police department's electrical bill."

She walked away, using that oddly appealing waddle pregnant women acquire. Hands clenched, neck rigid.

Milo said, "High-strung girl."

I said, "Not the best of mornings. Plus her marriage doesn't seem to be working too well."

"Ah . . . notice how I avoided telling her how you got here. No sense disillusioning the citizenry."

Most homicides are mundane and on the way to clearance within a day or two. Milo sometimes calls me on "the interesting ones."

This time, though, it was a matter of lunch.

Steak, salad, and scotch to be exact, at a place just west of Downtown. We'd both spent the morning at the D.A.'s office, he reviewing the file on a horrific multiple murder, I in the room next door, proofreading my witness statement on the same killings.

He'd tried to avoid the experience, taking vacation time then ignoring messages. But when Deputy D.A. John Nguyen phoned him at midnight and threatened to come over with cartons of week-old vegan takeout, Milo had capitulated.

"Sensible decision and don't even think of flaking on me," said Nguyen. "Also ask Delaware if he wants to take care of his business at the same time, the drafts just came in."

Milo picked me up at nine a.m., driving the Porsche 928 he shares with his partner, Rick Silverman. He wore an unhealthily shiny gray aloha shirt patterned with leering sea lions and clinically depressed angelfish, baggy, multi-pleated khakis, scuffed desert boots. The shirt did nothing to improve his indoor pallor, but he loved Hawaii so why not?

Solving the multiple had taken a lot out of him, chiefly because he'd nearly died in the process. I'd saved his life and that was something neither of us had ever imagined. Months had passed and we still hadn't talked about it. I figured it was up to him to broach the topic and so far he hadn't.

When we finished at the court building, he looked anything but celebratory. But he insisted on taking me out for a seventy-buck sirloin-T-bone combo and "all the Chivas you can tolerate, boy-o, seeing as I'm the designated wheelman."

An hour later, all we'd done was eat and drink and make the kind of small talk that doesn't work well between real friends.

I rejected dessert but he went for a three-scoop praline sundae drowned in hot fudge syrup and pineapple sauce. He'd lost a bit of weight since facing mortality, was carrying maybe two forty on his stilt-legged seventy-five inches, most of it around the middle. Watching him maximize the calories made it tempting to theorize about anxiety, denial, masked depression, guilt, choose your psychobabble. I'd known him long enough to know that sometimes gluttony was a balm, other times an expression of joy.

He'd finished two scoops when his phone signaled a text. Wiping his chin and brushing coarse black hair off his pockmarked forehead, he read.

"Well, well, well. It's good I didn't indulge in the firewater. Time to go."

"New case?"

"Of sorts," he said. "Bones buried in an old box under an older tree, from the size, a baby."

"Of sorts?"

"Sounds like an old one so probably not much to do other than trace ownership of the property." Tossing cash on the table, he got up. "Want me to drop you off?"

"Where's the property?"

"Cheviot Hills."

"No need to drive all the way to my place then circle back."

"Up to you," he said. "I probably won't be that long."

Back at the car, he tucked the aloha shirt into the khakis, retrieved a sad brown tweed sport coat from the trunk, ended up with a strange sartorial meld of Scottish Highlands and Oahu.

"A baby," I said.

He said nothing.

CHAPTER

5

Seconds after Liz Wilkinson left with the bones, Moe Reed beeped in.

Milo muttered, "Two ships passing," clicked his cell on conference.

Reed said, "Got all the deed holders, El Tee, should have a list for you by the time you get back. Anything else?"

"That'll do it for now, Moses. Regards from your inamorata."

"My what?"

"Your true love. She was just here."

"Oh," said Reed. "Yeah, of course, bones. She have anything to say?"

"Just that she thinks you're dreamy."

Reed laughed. "Let's hope she holds that thought 'cause we're going out tonight. Unless you need me to work late or something."

"Not a chance," said Milo. "This one won't earn overtime for any-one."

Reed was waiting outside Milo's office, holding a sheaf of paper and sipping from a water bottle. His blond hair had grown out a couple of inches from the usual crew cut, his young face was pink and unlined, belying his old-soul approach to life. Massive muscles strained the sleeves of his blue blazer. His pants were creased, his shoes spit-shined. I'd never seen him dress any other way.

"Just got a call, El Tee, got to run. Blunt force trauma DB in a bar on Washington not far from Sony Studios."

"Go detect."

"Doesn't sound like much detection," said Reed. "Offender's still at the scene, patrol found him standing on top of the bar yelling space demons made him do it. More like your department, Doc."

"Not unless I've offended someone."

He laughed, hurried off. Milo unlocked his door.

One of Milo's lieutenant perks, negotiated years ago in a trade-off deal with a criminally vulnerable former chief of police, is his own space, separate from the big detective room. Another's the ability to continue working cases, rather than push paper like most lieutenants do. The new chief could've abrogated the deal but he was smart enough to check out Milo's solve stats and though he amuses himself with chronic abuse of "Mr. So-Called Hotshot" he doesn't fix what isn't broken.

The downside is a windowless work space the size of a closet. Milo is long-limbed and bulky and when he stretches he often touches plaster. When he's in a certain mood the place has the feel of an old-fashioned zoo cage, one of those claustrophobic confinements utilized before people started thinking of animals as having souls.

He sank down into his desk chair, setting off a tirade of squeaks, read the list, passed it over.

Holly Ruche's dream abode was a thirty-one-hundred-square-foot single-family residence situated in what was then the Monte Mar-Vista Tract, completed on January 5, 1927, and sold three months later to Mr. and Mrs. Jacob Thornton. After ten years, possession passed to the Thorntons' daughter, Marjorie, who unloaded the property thirteen months later to Dr. and Mrs. Malcolm Crowell Larner.

The Larners lived there until 1943, when the deed was transferred to Dr. and Mrs. George J. Del Rios. The Del Rioses resided at the property until 1955, after which possession shifted to the Del Rios Family Trust. In 1961, ownership passed to the Robert and Alice Hannah Family Trust and in '74 Alice Hannah, newly widowed, took sole possession, a status that had endured until sixty days ago when her heirs sold to Mr. and Mrs. Matthew Ruche.

Initial purchase price: forty-eight hundred dollars. Holly and Matt had gotten a recession bargain at nine hundred forty thousand dollars, with a down payment of a hundred seventy-five thousand and the remainder financed by a low-interest loan.

Milo jabbed the list twice. "*Dr.* Larner to *Dr.* Del Rios. The time frame works, that box came from a hospital, and a shady white-coat fits with swiping medical equipment for personal use."

I said, "I'd start with the period of those newspaper clippings—post-'51. That narrows it to the Del Rioses' ownership."

"Agreed. Let's see what we can learn about these folk."

He plugged in his department password and typed away, chewing a cold cigar to pulp. Official databases yielded nothing on Dr. George Del Rios other than a death certificate in 1947, age sixty-three, natural causes. A search for other decedents with the same surname pulled up Del Rios, Ethel A., DOD 1954, age sixty-four, cancer, and Del Rios, Edward A., DOD 1960, age forty-five, vehicular accident.

"I like Edward A. as a starting point," he said. "The trust sold the house a year after he died, so there's a decent chance he was George and Ethel's boy and inherited the place."

I said, "A boy in his thirties who George and Ethel might've worried about, so they left the house in trust rather than bequeathed it to him outright. And even though the trustee didn't get it until '55, a son could have had access to the property before then, when Mama was living there alone."

"She goes to bridge club, he digs a little hole."

"Maybe their lack of faith was due to lifestyle issues."

"Eddie's a miscreant."

"Back then a well-heeled miscreant could avoid stigma, so 'vehicular accident' might've been code for a one-car DUI. But some stigmas you'd need to take care of yourself. Like a socially embarrassing out-of-wedlock birth."

He said, "Eddie's married and the mother's someone other than wifey? Yeah, that would be blush-inducing at the country club."

"Even if Eddie was a bachelor playboy, burying a social inconvenience could've seemed like a grand idea."

He thought. "I like it, Alex, let's dig dirt on this charmer. Pun intended."

He searched for obituaries on all three family members. Dr. George J. Del Rios's was featured in the *Times* and the *Examiner.* He'd been an esteemed, certain-to-be-missed cardiologist on staff at St. Vincent Hospital as well as a faculty member at the med school where I sometimes taught. No final bio for his widow. Nothing on her at all.

Father Edward Del Rios, director of the Good Shepherd Orphanage of Santa Barbara, had perished when a bus ferrying children from that institution to the local zoo had veered off Cabrillo Boulevard on July 6, 1960. Several of the children had been injured, a few seriously, but all had recovered. The priest and the bus driver hadn't been so lucky.

The *Santa Barbara News-Press* covered the crash on its front page, reporting that "several of the terrified youngsters describe the driver, Meldrom Perry, suddenly slumping over the wheel leading to the bus going out of control. The children also report that 'Father Eddie' made an heroic attempt to gain control of the vehicle. Both Perry, 54, of Vista, and Father Del Rios, just days from his 46th birthday, perished after being thrown free of the bus. But the man of God's valiant attempts may have prevented an even worse disaster. An investigation has begun into allegations that Perry suffered from a prior heart condition, a fact known to the bus charter company, an outfit with previous violations on record."

"Some playboy," said Milo. "Poor guy was a damn hero."

I said, "He lived in Santa Barbara so the house was probably rented out during his ownership."

"And try finding a tenant. Okay, time to canvass the neighborhood, maybe some old-timer will remember that far back."

"There's another reason the house could've been left in trust: Father Eddie was in charge but he had siblings."

"Seeing as he was Catholic?"

"Seeing as most people have siblings. If you can access any trust documents, they'll list who else benefited."

It took a while, but an appendix stashed in the bowels of the tax rolls finally yielded the data.

Two brothers, one sister, all younger than Father Eddie. Ferdinand and Mary Alice had passed away decades ago in their sixties, consistent with the genetic endowment bestowed by their parents.

The baby of the family, John Jacob Del Rios, was listed as residing in Burbank. Age eighty-nine.

Milo looked up his number and called. Generally, he switches to speaker so I can listen in. This time, he forgot or chose not to do so and I sat there as he introduced himself, explained the reason for calling as an "occurrence" at John J. Del Rios's old family home, listened for a while, said, "Thank you, sir," and hung up.

"Sounds young for his age, more than happy to talk about the good old days. But it needs to be tomorrow, he's entertaining a 'lady friend.' He also let me know he'd been on the job."

"LAPD?"

"Sheriff."

He typed some more. Commander John J. Del Rios had run the Sheriff's Correctional Division from 1967 through 1974, retired with pension, and received a citation from his boss for distinguished service. Further cyber-snooping pulled up a ten-year stretch at a private security firm. After that, nothing.

Milo made a few calls to contacts at the tan-shirts. No one remembered Del Rios.

I said, "Entertaining a lady friend? Maybe he's our playboy. He'd have been in his twenties, prime time for an active sexual life."

"We'll check him out tomorrow. Eleven a.m. After his golf game."

"Golf, women, the good life," I said. "A good long life."

"The priest dies young, the hedonist thrives? Yeah, I love when justice prevails."

6

The following morning, I picked Milo up on Butler Avenue and Santa Monica, just north of the West L.A. station.

The bones had made the morning news, print and TV, with Holly Ruche's name left out and the neighborhood described as "affluent Westside." Milo was carrying a folded *Times* by his side. He wore a lint-gray suit, algae-green shirt, poly tie the color of venous blood. The sun wasn't kind to his pockmarked face; that and his size and his glower made him someone you'd cross the street to avoid.

He appreciates the value of publicity as much as any experienced detective. But he likes to control the flow, and I expected him to be angry about the leak. He got into the Seville, stretched, yawned, said "Top of the morning," thumbed to the editorial pages. Scanning the op-ed columns, he muttered cheerfully: "Stupid, stupid, stupid, and big surprise . . . *more* stupid."

Folding the paper, he tossed it in back.

I said, "Any tips come in from the story?"

"Nothing serious, so far. Moe and Sean are working the phones.

The good news for Mr. and Mrs. Ruche is the dogs turned up nothing else, ditto for radar and sniff-tubes. Nothing remotely iffy in the house, either, so looks like we've got a lone antique whodunit, not a psycho cemetery."

He stretched some more.

I said, "You're okay with the leak."

"That's like saying I'm okay with earthquakes. What's my choice?"

He closed his eyes, kept them shut as I got on the 405. By the time I was over the hills and dipping down into the Valley and the 101 East, he was snoring with glee.

Burbank is lots of things: a working- to middle-class suburb, host to film lots and TV studios, no-nonsense neighbor to the mansions and estates of Toluca Lake where Bob Hope, William Holden, the Three Stooges, and other luminaries established a celebrity outpost that avoided the Westside riffraff.

The city also also butts up against Griffith Park and has its own equestrian center and horse trails. John Jacob Del Rios lived just northeast of the park, on a street of ranch houses set on half-acre lots. Paddocks were visible at the ends of driveways. The aroma of well-seasoned equine dung seasoned the air. A shortage of trees helped the sun along and as noon approached, the asphalt simmered and a scorch, like that of an iron left too long on wool, melded with the horse odors.

Del Rios's residence was redwood-sided, shingle-roofed, fronted by a marine-buzz lawn. An old wagon wheel was propped to the left of the door. A white Suburban with utility tires was parked at the onset of the driveway, inches behind a horse trailer. No paddock in view but a corral fashioned from metal piping housed a beautiful black mare with a white diamond on her chest. She watched us approach, gave two short blinks, flicked her tail.

I took the time to get a closer look. She cocked her head flirtatiously.

Glossy coat, soft eyes. Years ago, I'd take breaks from the cancer wards and ride up at Sunset Ranch, near the Hollywood sign. I loved horses. It had been too long.

I smiled at the mare. She winked.

Milo said, "C'mon, Hopalong, time to meet John Wayne."

The man who answered the door was more Gregory Peck than Duke: six five, and patrician, with a shelf of deeply cleft chin, a well-aligned arrogantly tilted nose, and thick hair as snowy as well-beaten egg whites. His eyes were clear blue, his skin clear bronze veneered by a fine mesh of wrinkles, his build still athletically proportioned save for some hunching of the shoulders and widening of the hips. Nearing ninety, John J. Del Rio looked fifteen years younger.

He wore a blue-and-white mini-check long-sleeved shirt, navy slacks, black calfskin loafers. The blue-faced steel Rolex on his left wrist was chunky and authoritative. Rimless, hexagonal eyeglasses gave him the look of a popular professor. Emeritus for years, but invited back to campus often.

Or one of those actors hired by health insurance companies to play Elderly-but-Fit on their scam commercials.

He proffered a hand larger than Milo's. "Lieutenant? J. J. Del Rios, good to meet you. And this is . . ."

"Dr. Alex Delaware, our consulting psychologist."

"I was a psychology major, myself, at Stanford." To me: "Studied with Professor Ernest Hilgard, I assume you've heard of him."

I said, "Of course."

He turned back to Milo. "I read about your 'occurrence' this morning. Least I'm assuming that's the case you're working. Is it?"

Milo said, "Yes, sir."

"Box of baby bones. Sad. The article said they were probably old, I figure you're here to pinpoint a likely offender using property tax rolls. Am I right?"

Milo smiled.

John J. Del Rios said, "Can't fault you for that approach, makes sense. But if it's an old 187, why the psych angle?"

Milo said, "Cases that are out of the ordinary, we find the input helpful."

"Psychological autopsy?"

"Basically. Could we come in, sir?"

"Oh, sure," said Del Rios. "No sense keeping you in the heat."

He waved us into a lime-green, beam-ceilinged front room cooled by a grumbling window A.C. Burnt-orange carpeting was synthetic, spotless, firm as hardwood. Blocky oak furniture from the seventies, the kind purchased as a suite, was placed predictably. Horse prints clipped from magazines were the concession to art. The only sign of modernity was a wall-mounted flat-screen, hung carefully so no wires showed. A pass-through counter led to a kitchen devoid of counter equipment. The house was clean and orderly, but ripe with the stale-sweat/burnt-coffee/Old Spice tang of longtime bachelorhood.

J. J. Del Rios headed for an avocado-colored fridge. "Something to drink? I'm having a shot of grape juice. Virgin Cabernet, if you will." He gave a bark-like chuckle. "Too early for my one-a-day booze infusion but the antioxidants in grape skin are good for you, you don't even need the alcohol." He brandished a bottle half full with magenta liquid. "Good stuff, no added sugar."

"Water'll be fine, sir."

" 'Sir.' Been a while since I heard that from someone who meant it." Another low, clipped laugh. "Don't miss the job but there was a nice order to it, everyone knowing their place."

"You ran the jail division."

"Big fun," said Del Rios. "Keeping lowlifes locked up, making sure they knew they weren't living at the Hilton."

"How long did you do it?" said Milo.

Del Rios returned with two waters in one huge hand, juice in the other. We all sat.

"What's this, small talk to gain rapport? If you know I ran it, you know for how long."

Milo said, "Didn't dig that deep, sir."

Del Rios snorted that off. "Tell me about your bones."

"Infant," said Milo. "Half a year old, give or take."

"That was in the paper."

"That's what we know so far."

"You've narrowed down the time frame to when my family owned the place?"

"Yes, sir."

"How?"

"Afraid I can't get into that, sir."

Del Rios smiled. "Now I'm not liking the 'sir' so much."

Milo smiled back.

The warmth generated by the exchange might've heated a baby gnat.

Del Rios said, "No sense drawing this out. My family had nothing to do with it but I can't tell you none of the tenants did. Nor can I give you a name, I have no idea who rented the place, stayed completely out of it."

"Out of real estate?"

"Out of anything that got in the way of having fun." Del Rios drank grape juice. Smacked his lips, dabbed them with a linen handkerchief. The resulting magenta stain seemed to fascinate him.

Milo said, "We've narrowed the time frame to the period your mother lived in the house."

"And what period might that be?"

"Nineteen fifty to '52."

"Well," said Del Rios, "I'm sure you think you're clever. Problem is you're wrong. After Dad died in '47, Mom did live there by herself, but only until she was diagnosed with both heart disease and cancer." The seams across Del Rios's brow deepened. "She was a devout woman, talk about a one–two punch from a benevolent God. It happened winter of '49, right after the two-year anniversary of Dad's death. She hung on for four years, the last two were a horror show, the only question was which disease would get her first. We tried having her stay in the house with a nurse but that got to be too much and by the spring of 1950 she was living with my brother Frankie, his real name was Ferdinand, but he hated it so he had us call him Frank. He and his wife lived in Palo Alto, he was in medical residency back then, orthopedics. That lasted until

the beginning of '52, when Mom had to be put in a home near Stanford. During her last year, she was basically vegetative, by '54 she was
gone. Before she moved up north with Frankie and Bertie, she put the
house in trust for the four of us. But none of us wanted to live there, it
reminded us of dead parents. Frankie was living in Palo Alto, my sister
Mary Alice was studying medicine in Chicago, and I, the rotten kid, the
dropout, was in the marines and couldn't care less. So Eddie—the oldest one, he was a priest—hired a management company and we rented
it out for years. Like I said, I can't tell you who any of the tenants were.
And everyone else is dead, so you're out of luck, son."

"Do you remember the name of the management company?"

"Can't remember something I never knew in the first place," said
Del Rios. "I'm trying to tell you: I had no interest in anything but fun.
To me the damn house was a source of moolah. Each month I'd get a
check from Eddie for my share of the rent and promptly blow it. Then
Eddie died in a bus accident and the three of us got rid of the place,
can't even tell you who bought it, but obviously you know."

He finished his grape juice. "That's the full story, my friend. Don't
imagine it makes you happy but I can't change that."

Milo said, "It clarifies things."

Del Rios removed his glasses. "A man who sees the bright side?
Funny, you don't give that impression."

He stood. We did the same.

Milo said, "Thanks for your time, Chief."

At the door, Del Rios said, "When I figured out what you were after,
the thought that my family was under suspicion annoyed me. Even
though if it was my case, I'd be doing the same thing. Then I realized I
couldn't help you and I started feeling for you, son. Having to dig that
far back." Winking. "So to speak. So here's one more tidbit that's probably irrelevant but I don't want you thinking J.J.'s not simpatico with a
fellow officer. Before my brother Eddie became a priest, he was a car
nut, an early hot-rodder, into anything with four wheels and a big engine. He even got Dad to buy him a Ford coupe that he souped up and

drag-raced. Anyway, one day Eddie and I were having lunch in the city. He was working as an assistant priest at St. Vibiana on Main Street, this was before he got transferred to Santa Barbara. During the time Mom was already living with Frankie. Anyway, Eddie says, 'Johnny, I drove by the house a few nights ago, making sure the managers were getting the lawn cut better than the last time, and you won't believe what was parked in the driveway. A Duesie.'"

I said, "A Duesenberg."

"In the flesh," said Del Rios. "The metal. It didn't mean much to me, I didn't care about cars, still don't, but Eddie was excited, going on about not just a Duesenberg but one with the big chrome supercharger pipes coming out of the side, apparently that's a big deal. He informs me this is the greatest car ever built, they were rare to begin with, twenty years later they're a treasure. He tells me a car like that would've cost more new than the house did, he's wondering how the tenant could have that kind of money, his best guess is she's got a rich boyfriend. Then he blushes, shuts his mouth, remembering he's a priest, no more gossip. I laughed like hell, told him he should get himself a hot rod on the sly, it bothers him he can confess about it. Meanwhile he can lay rubber right in front of the church, worst case the cardinal has a stroke. He laughed, we had our lunch, end of topic. Okay?"

"Female tenant."

"That's what he said," said Del Rios. "*She.* A woman fits with a baby. A rich boyfriend fits with an unwanted baby. What do you think, son?"

"I think, sir, that you're still at the top of your game."

"Always have been. Okay, good, now you have to get out of here, got a hot date and at my age getting ready is a production."

7

As I drove back to the city, Milo called a DMV supervisor to find out how far back car registrations ran.

"Inactive records are deleted after a few months, Lieutenant."

"What about paper archives?"

"Nothing like that, sir."

"No warehouse in Sacramento?"

"No such thing, Lieutenant. What exactly are you looking for?"

Milo told her.

She said, "With a subpoena, we could give you a list of currently registered Duesenbergs. That German?"

"American," he said.

"Really? I lived in Detroit, never heard of them."

"They haven't been manufactured for a long time."

"Oh," said the supervisor. "A historical vehicle. Would a list of current regs help?"

"Probably not, but if it's all I can get, I'll settle."

"Send me the proper paper and it's all yours, Lieutenant."

He hung up. I said, "Auburn, Indiana."

"What about it?"

"It's where Duesenbergs were built. Back in the day, cars were manufactured all over the country."

"My home state," he said. "Never knew that. Never saw anything exotic."

"You wouldn't unless you had rich friends. When Duesenbergs came out, they cost the equivalent of a million bucks and Father Eddie was right, they're prime candidates for the greatest car ever made. We're talking massive power, gorgeous custom coachwork, every screw hand-fashioned."

"Listen to you, amigo. What, you were once a gear-head?"

"More like a fantasizing kid." Who'd memorized every make and model because cars represented freedom and escape. Mentally cataloging all that information was a good time-filler when hiding in the woods, waiting out a drunken father's rage.

Milo tapped the tucked-leather passenger door. "Now that I think about it, this is kind of a classic buggy."

My daily ride's a '79 Seville, Chesterfield Green with a tan vinyl top that matches her interior leather. She rolled out of Detroit the last year before GM bloated the model beyond recognition, is styled well enough to help you forget she's Caddy froufrou over a Chevy II chassis. She loves her third engine, is dependable, cushy, and makes no unreasonable demands. I see no reason to get a divorce.

I said, "Bite your tongue. She thinks she's still a hot number."

He laughed. "So how many Duesenbergs were made?"

"I'd guess hundreds, not thousands. And chrome pipes means it was supercharged, which would narrow it down further."

"So getting that subpoena might be worthwhile . . . but then I'd need to backtrack the history of every one I find and the most I can hope for is some guy who visited the woman who lived in the house maybe at the time the baby was buried."

I said, "There could be a more direct way to identify her. If Father

Eddie noticed the car, other neighbors probably did. Anyone who was an adult back then is likely to be deceased, but in nice neighborhoods like Cheviot, houses get passed down to heirs."

"A kid who dug cars," he said. "Okay, can't postpone the legwork any longer. You have time?"

"Nothing but."

We began with properties half a mile either way from the burial site, encountered lots of surprise but no wisdom. Returning to the Ruche house, Milo knocked on the door, rang the bell, checked windows. No one home.

I followed him to the backyard. The yellow tape was gone. The holes where air-sniffing tubes had been inserted were still open. The chair where Holly Ruche had sat yesterday had been moved closer to the felled tree sections and a woman's sweater, black, size M, Loehmann's label, was draped over one of the massive cylinders. A few errant blond hairs stood out on the shoulders. Beneath the chair, a paperback book sat on the dirt. What to expect during pregnancy.

I said, "She came back when everyone left, wanting to check out her dream."

He said, "Location, location, location . . . okay, let's ask around some more about the car. Haystacks and needles and all that."

Expanding the canvass another quarter mile produced similar results, initially. But at a house well north, also Tudor but grander and more ornately trimmed than Holly and Matt's acquisition, a small, mustachioed man in his sixties holding a crystal tumbler of scotch said, "A Duesie? Sure, '38 SJ, blue over blue—navy over baby."

His mustache was a too-black stripe above a thin upper lip. The few hairs on his head were white. He wore a bottle-green velvet smoking jacket, gray pin-striped slacks, black slippers with gold lions embroidered on the toes.

Milo said, "What else can you tell us about it, sir?"

"Gorgeous," said the man. "True work of art. I saw it in . . . '50, so we're talking a twelve-year-old car. But you'd never know. Shiny, kept up beautifully. Those chrome supercharger pipes coming out the side were like pythons on the prowl. All that menace and power, I'm telling you, that was one magnificent beast."

"Who owned it?" said Milo.

The man shook his head. "I tried to get her to tell me, she'd just smile and change the subject."

"She?"

"Eleanor," said the man. "Ellie Green. She lived there—that brick place pretending to be this place, that's where the Duesie used to park. Right in the driveway. Not often, just once in a while. And always at night but there was a porch light so you could see it. Down to the color. Looking back, it had to be a boyfriend of hers, but I was a kid, five years old, it was the car that interested me, not her personal life. I'd never seen anything like it, asked my father about it. He knew everything about everything when it came to cars, raced at Muroc before the war."

He grinned. "Then he married my mother and she civilized him and he went to work selling Packards downtown. He's the one who filled me in on the Duesie. That's how I know it was a true SJ. Because he told me it wasn't one of those where someone retrofitted the pipes, this was the real deal."

"He never mentioned whose it was?"

"Never asked him," said the man. "Why, what's up? I saw all the commotion yesterday. What happened at that place?"

"Something was found there. What can you tell us about Ellie Green, sir?"

"She babysat me. Back before I started school, I was always sick. My parents got tired of never going out, so they hired her to watch over me. Couldn't have been fun for her, I was a runty piece of misery, had scarlet fever, bad case of the mumps, measles even worse, could throw up at will and believe me, I did when the devil told me to." He laughed. "At one point they thought I had diphtheria but it was just some nasty flu. But Ellie was always patient."

"How old was she?"

"Hmm . . . to a kid everyone looks old. Probably thirty, give or take? Why're you asking about her? What was found over there? I asked one of your guys in uniform but all he said was *an incident*."

Milo said, "Some bones were dug up in the backyard. It was on the news, Mr.—"

"Dave Helmholtz. I avoid the news. Back when I was a stockbroker I had to pay attention, now I don't. Bones as in human?"

"Yes, sir. A complete human skeleton. A baby."

"A baby? Buried in the backyard?"

Milo nodded.

Helmholtz whistled. "That's pretty grotesque. You think Ellie had something to do with it? Why?"

"We don't know much at all at this point, Mr. Helmholtz, but there's indication the bones were buried during the early fifties. And the only information we picked up about that period was that a Duesenberg was sometimes parked at the house."

"Early fifties," said Helmholtz. "Yup, that could certainly fit when Ellie was here. But why in the world would she bury a baby? She didn't have any kids."

"You're sure?"

"Positive. And I never saw her pregnant. Just the opposite, she was skinny. For back then, I mean. Today she'd be what's expected of a woman."

"How long did she live there?"

"She babysat me for close to a year."

"Did she have a day job?"

"Sure," said Helmholtz. "She was a nurse." He smoked, tamped, smoked some more. "Mom made a big deal about that—'a trained nurse.' Because I pulled a snit about being left with a stranger. I was a cranky runt, mama's boy, afraid of my own shadow. Trained nurse? What did I care? The first time Ellie came over, I hid under the covers, ignored her completely. She sat down, waited me out. Finally I stuck my head out and she was smiling at me. Bee-*yoot*iful smile, I'm talking movie-star caliber, the blond hair, the red lips, the smoky eyes. Not that

I care much about that, I kept ignoring her. Finally I got hot and thirsty and came out and she fetched me something to drink. I had a fever, that year I always had a fever. She put a cold compress on my forehead. She hummed. It soothed me, she had a nice voice. She was a nice person. Never tried to force anything, real relaxed. And a looker, no question about that."

I smiled. "You didn't care about her looks, you were concentrating on the Duesenberg."

Helmholtz stared at me. Broke into laughter. "Okay, you got me, I had a crush on her. Who wouldn't? She was nice as they came, took care of me, I stopped being upset when my parents went out."

"Obviously, someone else thought she was nice."

"Who's that?"

"The owner of the Duesenberg."

"Oh," said Helmholtz. "Yeah, Mr. Lucky Bastard." He laughed some more. "That's what Dad called him. Looking back it makes sense. Some rich guy wooed her, maybe that's why she left."

I said, "She never gave you any indication at all who he was?"

"I asked a couple of times, hoping maybe she'd figure out I loved the car, was angling for a ride. All she did was smile and change the subject. Now that I think about it, she never talked about herself, period. It was always about me, what I wanted, what I needed, how was I feeling. Pretty good approach when you're working with a spoiled little brat, no? I can see her doing great as a nurse."

He brightened. "Hey, maybe Lucky Bastard was a rich doctor. Isn't that why girls became nurses back then? To hook up with M.D.s?"

Milo said, "Is there anything else you can tell us about her?"

"Nope. I turned six, got miraculously better, went to school, made friends. Don't know exactly when Ellie moved out but it wasn't long after and instead of the Duesenberg we got a Plymouth. Big family with a Plymouth station wagon the color of pea soup. Talk about a come-down."

I said, "Could you estimate how many times you saw the Duesen-berg?"

"You're trying to figure out if she was entertaining some regular visitor, something hot and heavy going on? Well, all I can say is less than a dozen and probably more than half a dozen."

"At night."

"So how did a five-year-old see it? Because that five-year-old was a disobedient brat who'd sneak out of the house through the kitchen in the middle of the night and walk over to see the car. Sometimes it was there, sometimes it wasn't. The last time I tried it, I ran into my father. He was standing on the sidewalk in front of Ellie's house, looking at the car, himself. I turned to escape, he saw me, caught me. I thought he'd whack me but he didn't. He laughed. Said, yeah, it's fantastic, Davey, can't blame you. That's when he told me the model. 'Thirty-eight SJ. And what the pipes meant, the advantage of supercharging. We stood there together, taking in that monster. It was one of those—I guess you'd call it a bonding thing. But then he warned me never to leave the house without permission or he *would* tan my hide."

Helmholtz smiled. "I always felt he thought I was a sissy. I guess he didn't punish me because he assumed I was out there being a guy."

We continued up the block. No one else remembered Ellie Green or the Duesenberg.

Back at the station, Milo ran her name. Nearly two dozen women came up but none whose stats fit the slim blonde who'd lived at the bone house in 1951. He repeated the process with *Greene, Gruen, Gruhn,* even *Breen,* came up empty. Same for death notices in L.A. and the neighboring counties.

I said, "She worked as a nurse and the box came from the Swedish Hospital."

He looked up the defunct institution, pairing it with *Eleanor Green* and the same variants. A few historical references popped up but the only names were major benefactors and senior doctors.

He said, "Helmholtz could be right about Lucky Bastard being a medical honcho. Maybe even someone George Del Rios or his two

M.D. kids knew and Ellie Green came to rent the house through personal referral."

"Rich doctor wanting a stash pad for his pretty girlfriend," I said. "For partying or waiting out her pregnancy."

"Helmholtz never saw her pregnant."

"Helmholtz was a five-year-old, not an obstetrician. If she moved in before she started babysitting him, she could have already delivered."

"Rich doctor," he said. "Insert 'married' between those two words and you've got one hell of an inconvenience. Problem is, Ellie seems to have disappeared."

"Like her baby," I said.

"Lucky Bastard making sure to clean up his trail?"

"The baby was only found by chance. If her body was concealed just as skillfully, there'd be no official death notice."

"Nasty . . . wish I could say it felt wrong."

He got up, paced. "You know anyone who'd remember Swedish Hospital?"

"I'll ask around."

"Thanks." He frowned. "As usual."

8

Milo's request to find an old-timer got me shuffling the reminiscence Rolodex. The first two people I thought of turned out to be dead. My third choice was in her late eighties and still training residents at Western Pediatric Medical Center.

Salome Greiner picked up her own phone.

"Hi, Sal, it's Alex Delaware."

"Well, well," she said. "What favor does Alex Delaware need?"

"Who says I need anything?"

"You don't write, you don't call, you don't even email or text or tweet." Her cackle had the dry confidence of someone who'd outlived her enemies. "And yes, I am still alluring but I don't see you asking me on a hot date. What do you need?"

"I was wondering if you remembered Swedish Hospital."

"That place," she said. "Yes, I remember it. Why?"

"It's related to a police case."

"You're still doing that," she said.

"At times."

"What kind of police case?"

I told her about the bones.

She said, "I read about it." Chirps in the background. "Ahh, a page, need to run, Alex. Do you have time for coffee?"

"Where and when?"

"Here and . . . let's say an hour. The alleged emergency won't last long, just a hysterical intern. A man, I might add. Roll that in your sexist cigar, Sigmund."

"I'll be there," I said, wondering why she didn't just ask me to call back.

"Meet me in the doctors' dining room—you still have your badge, no?"

"On my altar with all the other icons."

"Ha," said Salome. "You were always quick with a retort, that's a sign of aggressiveness, no? But no doubt you hid it from patients, good psychologist that you are."

Western Pediatric Medical Center is three acres of gleaming optimism set in an otherwise shabby section of East Hollywood. During the hospital's hundred years of existence L.A. money and status migrated relentlessly westward, leaving Western Peds with patients dependent on the ebb and flow of governmental goodwill. That keeps the place chronically broke but it doesn't stop some of the smartest, most dedicated doctors in the world from joining the staff. My time on the cancer ward comprised some of the best years of my life. Back in those days I rarely left my office doubting I'd done something worthwhile. I should have missed it more than I did.

The drive ate up fifty minutes, parking and hiking to the main building, another ten. The doctors' dining room is in the basement, accessible through an unmarked door just beyond the cafeteria steam tables. Wood-paneled and quiet and staffed by white-shirted servers, it makes a good first impression. But the food's not much different from the fare ladled to people without advanced degrees.

The room was nearly empty and Salome was easy to spot, tiny, nearly swallowed by her white coat, back to the wall at a corner table eating cottage cheese and neon-red gelatin molded into a daisy. A mis-shapen sludge-colored coffee mug looked like a preschool project or something dreamed up by the hottest Big Deal grad of the hippest Big Deal art school.

Salome saw me, raised the mug in greeting. I got close enough to read crude lettering on the sludge. *To Doctor Great-Gramma.*

A blunt-nailed finger pinged ceramic. "Brilliant, no? Fashioned by Number Six of Generation Four. She just turned five, taught herself to read, and is able to add single digits."

"Congratulations."

"The Gee-Gees are entertaining, but you don't get as close as with the grandchildren. More like diversion from senility. Get yourself some coffee and we'll chat."

I filled a cup and sat down.

"You look the same, Alex."

"So do you."

"You lie the same, too."

Dipping her head, she batted long white lashes. I'd seen a photo from her youth: Grace Kelly's undersized sib. Her eyes were still clear, a delicate shade of aqua. Her hair, once dyed ash-blond, had been left its natural silver. The cut hadn't changed: jaw-length pageboy, shiny as a freshly chromed bumper, bangs snipped architecturally straight.

Born to a wealthy Berlin family, she was one-quarter Jewish, which qualified her to enroll in Dachau. Escaping to New York in the thirties, she worked as a governess while attending City College night school, got into Harvard Med, trained at Boston Children's where she did research on whooping cough. At thirty, she married a Chaucer scholar who never made much money but dressed as if he did. Widowed at fifty, she raised five kids who'd turned out well.

"Down to business," she said. "Tell me more about that skeleton."

I filled in a few more details.

"Ach," she said. "A fully formed baby?"

"Four to six months old."

"Intact."

"Yes."

"Interesting," she said. "In view of the rumors about that place."

She returned to her cottage cheese. It took me a moment to decode her remark.

"It was an abortion mill?"

"Not exclusively, my dear."

"But . . ."

"If you were a girl from a well-to-do family who'd gotten into a predicament, the talk was Swedish could be exceptionally discreet. The founders were well-meaning Lutheran missionaries, seeking to help the poor. Over the years, any religious affiliation was dropped and priorities changed."

"They went for-profit?"

"What else? One thing they *didn't* have was a pediatrics department. Or a conventional maternity ward. So I really can't see how a baby would ever come in contact with the place."

I described the blue box, asked if she knew what it was.

"I've never heard of such a thing. We wrap our bodies in shrouds, then bag them. Typically, mortuaries pick them up, there'd be no reason to use solid brass containers."

"Maybe it was designed for something else and whoever buried the baby improvised."

"Hmm," she said. "Yes, why not—how about storage for tissue samples? A precaution when dealing with infectious material. Back in those days all kinds of nasties were rampant—TB, polio. My old friend, pertussis. I don't see bronze serving any particular antiseptic purpose but someone could've had a theory."

"Makes sense. Did you know any of the staff?"

"My work was always here."

Not really an answer. I said, "But you know quite a bit about the place."

She smiled. "It's not only psychologists who know how to listen."

"Who did the talking?"

"A friend of mine attended there briefly."

"Why only briefly?"

She used her fork to section a perfect cube of Jell-O. "I'd imagine something drew his attention elsewhere."

"Was he bothered by what went on?"

She speared the Jell-O, ate, drank tea. "I can't remember what was related to me back in the Jurassic era."

"I'll bet you can, Salome."

"Then you lose the bet."

"Was it the abortions?"

Carving and piercing another cube, she withdrew the tines slowly. Red liquid oozed onto her plate. "I don't need to tell you, Alex. Those were different times. In any event, I can't see any direct link between Swedish Hospital and a full-term baby."

I said, "Eleanor Green."

The fork wavered. She put it down. "Who's that?"

"A pediatric nurse. She lived in the house where the bones were found."

"If you already have a name, why all the circumlocution? Go and track her down."

"She seems to have disappeared."

"Nurse on the run." She chuckled. "Sounds like a bad movie."

I said, "The friend who told you about Swedish—"

"Is gone, Alex. Everyone from my wanton youth is gone, leaving me the last woman standing. That's either my triumph or cause for clinical depression, take your pick."

"No peds, no ob-gyn," I said. "Besides abortions, what brought in the profit?"

"My guess would be the same kinds of things that bring it in now. Procedures—radiology, short-term surgery."

"Were the attending physicians from any particular part of town?"

She stared at me. "I appreciate your persistence, darling, but you're pressing me for data I simply don't have. But if we're still in a betting mood, I'd wager against Watts or Boyle Heights." She took hold of the fork, speared the abandoned Jell-O. Savored. "How have things been going for you, my dear? Doing anything interesting other than police work?"

"Some court work," I said.

"Custody?"

"Custody and injury. One more question, Sal: Did your friend ever mention a doctor who drove a Duesenberg?"

She blinked. "That's a car."

I said, "It's a very expensive car, made in the thirties and forties."

"I've never been much for automobiles, Alex. A fact that greatly distressed my boys when they wanted fancy-shmancy wheels and I insisted on no-frills functionality." She looked at her watch. "Oops, need to get going."

Standing on tiptoes, she pecked my cheek hard, marched away, stiff-shouldered, stethoscope swinging.

I called her name but she never broke step.

CHAPTER

9

Milo said, "Abortion mill. Plenty of those, back then."

I said, "This one served wealthy families."

"Good business model." He speared a massive forkful of curried lamb, studied the outsized portion as if daring himself. Engulfed, chewed slowly.

We were at Café Moghul, a storefront Indian restaurant on Santa Monica near the station. The bespectacled woman who runs the place believes Milo is a one-man strategic defense system and treats him like a god in need of gastric tribute.

Today, the sacrificial array was crab and chicken and the lamb, enough vegetables to fill a truck garden. The woman came over, smiling as always, and refilled our chai. Her sari was hot pink printed with gold swirls and loops. I'd seen it before. More than once. Over the years, I've seen her entire wardrobe but I have no idea what her name is. I'm not sure Milo does, either.

"More of anything, Lieutenant?"

"Fine for the time being." He snarfed more lamb to prove it, reached for a crab claw.

When the woman left, he said, "Anything else?"

"That's it."

"I go with Dr. Greiner's logic. No reason for a baby to be linked to a place like that. Same for Ellie Green, seeing as she worked with kids. Anyone with access to medical equipment coulda gotten hold of that box."

I said nothing.

He put the claw down hard enough for it to rattle. "What?"

"When I asked Salome if she recalled a doctor who drove a Duesenberg, she tensed up and terminated the conversation and walked out on me."

"You touched a nerve? Okay, maybe Duesie-man was the guy who worked at Swedish and he was more than a friend and she didn't want to get into details with you. Was Greiner married back then?"

"Yes."

"Happily?"

I thought about that. "Don't know."

"Kids?"

"Five."

"What was her husband like?"

"He wrote books about Chaucer."

"Professor?"

"Never got his Ph.D."

"How'd he earn a living?"

"He didn't."

"Real alpha male, Alex. So she was the breadwinner. So a fellow doc with hot wheels coulda been appealing. She doesn't want to dredge all that up, so she terminates the tête-à-tête."

"Why have a tête-à-tête in the first place?" I said. "Why not just talk over the phone?"

"She bothers you that much," he said.

"I'm not saying Salome did anything criminal. I do think she knows more than she let on."

"Fine, I respect your intuition. Now, what do you suggest I do about it?"

I had no answer, didn't have to say so because his phone began playing Debussy. Golliwog's Cakewalk.

He slapped it to his ear. "Sturgis . . . oh, hi . . . really? That was quick . . . okay . . . okay . . . okay . . . yeah, makes sense . . . could be . . . if I need to I'll try it . . . no, nothing else from this end. Thanks, kid."

Clicking off, he snatched up the crab claw, sucked meat, swallowed. "That was Liz Wilkinson. She dates the bones consistent with the clippings. No new evidence of trauma, internal or external, not a single deformity or irregularity. She didn't find any marrow or soft tissue but will ask DOJ to try to get DNA from the bone tissue. Problem is between budget cuts and backlog, this is gonna go straight to the bottom of the pile. If I want to speed it up, she suggested I ask Zeus to descend from Olympus. Only thing that'll motivate him is if the media continue to cover the case. And Liz just got a call from a *Times* reporter."

"The press contacts her but not you?"

"When did you hear me say I wasn't contacted?" His tongue worked to dislodge food from a molar. Placing the crab claw on a plate piled with empties, he scrolled his phone through a screen of missed calls. The number he selected was from yesterday afternoon.

"Kelly LeMasters? This is Lieutenant Milo Sturgis returning your call on the bones dug up in Cheviot Hills. Nothing new to report, if that changes, I'll let you know."

He returned to his food.

I said, "So we forget about Swedish Hospital."

"I don't see it leading anywhere, but feel free to pursue. You come up with something juicy, I'll say it was my idea in the first place."

An innocuous chime sounded in my pocket. My phone's turn to join the conversation.

Milo said, "The ringtone era and you're living in a cave?"

I picked up.

"Hi, Doctor, Louise at your service. Just took one from a Holly Ruche. She said no emergency but to me she sounded kind of upset so I thought I'd be careful."

"Thanks, Louise."

"All these years talking to your patients," she said, "you pick things up. Here's her number."

I walked to the front of the restaurant, made the call.

Holly Ruche said, "That was quick. I'm sorry, I didn't mean to bother you."

"No bother. What's up?"

"Is there anything new on the . . . on what happened at my house?"

"Not yet, Holly."

"I guess these things take time."

"They do."

"That poor little thing." Sharp intake of breath. "That *baby*. I was all about myself, didn't even think about it. Now I can't stop thinking about it. Not that I'm OCD or anything."

"It's a tough thing to go through, Holly."

"But I'm fine," she said. "I really am . . . um, would you have time to talk? Nothing serious, just one session to clear things up?"

"Sure."

"Oh," she said. "Well, thank you. I couldn't do it tomorrow. Or the day after."

"What works for you, Holly?"

"Um . . . say in three days? Four? At your convenience."

I checked my calendar. "How about three days, one p.m.?"

"Perfect. Um, could I ask what your fee is?"

"Three hundred dollars for a forty-five-minute session."

She said, "Okay. That'll work. Seeing as it's only once. Where's your office?"

"I work out of my home." I told her the address. "Off of Beverly Glen."

"You must have fantastic views."

"It's nice."

"Bet it is," she said. "I'd have loved something like that."

CHAPTER

10

There are many reasons I became a psychologist. Some I understand, some I'll never even be aware of.

One motive I think I do get is the urge to protect, to make up for the abandonment that ruled my childhood. It's a trait that usually fits the job well, earning patient gratitude and delusions of godliness.

Sometimes I get heavy-handed, offering armor-plate when a thin sweater will do. That's why figuring out how much to tell Robin about the bad stuff has always been an issue. I've learned to include her, but I'm careful about the details.

On this one, I didn't even know how to start.

Robin's an only child. Her mother's a difficult woman, emotionally stingy, self-centered, competitive with her daughter. The loving parent was her dad, a master carpenter. He taught her what he knew about wood and the joy of craft, died when Robin was young. Now she works with power tools, doesn't take well to being smothered by testosterone, no matter how well intended.

For all the support I got from my older sister, I might as well have been a singleton. Mom was too up and down mood-wise to be of use when Dad drank and went hunting for prey. I learned to value solitude because alone meant safe. Inherently a friendly child, I learned to be sociable and genuinely empathic, but more often than not any group of people makes me feel alienated.

Two people like that and you can see how it would take time to work out Relationship 101.

I believe Robin and I have done a pretty good job. We've been together for a long time, are faithful without strain, love each other madly, press each other's erotic buttons. All that bliss has been ruptured twice by breakups, neither of which I understand fully. During one separation, Robin got pregnant by another man. The pregnancy and her time with him ended badly. I've worked with children my entire adult life but have never been a father. Robin and I haven't talked about that in ages.

I hope she doesn't spend too much time wondering.

I drove home thinking about tiny bones, a life barely lived, a nurse who could be anything between saint and monster. I still hadn't figured out what to divulge when I reached the top of the old bridle path that snakes up to our property.

To look at the house, free of trim or artifice, high white stucco walls sliced into acute angles where the trees don't shroud, you'd think emotionally distant people live here. The original structure, the one I bought for myself as soon as I had a bit of money, was tiny, rustic, all wood and shingle and quirk and creak. A psychopath burned it down and when we rebuilt we were looking for change, maybe a fortress.

Inside, matte-finished oak floors, comfortable, slouchy furniture, and art biased toward pretty rather than politics combine to warm things up. The square footage isn't vast but it's more than two people and one small dog need, and my footsteps echo when I cross the living room and head up the skylit corridor to my office.

Robin's truck was parked out front but no sign of her in the house, so she was out in her studio, working. I postponed a bit, checking email, paying bills, scanning news sites and reassuring myself that the world continued to spin with all the logic of a grand mal seizure.

By the time I poured a mug full of coffee in the kitchen and walked down to the garden where I stopped to feed the koi, I was still unresolved about what to say.

"Baby bones," I told the fish. "Don't even know if it was a boy or a girl."

They slurped in gratitude.

I was dawdling by the water's edge when the door to the studio opened. Blanche, our little French bulldog, trotted toward me, twenty pounds of blond charm and Zen-serenity. The breed tends to be stubborn; Blanche isn't, preferring diplomacy to artillery. She nuzzled my pant leg, snorted coquettishly. I rubbed her head and she purred like a cat. She'd rolled on her back for a belly tickle when Robin emerged, fluffing her mass of auburn curls and brushing sawdust from her favorite red overalls.

Mouthing an air kiss as she hurried toward me, she arrived smiling, planted a real smooch on my lips. Her breath was sweet with cola, the black T-shirt under the overalls fragrant with wood dust. Spanish cypress, a material that holds on to its perfume for centuries. The feather-light flamenco guitar she'd been working on for weeks.

I kissed her back.

She said, "What's the matter?"

"Who says anything?"

She stepped back, studied me. "Honey?"

"What was the tell?"

"The shoulders," she said. "It's always in the shoulders."

"Maybe it's just a kink."

Taking my hand, she guided me toward the house. Blanche trotted at our side, checking me out every few seconds. Between the two of them, I felt like a patient. As we reached the door, Robin said, "The new case?"

I nodded.

"Especially bad?"

"Maybe."

She put her arm around my waist. When we got in the kitchen, I offered her coffee.

"No, thanks, just water." She fetched a bottle from the fridge, sat down at the table, propped her perfect chin in one hand. Chocolate eyes were soft, yet searching. Her lips parted. The slightly oversized central incisors that had turned me on years ago flashed into view.

I filled a second mug, joined her. "A baby. A baby's skeleton."

She winced. "That must have been terrible for everyone involved." She stroked my fingers.

I told her everything.

When I was through, she said, "One of the girls at that hospital changed her mind and had her baby? Gave it to that nurse to take care of and something went wrong?"

"Could be."

"*Wrong* doesn't have to mean a crime, Alex. What if the poor little thing died by accident? Or from a disease and it couldn't be buried legally because officially it didn't exist?"

A new tremolo colored the last three words.

She said, "A thing; *it.* Can they do DNA, find out the sex?"

"Theoretically." I told her about the case's low priority.

She said, "Every generation thinks it invented the world, no one cares about history."

"Are you sorry I told you?"

"Not at all." She stood, got behind me, kneaded my shoulders. "You are one block of iron, darling."

"Oh," I said. "Perfect. Thanks."

"Full-service girlfriend." She worked on my muscles some more, stepped away, unsnapped the overalls, let them fall to the kitchen floor. The black T-shirt and a navy blue thong contrasted with smooth, tawny skin. She stretched, flexed each lovely leg. I stood.

"I'm filthy, hon, going to shower off. After that, we can figure out what to do about dinner."

I was waiting when she emerged from the bathroom, armed with a few restaurant suggestions.

She unpeeled her towel, folded it neatly, stood there naked. Holding out a hand, she led me to the bed. "Time for you to be a full-service boyfriend."

Afterward, she ran her nails lightly over my cheek. Bobbled my lips with the side of an index finger the way kids do when they're goofing. I let out a high-pitched moan, did a fair imitation of a leaky drain. When we both stopped laughing, she said, "How are you doing now?"

"A lot better."

"High point of my day, too. How about Italian?"

11

'd heard nothing new about the bones for two days when the *Times* ran a follow-up piece.

The article was stuck at the bottom of page 15, trumped by water issues and legislative ineptitude, a shooting in Compton, the usual petty corruption by various civic employees. The byline was Kelly LeMasters, the reporter Milo had belatedly called.

The coverage boiled down to a space-filling rehash ending with the pronouncement that "A priority request to analyze the bones for DNA at the state Department of Justice lab is LAPD's best hope for yielding fresh information on a decades-old mystery."

The newspaper was in Milo's hand when he rapped on my door at ten a.m.

I said, "Pleasant surprise."

He strode past me into the kitchen, flung the fridge door open, did the usual bear-scrounge, and came up with a rubbery-looking chicken leg that he gnawed to the bone and a half-full quart of milk that he chugged empty. Wiping the lacto-mustache from his nearly-as-pale face, he thrust the *Times* piece at me. "Compelling and insightful, call the Pulitzer committee."

I said, "Pulitzer was a tabloid shlock-meister."

He shrugged. "Time heals, especially with money in the ointment." He flung the article onto the table.

I said, "So you spoke to LeMasters."

"Not quite. I spoke to His Grandiosity's office begging for DOJ grease. That was yesterday afternoon. Next morning, voilà."

"The chief leaks?"

"The chief plays the press like a harmonica. Which is fine in this case because everything's dead-ended. Social Security can't turn up records of our Eleanor Green, and I can't find dirt on Swedish. Even the oldest vice guy I know doesn't remember it, one way or the other. So if they were breaking the law, they were doing it discreetly."

He got up again, searched the pantry, poured himself a bowl of dry cereal. Midway to the bottom, he said, "The bones aren't why I'm here. I never really thanked you for last year."

"Not necessary."

"I beg to differ." He flushed. "If ensuring my continuing survival doesn't deserve gratitude, what the hell does, Alex?"

"Chalk it up to the friendship thing."

"Just because I didn't get all sentimental doesn't mean I'm not aware of what you did." Deep breath. "I've been thinking about it every damn day."

I said nothing.

"Anyway." He used his fingers to grasp the last few nuggets of cereal. Drawing his big frame to its feet a second time, he loped to the sink, washed the bowl. Said something I couldn't hear over the water.

When he turned off the spigot, I said, "Didn't catch that."

"The T word, amigo. Gracias. Merci. Danke schoen."

"You're welcome."

"Okay . . . now that we've got that out of the way . . . how're Robin and the pooch? She working out back?"

"Delivering a mandolin."

"Ah."

His jacket pocket puffed as his phone squawked.

Moe Reed's pleasant voice, tighter and higher than usual, said, "New one, boss."

"I could use something fresh, Moses."

"It's fresh all right," said Reed. "But I'm not sure you'll like it."

"Why not?"

"More bones, boss. Same neighborhood. Another baby."

A city worker, part of a crew planning a drainage ditch at the western edge of Cheviot Hills Park, had spotted the scatter of white.

Unruly toss, strewn like trash, barely concealed by bushes. What might pass for dried twigs at a distance was an assortment of tiny skeletal components.

This baby appeared even smaller than the one unearthed in the Ruches' backyard. The skull was the size of an apple. Some of the bones were as thin as drinking straws and some of the smallest—the phalanges of the hand—were thread-like.

These remnants were clean-looking. Silvery white, luminous in the sunlight.

I thought: Scrubbed clean, maybe polished. *Prepared?*

The orange-vested laborer who'd found them was a huge, muscular guy named George Guzman who kept dabbing tears.

Moe Reed stood next to him, pad in hand. His expression said he'd been offering continuous sympathy, wasn't sure he liked that gig. At Reed's other side stood Liz Wilkinson, impassive but for soft searching eyes, tool cases on the ground next to her, white coat draped over one arm. Ready to have a go at the skeleton but waiting for the coroner's investigator to release the victim for further analysis.

The C.I. hadn't shown up yet. Neither had the crime scene techs, but Liz had gloved up in anticipation. She stood right up against Moe, hips pressed against his. Hard to say who was supporting who.

Guzman stared at the white bones and sniffled.

Reed's mouth twisted. "Okay, thanks, sir."

"For what?"

"Calling us."

"There was a choice?" said Guzman. He took another look. "Man."

Reed said, "You can go, now."

Guzman said, "Sure," but he lingered. Reed prompted his exit by pointing at the yellow tape.

Guzman said, "Sure, sure," took a step, stopped. "I'll never forget this. We just had one."

"One what, sir?"

"Baby." The word came out strangled. "George Junior. We waited a long time for him."

"Congratulations," said Milo.

Guzman looked at him.

Reed said, "This is my boss, Lieutenant Sturgis. Sir, Mr. Guzman is our first arriver. He called it in."

Guzman said, "I'm always here first. Since we started the job, I mean."

"What's the job?" said Milo.

"Making sure water doesn't collect and ruin the roots of all those trees." Guzman pointed. "We need to check out the entire area, taking samples of what's below, then if we need drains, we put 'em in. Few years ago it was done wrong, flooded the archery field."

"It's your job to get here before anyone else?"

"No, no, not officially," said Guzman, "but that's what happens, I make it at seven ten, fifteen, the other guys not till seven thirty. 'Cause I take my wife to work, she waitresses at Junior's on Westwood. I drop her off, she gives me coffee, I drive a couple minutes and I'm here."

Guzman's eyes drifted back to the bones. "I thought it was a squirrel or something. Dead animals, we see plenty of that. Then I got close and . . ." He blinked. "It's definitely human?"

Everyone turned to Liz Wilkinson. She said, "Unfortunately."

"Damn," said Guzman, biting his lip. His eyes misted.

Milo said, "Appreciate your help, sir. Have a nice day."

His prompt was more directive than Reed's, a nudge to Guzman's elbow that got the giant in motion. Guzman plodded toward the tape, ducked under with effort, walked several yards, and joined another group of orange-vests hanging near a yellow city truck. The group stayed there, listening as Guzman regaled them.

Milo said, "There's one who likes attention. You pick up anything about him that fills your nostrils, Moses?"

"Kind of a crybaby," said Reed, "but nothing overtly creepy."

"Run him through, anyway."

"Already done, boss. Clean."

"Good work, kid, that's why you get the big bucks. Any anthropological impressions, Liz?"

Wilkinson said, "By its size, this child might be younger than the first. The teeth will help me judge but I haven't inspected them because the way the skull's positioned the mouth is in the dirt."

"We'll get you access soon as the C.I. okays it." To Reed: "Any word from the crypt?"

"Held up in traffic. Best guess is within the hour."

"What about Crime Scene?"

"They should've been here already."

Milo turned to Liz. "You were notified by the crypt crew?"

She smiled. "By Moe."

Reed fidgeted.

Milo laughed. "Anything for a date, Detective Reed?"

"I'll take what I can get."

Liz said, "I think that's a compliment."

Milo said, "Anything else of a scientific nature, Dr. W?"

"These bones look considerably fresher than the first, so you could have a fairly recent crime. But that could also be the result of cleaning or bleaching. From what I can see so far, they appear totally de-fleshed. As to how that was done, I'm a bit puzzled. The most common methods would be mechanical—scraping—or chemical—corrosives, boiling— or a combination of both. But all that seems to be lacking here."

"How can you tell?"

She let go of Reed's hand, walked closer to the bones. "Don't tattle on me to the crypt folk, Milo, but I crouched down and had a good close look." She held up a gloved hand. "Then I put these on and touched several of the bones because the freshness intrigued me. I was careful not to move anything, there was no disruption of the crime scene. But I wanted to see how they responded to tactile pressure. I also used a magnifying loupe and couldn't find any of the tool marks you'd get from scraping, or the pitting and cloudiness you'd get from a corrosive bath. More important, the bones felt relatively rigid, as firm as an infant skeleton could be, and with boiling you'd expect them to turn at least a bit rubbery. Especially the smaller bones, those could be as pliable as cooked noodles. It's possible there's a new chemical able to do the job without leaving traces but I haven't heard of it. Maybe something'll turn up in the analysis."

"De-fleshed," said Milo, "but no sign of trauma. So maybe this one *is* a lab specimen, Liz. Some sick wiseass reads about the first case, decides to prank us with a medical souvenir he buys on the Internet."

"Anything's possible but I don't think so. For the same reason as with the first: You'd expect holes for wires."

Milo went over to the bones, squatted, a Buddha in a bad suit. "Almost like plastic, with that shine."

I said, "Is it possible they were coated with something that's obscuring the tool marks?"

Liz said, "I thought about some kind of lacquering but it would have to be super-thin because normal anatomical irregularities are visible."

Milo said, "Call the C.I. again, Moses, get a fix on ETA."

Reed complied. "Half an hour, minimum."

"Wonderful."

I said, "Sick joke or murder, with the dump being so close to the first bones, this reeks of copycat."

Milo inhaled, gut heaving. "Two in Cheviot Hills. Can't remember the last time we had a murder here."

Liz said, "The distance to the Ruche home is less than a mile—point nine three to be exact."

Milo smiled. "Geography's in your job description?"

Reed said, "She clocked it 'cause I asked her."

"You did me a favor, honey. Distracted me from thinking about two dead babies." Ungloving, she took out her phone, walked a few feet to the side.

Milo said, "Moe, soon as the techies and the crypters get here, you and I are heading back to the office to run a search on missing infants. Meanwhile, call Sean. I'll be wanting him to canvass the neighborhood."

Moe left a message for Binchy.

Liz returned. "Just spoke to one of my old profs. He's never seen a specimen without wires and he's not aware of any lacquer that's commonly used. But no one knows everything so I'll stay on it. One bright spot: If these are relatively fresh, DNA's likely. Speaking of which, what's the status with the first set? DOJ hasn't instructed me to send them yet."

"Start the paperwork, kid."

Reed's phone rang. He said, "Hey, Ess-man, whusup? *What?*"

As he listened, his hand tapped the butt of his service gun. When he clicked off, his face was tight. "You're not going to believe this, they just found another."

Liz said, "Another *baby?*" Her voice caught. All pretense of scientific detachment ripped away like a dangling scab.

Reed said, "Another DB, adult female, gunshot wound, right here in the park, the southern edge."

Milo's face was as animated as a frozen chuck roast. He waved a uniform over.

"Keep this area tight, Officer. No one but the techies and the C.I. gets in."

"Yessir. That mean you're finished here?"

"Not even close."

CHAPTER

12

The woman was late twenties to early thirties, dark-haired, medium height, slightly heavy at arms, hips, and ankles. She lay on her right side, the front part of her body shaded by shrubbery. Her dress, short-sleeved and knee-length, was patterned in a pale green mini-paisley with old-fashioned cap sleeves.

One leg rested atop the other, a position that almost resembled peaceful sleep. No disruption of clothing, no obvious sexual posing, but Milo pointed out faint pink rings around her wrists that were probably the residuals of being bound.

A rubber-soled brown loafer encased her right foot. Its mate lay a couple of feet away to the north. Her hair was trimmed short enough to expose the nape of her neck. The bullet hole was a red-black mini-crater at the junction of cranium and spine.

A single shot, fired at close enough range to leave light stippling, entering the medulla oblongata and cutting off the respiratory functions marshaled by the lower brain.

What the papers like to call execution-style, but there are all sorts of ways to execute someone and what this wound and the wrist marks said was a killer in total control leaving nothing to chance.

The two uniforms guarding the scene said she'd been spotted by a jogger. Her bare foot, clean and white amid the greenery, had been the attention-getter.

No jogger in sight. Milo didn't comment on that as he explored the edges of the scene.

Even without her foot protruding, the woman would've been noticed soon enough. This part of the park was relatively secluded but could be reached by any number of pathways or a simple walk across rolling lawn, followed by a brief pass through a planting of gum trees. The jogging trail was a well-worn rut that paralleled the park's southern border. Where the body lay, the trail veered especially close, maybe three feet away.

Intending for her to be found? A methodical killer eager to show off?

Milo kept looking at the woman. I forced myself to do the same. Her mouth was agape, eyes half open, filmed like those of a hooked fish left too long on deck. Crusts of dried blood leaked from her ears, nose, and mouth. That and the size of the bullet hole said a small-caliber slug had bounced around her brain like a pinball.

No purse, no jewelry, no I.D. Whatever bare skin was visible was free of tattoos, scars, distinguishing marks.

I spotted additional blood speckling dirt, leaves, a rock. No need to point it out; Milo crouched like a silverback gorilla, examining one of the larger splotches.

He moved to a spot just north of the woman's legs and pointed. A broken chain of footprints appeared to lead up to the body. A second series pointed in the opposite direction.

Large, deep impressions for both. The same person, a heavyweight. The tracks revealed none of the corrugations you'd see with an athletic shoe or a hiking boot, just your smooth heel-sole imprint lacking trademark or label or idiosyncrasy.

Both sets of prints vanished as soil gave way to grass. Tough park turf had sprung back hours ago, concealing the killer's entrance and exit.

Milo circled a couple more times, wrote something down in his pad, showed me a pair of depressions in the grass, slightly to the left of the corpse.

Shallow indentations, as if two weighted bowls had been placed there. Easy to miss but hard to ignore once you saw them. The resilient lawn had tried but failed to mask them completely.

I said, "On her knees."

"Has to be," he said. "Then he shot her and she fell over."

"Or was pushed."

"No bruising or dirt on her face."

"He could've cleaned her off before he arranged her."

"You think she looks posed? He didn't put that other shoe on."

"It was dark, maybe he didn't notice."

He crouched, took out his flashlight despite ample sun, aimed the beam between her teeth.

Victim on her knees, check for oral rape.

I said, "Anything?"

"No obvious fluid but I am seeing little white specks on her gums."

He showed me.

I said, "Looks like fabric. Bound *and* gagged."

He waved the uniforms over. Both were young, male, clean-featured, with gym-rat swaggers. One was sandy-haired and freckled, the other had a dark buzz cut and suspicious brown eyes.

"You guys check for casings?"

Sandy said, "We did, sir, nothing."

Milo did his own search, took his time but came up empty-handed. Careful shooter or a revolver.

The uniforms had returned to their original positions. He waved them back. "Who called it in?"

"Like we said, the jogger," said Sandy. "A girl."

"Where is she?"

Buzz said, "We got her information and let her go home. Here you go, sir."

Milo took the paper. "Heather Goldfeder."

Sandy said, "She lives just a few blocks away. With her parents."

"We talking a minor?"

"Barely a major, sir. Eighteen last month, she was pretty traumatized."

"Who made the judgment to let her go?"

The cops looked at each other. Buzz said, "Sir, it was a joint decision. She's maybe five two, hundred pounds, so she's obviously not the offender."

Milo said, "Teeny toon."

"Student at SMC, sir. She was really distraught."

Milo said, "Thanks for the psychological profile."

"Sir," said Buzz, "she told us she runs here three times a week, never saw your victim before. Ever."

Sandy said, "Sir, if we did something wrong by letting her go, we're sorry. She was totally emotional, we made the judgment that babysitting her would distract our attention away from what needed to be done."

"Which was?"

"Securing the scene, sir."

Milo ushered me several yards away. "Everyone's a damn therapist. So what does a real shrink have to say about this one being connected to the new bones?"

I said, "Two bodies in the park, same approximate time?"

He nodded. "So what do we have, Mommy and Baby?"

"If so, Baby died first. Days or weeks or months ago."

"Maybe Mommy got blamed for that by Daddy?"

"That would be a good place to start."

"On the other hand, if Daddy's so devoted, why would he dump his kid's bones?"

I thought about that. "We could be talking about someone with serious psychiatric issues—paranoia, an active delusional system that got kicked up by the baby's death. That could also explain the bones

being preserved. He elevated them to an object of worship—some sort
of icon. It also fits with leaving them in the park on the night he killed
the person he deems responsible. This is what *she* did, this is what *I* did
to *her.*"

"Some nutter de-fleshing his own kid's skeleton? What's next, he
walks into traffic with an AK?"

"Delusional doesn't have to mean a raving lunatic," I said. "There's
nothing disordered about the woman's murder, so you could be dealing
with someone who keeps it under wraps pretty well."

"Till he doesn't." He phoned Reed, found out the coroner's investigator had arrived, done a quick visual, authorized Liz to take possession of the bones, and left. The crime scene techs were doing their thing
but had turned up nothing, so far.

Returning to Sandy and Buzz, he said, "We're heading back to the
other scene. You stay here."

"How is that one, sir?" said Sandy.

"What do you mean?"

"The other scene. We heard bones over the radio. Whose?"

"Someone dead."

Sandy flinched.

Buzz said, "They have something to do with each other? Have to
be, no?"

Milo rocked on his heels. He spoke between clenched jaws. "Here's
what has to be: Guard this scene as if it was your best set of barbells.
Don't let anyone but the C.I. and the C.S. crew within fifty yards of the
body—make that a hundred. Stand right there. Don't wander off.
Don't answer any questions. Of any sort. From anyone. At any time. If
you're considering thinking, don't do that, either."

Buzz stood straighter. "Sir. We're all about proper procedure."

Milo saved his laughter until we were well away. Not a pleasant
sound, quick and harsh as a gunshot.

Liz Wilkinson stood just outside the perimeter of the bone-dump. A
team of three crime scene techs had nailed up an inner cordon on

stakes, was photographing, bagging and tagging. Moe Reed stood near enough to observe, far enough to avoid getting in their way.

Liz said, "Got some new data for you. The front of the face exhibits no breakage or damage of any sort. No erupted teeth on either jaw, the buds are barely visible, I'm estimating age at around two months. And Alex, you were right about the bones being coated. When I got up close I could smell beeswax, it's got a distinct aroma. My father collects antique tea caddies and he uses it to shine them up. So maybe we're dealing with another type of collector. Some sort of fetishist."

Milo repeated the enraged-father theory.

She said, "A father preserving his own child's bones?" She looked at me.

I said, "You know the drill: Anything's possible."

"God, I hope that's not how it turns out. These past few days are already testing my detachment mettle."

"If there were faint tool marks could they be spotted under the wax?"

"I think so but I'll find out when I get them magnified. I'll x-ray every single one, maybe we'll get lucky and internal damage due to disease will show up, or a subtle injury. The nice thing—God, that sounds horrible—is that fresh infant skeletal remains have the best chance of yielding genetic material."

Milo said, "Fresh, as opposed to the first ones."

"DNA's been extracted from eons-old tissue so I'm guardedly optimistic on those, as well.".

"That like nervously calm?"

She grinned. "Kind of. Anyway, Mommy and Baby should be easy enough to verify."

"Good," said Milo. "I like answers."

13

Milo and I drove back to his office, where he searched missing persons for a match to the dead woman. By three p.m., twenty-eight possibilities had surfaced. By six, each lead had fizzled. An initial foray into one of the national data banks proved fruitless but there were other lists. So many women unaccounted for.

My phone rang. Service operator letting me know that Holly Ruche had canceled her appointment.

"Any reason given?"

"No, Doctor, but she did sound kind of tense. You'd think that would be a bad time to cancel, huh?"

I agreed and amended my date book.

Milo was staring at a phone-photo he'd taken of the dead woman. He said, "Even if her main squeeze doesn't miss her, someone will. Time to go back to the media. Starting with that reporter." He checked the blue-bound murder book he'd begun on the old bones, found what he was looking for. "Kelly LeMasters, you're my new girlfriend. And that's saying a lot."

He punched numbers, barked, "Sturgis, call me." Moments later, his office phone rang.

I said, "That was quick."

"The old charm kicking in." He switched to speaker.

Deputy Chief Maria Thomas said, "How's it going on the two you picked up today?"

"Just started, Maria."

"Run the details by me." Not sounding the least bit curious.

He gave her basics.

She said, "How are you planning to I.D. your adult vic?"

"The usual way."

"Meaning?"

"Our pals in the press. Just left a message for the *Times* reporter."

"What message?"

"To call me back."

"When she does," said Thomas, "undo it."

"What?"

"Tell her you were just touching base on the old one, don't give her anything on the new ones."

"Why would I touch base without new info?"

"Figure something out."

"What's going on, Maria?"

"You know the answer."

"Actually, I don't."

"Think."

"Edict from on high?"

"An administrative decision has been made."

"Why?"

"Can't get into that, nor can I advise you how long it'll be operative."

"On the first bones you couldn't wait to play *Meet the Press*. In fact, you did it without letting me—"

"Flexibility," said Thomas, "is the hallmark of good management."

"What the hell changed?"

"Nothing changed. The cases aren't the least bit similar."

"Exactly, Maria. The first one *was* ancient history. With these new ones I might actually get a lead by going public."

"Or not," said Thomas.

"What's the risk?"

"As I said, the cases are structurally different. The first bones were perceived as a human-interest story. Historical, quaint, however you want to put it."

"A dead baby is quaint?"

"No one likes a dead baby, Milo, but the consensus is that we probably don't have a *murdered* baby, are most likely dealing with natural causes, some sort of extreme grief reaction. The consensus is also that lacking media input you'd never close it, but that with media exposure you had a minimal chance. Obviously, that hasn't panned out, so much for good press for the department."

"This is about P.R.?"

"Have you seen the latest city council budget proposals?"

"I avoid smut."

"Some of us don't have that luxury and trust me, it's bad, we're talking across-the-board slash-and-burn like I've never seen before. Given that, some touchy-feely closure on a poor little baby would've been nice."

"That doesn't answer my first question, Maria. Why a blackout on the new ones? Closing real murders is gonna make us look even better."

"Whatever," she said. "Meanwhile, do not talk to the *Times,* or anyone else in the media."

"How do I I.D. my adult victim, let alone a sack of bones?"

"Did your adult victim appear homeless or otherwise a lowlife?" said Thomas.

"No, and that's exactly why I figured—"

"If she's not a throwaway, someone will report her missing."

"So I wait."

"You do your job and obey directives."

"Whose secret are we keeping, Maria?"

"Stop whining. Some things are better left unsaid."

"Not in my business."

"We're in the same business."

"Are we?" he said.

She snickered. "It didn't take long, did it? The outrage, the self-righteousness, the lonely warrior tilting against windmills."

"Who's tilting? I just want to—"

"Listen and listen well because I'm only going to explain it one more time: There's a strong desire among those responsible for the decisions that govern your professional life to avoid getting lurid with this particular case at this particular juncture."

"Lurid as in . . ."

"Yuck-stuff," she said. "As in more baby bones start popping up all over the place because psychotics get stimulated by coverage. Go ask your shrink friend, he'll tell you about that kind of thing."

"Yuck-stuff," he said, "that just happens to take place in a high-end neighborhood. A dead woman and baby bones in Nickerson Gardens would be a whole different story."

"Discussion over," said Thomas.

Click.

Milo swiveled and faced me. "You're an ear-witness. That actually happened."

I said, "Your point about which neighborhood got to her. May I?"

As I pulled my chair up to his computer, he rolled his back to give me room.

A check of *viprealestate.net* subheaded *cheviot hills* pulled it up in nanoseconds.

Last year, Maxine Cleveland, a recently retired county supervisor, had purchased a "thirteen room Mediterranean manse" on an oversized lot on Forrester Drive in the "leafy upscale district of Cheviot Hills."

A onetime public defender long considered hostile to cops, Cleveland had morphed into a law-and-order stalwart following the chief's endorsement of her reelection and some well-placed fund-raisers arranged by the chief's retired-anchorwoman wife.

Cleveland and her labor-lawyer husband had only lived in the Cheviot house for seven months before putting it up for sale. Both had accepted jobs in D.C., she as an assistant attorney general, he as chief counsel for the Occupational Safety and Health Administration.

Cleveland's first assignment would be heading a task force on financial shenanigans in the banking arena and the real estate website wondered if she could be objective, given a drop in the value of her investment due to the recession. An economic slump brought on, in part, by Wall Street's addiction to junk mortgages.

I said, "Toss in two DBs a short hop away and it won't be much of a broker's carousel."

"Idiots," he growled. "Okay, go home, no sense sitting and watching me type."

I moved out of the way and he bellied up to his keyboard. Entering his password, he logged onto NCIC. The screen froze. He cursed.

I said, "What about the jogger—Heather Goldfeder?"

"What about her? My resident geniuses said she didn't know the victim."

"She didn't know the victim but the way the bones and the body were dumped suggests a bad guy familiar with the park. She runs there regularly so it's possible she's seen something or someone she doesn't realize is relevant. A man casing the area or loitering near the jogging path."

He loosened his tie, yanked it off. "I was going to get to her once I finished with missing persons."

His phone rang again. Kelly LeMasters sounding excited about "touching base."

Instead of picking up, he sat there and listened as LeMasters emphasized her interest in the old bones, offered an additional cell number, and hung up.

"Okay," he said, "let's do it."

"Do what?"

"Check out little Heather."

"You changed your mind."

"I hate typing."

He phoned the Goldfeder home. Heather's father picked up, Milo introduced himself then listened for a while.

"Yes, I know that had to be difficult, Mr. Goldfeder . . . *Doctor* Goldfeder, sorry . . . yes, I'm sure it was. Which is one reason I'm calling you. We happen to have an expert psychologist and he's available to offer some crisis . . ."

He hung up shaking his head.

I said, "No-go?"

"Quite the contrary, definite yes-go. 'About time you people considered the human factor.'"

"Thanks for calling me an expert."

"Onward."

14

I pulled up in front of the Goldfeder home at ten the following morning. Going it alone because Milo felt "the pure psych angle would work best."

The two-story Spanish Colonial was three blocks south of the dead woman's dump site. Two white Priuses shared the driveway with an identically hued Porsche Cayenne SUV. One of the hybrids bore a Santa Monica College decal on the rear window. That vehicle was dust-streaked, its interior a jumble of paper, empty bottles, rumpled clothing. The other two were spotless.

I climbed a geranium-lined walkway to a stout oak door, raised a brass lion's-head knocker and let it drop gently onto the wood. The man who answered wore green surgical sweats, baggy in most places but snug around bulky shoulders and lifter's arms. Fifty or so, he had thinning dark hair, a small face conceding to gravity, a gray goatee more stubble than beard.

"Dr. Delaware? Howard Goldfeder." The hand he offered was out-sized, smooth at the palms, pink around the cuticles from frequent washing. I'd looked him up last night: ENT surgeon with a clinical professorship. Same for his wife, Arlene, Department of Ophthalmology.

Heather's Facebook page had showed her as a pixie-faced cutie nearly overwhelmed by a storm cloud of dark hair. The page was thinly utilized, with only a smattering of friends. Favorite activities: running, more running. Phys. ed. major at SMC.

"Doctor," I said.

"Howard's fine."

"So is Alex."

"Given the context, I'll stick with Howard and Dr. Delaware."

"What context is that?"

"You're here to work, I'm here as Heather's dad. Speaking of which, how about we get things straight from the outset: Are you here to counsel my daughter about finding a corpse or to pry information out of her for the police? I'm asking because I thought it was a little weird for that lieutenant to offer the services of a psychologist out of the clear blue. Also, I did a little checking and you're a serious guy, we're both faculty crosstown. Why would someone with your credentials work for the cops? Do you have some sort of research project going on?"

I said, "I work with them, not for them, because I find it satisfying. In terms of your main concern, which is understandable, Lieutenant Sturgis would love any new information but my focus is going to be on Heather's well-being. How's she doing?"

Howard Goldfeder studied me. "Okay, I guess."

"You have your doubts?"

"She can be a high-strung kid. C'mon in."

"Anything else I should know before I talk to her?"

"My opinion is she exercises too much."

The living room was vault-ceilinged, furnished in overstuffed chenille, suede, and brass-accented mahogany. A U-shaped staircase rose to a landing. Rails, risers, and newel posts gleamed. The furniture looked as if it was rarely used, every pillow plumped and dimpled, as if styled for a photo shoot. Persian rugs lay as flat as if they'd been stenciled onto the wide-plank floor. Mullion windows sparkled, fireplace tools glinted. If dust was present, it was hiding in fear.

Howard Goldfeder said, "My wife's working, she's an eye surgeon. I'll go get Heather; if you need me, I'll be in my study. How long do you figure this will take?"

"Probably no more than an hour."

"I can handle that."

I said, "What did Heather tell you about finding the body?"

"She was running," said Goldfeder. "Like she usually does. Every day, rain or shine, she's out the door between seven and nine, depending on her class schedule, does her six miles religiously. Sometimes she ups it as high as ten a day."

"Rigorous."

"That's just morning, her afternoon run's another three, four. That she does at the track at school."

"Was she a high school athlete?"

"Not even close, couldn't get her involved in anything extracurricular, she started after she graduated." His lips pursed. "Obviously, you're wondering if she's got an eating disorder and honestly, we don't think so. She doesn't take in a lot of calories, true, and she's vegan, I'm always on her to get more iron. But she's always been a small eater and we have plenty of meals together so we can tell what she's ingesting. In terms of bingeing and bulimia, there's absolutely no sign of that. Her teeth are as perfect as the day her braces came off and I had her pediatrician look at her electrolytes just in case I was missing something and she's in peak condition. Yes, she's on the thin side, but she's always been that way, just like my wife and my wife's entire family. My side's all the fatties, which is why I need to watch."

Patting a flat abdomen. "Make yourself comfortable."

"In terms of finding the body—"

Goldfeder's meaty shoulders drooped. "That was some drawn-out answer to a simple question, huh? I guess I'm not too concerned with a onetime thing like the body. It's the general stuff that concerns me. Like the fact that she's incredibly compulsive about her running but with everything else she slacks off totally. I won't even tell you her GPA, it's clearly way below what she's capable of. That's why she's at SMC instead of the U."

"Not much for academics."

"Never reads, never shows any interest in—but she's a good kid . . . never had a boyfriend, either. Never dated. Ever. I guess we should be grateful she's never gotten into any sort of trouble with boys . . . but now that she's in college . . . also, she doesn't share much."

"About?"

"What's going on with her, her feelings. Her life. She used to share, everything's lip service, now. Love you Daddy, love you Mommy, then she's off by herself."

"But her mood's okay."

"She seems happy to me," said Goldfeder.

"So she likes her privacy."

"I guess, but I can't stop wondering if she's holding back. She's an only child, we put a lot into her—this all probably sounds neurotic, maybe it is, I don't know."

I said, "Sounds like parental concern."

"I guess I should stop being a pain—you'll meet her, you be the judge. Okay, back to your question: She didn't say much about what happened yesterday, just that she was running and saw it. She could tell right away it was dead from the color and the blood, some flies were already there. She said that freaked her out the most, the flies, the noise they made. She felt light-headed but she didn't faint, she kept her wits about her, called 911 and stuck around. Overall, I'd have to say I'm proud of how she handled it."

"You should be."

"Basically, she's a *great* kid . . . I'll go get her."

The girl who preceded him down the stairs seconds later had lopped off most of her hair since posting her Facebook shot, massive mane giving way to a crew cut. Her features were delicate and symmetrical. Huge, deep blue eyes connoted wonder.

She smiled and waved as she bounced down on stick-legs, seemed to take flight only to alight with grace. I thought: *Tinker Bell.*

Her father worked to keep up with her.

When she reached the bottom, she kissed his cheek. "Go back to work, Daddy, I'm fine."

"I've got paperwork to do in the study."

"Oh, Daddy. *Really.* He looks like a nice man. I don't need a chaperone."

"I'm not trying to be one, baby, there are bills to be paid."

"So organized." She giggled. "Okay, go to your study but close the door."

"I intended to."

"Sure you did."

Howard Goldfeder's reply was inaudible as he headed up the hall. Looking back for a second, he shut his door.

Heather said, "He's protective 'cause he loves me," and sat down perpendicular to me. She had on an oversized, sleeveless white blouse, khaki shorts, flat sandals. Skinny limbs but none of the ropy dehydration of severe anorexia. Lovely teeth, as her father had claimed. No evidence of breast development but the shirt would hide a less-than-generous bust.

"Well," she said, "my therapy begins."

I laughed.

"What's funny?" she said.

"You're pretty organized yourself."

"Oh, I'm not, trust me, I'm a total slob."

"Your dad tells me you're quite a runner."

"What he means is I'm a freak. My mother thinks so, too, 'cause I like to get down at least three hundred miles a month, more if I have time."

"Impressive."

"They think it's nuts. Like an OCD thing, even though they bugged me to do sports in high school. Even though she's at the gym six times a week and he's there like three, four times, lifting weights and hurting himself all the time. I run 'cause I'm good at it. First time I tried I could go five miles without even breathing hard. I thought it would take time but it was easy. Felt amazing. Still does. When I run, it's like I'm flying, nothing else makes me feel that way. That's why I switched from Spanish to P.E. I want to be a coach or a personal trainer."

"Makes sense."

"So," she said. "What should we talk about?"

"Whatever you'd like."

"Would you like me to talk about yesterday?"

"If you want."

"What do *you* want?" she said. "Being with the police."

"I'm not here as a police representative."

"Then what?"

"To make sure you're okay after what happened."

"Okay? Sure I'm okay. It was a great experience, seeing a dead person, let's do it again tomorrow."

She looked at the carpet. "Will talking to you help with my dreams?"

"You're having nightmares?"

"Just last night. First I saw her face, then it kind of blended into a skeleton. Then I saw babies, tons of babies, with teensy little faces, all looking at me. Like they needed help. Then *they* turned into skeletons, it was like a mountain of skeletons."

"Babies," I said.

"Babies turning into skeletons. They told me about the skeleton across the park and it probably got stuck in my brain. Don't you think?"

"Who's they?"

"The two cops that showed up. They said there'd been another case across the park, a baby skeleton, maybe it was connected to the woman. Till then I was holding out pretty good. But a baby? Just thinking about it freaked me out."

She smiled broadly. Burst into tears.

I fetched tissues from a spotless powder room left of the front door, waited until she'd composed herself.

"Wow," she said. "I really thought I was okay. Guess I wasn't."

"Crying doesn't mean you're not okay, Heather. Neither does dreaming. Yesterday was a lot to deal with."

"It's weird," she said. "Seeing her again. It's not like I knew her but now I feel I kind of do. Like finding her made us . . . connected us. Like her face will be with me forever. Who was she?"

"We don't know yet."

"She looked like a nice person." Laughing. "That's a stupid thing to say."

"Not at all, Heather. You're searching for answers. Everyone is."

She sat there for a while, shredding the tissue, letting flecks fall to the immaculate rug. "I saw the hole in her head. She was shot, right? I asked the cops but they wouldn't tell me."

"She was," I said. "How'd the topic of the baby come up?"

"Soon after they finished asking me questions one of them got a call on his doo-what, his radio, then he hung up and the two of them started discussing something. They looked nervous so I asked them what's up. They didn't want to tell me but I cried and bugged them. Because that always works with my parents. Finally they told me. Was it *her* baby?"

"We don't know."

"Don't you think it was? Why would both of them get killed the same time in the park? Nothing ever happens in the park. I've been running for months and the worst thing I ever saw was a coyote, that was way back when I first started. Just standing there, all bony and hungry-looking. I screamed and it ran away."

"Spotting the body was a lot tougher."

"The flies," she said. "That was the grossest. At first I thought it was one of those dummies in the department store—a manikin." Giggle. "They should call it a womanikin, right? She had one bare foot and that's what got my attention, real pale, almost like plastic. Then I saw the rest of her, then I heard the flies." She sighed. "I guess someone had to find her."

"Keeping your wits about you and calling 911 took presence of mind."

"Actually my first thought was to book as fast as I could, but then I thought what if someone's still around and they try to shoot *me*? So I took a second to look around, check out the area, figure out the best escape route. The park was so quiet and that kind of made it even freakier. A nice morning, the sky was blue, and she's just *lying* there. When do the cops think they'll know who she is?"

"There's no way to tell, Heather."

"That sucks. So . . . my dreams don't mean I'm a head-case?"

"Your brain's using sleep to take in what happened and give your mind time to integrate. And yes, talking about it can help. Because one way or the other people need to express themselves."

She finished destroying the tissue. Deliberately sprinkled the fragments onto the floor. "Is this talk totally secret?"

"Absolutely."

"No one finds out? Not the cops? Not my parents?"

"You have total confidentiality."

"What if I want you to say something to someone?"

"Your choice."

"I'm in control."

"Yes."

"That's . . . interesting."

She got up, spent a long time gathering the shredded tissue, found every single speck, threw the collection out in the powder room. When she returned, she remained on her feet. Her mouth was tight. "So . . . can I get you something to drink?"

"No, thanks."

"You're sure?"

"I'm fine."

"Okay . . . I guess that's it. Thanks for talking to me."

I said, "Your question about confidentiality."

"What about it?"

"So far you haven't told me anything your parents and the cops don't already know."

She turned her back on me. Gave a half turn, reversed it. Rotated a bit more and revealed a tight-jawed profile.

"No, I haven't," she said.

I sat there.

She said, "I like girls, okay? Like that Katy Perry song, I kissed one and it was more than cherry ChapStick that made me do it? Now I'm in love with someone and that gives me *good* dreams."

She faced me. "Do you think I'm weird?"

"Not in the least."

"*They* will. The cops will."

"Can't speak for your parents but the cops won't know or care."

"It's no one's business anyway, Doctor. Just mine and Ame— I don't want my parents to know. Ever."

"I can understand that."

"But that's not realistic, is it?" she said. "I'm their kid."

"You're an adult, Heather. What you tell them is your decision."

"Ha," she said. "I mean the part about being an adult. Like I'm even close."

"Legally you are."

"So if my birthday was next month instead of last month, I'd still be a kid and you could tell them?"

"It can get complicated," I said. "But I'd never tell them, anyway."

"Why not?"

"It's your personal business."

"But now I am an adult. Cool." Giggle. "I guess that sucks if it means I have to pay for stuff."

She turned serious. Touched her cropped hair. "I cut it all off last month. I feel like wearing boy clothes but I don't have the guts. Think I can get away with boy clothes like in a cute way? So they'll think it's just a fashion thing?"

"Keep it subtle enough? Sure."

"Like what?"

"Don't show up in a business suit and a tie. And I'd forget the pencil mustache."

She laughed. "You seem okay but no offense, I don't think I need you. I already started therapy with someone at student counseling. She's a total dyke—compared with her, I'm Super-Femme."

"I'm glad you've found someone you trust."

"I don't know if I trust her yet. But maybe, we'll see. So anyway, thanks for trying to help me."

"Thanks for being open to it."

"Honestly," she said, "the only reason I agreed to talk to you was Dad and Mom were bugging me to do it, saying they were finally getting something from their tax dollars. I try to do what they ask if it's only a small hassle. No offense."

"Picking your battles."

"That way I can do what I want when it's important."

"Sounds like a good strategy." Same one I'd used throughout my childhood. Up to the day I turned sixteen and bought an old car and began my escape from Missouri.

She said, "You think it's okay to play them like that?"

"You're not playing them, you're being selective."

"Sometimes I wonder if I should just be honest—this is who I am, deal."

"One day you may be able to do that."

"That's kind of scary," she said.

"One day it may not be."

A creak came from up the hall. The door to Howard Goldfeder's study opened and he stuck his head out.

Heather said, "I'm fine, Daddy."

"Just checking."

"Thank you, Daddy."

He didn't budge.

"Daddy."

He went back inside but the door remained ajar. Heather trotted over, pushed it shut, returned. "Do me a favor, Dr. Delaware. Before you leave tell him I look normal. So he doesn't think I need some Beverly Hills shrink."

"Will do," I said.

"You don't think I need that, right?"

"You're the best judge of that."

"Are you saying I'm screwed up but you don't want to piss me off?"

"Everything you've told me says you're reacting normally. The fact that you're already in therapy says you know how to take care of yourself."

"What about my running?"

"Sounds like you like to run. So do I."

"That's it?"

"Do you eat normally?"

"Yes."

"Do you binge and gag yourself in secret?"

"No."

"In general, do you think life's going okay?"

"Yes."

I shrugged.

She said, "Are you like . . . super-supportive to everyone?"

"I don't read minds, Heather, so all I can go on is what you tell me and what I observe about you. If there's some secret problem you're not telling me about, I could be missing something. But so far you're not setting off any alarms."

"Okay . . . do you like talk directly to the police?"

"Not about what patients tell me—"

"No, no, that's not what I meant," she said. "I'm talking about crimes. Like if someone tells you something and *wants* you to tell the cops, what do you do, just get on the phone?"

"You bet."

"And then the police come to see that person?"

"Sometimes," I said. "But the police can't force anyone to talk to them. Even a suspect."

"Like on TV. You have the right to remain silent."

"Exactly."

She sat back down. "Okay. I have something. It's probably not important, I was going to call them, then I said why bother, it's probably nothing. Then I wasn't sure if I was doing a wrong thing. But since you're here, anyway . . ."

She exhaled. "It's *not* some big clue or anything but the night before, I was near the park. Pretty close to where I found her but outside the park, on the other side of the fence."

"On the street."

"I wouldn't think anything about it, but with what happened . . . I mean it was so close. If you could walk through the fence, you'd be right there in seconds."

Her right hand tugged at the fingers of her left. "I was with someone. Parked in my car. My parents were out late, a party in Newport Beach. I figured it would be a good time to . . . then I chickened out of using the house so we went driving and we parked. Not that we were doing anything, we were just talking." She colored. "Kissing a little, that's it. Just hanging out, it was nice. Until someone drove by and slowed down. Then they drove away and came back and slowed down again. Like they were checking us out. We got the frick out of there. Think we were in danger?"

"I think you were smart to be careful."

"I figured I should tell the cops," she said. "But the person with me can't . . . she's got commitments, okay? This could screw things up."

"I understand."

She punched the arm of her chair. "I'm *trying* to do the right thing but I also need to do the right thing for her."

"I don't see a problem with that, Heather."

"You promise she won't get hassled?"

"She doesn't need to get involved at all if you know everything she does."

"I do, I was in the driver's seat, had a better view."

"Then I don't see any need for her to be interviewed."

"I need to be interviewed?"

"At the most Lieutenant Sturgis will follow up with a phone call and have you repeat what you just said to me so he can have an official statement."

"That's it? You promise?"

"I do."

"I don't mind talking, it's just Amelie—I care about her."

"So you want me to pass this along to Lieutenant Sturgis?"

"I guess."

"I need you to be sure."

"Fine, I'm sure."

"Is there anything else you want to say about the car that checked you out?"

"Not a car, an SUV, that's all I know, I don't know brands."

"Can you recall any details?"

"It wasn't the same as my dad's SUV, his is a Porsche, this was bigger. Higher up."

"What about color?"

"Dark, can't tell you a color."

"Unusually high? Like it had been raised?"

"Hmm," she said. "Maybe . . . yes, I'd say so. I definitely felt we were being looked down on—oh, yeah, it had shiny rims."

"Did you see who was inside?"

"No, it was dark and honestly, we didn't want to know, we just got out of there."

"What did the SUV do?"

"It didn't follow us," she said. "Maybe it stayed there, I don't know. Which would be weird, when the next morning . . ."

"Someone checking out the park."

"I mean you can see right through the fence, it's not wood, it's just chain link. Do you think I'm making a big deal out of nothing?"

"One pass might be someone driving by, Heather. Coming back a second time's more troublesome. Whatever the intention, you were right to leave."

"Oh, man . . . city full of freaks. I don't know if I'll ever step foot in the park again."

"What time did this happen?"

"Late," she said. "Like one a.m. I know 'cause I called my parents at twelve forty-five, they were just about to leave, I figured we had half an hour more. But after the SUV freaked us out, I drove her to her car and went home."

"Any chance you saw even part of the SUV's license plate?"

"Uh-uh."

"Anything else you remember?"

"No," she said. "Oh, one more thing: The police guy can call me but use my personal cell, not the landline where they pick up."

I copied down the number.

Howard Goldfeder emerged from his office. "How we doing?"

"We're doing great, Daddy."

He said, "Doctor?" As if his daughter hadn't spoken.

I said, "She's terrific."

Goldfeder said, "I could've told you that."

Heather smiled, hiding it from him but allowing me a glimpse of her satisfaction.

15

Milo cursed. "Geniuses. They give a witness info then let her leave the scene before I have a chance to talk to her."

"It could work in your favor," I said. "Hard to keep secrets with that level of professionalism, so Maxine Cleveland's squeeze play may be exposed. You ever touch base with that reporter?"

"We keep missing each other, wink wink. Meanwhile, no one's reported my vic missing."

"Maybe she hasn't been gone long enough."

"Always the optimist," he said. "The prelim from the coroner just came in. She's had good dental care, maybe orthodontia. Her blood's clean, no booze, drugs, or disease, and her body's free of needle marks, scars, iffy tattoos, or any other sign of a rough life. Dr. Rosenblatt said she looked like someone who shouldn't have ended up on his table. And yeah, I know that's politically incorrect but truth is truth, right?" He pounded his hand with his fist. "Someone has to be looking for her."

He gulped a big chunk out of the egg bagel I'd just turned down. A bag that had once held a dozen mixed leaned against his computer. The crumbs of the jalapeño and the onion that he'd finished littered his desktop. "In terms of LeMasters, it's all I can do not to call her and leak but when the air turns brown and the fan gets filthy, you know who the brass will be chasing down."

"Want me to call her?"

"Oh, yeah, *that* would be subtle. So little Heather and her girl-friend got spooked by a dark SUV—not a Porsche—no info on the tags, no view of the driver. That narrows it to half the vehicles on the Westside."

"Even without more info, it's interesting, no?"

"Somebody casing the park? Hell, yeah."

The egg bagel disappeared down his gullet. He washed it down with cold coffee from the big detective room. We were in his office, the tiny space humid from poor ventilation and discouragement. I'd arrived just before noon, honoring his early-morning request for a "sit-down." He'd sounded anxious. I'd been there for a quarter hour, still had no idea exactly what he wanted.

He brushed crumbs into his wastebasket. "One pass by the SUV might not mean much but coming back a second time's a bit more ominous. But ominous doesn't mean it's connected to my murders, there are all kinds of night-crawlers out at that hour. And showing himself that openly doesn't fit an offender who picks up his casings, leaves nothing serious behind."

"Or he used a revolver and got lucky."

"Hey," he said, "you're supposed to see the good in everyone. Yeah, that's possible but the overall picture's organized, you said so yourself. Someone like that's planning a shoot-and-dump, he's gonna advertise his presence the night before to a coupla jumpy girls?"

"True," I said.

"Don't do that."

"What?"

"Agree so readily. It scares me."

"Keep living, you'll have plenty of opportunity for terror."

He grinned, stretched, pushed lank black hair off his mottled forehead, sank as low as the chair would allow. "This guy's an exhibitionist, right? Showing off his work, look how clever I am. Having a grand old time."

"He could be bragging," I said. "Or his message is something not so obvious. Specific to his mode of thinking."

"He's crazy?"

"Not to the point where he can't function, but his mind's probably a scary place. Whatever his motive, it's personal."

"Woman and child, a family thing? Yeah, I know we talked about that but I'm having my doubts, Alex. I just can't see a father processing his own kid's bones then strewing them like garbage. Speaking of which, Liz Wilkinson called me just before you got here, totally beating herself up. Apparently, there's a technique for cleaning bones that she missed."

He pulled two sheets of paper out of his printer. One contained a pair of split-frame photos: on the left, half a dozen small, glossy, hard-shelled brown insects, to the right a single, spiky, caterpillar-type creature.

The second sheet was an order blank for "high-grade, mite-free dermestid beetles" from a lab supply company in Chicago.

I said, "Flesh-eating bugs?"

"Flesh, hair, wool carpeting, any sort of animal matter, wet, dry, or in between. Not bone and teeth, because the little buggers' jaws can't handle anything that hard, but anything short of that. The adults like to snack, but it's the larvae—the ones with the whiskers—that are the serious gourmets. Set 'em loose and they can munch a bear skull sparkling clean within twenty-four hours, inflict no damage on the skeleton. Which is exactly why taxidermists and museums and scientists use 'em to spruce up specimens. Liz called it anthro for dummies, said two babies in a row probably clouded her judgment."

He swung his feet onto the desk. "Does the use of creepy-crawlies spark any ideas?"

I said, "Set the beetles, then wax and buff? It's starting to sound ritualistic."

"Beetles and *bees*wax," he said. "Maybe I should be looking for a deranged entomologist."

"Or one of those guys who like to mount heads over the mantel. Her I.D. was missing, same for jewelry, if she was wearing any."

"Trophy-taking."

"Maybe not in the sense of a sexual sadist evoking a memory," I said. "If that was his aim, he'd have held on to at least some of the bones. Family or not, this one's rooted in intimacy and specific to these victims. Can purchasers of the beetles be traced?"

"If only," he said. "They're legal and not protected like toxic chemicals so anyone can buy them. No way could I get a subpoena that broad."

"You could narrow the search," I said.

"How?"

"Order your two geniuses not to leak the information then sit back as the tips pour in."

He started with laughter, ended with a coughing fit. When he recovered, he said, "How do you see the first bones fitting in, if at all?"

"Reading about them could have been the trigger that got our bad guy to dump his bones nearby."

"And shoot and dump the woman the same night. What, he got a message from God? Time to take out the garbage?"

"Or hearing about the first bones jelled things for him," I said. "Maybe he'd been holding on to them, trying to achieve mastery by transforming them. That didn't work. Or it did. Either way, he had no further use for them."

"I still can't get past a father doing that to his own kid."

"We could be dealing with a stepfather or a boyfriend. Maybe even someone who thought the baby was his until he learned differently and grew enraged. Infanticide's not that rare among primates and that includes us. One of the most frequent motives is eliminating another male's offspring. Our offender may have believed that getting rid of the baby would solve his problems, he'd be able to forgive her, move on. That didn't happen so he got rid of her, too. Flaunted both victims as a final flourish: Now I'm the master of my own destiny. And by leaving the bodies in proximity he made sure they were connected: This is what she did, this is why she died."

"So why not leave her right next to the bones?"

"Don't know," I said.

"Guess."

"By placing his kills at opposite ends of the park he could've been symbolically laying claim to the entire area. Or I'm over-interpreting and it was a simple matter of expediency: He got distracted or alarmed by someone."

"You guess pretty fast."

"Used to get into trouble in school for that."

"Thought you were Mr. Straight A."

"That annoyed the teachers even more."

This time he produced a complete laugh. "A stepdad, yeah, I like that. But holding on to the bones and fooling with them, you see Mommy going along with that?"

"Who says Mommy knew?"

"She has a baby one day, next day it's gone?"

"What if he forced her to give it up for adoption? As a condition of staying together. Told her he'd handle it and took care of business in a horrible way. Even if she suspected, she could've been too passive or guilty or frightened to do anything about it. Back when I worked at the hospital I can't tell you how many cases I saw where mothers stood by as stepfathers and boyfriends did terrible things to their children, including torture and murder. Any word on the DNA?"

"Maria Thomas emailed an hour ago, wanting me to know she got it prioritized. Like I'm supposed to feel grateful for her allowing me to do my job. Looks like under a week for basic analyses but fancy stuff will take longer."

He took out a cold cigar, propped it between his index fingers. "You ever feel you've had enough of the garbage I send your way?"

"Nah, keeps life interesting."

"Does it?"

"Why the question?"

"Just wondering." He got up, opened the office door, stood gazing out to the corridor, his back to me. "What about Robin? She's okay with it?"

All these years, first time he'd asked.

"Robin's fine."

"And the pooch?"

"Perfectly content. So are the fish. What's going on, Big Guy?"

Long silence.

Then: "What you did for me . . . I'm not gonna forget it."

That sounded more like complaint than gratitude.

I said, "Let's not forget the times you saved my bacon."

"Ancient history."

"Everything ends up as history."

"Then we die."

"That, too."

We both laughed. For lack of anything else.

16

The new murders had nudged the first set of bones off Milo's screen. But I couldn't let go of the baby in the blue box. Kept thinking about Salome Greiner's tension when I'd asked about a Duesenberg-driving doctor.

DMV kept no records of old registrations but a car that rare and collectible couldn't be hard to trace.

Back home, I went straight to my office. The Auburn Cord Duesenberg Club in Indiana had a museum, an online store, and an energetic members forum.

A woman answered the phone, sounding cheerful. I told her what I was looking for and she said, "You're in California?"

"L.A."

"The top Duesenberg expert is right near you, in Huntington Beach."

"Who's that?"

"Andrew Zeiman, he's a master restorer, works on all the serious cars, here's his shop number."

"Appreciate it."

"Was a Duesie involved in a crime?"

"No," I said, "but it might lead to information about a crime."

"Too bad, I was hoping for something juicy. Lots of colorful characters owned our babies—Al Capone, Father Divine, Hearst—but nowadays it's mostly nice people with money and good taste and that can get a little routine. Good luck."

A clipped voice said, "Andy Zeiman."

I began explaining.

He said, "Marcy from ACD just called. You want to locate an SJ for some sort of criminal investigation."

Statement, not a question. Unperturbed.

I said, "If that's possible."

"Anything's possible. Date and model."

"We've been told it was a '38 SJ, blue over blue."

"SJ because it had pipes, right? Problem is you can put pipes on anything. Real SJs are rare."

"Aren't all Duesenbergs?"

"Everything's relative. Total Duesenberg production is four hundred eighty-one, SJs are less than ten percent of that. Most were sold on the East Coast until '32, then the trend shifted out here because that's where the money and the flamboyance were."

"Hollywood types."

"Gable, Cooper, Garbo, Mae West, Tyrone Power. Et cetera."

"How about we start with the real SJs. Is there a listing of original owners?"

"Sure."

"Where can I find it?"

"With me," said Zeiman. "What year does your witness think he saw this supposed SJ?"

"Nineteen fifty, give or take."

"Twelve-year-old car, there'd be a good chance of repaint, so color might not matter. Also, it wasn't uncommon to put new bodies on old chassis. Like a custom-made suit, altered to taste."

"If it helps to narrow things down, the owner may have been a doctor."

"Give me your number, something comes up I'll let you know."

Seven minutes later, he called back. "You might have gotten lucky. I've got a blue/blue Murphy-bodied Dual Cowl Phaeton ordered by a Walter Asherwood in '37, delivered November '38. Murphy body with later enhancement by Bohman and Schwartz. Both were L.A.-based coachbuilders."

"The car started out on the West Coast."

"Yup. Walter Asherwood held on to it until '43, when he transferred ownership to James Asherwood, M.D. Nothing else in the log fits, so it's either this one or your person didn't see a real SJ."

"Where did the Asherwoods live?"

"Can't give you the address because for all I know family members are still living there and we respect privacy."

"Can you give me a general vicinity?"

"L.A."

"Pasadena?"

"You can fish but I won't bite," said Zeiman. "You've got a name, that should be sufficient."

"Fair enough," I said. "Can you tell me who owns the car, now?"

"One of our members."

"Did he or she buy it from Dr. Asherwood?"

"There's a complete chain of ownership but that's all I can say. Why do you need the current owner, anyway?"

"We're trying to trace a dead baby's mother."

"What?"

"The car was seen parked in the driveway of a house where an infant was buried decades ago. The bones were just dug up."

"Dead baby?" said Zeiman. "So we're talking murder."

"That's not clear."

"I don't get it, either it's murder or it's not."

I said, "Depends on cause of death."

"Hold on," he said. "My wife mentioned something about that, she'd heard it on the news. Made her cry. Okay, I'll make some calls."

"Thanks for all the help."

"Most interesting request I've had since two months ago."

"What happened two months ago?"

"Shifty Mideastern type walks into my shop, flashing cash, wants me to build a Frankencar out of retools that he can sell as genuine to a sucker in Dubai. I said no thanks, phoned the Huntington Beach cops, they told me intent's no felony, until a crime was committed there's nothing they can do. That felt wrong to me so I tried the FBI, they didn't even return my call. At least you do your job. So I'll help you."

It took just over an hour to hear back from Zeiman. By then I'd made progress on my own.

A search of *38 duesenberg dual cowl phaeton murphy body* had produced three possibilities. The first was a "barn find" up for auction in Monterey. The once-sleek masterpiece had been the victim of a 1972 engine fire during careless storage in Greenwich, Connecticut. Hobbled by engine rot, char scars, metastatic rust, and a broken axle, it was deemed "ripe for restoration to show condition" and estimated to fetch between six and eight hundred thousand dollars. The auction company's catalog presented a history that included a California stint, up north, under the stewardship of a Mrs. Helen Bracken of Hillsborough. But subsequent owners included neither Walter nor James Asherwood and the original color, still in evidence through the blemishes, was claret over scarlet.

Candidate number two, a black beauty, due to go on the block in Amelia Island, Florida, had accumulated a slew of awards during a pampered life. Five owners: New York, Toronto, Savannah, Miami, Fishers Island.

Bingo came in the form of a car that had taken first place at the Pebble Beach Concourse d'Elegance ten years ago, a gleaming behemoth benefiting from a six-year frame-off restoration by Andrew O. Zeiman.

Program notes from the award ceremony noted that care had been taken to replicate the car's original cerulean/azure paint job as well as the "precise hue of its robin's egg blue convertible roof, now replaced with modern but period-reminiscent materials."

The proud owners were Mr. and Mrs. F. Walker Monahan, Beverly Hills, California. A winners' circle photo showed them to be mid-sixtyish, immaculately turned out, flanked by a burly, white-bearded man. Andrew Zeiman was clad, as was Mr. Monahan, in a straw Borsalino, a navy blazer, pressed khakis, conservative school tie.

I had my eyes on Zeiman's photograph when the phone rang. "It's Andy again." Low-tech Skype. "You must be one of those fortunate sons, maybe we should hit the blackjack tables."

"The case resolves, I might just take you up on that."

"The current owners agreed to talk to you. They're good people."

"Do they remember the Asherwoods?"

"Talk to them," said Zeiman.

CHAPTER

17

Researching the person you're trying to influence is a handy tool when peddling gewgaws, pushing con games, and practicing psychotherapy.

The same goes for witness interviews; before reaching out to the F. Walker Monahans of Beverly Hills, I searched their names on the Web.

Mister sat on the board of two banks and Missus, a woman named Grace, occupied similar positions at the Getty, the Huntington, and the volunteer committee of Western Pediatric Medical Center.

The hospital affiliation made me wonder if she'd be the link to Dr. James Asherwood.

A search of his name pulled up nothing but a twelve-year-old *Times* obituary.

Dr. James Walter Asherwood had passed away of natural causes at his home in La Canada–Flintridge, age eighty-nine. That placed him at forty or so during the period Ellie Green had lived at the house in Cheviot Hills. Easily feasible age for a relationship. For unwanted fatherhood.

Asherwood's bio was brief. Trained at Stanford as an obstetrician-gynecologist, he'd "retired from medicine to pursue the life of a sportsman and financier."

The *Times* hasn't run social pages in a while and being rich and well-born no longer entitles you to an obit. At first glance, nothing in Asherwood's life seemed to justify the paper's attention, but his death was the hook: "A lifelong bachelor, Asherwood had long voiced intentions to bequeath his entire estate to charity. That promise has been kept."

The final paragraph listed beneficiaries of Asherwood's generosity, including several inner-city public schools to which Asherwood had bequeathed a hangarful of vintage automobiles. Western Peds was listed midway through the roster, but unlike the cancer society, Save the Bay, and the graduate nursing program at the old school across town, the hospital wasn't singled out for special largesse.

Fondness for the nursing school because he remembered one particular RN?

Had ob-gyn skills meant detour to a career as an illegal abortionist? Did dropping out of medicine imply guilt? A legal concession as part of a plea deal?

Lifelong bachelor didn't mean loveless. Or childless.

Doctor to financier. Moving *big* money around could mean the ability to purchase just about anything, including that most precious of commodities, silence.

No sense wondering. I called the F. Walker Monahans.

A beautifully inflected female voice said, "Good evening, Doctor, this is Grace. Andy told us you'd be phoning."

No curiosity about a psychologist asking questions on behalf of the police. "Thanks for speaking with me, Mrs. Monahan."

"Of course we'll speak with you." As if a failure to cooperate would've been unpatriotic. "When would you care to drop by?"

"We can chat over the phone."

"About cars?" Her laugh was soft, feline, oddly soothing.

"About a car once owned by Dr. James Asherwood."

"Ah, Blue Belle," she said. "You do know that we've sold her."

"I didn't."

"Oh, yes, a month ago, she'll be shipped in a few weeks. Immediately after Pebble Beach we were besieged with offers but refused. Years later, we're finally ready. Not without ambivalence, but it's time to let someone else enjoy her."

"Where's she going?"

"To Texas, a natural gas man, a very fine person we know from the show circuit. He'll pamper her and drive her with respect, win-win situation for everyone."

"Congratulations."

"We'll miss her," said Grace Monahan. "She's quite remarkable."

"I'll bet."

"If you'd like to pay your respects before she leaves, that can be arranged."

"Appreciate the offer," I said. "If you don't mind, could we talk a bit about Dr. Asherwood?"

"What, in particular, would you like to know?"

"Anything you can tell me about him. And if you're familiar with a woman he knew named Eleanor Green, that would be extremely helpful."

"Well," she said, "this is a person we're going to discuss and that deserves a more personal setting than the phone, don't you think? Why don't you drop by tomorrow morning, say eleven? Where are you located?"

"Beverly Glen."

"We're not far at all, here's the address."

"Thank you, Mrs. Monahan."

"You're quite welcome."

Board seats and ownership of a multimillion-dollar show car had led me to expect residence in Beverly Hills' uppermost echelons. A manse at the northern edge of the flats, or one of the mammoth estates nestled in the hillocks above Sunset.

The address Grace Monahan gave me was on South Rodeo Drive, a pleasant but low-key neighborhood well away from the try-too-hard glitz and glassy-eyed tourism of the twenty-four-karat shopping district.

The numbers matched a nondescript, two-story, not-quite-Colonial apartment building on a block of similar structures, shadowed by the white marble monument on Wilshire that was Saks Fifth Avenue.

Monahan: 2A. A once-wealthy couple who'd fallen on hard times? The real reason for selling the blue Duesenberg?

I climbed white-painted concrete steps to a skimpy landing ringed by three units. The wooden door to 2A was open but blocked by a screen door. No entry hall meant a clear view into a low, dim living room. Music and the smell of coffee blew through the mesh. Two people sat on a tufted floral sofa. The woman got up and unlatched the screen.

"Doctor? Grace."

Five and a half feet tall in spangled ballet slippers, Grace Monahan wore a peach-colored velvet jumpsuit and serious gold jewelry at all the pressure points. Her hair was subtly hennaed, thick and straight, reaching an inch below her shoulder blades. Her makeup was discreet, highlighting clear, wide brown eyes. The Pebble Beach photo was a decade old but she hadn't aged visibly. Nothing to do with artifice; smile lines and crow's-feet abounded, along with the inevitable loosening of flesh that either softens a face or blurs it, depending on self-esteem at seventy.

The duration and warmth of Grace Monahan's smile said life was just grand in her eighth decade. One of those women who'd been a knockout from birth and had avoided addiction to youth.

She took my hand and drew me inside. "Do come in. Some coffee? We get ours from Santa Fe, it's flavored with piñon, if you haven't tried it, you must."

"I've had it, am happy to repeat the experience."

"You know Santa Fe?"

"Been there a couple of times."

"We winter there because we love clean snow—have a seat, please. Anywhere is fine."

Anywhere consisted of a pair of brocade side chairs or the floral sofa where her husband remained planted as he continued watching a financial show on the now muted TV. Still canted away from me, he gave an obligatory wave.

Grace Monahan said, "Felix."

He quarter-turned. "Sorry, just a second."

"Felix?"

"A sec, sweetie, I want to see what Buffett's up to, now that he's a celebrity."

"You and Buffett." Grace Monahan completed the three steps required to transition to a tiny kitchenette. She fiddled with a drip percolator.

I sat there as Felix Walker Monahan attended to stock quotes scrolling along the bottom of the screen. Above the numbers, a talking head ranted mutely about derivatives. Watching without sound didn't seem to bother Felix Monahan. Maybe he was a good lip-reader. The same tolerance applied to TV reception that turned to snow every few moments. The set was a convex-screened RCA in a case the size of a mastiff's doghouse. Topped by rabbit ears.

The room was warm, slightly close, filled with well-placed furniture, old, not antique. Three small paintings on the walls: two florals and a soft-focus portrait of a beautiful, round-faced child. Great color and composition and the signature was the same; if these were real Renoirs, they could finance another show car.

The blowhard on the screen pointed to a graph, loosened his tie, continued to vent. Felix Walker Monahan chuckled.

His wife said, "What can you get out of it without hearing it?"

"Think of it as performance art, sweetie." He switched off, swiveled toward me.

Unlike his wife, he'd changed a lot since Pebble Beach: smaller, paler, less of a presence. Scant white hair was combed back from a wrinkled-paper visage that would've looked good under a powdered wig or gracing coinage. He wore a gray silk shirt, black slacks, gray-black-checked Converse sneakers sans socks. The skin of his ankles was dry, chafed, lightly bruised. His hands vibrated with minor palsy.

He said, "Jimmy Asherwood, fine man. Better than fine, first-rate."

"Did you buy the Duesenberg from him?"

He grinned. "Even better, he gave it to us. To Gracie, actually. She was his favorite niece, I lucked out. When I met her I knew nothing about cars or much else. Jimmy's collection was quite the education."

His wife said, "I was his favorite niece because I was his only niece. My father was Jack Asherwood, Jimmy's older brother. Jimmy was the doctor, Dad was the lawyer."

Felix said, "If Jimmy had twenty nieces, you'd still be his favorite."

"Oh, my." She laughed. "I already give you everything you want, why bother?"

"Keeping in practice for when you finally say no."

"Scant chance—here's coffee."

"Let me help you," he said.

"Don't you dare be getting up."

"Oh, boy," he said. "Starting to feel like a cripple."

"The difference, Felix, is that cripples remain crippled while you can be up and around soon enough. *If* you follow orders."

"Hear, hear," he said. To me: "Had surgery five weeks ago. You don't want to know the details."

Grace said, "He certainly *doesn't.*"

"Let's just say plumbing issues and leave it at that."

"*Felix.*"

He rotated his arm. "They cored and bored me, like an engine. Roto-Rooter wasn't picking up their messages so I had to go to a urologist."

"*Fee-lix!* TMI."

"What's that mean, sweetie?"

"Don't play innocent with me, young man. The grandkids always say it when you're overdoing."

"Ah," he said. "Too Many Issues."

"Exactly." She brought a silver tray holding three coffees and a box of cookies. "Pepperidge Farm Milano Mints, Doctor. Cream?"

"Black's fine."

Pouring, she sat down next to her husband. They lifted their cups but waited until I'd sipped.

I said, "Delicious. Thanks."

Felix said, "Here's to another day aboveground."

"So dramatic," said Grace, but her voice caught.

I said, "Nice paintings."

"They're all we have room for, I don't like crowding, art needs room to breathe." She sipped. "In Santa Fe we have oodles of wall space but not being there much of the year we don't like to hang anything too serious."

"In S.F., we patronize the local artists," said Felix. "Nice level of talent but not much in the way of investment."

"Life's about more than compound interest, dear."

"So you keep telling me."

I said, "Have you lived here long?"

"Ten years."

"Bought the building fifteen years ago," said Felix. "Followed it up by buying the rest of this side of the block."

"There you go again," said Grace. "Making like a tycoon."

"Just citing facts, sweetie." Working to steady his hand, he put his cup down. Bone china rattled. Coffee sloshed and spilled. His lips moved the same way Milo's do when he wants to curse.

Grace Monahan bit her lip, returned to smiling at nothing in particular.

Felix Monahan said, "The original plan was to tear the entire block down and build one big luxury condo but the city proved obdurate so we kept the block as is and went into the landlord business. The last thing on our minds was actually moving here, we had a fine Wallace Neff on Mountain Drive above Sunset. Then our daughter moved to England and we said, what do we need thirty rooms for, let's downsize.

The house sold quickly, those were the days, caught us off-guard and we hadn't found a new one. This apartment was vacant so we said let's bunk down temporarily."

Grace said, "We found out we liked the simplicity and here we are."

"Tell him the real reason, sweetie."

"Convenience, darling?"

"Walking distance to shopping for someone who's not me. By the way, Neiman phoned. They're prepared to offer you a daily chauffeur if strolling three blocks proves too strenuous."

"Stop being terrible, Felix." To me: "I buy only for the grandkids. We're in our post-acquisitional stage."

I said, "Perfect time to sell the car."

Felix said, "On the contrary, perfect time to keep it. And all the others. One day the entire collection will go to a deserving museum, but Blue Belle is taking her leave because we believe cars are to be driven and she's gotten too valuable for that." His eyes softened. "She's lovely."

I said, "Dr. Asherwood was a generous man."

"*Generous* doesn't do him justice," said Grace. "Uncle Jimmy was selfless and I mean that literally. Nothing for himself, everything for others. He left every penny to charity and no one was resentful because we respected him, he'd given us so much during his lifetime."

"I read about the donations in his obituary."

"His obituary doesn't begin to describe it, Dr. Delaware. Well before Jimmy passed he was giving away money and things."

I said, "I used to work at Western Pediatric and I noticed the hospital on the list of beneficiaries. Did he attend there?"

"No," she said, "but he cared about the little ones." Scooting back on the couch, she sat up straight. "Why are you curious about him?"

Her voice remained pleasant but her stare was piercing.

Know the person you want to influence. The real reason *she'd* wanted a face-to-face.

I said, "Did you read about a baby's skeleton being dug up in Cheviot Hills?"

"That? Yes, I did, tragic. What in the world would Jimmy have to do with such a thing?"

"Probably nothing," I said. "The burial date was traced to a period when a woman named Eleanor Green lived in the house."

I waited for a reaction. Grace Monahan remained still. Felix's hand seemed to shake a bit more.

He said, "You think this woman was the mother?"

"If we could learn more about her, we might find out," I said. "Unfortunately, she seems to be somewhat of a phantom—no public records, no indication where she went after moving. Dr. Asherwood's name came up because his Duesenberg was spotted parked in her driveway on more than one occasion."

Grace said, "Eleanor Green. No, doesn't ring a bell." She turned to her husband.

"Hmm . . . don't believe so."

His palsy had definitely grown more pronounced. Her fingers had stiffened.

She said, "Sorry we can't help you, Doctor. Jimmy knew lots of women. He was an extremely handsome man."

She crossed the room to a low bookshelf, took out a leather album, paged through and handed it to me.

The man in the scallop-edged black-and-white photo was tall, narrow, fine-featured, with a downy pencil mustache under an upturned nose and pale, downslanted eyes. He wore a cinch-waisted, pin-striped, double-breasted suit, black-and-white wingtips, a polka-dot handkerchief that threatened to tumble from his breast pocket, a soft fedora set slightly askew. He'd been photographed leaning against the swooping front fender of a low-slung, bubble-topped coupe.

"Not the Duesenberg, obviously," said Felix Monahan. "That's a Talbot-Lago. Jimmy brought it over from France immediately after the war. It was decaying in some Nazi bastard's lair, Jimmy rescued it and brought it back to life."

Grace said, "He was barely out of med school when he enlisted, was assigned to an infantry unit as a field surgeon, served in the Battle of the Bulge, raided Utah Beach. He was injured on D-Day, earned a Purple Heart and a host of other medals."

"A hero," said Felix. "The real deal."

Grace said, "Now, would you like to see Blue Belle? She's downstairs in the garage."

As smooth a dismissal as any I'd heard. I said, "She's here?"

"Why not?" said Felix. "A garage is a garage."

"Is a garage," said Grace. "To paraphrase Alice B. Toklas."

I said, "I'd love to see the car but could we talk a bit more?"

"About what?"

"Your uncle's medical practice."

"There's nothing to talk about. After his wounds healed, he delivered babies."

"Then he quit," I said.

"No," she said, "he retired. Quitting implies a character flaw. Jimmy left medicine because his father, my grandfather Walter, was ill and his mother, my nana Beatrice, was terminal. Someone had to take care of them."

"Jimmy had no wife or children."

Quick glances passed between them.

"That's true," said Grace. "If you ask me why I'll tell you I don't know, it was none of my business."

"Never met the right woman," said Felix. "That would be my guess."

"That's not what he's after, darling. He's looking for dirt on poor Jimmy."

"Not at all, Mrs. Monahan."

"No?" she said. "You work with the police, they dig dirt—granted it's generally for a good cause. You've been involved in over a score of very nasty cases, have probably come to see the world as a terrible place. But that doesn't apply to Jimmy."

A score. Serious research on her part.

I said, "I'd like to think I keep a pretty balanced view of the world."

Rosy spots radiated through her makeup. "Forgive me, that was rude. It's just that I adored Uncle Jimmy. And—I confess to being a bit of a snoop myself, Dr. Delaware. After you called, I inquired about you at Western Peds. We donate there. Everyone had good things to say about you. That's why we're talking." She caught her breath. "If that offends you, I'm sorry."

"Girl Scout heritage," said Felix. "Be prepared and all that."

"Brownie," she corrected. "But yes, I do respect a logical plan. As I'm sure you do, Dr. Delaware. But trust me, Jimmy led a quiet, noble life and I can't have his name sullied."

"Mrs. Monahan, I'm sorry if I—"

"Actually," Felix broke in, "it's Doctor Monahan."

"No, it's not!" she snapped.

He flinched.

She said, "Sorry, darling, sorry," and touched his hand. He remained still. "Forgive me, Felix, but all this talk about Uncle Jimmy has made me edgy."

He said, "Nothing to forgive, sweetie." To me: "She doesn't like tooting her own horn but she *is* a doctor. Full M.D., trained and qualified. Women's medicine, same as Jimmy."

"Not to be contentious," she said, "but a doctor is someone who doctors. I never practiced. Got married during my last year of residency, had Catherine, said I'd go back but I never did. There was more than a bit of guilt about that, I felt I'd let everyone down. Especially Jimmy because it was he who'd written a personal letter to the dean, back then women weren't exactly welcomed with open arms. After I decided to eschew medicine, it was Jimmy I talked to. He told me to live my life the way I wanted. In any event, if you need me to tend to your ills, you're in trouble. Now, since you probably have no serious interest in seeing Blue Belle—"

"I do."

"Don't be polite, Dr. Delaware, we don't force our enthusiasms on anyone."

"Never seen a Duesenberg," I said. "I'd be foolish to pass up the opportunity."

Felix Monahan stood with effort. "I'll take him, sweetie."

"Absolutely not," said Grace. "I can't have you—"

"I'm *taking* him. *Darling.*"

"Felix—"

"Grace, I have yet to convince myself I'm a fully functional human being but if you could pretend it would be an enormous help."

"You don't need to prove anything—"

"But I do," he said in a new voice: low, flat, cold. "I most certainly do."

He walked toward the door, slowly, overly deliberate, like a drunk coping with a sobriety test.

Grace Monahan stood there, as if daring him to continue. He opened the door and said, "Come, Doctor."

She said, "Hold his arm."

Felix Monahan turned and glared. "Not necessary. *Sweet*heart."

He left the apartment. I followed.

Grace said, "Men."

I trailed Felix Monahan down the stairs to the sidewalk, sticking close and watching him sway and lurch and intentionally ignore the handrail.

Midway down he tripped and I reached out to steady him. He shook me off. "Appreciate the offer but if you do it again, I might just acquaint you with my left jab."

Laughing but not kidding.

I said, "You boxed?"

"Boxed, did some Greco-Roman wrestling, a bit of judo."

"I get the point."

"Smart man."

When we reached the street, he continued south, turned the corner at Charleville, and entered the alley behind his building. Six garages, one for each unit, each furnished with a bolt and a combination lock.

The third garage was secured with an additional key lock. Keeping me out of view, Monahan twirled, inserted a key, stood back. "Slide it up, I'm smart enough to know my limitations."

The door rose on smooth, greased bearings, curved inward and upward, exposing two hundred square feet of pristine white space filled with something massive and blue and stunning.

A gleaming vertically barred grille stared me in the face. The radiator cap was a sharp-edged V aimed for takeoff.

The car was huge, barely fitting into the space. Most of the length was taken up by a hood fashioned to accommodate a gargantuan engine. Headlights the size of dinner plates stared at me like the eyes of a giant squid. Hand-sculpted, wing-like fenders merged with polished running boards topped by gleaming metal tread-plates. A side-mounted spare matched four wide-wall, wire-wheeled tires. The car's flanks were fluid and arrogant.

"Supercharged," said Felix Monahan, pointing to a quartet of chrome pipes looping out of a chrome-plated grid. Thick and sinewy and menacing as a swarm of morays. "We're talking zero to sixty in eight seconds in the thirties."

I whistled.

He went on: "She cruises at one oh four in second gear and that's without syncromesh. Max speed is one forty, and back when she was born you were lucky to get fifty horsepower out of a luxury car."

"Unbelievable," I said.

"Not really, Doctor. What's unbelievable is how a country that could create this can't come up with anything better than plastic phones that die in six months. Put together by peasants living on gruel."

I'd come to see the car in the hope that I might pry more info from him. But the Duesenberg's beauty held me captive. The paint, a perfect duet of convivial blues, was a masterpiece of lacquer. The interior was butter-soft, hand-stitched leather whose pale aqua hue matched the spotless top. More artisanal metalwork for the sculpted dashboard. The rosewood-and-silver steering wheel would've looked dandy on a museum pedestal.

Even silent and static, the car managed to project an aura of ferocity and mastery. The kind of queenly confidence you see in a certain type of woman, able to work natural beauty to her advantage without flirting or raising her voice.

I said, "Thanks for giving me the opportunity."

Felix Monahan said, "You can thank me by dropping the whole notion of Jimmy Asherwood being some sort of criminal. A, he isn't, and B, I don't like anything that upsets my wife."

"No one's out to—"

He stopped me with a palm. "That woman you mentioned—Green—I can't tell you about her because I don't know her and I'm sure that applies to Grace. However, I did know Jimmy and there's zero chance he fathered that baby or had anything to do with its death."

"Okay."

"That doesn't sound sincere."

"I—"

"When Grace inquired about you, she was told you're quite the brilliant fellow, had a promising academic career that you traded, for some reason, for immersing yourself in the lowest elements of society—hear me out, I'm not judging you, as Jimmy told Grace, everyone should live their own life. But now I see you as intruding on Grace's life and that worries me because of something else your former colleagues said: You never let go."

I kept silent.

He said, "Close the garage."

After he locked up, he faced me. His eyes were slits, and the tremor in his hands was mimicked by quivers along his jawline.

"Mr. Monahan, I'm—"

"Listen carefully, young man: Jimmy didn't father that child or any other. He was incapable."

"Sterile?"

"Grace doesn't know. But I do, because Jimmy was like an older brother to me and he could confide in me in a way he couldn't with Grace because I was able to keep my emotions in check. He and I used to motor together, drive out to where he stored his cars, pick one on a whim and go hit some great, dusty roads. One day we were out in his '35 Auburn Boattail Speedster. Motoring in Malibu, up in the hills, in those days it was brush and scrub. The Auburn chewed up the asphalt, glorious thing, Jimmy and I took turns behind the wheel. We stopped for a smoke and a nip—nothing extreme, a taste from the hip flask and a couple of fine Havanas at a spot where the ocean was visible. Jimmy seemed more relaxed than I'd ever seen him. Then all of a sudden, he said, 'Felix, people think I'm homosexual, don't they? Because I like art and going to the ballet and have never married.' What do you say to something like that? The truth was he was right. Jimmy was regarded as what was then called 'sensitive.' Apart from cars, his interests were feminine."

"The paper described him as a sportsman."

"The paper relied on information provided by Grace. The only sport I ever saw Jimmy engage in was a spot of polo in Montecito and not much of that. Now, there's nothing wrong with liking *Die Fleder-maus,* but combine that with his never marrying—never showing interest in women—it was a reasonable conclusion. But what I said was, 'Jimmy, that's rot.' To which he said, 'You're not a fool, Felix. You never wondered?' I said, 'Your business is your own, Jimmy.' To which he replied, 'So you believe it, too.' I protested and he laughed that off, stood and proceeded to unbuckle his belt and lower his trousers and his shorts."

His eyes clamped shut. "Terrible sight. He'd been mangled. Shrapnel flyoff from a land mine on D-Day. Larger pieces and he'd have been sheared in two, fortunately he survived. However, the shards that did find their way into his body left hideous scars on his legs. And nothing much in the way of manhood."

"Poor man."

"When I saw it, Dr. Delaware, I couldn't help myself, I cried like a baby. Not my style, when my *mother* passed I held myself in check. But Jimmy like that?"

Long sigh. "He pulled up his trousers and smiled and said, 'So you see, Felix, it's not for lack of interest, it's for lack of equipment.' Then he took a long swallow from the flask—emptied it—said, 'You drive home.'"

Monahan placed both hands to his temples. "Jimmy was a man's man. And you need to honor that and vow to not repeat this to anyone because if Grace ever learned the truth and that I was the one who told you, it would destroy her and do irreparable harm to my marriage."

"I promise, Mr. Monahan. But there's something you need to consider: The lieutenant I work with is honorable and discreet, but he's also extremely persistent and left to his own devices he may eventually trace the car back to Jimmy, as I did. I have credibility with him and if I'm allowed to give him some basic details, it's unlikely you'll ever hear from him."

"Unlikely," he said. "But you can't guarantee."

"I'm being honest, Mr. Monahan."

"You're a psychologist, sir. Your allegiance should be building people up, not tearing them down."

"I agree."

"What would you like to tell this policeman?"

"That Jimmy was a good man whose war injuries prevented him from fathering a child. That most of his life seems to have centered around good deeds."

"Not most," said Felix Monahan. "All. A purer soul never walked this earth."

His eyes swept over my face, thorough as a CAT scanner. "I choose to consider you a man of honor."

"I appreciate that."

"Show your appreciation by doing the right thing."

18

A call to the development office at Western Peds added focus to Dr. James Asherwood's generosity. Back in the sixties he'd endowed a small fund for the neonatal ICU.

Special concern for problem newborns on the part of a man unable to father children. A man who worked ob-gyn at a place where covert abortions were standard operating procedure.

How that connected to a baby buried under a tree eluded me.

That night the big blue Duesenberg didn't appear in my dream but a cream-colored Auburn Boattail Speedster did. No reason to believe Jimmy Asherwood's had been that color but I'd pulled up images on the Web, supplied my own script and scenery.

In the dream, Asherwood and a young Felix Monahan, who bore a striking resemblance to me in my twenties, roared up a series of dusty, sun-splotched canyons that snaked through the Santa Monica Mountains.

The ride ended with a smoke and a nip from a silver flask at a spot where the ocean grew vast. Then a return ride that felt more like aerial gliding than motoring.

When Asherwood dropped me at the dingy apartment building on Overland that had housed me during starving-student days, he tipped his fedora and saluted and I did the same and I assured him I'd never betray him.

His smile was blinding. "I trust you, Alex."

The following morning Milo dropped in at nine o'clock.

Robin had left early for a trip to Temecula, visiting an old Italian violin-maker who'd finally retired and was parting with maple, ebony, and ivory. I was sitting at the kitchen table reviewing a custody report that had a decent chance of being read because the judge was a decent human being. Blanche curled at my feet relishing the shallow sleep of dogs, snoring gently. She sensed Milo's presence before the door opened, was up on her feet waiting for him.

He said, "Ah, the security system," patted her head, placed his attaché case on the table, and sat down.

No fridge-scavenge. Maybe he'd eaten a big breakfast.

"Time for current events, class." Out of the case came a rolled-up newspaper. The masthead read:

The Corsair
The voice of Santa Monica College

A pair of articles shared the front page: a feature on renewed interest in the benefits of high colonics and "SMC Student Plays Crucial Role in Westside Murder."

Heather Goldfeder's headshot was accurately elfin. The slant was her "extreme bravery after coming across a hideously slain homicide corpse as she trained for a marathon in Cheviot Park. 'What made it worse,' said the SMC freshman, 'was this wasn't the first murder in my neighborhood, a little baby skeleton was also found in the park and there was also another baby dug up real close to where I live. Though I heard that one was real old.'"

I said, "Let's hear it for freedom of the press. Maria know yet?"

"She woke me at six, was spewing like I've never heard her. I told her it hadn't come from me, she said she didn't believe me, I said feel free to waste time investigating. Then she started in on how it was my responsibility to muzzle my witness and I said last I heard gag orders came from judges."

He put the paper away. "The one who's *really* got steam coming out of her ears is that *Times* gal, LeMasters. She left a message an hour ago using naughty words and accusing me of allowing *this* august publication to scoop her, probably because I have a kid who goes there."

He went to the fridge, searched a top shelf.

I said, "Any tips come in?"

"Nothing serious yet, and I don't think there will be unless Flower Dress's picture goes public. Still waiting to hear back from Maria on that."

He tried a lower tier. "What's with you guys, no leftovers?"

"We've been eating out."

"Not even a doggie bag? Oh, yeah, that's not a dog, it's an alien princess who won't touch her foie gras unless it's been consecrated by a celebrity chef. Am I right about that, mademoiselle?"

Blanche trotted up to him, cocked her head to the side.

Grumbling about his back, he bent low to rub behind her ears. She rolled over and exposed her belly. He murmured something about "Entitlement." She purred. "Nice to see my charm transcends gender."

I said, "She's a happy girl. Had lamb chop leftovers last night."

"Don't gloat, Dr. De Sade." He foraged some more, returned with a half pint of cottage cheese and a bottle of KC Masterpiece Original Barbecue Sauce that he glurped directly into the container, concocting a mélange that evoked something you'd find at a shotgun homicide.

Three tablespoons later: "Got the DNA results on everything. Nothing in the old bones, too degraded, but plenty in the new bones: The baby's mommy had some African American heritage so Flower Dress wasn't her. So much for the mother-child-bad-daddy theory. Any suggestions?"

"Nothing that would make you feel better."

"Try me."

"Take away the family angle and you could have an offender who murders all kinds of people for motives you won't understand until you catch him."

"A pleasure killer," he said. "Gets off on amateur taxidermy. I was hoping you wouldn't say that, knew you would." His eyes dropped to the cottage cheese container. He downed another spoonful of clotted red soup. First time I'd seen him grimace after ingesting anything.

Dumping the mixture in the trash, he drank water from the tap. "So what's my plan, just wait and hope this nutcase screws up on the next one?"

"You could put the park under surveillance."

"You think he'd actually go back?"

"Nothing succeeds like success."

"Well," he said, "the best I can do for surveillance is a couple of additional drive-bys per shift by sector cars. I know 'cause I've already asked, great minds and all that . . . maybe I'll do an all-nighter . . . God, I'm hungry, how long will it take you to defrost a steak? Or a roast? Or half a cow?"

His phone chirped Ravel's "Bolero." He picked up, flashed a V. "That's great, sir, I apprec—" The victory sign wilted as he listened for a long time.

He put the phone down and drank more water at the sink.

I said, "His Godliness ranting?"

"Lower the volume, it woulda been a rant. 'Well, Sturgis, looks like your fucking victim is gonna be a fucking reality star for fifteen fucking minutes so get a decent fucking photo of her fucking dead face because you've got one fucking shot at this. And you better fucking be able to do something with it because I just swallowed a whole lot of fucking bullshit from a fucking piece-of-shit politician who's got fucking White House connections.' "

I said, "When will the photo run?"

"Tonight at six. If I get my fucking ass in gear." He smiled. "I believe I will."

◆

Ten-second flash at the tail end of the news. Three hours later, Milo phoned, exuberant. "Her name's Adriana Betts and she's originally from Boise. A cousin from Downey saw it and recognized her, called Adriana's sister back in Idaho, the sister called me, emailed a photo. She's flying down tomorrow, I booked Interrogation B at the Butler Avenue Hilton."

"Did the sister have anything interesting to say about Adriana?"

"Wonderful person, not an enemy in the world, how could this happen, why do bad things happen to good people."

That got me thinking about Jimmy Asherwood and I was hit with a strange, aching sympathy for a man I'd never known.

"Alex? You there?"

"Pardon?"

"I asked if you can make it tomorrow for the sister and you didn't answer. Three p.m."

"Yes," I said.

"My favorite word."

19

No DNA was needed to link Helene Johanson's chromosomes to those of Adriana Betts.

Four years older than Adriana, Helene had a pleasant, square face, solid build, and chestnut hair that made her a near-twin to her sister. Watching her step into the interview room was unsettling: a dead woman come to life.

The match didn't extend to style. Adriana had been found wearing a loose dress and budget shoes, both tagged by the coroner as "Walmart, made in China." Helene's preferences ran to designer jeans with rhinestone accents, a formfitting black ribbed top under a fringed caramel suede jacket, snakeskin cowboy boots. Her nails were polished rose-pink. The diamond studs in her ears looked real. So did the Lady Rolex on her left wrist and the Gucci bag from which she pulled out a silk, lace-edged handkerchief.

HAJ monogram on one corner. She took in the room, dried a corner of one eye.

Milo said, "Thanks for getting here so quickly, Ms. Johanson. I'm sorry it had to be for such a terrible reason."

Helene Johanson said, "I'm sure you hear this all the time but I can't believe this is real."

"I hear it often, ma'am, but that doesn't make it any less true. Are you able to talk about Adriana?"

"I'm here," she said, with no conviction. "I guess it's better than watching the bulls get castrated."

"Pardon?"

"We ranch beef cattle outside of Bliss. Red and Black Angus for the organic market. This is the week some of the boys become less-than-boys. The noise and the smell are terrible, I always leave. But I'd rather be doing that than *this*." She slapped the handkerchief on the table. "Lieutenant, what happened to my *sister*?"

"What we know so far is she was shot in a park."

"During the day?"

"At night, ma'am."

"That makes absolutely no sense," said Helene Johanson. "What would Adriana be doing in a park at night? Did she make a wrong turn into a slum or something?"

"Actually, it's a very nice neighborhood. A place called Cheviot Park. Did Adriana ever mention it?"

"No, she didn't mention L.A., period. Why would she? She lived in San Diego."

"Really," said Milo. "When did she move there?"

"Around a year ago. Before that, she was a year in Portland. Why would she be in a park in L.A.?"

"Did she know anyone here?"

"Not that she ever mentioned."

"What brought her to San Diego?"

"Same thing as Portland," said Johanson. "A job. Babysitting. Not like a teenager doing it part-time, a real job, working for a family. She loved it. Loved children." Her face crumpled. "Now she'll never have any of her own—can I call my husband?"

"Sure," said Milo.

She took a while to locate her cell in her purse, speed-dialed, spoke to "Danny" and cried.

When she hung up, Milo said, "Ms. Johanson, anything you can tell us about Adriana will be helpful. The kind of person she was, who her friends were."

"The kind of person she was . . . is a good person. A wonderful person. There wasn't a mean cell in Adriana's body. She was kind and sincere. Very religious. We were brought up Methodist but she went for something more intense. Religion was important to her. She taught Sunday school. Preschoolers—she *always* loved the little ones."

"In terms of her friends—"

"Her church group. Even before she switched. She always hung with the good kids."

"Who'd she hang with in California?"

She twisted a diamond stud. "I guess this is the point where I tell you we weren't close. And feel crappy about it. The entire flight I was thinking of why I didn't pay Adriana more attention. Even if she didn't ask for it, I should've included her more . . . I'm sorry, I don't know. Don't know much about her life since she left Idaho."

"Why'd she leave Portland?"

"The people she worked for couldn't afford her. Adriana had grown attached to the little boy but there was no choice."

"Did she get her jobs through an employment agency?"

"Couldn't tell you."

Milo said, "Do you have her address? In Portland, as well, if you recall."

Head shake. "Sorry."

"What about a phone number?"

"All she gave me was her cell." She scrolled her own phone, read off the number. Not committed to memory; the sisters hadn't talked often.

Milo said, "Did she tell you anything about her San Diego employers?"

"They were doctors—medical professors."

I said, "At UC San Diego?"

"All she told me was one of them did research on cancer, Adriana was impressed by that. But I can't tell you if it was the husband or the wife."

"Was she happy with the job?"

"Adriana was happy about everything, she was a happy person—oh, here's something, the little girl was adopted. Korean or Chinese, some kind of Asian." Her eyes brightened. "Oh, yeah, her name was May, Adriana said she was adorable."

"How long ago did you have that conversation?"

Helene Johanson's eyes wandered. "Too long ago. Right after she started."

Milo said, "This may sound like a stupid question, ma'am, but did Adriana have any enemies?"

"No, everyone loved Adriana. And I can't see her falling in with a bad crowd, that wasn't her. She liked quiet things, reading, crocheting—she'd make blankets for her church friends' babies."

"What about her personal relationships?"

"With men?"

"Yes."

"She had a boyfriend in high school. Dwayne Hightower, his family farmed a big spread near where Danny and I run our Angus. Great family, everyone thought Dwayne and Adriana would be married after high school graduation. Then Dwayne got himself killed in a tractor accident and Adriana never wanted to date." She sniffled. "All those years doing for others. It's so unfair."

"I'm sorry, ma'am."

"When Dwayne died, it's like Adriana pulled away. Drew into herself. But then she came out of it and it was the same old Adriana, cheerful, happy, helping others."

"Resilient," I said.

"You bet."

"But no interest in dating."

"It wasn't for lack of guys trying. Then they stopped, I guess they got the message."

"Was there anyone in particular who might've felt rejected?"

"One of those crazy stalker things? No way."

"Would your parents have any additional—"

"They're gone," she said. "Cancer, both. Danny thinks it was the radon in the basement and I think he might be right. Because Mom and Dad went within nineteen months of each other and there was definitely radon, Danny had it measured. So we'd know if our kids could be safe. They didn't find a lot but there was some. I wanted Adriana to sell the house and keep all the money. Danny and I sell every pound of meat we raise and we're also getting good money for bones and skin and renderable fat. So I wanted Adriana to get the house but she said it belonged to both of us by right, she wouldn't take extra."

"What happened to the house after Adriana moved to Portland?"

"We sold it, by the time taxes and the mortgage were paid, there really wasn't much left."

I said, "Any reason Adriana took jobs outside of Boise?"

"She told me it was time to travel, see what was out there. I said, why don't you go all the way, do something crazy, check out Europe? Danny and I love to travel, we cruise, last year we saw the coast of Italy, it was amazing." She smiled. "I guess the West Coast was adventure enough for Adriana." She bit her lip. "Now I guess I have to look? To identify her?"

"That won't be necessary, Ms. Johanson."

"No?"

"We know who she is."

"Oh, okay, so how does it work? Do I take her back with me?"

"Eventually but not quite yet, Ms. Johanson."

"She's being autopsied?"

"Yes, ma'am."

"When will that be finished?"

"Within a few days."

"Then what?"

Milo said, "You'll be informed and given a list of local undertakers who can help you through the process. They'll take care of everything."

"I guess I'll bury her next to Mom and Dad . . . there's a space. Two, one for each of us."

I said, "No other sibs?"

"Nope, just Adriana and me . . . I'll tell her pastor, I'm sure he'll want to do some kind of memorial."

Milo said, "Could we have his name, please?"

"Pastor Goleman. Life Tabernacle Church of the Fields. Any recommendations for picking an undertaker, Lieutenant Sturgis?"

"They're all good, ma'am."

"Six of one, half dozen of the other? Okay, I guess I'll fly back, you tell me when I can have my sister."

"Do you need a ride to the airport?"

"No, I reserved a car and driver for all day."

"When's your flight?"

"Whenever I want." She looked away. "I'm leaving from Van Nuys, we own a small plane—a tiny little jet, you can't even stand up in it, nothing fancy. We use it for business, visiting the various cattle auctions and semen dealers and whatnot."

"Makes sense," said Milo.

"Efficient. That's what Danny says, though between us, I think he just wanted his own plane. I thought I'd be bringing Adriana back with me, talked to the pilot about there being room in the hold, he said there was." She swiped at her eyes. "I guess I'll be going home alone."

20

Adriana Betts's cell phone registration traced to an address in Portland but her recent billing had gone to a Mailboxes Galore in a La Jolla strip mall. Milo began the paperwork for subpoenaing the records, then tried the mail drop.

The clerk said, "Let me check . . . here we go, Betts. Closed three months ago."

"Any idea why?"

"We don't ask."

"She leave a forwarding?"

"Let me check . . . nope, just a close-down."

"Was she all paid up?"

"To the day," said the clerk. "That's pretty cool."

"What is?"

"Someone being honest."

I said, "La Jolla makes sense if she was working for two doctors. Big medical town. And a pair of physicians would be less likely to run out of nanny money."

"Med school's a big place," he said. "You have any contacts?"

"A few in Pediatrics, but the sister said cancer research so I'd try Oncology first."

"Sister didn't know much, did she? Maybe Adriana didn't want her to. Why would a church girl need a P.O.B.?"

I said, "Church girl with a secret life?"

"She didn't die pretty."

An outraged activist might call that blaming the victim. Anyone with homicide experience would call it logic.

He read off the Portland address on the cell registration. "Let's talk to these people, first."

Susan Van Dyne worked as a reference librarian at the Multnomah County Library, Main Branch. Bradley Van Dyne was in human resources at a start-up software company. Both had Facebook pages that showed them as bespectacled towheads with an interest in snow sports. Their only child was a three-year-old named Lucas, already wearing glasses. In one of several posted photos, Adriana Betts could be seen holding the boy on her knee.

Everyone smiling, Adriana's grin the widest. She had on the same dress she'd died in. Lucas grasped her finger with a tiny hand. Child and nanny appeared in love. So far, I believed everything Adriana had told her sister.

The Van Dynes' number was listed. They gasped in unison when Milo told them about the murder.

"My God, my God," said Susan. "Adriana was a gem. We so regretted having to let her go."

"Why did you?"

Bradley said, "Lost my job, couldn't afford her anymore. When the HR department gets reamed, you know the company's terminal. And guess what? They bellied up ten days after I got my pink slip."

Susan said, "With Bradley staying home it didn't make sense."

"I became Mr. Mom," said Bradley. "Not my finest hour, I'm finally bringing in a paycheck again. Poor Adriana, I can't believe anyone would hurt her. Was it a random thing? 'Cause it's not like she traveled the fast lane."

"No partying?" I said.

"Her? She made us look like night-lifers and trust me, we're not."

Susan said, "She had her evenings to herself but never went out. All she wanted to do was read and watch TV and crochet. She made three lovely blankets for Lucas. Oh, God, he'd be so sad if he knew."

Milo said, "Did Adriana have any friends?"

"None that we ever met."

Bradley said, "She actually told me her best friend was Lucas."

Susan said, "She and Lucas really bonded. She had great instincts, could get down and play at his level. He still asks about her. Letting her go wasn't easy."

"How'd she react to that?"

Bradley said, "No drama, it was like she'd expected it. I'd been bitching for a while about the company having problems."

Susan said, "To tell you the kind of person she was, we offered her an extra month's severance. She refused to take it, said we needed it to tide ourselves over."

I said, "That's pretty close to saintly."

Bradley said, "You could describe her as saintly. That's why it doesn't make sense, someone killing her."

Susan said, "Maybe not, Brad."

"What do you mean?"

"Saints get martyred."

"Oh," he said. "Yeah, I guess so."

I said, "Any idea who'd want to martyr Adriana?"

"Of course not," said Susan. "We haven't been in touch for over a year."

"Do you know who she went to work for?"

"Of course," she said. "The Changs."

"You know them?"

"No, but Adriana gave us their address so we could forward mail. They're doctors."

"Better financial bet," said Bradley.

Milo said, "Did she get much mail for forwarding?"

"Actually, not a single piece. Even when she lived here it was just junk—coupons she gave to us. Oh, yeah, she also got occasional correspondence from her church back in Idaho."

Susan said, "Tabernacle Something. I guess she was a fundamentalist. But it's not like she was heavy-handed, some kind of Jesus freak."

"Did she find a church in Portland?"

"She went every Sunday," she said. "Ten to noon, that's the only time she left for any stretch. Can't tell you where the church was, though, because we never asked and she never said."

"Anything else you think would help us?"

Bradley said, "Sue?"

Susan said, "No, sorry."

Milo said, "How about the address in La Jolla?"

Susan said, "Hold on, I'll find it."

Seconds later, she was reading off the P.O.B. Milo had just called.

He gestured obscenely. "One more question: Did you find Adriana through an agency?"

"Nope," said Bradley, "through an ad we ran in the paper."

"It wasn't as risky as it sounds," said Susan. "We ran a background check through a friend, he does security for one of the hotels. He said she came up absolutely spotless."

"Could we have his name?"

Silence. "That's absolutely necessary?"

"There's a problem, ma'am?"

"Well," said Susan, "actually, he's not a friend, he's my brother and I'm not sure he's allowed to freelance with the hotel account."

"I promise not to get him in trouble, Ms. Van Dyne, just want to find out anything I can about Adriana."

"Okay. Michael Ramsden. Here's his number."

"Appreciate it and if you think of anything, here's mine."

"It really makes no sense," said Bradley. "Whoever did this has to be mentally ill or something."

"Absolutely," said Susan. "Adriana was so stable, Lucas adored her. I am *not* going to tell him what happened."

Michael Ramsden was caught off-guard by the call from Milo.

He said, "Who?"

"Adriana Betts."

"Never heard of her."

"Hmm," said Milo. "So I guess your sister lied."

"Hold on—let me switch to another phone." Moments later: "Are we talking the housekeeper?"

"Susan said you backgrounded her."

"All I did was the basics, nothing anyone couldn't do online, so I'd appreciate your not making a big deal of it."

"Doing it on company time."

"Coffee-break time," said Ramsden. "My personal laptop, my sister was satisfied. You're saying someone killed this girl?"

"Yes."

"Whoa," said Ramsden. "Well, there was nothing in her record to suggest that might happen."

"Spotless?"

"That's what the computer said."

A scan of the UCSD med school faculty revealed that Donald Chang, M.D., was a fellow in vascular surgery and Lilly Chang, Ph.D., worked in Oncology as a cell biologist. He was in the operating room. She answered her extension.

"Adriana? Oh, no, that's terrible. In L.A.?"

"Yes, Doctor."

"Well," she said, "I suppose that might explain it."

"Explain what, Dr. Chang?"

"Her flaking on us," she said. "At least that's what we assumed. Not at the outset, mind you. Our initial worry was something had happened to her, because she'd always been so reliable, never even went out at night. Then about three months ago she said she was meeting a friend for dinner and never came back. We called the police, checked E.R.'s, were really worried. When she didn't answer her phone we figured she'd bailed and got pretty irate, I have to tell you. Both of us work all day and now there was no one for May. We complained to the agency and they gave us a discount on her replacement."

"What about her car?"

"She didn't have one, used the bus or walked. Obviously that would restrict her but as I said, she wasn't much for going out."

"Until she was," said Milo.

"Well, yes," said Lilly Chang. "I'm so sorry to hear what happened to her. It happened in L.A.? That's where she went?"

"Did she ever talk about L.A.?"

"Never," said Lilly Chang.

"What agency did you get her from?"

"Happy Tots. They were highly apologetic."

"What happened to Adriana's personal effects?"

"The little she had we boxed and stored. It's still there because, frankly, we forgot about it."

"We'd like to come down and pick up the boxes."

"Sure, they're just sitting in our storage unit. There really wasn't much."

"How about we come down today?"

"This evening would be okay, I guess. After seven thirty, I've got meetings until six thirty, want to put May to bed myself."

"No problem, Doctor. While we're there, if we could chat a bit more with you and your husband that would be great."

"There really isn't anything to chat about."

"I'm sure, Doctor, but this is a homicide and we need to be thorough."

"Of course. But if you want Donald, it'll have to be even later—no earlier than nine, probably closer to ten."

"He keeps long hours."

"Long would be good," said Lilly Chang. "More like infinite."

◆

Milo phoned Happy Tots Child Care Specialists, spoke to a woman named Irma Rodriguez who sounded as if she was wrestling with abdominal pain.

"That one," she said. "She sure fooled us."

"About what, ma'am?"

"Thinking she was reliable. What trouble's she gotten herself into?"

"Death," said Milo.

"Pardon?"

"She was murdered."

"Oh good Lord," said Rodriguez. "You're kidding."

"Wish I was, ma'am. How'd Adriana come to register with you?"

"She phoned us, emailed references from her previous employers, was lucky the job with the Changs came up right then. That's a good solid job, I was p.o.'d at Adriana for treating them so shabbily."

"What was Adriana like?"

"Well," said Rodriguez, "usually I meet applicants face-to-face but with the quality of her references and the perfect background check, I figured she'd be okay."

"Who supplied the references?"

"Hold on."

Several moments of dead air before she returned. "Only one but it was good. Mr. and Mrs. Van Dyne from Portland, Oregon. Someone killed her, huh? You just never know."

I called Robin, told her I'd either be home late or spend the night in San Diego, explained why.

She said, "A nanny. Everything seems to revolve around little ones."

"Seems to," I said, picturing a paper-doll chain of tiny skeletons.

"If you do come home tonight, wake me, no matter how late."

"You're sure?"

"Positive. I miss your feet in the bed. The way you end up in some weird position and I'm stretching and groping to find you."

"Love you."

"That's another way of saying it. Whoever drives, be careful."

◆

We left the station at five fifteen. Rather than brave rush-hour freeway traffic, Milo took surface streets to Playa Del Rey, where we had dinner at a dockside Italian place with C décor and A food.

He said, "Leave the driving to moi, you can have wine, Mr. Wing-man."

We both drank coffee and by seven thirty I was feeling keyed up but no clearer on who'd want to kill a near-saintly woman. Once we got on the 405 South, Milo turned quiet and I picked up my messages.

Holly Ruche had phoned at six, apologizing for canceling and wanting another appointment. I left her a message saying okay. A hundred and ten minutes later, we rolled into La Jolla.

21

Donald and Lilly Chang lived a brief stroll from the UCSD campus in a massive, gated complex called Regal Life La Jolla. Four-story brown-and-beige apartment blocks were surrounded by Torrey Pines. So was most of the beach town, where land didn't nudge blue Pacific.

Gorgeous place, warm night. A lot more temperate than Portland though I doubted Adriana Betts had weather on her mind when she'd moved.

Searching for the right kind of job: caring for other people's little treasures.

I knew all about that.

Milo rolled up to the Regal Life guardhouse. No need to flash the badge, Lilly Chang had left his name. We parked in a visitors' area, walked past fountains, flagstone roundabouts, perfect palms and pines and coral trees, precise sections of velvet lawn.

It took a while to locate the building but we got buzzed through the security door immediately.

A redheaded, exuberantly freckled woman wearing enormous

blue-framed eyeglasses, a black T-shirt, and baggy green linen pants responded to Milo's knock. Her feet were bare. The shirt read *I May Look Lazy but on a Cellular Level, I'm Quite Busy.*

"Hi, I'm Lilly, c'mon in. Donald's showering, he'll be right with you."

Dr. Lilly Chang was five six and lanky with a loose walk that caused her ginger mop of hair to shudder as she led us into her living room.

Despite the exterior luxe, the apartment was small, white, generically bland, a status unrelieved by the obligatory granite kitchen outfitted with the requisite brushed-steel appliances. What passed for a Juliet balcony offered an oblique view of a brown wall. The furniture looked as if it had been rescued from a dorm. The sole artwork was a poster featuring a cartoon human brain. The legend beneath the drawing read *Software: Sometimes You Don't Have to Buy It.*

No need for paintings or prints; the walls were pretty much taken up by photos of a beautiful almond-eyed baby with blue-black hair. In some of the shots, May Chang had been propped up for a solo pose. Her reaction to stardom ranged from stunned disbelief to glee. In other pictures, she sat on Lilly Chang's lap or that of a balding Asian man who looked close to forty.

A white plastic baby monitor breathed static from atop a black plastic end table. Above the table hung the largest portrait of May, gilt-framed.

Lilly Chang said, "I know, we're a bit too in love."

I said, "She's adorable. How old is she?"

"Twenty-two months. She's our joy."

She fingered the hem of the T-shirt. One of those smooth-faced women whose age was hard to determine. My guess was early thirties.

"Please, sit," she said. "How was your drive?"

Milo said, "Piece of cake."

"My parents live in L.A., I try to see them every five, six weeks. Sometimes it can get pretty hairy." She smiled. "Though I guess you guys could use your siren to speed through."

Milo said, "That would be nice but unfortunately it's a big no-no."

"Figures," she said. "Can I get you some coffee or juice?"

"No, thanks, Dr. Chang."

"Lilly's fine."

I said, "Where do your parents live?"

"Sherman Oaks. I was the original Valley Girl." Showing teeth. "Gag me with a spoon. Fer sure." She turned grave. "So we're here to talk about poor Adriana. I'm still integrating the news, it's so dreadful."

"It is," said Milo.

"May I ask where it happened?"

Milo said, "Cheviot Park."

"Wow," she said. "My family used to go there for Fourth of July fireworks. It always seemed like a safe place."

"It generally is."

"Wow," she repeated. "After we spoke I tried to think if there was anything I could remember that might help you. The only thing I came up with, and it's probably nothing, is four, five months ago, Adriana came with us on a trip to see my parents. We offered her the day off but she said she didn't need it, just in case Donald and I wanted to go out to dinner she'd be available to babysit."

I said, "Your parents couldn't babysit?"

"Of course they could. I sensed that Adriana wanted to come along so I said sure. My mother had cooked dinner so we stayed in. When Adriana heard that, she asked if we minded if *she* went out. To meet a friend for dinner. I know I told you over the phone that she didn't have friends but I was thinking of down here and the L.A. thing slipped my mind. Anyway, we said sure, go have fun. She made a call and soon after someone picked her up and she was gone for a couple of hours. Now I'm wondering if her real reason for tagging along was she'd planned on a date."

Milo said, "A man picked her up?"

"No idea, all I can tell you is it was a red car and the only reason I remember that was the color shined through the lace curtains over the picture window. I do remember thinking, *Pretty flashy for Adriana, maybe she's got a secret boyfriend.* But then she never went out again. And I mean never."

I said, "What was her mood when she returned?"

"Normal," she said. "Not upset, not ecstatic. She was always kind of quiet. To tell the truth, I wasn't paying attention because I was exhausted and dreading two more hours on the freeway. Donald had been on call and he was just zonked out and Adriana didn't have a license. So I was stuck with the driving."

"You did a great job," said a voice from the doorway.

Since being photographed with his daughter, Donald Chang had shaved his head and grown a drooping mustache. Broad-shouldered and slim-hipped, he had taut skin and bright black eyes. I revised my age estimate a few years downward.

We shook hands. His skin barely touched mine. Surgeon's caution. I'd anticipated that and was careful not to squeeze. Milo's touch was even lighter, a bare graze of fingertips. Courtesy of all those years living with Rick, whose name for the policy was "Don't scratch the Stradivarius."

Donald Chang sat next to his wife, placed a hand on her knee.

"Terrible about Adriana," he said. "She was a really nice person. Not the most social person, but I don't mean that in a weird way. I just never saw her desirous of any prolonged interaction with anyone but May."

Lilly said, "Except for that time in Sherman Oaks."

"What time?"

"When we were with my folks and she went out?"

"Oh," said Donald. "That is true. But it never happened again, did it?"

She shook her head.

I said, "She enjoyed her time with May but wasn't much for adult conversation."

"I wouldn't imply immaturity from that," said Donald. "She was a serious person. But yes, she definitely preferred to be with May and the moment May was asleep, she'd retire to her room."

Lilly said, "Not to evade housework, during the day she managed to clean and straighten up beautifully. Even though that's not what she was originally hired for, the plan was to get a maid twice a week."

Donald said, "Adriana insisted it wasn't necessary, the place isn't big, she could handle everything. We offered to pay her whatever we were going to pay the maid but she refused. We didn't want to take advantage of her and insisted she get something extra. Finally, she agreed to an additional hundred dollars a week. Which was a huge bargain for us. So when she considered her day over and went into her room, that was fine."

Lilly said, "Right from the get-go, she was great with May, but we were careful anyway, installed hidden baby cams. Watching the recordings reassured us. She couldn't have been more patient or loving or attentive."

Milo said, "Do you have the recordings?"

"Sorry, everything was uploaded to my computer at work and once I was confident Adriana was okay, I deleted the file and got rid of the system."

Donald said, "We removed the cameras when Adriana was out walking May. We didn't want her discovering them, thinking we hadn't trusted her. Though, of course, we hadn't. Trust needs to be earned."

I said, "And Adriana earned it."

"In spades," said Lilly. "She was a gem."

Same term Susan Van Dyne had used.

Donald said, "For someone like that to be murdered is astonishing. Do you have any idea who did it?"

"Not yet, Doctor," said Milo. "What else can you tell me about her?"

Donald turned to his wife. She shook her head.

I said, "Where did she sleep?"

"In the spare bedroom."

"Could we see it?"

"There's nothing of hers left in there, it's all the current nanny's stuff and she's sleeping in there."

"How's the new nanny working out?"

"She's nice," said Lilly.

I said, "But no Adriana."

"Corinne's pleasant, May seems to be attaching to her. But Adriana had something special. A real kid person."

Donald said, "Corinne's also not much for cleaning, now we do bring a maid in once a week."

I said, "Did Adriana talk about herself?"

"Not really," said Lilly. "She wasn't rude but she had a way of . . . I guess *deflecting* would be the right word."

"How so?"

"With ambiguous answers, then changing the subject. 'Oops, there's a stain on the counter,' and she'd get busy cleaning. I wondered if her personal history was painful, maybe a past relationship that had hurt her."

Donald stared at her. "Really?"

"Yes, darling."

He said, "I always thought she was just shy. What specific evidence of being hurt did you pick up?"

She smiled. "No evidence at all, it was just a feeling."

I said, "Did you pick up signs of her worrying about anything?"

Lilly thought. "Like depression?"

"Depression, anxiety, or just plain worry."

"No, I couldn't say that, she wasn't moody at all. Just the opposite, she was even-tempered, never raised her voice. I just felt she wanted her privacy and I respected that."

"Unemotional," said Milo.

"No, I wouldn't say that, either. Her default mood was . . . *even* is the best word I can come up with. Going through her day, pleasant, never complaining. Once in a while—infrequently—I'd catch her with a remote look on her face. Like she was remembering something troubling. But, honestly, it was nothing dramatic."

I said, "She lost a fiancé to a farm accident."

"Oh, my. Well, that could be it, then."

Donald put his arm around Lilly's shoulder. "Honey, you're an emotional detective. I'm impressed."

A beep sounded on the monitor. Both Changs turned to the machine.

Silence.

"Back to sleep," said Donald, crossing his fingers.

Lilly said, "That's really all I can tell you about Adriana. Would you like to collect her belongings?"

Donald said, "So to speak."

Milo said, "Not much in the way of worldly possessions?"

"Let's put it this way, guys. Everything fit into two boxes and one of them's small. That's not much of a life, is it?"

22

Donald Chang took us down in the elevator to a parking garage filled with vehicles save for a section cordoned by a mesh gate. Behind the mesh was a wall lined with storage lockers.

Chang unlocked the gate and one of the lockers and stood back. "The two in front are Adriana's, everything else is our stuff."

Milo drew out a cardboard wardrobe and a carton of the same material, around two feet square. Both boxes had been sealed cleanly with packing tape and neatly labeled *Adriana Betts's Belongings*.

Chang said, "Can't tell you what's in there, Lilly packed. Do you want to go upstairs to look at them?"

"Thanks, but we'll take them back to L.A."

"Forensic procedure and all that? Makes sense. Good luck, guys."

Milo gave him a card. "In case you or your wife remember something."

Chang tugged a mustache end. "I don't want to demean the dead but my opinion is Adriana was a bit odder than you just heard from Lilly."

"How so, Dr. Chang?"

"My wife sees the good in everyone, puts a gloss on everything. The way I perceived Adriana she was a total loner, no life at all other than caring for May and cleaning like a demon."

I said, "Except for that one time the red car picked her up."

"Yes, that would be the exception, but outliers don't necessarily say much, do they?"

Milo said, "When she got back from the date she looked okay."

"Nothing stood out but bear in mind that neither of us was psycho-analyzing Adriana, our priority was that May stay calm during the drive home."

Another mustache tug. "I certainly don't want to put Adriana down just because she stuck to herself, lots of the people I worked with in computer sciences at Yale were like that. And I'm not complaining about her work, as Lilly said Adriana was a dream employee, great with May. But once in a while, I wondered about her."

"Wondered about what?"

"Her being too good to be true. Because I've observed people like that—the ones who come across totally dedicated to the job, single-minded, no outside life. Sometimes they're fine but other times they end up cracking. I've seen it on high-pressure wards, your saintly types can turn out to be horrid."

I'd learned the same lesson working my first job as a psychologist: the plastic bubble unit on the Western Peds cancer ward where I finally figured out the most important question to ask prospective hires: *What do you do for fun?*

Milo said, "So you were waiting for the shoe to fall, huh?"

"No, I'm not saying that, Lieutenant. Not even close, I liked Adri-ana, was pleased with the order she brought to our lives. I'm just a curi-ous person." He smiled. "Maybe overly analytic. I didn't want to say any of this in front of Lilly. She was totally enamored of Adriana, hear-ing about the murder was pretty traumatic for her. I know she looked fine to you but two hours ago she was sobbing her heart out. It's an especially soft heart, my wife likes to believe in happy endings."

I said, "You're a bit more discriminating."

"Maybe I'm just a distrustful bastard by nature, but when Adriana flaked on us—what we thought was flaking—Lilly was surprised but I wasn't."

Milo said, "You figured something stressed her out."

"I figured she was like everyone else: Something better comes up, you bail." Chang smiled again, wider but no warmer. "That's a California thing, right?"

We placed the boxes in the back of the unmarked and headed back to L.A.

Milo swerved into the carpool lane and kept up a steady eighty-five per, jutting his head forward, as if personally cutting through wind resistance.

At Del Mar, he said, "Adriana goes on her one and only date with someone in a red car. So maybe the SUV little Heather saw isn't relevant. Hell, what's to say any of it's relevant?"

I said, "Something drew Adriana to that park."

"Something drew her to L.A., amigo. I'd say a better gig but bailing on the Changs for extra dough doesn't sound in character."

"A friend in need might have lured her. Someone with a baby."

"It was Mama in a red car, not a date?"

"Mama in a red car who called Adriana for help because something scared her. If those fears were justified, Adriana could have lost her life because she got too close to the situation."

"Bad Daddy."

"Major-league monster Daddy who murdered the mother of his child and the child, held on to the baby's skeleton as a psychopathic trophy. That ended when he read about the bones in Holly Ruche's backyard and decided to ditch his collection nearby. Mom had already been taken care of and Adriana, suspicious after her friend disappeared, followed him. Unfortunately, he spotted her."

He drove for a while. "Charming scenario. Too bad I've got nada to back any of it up."

"You've got Adriana's personal effects."

"There was anything juicy in those boxes, the Changs—being trained observers—would've noticed and said something."

"That's assuming they snooped."

"Everyone snoops, Alex."

"Not busy people."

"Okay, fine. I'll burn some incense to the Evidence Gods, pray a hot lead shows up in the boxes. I was a less pro-*fessional* detective, I'd pull into the next truck stop and do an impromptu forensic."

"Everything goes straight to the lab?"

"Hell, no," he said. "Finders keepers, but I'm doing it by the book."

We got off the freeway at Santa Monica Boulevard at 1:36 a.m. For all its rep as a party town, most of L.A. closes down early and the streets were dark, hazy, and empty. That can stimulate the creepers and the crawlers but Milo's police radio was calm and back at the station the big detective room was nearly deserted, every interview room empty.

He used the same room where Helene Johanson had cried, dragged in an additional table and created a work space. Spraying the surfaces with disinfectant, he gloved up, used a box cutter to slit the wardrobe open, emptied the contents.

Clothing. More clothing. A peer at the bottom evoked a disgusted head shake. He examined the garments anyway.

A couple more bland dresses similar to the one Adriana Betts had died in, two pairs of no-nonsense jeans, seven nondescript blouses, cotton undergarments, T-shirts, a pair of sneakers, black flats, cheap plastic sunglasses.

"No naughty secret-life duds, amigo." He sniffed the garments. "No secret-life perfume, either. Adriana, you wild and crazy kid." Shutting his eyes for several moments as if meditating, he opened them, repacked the clothes, sealed the box and filled out a lab tag.

The smaller box yielded a hairbrush, a toothbrush, antacid, acetaminophen, a blue bandanna, and more garments: two pairs of walking shorts and a wad of white T-shirts. Milo was about to put everything back when he stopped and hefted the shirts.

"Too heavy." Running his hands over each tee, he extracted a shirt from the middle of the stack and unfolded. Inside was a brown leatherette album around six inches square, fastened by a brass key clasp.

"Looky here, Dear Diary." He pressed his palms together prayerfully. "Our Father Who Art in Heaven, grant me something evidentiary and I'll attend Mass next Sunday for the first time in You know how long."

The clasp sprang free with a finger-tap. A pulse in his neck throbbed as he opened the book.

No diary notations, no prose of any sort. Three cardboard pages held photographs moored by clear plastic bands.

The first page was of a teenage Adriana Betts with a boy her age. Bubbly cursive read:

Dwayne and Me. Happy Times.

Dwayne Hightower had been a huge kid, easily six six, three hundred, with a side-of-beef upper body and thick, short, hairless limbs. His face was a pink pie under coppery curls, his smile wide and open as the prairie. He and Adriana had posed in front of hay bales, barns, a brick-faced building, and a green John Deere tractor with wheels as tall as Adriana. In each shot, Hightower's heavy arm rested lightly on Adriana's shoulder. Her head reached his elbow. She clung to his biceps. Their smiles were a match in terms of innocence and wattage.

The following page began with more of the same but ended with shots from Dwayne Hightower's funeral. Adriana in a black dress, her hair tied back severely. Wearing the cheap sunglasses from the wardrobe.

The final page was all group shots: Adriana and several other young adults in front of a red-brick church. The edifice that had backdropped her and Dwayne. Had they planned to wed there?

Not a single tattoo, body pierce, or edgy hairdo in sight. These pictures could've dated from the fifties. Heartland America, unaffected by fad or fashion.

In some of the shots, a portly white-haired man in his sixties wearing a suit and tie stood to the left of the group.

In most of the pictures, Adriana, though not particularly tall, had positioned herself at the back. Not so in the last three, where she posed front-center, next to the same person.

Young black woman with short, straightened hair and a heart-shaped face. Extremely pretty and graceful despite a drab smock that could've come out of Adriana's closet.

A single chocolate dot in a sea of vanilla.

The bones in the park had yielded African American maternal DNA.

I didn't need to say anything. Milo muttered, "Maybe." Then he pointed to the older man in the suit. "Got to be the pastor, whatever his name is."

"Reverend Goleman," I said. "Life Tabernacle Church of the Fields."

He turned to me. "You memorize everything?"

"Just what I think might be important."

"You figured the church might be important? Why didn't you say so?"

"There's *might* and there's *is*," I said. "No lead before its time."

"You and that party wine from when we were kids—the Orson Welles thing."

"Paul Masson."

"Now you're showing off."

I reexamined the photos that included the black woman. "Adriana stands nearer to her than she does to anyone else. So let's assume a close relationship."

"The pal in the red car?"

"What we've heard about Adriana says she had a moral compass, would never have bailed on the Changs without a good reason. Helping a good friend might qualify."

"If she was murdered because she knew too much, why dump the bones near her and risk the association?"

"He's a confident guy."

"Talk about a poor choice for your baby's daddy. And that leads me back to the problem I had before. Child abuse, even murder, something rage-related, happens all the time. But I'm still having trouble seeing anyone, even a psychopath, taking the time to clean and wax his own offspring's bones then tossing them like trash."

I have no trouble seeing anything and that turns some nights hellish. I said, "You're probably right. The first step is I.D.'ing this woman."

He looked at his watch. Close to three a.m. "Too early to rouse Reverend Goleman in Idaho." Separating the photo album from the cartons, he dropped it into an evidence bag. We carried both boxes to the big D-room, where he secured them in a locker. Returning to his office, he wrote an email to the crime lab. Leaning back in his chair, he yawned. "Go home, sleep late, kiss Robin and pet the pooch. Have a nice breakfast tomorrow morning."

"You're not going home."

"There's a sleeping room near the holding cells. I may just bunk out so I can be ready to phone Boise in four hours. Hopefully a devout fellow like the Rev will be cooperative."

"Speaking of devout," I said, "where will you be attending Sunday Mass?"

"What? Oh, that. I said evidentiary, not suggestive."

"Driving a tough bargain with the Almighty?"

"He wouldn't respect me otherwise."

23

I slipped into bed just after three thirty a.m., careful not to rouse Robin.

She rolled toward me, wrapped her arms around my neck, murmured, "Morning."

"Not enough morning. Go back to sleep."

One of her eyes opened. "Anything new?"

"I'll tell you about it when we wake up."

"We're awake now." She propped herself up.

I gave her a rundown.

She said, "Mothers and babies," sighed and slid away from me, was breathing evenly within seconds. Sometimes she talks in her sleep when she's upset. This time she remained silent until daybreak. I knew because I watched her for a long time.

An internal prompt woke me at seven a.m. I should've been wiped out; instead I was hyped, eager to know what Milo had learned from the Right Reverend Goleman. I waited for him to call and when he hadn't by seven thirty, I took a robotic run, showered, shaved, brought coffee out to Robin in her studio.

No saw buzz or hammer percussion as I approached. Maybe she'd dozed less soundly than I'd thought, didn't trust herself with sharp things.

She was sitting on her couch, Blanche a little blond pillow under her arm, studying a beautiful book showcasing a collection of vintage guitars. One man's monomania. I'd bought it for her last Christmas.

I said, "Inspiration?"

"Aesthetics. You get any decent sleep?"

"Sure," I lied.

"Hear from Big Guy?"

"Not yet."

I held out the mug. She said, "Let's go outside," and we sat near the pond, tossing pellets to the koi and drinking coffee and not saying a thing.

Eleven minutes of uneasy serenity before I heard from Big Guy.

For someone who hadn't slept at all, Milo sounded chipper.

"The bad news: Reverend Goleman is away from the office. The good news: He's right here in SoCal, attending a convention in Fullerton. We're meeting at my office at noon."

"He give you the name of Adriana's friend?"

"Yes," he said, "but it's complicated. See you when the sun's high?"

"Wouldn't miss it."

I arrived a few minutes early, encountered Milo as he was locking up his office. "According to Goleman, the friend is Qeesha D'Embo. Unfortunately, that doesn't match anything in the databases."

"Alias? She was hiding something?"

"Maybe—this looks like our clergy-type."

A tall rotund man accompanied by a smallish female officer headed our way.

Milo said, "I'll take it from here, Officer," and shook Goleman's hand. Goleman's suit was plaid, deep blue with a pale pink crosshatch. His white hair was shorter than in the church photos, cropped nearly to the skin at the sides, bristly and uncooperative on top. Heavy build but hard-fat, no jiggle when he moved. One of those thick sturdy men built for hours behind the plow.

"Thanks for meeting with me, Reverend."

"Of course," said Goleman. His voice was deep and mellow, easy-listening at sermon time. He reached out to grip my hand. His paw was padded and callused, just firm enough to be sociable.

Milo led him to the same interview room, minus the extra table.

When Goleman sat, he overwhelmed the chair. He tugged up his trousers, revealed high-laced work boots.

"Something to drink, Reverend?"

Goleman patted his belly. "No thanks, Lieutenant, I had breakfast at the hotel including way too much coffee. Big buffet and I overdid it with the huevos rancheros. As usual."

Milo said, "Know what you mean."

Goleman smiled faintly. "It's tough for us big guys with healthy appetites. I don't even make resolutions anymore because I'm weary—and wary—of failing my Savior." He began crossing a leg, changed his mind, planted his foot back on the linoleum. "I'm in despair over Adriana. She was a wonderful girl, not a mean bone in her body. I say that as more than her pastor. I knew her personally. She dated my nephew."

"Dwayne."

Goleman's lips folded inward. "You know about Dwayne."

"He came up in the course of trying to learn about Adriana."

"Terrible, terrible thing," said Goleman. "Farmwork's always dangerous but when it actually happens . . . I have no doubt Dwayne and Adriana would've married and raised wonderful, warmhearted children." His voice caught. "Now it's Adriana we're mourning. Do you have any idea who did this?"

"No, Reverend."

"This is the kind of ordeal that tests one's faith and I'm not going to tell you I passed with flying colors. Because when I heard about Adriana from her sister—wanting me to conduct the service—I couldn't dredge up an ounce of faith."

Milo said, "Bad stuff can do that, Reverend."

"Oh, it can, Lieutenant. But that's the point of faith, isn't it? Believing when everything's rolling along hunky-dory is no challenge." Goleman massaged double chins. "And now you've implied Qeesha might be in trouble."

"I didn't find any record of any Qeesha D'Embo."

"I'm not surprised," said Goleman.

"You figured it for an alias?"

"Qeesha was always quite secretive, Lieutenant, and given her circumstances I can't say I blamed her. She came to us two years ago as part of a group of fire survivors, a conflagration in New Orleans. Poor, desperate people who'd survived Katrina only to see their homes go up in flames. Several churches in our city collaborated to take some of them in and we got Qeesha. She was a lovely girl. Hardworking when it came to church activities. And the fire's not all I was referring to as her circumstances. Not only had she lost her mother and her house, she was forced to run from someone who'd terrorized her."

"Terrorized her how?"

"Domestic violence," said Goleman. "One of those stalking situations. This fellow—she only referred to him by his first name, Clyde—had become obsessed with her, wouldn't take no for an answer. Mind you, I never heard this from Qeesha. Adriana told me after I voiced my concerns about Qeesha's reluctance to talk about her ordeal, suggested bottling everything up might not be the best idea, perhaps counseling would help. Adriana explained to me that Qeesha was dealing with more than the fire, was too overwhelmed to handle counseling."

I said, "Instead, she confided in Adriana."

"Adriana opened her home to Qeesha, they grew close very quickly. Inseparable, really, it was rare to see one without the other, Adriana was our best preschool teacher and Qeesha served as her aide. They were terrific with the little ones. Then one day Qeesha didn't arrive with Adriana and Adriana told me she'd moved to California."

"Running from Clyde?"

"I don't know, Lieutenant. Adriana seemed to be surprised herself. Apparently, Qeesha had moved out in the middle of the night without explanation."

Same thing Adriana had done with the Changs. "How long ago was this?"

"Qeesha was only with us for a short while—I'd say a couple of years ago, give or take."

"Reverend," said Milo, "when a homicide occurs, we need to ask all sorts of questions. You just said Adriana and Qeesha grew inseparable. Could there have been more than friendship?"

"Were they lovers?" said Goleman. "Hmm, never considered that. There were certainly no signs. And we do have gay people in our church, there wouldn't be any official stigma. Though I'm sure some of our parishioners might look askance. But no, I never saw that. Not that I'm an expert."

"What kind of church is it?"

"Nondenominational, fairly fundamentalist in terms of how we read Scripture. And yes, I do have my personal views on homosexuality but I keep them to myself because our emphasis is on faith, prayer, careful study of both Testaments with an emphasis on textual exegesis, and, most important, good works. We're a community of doers."

"Charity," said Milo.

"Charity implies one person doing a favor for another, Lieutenant. Our view is that the giver gets as much out of the gift as the taker. I'm sure that sounds self-righteous but in practice it works out quite well. All of our members tithe and most everyone takes on some kind of good work. We're not a wealthy tabernacle but we do our best to provide shelter and sustenance to the needy."

Milo nodded. "Back to Clyde, if we might?"

Goleman said, "The only thing I can tell you other than his first name—and I must say I found it appalling—is that he's a police officer."

"From New Orleans."

"Adriana never specified but I assumed that to be the case. She told me that contributed to Qeesha's fear: Clyde was a law officer, she felt he could get away with anything."

"Was there any indication Clyde had located Qeesha?"

"No, sir," said Goleman. "May I assume from your questions that you believe she's also been a victim?"

"The investigation has just begun so we don't believe anything, Reverend. Did Qeesha have a vehicle?"

"No, she—all the New Orleans people—arrived with virtually nothing."

"Did Adriana drive?"

"Of course. Why do you ask?"

"Because she didn't drive in California."

"Really," said Goleman.

"Really."

"Well, I can't explain that, Lieutenant. What she drove in Boise was Dwayne's truck. His parents—my sister and brother-in-law—insisted Adriana have it. But when she left to take the job in Portland, she insisted on returning it to Nancy and Tom and left on Greyhound. Truth is, my sister never wanted to see the truck again. Dwayne's high school sticker was still on the rear window and Adriana hadn't cleaned out his personal effects from the glove compartment. But Adriana insisted."

I said, "Why'd Adriana leave Boise?"

"She never told me," said Goleman. "I assumed she'd had enough."

"Of what?"

"Grief, memories. A life that needed changing."

24

Milo and Goleman exchanged cards and Goleman extracted a promise from Milo to let him know "once you've solved it."

As we watched him barrel away, Milo said, "Optimism of the righteous." We returned to his office, where he called Delano Hardy's home number in Ladera Heights.

Milo's initial partner at West L.A., Hardy had retired a few months ago. The department's logic back then was a pairing of outsiders: gay D with black D. The partnership had worked well until Del's wife pressured him not to spend his days with "someone like that."

That same wife answered.

"Martha, it's Milo. Del around?"

"Milo, how nice." Her voice was Karo syrup. "He's out gardening. How've *you* been doing?"

"Great, Martha."

"Well, that's *good.* Everything just coasting *along?*"

"The usual, Martha."

"That's really good, Milo. Hold on."

Del came on. "What's the occasion?"

"High intrigue in New Orleans. You garden?"

"Yeah, right. I'm weeding her flower beds, big-time fun," said Hardy. "The old country, huh?" He'd moved to California as a teen but had grown up in one of the parishes swept away by Katrina. The division had passed around the hat for some of his relatives. I kicked in a couple hundred bucks, received a personal call from Del. I'm sure he did the same in response to Milo's thousand-dollar donation.

"So what can I help you with, Big Guy?"

Milo explained about Qeesha D'Embo and a scary cop named Clyde.

Hardy said, "Only connection I might conceivably still have is Uncle Ray—not my real uncle, my godfather Ray Lhermitte, did patrol with Daddy, worked his way up to captain. But he's a lot older than us kids, Milo. For all I know he's passed."

"This point, I'll take anything, D.H. Got a number for him?"

"Hold on, I'll go find it. You want, I can prime the pump by calling him first."

"Thanks."

"I should be thanking you," said Hardy.

"For what?"

"Letting me pretend I'm half useful. This retirement business is like dying on your feet."

Eighteen minutes later, a call came in from Commander Raymond Delongpre Lhermitte (Retired). In a bass voice that alternated between rasp and molasses, Lhermitte said, "Tell me why you need this, son."

Milo obliged.

"Okay," said Lhermitte. "You present your case well. Problem is, we've been dealing with some pretty bad corruption issues here. Hurricane agitated it, the waters are still roiling, and even though I'm off the job I have no desire to stir up more."

"Me neither, sir."

"But you're working a whodunit so to hell with anything else."

"That's true."

"As it should be," said Lhermitte. "Fact is, I shouldn't even care, I'm growing orchids and shooting nutria for sport, but I can't break the bonds. To the department as well as to my beautiful, crazy city. Never found a better place to live but sometimes it seems we've irritated the Almighty."

"Gotta be rough," said Milo.

"So," said Lhermitte, "this girl was one of the fire survivors? That was a bad one, started in a hotel and took down an entire block of old wood buildings. What was that name again?"

"Qeesha D'Embo."

"Sounds African-phony to me, son. No, afraid I'm not aware of anyone by that name."

"Wouldn't expect you to know everyone, sir."

"I know a lot of people," said Lhermitte. "Including Clyde Bordelon."

"A cop?"

"Unfortunately, son. Ugly piece of psychology, I'd like to think the regs we got in place now he'd never have gotten hired. But who knows, nothing's perfect."

"He's still on the force?"

"No, he's lying under dirt. Shot with his own poorly maintained service gun in the backyard of his own poorly maintained house."

"When?"

"Coupla years ago. Still an open case."

"Any suspects?"

"Too many suspects, son. Nasty individual that he was."

"What kind of nasty?"

"Clyde was what's known as an individual of loose morals. By that I don't mean transgressions of a sexual nature, though if you told me Clyde had congress with a herd of cocaine-blinded goats I wouldn't gasp in amazement because bottom line, the man was amoral, rules just didn't apply to him. But the sins the *department* suspected were of a monetary nature: payoffs, bribes, hijacking cigarette and liquor trucks, consorting with the criminal element on a variety of projects. So you can see what I mean about a plethora of suspects."

"Any of them stand out?"

"A girl," said Lhermitte. "A dancer, not a church-girl. But her name wasn't Qeesha, it was Charlene Rae Chambers."

"By dancer—"

"I mean stripper. Her stage name was CoCo. Like the dress designer. Pretty little thing, not one of ours, she was a Yankee, came up from somewhere in New York to work the pole at the Deuces Wild. One of Clyde's favorite after-hour spots. After she started there it became his only after-hour spot."

"Obsessed?"

"You could say that."

"Why was she the prime?" said Milo.

"Because she was the last person seen with Clyde when he was alive and talk was he'd stalked her, wouldn't take no for an answer. Despite her claim of being bothered, witnesses have her getting into his car that night and riding away. It took a while for our detectives to talk to her. So many suspects and all. By the time they reached her it was too late for a GSR and she had an alibi. Clyde took her straight home, she showered and slept for eight hours. Her roommate, another dancer, verified it."

"Not exactly ironclad."

"Oh, there's a good chance she did it," said Lhermitte. "Or had someone else do it for her. Matter of fact, I'd bet on her being responsible. Two days after she was interviewed, she was gone, no forwarding."

"I'd like to send you a picture of Qeesha—"

"Then you'd have to do it by what my grand-babies call snail mail. Got no computer, no fax machine, only one phone in the house, a rotary, as old as me, made of Bakelite. Tell you what, though, I'll make a call and see if someone still on the job can help you."

"Appreciate it, sir. Did Charlene actually live in the fire zone?"

"Don't know if she did or she didn't," said Lhermitte. "I'll ask about that, too."

"Thank you, sir."

"Pleasure's all mine."

By the time a New Orleans detective named Mark Montecino had emailed asking for Milo's fax number, Milo had already pulled up two NCIC mug shots of Charlene Rae Chambers, female black, brown and brown, five four, one oh two. A DOB that would make her twenty-seven.

Her record was unimpressive: five-year-old bust for soliciting prostitution, four-year-old bust for battery on a peace officer, both filed at a precinct in Brooklyn. Dismissal on the first, four days in jail for the second.

"Couldn't have been heavy-duty battery," he said.

Even disheveled and wild-eyed with fright, Charlene Chambers had photographed pretty.

I said, "She looks scared."

"That she does."

His fax beeped. Out slid a solicitation mug shot from New Orleans. Now she was beautiful and more composed than during her previous arrests. On the paper Mark Montecino had written, *She didn't live near the fire.*

Milo ran her through the data banks. She'd never paid taxes or registered for Social Security in New York, Louisiana, Idaho, or California. No driver's license, no registered vehicle, red or otherwise.

"Running away," he said, "but not because she was scared of Clyde. She was worried she'd be collared for his murder. Church folk in Idaho were charitable so she took advantage. An opportunity came up here in L.A., and she was gone."

I said, "I know it's a stereotype but New Orleans and voodoo aren't strangers and waxy bones sounds like something that could be part of a hex."

"Let's find out," he said, turning back to his screen. "First time in a long time *I'm* not feeling hexed."

25

Websites on New Orleans voodoo pulled up nothing about waxed infant skeletons. The closest match was a Day of the Dead offering to the ancestral spirit Gede that sometimes included bones.

Milo looked up the date of the rite. "November first. Months off."

I said, "People improvise."

"Some local whack concocted his own private sacrifice?"

"Making it up's a lot easier and more lucrative than studying theology, Big Guy. Do-it-yourself religion's the SoCal way."

"Another Charlie Manson. Wonderful."

"To a devout woman like Adriana, black-arts worship would've been the worst kind of heresy. But Qeesha could have been attracted to an occult group because it reminded her of her time in New Orleans. If it started to bother her and she wanted out and told Adriana about it, I'm betting Adriana would've jumped at helping her."

"It was Qeesha picking her up in that red car."

"Doesn't sound as if unregistered wheels would be a problem for Qeesha."

"Coupla old friends trying to escape the zombie horde."

I said, "What if Qeesha's involvement with the horde included getting pregnant? With Daddy being a loony warlock who ended up killing her and the baby? Adriana went looking for them, paid for her loyalty."

"Adriana bailed on the Changs three months ago but she got shot a few days ago. What happened during the interim, Alex? Are we talking about a patient bunch of freaks? Because there's no evidence she was confined. Zero signs of abuse on her body and those lig marks were relatively fresh."

"Maybe she was careful, snooping around without showing herself. Until she did."

He rubbed his face. "A picture just flashed in my head."

"Black-robed ghouls chanting ominously in the moonlight?"

"You're getting a little scary, dude."

"You don't know?"

"Know what?"

"Ph.D.'s in psych," I said. "The state grants us a license to mind-read."

"What am I thinking now?"

"You're back in Bizarro World with no damn leads."

"Oh, man," he said. "This case ever closes, we're definitely playing the stock market."

His desk phone jangled.

Dr. Clarice Jernigan said, "New lab result. Your victim Adriana Betts was dosed up before she was shot. Nothing illegal, her blood showed high concentrations of diphenhydramine. Your basic first-generation antihistamine, what they put in Benadryl."

"How much is high, Doc?"

"Not a lethal dosage but enough to sedate her profoundly or put her out completely."

"She was knocked out first, then shot."

"That's the sequence, Milo. To me it says a calculated offender operating in a highly structured manner. Seeing as her murder is probably related to that infant skeleton, we're obviously dealing with someone who operates on a different psychiatric plane. Have you spoken to Delaware recently?"

I said, "Right here, Clarice."

"Hi, Alex. I'm thinking a sociopath with some looseness of thought around the edges, or someone downright deranged who manages to keep his craziness under wraps. Not necessarily schizophrenic but maybe an isolated paranoid delusion. Make sense?"

"It does, Clarice. I'm also wondering if we've got a killer who lacks physical strength."

"He uses a downer to incapacitate her? Sure, why not? What's your take on the baby?"

"Beyond cruel."

"Sorry I asked."

After she hung up, Milo said, "Lack of physical strength. As in female?"

"Ray Lhermitte pegs Qeesha as a likely murderer. What if she acquired a taste for power and became a cult queen?"

"No warlock," he said, "a nasty little witch. *That's* turning it a whole new way. You're saying she killed Adriana? What's the motive? And why bring Adriana back to L.A. to do it?"

"Could've been something religious," I said. "Uncomfortable truths about the cult. Adriana was outraged, threatened to go to the cops. That could explain the diphenhydramine. A relatively humane way to eliminate a former friend."

"Then why shoot her in the head? Why not just poison her straight out?"

I had no answer for that.

He said, "Qeesha as Devil Spawn. We keep jumping around like frogs on a griddle. Sit around long enough, we can probably come up with another hundred scenarios."

He stood, hitched his trousers. "One way or the other, I need to look for Ms. D'Embo aka Chambers aka God-Knows-Who-Else."

I said, "If she's driving unregistered wheels she could wrongly assume that's another layer of security."

"So focus on the car, maybe it's stolen."

"Starting with people who frequent the park."

"And there's restricted parking at night, so check for citations. Yeah, I like it, it's damn close to normal police work."

Moe Reed and Sean Binchy reported nothing fruitful from the canvass of park employees, patrons, and nearby residents. Both would re-inquire about red cars and dark SUVs.

While Milo checked the grand theft auto file I stepped into the hall and phoned Holly Ruche.

She said, "I hope you're not mad at me. For canceling."

"I'm sure you had a good reason."

"I—I'll explain when I come in. If you'll take me."

"No problem."

"Just like that? Do you have time tomorrow?"

I checked my book. "Eleven a.m. works."

"Wow," she said. "You're not that busy, huh?"

"Looking forward to seeing you, Holly."

"I'm so sorry. That was bratty."

"How's the house going?"

"The house?"

"Remodeling."

"Oh," she said. "Nothing's really happening . . . I'll tell you everything tomorrow. Eleven, right?"

"Right."

"Thanks again, Dr. Delaware. You've been incredibly tolerant."

I returned to Milo's office. He said, "No vehicles were ticketed that night. These are the theft stats, not as bad as I expected."

He showed me his notes. Sixteen thousand GTAs in the city of L.A. over the past year. The three-month total was three thousand, eight hundred fifty-four. Of those, six hundred thirty-three were red. Westside red GTAs numbered twenty-eight. Ten of those had been recovered.

Milo got on the phone and questioned the detectives assigned to the eighteen open cases. Seven were suspected insurance scams, all from a section of Pico-Robertson, with the reporting individuals members of a small-time Ukrainian gang. Of the remaining eleven cars, one was a four-hundred-thousand-dollar Ferrari lifted from the Palisades, the other a comparably priced Lamborghini taken in Holmby Hills, both deemed improbable choices for the car Lilly Chang had seen because of their conspicuousness and the engine noise they'd generate.

The D handling the exotics was a woman named Loretta Thayer. She said, "If your witness didn't hear a roar that set off the Richter scale it wasn't one of those. Same for a red Porsche Turbo I just picked up that's not in the files yet."

Milo said, "Spate of red hotwheel heists?"

"Interesting, no?" said Thayer. "My hunch is they're going to the same collector overseas, probably Asia or the Mideast."

"Toys for some oil sheik's twelve-year-old to roll around the desert in."

"At that age," said Thayer, "I was happy to have roller skates."

Milo emailed photos of Charlene Chambers/Qeesha D'Embo to Thayer and two other detectives, asked them to show the images to their victims.

Thayer called back an hour later. "Sorry, no recognition."

"That was fast."

"Protect and serve, Lieutenant. It helps being on the Westside, everyone's got a computer or an iPhone, I reached them electronically."

No calls back from the other D's for the next half hour. Milo worked on some overdue files and I read abstracts of psych articles on his computer.

He looked at his watch. "More I think about it, more of a waste of time the car angle seems. It could be unregistered but not stolen. Or Lilly Chang remembers wrong and it wasn't even red—hell, maybe it was a scooter. Or an RV. Or a horse and buggy."

I said, "Power of positive thinking."

"Wanna hear positive? Time for lunch."

"The usual?"

"No, I'm craving vegan. Just kidding."

We drove to a steak house a mile west of the station, sawed through a couple of T-bones, and drove back to his office where he picked up replies from the remaining auto theft detectives. None of their victims recognized Qeesha but a D II named Doug Groot said, "It's possible one of my victims lied."

"Why do you think that?"

"The usual tells," said Groot. "Looking everywhere but *at* me, too quick on the draw, like he'd rehearsed it. Also, he just gave me a feeling from the beginning. The car was a nice one, BMW 5 series, all tricked out, only a couple of years old, low mileage. But he didn't seem that bugged about having it boosted. Made the right speech but no emotion—again, like he'd rehearsed."

"Insurance thing?" said Milo.

"He filed with his carrier the day after I interviewed him."

"When did it happen?"

"Nineteen months ago."

"What were the circumstances?"

"Taken from his driveway sometime during the night," said Groot. "It's not impossible, his building's got an open carport. But supposedly he'd left it locked with the security system set and I talked to the neighbors and no one heard any alarm go off. He seemed so hinky I actually ran a check on him. But he had no obvious ties to any scammers, no record of anything."

"What's this solid citizen's name?"

"Melvin Jaron Wedd, like getting married but two 'd's."

"This guy really twanged your antenna, huh?"

"You know what it's like, El Tee. Sometimes you get a feeling. Unfortunately none of mine led anywhere. The car's never shown up."

"Loretta said nice red wheels might be going to the Mideast."

"Two-year-old Bimmer's nice," said Groot, "but probably not nice enough for that. Mexico or Central America, maybe. For all I know it's being used to ferry around Zeta hit men."

"What line of work is Wedd in?"

"Something showbizzy. Can I ask what your curiosity is about the car and this Chambers woman?"

"She might be a really bad girl," said Milo. "Or a victim. Or neither and I'm spinning my wire wheels."

Groot chuckled. "The job as usual. You want to follow up with Wedd?"

"Might as well."

"Here's his info."

Milo copied, thanked Groot, clicked off. Seconds later, he'd pulled Melvin Jaron Wedd's driver's license.

Male white, thirty-seven, six two, one ninety, brown, brown, needs corrective lenses.

Wedd's photo showed him with a pink, squarish face, smallish eyes, thin lips, a dark spiky haircut. He'd posed in a black V-necked T-shirt. Black-framed glasses gave him the hipster-geek look of any other West-side guy working a Mac at a Starbucks table.

"Doesn't look like a warlock," said Milo.

I said, "More like Clark Kent at leisure."

He ran Wedd through the banks just in case something had popped up since Groot's search. No criminal record, a scatter of parking tickets, the most recent thirty months ago. All paid in a timely fashion.

Then he switched to the DMV files and said, "Well, looky here."

Wedd's new registered vehicle was a black Ford Explorer, purchased brand-new, three weeks after the theft of the red BMW. "Be interesting if he jacked it way up and stuck on fancy rims."

He shifted to the Web, called up an image of an Explorer enhanced that way, sent the picture to Heather Goldfeder, and asked if it resembled the SUV she'd seen.

Seconds later: *cud b cant say 4 sure how r u.*

He sent back a happy face emoticon.

Her instant response: *me 2 xoxoxo.*

◆

The landline and cell phone Groot had given for Wedd were unresponsive to Milo's calls. No message machine on either.

He said, "A fellow who likes his privacy. Let's invade it."

The address was an apartment west of Barrington and just north of Wilshire. Officially Brentwood, but not what you thought of when someone said Brentwood.

Quarter-hour drive from the station under the worst circumstances. Circumstances were favorable: i.e., Milo's leaden foot. We made it in eight.

26

Back in the fifties, someone thought it was a nifty idea to erect a two-story box with the top floor cantilevered over a concrete carport, the entire structure slathered with pimply aqua stucco, the squat, expressionless face embellished by a five-foot starburst spray-painted gold and the proclamation *Dawn-Lite Apts* in that same gaudy tint.

Several decades later someone thought restoring the dingbat to its original glory was historical preservation.

As we pulled up to Melvin Jaron Wedd's building, a white-garbed painter was regilding the star, his compadre patching thin spots of aqua.

Milo said, "Misdemeanor, maybe a felony."

I said, "You don't like midcentury?"

"Depends on the century."

"Didn't know you were into architecture, Big Guy."

"Rick is. I imbibe through osmosis."

We got out and inspected the carport from which the BMW had been lifted. Six stalls, one occupied by a dusty brown Acura. No tenant names, not even a unit number. The mailbox at the foot of the grubby stairs that led up to the second story listed J. Wedd as residing in 3.

Each apartment was accessed through an open landing. Number 3 was ground-floor rear. Cheap vertical blinds blocked the single window. A dead plant in a terra-cotta-colored vinyl pot squatted near the door. So did several piles of junk mail. Milo pushed a button. The resulting buzzer sounded like flatulence.

No answer. He tried again. Rapped hard with detective-callused knuckles.

The door to the adjoining unit opened and a dreadlocked head emerged, bleached-blond with dark roots. Matted strands trailed to a black-shirted shoulder. The face below the hair was bronze, seamed, craggy, hazed by three days of dark stubble. Sagging eyes were wary. A bass voice said, "Police, right?" and the eyes turned friendly.

Milo said, "Yes, sir."

"My brother's a cop." Six feet of sun-damaged sinew stepped out onto the landing. The black shirt was a body-conscious tee that said *Think: It's Not Illegal Yet.* Below that, baggy shorts printed with leaping dolphins ended at knees enlarged by random bumps. Bare feet sported ragged nails and more protrusions. Calcium deposits, your basic surfer knots.

He looked around thirty-five, accounting for sun damage. A thumb hooked toward Melvin Jaron Wedd's door. "He do something?"

"We're here to talk to him."

"He hasn't been here for days."

"Any idea where he's gone?"

"He's gone all the time. Obviously, he's got somewhere else to crash."

"When's the last time you saw him, Mister . . ."

"Robert Sommers." Cornrow grinned crookedly, as if his name provided unceasing amusement. "The last time was . . . a couple of weeks ago? I'm not good with time. Except for the tide tables."

"Chasing waves?" said Milo.

"Whenever I can," said Sommers.

"Follow the big ones?"

Sommers grinned. "Not to Peahi or anything like that, I'm only Laird Hamilton in my dreams. My folks have a place in Malibu, sometimes I bunk down with them." Wider grin. "Dump some laundry, too. Mom claims she still misses me."

"Nice to have that kind of freedom."

"I'm a Web designer so I'm flexible."

"We heard Wedd does something in show business."

Sommers huffed. "That could mean he's part of a catering crew."

"How long have you been living next to him?"

"I've been here around three years, he moved in later, maybe two, two and a half. I don't have problems with him, he keeps to himself. Not your friendly type, though. He'll never be the first to say hi and when he answers it's like he's being forced to do it. Guess that makes him your basic loner. My brother says that can be a danger sign but I can't say anything weird goes on here."

Milo said, "Your brother a detective?"

"Malibu Sheriff, rides a cruiser up and down PCH. One time he stopped me, made like he was going to ticket me. Revenge for all those times I kicked his ass."

Milo said, "You got a warning instead."

Sommers flexed a muscle and laughed. "More like I warned him."

"Do you recall when Mr. Wedd's car was stolen?"

"So that's what you're here about. What, you recovered it?"

"Not yet."

"Oh," said Sommers. "That little Bimmer was sweet, I wouldn't replace it with a Monstro-mobile."

"The Explorer."

"Explorer all ghettoed up with crazy wheels, black paint job, black windows."

"What kind of crazy wheels?" said Milo.

"Big," said Sommers, drawing a wide circle with his hands.

"Chromed, reversed, had to be serious cash. And the whole thing's jacked up. Maybe he's got hydraulics to lowride it, never seen him do it, but people get crazy with their cars."

"Big wheels, jacked and black," I said. "Pretty macho."

"My ex-girlfriend says you're secure in your masculinity, you don't need to pimp your wheels." Sommers laughed. "But maybe she was just making me feel good about my turdmobile."

"Brown Acura?"

"That's a nice way to put it," said Sommers. "Used to be my parents' cleaning lady's. She got a new one, I glommed El Crappo. You guys suspect Clark of a rip-off, like an insurance scam?"

"Clark?"

"He looks just like Clark Kent plus dude's attitude is kind of . . . I guess you'd say self-righteous."

I said, "Takes himself seriously."

"Jump in the phone booth and save Metropolis," said Sommers.

"Who does he hang out with?"

"No bros but lots of girls. Mostly I hear them rather than see them."

"Thin walls."

Sommers laughed. "Not that, at least that would be entertaining. More like they talk, wake me up. Like it's the morning and I'm hearing chick voices. I keep flexible hours because I have clients in Asia, try to catch Z's whenever I can. When he's here it's like Chick Central. And chicks *talk*."

Milo clucked sympathetically as he drew out a photo of Charlene/ Qeesha. Any hint the image was a mug shot had been removed. Still, she didn't look happy to be posing.

"Robert, ever see this girl with Wedd?"

"Not for a while."

"But you have seen her."

"Sure," said Sommers. "I remember her because she was the only black chick. Also, she was pregnant, like out to here, I'm like whoa, Clark thinks he's a superhero but he forgot the condom. I kinda felt sorry for her because she was in and out a lot—more than the others. And he's playing around with other chicks when she's not here."

"When's the last time you saw her?"

"Hmm . . . maybe a half year ago? It was a while."

"You ever see any conflict between them?"

Sommers said, "You know, one time, guess it was the last time, I heard the door slam and I looked out the blinds and saw her leaving, she's walking real fast. But he didn't go after her and I didn't hear them hassling, so I don't know, is that conflict—is that like from a mug shot?"

Milo said, "It is, Robert."

"She's a criminal type? Her and Clark are doing car scams together?"

"She was here more than the others?"

"Definitely. Most of the chicks you saw them once, twice." Sommers twirled a dread. "The black chick I saw maybe . . . six times, seven times?"

I said, "He's into one-night stands."

"Guess so." He snorted. "Playah Clark."

Milo showed him a picture of Adriana Betts.

"Her I never saw. She part of the scam gang? Looks kinda shady." His hand gathered up several clumps of hair. "More I think about it, more I'm pretty sure she was pissed at him—the black chick. Walking fast, like she couldn't wait to get away from him. Maybe it was hormones, you know? Baby hormones. That happened to my girlfriend when she was with child. The bigger she got, the grumpier she turned, kind of hellish."

"You have a kid?"

"Nope, she terminated. Her decision, she'd rather go to law school." Sommers shrugged. "I thought it might be cool. Being a daddy. But she had to do what she had to do."

27

Milo gave his card to Sommers, asked him to call if Wedd showed up.

Sommer said, "Sure, but like I said, he's not here too much."

We tried the remaining four apartments in Wedd's building. No answers at the first three units. A woman came to the fourth door towing an I.V. line on wheels. Something clear and viscous dripped into her veins. Her hair was a gray tangle, one shade darker than her face.

"Sorry . . ." She paused for breath. "I never leave . . . don't know anyone."

"He lives downstairs in Three," said Milo. "Had his car stolen a while back."

"Oh . . . that." Her jaws worked. She could've been any age from fifty to eighty. "People were . . . surprised."

"Why's that, ma'am?"

She inhaled twice, braced herself in the doorway. "At nights . . . the lights are . . . super-bright."

"Anyone trying to break into a car would be conspicuous."

"Yes . . . funny."

She labored to smile. Succeeded and hinted at the beautiful woman she'd once been. "It . . . happens."

We returned to the unmarked. Milo put the key in the ignition but didn't start up.

"Groot's instincts were good, the Bimmer's a likely scam and Clark Kent's shaping up like a bad boy with a second pad. Think he's the daddy?"

I said, "He's got women coming in and out constantly, but Qeesha's the only one seen more than once or twice. That says beyond casual and the last time Sommers saw her, she was conspicuously pregnant and looked angry. Maybe because Wedd wanted her to terminate? If she was pressing Wedd for money, it could've motivated the car scam: He finds her wheels, gets her temporarily out of his hair, uses the insurance money for his own new drive. A pimped-up SUV just like Heather saw at the park that night."

"At the park 'cause he's doing advance work, taking care of business. Qeesha hassled him, he killed her and the baby. Ditto Adriana, because she knew too much. Clark's sounding like a *real* bad boy." He frowned. "With no criminal record."

"The timing works," I said. "Qeesha left Idaho a couple of years ago, plenty of time to hook up with Wedd, get pregnant. What I find interesting is Adriana didn't follow her to L.A. but she did leave home, right around the same time. Reverend Goleman suggested she needed a life change. Meeting Qeesha, seeing her independence, might've inspired Adriana. She'd run the day care at the church. She found child-care work with the Van Dynes, then the Changs. San Diego's close to L.A. so it's not illogical she and Qeesha would reconnect. Maybe that post office box of hers was her own bit of naughty intrigue, allowing the two of them to correspond in secrecy. Allowing her vicarious entry to Qeesha's world without actually participating. But four, five months ago that changed when Qeesha called for help and Adriana went down to L.A. with the Changs—a break of her usual routine. That's the same time Sommers saw Qeesha pregnant and unhappy. What if Qeesha sensed she was in danger—she'd seen something frightening in Wedd's attitude—and wanted support? Or a witness?"

He looked over at the building. The painters had paused, were sitting at the curb eating burritos. ". . . Those bugs. Wax. If Wedd's our guy, he's something other than human." Head shake. "All those women, he's got some kind of charisma going."

"Women who aren't seen more than once or twice."

He stared at me. "Oh, no, don't get imaginative. Too early in the day."

He started the car but kept it in Park. His left hand gripped the steering wheel. The fingers of his right hand clawed his knee. He rubbed his face.

I said, "Sorry."

"No, no, now it's *my* head's going in bad directions. What if the baby wasn't unwanted, Alex? What if it was wanted in a bad way? Literally. For some kind of nut-cult ritual."

His normal pallor had leached to an unhealthy off-white. I felt my own skin go cold.

He said, "Dear God in Heaven, what if that poor little thing was *farmed*."

28

A woman stood near the entrance to the division parking lot. Tall, lanky, long-legged with frizzy yellow hair, wearing a maroon pantsuit with shoulder pads a couple of decades too big, she consulted a piece of paper as she checked out entering vehicles. A badge was clipped to her lapel.

I said, "Department bean counter?"

Milo said, "Your tax dollars at work." He rolled up behind a black-and-white and a blue Corvette that was someone's civilian ride. Both cars passed the frizzy-haired woman's scrutiny. When Milo pulled up to the keypad, she looked at him, waved the paper.

"Lieutenant Sturgis?" She approached the driver's side.

Milo said, "Another survey? Not today," began rolling the window up.

"Don't do that!" Her protest was more screech than bellow. Her pantsuit was the color of pickled beets, some fabric that had never known soil or harvest. She wore glasses framed in pale blue plastic, rouge that was too bright, lipstick that wasn't bright enough. Had one of those rawboned bodies that abhor body fat. Nothing masculine about her, but nothing feminine, either.

She pressed a hand on the half-rolled window. Picture on her badge; I was too far to read the small print. She showed Milo the paper in her hand: On it was a full-page, color photo of him.

He said, "Never seen the guy."

"C'mon, Lieutenant."

He rolled down the window. "What can I do for you?"

"You could stop avoiding me." She unclipped the badge, showed it to him. "Kelly LeMasters, L.A. *Times*."

Milo didn't oblige her with a response.

She said, "That's the way it's going to be? Fine, I'll grovel for every crumb. Even though I shouldn't have to 'cause I'm with the paper of record and I've been calling you all week on those skeletons and you've been shining me on like I'm your ex-wife filing for more spousal support."

She smiled. "Or in your case, ex-husband."

Milo said, "A comedian."

"Anything that works," said Kelly LeMasters. Her tone said she was used to rejection. But not inured to it.

A car pulled up behind us. Large black man at the wheel of a brand-new Chevy unmarked. Dark suit, white shirt, red tie. Scowl of impatience. Horn-beep.

Milo said, "That's a captain behind me, so I'm going to pull into the lot. It has nothing to do with avoiding you."

"You couldn't avoid me if you wanted to, I'll be right here when you come walking out."

True to her word, she hadn't budged a foot. Looking at me, she said, "This is the psychologist. He advise you to shine me on?"

"No one's shining you on. Sorry if it came across that way."

"Ma'am bam thank you *not,*" she said. "What, you're allergic to cooperation?" She looked me over, top-to-bottom. "Good angle, grizzled homicide cop and dashing shrink." Blue eyes shifted back to Milo. "Delete *grizzled*, insert *rumpled*."

He reached for his tie, lying crookedly across his paunch. The reflexive move cracked up Kelly LeMasters. She slapped her knee with glee. Long time since I'd seen anyone do that. Not since my last drive through the Ozarks.

Milo said, "Glad to be amusing."

Kelly LeMasters said, "See? You're human. Have your vanities like everyone else. So why in the world would you refuse to cooperate with me? I could make you famous. At least temporary-famous and that's pretty cool, no?"

"Thanks but no thanks."

"Playing hard to get? Why run from stardom, Milo Sturgis? In addition to being a sexual-preference pioneer, for which you've never received just credit, you're darn good at what you do. According to my sources, over the past twenty years you've closed proportionately more murders than any other detective. And yet no one really knows about the totality of your accomplishments because you refuse to maintain any sort of media presence. Sure, you pop up from time to time, giving pithy little quotes. But more often than not you let some boss-type get the credit for your work."

"Aw shucks."

"Fine, you're the gay Jimmy Stewart but why shut me out on these baby cases? What is it? My breath?"

She leaned close, exhaled noisily. "See? Minty fresh?" I was favored with a second blast of herbal aroma. "Back me up on that, Doctor."

Milo and I laughed.

"See," she said, "I'm a funny girl. Reward me, Milo Sturgis."

"It's complicated."

"So what isn't?" Her hand shot out. A white-gold wedding band circled one of ten bony fingers. Her nails were short, unpolished. But for the ring, she wore no jewelry.

Milo said, "Now we shake?"

"We sure do," said Kelly LeMasters. "Seeing as we're going to be warm, nurturing, mutually advantageous buddies."

A car approached from Santa Monica Boulevard. Shiny unmarked, new enough to lack plates.

Milo motioned LeMasters away from the lot entrance, turned his back to the oncoming vehicle.

"Who's that?" she said.

"Doesn't matter. Let's not talk here."

Kelly LeMasters said, "No prob. That Indian place you like?"

He glared at her. "*Nowhere* I like, I don't want to be seen with you. Minty fresh notwithstanding."

"Fine," she said. "If it means you're going to give me something juicy."

"No obligations."

"That's what they all say."

We headed up the block into the residential area south of the station. Milo and LeMasters walked abreast as I trailed two steps behind. A few turns later he stopped in front of a dingbat apartment building. White stucco instead of aqua but stylistically not dissimilar from Melvin J. Wedd's part-time residence.

Milo's idea of a private joke? Nothing about him suggested mirth as he drew himself up to max height, the way he does when he's out to intimidate.

If that was the goal, it failed with Kelly LeMasters. She took a notepad and pen out of her bag and said, "Go for it."

Milo said, "Put that away, we're off the record. If you guys still respect that."

"Milo, Milo," she said. "If nothing's on the record, what use are you to me?"

"This may come as a shock, *Kelly:* Being useful to you isn't my priority."

"Of course not, solving nasty old murders is, yadda yadda yadda. But you know as well as I do that those things go together. How many of your closed files would still be open if you didn't get media exposure when you needed it?"

"I appreciate the value of a free press. But my hands are tied."

"By?"

"Off the record?"

"Regarding that small point?" she said. "Sure."

"Bureaucracy."

She said, "You've got to be kidding. *That's* the staggering secret? We all deal with red tape, you think my employer's all Bill of Rights and no bullshit?"

"Glad you empathize."

"I don't need you to tell me why your stupid, venal bosses closed you up on the second skeleton: politics as usual, the whole Maxine Cleveland real estate thing. You ever meet her? Brain-dead and clueless, should be a perfect fit in D.C. That ploy was stupid, where did it get her?" She removed her glasses. "Your idiot bosses let me get scooped by a *damn student paper.*"

"You want to complain, I can give you some phone numbers."

"How far would that get me?"

"Exactly my point, Kelly. It's like talking to dust."

She studied him. "You're a crafty one, aren't you? Okay, we go off the record, as long as at some point it goes on the record and I don't mean months."

"Nope, can't give you a deadline."

"I don't want a deadline, I just want you to be reasonable." She put her glasses back on. Wrote something in her pad, angling the page so he couldn't see. I've seen him do the same thing with witnesses, trying to kick up the intrigue, establish dominance.

The two of them would make an interesting bridge twosome.

"Define *reasonable,* Kelly."

"Use common sense, cut the crap, however you want to define it. I am *not* going to remain mute for eternity only to have every moron on TV and the Internet going with the story."

Bony hands slapped onto bony hips. "Got it?"

"Got it."

"Fine." Her pen poised. "Shoot."

"Put the pad away."

"You don't trust me to keep it under wraps?"

"You just said your patience couldn't be guaranteed."

"We're wasting each other's time," she said. "This is bullshit."

"Then how about we table the proceedings? Something opens up, I promise to let you know."

"Why would you do that?"

"Because you're right," he said.

She studied him. "You're shitting me. Nice try."

"I'm not. You're right."

"Admitting you made a mistake? Have you checked your Y chromosomes recently?"

"If it was up to me, Kelly, I'd have lots to tell you and it would hit the paper tomorrow. Not because I care about you or your job but because it could be in my best interest. Unfortunately, by pulling that stunt at the parking lot, you made sure anything you write is going to be traced right back to me."

"I . . . maybe that was poor judgment but what was my choice?"

Milo shrugged.

Kelly LeMasters said, "Okay, fine, no notes and I swear to protect your identity." The pad and pen returned to her bag.

Milo said, "Same for the tape recorder you've got in there."

"How . . . fine, you're an ace detective." She produced the machine, switched it off.

He took it, removed a mini-spool that he pocketed, returned the recorder.

Her nostrils flared. "You're going to keep that?"

"For both our sakes."

"Want to check if I've got a nuclear-laser thought-reader in here?"

"Nah, those are so twentieth century. So what do you want to know, Kelly?"

"After all that I have to ask questions? Just tell me what you've learned about those baby skeletons."

"The first skeleton may not be related to a crime."

"What makes you say that?"

"No signs of trauma or injury."

"Maybe it was smothered or something."

"Anything's possible but I need evidence."

"A body buried under a tree is evidence," she said. "If no crime was committed why conceal it?"

"Could've been a death due to natural causes that someone wanted to cover up."

"What kind of death is natural for a baby?"

"Disease."

"Then why cover it up?"

"Wish I knew, Kelly. I may never know."

"Why the pessimism?"

"Too old, too cold."

"I assume you've traced the owners of the house."

"You assume correctly. No leads, there."

"I know," said LeMasters. "I looked into it, myself. Found that old guy in Burbank, the whole John Wayne thing, he had nothing to say. Neither did anyone in Cheviot Hills. Including that kid who blabbed to the SMC paper. Her thing was *I talk to Lieutenant Sturgis, no one else.*"

Milo said, "Power of the press."

"Yeah, we're real popular—so I should just forget about the first one."

"Probe to your heart's content, Kelly. You learn anything, I'll be grateful." Sounding sincere. Not a word about Eleanor Green, a big blue Duesenberg.

Nothing from me to either of them about Dr. Jimmy Asherwood.

Kelly LeMasters said, "Okay, let's get to the juicy one."

"Once again, Kelly, there's no evidence of trauma but I'm assuming homicide, because of the dead woman who was found across the park. Also, we've done prelim DNA on the bones and the baby was a girl."

Kelly LeMasters didn't emote. "Okay, go on."

"By the state of her dentition two or three months old."

"That's it? What about the woman?"

Milo said, "Does it bother you at all?"

"What?"

"A baby."

Her jaw tightened and her arms grew rigid. "Does it bother *you*?"

"You bet."

"Well, me, too," she said. "So it's settled, we both make our livings off other people's misery but we're still human." She turned to me. "Guess that applies to you, too—the misery part. Tell me, did you coach him in all this psychological warfare?" She faced Milo again. "Does it *bother* me? Let's put it this way: I've got one kid and it took me three miscarriages to get him, so no, I don't get a thrill out of dead babies, don't find them the least bit entertaining. Now what the hell else do you want to know?"

Milo said, "Sorry."

"Screw the apology. Give me some meat to chew on."

"We've identified the adult victim. Nothing in her past predisposes her to being murdered."

"Name," said LeMasters.

"Adriana Betts, originally from Idaho. She was religious, had no bad habits, worked as a nanny."

"She took care of kids?"

"Yes."

"That include babies?"

"In some cases."

"That doesn't sound like a connection to you?"

"Theoretically? Sure, Kelly, but we interviewed her employers and all their kids are alive and well. No one has a bad word to say about her."

"Religious types can be hypocrites."

"Anyone can."

"What, you're a Holy Roller? Despite what the church says about people like you?"

"Let's stick with the case, Kelly."

"I can't see it," said LeMasters. "Being Catholic and gay." She laughed. "Unless you're a parish priest."

"You're Catholic?"

"Once upon a time."

"Nice to know you've got no biases."

She frowned. "Where will you be taking the investigation?"

"Hard to say."

"No, it's not," she said. "Everyone says you're methodical as well as intuitive, always come up with a plan. So don't hold back on me. What's next?"

"Same answer, Kelly."

She folded her arms across her chest. "I go off-record and you give me generalities?"

"That's because generalities are all I've got. I could feed you stuff that would spark your prurient interest, set you off on a useless maze-run. But it wouldn't help my case, could even hurt it if you printed fallacious crap."

"I thought we were working on trust here."

"We are," he said. "Have we reached our goal?"

"Of what?"

"Mutually advantageous buddy-hood."

"Not even close," she said. "I promised to keep everything under wraps and you gave me squat."

He creased his brow. "I'm going to tell you something else but you have to pledge not to use it until I say otherwise. I mean that, Kelly. It's essential."

"Fine, fine. What?"

"Though of apparently sound moral character, Adriana Betts may have somehow gotten mixed up with bad people."

"What kind of bad people?"

"This isn't fact-based," he said, "but possibly cult members."

"Not fact-based? Then what?"

"Inference."

"Yours or Dr. Delaware's?"

"Mine."

"You inferred from the body?" she said. "Some sort of ritual mutilation? I heard she was just shot."

"Sorry, that's all I can say, Kelly."

"Church-girl in the clutches of Satan worshippers? Any freakos in particular?"

"Not even close," he said. "I'll be looking into that world, would welcome your input on the topic."

"I don't know squat about cults."

"That makes two of us, Kelly."

Her arms relaxed. Her eyes brightened. "Are we talking another Manson thing?"

"I sure hope not."

"This town," said LeMasters, "is Weirdo Central. Can you narrow it down at all?"

"Wish I could, Kelly, and you need to make sure no one knows we had this talk."

"Like I said, I protect my sources."

"I'm not talking legally, I mean total blackout." His turn to move closer to her. Big black eyebrows dipped. He loomed. Kelly LeMasters shrank back. He filled another few inches of her personal space. She tried to stand her ground but the primal fear of something big and aggressive caused her to step back.

"Total," he repeated. "You screw that up, I'll never talk to you again and neither will anyone in the department."

He'd lowered his voice. The resultant half whisper was movie-villain ominous.

LeMasters blinked. Forced herself to smile. "You're threatening me?"

"I'm stating a contingency, Kelly. And here's another one, just to show you what a nice guy I am: If you stick to your part of the deal, you'll be the first one to know if I close the case."

"*If,* not *when?*"

"Appreciate the vote of confidence, Kelly. Either way, you'll scoop everyone. I promise."

"How much lead time will I get?"

"Enough to close everyone out."

"You can guarantee that?" she said. "What about your bosses?"

"Fuck 'em," he growled.

His eyes were green slits.

Kelly LeMasters knew better than to argue.

We walked her back to Butler Avenue, watched her diminish to a beet-colored speck that turned east on Santa Monica and disappeared.

I said, "To paraphrase Persistent Kelly, what's next?"

"I look into Mr. Wedd and you go about your normal life."

"Whatever that means."

"It means have a nice day. Relatively speaking."

29

Holly Ruche showed up six minutes late. Blanche and I greeted her at the door. She said, "I generally don't like dogs. But I've been thinking of getting one. For the baby."

Worst reason in the world. I said, "I'm happy to keep her out of the office."

"She's like a therapy dog?"

"Not officially but she's got enough credits for her own Ph.D."

She looked down at Blanche.

Blanche beamed up at her.

She said, "What's her name?"

"Blanche."

"She's kind of cute . . . almost like she's smiling. Okay, I guess she can be there."

"Up to you, Holly."

"It's okay. Yes, it's definitely okay, she's well behaved." She took in the living room. "Stylish. You're into contemporary."

After a psychopath burns down your first house simplicity can be a tonic.

I smiled.

She said, "Have you been here long?"

"A while."

"This neighborhood. Must've cost a fortune."

"Let's go to my office."

Seated on the battered leather couch, she said, "Sorry. That crack about a fortune. No business of mine. I guess I'm just hyper about how much things cost. Especially real estate."

"The decorating's at a standstill?"

"Still in the talking stages."

"You and Matt."

She knitted her hands, gazed down. "Mostly me and me."

"Kind of a monologue."

She stroked her belly. She'd put on some girth and her face had grown fuller. Her hair was tied back functionally, tiny pimples paralleled her hairline. "I guess that's part of why I'm here. He's not available. Physically or emotionally. They go together, I guess. He works all the time."

"Is that something new?"

Her lower lip curled. Tears seeped from under her lower lids and trickled onto her cheeks.

"I guess not," she finally said. "I guess that's the real problem. Nothing's changed."

I handed her a tissue. Kleenex should pay me a commission. "Matt's always been work-oriented."

"I respect that, Dr. Delaware. He's super-responsible, that's a big deal, right? He could be a slacker."

"Sure."

"He thinks it's manly. Taking care of business. I guess it is. I *know* it is."

I said, "It's part of why you were attracted to him."

"Yes—how'd you know that?"

"Educated guess."

"Well, you're right, that was a big part of it. It's just—I guess you need to know more about my father. Like the fact that I didn't have one."

I waited.

She said, "I never knew him. I'm not sure my mother knew him." Her fingers closed over the tissue. "This is hard to talk about . . . but I need to be honest, right? I mean this is the place for that."

Her fingers relaxed. She dropped the tissue in a wastebasket. "Being pregnant has made me think about all sorts of things I told myself I'd never have to think about."

"Your own family."

"If you can call it that."

"There wasn't much in the way of family."

"Just me and my mother and she was . . ."

She sat for a while. "There's no two ways about it, Mom was loose. Morally, I mean. Not to me, to me she was just Mom, but looking back . . . she was a cocktail waitress—I'm not saying that was bad, she worked incredibly hard, she took care of me, put food on the table. But she also . . . supplemented her income. By bringing men home, when I was little I thought it was normal. Locking me in my room with cookies and candies."

She bit her lip. "That didn't stop me from seeing some of them. Hearing them. All kinds of men, different ages, races, it was like . . . she called them her friends. 'Time for quiet time with these Oreos and Kit Kats, sweetie. I need to spend time with my friends.'"

I said, "At some point you realized that wasn't typical."

"I realized it when I started kindergarten and saw how other kids lived. My first years were kind of isolated, we lived in a trailer park. Don't get me wrong, it was a nice trailer, Mom kept it up, planted flowers all around, there was a little birdbath where sparrows and finches would come. We were pretty close to a nice neighborhood, working class, solid people, lots of religious types. It didn't take me long to catch on that other mothers didn't do what mine did. I never said anything because Mom loved me, took care of me, I always had nice clothes and good food. The same things other kids had, who was I to be ungrateful?"

More tears. "I shouldn't have said that. Calling her loose, that was wrong, really mean."

Another tissue interlude.

She said, "She's gone, can't defend herself . . . I just feel it's time to be honest, you know? Confront reality. So I can understand myself."

"Now that you're becoming a mom."

"I don't want to be like her," she said. "I mean in some ways I do, I want to be loving, to take care of my Aimee, to give her everything. That's why I married Matt, he's a totally great provider."

"When I talked to you at your house you said you'd worked most of your life, had a career until recently."

"That's true."

"You set out to be independent."

"Yes. So?"

"So even though Matt's maturity and industriousness were qualities you found attractive, you never intended to rely upon him totally."

"I . . . yes, that's true, I guess you're right. You're saying Mom made me tough?"

"I'm saying you're an obviously capable, thoughtful person. Does your mother get some of the credit? Sure, but in the end you made your own decisions."

"I guess I did . . . but I'm still sorry. For saying that about Mom. I miss her so *much*!"

She burst out weeping, took a while to compose herself. "She passed three years ago, Doctor, she suffered so much. I guess I've been angry at her for leaving so young, she was fifty-four. Even though that's not rational. I was being selfish, I'm too selfish, period, I shouldn't have *said* that."

"Did you treat her unkindly when she was alive?"

"No, of course not. When she had to go to hospice—she had ALS,

Lou Gehrig's disease—I was always there for her. It was terrible, she hung on for three years. I paid for whatever Medi-Cal and insurance didn't cover. I was there all the time. Her mind was still working but nothing else was, that's what made it so horrible. At the end, she could still move her eyes, I could see the love in them. So how could I *say* that?"

"Your life's in flux, Holly, it's normal for old feelings to come back. You love your mother but some of the things she did frightened and embarrassed you. You've never expressed how you felt about it. It's okay."

"You're telling me it's okay to say things like that? Calling her *loose*?"

"It's a word, Holly. Your actions spoke much louder."

Long silence. "You're so nice. Your wife is lucky—are you married?"

I smiled.

"Sorry, sorry, I need to mind my own business."

"It's not that, Holly. This is about you."

She smiled. "That's sure different. Being the star. Though I guess I was the star to Mom. She never had any more kids. I guess one whoopsie baby was enough."

"You know for sure you were an accident."

"Why wouldn't I be?"

"Your mother sounds like an organized person."

"You're saying she intended me?"

"Did she make any other whoopsies?"

She pulled at the tissue. Tugged at her ponytail. "I see what you mean. She always told me I was the best thing ever happened to her."

"I'm sure you were."

She glanced at Blanche. I gave the *okay* nod and Blanche waddled over to the couch.

Holly said, "Is she allowed up here?"

"Absolutely."

"If you want you can come up, cutie." Blanche leaped effortlessly to her side, moved in close for a snuggle. Holly stroked the folds of her neck. "She's so soft. Like a stuffed animal."

"As cute as a toy," I said, "and a whole lot smarter."

"You've got it all, don't you," she said. "The house, the dog. Maybe a wife—sorry . . . so maybe that's why you think I was a deliriously desired baby. Okay, I'll go with that. My Aimee's wanted, that's what's important. Let me ask you something: Do you think permissive's the best way to go or keep up the discipline?"

"Depends on the child."

"Some kids need more discipline."

I nodded.

She said, "Matt sure doesn't need any more, he's the most self-disciplined person I've ever met."

"How about you?"

"I'm okay . . . I guess I know how to take care of myself . . . I wonder what Aimee will be like. Not that I'm trying to box her in with expectations. I mean obviously I'd like her to be beautiful and brilliant—healthy, that's the most important thing. Healthy. So you're saying I need to get to know her before I work out my plan."

"You may not need a plan," I said.

"No?"

"A lot of people have good instincts."

"But some don't."

"How about your mother?"

"She had excellent instincts," she said. "The best." Wide smile. "Now I feel better. Saying something nice to make up for the other thing."

She crossed her legs. "That was your plan, right? To guide me to say something nice."

"Like I said, Holly, sometimes a plan isn't necessary."

"You knew me well enough to just let me go on."

"You know yourself."

"I guess I do, Dr. Delaware." She placed a hand on her belly. "This is mine, I own it. I'm not saying Aimee's not a separate person, I get that. I'm talking about the process. Carrying her, nurturing her with my body. A woman needs to feel she owns that . . . I feel much better now. If I need you can I call?"

"Of course."

"I don't care anymore about the house or the remodeling or any material crap," she said. "That kind of ownership doesn't matter."

CHAPTER

30

I made a couple of tuna sandwiches, brought them to Robin's studio.

She said, "The perfect man," washed sawdust from her hands, gave me a kiss. We ate near the pond, talked about everything but work, returned to work. Blanche chose to stay with Robin but she licked my hand first.

I said, "Master diplomat."

Robin held out the half sandwich she'd wrapped in a napkin. "More like I've got the goodies."

"Definition of diplomacy."

I sat wondering what Adriana Betts had done for money and lodging during the months between leaving La Jolla and showing up dead in the park.

Maybe she'd saved up enough to coast. Or perhaps she'd resorted to what she knew best: taking care of other people's offspring. I printed a list of every employment agency in L.A. County that advertised nannies, au pairs, governesses, any sort of in-house staff.

For the next hour, my lie was glib and consistent: I was Adriana's potential employer and she'd listed the agency as having handled her in the past. I must have been pretty convincing because I encountered a lot of outrage at the falsehood. Several people said I was lucky to learn about Adriana's poor character early on. Most made sure to let me know they had far superior candidates.

With a dozen calls to go, I took a coffee break and checked with my service. A family court judge had left a message thanking me for a "helpful" custody report, ditto one of the attorneys on the case. Third was Holly Ruche offering her gratitude, no specifics.

The service operator, a woman I'd never talked to before, said, "You have teenagers by any chance, Doctor?"

I said, "Why?"

"Everyone seems to appreciate you. If you tell me your teenagers do, I may make an appointment, myself."

I laughed.

She said, "You sound cheerful, so that's my answer. You don't have any."

I'd whittled the agency list to four companies when the man who answered at Gold Standard Professionals in Beverly Hills listened to my pitch but didn't reply.

I said, "You know Adriana?"

He said, "Hold on for a moment, please." Deep, mellifluous voice.

As I waited, I examined the company's Internet ad. The pitch featured twenties-style cartoons of butlers, footmen, chefs in toques, maids in lace uniforms, lettering in an angular art deco font. Boldface motto: *The ultimate in classic service, beyond the ultimate in classic discretion.*

Maybe discretion was what kept me on hold for seven minutes before the connection was cut.

I redialed, got voice mail. After fielding more indignation at the remaining three agencies, I gave Gold Standard another try.

This time no one answered.

I Googled the company. A single reference popped up, a piece from the *Beverly Hills Clarion* that could've been a paid ad or least-resistance journalism. Gold Standard's owners were Jack and Daisy Weathers, "former performers, now entrepreneurs in the field of high-end service," who'd parlayed their knowledge of "the unique demands of the industry with post-graduate training in human factors and development."

For Jack that meant a master's degree from a "university" I knew to be a correspondence mill. No educational specs for Daisy. The accompanying photo showed the Weatherses to be white-haired, tan, wearing matching pink shirts and smiles crammed with post-graduate dental work.

The smooth voice could easily have been that of an actor, so maybe I'd talked to the boss. Gold Standard's address was a P.O.B. in Beverly Hills, 90211. South end of the city, maybe a mail drop.

Was there no need for an office because clients of sufficient importance merited house calls? Or did one have to pass muster before being favored with private-club status? If the latter was the case, I'd flunked. Maybe that had nothing to do with Adriana, just disdain for an obviously undeserving plebe with no link to "the Industry." But no other agency had reacted that way.

I put in a call to Milo. He said, "I was just going to call you. Eat, yet?"

"Had a sandwich."

"That's a snack not a meal. The usual place."

"No reporter in tow, huh."

"Speaking of Lois Lane, I may have created a monster. I'm walking over right now, gonna start grub-festing without you. Seeing as you already had a *sandwich*."

I found him at his usual corner table at Café Moghul, perched like a potentate behind platters of lamb, chicken, lobster, and crab, some kind of meatball big enough to hurl at Dodger Stadium, the usual Himalaya of naan and vegetables, bowls of mystery sauce.

Be nice if synchrony ruled the world and there was a master detective in Mumbai stuffing his face with burgers, fried chicken, and pizza.

Unlike every other time I'd been in the restaurant, the dining room was nearly full. The new patrons were uniformed cops and plainclothes detectives. Everyone chowing down on generous portions but none of the wretched excess left at the Altar of Milo.

I sat down. "Looks like the world's caught on."

"What they caught on to is a special lunch deal, half price on everything."

A detective I recognized waved and brandished a lobster claw. Milo muttered, "Bargain-hunting vulgarians."

The bespectacled woman brought me iced tea and a clean plate. She looked exhausted.

I said, "Busy."

She beamed at Milo. "They listen to him."

He said, "You've got to believe me, it was the flyer you left at the station."

Her smile widened. Knowing she'd encountered a deity and figuring humility was one of his divine attributes.

I said, "What's up, Mahatma?"

He leaned in close, lowered his voice. "Ol' Kelly's digging like a gopher. So far I've received about fifty pages of attachments on infanticides, none of which is relevant. Meanwhile, zip on Adriana, Wedd, or Charlene Chambers as herself or as Qeesha D'Embo. And none of the cult sites I've found seems to fit. Including their photos."

"Cults post publicity photos?"

"You better believe it, they're proud of themselves. Basically, it's a party scene, Alex, lots of nudity and naughty groping. Weirdest thing I found was a Beelzebub-worshipping bunch that gets off by smearing themselves with food, the prime sacramental offering being baked beans. Vegetarian, of course."

I said, "Someone's engaged in truly ugly behavior, why advertise?"

Nodding, he downed half a plate of lamb, wiped his hands and mouth, scanned the room, switched to a low-volume leprechaun brogue. "I *was* a wee bit *impish,* laddy. Gave Ms. LeMasters the name and number of one Maria Thomas and told her it wouldn't displease me if she harassed the brass about going public on selective info."

"Selective as in what you decide."

"Is there another definition?"

"Maria's not going to make the connection to you?"

"The story Kelly's telling her is she's fed up with me because I keep stonewalling her so she's decided to go over my head. If Maria gives her the okay, no problem. If Maria tells her no, she'll publish a follow-up piece on the park murders, anyway. To my great apparent chagrin."

I said, "Impressively devious."

"When in Nome, do as the Ice Queen does. Meanwhile, no cult link to Wedd but I have learned a few things about him, most of it disappointing. Not only does he lack a criminal record, according to his landlord he's a model tenant, pays on time, never complains. As opposed to Surf-Boy Sommers who's chronically late with his rent and bitches about everything and who the landlord sees as a druggie. So I'm not sure he's gonna work as a witness. I also found out that an A.C. company was in Wedd's place to install new thermostats two weeks ago, landlord let them in, the place was neat, clean, nothing out of the ordinary."

"Landlords have to notify tenants about service calls, so Wedd would've had time to clean up."

"In this case the landlord got phone authorization from Wedd the same day. He did say from the look of the place Wedd didn't seem to use it much. Which backs up the dual-crib theory. I was able to get Wedd's cell number and email, as well as the work history Wedd listed on his application."

He pulled out his pad. "Steadily and gainfully employed for over three years at a company called CAPD, Inc. The intriguing factoid in this whole data storm is CAPD has no listed address. The 'PD' part made me wonder if they're trying to sound police-like, a hush-hush private security outfit. But there are no business listings in the county under that name and when I called the number Wedd listed I was automatically transferred to a company of the same name on Grand Cayman Island and their answer was an electronic beep that then cut off midsentence. And when I searched for an island address, there was none."

I said, "The Caymans are big on offshore banking."

"That was hypothesis two, some shady financial scam, and Qeesha being a naughty girl mighta had a history with them. So I called Ray Lhermitte in New Orleans but CAPD meant nothing to him."

"Wedd told Sommers he worked in the industry. I just fielded my own bit of intrigue, based on that."

I told him about my agency calls, the evasive response at Gold Standard.

"Maybe he just didn't like the sound of my voice but my gut says he was hiding something."

A cop across the room flashed a thumbs-up. Milo growled, "Rank conformist." To me: "Gold Standard. Why not Platinum? Okay, let's ditch these bandwagon-jumpers and see what *Gold* Standard's all about."

He threw cash on the table. The woman in the sari rushed over and tried to return the money. "For your commission!"

"Give it to charity," he said.

"What charity, Lieutenant?"

"Something kind and gentle."

"Like you."

He stomped out of the restaurant.

The woman said, "Such a wonderful man!"

One of the cops called out, "Pardon, could we have some more of that spinach?"

CHAPTER

31

As we drove to the south end of Beverly Hills, I thought of something. "Sommers said Wedd avoided conversation. How'd he know Wedd was an Industry guy?"

"Let's find out."

Sommers answered his phone. "He used to get *Variety* delivered."

"Used to?"

"Haven't seen it for a while. Also the way he walked was a tip-off. Full of himself. Like 'I'm a dude who *knows* people.' He do something bad to those girls?"

"No evidence of that, Robert."

"Meaning maybe he did," said Sommers. "Okay, if he shows up I'll let you know."

Gold Standard's address matched a two-story building clad with salmon-colored granite. Quick 'n Easy Postal and Packaging took up the street-level space. The female clerk working the counter was young and cute with doe eyes and a fox-face. Her hair was a red tsunami.

Sleeve tattoos and a steel stud jutting from her chin said pain wasn't an issue for her. Neither was discretion.

Milo said, "Where can I find the people who rent Box Three Thirty-Five?"

"Go outside and up the stairs."

I'd been wrong about a mail drop. Was glad to be humbled.

"If their office is right here why do they need you?"

The clerk said, "Hmm. 'Cause I'm cute?"

He squinted to read her name tag. "Well, sure, I can see that, Cheyenne. Is there any other reason?"

She twirled the chin stud. It caught for an instant, made her wince, finally rotated. "The building owner doesn't provide mail slots for the tenants."

"How come?"

"'Cause that was the deal in order for us to move in. It worked, most of them rent from us. Are those guys in trouble or something? 'Cause they don't seem like the type."

"What type is that?" said Milo.

"They're kinda . . . like old?" She inspected us. "I mean serious old."

"Grandma and Grandpa."

"Not like my Gram-peeps. *They* don't have a clue."

"These guys do."

"These guys are like cool dressers. In an old way."

"These fashion plates have a name?"

"Plates?" she said.

"What are their names, Cheyenne?"

A fingernail pinged the stud. A speck of blood seeped from between steel and skin. A tiny red bubble formed. She flicked it away. "They *are* in trouble? Wow."

"Not at all, Cheyenne. We just need to talk to them."

"Oh. They're Daisy and Jack. She used to act on TV and he was like a musician."

"They told you that."

"Yeah, but it's true, I saw her acting."

"Where?"

"On TV," she said. "One of those movies, cowboys and horses. She was like the girl he loved."

"The main cowboy."

"Totally. He put her on the horse and they did a lip-lock. She was hot."

I said, "Was Jack playing guitar in the background?"

"Huh? Oh, no, he was like into trumpets or something. In a TV band."

"One of those late-night shows?"

Blank look. If I was a network head I'd be worried about longevity.

Milo said, "So what kind of business do Daisy and Jack run upstairs?"

"I dunno."

"What kind of mail do they get?"

"Dunno that either."

He smiled. "You never look?"

"Mail comes in the morning," she said. "I get here at noon. Why don't you just go up and talk to them if you're so interested?"

"They're in?"

"Dunno."

"Okay, thanks, Cheyenne."

"So maybe they're in trouble, huh?"

Stairs carpeted in cheap blue low-pile polyester led to a windowless foyer rimmed by five slab doors. No sound from behind any of them. Gold Standard Professionals' neighbors offered electrolysis, bookbinding, tax preparation, and gift counseling.

Milo said, "Gift counseling? What the hell does that mean?"

I said, "Maybe they tell you who's been naughty or nice."

"Next there'll be laxative counseling. 'We open new channels of communication.' Okay, here goes nothing." He rapped on Gold Standard's door. A male voice said, "Who's there?"

"Police."

"What?"

"Police. Please open up."

Another *"What?"* but the door cracked.

Jack Weathers had added a clipped white mustache and some wrinkles since his *Clarion* interview. He was tall, well built, seventy to seventy-five, wore a white polo shirt under a sea-green cashmere V-neck, taupe linen slacks, calfskin loafers sans socks. His skin was shiny and spray-bronzed, his eyes a deeper tan. A wedding band crusted with pavé diamonds circled his left ring finger. One pinkie hosted a white-gold emerald ring, the other a rose-gold creation dominated by a massive amethyst. The gold chain around his neck was curiously delicate.

He said, "Police? I don't understand."

Milo flashed the badge. "Could we come in, please, Mr. Weathers?"

"Do I have a choice?"

"Of course, sir."

A female voice said, "Jack? What's going on?" Before Weathers could answer, a woman came up behind him and shoved the door wide open.

A foot shorter than her husband, Daisy Weathers had on a black jacquard silk top, cream gabardine slacks, red stilettos that advertised a virtuoso pedicure. Serious bling glinted at all the predictable spots. The white in her hair verged on silver-plate. The style was some cosmetologist's ode to meringue. Her eyes were glacier-blue, oddly innocent. Small bones and a sweet face had kept her cute well beyond the expiration date.

Jack Weathers said, "They're the police."

Daisy Weathers said, "Hi, boys. Collecting for the law enforcement ball? We give every year." Sultry voice. She winked.

Milo said, "Not exactly, ma'am."

Jack Weathers said, "They don't send guys in suits for the ball, Daze. They send kids—scouts, cadets, whatever you call 'em."

Daisy Weathers said, "Cute kids, they're making 'em bigger nowa-days. What can we do for you boys?"

Milo said, "We'd like to talk about Adriana Betts."

She looked puzzled. "Well, I can't say I know who that is."

Jack Weathers's face darkened. A fist punched a palm. "*Knew* it—it was one of you who called earlier, right? If you'd left a number, I'd have called you back."

I said, "Got cut off, couldn't get through after that."

His eyes danced to the right. "Well, I don't know about that. Our phones are working fine."

Daisy said, "Jack, what's going on?"

"All they had to do was call, this really isn't necessary."

"He says he did."

"Well, all he had to do was try again." Maybe Weathers was usually truthful, because lying didn't sit well with him. I counted at least three tells in as many seconds: lip-gnaw, brow-twitch, foot-tap. Then his eyes got jumpy.

"Anyway," I said, "we're here, so no harm, no foul."

Milo moved toward the doorway. Jack Weathers considered his options and stepped aside.

Daisy Weathers said, "What was that name, boys?"

Milo said, "Adriana Betts."

"Is that someone I'm supposed to know, Jack?"

The eyes turned into pinballs.

She touched his wrist. He jerked reflexively.

"Jackie? What's going on?"

"It's nothing, baby."

I said, "So she did work for you."

"No one works *for* us," said Jack Weathers. "We're facilitators."

"Ja-ack-ee?" said his wife. "Again?"

Weathers looked away.

"Jack!"

"No big deal, Daze."

"Obviously it is a big deal if the police are here."

He cursed under his breath.

She said, "You boys better come in and straighten this out."

The single-room office was furnished with two cheap desks and three hard-plastic chairs. The walls were hospital-beige and bare. A lone window half covered by warped plastic blinds looked out to an alley and the brick wall of the neighboring building. One desk was set up with a multi-line phone, a modem, a computer, a printer, and a fax machine. The other held a collection of bisque figurines—slender, white-wigged court figures engaged in spirited nonsense. Daisy Weathers took a seat behind the porcelain and lifted a lute-playing lady in a ball gown. One of her six rings clinked against the doll. Her husband winced.

Then he slipped behind the bank of business machines and eased his long body as low as he could manage.

Milo said, "Tell us about Adriana Betts."

Daisy said, "Yes, do, dear."

Jack said, "She came with good recommendations."

"Did you do the screening, Jackie?"

"It was an urgent one, Daze."

She slapped her forehead. "Bending rules. What a shock." To us: "My sweetie pie, here, has a heart softer than a ripe persimmon." That sounded like a line from a movie.

Jack said, "Someone comes to me in need, I try to help."

"He really does, boys. I wish I could get mad at him but you need to know him, he's a people-pleaser."

Milo said, "What kind of screening do you usually do?"

"Comprehensive screening," said Jack. "Just what you do."

"What we do?"

"Er . . . what I'm sure you do when you hire police officers." Weathers's smile was a pathetic grope for rapport. "To ensure the best fit, right? Everyone knows BHPD's the best."

"I'll pass that along to them," said Milo. "Actually, I'm LAPD."

"Oh," said Jack Weathers. "Well, I'm sure the same applies to you, we used to live in Los Angeles. Hancock Park, lovely, we had a gorgeous Colonial with a half-acre garden, the police were always helpful."

"Great to hear that, sir. So with Adriana Betts you decided to forgo the usual screening."

Daisy let out a prolonged sigh. Jack shot her a look that could've been a warning. Or fear.

"As I said, there was urgency."

I said, "Someone was in need."

"That's what we do," said Jack. "We fill needs."

"In Ms. Betts's case, child-care needs?"

He didn't answer.

Daisy said, "No matter who you are, finding the right people is always a challenge."

I faced Jack. "Meaning someone important. Who'd you send Adriana to?"

He shook his head.

Milo said, "Sir?"

Jack Weathers said, "What exactly are you claiming happened? Because I absolutely refuse to believe it was anything serious. I pride myself on being an excellent judge of character and that young lady had obviously fine character. She was *religious,* had a letter from her pastor."

Milo pulled out one of Qeesha's mug shots. "What about this young lady?"

Daisy blurted, "Her?"

Jack tried to hiss her silent.

She said, "I'm really at sea over this. Will someone please tell me what's going on?"

Jack folded his arms across his chest.

Milo said, "You'd placed Qeesha D'Embo where you sent Adriana."

Silence.

I said, "Qeesha vouched for Adriana. That's why you didn't feel the need to screen her."

Daisy said, "Normally, we'd still screen. But if it was urgent—"

"They *get* it," said her husband.

She pouted. "Jackie?"

"We're not saying anything more, gentlemen. Not without advice of counsel."

Milo said, "You want a lawyer to answer routine questions?"

"You bet."

Daisy put the figurine down. No visible tremor but the base rattled on the desktop.

Milo said, "You're not being accused of any crime, Mr. Weathers."

"Even so," said Jack.

"You didn't screen Adriana but you did screen Qeesha."

Daisy said, "I've never heard of Qeesha, we knew her by another name—what was it again, Jackie?"

Weathers shook his head, drew his finger across his lip.

"She's a beautiful girl," said Daisy. "The way those black girls can be with their big dark eyes. What *was* her name . . . something with an 'S,' I believe, I'd have to check the—"

"Shut *up,* Daze!"

Daisy Weathers stared at her husband. One hand bounced on her desktop. The other rose to her face, pinched cheek-skin, twisted. Her eyes turned wet.

Jack Weathers said, "Oh, baby."

Daisy sniffled.

He turned to us. "Now look what you've done—I need you to leave."

Standing, he pointed to the door.

Milo said, "Suit yourself, Mr. Weathers," and got up. "But here's what puzzles me. You run a business based on the ability to judge character. You said before that whatever happened to Adriana wasn't a big deal because she was a woman of good character. But from what I can tell, you're only batting five hundred, sir. Good for baseball, not so good for job placement."

"What are you *talking* about?"

"You were right about one thing, wrong about the other. Yes, Adriana seems to have been a woman of excellent character. But what happened was a really big deal."

"What happened?" Weathers demanded.

"Your lawyer can tell you. After we return with your friends at BHPD armed with a search warrant for all of your records."

"That's impossible!" Weathers shouted.

"Jack?" said Daisy.

"It's not only possible," said Milo, "it's probable."

"You're not making sense!" said Weathers. "Adriana had excellent character but she still committed some kind of . . . bad deed?"

"She didn't do anything, Mr. Weathers. Something was done *to* her."

"She's hurt?" said Daisy.

"She's dead, ma'am. Someone murdered her."

"Oh, no!"

"I'm afraid yes, Mrs. Weathers."

"I never even knew her, Jack hired her. Poor thing." She cried. It seemed genuine, but who could be sure about anything on the Westside of L.A.

Her husband remained dry-eyed.

Milo said, "Care to fill us in, sir?"

"Not on your life," said Jack Weathers. "Not on one blessed second of your blessed life."

32

We lingered outside the door Jack Weathers had just shut. Conversational noise began filtering through the wood: Daisy Weathers's higher-pitched voice, plaintive, then demanding. No response from Jack. Daisy, again, louder. A bark from her husband that silenced her.

Several seconds later his voice resumed, softer, less staccato. A long string of sentences.

Milo whispered, "On the phone, now it's a lawyer game."

We left the building.

Milo drove a block, U-turned, found the farthest spot that afforded a view of the marble-clad building. Red zone but until a B.H. parking Nazi showed up, the perfect vantage point.

I said, "Waiting for Jack to leave?"

"Maybe I stirred up enough for him to meet with legal counsel. I tail him, find out who I'll be dealing with. Without that I can't approach him."

"No warrant party with BHPD?"

"Yeah, right. On what grounds?"

"Jack's demeanor."

"He got agitated? To a psychologist, that's grounds. To a judge, you know what it is." He stretched, knuckled an eyelid. "Any way it shakes out, he's toast. Runs a business based on image and trust and hires one woman with a police record, another who ends up getting killed. And who was referred by the bad girl. Screening my ass."

I said, "Maybe it goes beyond that. Weathers bills himself as a Hollywood insider so maybe he also placed Wedd. At the same client who employed Qeesha and Adriana. Someone powerful enough to shelter income in the Caymans and to scare Weathers straight to legal counsel."

"CAPD," he said.

"Let's try to find out who they are."

"Easier said than done."

"Maybe not."

I pulled out my cell, punched my #1 preset.

Robin said, "Hi, hon, what's up?"

"Got a spare minute for some research?"

"About what?"

"Ever hear of CAPD?"

"Nope."

"Who would you call if you needed info on a big-time showbiz-type?"

"What's this about, Alex?"

I told her.

She said, "Interesting. I'll see what I can do."

Most of Robin's guitars and mandolins are commissioned by professional musicians and collectors who play seriously. A few end up stashed in the vaults of rich men seeking trophies—lucky-sperm recipients, real estate tycoons, Aspergian algorithmers, movie stars.

Plus the lampreys who get rich off movie stars. I rarely think of my girl as a Hollywood type but she's the one who gets invited to all the parties we seldom attend.

Six minutes later, that paid off. "Got what you need."

"That was quick."

"I looped in Brent Dorf."

Dorf was a luminary at a major talent agency. I'd met him last year when he picked up a replica of an eighteenth-century parlor guitar that would end up hanging on a wall. When he found out what I did for a living, he reminisced about being a psych major at Yale, regretted that he hadn't pursued it because his "primary passion" was helping people. My experience is people who talk about being passionate seldom are.

Brent had impressed me as the perfect political type—a mile wide and an inch deep, programmed to banter on cue. His jokes were clever, his attention span brief. Whatever charm he managed to project was diluted by the flat eyes and sanguinary grin of a monitor lizard. At least he paid his bills on time.

I said, "Dorf knew about CAPD?"

"Boy did he, honey. Unfortunately, Big Guy's life is going to get really complicated."

She explained why.

I told Milo.

He said, "Oh."

Then he swore.

33

P rema-Rani Moon was Hollywood royalty. As is the case with real royalty, that meant a mixed bag of privilege and decadence.

Grandpa Ricardo (né Luna) had been nominated for an Oscar but didn't win the statuette. Grandma Greta's success rate was one for three. Uncle Maximilian's average over a forty-year career was the best: a perfect two out of two.

Daddy Richard Jr.'s star had glittered, then sputtered, with seven forgettable pictures followed by a descent into the gummy haze of heroin addiction. Rick Moon's final attempt at rehab was a stint at a Calcutta ashram run by a guru later proved to be a rapist. Flirtation with fringe Eastern philosophy led Moon to endow his only child with a hybrid Indian name: Prema, a Sanskrit word for "love," and Rani, "queen" in Hindi.

By the time the little girl was five, all traces of religion in her father's muddled consciousness had been banished and he was living in Montmartre with the little girl's mother, a second-tier Chanel model turned semi-famous by her marriage to the handsome, tormented American film scion.

A coke-induced heart attack claimed Rick's life at age thirty-eight. Lulu Moon claimed she'd tried to revive her husband. If so, the powder she'd crammed up her nose hampered the process. Fourteen months later, she was buried next to Rick at Père Lachaise cemetery after slashing her wrists while her daughter slept in an adjoining bedroom.

Prema, as she was now known, discovered the body. Never schooled, she couldn't read the barely literate suicide note that belied Lulu's claims of attending the Sorbonne.

Shipped back to Bel Air, the child was raised by her grandparents, which translated to a stream of boarding schools where she failed to fit in. The child-rearing ethos on Bellagio Road was less-than-benign neglect. Ricardo and Greta, still working occasionally in character roles, were gorgeous alcoholics and compulsive plastic surgery patients who had no interest in children—in anyone other than themselves. By the time Prema was fourteen her grandparents were pickled in Polish vodka and resembled wax figures molded by addled sculptors. Two years later, Ricardo and Greta were dead and Prema was an adolescent heiress whose considerable assets were managed by a private bank in Geneva.

With no other option, Maximilian Moon, now knighted and living in London, took on the task of serving as his niece's guardian. That translated to a two-room suite on the third floor of Sir Max's Belgravia mansion, Prema enduring her uncle's abysmal piano playing and getting to know the coterie of young lithe men he labeled his "paramours."

When Prema was sixteen, a poobah at a major modeling agency noticed the tall, slender blond girl with the scalpel-hewn cheekbones, the ripe-peach lips, and the huge indigo eyes standing in a corner at one of Max's parties with an unlit joint in her hand. The offer of a contract was immediate.

Prema yawned her way down the runway as a Gaultier clothes-hanger, rented herself a garret off Rue Saint-Germain, never bothered to visit her parents' graves. The combination of passive income and modeling fees allowed her to regularly score chunks of hashish the size of soap bars from Tunisian dealers near the flea market, a treat she shared with her fellow ectomorph beauties.

Her apathy during Fashion Week made her all the more attractive. *Elle* and *Marie Claire* vied to feature her as the next *jeune fille* sensation. Prema turned them down and abruptly abandoned modeling because she found it "stupid and dull." Back in London, she occasionally ran with a crowd of similarly bored kids but preferred solitary time for smoking weed.

One day, Uncle Max paused long enough in his butchery of Rachmaninoff to suggest his now gorgeous niece attend university. When Prema laughed that off, he offered her a stint as a fairy in a Royal Shakespeare Company production of *A Midsummer Night's Dream* in which he was slated to play Oberon.

Prema agreed.

She loved being someone else.

The rest is fan-mag history.

Donald Lee Rumples was born in Oklahoma City where his father worked as a pipe fitter and his mother stayed home raising five kids. Preternaturally handsome but lacking the coordination for athletics enjoyed by his brothers and the attention span for scholarship displayed by his sisters, he dropped out of high school at seventeen, worked as a janitor, then a gutter at a meatpacking plant, gave that all up and hitchhiked to L.A. where he swept up a 7-Eleven on Western Avenue in Hollywood.

That career lasted four months, at which time he wangled a day job as a golf caddie supplemented by a nighttime gig sweeping up a pizza joint in Brentwood. It was there that the wife of a TV producer took a shine to the black-haired, black-eyed kid tidying up the pepperoni and offered him a position as a houseboy at her manse in Holmby Hills.

A year of not-so-clandestine bedding of the somewhat large lady of the very large house led to Donald's being spotted while serving hors d'oeuvres at his host's Christmas party. The spotter was a casting agent and the offer was a walk-on part in a low-budget horror flick.

Once on the set, Rumples caught the eye of a female assistant director. The following day he'd moved into her Venice apartment. Weeks
after that, he traded up to the Encino compound of her boss, the male
director. Months later he was the toy of a studio executive with a spread
in Bel Air who got him an agent. That led to a speaking part in a dog
food commercial. The spot sold a lot of kibble and Donald scored a
speaking part in an action film and a legal name change. His face and
physique were adored by the camera and if he had enough time he
could memorize a few lines.

The action flick was marketed to teenage boys but women loved it
and marketing surveys revealed the reason: "strong but sensitive"
black-haired, black-eyed Ranger Hemos, played by Donny Rader. A
curious slurred delivery that would have been judged clumsy in a
homely man was labeled sexy by legions of female admirers.

One of those admirers was Prema Moon, now thirty-four and an
established star. She summoned the younger man with the strangely
appealing mumble to her compound off Coldwater Canyon. Donny
had just begun living with his last costar, a sweet-tempered B-list actress
with the IQ of adobe. Prema couldn't have cared less about prior commitments. In what *People* termed "a disarming burst of candor" she
described the courtship as "the boy was fresh meat. I swooped down
like a raptor."

Donny moved to the estate. Bigger and better roles came his way.
Two years into their relationship, he and Prema were each pulling
twenty million a picture and lending new meaning to the term "power
couple." Paparazzi got rich peddling candid shots of the duo. Donny
and Prema took it to the next level, costarring in three pictures. Two
stylish comedies tanked but the dystopian sci-fi epic *Wizardine* grossed
north of two billion internationally.

At age thirty-seven, Prema Moon announced her desire for a qui-
eter life, adopted an orphan from Africa and two from Asia, became the
spokesperson for a slew of human rights organizations, caused diplomats to squirm as their shorts rode up when she addressed the U.N. in
her trademark sultry voice.

At forty, she added a baby girl to her "tribe."

Donny Rader, ten years his wife's junior, dropped out of the limelight.

The couple's net worth was rumored at three hundred million. Everyone figured they'd resurface. A hack at *The Hollywood Reporter* termed them "far greater than the sum of their parts," and dubbed them Premadonny.

The sobriquet stuck. How could it not?

Milo said, "CAPD, Creative Aura of Prema and Donny. Sounds like something you'd doodle while zoning out in class."

I said, "Along with goofy drawings of rocket ships. Robin's source says it used to be one of their holding companies but it got dissolved, something to do with changes in the tax code."

"Lord Donny, Lady Prema, top of the Industry food chain. Jack's probably mainlining blood pressure meds."

"Working for them could be why Wedd doesn't use his apartment much. Their compound is ten acres, probably includes staff housing."

His phone played "Hungarian Rhapsody." Kelly LeMasters said, "I feel for you. Having to deal with that bitch."

"Maria was her usual charming self."

"Maria," she said, "is one of those automatons who delude themselves they're capable of independent thought."

"She stonewalled you, huh?"

"She sure tried," said LeMasters. "I told her I'd run a follow-up story hell or high water and would harass you to the point of stalking and she waffled just like you said. The way we left it is she'll call you to work out the 'proper data feed' and get back to me."

"Good work, kid."

"Now we're buddies?"

"Common enemy and all that, Kelly."

Click.

He said, "Ten acres. Didn't know you were interested in movie stars."

"A couple of years ago a man representing them called for an appointment for a 'family member' but claimed he didn't know who. I asked him who'd referred them to me. He had no idea about that, either, was just following instructions, asked if I could make a house call. I said okay if payment would be portal-to-portal. He said money was no object, gave me the address. I was intrigued so I did some research, including Google Maps. The next day, a call came into my service canceling. When I phoned to ask why, I couldn't get through. I tried again, same result."

"They hire another shrink?"

"I have no idea."

"Lucky me," he said. "If you'd actually seen them or their kids, you'd have to recuse yourself. No actual contract or contact, no confidentiality, right?"

"Right, but if someone that powerful wanted to sue me, they'd do it anyway."

"You're staying out of it?"

"Hell, no."

We'd watched the marble-clad building for nine minutes when Maria Thomas called.

"Just had an obnoxious conversation with a *Times* reporter who brags she's been dogging you."

Milo said, "Kelly LeMasters, Olympic gold medalist in the Pestathlon."

"She getting in the way of the job?"

"If it goes any further, she will," he said. "At this point she's just an annoyance."

"Well," said Thomas, "she's threatening to hound you to the ground unless you feed her exclusive info and if you don't give her anything, she'll dig for alternative sources and go public. And we both know she'll find alternatives, all those loose-lipped idiots floating around the department."

"That's my problem, Maria?"

"Now it is."

Milo groaned. Turned to me and gave a thumbs-up and grinned like a drunk.

"Way I see it," Thomas continued, "you can neutralize her by being selective."

"Easy for you to say, Maria. You're not the one getting dogged."

"Yeah, yeah. Anyway, that's the way it's going to be. You're instructed to meet with her A-sap and offer her judicious info."

"Define *judicious*."

"At this point," said Thomas, "Moron Maxine's real estate deal's totally screwed so feel free to play with the Cheviot Hills angle. Give her anything that doesn't compromise the investigation."

"I've been shutting her out completely," he said. "Now I do a total about-face."

"Flexibility," said Thomas. "It's a sign of psychological strength, ask Delaware."

"I see him, I might just do that."

"Whatever. Now go meet with the bitch and stay in control. Any progress on the case?"

"Not much."

"Then it's no big deal. Feed her a steaming mound of bullshit, press-types are born with taste buds for it."

Click.

I said, "Didn't know Machiavelli was Irish."

He laughed. "When you're in love, laddie, everyone is Irish." His head swiveled toward Beverly Drive. A car had pulled up in front of Gold Standard's building.

Iron-gray Mercedes sedan. A curly-haired, middle-aged man in a navy suit got out and remote-locked the car. Bypassing the mailbox outfit, he opened the door to the second floor, stepped in and up.

Milo said, "Maybe he's someone needs gift counseling but I'm smelling the musty aroma of lawyer."

He swung another U, got behind the Mercedes, copied the tags. Continuing south into L.A., he crossed Pico, turned left on Cashio Street, parked, ran the numbers.

Floyd Banfer, home address on South Camden Drive in B.H.

A 411 call obtained Banfer's professional listing: attorney-at-law, office on Roxbury Drive just north of Wilshire in B.H.

"Keeping it local," said Milo. "Should I go back in there and confront them or give myself time to plan? I'm leaning toward wait and see."

"Sounds like you know what to do."

"Spoken like a master therapist."

We headed back to the station. He continued past the staff lot, stopped where I'd parked the Seville, kept the engine running.

I said, "Playdate's over?"

"I'd better get the meeting with LeMasters out of the way. I'd bring you along but she'll probably make a big deal about the cop-shrink thing and I figure you don't want the exposure."

"More important, it'll be good for Kelly to feel she's getting your undivided attention."

"That, too."

"Anything I can do in the meantime?"

"Clean up your room and stop sassing your mother. What can you do . . . okay, here's something: Figure out a way I can get into Premadonny-Land to look for Mr. Wedd."

"Maybe you won't need to," I said. "If he's holed up there, eventually he'll leave."

"Start surveillance on the place?" Out came his pad. "You remember the address?"

"No, but it's easy to find. Coldwater north, about a mile past Mulholland on the west side of the road there's an unmarked private road that leads up to a gate."

"Your research included driving up there?"

"I'm an empiricist."

"Some rep called you, huh? Wouldn't it be something if it was Wedd?"

"It would," I said.

"You've already thought about that."

I wished him well, got out of the car.

He said, "Hooray for Hollywood." Roared away.

35

My research on Premadonny had involved more than I'd let on to Milo.

After the call from the stars' rep, I'd picked among millions of Web citations. Bios composed early in their careers aired bins of dirty laundry. Everything subsequent was P.R. pap programmed as carefully as a laugh track.

Clips from their films left no question about their physical perfection. A Renaissance artist would've submitted to indignity, if not outright torture, in order to paint them.

Prema Moon came across as a competent, occasionally impressive performer who could amplify or lower her sexuality as if equipped with an erotic rheostat. The only mention she made of her children was on a press release announcing her "hiatus from film work in order to concentrate on being a full-time mom." Donny Rader lent his support to that move, calling his wife "the ultimate earth mother, protective as a mama lion."

Rader's acting was surprisingly one-note. His default mannerisms were the slow, theatrical lowering of hooded eyes and the tendency to slur his words.

The man who'd requested the appointment had begun talking in a choppy, agitated delivery but had shifted quickly to mumbly diction.

I replayed a few of Rader's clips, heard the same elisions, over and over. If not identical to the man on the phone, awfully close.

Had it been a worried father phoning me about his child but choosing to hide that fact? Because A-list celebs weren't supposed to do things for themselves?

Or was there a deeper motive for the deception?

Whoever the "representative" was, he'd skated away from naming the child in question, assuring me I'd find out soon enough then hanging up. His tension had been notable, and that could mean an especially worrisome problem.

I'd keyworded *premadonny children.*

Millions of hits on the parents but almost nothing on the kids.

An image search pulled up a solitary photo gone viral: a shot taken a few months before in New York of Prema and her kids attending a Broadway Disney musical.

Red-velvet, gilt-molded walls in the background supported the caption's assertion that the group had been photographed in the theater lobby. But the space was otherwise unpopulated, which was odd for an SRO hit, and the lighting was dim but for a crisp, klieg-like beam focused on the subjects. Maybe Prema and her brood had been let in early. Or they'd arrived on a Dark Monday in order to be posed as carefully as a Velázquez royal sitting.

I studied the shot. Prema Moon, wearing a conservative, dark pantsuit that set off cascades of golden hair, stood behind the four kids. The lighting was gracious to her heart-shaped face and her perfect chin and her beyond-perfect cheekbones.

The oldest child, a boy of ten or eleven, had fine features and ebony skin that evoked Somalia or Ethiopia. A doll-like Asian girl around eight and a grave Asian boy slightly younger flanked a platinum-haired, pouting toddler with cherubic chubby cheeks and dimpled knuckles.

All of them were dressed in matching white shirts and dark pants, as uniformly clad as parochial school students. No names provided, just "Prema and her pretty quartet."

"Pretty" was an understatement; each child was gorgeous. All but the youngest smiled woodenly. The collective posture, again excepting the toddler, was military-rigid.

Prema graced the photographer with the faintest smile—just enough parting of moist, full lips to imply the theoretical possibility of mirth. Her eyes refused to go along; laser-intense, they aimed at some distant focal point.

No physical contact between her and her progeny; her arms remained pressed to her sides.

I searched the kids' faces looking for anything that might tell me whom I was scheduled to see. Not much of anything emotion-wise, which in kids meant plenty was going on.

Intrigued about what I'd encounter once I got behind the gates of the compound, I logged off.

A day or two after the cancellation, I remained curious. Then my calendar booked up the way it usually does and I was concentrating on murder victims and patients who actually showed up.

Now, nearly two years later, I drove home, curiosity re-ignited.

This time the computer was a bit more cooperative and I found a couple of hundred references to the children, including their names.

Kion, thirteen.

Kembara, eleven.

Kyle-Jacques, eight.

Kristina, four.

But not a single image. The theater-lobby shot had been expunged.

A closer reading of the citations proved disappointing. All of them discussed how zealously Premadonny protected their progeny's privacy. A few snarky types bemoaned the couple's "CIA approach to parenting," but most of the chatterers and bloggers and gurus of gossip were supportive of the attempt to prevent the children from becoming "grist for the paparazzi mill."

Maybe so, but there was another reason for isolating children.

Milo was concentrating on Melvin Jaron Wedd's link to the compound on Mulholland Drive. My mind was going in a completely different direction.

I made some coffee, added foamed milk and cinnamon, brought a mugful to Robin's studio.

She put down her chisel and smiled. "This is becoming a regular thing."

Blanche's little flat nose quivered as she inhaled the aroma. I fetched her a bacon-bone from the box Robin keeps at hand. She took the treat from my fingers with her usual delicacy, trotted over to a corner to nosh in peace. Robin sipped and said, "You even girlied it up for me, what a good boyfriend."

"Least I can do."

"You owe me for something?"

"Cosmically, I owe you a ton. When you call Brent Dorf a second time, my gratitude will blossom further. Ask if I can talk to him in person about Premadonny. If he has nothing to offer, maybe he can refer me to someone who does."

"You actually suspect those two of something?"

"It hasn't gotten that far, but a murder victim worked for them and maybe so did a prime suspect. Toss in Qeesha D'Embo, who could be victim or suspect, and it's well beyond interesting."

"Weird goings-on behind the gates," she said. "Maybe they just hired the wrong people."

"Maybe," I said, "but all of this has stirred up something that happened a couple of years ago."

I told her about the canceled referral, my suspicion that Donny Rader had tried to hide his identity. "Back then my gut told me there was a serious problem with the family. Now I'm wondering if that meant a child disturbed enough to hurt a baby."

She put her cup down. "That's horrible."

"Horrible and worth covering up. Prema Moon gave up her career and recast herself as a devoted, protective mother. Both of them have. Can you imagine the repercussions if it turned out they'd raised a murderous child? Even if the baby's death was accidental—kids horsing around, something unfortunate happened—that kind of disclosure would be disastrous. Any mother would have good reason to go to the cops. But Qeesha D'Embo was no stranger to deceit and working the angles, so she might've put a serious squeeze on. We know she had conflict with Wedd, assumed it was a romantic issue. But Wedd could've been Premadonny's paymaster, so maybe the problem between them was business."

"She wanted more, he said no, she's dead, too."

Her nails pinged the coffee mug.

I said, "Sorry to pollute your day."

"I'm fine—the car scam, Alex. Why would Premadonny stoop to insurance fraud?"

"That could've been Wedd improvising so he could pocket the payoff money."

"Or he really is the only bad guy and they had the misfortune of hiring him. What exactly does he do for them?"

"Don't know, the agency's clammed up."

"A murderous child," she said. "How old are the kids?"

"Four, eight, eleven, thirteen."

"So the oldest," she said.

"Most likely."

"Boy or girl?"

"Boy."

"What else do you know about him?"

"Nothing, they've all been swept out of sight, I'm talking utter invisibility. There are good reasons for keeping your kids out of the public eye. But there are also bad ones."

"Protecting a homicidal thirteen-year-old."

"Protecting the alternative universe that created a homicidal thirteen-year-old. Rob, when I come across unusually secretive, isolated families, there's almost always major pathology at play. The most common factor is abuse of power—a cult-like situation. Sometimes that stops at eccentricity. Sometimes it leads to really bad things."

She drank more coffee, placed the mug on her desk. "Okay, I'll call Brent right now."

"Thanks, babe. Let him know I need him because he's dialed in."

"Brent's all about being Mr. Inside, that's the perfect approach." She smiled. "But of course you knew that."

36

Brent Dorf had just left for New York on business. His assistant claimed a return date hadn't been set but promised to deliver the message.

Robin said, "Brent'll be interested in what I have for him, I'm counting on you, luv."

She hung up.

I said, "Luv?"

"Charles is British and gay but he likes flirting with girls. Brent's gay, too, for that matter. But he has absolutely *no* interest in girls."

She laughed. "I can just imagine him and Milo taking lunch at the Grill on the Alley."

"They allow polyester?"

"On alternate Tuesdays."

"We haven't been there in a long time."

"I don't think we've ever been there."

"There's another reason to go," I said. "Tonight sound good?"

"You're in the mood?"

"For time with you, always."

"Meaning you're tired of thinking."

I told her that's not what I meant at all and that I loved her and went back to my office.

Dinner was a two-hour respite and when we left the Grill shortly after ten p.m., I felt loose and content. The night air was clean and warm, an invitation to walk. Rodeo Drive's around the corner from the restaurant and once the tourists go to bed, it's a peaceful stroll. Robin held my arm as we strolled past windows showcasing stuff no one could afford. We made it home by eleven.

Making love was a great next step in the quest for distraction but when you're compulsive and addicted to the bad stuff, you inevitably return to that dark place. I lay next to Robin as she slept peacefully, unanswerable questions eddying in my head.

The following morning, as she showered, I took Blanche outside for her a.m. toilette and retrieved the paper from the driveway. Leafing through, I came across Kelly LeMasters's follow-up story on the park murders.

Page 10, maybe five hundred words, but she'd scored above-the-crease placement.

Milo had lured her with the promise of something juicy but nothing close to that appeared in the article, leaving LeMasters to play with human-interest filler: the mystery trajectory that had taken Adriana Betts from church-girl to murder victim, the impact of two Cheviot Hills murders upon affluent citizens.

Adriana's sister, Helene, and the Reverend Goleman were quoted but their comments were no more revelatory than their station-house interviews. The sad mystery of a "strewn infant skeleton" was noted as was the "eerie parallel" to the bones found under Matt and Holly Ruche's cedar tree. Nothing about the park baby's racial makeup or parentage.

Milo's name didn't come up until the final paragraph, where he was described as "a veteran homicide detective left baffled." The piece ended with an "anyone with information" message and his landline.

I figured he'd be busy all morning fielding leads, was surprised when he phoned at nine.

"Taking a break from the tipsters?"

"Got Moe and Sean on that, I need to roll. Just got a call from Floyd Banfer, Jack Weathers's lawyer. He wants to meet, an hour and a half, B.H. parkway, corner Rexford."

"Right near City Hall."

"Banfer's serving papers at BHPD, said he'd walk over."

"He's suing the police?"

"Some sort of workers' comp deal on behalf of a fired officer. Nothing, he assured me, that I'd find objectionable."

"What's on his mind?"

"He wouldn't say but he's definitely antsy, Alex. I like that in attorneys. Makes them seem almost human."

Milo and I arrived at ten twenty, found a bench on the north side of the parkway with a clear view of the Beverly Hills government complex. The original city hall is a thirties Spanish Renaissance masterpiece. The civic center complex built fifty years later tried to work deco and contemporary into the mix and ended up looking tacked on. A degraded granite path, Chinese elms, and lawn separated us from Santa Monica Boulevard. Traffic howled in both directions. An ancient man accompanied by a husky attendant inched a walker past us. A trio of Persian women in Fila tracksuits bounced by chatting in Farsi. A young woman who could have been a Victoria's Secret model if the company raised its standards raced past all of them looking miserable.

Directly in front of us was a six-foot-by-ten-foot mound of lumpy chrome-plate.

Milo said, "What the hell is that?"

"Public art."

"Looks like a jumbo jet had digestive problems."

At ten twenty-six Floyd Banfer exited the police station, crossed the street, and headed toward us. When he arrived, he was flushed and smiling, a compact man with a peanut-shaped head, bright blue eyes, and the kind of white stubble that Milo calls a "terrorist beard."

"Punctual," he boomed. "Nice to be dealing with professionals." Compact man with an expansive bass voice.

A hand shot out. "Floyd Banfer."

"Milo Sturgis, this is Alex Delaware."

Shakes all around. Banfer's grip was a mite too firm, his arm remained stiff, his eyes wary. The smile he'd arrived with seemed glued to his face. "Pretty morning, eh?"

"Don't imagine Beverly Hills would allow anything less, Counselor."

Banfer chuckled. "You'd be surprised." His suit was the same dark gray we'd seen yesterday, a slightly shiny silk-and-wool. His shirt was a TV blue spread-collar, his tie a pink Hermès patterned with bugles. Fifty to fifty-five, with thin, wavy hair tinted brown and throwing off red highlights the way men's dyed hair often does, he radiated an odd mix of good cheer and anxiety. As if he enjoyed being on edge.

Milo motioned to the space we'd created between us on the bench.

Banfer said, "Mind if we walk? That piece of shit they call art makes me queasy and any chance to exercise is welcome."

"Sure."

The three of us headed west. The granite pathways are supposed to resist dust but Banfer's black wingtips turned gray within seconds. Every few yards, he managed to wipe the shoes on the back of his trousers without breaking step. At Crescent Drive we paused until cross-traffic cleared. A helmeted bicyclist rounded the corner and sped toward us and Banfer had to step to the right to avoid collision.

"Totally illegal," he said, still smiling. "No bikes allowed. Want to chase him down and give him a ticket, Lieutenant?"

Milo hadn't told Banfer his rank. Banfer did his homework.

"Above my pay grade, Counselor."

Banfer chuckled again. "So why did I ask for this meeting?"

He paused, as if really expecting an answer.

Milo and I kept walking.

Banfer said, "First off, thanks for being accommodating, got a tough week, if not now, it would have to wait."

"Happy to oblige, Mr. Banfer. What's on your mind?"

"Floyd's fine. Okay, let me start with a given: Jack Weathers is a good man."

Milo didn't answer.

Banfer said, "You kind of scared him, popping in like that."

"Not my intention."

Banfer picked up his pace. "Be that as it may, Lieutenant, here's the thing: Jack and Daisy are good people, run a good business, perform a good service—did you know they used to be in the Industry? Small screen mostly, Jack played music and acted, did a whole bunch of *Hawaii Five-O*'s, some *Gunsmoke,* couple of *Magnum*s. Daisy was on *Lawrence Welk* for years. Then Jack did real estate out in the Valley and Daisy did some dance teaching, she was a dancer before she was an actress, performed with Martha Graham, knew Cyd Charisse, I'm talking talent."

"Impressive," said Milo.

"I'd say."

Several more steps. A group of younger Persian women glided past, trim in black velour, wearing pearls and diamonds, listening to iPods.

Banfer said, "What I'm trying to get across is these are decent, honest people, been working all their lives, neither of them came from money, they found a niche, developed it, thank God they've been doing well, can even possibly think about retiring. At some point. Though I don't know if they will, that's up to them."

"Makes sense."

"What does?" said Banfer.

"Making their own decision about retirement."

"Yes. Of course. My point here is that we're talking good people."

"I'll take your word for it, Floyd."

"Good. Anyway, in case you don't know how the Industry works, let me cue you in, it's all hierarchy. Bottom of the pyramid up to the top, we're talking highly structured, who you know determines how you do, things can change in a snap." He paused to breathe. "Who'm I preaching to, this is L.A., you're pros."

We reached Canon Drive. A homeless man shuffled toward us, leaving a wake of stench.

Banfer wrinkled his nose. "No more vagrancy laws. I'm ambivalent about that, would like to see them taken care of properly but you can't just go scoop them up out of the park the way I saw in Europe when I was a student backpacking in the eighties. Made me think of storm troopers."

Milo made no effort hiding the glance at his Timex.

Banfer said, "Time to cut to the chase? Sure, makes sense."

But he offered no additional wisdom as we continued walking.

Halfway to Beverly Drive, Milo said, "Floyd, what exactly can I do for you?"

"Accept the data I'm going to proffer in the spirit with which it's offered."

"Meaning?"

"Jack and Daisy need to be kept out of any homicide investigation, nor will their contract client—the client in question—be notified of their input to the police."

"CAPD," said Milo. "Creative Aura of Premá and Donny."

Banfer's chin vibrated. "So you know. Okay, now you see what I mean."

"You go to court much, Floyd?"

The question threw Banfer off-balance and he stiffened his arms. "When it's necessary. Why?"

"Just curious."

"You're saying I'm long-winded? Would bore a jury? Don't worry, I do just fine. Am I being a bit . . . detailed? Maybe I am, yes, I am. Because I told Jack and Daisy I'd take care of it and darned if I'm going to go back to them and tell them I didn't. They're good folk."

"Which one are you related to?"

Banfer turned scarlet. "Why would you assume that?"

"You seem unusually dedicated but sorry if I presumed."

"Let me assure you, I'd do the same for any client, Lieutenant." A beat. "But if you must know, Jack was married to my mother's sister and then she died and he married Daisy. So technically, Daisy's my step-aunt but I think of her as my full aunt, she's dear to me, she's a dear woman."

"She seemed very nice."

"Jack's nice, too."

"No doubt."

"So do we have a deal?"

"That depends on what you have to offer."

"I have the truth to offer, Lieutenant Sturgis—may I call you Milo?"

"Sure."

"Milo, this can be extremely simple if we go the simplicity route. I give you information and you use it as you see fit in your criminal investigation but you don't draw Jack and Daisy into it."

"I have no desire to complicate their lives, Floyd, but I need to be up front with you. If they've got crucial information, it could find its way into the case file."

"Not true," snapped Banfer. "Just call them confidential informants and everything will go smooth as silk."

"I can do that but I can't promise that at some point a prosecutor's not going to want to know their identity."

"If that happens, you say no."

"It doesn't work that way, Floyd."

"Then we . . . have a problem."

"You may have all kinds of problems if Jack and Daisy don't co-operate, Floyd. I don't need to tell you about all the unpleasant legal maneuvers at the D.A.'s disposal."

"I'll fight each and every one."

"That will toss Jack and Daisy right into the limelight."

Banfer slanted forward, walked faster.

Milo said, "All this hassle just to make sure Premadonny doesn't get mad at them?"

"It's not a matter of mad," said Banfer. "It's a matter of excommunication. Do you know how powerful those two are?"

"A-list."

"Oh, no, no, no." Banfer's hand arced above his head, like a kid playing airplane. "*Miles* above A-list. It's like pissing off the queen of England."

"Last I checked the queen hadn't excommunicated anyone, Floyd."

"Okay," said the lawyer, "perhaps I engaged in a bit of hyperbole, but still. If word gets out that Jack somehow violated a confidence, the results could be professionally and financially devastating."

"Jack and Daisy signed a gag clause."

Banfer frowned. "Standard operating procedure when dealing with clients at that level."

"Maybe so, but we already know Jack sent Adriana Betts to work at Premadonny's compound and we're fairly certain he did the same for a couple of other people who may be connected to Adriana Betts's murder. Did you read today's *Times*?"

"Of course," said Banfer. "That's why I called you."

"The reporter's itching for anything I can give her. I've been holding her off but that could change."

"You're threatening to leak my clients' identities?"

"You called the meeting, Floyd. I'm letting you know how things stand."

Banfer clicked his teeth. "Lieutenant Sturgis," he said, as if hearing the title for the first time. "Do you by chance have legal training?"

"I'll take that as a compliment though I'm not sure I should. The answer is just what I've learned on the job."

"Well, you're a wily man, Milo. Not what I'd expect. Because frankly most of the cops I encounter aren't what you'd call intellectual giants."

"You encounter a lot of cops?"

"I do my share of workers' comp, have represented several of your compatriots, learned how they tick. Typically their long-term goals don't stretch beyond a brand-new motorcycle and a Hawaiian vacation."

"Oh, those crazy kids in blue."

"It was meant as a compliment. You seem different, Milo. A careful planner."

"Accepted and appreciated, Floyd. So what is it you'd like to tell me in the hope that Jack and Daisy remain bulletproof?"

Banfer stopped, took hold of the bulb at the end of his nose and twisted. His breath had grown ragged. He said, "Let's sit down."

37

Beverly Hills park benches are complex creations, curvy and black and wrought iron with a center divider that makes it difficult for more than two people to sit. Milo motioned Banfer to the left. A flick of his head directed me to the right.

Leaving him on his feet, looming.

Another homeless man shambled by, eyes rolling, stumbling.

Banfer said, "That's probably where they got the idea for that picture—*Down and Out in Beverly Hills.* They prettied it up, but that's the Industry . . . okay, back to business: Jack and Daisy are—"

"Wonderful people. Acknowledged, Floyd."

"Ethical people," Banfer corrected. "Jack made some mistakes, granted, but the basic core is ethical so there's no reason for you to worry about them."

"Mistakes as in hiring Adriana Betts without vetting her."

Banfer rubbed his temples. "Facts can only tell you so much when you're dealing with human beings, Milo. Jack's come to trust his instincts and Ms. Betts impressed him as a decent young woman."

I said, "Plus it was an urgent situation."

Banfer clicked his teeth again. "Allegedly."

"You have your doubts?"

"The origin of that supposition was a call Jack received from another employee at the compound. Someone he'd placed a while back. She—there was an assertion that the clients needed additional child care as soon as possible, Jack was to come up with someone immediately. This individual knew someone who fit the bill perfectly—the right training and experience. Jack's a people-pleaser, he got into the business to fill human need. It seemed like an ideal arrangement."

Milo said, "Don't see a big problem there, Floyd. If he had checked Adriana out he would've learned she was squeaky-clean."

Banfer crossed his legs, tugged a sock up a hairless shin. "Well, that's good to hear."

"On the other hand, Floyd, if the employee who recommended her was Qeesha D'Embo, that complicates matters."

"I'm not familiar with that name."

"How about Charlene Chambers?"

"Nor that one."

Milo produced the mug shot.

Banfer sagged.

"How do you know her, Floyd?"

"She represented herself to Jack and Daisy as Simone Chambord. That's the name Jack and Daisy used to check her out and she came up spotless."

"When was she hired?"

"Twenty-three months ago."

Soon after leaving Boise.

I said, "What was she hired for?"

The question seemed to puzzle Banfer. "Child care, of course." He tapped the photo. "After you showed that to Jack and he called me in a panic, I took a closer look at her. Specifically, I traced the Social Security number she'd used when she applied for the job. It matches a Simone Chambord, all right, but that person turns out to be an eighty-nine-year-old woman living in a rest home in New Orleans. I called over there and the director informed me Mrs. Chambord had advanced Alzheimer's, had been that way for five years."

"Jack and Daisy's search didn't pull that up?"

"They were focused on relevant criteria. Criminal record, poor credit."

"Good point," I said. "Advanced Alzheimer's would sure inhibit criminality."

Banfer shook his head. "The potential ramifications for Gold Standard are obvious but no harm was intended."

Milo said, "Your clients provided a con artist as a nanny for movie stars' kids, did the same for a woman who ended up dead. Yeah, I'd say those are ramifications."

"That's a tiny proportion of all the wonderful people Jack and Daisy have connected with wonderful clients."

Recited with all the conviction of a gulag loyalty pledge.

I said, "Unfortunately, you're only as good as your last picture."

Banfer sighed. "I've advised Jack to sit tight, but obviously he's on pins and needles. To make matters worse, Daisy knew nothing about any of this."

Milo said, "Unhappy wife, unhappy life."

"It's a mess, all right. By the way, I did check out Ms. Betts's Social Security and it comes back to her. Have I missed something? Because she and Chambord seem an unlikely pairing."

Milo said, "Nothing crooked has turned up on Adriana."

"That baby found at the park—those bones—what's the connection?"

"Don't know yet, Floyd. That's why we wanted to talk to Jack and Daisy."

"Well, they certainly can't tell you anything about *that*."

"Qeesha—Simone—was hired twenty-three months ago. What about Adriana?"

"Recently. Around three, four months ago according to Jack."

"He can't be more precise?"

Banfer stared straight ahead.

Milo said, "He destroyed the files?"

"I can't get into that."

"Your client got rid of potential evidence. If you advised him to do that you could be facing obstruction charges."

"Same answer, I'm afraid."

Banfer turned to Milo. Milo glared and Banfer faced forward again. "Let's put this in context: I've been more forthcoming than I need to be, given the circumstances."

"What circumstances are those, Floyd?"

"No charges have been filed against anyone, you're at the supposition stage, fishing around, and neither I nor my client is obligated to talk to you about anything. However, we *chose* to cooperate volitionally because we're *not* obstructionistic. And in terms of files, I'm unaware of any statute requiring a small businessman to cope with needless paper buildup."

"Fair enough," said Milo.

Sudden switch to an easy, amiable tone. Banfer risked another try at eye contact. Milo smiled.

"Well," said the attorney, "it's good to see we've reached a meeting of the minds."

"I agree. Now how about we talk to Jack, directly."

"You feel that's necessary?"

"Wouldn't ask if I didn't, Floyd."

Banfer sighed again, punched numbers on his cell phone. "Hey, it's me . . . as well as can be expected . . . I told them that . . . they still want to talk to you . . . I'll stay right here, not to worry . . . might as well, you've got nothing to hide . . . sooner's better than later, Jack, let's get it over with and move on . . . we're on the parkway between Beverly and Camden . . . good idea." Clicking off, he studied the traffic. "On his way."

Jack Weathers wore a blue cashmere blazer, a white silk shirt, dove-colored slacks, blue suede loafers with gold buckles. If they recast *Gil-*

ligan's Island, he'd be great for Thurston Howell the Third. Except for the defeated, sagging shoulders, the bags under his eyes, the wrinkles that had deepened during the twenty-four hours since we'd last seen him.

The shuffling gait of an old, weary man.

I got up and vacated the space next to Banfer. Weathers hesitated.

Milo said, "Take a load off, Jack."

Weathers's jowls quivered. Pink capillaries laced the whites of his eyes. A couple of cuticles were rubbed raw, detracting from an otherwise perfect manicure.

He sat down heavily and Banfer filled him in on what we knew. When Banfer wanted to, he could be concise.

Jack Weathers laced his hands together, stared at his knees.

Milo said, "Tell me everything you remember about the woman who called herself Simone Chambord."

"What's her real name?" said Weathers.

"Why don't you let me do the asking so you can do the answering."

Weathers's head snapped back.

Floyd Banfer said, "Let's keep it streamlined, Jack, and they'll be out of your hair."

Weathers said nothing. The group of younger Persian women returned. His attention shifted to shapely rears, and that seemed to relax him.

He said, "Good-looking girl, black but lightish. I figured her for a wannabe actress."

"Because of her looks."

"That and she had a way about her."

"What way was that, Jack?"

"Vivacious," said Weathers. "Theatrically vivacious."

"Like she was playing a role."

"This town, everyone plays a role. What I'm getting at is everything was just a little bit exaggerated." He studied Milo. "You're kind of central-casting yourself."

"So you figured Simone for a wannabe."

"But she had the right credentials for the child-care job. Experi-ence, letters of reference."

"From who?"

"Previous employers."

"How about some names?"

"Don't recall," said Weathers.

"How about checking the file?"

"No file." Weathers colored. "We turn everything over regularly."

"Paper buildup."

Floyd Banfer rubbed one leg against the other.

Jack Weathers said, "Exactly."

"Okay," said Milo, "but when she applied you must've called her references. Any memories of who they were and what they told you?"

"Nah, I've got so many applications, nothing stands out."

"Business is good."

"Can be," said Weathers. "All I can tell you is she checked out."

"Wannabe actress," said Milo. "Guess you see a lot of that."

"I go in assuming the real agenda is advancing their careers. Or so they believe."

Milo said, "Doesn't work that way?"

"Works against them."

"Why's that?"

"Because once someone's seen as being in a service position they tend to be . . . always seen that way."

"They're viewed as inferior?"

"Not inferior," said Weathers. "Different."

"Donny Rader started off as a golf caddie and houseboy for a pro-ducer."

"That's the official story."

"Not true?"

Weathers sneered. "I don't know what's true, what's not. I don't know anyone's narrative."

Floyd Banfer said, "It's all a matter of information control. We hear what they want us to hear."

"Stars," said Milo.

"Anyone in power."

I said, "So you have no problem hiring wannabes."

Jack Weathers said, "Not if they learn their proper place and do the damn job."

"Did Simone Chambord learn?"

"Never heard about problems."

"Far as you know, she's still working for Premadonny."

"I'd assume."

"What else do you remember about her?"

"Good-looking," said Weathers. "Extremely attractive. In that fresh way. Great figure . . . she could carry on a conversation, said she loved kids, showed me a child-development book she was reading."

"She was hired as a nanny."

"No," said Weathers. "As a child-care assistant."

"What's the difference?"

"Pay scale, for starts. When the client insists on an official nanny, we hire British girls who take formal training at one of the schools they have over there. They've got the book learning but some of them can be a little uptight. Some clients like that. Others want something more relaxed."

"Prema Moon and Donny Rader have a relaxed attitude."

"I'd assume."

"How many other people have you sent to them?"

"Couldn't say," said Weathers.

Milo said, "Wild guess."

Weathers looked at Banfer. Banfer nodded.

"Wild guess? I'd say half a dozen."

"What jobs did you fill for them?"

"I believe there were a couple of domestics. Housekeepers. We don't do that anymore, can't compete with the domestic-specialty agencies, all those ads they run in the Spanish papers. But back then we did, so probably that's it. Couple of domestics."

He turned to Banfer. "This is okay?"

"So far, Jack."

Milo said, "You're worried about Premadonny's gag clause?"

"Hell, yeah," said Weathers. "We're talking damn stringent."

"As opposed to . . ."

Banfer said, "Clauses that are less stringent." He smiled at his own obfuscation.

Milo said, "Educate me, Counselor."

"It's nothing complicated, Milo. Default is generally a ban on talking to the media, publishing a book, that kind of thing. This particular clause covers virtually every single syllable uttered about Premadonny to anyone on any topic. Is it legally binding? Probably not, but testing that theory would bring considerable anguish. In any event, Jack's told you everything he knows about the Chambord woman and Ms. Betts."

"Then on to the next topic," said Milo, pulling out the enlargement of Melvin Jaron Wedd's DMV photo.

Floyd Banfer's face remained blank.

Jack Weathers said, "Oh, shit."

38

Floyd Banfer placed a hand on Jack Weathers's cashmere sleeve. "He's also one of yours?"

Milo said, "Who is he, Jack?"

Weathers wrung his hands. "A guy . . . M.J."

Milo said, "Melvin Jaron Wedd. When did you place him at the compound?"

Weathers muttered something.

"Speak up, Jack."

"Three years ago. Give or take."

"What's his job title?"

"Estate manager," said Weathers. "I'd placed him before, similar thing."

"Whose estate did he manage before?"

"Saudi family, gigantic place in Bel Air. Four, five years ago."

"And before then?"

"No, that was the first. They had no problems with him—the Arabs. They moved back to Riyadh."

"So you sent him to Premadonny."

"Yeah, yeah."

"Who solicited your help?"

"Business manager."

"Who's that?"

Weathers's eyes traveled to the right. "Not the manager directly, some assistant."

Floyd Banfer said, "Or some assistant's assistant."

Weathers regarded his nephew crossly. "That's the way it goes with people at their level."

Milo said, "Who's their business manager?"

"Apex Management. They handle a lot of the biggies."

"What do you remember about M.J.?"

"A guy," said Weathers. "I think he had some bookkeeping experience. Him I *did* check out. What's the problem with him?"

"Maybe nothing, Jack."

"Maybe nothing but you're carrying around his picture?"

"His name came up."

"Meaning?"

"His name came up."

Weathers waved a hand. "Frankly, I don't want to know. Now can I go and try to pay some bills? I'm no civil servant, got no cushy pension and overtime."

Milo said, "Sure. Have a nice day."

"Sure?"

"Unless you've got something more to tell us, Jack."

"I've got nothing. To tell or to hide or to relate or report. I'm in the service business, I find service people for clients who need service. What they do once they're hired is their business."

Bracing himself on the bench's center divider, he got to his feet, buttoned his blazer. Banfer stood and took him by the elbow. Weathers shook off the support with surprising fury. "Not ready for a scooter yet, Floyd, let's get breakfast, Nate 'n Al, Bagel Nosh, whatever."

Working hard at casual.

Banfer tapped his Rolex Oyster. "Sorry, appointments."

"Busy guy," said Weathers. "Everyone's busy. I should be busy."

He hobbled away.

Banfer said, "His blood pressure's not great, I hope the stress doesn't cause problems."

Milo winked. "That sounds like prep for a civil suit."

"Not funny, Lieutenant. Are we through?"

Before waiting for an answer, Banfer headed east on the parkway. A curvaceous female jogger came heading his way. He didn't bother to look.

Milo sat down on the bench. "I drove by that private road this morning. Like I thought, tough surveillance. The county registered the compound as eleven acres, divided into three legal parcels, all registered to another holding company called Prime Mayfair. Tried a trace-back, it dead-ends at a paper-pusher who works for Apex Management."

I said, "A lot of plot to thicken."

He looked up Apex's number. Got transferred a few times. Hung up, shaking his head.

"Got stonewalled by an assistant's assistant's walking-around-guy's gopher's peon's underling slave. Not that anyone would tell me anything even if I could get through. Weathers's destroying his files doesn't help, want to take bets he'll be torching Wedd's soon as he gets back from breakfast? And for all the tough talk to Banfer, there's nothing I can really do about it."

"At least you've got confirmation that all three of them worked together."

He kicked a leg of the bench. Unfolded Wedd's DMV shot and stared at it for a while. "I need face-time with this prince but getting into that compound's as likely as being invited to an Oscar after party." He smiled. "Actually, Rick was invited to one a few years ago. After sewing up the DUI daughter of some hoo-hah producer who drove her Aston into a wall."

"Did you go?"

"Nah, both of us were on call that night . . . okay, I'll figure out a way to watch the place. After I recanvass the park, see if the staff or the regulars remember anything."

He checked with Reed and Binchy to learn if Kelly LeMasters's story had pulled up anything solid. It hadn't. Same for the anonymous Crime Stoppers line.

I said, "Breakfast? Nate 'n Al, Bagel Nosh?"

"No, thanks, already ate."

Prior meals had never deterred him before.

I said, "Hope you feel better."

Back home I put in a call to Dr. Leonard Coates.

Len and I were classmates in grad school, worked together for a year at Western Pediatric. I stuck around at the hospital, putting in time on the cancer wards while Len shifted to a Beverly Hills private practice.

Soon after hiring a publicist, Len began getting quoted in the popular press. It didn't take long to acquire a celebrity patient load, and a few years in he'd taken over the penthouse floor of a building on Roxbury, was overseeing half a dozen associates. While suffering from a serious case of Hollywood Sepsis.

It's a progressive condition, also known as Malignant Look-At-Me Syndrome, leading to excessive dependency on public exposure, self-invention, and the narcosis of fame.

Len's addiction had led him to write a useless pop-psych book, peddle countless treatments for screenplays and reality shows, obsess on getting his picture taken at certain parties in the company of eye candy. Tall and slim and meticulously bearded, he plowed through a succession of women. I'd stopped counting his marriages at four. He had two kids that I knew of and the few times I saw them they both looked depressed. The last time Len and I had run into each other was at a hospital fund-raiser. Smiling all the while and checking out the crowd nonstop, he'd spent a lot of time griping about "ungrateful brats. Just like their mothers, you can't fight genetics."

His service operator put me on hold. The audio track was a sales pitch for "Dr. Coates's compelling new book *Putting Your Life in Balance*."

The operator broke back in as a synopsis of chapter 1 was ending. The gist was "Stop and Smell the Roses." I'd never known Len to have a hobby.

She said, "Sorry, Doctor's unavailable but he'll get the message."

I said, "How's the book doing?"

"Pardon?"

"Dr. Coates's new book."

She laughed. "I just sit here in a small room and answer the phone. Last thing I read was a utility bill."

To my surprise, Len called my private line nine minutes later.

"Hey, Alex! Great to hear from you! How's life treating you?"

I said, "Well, Len. You?"

"Off-the-chart busy, it never stops. But what's the alternative? Stagnation? We're like sharks, right? We need to keep moving."

"Congratulations on the book."

"Oh, you heard the tape? We'll see how it does. I calculated my hourly fee writing it. Somewhere south of ten bucks an hour but my agent claims it's a stepping-stone. She's been getting nibbles for a talk show, says I've got more people-warmth than you-know-who, so maybe. What's up?"

"What do you know about Prema Moon and Donny Rader?"

A beat. "May I ask why you'd care about people like that?"

"Hollywood types?"

"Shallow types," he said. "That's my bailiwick, you're not going to encroach on my territory, are you, Alex?" He laughed. "Just kidding, you want 'em, they're yours. Though you have to admit, I'm better suited to that kind of thing because we both know I'm about as deep as a rain puddle in August. You, on the other hand . . . please don't tell me you've sold out, Alexander. I've always thought of you as my positive role model."

Guffaws, rich, loud, audio-friendly.

"You're selling yourself short, Len."

"Not in the least. Know Thyself is my first commandment. Meanwhile, I just bought myself a new Audi R8, the convertible. Tuned it up so the compression's insane, real beast, and trust me, that didn't come from listening to whiny mothers. Bet you're still with the old Caddy, right?"

"Right."

"There you go," he said. "Loyalty and solidity. Maybe one day it'll be a classic."

"I can hope."

"So what's with the sudden interest in the Golden Gods?"

"You know them?"

"If I did, would I be talking about them? No, I don't know them personally but after all these years . . . how can I put this—okay, let's just say if someone told me either of them had Proust on the nightstand I'd figure it was for a drink coaster."

"Not intellectuals."

"*None* of them are," he said, with sudden fury. "They're genetic freaks—bipedal show-dogs able to memorize a few lines. Sit heel stay emote. Even if they start out with some native intelligence they're egregiously undereducated so they never *know* anything. I had one—obviously I won't tell you her name—who came in to talk to one of my staff about a problem kid. But only after she was turned down by the Dog Whisperer. Why'd she go to him first? Probably to get on TV. But the reason she gave us was all animals are the same, right? It just takes the proper vibrations to make everything perfect."

I laughed

"Sure it's funny," said Len, "except we're talking about a five-year-old with enough problems to fill the DSM and Mommy wants to treat him like a pug. Anyway, no, I'm not personally intimate with either Prema or Donny but I have heard that he's borderline IQ and she basically runs things. Now, same question: Why the curiosity?"

"Be my therapist, Len."

"Pardon?"

"I need you to keep this in confidence."

"Of course. Sure."

I told him about the broken appointment two years ago, the surfacing of Premadonny's compound in a current criminal investigation.

He said, "Oh, my. See what you mean about tight lips. And even without the whole ethical thing, no sense getting on the bad side of people like that."

"They're that powerful?"

"That's the town we live in, Alex. You didn't grow up here, right? You're from some wholesome flyover place—Nebraska, Kansas?"

"Missouri."

"Same difference. Well, I was born in Baja Beverly Hills, my dad was an aerospace engineer, back then the studios had their influence but it was mostly about rockets and planes, real people making real product. Not the bullshit-purveying company town it is now. So good luck."

"He's no genius and she runs the show."

"Supposedly he's close to retarded—'scuse me, developmentally disabled. And living with Stupid, she'd need to run things, no?"

"She sounds like the perfect political spouse."

"Ha! There it is—that acid wit Alexander occasionally allows himself to indulge in. I used to dig when you did that in school. Made me feel better about my own uncharitable cognitions. I used to dig our time in school, period. Western Peds, too, Alex. They worked us like galley slaves but we knew we were doing good every day and it was exciting, right? We never knew what each day would bring."

"That's for sure."

"Like the time we were trying to have lunch, I remember like it was yesterday, we've got our tuna salad and our coffee on our trays, are about to finally take ten minutes and you get paged and this look comes over your face and you just leave. Later, I run into you and you tell me some patient's father brought a gun onto the onco ward, you spent an hour talking him down."

"Good times," I said.

"They *were,* man. Especially 'cause I ate your tuna." He laughed. "Imagine that, today—shrink gets a call, handles it, finito. Nowadays there'd be a mass panic, some gross overreaction due to protocol, and someone would probably get hurt. I did some of that shit myself when I was there, Alex. Crisis interventions no one heard about because they were successful. Those were *great* times."

"They were, Len."

"But get real and move on, huh? I *do* love my R8. How many miles on the Caddy?"

"Lost count by the third engine."

"Beyond loyal, we're talking commitment. Well, good for you. And great to hear from you, friend, we need to do lunch."

39

Itrolled gossip sites and the links they sent me to for personal sightings of Prema Moon and/or Donny Rader.

They'd been highly visible until four, five years ago, showing up at clubs, screenings, premieres, charity events, shopping sprees. Audiences with heads of state. But the two hits I found covering the last eighteen months featured Prema only, both times in L.A.: World Affairs Council symposium on African famine, Banish Hunger luncheon where the actress received an award.

Time to give my personal conduit to Glitz-World another try. Robin was sweeping her workbench. Pads for applying French polish sat in a wastebasket. The flamenco guitar hung drying.

"Gorgeous."

"You can test-drive it for me in a couple of days."

"Perks of the job," I said. "Do you still have a way of contacting paparazzi?"

"I'm sure some of my clients do."

"Could you call one of them?"

"Looking for a lead on the *staaahs*?"

I told her about the sudden drop in sightings.

"Burrowing because they've gotten weird?" she said. "Okay, I'll try Zenith. He's not so big anymore but he hangs with the biggies and his current flame's that actress on the doctor show and she's always good for a cleavage shot."

Zenith Streak né James Baxter professed ignorance of "all that bullshit" but he connected her to his publicist who punted to another rock star's personal manager. It took three additional calls before she obtained the number of a paparazzo named Ali, whom she sweet-talked before passing the phone to me.

I introduced myself.

He said, "Hey, dog, whusup?" in a Middle Eastern accent.

"Haven't seen much on Premadonny lately."

His voice climbed three notes up the scale. "Whu, you know 'em?"

"No. I was just wondering why."

"Aw, man . . . so why you— They pissing me off, man."

"Why?"

"Whu you think? For not *being,* know muh saying?"

"No more photo ops."

"Got to eat, dog, they the meat, dog. We don' hassle 'em, we they friends with the lens."

"So no idea why—"

"They used to *be,* man. Like a clock, we getting the call, they there smiling, waving, smiling, waving. We shooting and booting and sending. Then we spending."

"They orchestrated everything."

"Huh?"

"It was all prearranged."

"Sure, man, what you think?"

"You ever get pictures of their kids?"

"Nah, just them. Pissing me off, know what a baby brings? Hot tot shot's the mostest lot."

"Any idea why they don't call anymore?"

"They crazy."

"How so?"

"They not callin, they crazy. You not there, no one care. So what, you're like a music person's si-nificant other?"

"Yup."

"You know Katy?"

"Sorry, no."

"Taylor?"

"No—"

"Adam, Justin—you know even Christina, that's cool—how bow Bono? You know anyone, I slip you a share of what's there."

"Sorry—"

"You don know *no one,* dog?"

I chose to answer philosophically. "Not really."

"Then we done."

Robin said, "So they really are playing ground squirrel." Her smile was sudden, mischievous. "Or they've just opted for the simple life."

I said, "Growing their own vegetables, and raising hyperintellec-tual organic cattle. For the milk."

She said, "Don't forget hand-stitched hemp duds."

We both laughed. I tried to put my heart into it.

Holly Ruche had phoned while I was in the studio. I called her back, figuring single-session euphoria had faded, the way it often does.

But when she answered, her voice was fat with pleasure. "Thanks so much, Dr. Delaware. For what you've accomplished."

Not sure what I'd done, I said, "Glad everything's going well."

"Everything's going great, Dr. Delaware. Matt's talking. Really talk-ing, not just the hello how are you we used to do."

"That's great, Holly."

"Turns out what he needed was for me to *tell* him I valued what he had to say. Because his parents *discouraged* talking, his father actually used to say 'Children should be seen, not heard.' Can you believe that? Anyway, I did. Tell him. It just opened him up. Me, too. About my issues. And he was surprised to know how I felt about my mom. Which makes sense, I never talked about her until you led me in the right path. Anyway, Matt listened, nonjudgmental. *Interested.* Then he told me more about his childhood. Then we . . . everything kind of kicked up to a new level. I'm feeling in control, like I *really* own this pregnancy. Own my entire life."

"That's terrific, Holly."

"Couldn't have done it without you, Dr. Delaware."

My line of work, things like praise from patients aren't supposed to affect you because it's all about healing them, not your ego.

To hell with that, I take what I can get. "I really appreciate your telling me, Holly."

"Sure," she said. "Do you have another second?"

"What's up?"

"In terms of . . . what happened . . . to the baby. I'm assuming they haven't found anything out? Because I did read about that other poor little thing, it made my heart ache, I cried, Dr. Delaware."

"Sorry, Holly, no progress, yet."

"Something so long ago, I imagine it would be difficult to solve. And this probably won't help but that box—the blue hospital box? For some reason it bothered me. Someone putting a baby in something like that."

Her voice caught. "This is going to sound weird but I've been going online and searching for something like it and finally I found it. A box just like it at a collectibles site called OldStuff.net. From the same hospital—Swedish, the seller calls it a bank box, for depositing money, she has others for sale, from other hospitals. I called her up and she told me back in the day they used metal boxes for extra security when they brought cash to the bank. Before the armored cars were safe enough so you could use bags."

"Interesting."

"Could it be important?"

"At this point, any information's valuable."

"Great, Dr. Delaware. Then I feel good about all the time I spent online. Bye."

I logged onto the site. Identical blue box. No additional wisdom.

Robin knocked on my office door. "Going to keep working for a while?"

"Nah, let's have some fun."

She looked at the screen. I explained.

She said, "Never thought of hospitals as cash businesses."

"Place was an abortion mill back when abortion was a felony. Illegal means high profit margins."

I logged off.

She said, "Fun sounds okay." Utter lack of conviction.

I put my arm around her. "C'mon, life's short, let's own ours. How about music?"

"Sounds good."

"Let me check the Catalina . . . here's their calendar . . . Jane Monheit."

"Like her," she said. "If we can get tickets, let's do it."

Monheit was in fine voice backed by a band that never stopped swinging, the food at the club was decent, a couple of generous Chivas pours went down well.

We got home and beelined to bed and afterward I plunged into sleep, stayed out for an atypical seven hours, woke up with an aching head that filled quickly with words and pictures.

When I got to my office my cell phone was beeping and my landline message machine was blinking.

A pair of calls, less than a minute apart. I punched Play on the machine.

Milo's voice said, "Found my boy Wedd. Call."

"Sturgis."

"Congrats."

"Hear what I have to say first."

40

Melvin Jaron Wedd had been found in the passenger seat of his pimped-up black Explorer. Single gunshot wound to his left temple. The entry hole said large-caliber. The stippling said up close and personal, though probably not a contact wound.

Brain matter clotted the back of his seat. A Baggie of weed sat between his splayed knees. A glass bong glinted on the floor near his left shoe. The impact had caused him to slide down, leaving his corpse in an awkward semi-reclining state that wouldn't have been comfortable in life.

His mouth gaped, his eyes were shut, his bowels had emptied. Rot and insect activity said he'd been there days rather than hours.

Masked and gloved, a C.I. named Gloria was going through his pockets. She'd already procured his wallet, pulled out a driver's license, credit cards, eighty bucks in cash. Milo didn't need any of that to know who the victim was. A BOLO-find on Wedd's Explorer had shown up in his office email shortly after six a.m. He'd been online an hour before, "eating futility for breakfast."

Blood in the SUV said the Explorer was the murder scene. The vehicle had been left at the rear of a construction site east of Laurel Canyon, four hundred feet up a quiet street just north of the Valley. Nice neighborhood; a while back, Milo had caught a case not far from here, a prep school teacher left in a bathtub packed with dry ice.

A large, elaborate house had been framed up on the lot. Weathered wood marred by rust streaks below the nails said it had been a while since the project was active. Care had been taken to preserve the assortment of mature eucalyptus at the rear of the lot. The trees hadn't been trimmed and some of their branches drooped to the ground and continued trailing along the dirt, shaggy and green, like oversized caterpillars. The foliage had served to partially shield the Explorer but if anyone had been working on the site, they'd have noticed the vehicle immediately.

I said, "Foreclosure?"

Milo said, "Yup, last year. Guy who found the body goes around checking out bank-owned properties. The former owners are a nice older couple from Denver, moved here to be with their grandkids, tried to build their dream house, got taxed out of their dry-cleaning business. I had Denver PD talk to them. They've never heard of Wedd and they come up antiseptic-clean. And there goes my case on Adriana because ol' Melvin ain't ever talking."

Gloria called out his name. We approached her, tried to stand sufficiently back to avoid the wafting of death fumes.

"This was in his jacket, Milo. Upper inside pocket."

She held out a matchbook, white cover, unmarked. The kind you get with cigarettes at the liquor store.

Milo said, "So he had a fuel source for his dope."

Gloria opened the book. No matches left, just fuzzy stubs. Inside the book's cover, someone had scrawled in blue ballpoint. Tiny, cramped cursive.

Milo put on reading glasses, gloved up, took the book.

I read over his shoulder.

This is guilt.

Gloria said, "Can I theorize a little?"

"Sure."

"If we'd found a gun, I'd look at this as maybe a suicide note. Seeing as it's clearly a homicide, either your victim had remorse for something and wrote this himself or someone else thought he should pay for something."

"Have you checked his other pockets yet?"

"Twice. I even looked in his underwear." She wrinkled her nose. "I'm dedicated up to a point. Any idea what Mr. Wedd could be guilty of?"

"Before this I had a few ideas." He shook his head. "Anything else?"

"The driver's-seat adjustment seems to roughly fit Wedd's height, so either he was driving and moved to the passenger side or your offender's around the same size. I guess the weed and the bong are meant to imply a drug party. But with no matches in the book or anywhere else, same for ashes or residue?"

"It looks staged to you?"

"That or there was an interruption before the party got going," she said. "Was Wedd involved in that world?"

"Not that I know," said Milo. "But I don't know much, period."

He stepped away from the stench. Gloria and I followed. She said, "I'll do my best to rush DNA on the bag and the pipe, see if any chemistry other than his comes back. You saw those prints the techies pulled from the car. They've already gone to the lab, maybe you'll get lucky."

He said, "That's my middle name."

"Lucky?"

"Maybe."

A tow truck arrived to hook up the SUV. Neighbors had begun to emerge and uniforms were doing their usual blank-faced centurion thing, easing concerned citizens away from the scene with no thought to reassurance.

Milo looked at the white-bagged body being gurneyed away. "Melvin, Melvin, Melvin, so now you're another victim." To me: "All those women he had coming in and out, there could be a horde of angry husbands, boyfriends." Back at the corpse: "Thanks a bundle for your dissolute lifestyle, pal."

I said, "You see Wedd getting into a car with an angry husband? Letting him drive?"

"Someone with a gun? Sure. Or the offender's a jilted female, hell hath no fury and all that."

"Tall girl."

"Plenty of those in SoCal—what, you don't like the jealousy angle?"

"It's a common motive."

"But you have a better idea."

I told him my growing suspicions about Premadonny, leaving out the possibility of a violent child.

He said, "Creepy-World flourishes in Coldwater Canyon? What's the motive for doing two, maybe three employees, Alex? They're abusing their kids and bumping off the staff to keep them quiet?"

"Put that way, it sounds pretty weak."

"No, no, I take every product of your fertile mind seriously, it just came out of left field. Okay, let me focus for a sec: They bug you because they isolate their kids. Maybe they got tired of the hustle, had enough dough, said screw it."

I said, "That could be it."

"But," he said.

"No buts."

Gathering the flesh above his nose with two fingers, he deepened the fissure that time and age had provided. "Dealing with suspects like that. God, I hope you're wrong."

"Forget I brought it up."

His cell squawked Tchaikovsky. He said, "Okay, thanks," dropped the phone back in his pocket. "Prints from two individuals in the car: Wedd's and an unknown contributor with no match to AFIS. Unknown's was on the driver's side of the center console, Wedd's showed up on the trunk latch and the interior of the trunk. To me that says our movie stars *aren't* involved."

"How so?"

"Someone at that level chauffeuring the help? More likely some disreputable who Wedd pissed off did this. Not that it makes a difference in terms of Adriana and the baby getting icier by the second."

He left me standing there, headed toward the SUV, stopped, returned. "That canceled appointment, any hint about what kind of problem their kid was having?"

"The guy I spoke to wouldn't even tell me which kid it was."

"Okay, they're weirdly secretive. Maybe shitty parents—no shock, given all the money, no one getting told no. But that's a long way from linking them to my murders and I've still got Qeesha, a confirmed criminal and likely a killer herself. And Wedd, a guy who defrauded insurance, and Adriana, who might've had a secret life. Toss in ingredients like that and no telling what'll cook up."

I said, "Felony gumbo."

"You figure I'm in denial. Hell, yeah, sure I am. But aren't you the one says denial can be useful?"

"I love being quoted."

"Hey," he said, "it's either you or the Bible and right now I'm not feeling sufficiently pious to invoke Scripture. C'mon, I'll walk you to your car."

41

Obsessiveness and anxiety are traits that can clog up your life. But the way I figure, they've got plenty of evolutionary value.

Think of cave-people surrounded by predators. Jumpy, annoyingly picky Oog sleeps fitfully because he's mindful of creatures that roar in the night. More often than not, he wakes up with a dry mouth and a pounding heart.

Easygoing Moog, in contrast, sinks easily into beautiful dreams. One morning he fails to wake up at all because his heart's been chewed to hamburger and the rest of his innards have been served up as steaming mounds of carnivore candy.

The blessing-curse of an overly developed attention span helped me escape a family situation that would've continued to damage me and might've ended up killing me. Since then, over-the-shoulder vigilance has saved my life more than once.

So I'll sacrifice a bit of serenity.

Milo was right; denial could be the right way to go but this morning it felt wrong and I got home itching to focus.

An hour on the computer gave way to double that time on the phone. My pitch grew better with repeated use but it proved useless. Then I switched gears and everything fell into place.

By four p.m. I was dressed in a steel-gray Italian suit, open-necked white shirt, brown loafers, and hanging near the southwest corner of Linden Drive and Wilshire.

Busy stretch of impeccable Beverly Hills sidewalk, easy to blend in with a light pedestrian parade as I repeated a two-block circuit while pretending to window-shop.

The Seville was parked in a B.H. city lot. Two hours gratis, so shoppers could concentrate on consumer goods and cuisine.

I wasn't planning to buy anything; I had something to sell. Or trade, depending on how things worked out.

Apex Management was headquartered in a forties-era three-story brick building that looked as if it had once housed doctors and dentists. A few months ago, I'd read about the Beverly Hills city council wanting to clamp down on medical offices because health care attracted hordes of—surprise!—sick people who took up too many, parking spaces and failed to spend like tourists.

Entertainment ancillaries like Apex, on the other hand, churned expense accounts at the city's truffled-up eateries and attracted publicity magnets and the paparazzi and there's no such thing as bad publicity.

I was facing a collection of psychotically priced cashmere sweaters and wondering if the goats who'd donated their hair were having a rough winter when the first human outflow emerged from behind Apex's carved oak doors.

Three men in their twenties and thirties, then four more, all wearing Italian suits, open-necked dress shirts, and loafers. Industry-ancillary uniform. Which was the point.

Next came a man and two women in tailored pantsuits, followed by a pair of younger women similarly but less expensively attired. Those two let the door close on the next person out: a tired-looking older man in a green janitor's uniform.

Three minutes later the prey came into view.

Tall, late twenties, crowned by a thick mop of blond-streaked, light brown hair, he wore black-framed geek eyeglasses that stretched wider than his pasty, bony face. In the firm's Christmas party photos he'd worn wire rims.

He'd also tended to pose standing slightly apart from his co-workers, which had led me to hope he was a loner.

Wish fulfilled: all by himself and looking worn out and distracted.

The perfect quarry.

I watched him stop and fidget. His suit was black with a pink pin-stripe, narrow-lapelled, snugly fitted. Cheaply cut when you got close, as much hot glue as stitching in play. A Level Two Service Assistant's salary wouldn't cover high-end threads.

I walked toward him, noticed a loose thread curling from one shirt collar. *Tsk tsk.*

We were face-to-face. He was concentrating on the sidewalk, didn't notice. When my shadow intruded on his, his head rose and he gave a start and tried to move past me.

I blocked him. "Kevin?"

"Do I know you?"

"No, but you do know JayMar Laboratory Supplies."

"Huh?"

I held my LAPD consultant I.D. badge close to my thigh, raised it just enough so he had to strain to read the part I wasn't covering with my thumb.

Showcasing the always-impressive department seal while conceal-ing my name and ambiguous title.

"Police?"

I said, "Could I have a moment of your time, Kevin?"

His mouth opened wide. So did the carved oak door, ejecting more suits, male and female, a large group buoyant with liberation, headed our way, laughing raucously.

Someone said, "Hey, Kev."

The quarry waved.

I said, "I can show them the badge, too."

His jaws clenched. "Don't."

"Your call, Kev." Walking back to Wilshire, I returned to the sweater display, kept my eye on him while pretending to study my cell phone.

Co-workers coalesced around him. A woman said something and pointed across Wilshire. Smiling painfully, he shook his head. The group continued on, merry as carolers. Crossing the boulevard, they continued toward a restaurant on the ground floor of a black-glass office building.

El Bandito Grill.

A banner proclaimed *Happy Hour!!!*

Not for Kevin Dubinsky.

As I waited for him, he kicked one heel with the other. Contemplating an alternative. Failing to come up with one, he removed his glasses and swung them at his side as pipe-stem legs propelled him toward me.

When he got close, he mumbled, "What's going on?"

I said, "How 'bout we walk while we chat?"

"Chat about what?"

"Or we could talk right here, Kevin." I pulled out the photocopied order form.

JayMar Laboratory Supplies, Chula Vista, California

Five hundred dermestid beetles and a set of surgical tools, including a bone saw, purchased four months ago.

It had taken me a while to get the info. Call after futile call using the address of the compound off Coldwater Canyon.

The pitch: "I'm calling to renew an order for dermestid beetles . . ."

No one knew what I was talking about. Then I realized I'd goofed big-time. People like that didn't do things for themselves. After substituting Apex Management's shipping address—a warehouse in Culver City—I had confirmation by the seventh call, a nice clean fax of the form.

Kevin Dubinsky's name at the bottom as "purchaser."

Facebook and LinkedIn supplied all I needed to know about him. Let's hear it for cyber-truth.

He turned away from the order form. "So? It's my job."

"Exactly, Kev. Your job's what we need to discuss."

"Why?"

"You buy flesh-eating insects and scalpels regularly?"

"I figured it was . . ." He shut his mouth.

"It was what?"

"Nothing." Flash of bitter smile. "I'm not paid to think."

"Are you paid *not* to think?"

No answer.

"What you take home, Kev, you might want to reconsider your priorities."

"There's a problem?"

"Only if you don't cooperate."

"With what?"

"Better I ask the questions."

"Something bad happened?"

"I don't visit people to talk about jaywalking, Kev."

"Oh, shit—what's going on?"

"Like I said, Kev, the less you know the better."

"Shit." He licked his lips, began walking east on Wilshire. I kept up with his long stride. All those years with Milo, great practice.

I said, "Tell me about it."

"I don't remember specifics."

"You buy what you're told, all part of the job."

"That *is* the job. Period."

"Service assistant."

"Yeah, it's stupid, I know. I need to eat, okay?"

"You get a call to—"

"Never a call, always email."

"Buy me bugs."

"I order all kinds of things. That's what I'm paid to do."

"You do all the purchasing for the Premadonny compound?"

"No, just . . ." Head shake.

"Just things they don't want their name on?"

Silence. Wrong guess. I'd try the same question later.

"So how many times have you ordered beetles and knives?"

"Just that once."

"You didn't find it weird?"

"Wondering wastes time."

"Busy guy," I said. "They work you hard."

"Like I said, I like to eat."

"Don't we all."

He stopped. "You don't get it. I don't ask questions and I'm *not* allowed to answer any."

"About . . ."

"Anything. Ever. That's Rule Number One. Numbers Two through Ten say refer back to One."

"That sounds like something your boss told you."

No reply.

I said, "Privacy's a big deal for Premadonny."

"They're all like that."

"Stars?"

"You can call 'em that."

"What do you call 'em?"

"The gods." His lips turned down. A sneer full of reflexive disdain. The same flavor of contempt I'd heard in Len Coates's voice.

Perfect opening for me.

"Funny, Kev, you'd think they'd want nothing *but* attention."

"They want it, all right. On their terms." Long slow intake of breath. "Now I'm fucked, I already said too much."

I said, "Service assistant. That could mean anything."

Kevin Dubinsky emitted a high, coarse sound that didn't approach laughter. "It means fucking *gopher.* Know what they actually pay me?"

"Not much."

"Less than that." He laughed.

Resisting the urge to pluck the loose thread from his collar, I said, "That's the way the Industry works. The gods perch on Olympus, the peasants grovel."

"Better believe it."

"So no sense getting screwed on their account, Kevin."

"I like to *eat,* man."

"I'm discreet. Tell me about the job."

"What's to tell? I order stuff."

More eye movement. Time to revisit his first evasion. I said, "Not for the entire compound."

He gnawed his lip.

"Eventually we're going to find out, Kevin, no sense complicating your life by getting tagged as uncooperative."

"Please. I can't help you."

"Who'd you buy that crap for?"

Silence.

I said, "Or maybe we should assume you bought it for your own personal use, that could get *really* interesting."

"Her, okay? I only buy for her, he's got his own slave."

"Who's that?"

"Like I know? I do what I'm told."

"You buy stuff she doesn't want traced back to her."

"I buy for her because she can't dirty her hands being a real person." He laughed, patted a trouser pocket. "I use a Centurion—a black card—just for her swag. Get to pretend every day."

"Must get interesting."

"Nah, it sucks."

"Boring purchases?"

"Boring expensive purchases." He mimed gagging himself with a finger.

I said, "You buy, the stuff ships to Culver City, the paperwork gets filed somewhere else, so if someone goes through her garbage they can't figure out what she's into."

"Maybe that's part of it," he said. "I always figure, it's God forbid they do anything for themselves."

"Do you handle groceries and stuff like that?"

"Nah, that goes through her staff at the compound."

"What do you buy?"

" 'Special purchases.' "

"Meaning?"

"Whatever she feels like."

We walked half a block before he stopped again, drew me to another display window. Manikins who'd have to plump up to be anorexic were draped in black crepe garments that might be coats. Blank white faces projected grief. Nothing like a funeral for selling product.

He said, "I'm going to tell you this so you'll understand, okay? One time—I don't know this personally, I was told it—they actually set up a scene so she could fill her car up and look like a regular person. They picked a gas station in Brentwood, Apex paid to clear the place out for a day, masked it off with those silver sheets photographers use so no one could see what was going on. They gave her a car that wasn't hers, something normal, and she pretended to fill it up."

I said, "For one of those stars-are-just-like-us deals."

Another contemptuous look. "Five takes for her to get the hang of putting gas in a fucking car. She had no fucking clue."

"Unreal."

"Her life is unreal, man. So what'd she need those bugs for?"

I smiled.

"Okay, I get it, shut up and cooperate."

"Do your purchases get audited?"

"Every month a prick from accounting goes over every damn thing. I charge a pencil that can't be explained, my ass is grass. A girl who used to work in the next cubicle, she bought for—I can't tell you who—she got busted for a bottle of nail polish."

I said, "Sucks. So what's the most expensive item you've ever bought for her?"

"Easy," he said. "Last year, time share on a Gulfstream Five. Seven figures up front plus serious monthly maintenance. She never uses it."

I whistled.

"That's the point, dude. Doing stuff no one else can do, to show you're God. One day I'm going to find a real job."

"How long have you been at Apex?"

"Little over three years," he said. "Started out doing messenger shit. Which was basically bringing envelopes from one schmuck boss to another, picking up lunch, all kinds of scut. When I signed up, I figured it would be temporary. So I could save up enough and go back to school."

"What were you studying?"

"What do you think?"

"Acting."

He chuckled. "They taught you to detect pretty good. Yeah, I was like every fool comes to L.A., thought because I was Stanley in high school and my drama teacher loved me I could live . . . atop Olympus." He shook his head. "My crib's a barf-hole in Reseda, I'm barely getting by, and now I got cops talking to me. Maybe it's time to go back and study something real. Like real estate. Or online poker."

He reached for my sleeve, retracted his hand before making contact. "Please don't screw me, dude. All I did was what I was told."

"If that's true, I don't see you as having any liability, Kevin."

"I don't mean problems with you, I mean the job. Rule One."

"I'll do my best to keep you out of it."

"The way you said that scares me."

"Why?"

"It could mean anything."

"What it means, Kev, is that we need each other."

"How?"

"You don't want me talking about you and my bosses can't afford you telling anyone about this meeting because there's an ongoing investigation."

"No prob, I won't say a word."

"Then we're cool."

I held out my hand. We shook. His skin was clammy.

"Thanks for talking to me, Kev."

"Believe me, my yap is permanently shut. But can I ask one thing? Just for my own sake?"

"What?"

"Did she do something bad with that shit? I figured it was for the kids, some sort of science project, you know? She's always getting stuff for the kids."

I said, "Ever hear of the Lacey Act?"

"No, what's that?"

"Protection for endangered species."

"That's what this is about? Those stupid bugs were illegal?"

"Protected." I ran a finger across my lips. "Like this communication. Have a nice day, Kevin."

"I'll try," he said. "Getting harder, but I'll try."

CHAPTER

42

The morning after meeting Kevin Dubinsky, I dressed in sweatpants, a T-shirt, running shoes, and a Dodgers cap, was ready to leave by eight. Blanche, figuring it was time for a stroll, bounced up to me and smiled.

I said, "Sorry, honey," fetched her a consolation strip of bacon that she regarded with sad eyes before deigning to nibble, carried her to Robin's studio, and left the house.

I drove up Beverly Glen, turned right at Mulholland, passing the fire station near Benedict Canyon, stopping once to pick up a nice-sized branch that had fallen off an ancient sycamore. Sailing through pretty, dew-livened hills I reached the Coldwater Canyon intersection, across from TreePeople headquarters.

A little more than half a mile south of the private road that led to the Premadonny compound.

I drove two miles north of the property, found a patch of turnoff not meant for long-term stay, left the car there, anyway. Stick in hand, I returned south on foot.

Crows squawked, squirrels chittered, all kinds of animal noises became evident once you listened. I spotted a deer munching dry grass then speeding toward a McMansion that blocked far too much canyon view, came upon the desiccated remains of a gorgeous red-and-yellow-banded king snake. Juvenile, from the size of it. No signs of violence to the little reptile. Sometimes things just died.

I kept going, using the branch for a walking stick that I hoped would imply Habitual Hiker. Nice day to be out walking, if you ignored the occasional car roaring toward you, oblivious or hostile to the concept of foot travel. Fools texting and phone-yakking and a notable cretin shaving his face made the journey an interesting challenge. More than once I had to press myself against a hillside to avoid being pulverized.

I kept up a steady pace, tapped a rhythm with the stick, pretended to be caught up in pedestrian Zen. In L.A., that makes you strange. In L.A., people ignore strange.

When I reached my destination, I found a tree-shielded spot across the road and had a look at the entry to the compound. A discreet sign warned against trespassing. An electric gate ten or so yards up blocked entry. The road to that barrier was a single lane of age-grayed asphalt in need of patching, shaded by bay laurels and untrimmed ficus. A stray plastic cup lid glinted from the shrubbery. Appropriately secluded but a little on the shabby side; not a hint this was Buckingham West.

I continued walking, searched for police surveillance. None that I could see; maybe Milo hadn't gotten around to arranging it.

I hadn't heard from him since the meet at Melvin Wedd's crime scene. Probably inspecting Wedd's apartment, locating next of kin, all that logical detective procedure.

Correspondence with Wedd's family would be an exercise in deception: prying out dirt about a victim/possible suspect under the guise of consolation. Milo was good at that, I'd seen him pull it off plenty of times. Later, he'd mutter about the power of positive hypocrisy.

I covered another mile, reversed direction, took a second look at the access road to the compound, repeated the process several times, never encountering another person on foot.

They say walking's the best exercise, if we had time to do enough of it, we wouldn't need to jog or run or tussle with implements of gym-torture. By the time I got back in the Seville my feet were starting to protest and I guessed I'd covered at least ten miles.

It had been a learning experience. Body and mind.

When I was minutes from home, Robin called. "Guess what, Brent's back in town, can't wait to talk to you."

"Eager to do his civic duty?"

She laughed. "More like his un-civil duty. He hates them, Alex. Quote unquote. He's lunching, guess where?"

"Spago."

"Grill on the Alley. Karma, huh?"

"Last time I was there the company was a whole lot cuter."

"But nowhere near this informative, baby. Good luck."

The Grill bustles pleasantly at dinnertime. During lunch it roars, filling up with Industry testosterone, every power booth occupied by movers and shakers and those too rich to bother doing either. Each bar stool is occupied but no one gets drunk. Platters of food are transported smoothly by an army of white-jacketed waiters who've seen it all. Sometimes tourists and others naive enough to venture in without a reservation bunch up at the door like immigrants seeking asylum. A trio of hosts seems genuinely remorseful when they reject the unschooled.

My hiking duds were far below the sartorial standard but you'd never know it from the smile of the woman behind the lectern. "May I help you?"

"I'm meeting Brent Dorf."

"Certainly." She beckoned a waiter with an eyebrow lift and he led me to a table on the south side of the restaurant, concealed by the center partition.

Far from the see-and-be-seen; Brent's clout was beta.

◆

He was hunched over a Caesar salad, forking quickly as if he needed to be somewhere else yesterday. When he saw me, he didn't stop eating. A millimeter of white wine remained in his glass.

The waiter said, "Cocktail? Or Chardonnay like Mr. Dorf?" and handed me a menu.

I said, "Iced tea's fine. I'll also have a Caesar."

"No croutons, dressing on the side, like Mr. Dorf?"

"Dressing and croutons are fine. Anchovies, too."

The waiter smiled approvingly, as if someone finally had the sense to do it right.

Brent said, "Lay on the calories and the sodium, easy for you skinny folk."

He was thinner than me, had the wrinkles and sunken cheeks to show for it. His head was shaved, his oblong hound-dog face had been barbered so closely that I wondered about electrolysis. Last time I'd seen him he'd been thirty pounds heavier and sported a soul patch.

I said, "You're not exactly obese, Brent."

"Good tailoring, you don't want to see me naked." He looked at the ramekin of salad dressing at his right elbow, considered his options, pushed it away. "I'm under pressure, my friend."

"Tough job."

"Not that pressure, body pressure."

"Honestly, you look good, Brent."

"Yeah, yeah, everything's relative," he said. "Got myself a twenty-eight-year-old dancer with statue-of-David definition, I'm talking physical perfection." He sighed. "Todd claims he loves me but we both know he's out for the good life. By both of us, I don't mean him and me, I mean you and me. Seeing as you're a mental health sage."

My tea came.

Brent said, "How's *your* gorgeous other?"

"Terrific."

"Robin, Robin," he said. "I always thought she was special. A knockout who knows how to use power tools? Sexy."

"No argument, Brent."

His eyelids descended, half hooding irises the color of silt. He looked around the room, bent closer, lowered his voice. "So you want to know about Lancelot and Guinevere."

"Anything you can tell me."

"Funny," he said, "I figured *you* could tell *me*."

"Why's that?"

"Because I sent them to you. Referred them. Figured by now you'd have all the insights."

"That was you?" I said. "They canceled, never saw them."

"Figures," he said. "They're big on that."

"Canceling?"

"Reneging." His hand tensed, gave a small wave and brushed against his glass, knocking it over. The minuscule amount of wine was no threat as it dribbled to the tablecloth, but he flung himself back as if escaping an avalanche. High-strung type.

When the waiter came over to help, he barked, "I'm fine, just bring his food."

"Yes, sir."

I drank tea as Brent checked out the adjoining booths. No one paid attention to his scrutiny.

"So they never showed up," he said. "Well, they fucked me over big-time, that's why I'm happy to give you dirt. But first tell me why you need to know about them."

"Can't."

"Can't?"

"Sorry, that's all I can say, Brent."

"Ooooh, big giant *police* mystery? Got to be juicy if that cop has you on it." He winked. "Another O.J. thing? Blake? Something better?"

"Not even close, I was hoping you'd get me closer."

"I do the giving, you do the taking?" He laughed. "So you've met Todd."

My salad arrived. Brent lifted an anchovy from my plate, chewed, swallowed. "Blood pressure's probably through the roof now, but yummy."

"So how'd you come to refer them to me?"

"I was doing a deal and the issue came up. I think kid-shrink, I think you."

"What kind of problem were they having?"

"How should I know? I never talked to them."

"Your people set it up with their people. Then you took lunch."

"Ha ha ha. As a matter of fact, yes, that's what happened. But high-level people. People authorized to make decisions. We were at that stage by then, I thought I had the deal nailed."

An index finger massaged the empty wineglass. Reassuring himself he was steady. He said, "My house has a wine cellar, I've got twelve hundred bottles, more than I'll be able to drink, and Todd doesn't touch alcohol."

"Embarrassment of riches."

"Yeah . . . anyway, that's it. Someone asked about a therapist, I said I knew someone."

"They asked for a child therapist, specifically."

"Hmm," he said. "I think so—this was what, two years ago?"

"Just about."

His eyes drifted toward the bar, followed the entry of four men in suits and open-necked shirts. And loafers. He started to wave, stopped when they failed to notice him. Or ignored him. They continued to a corner booth. He finished his wine.

I said, "No hint about what the problem was."

"Ri . . . ight." Still checking out the room.

I ate salad as he gave the anchovies an occasional lustful look. "I need to be honest, Alex. It wasn't something I thought much about, I was concentrating on the deal. Besides, I get that kind of thing all the time."

"Requests for referrals."

"Doctors, dentists, chiropractors, masseuses. All part of the job."

"Knowing the right people."

"Knowing the right matches, who fits with who. I figured you'd be okay for them because you have all the right paper, probably wouldn't fuck up."

I smiled. "Thanks for the endorsement, Brent."

"They canceled, huh? So what else is new."

"Why'd they bail on your deal?"

"Not *my* deal, a deal between titans, I'm talking A-est of the A-list, something that could've been *huge*. I set it up elegantly, if it had gone through, I'd never have to think about anything for the rest of my life."

"Blockbuster."

"Blockbuster times a quintzillion, Alex. I'm talking action, romance, long and short arcs, merchandising potential up the wazz, sequels that would've gone on for infinity. I'm talking the biggest thing they'd do together, *wa-aaay* bigger than *Passion Power* and that piece of shit pulled in heavy eight figures with overseas distribution. The upside would've been astronomical. More important, I staked my word on it, staked my fucking soul. Everything was in place, contracts drawn, clauses hammered out, legal fees alone cost more than entire pictures used to rack up. We were set up for a signing, going to make a big thing about it, press conference, photo ops. The day before, they change their mind."

"How come?"

"People like that have to give a reason?" His fist hit the table. The wineglass bounced. He caught it. "Gotcha, you little bastard."

Beckoning the waiter, he brandished the glass. "Take this away, it's annoying."

"Yes, sir."

Flecks of foam had collected at the corners of Brent's mouth. He made claws out of his hands, scratched air. "I put everything into it, Alex. Hadn't taken on another client the entire year and I'm talking names, people pissed off at me. Everything else came my way, I delegated to other agents at the firm. So of course, my alleged friends and colleagues held on to everything after I got . . . after the deal got murdered and I had nothing, was starting from fucking scratch and my credibility's worse than a politician. Everything changed. I got moved to a new office. Want to take odds it was bigger? Don't." Long sigh. "But I'm getting back to a good place in my life, every day's progress."

He shoved his plate to the side. "The deal was perfection, every *meeting* was perfection. And for a bullshit reason like that? Give me a fucking break."

I said, "Thought they didn't give you a reason?"

"I said that? I never said that. What I said was people like that don't *have* to have a reason. Yeah, they gave an excuse. Family matters. And that's *after* I referred them to you, so what the fuck was their problem?"

His eyelids dropped farther. "Here's a confession, Alex. For a while I got paranoid. About you. Did they go see you and you laid some shrink crap on them—spend more time with the kids, whatever—and *that's* what fucked things up? For a while I had . . . thoughts about you. Then I realized I was getting psycho, if I didn't watch out I'd go totally psycho."

He reached across, patted my wrist. "I have to be honest, that's one reason I wanted to meet with you. To find out what the fuck happened. So now I find out you don't *know* what the fuck happened and you're asking *me* what the fuck happened. Funny. Ironic. Ha ha ha. And they're in some kind of trouble. Good. I'm happy. They should rot in hell."

"What kind of people are they?"

"What kind do you think? Selfish, narcissistic, inconsiderate, he's an idiot, she's a controlling bitch. You buy that Super Mom–Super Dad crap? It's just part of the façade, everything about people like that is a façade. You ever hear him talk? Dluh dluh dluh dluh. That's what passes for James Dean, now. Welcome to my world."

The waiter came over. "Anything else, gents? Coffee?"

Brent said, "No. Check."

I paid.

Brent said, "Good man."

43

I reached Milo at the coroner's.

"Just watched a .45 slug get pulled out of Wedd's head, a weapon ever shows up, it's early Christmas. His apartment was vacant except for a mattress on the bedroom floor and some over-the-counter pharmaceuticals in the john. He used to get heartburn and headaches, now he's passed both along to me. Had the place dusted, sent the meds and the mattress to the lab, located one relative, Wedd's brother, cowboy-type in Montana where Wedd's originally from. No contact with Brother Mel for years, was appropriately shocked about the murder, said Mel was always the wild one but he never figured it would get that bad."

He paused for breath.

I said, "Wild but no criminal record."

"Minor-league stuff when he was young—joyriding, malicious pranks, neighborhood mischief, a few fights. No criminal record because the sheriff was his uncle, he'd bring Mel home and Mel's dad would whup him. Then Mel got bigger than Dad and the parents basically gave up."

"When did he come to L.A.?"

"Ten years ago, brother's had no contact with him since. He wasn't surprised to know Mel had gone Hollywood. Said the only thing Mel liked in high school was theater arts, he was always getting starring roles, could sing like Hank Williams, do impressions. John Wayne, Clint Eastwood, you name it."

"I've got something. You might even think of it as progress."

I told him about the order from JayMar Lab, my talks with Kevin Dubinsky and Brent Dorf. Leaving out Len Coates because everything he knew was secondhand.

Milo said, "Knives and beetles. Her."

"Purchased right around the time the baby was born. Poor little thing might've been targeted in utero."

"I need to digest this . . . got time? My office, an hour."

Midway through the drive to the station, I got a call from Len.

"Alex, I can't tell you where I got this, so don't ask, okay?"

"Okay."

"The client we discussed did in fact opt for a therapist other than yourself. But the contact was limited to a single visit so obviously there was some serious resistance going on, don't take it personally."

"Thanks for the reassurance, Len."

"Well," he said, "we have feelings, too, no one likes to be passed over."

"Agreed. One visit for what?"

He cleared his throat. "Here's what I can tell you, please don't ask for more: Client shows up late, can't seem to articulate a good reason for being there, leaves before the session is over."

I said, "Trouble focusing." Thinking of Donny Rader's voice on the line, his reputation as a barely literate dullard.

Then Len slipped and changed all that. "She . . . there was a lot of generalized anxiety, no ability to . . . explicate. Basically, it amounted to nothing, Alex, so I don't see anything you can do with it."

She.

"I'm sure you're right, Len. Thanks."

"Law enforcement issues notwithstanding, Alex, none of this can ever be repeated to anyone."

"I get it, Len. You have my word."

"Good . . . you still taking patients?"

"Infrequently."

"I'm asking because sometimes I get run-over. Good cases, not bullshit ones, things get crazy-busy, I could use backup."

"Beyond your associates."

"They're kids, Alex. We're vets. You interested?"

"Something short-term, in a pinch, I might be able to help."

"Pretty busy, yourself."

"It can get that way."

"Playing Sherlock, huh? Ever think of selling yourself to TV? Make a good series."

"Not really."

"No interest at all?"

"I like the quiet life."

"Think about it anyway, I'd produce in a heartbeat. And don't be a stranger."

I continued toward the station, thought about Donny Rader setting up an appointment, Prema Moon showing up late and leaving early, unable to explain what she was after.

A couple of nervous, caring parents? That didn't fit with the notion of cold-blooded baby killers. Something was off. I was struggling with that when Milo rang in.

"Almost there," I said.

"Change of plans."

He laid them out. I got on the freeway, sped downtown.

44

The chief had opted to hide in plain sight, designating the meet at Number One Fortune Dim Sum Palace, one of those arena-sized places in Chinatown that still feature gluey chop suey, oil-drenched moo goo gai pan, and seafood of mysterious origin.

The air was humid with steam, sweat, and MSG. Linoleum floors had been pounded dull by decades of feet. The walls were red, green, more red, raised panels embossed with gold dragon medallions and outsized renderings of birds, fish, and bats. Chinese lettering might have meant something. Hundreds of lunchers were crammed into vault-like dining rooms, tended by ancient waiters in black poly Mao suits and tasseled gold beanies who moved as if running for their lives.

Enough clatter and din to make the Grill seem like a monastery. If there was a caste system behind this seating scheme, I couldn't decipher it, and when Milo asked to be directed to the chief's table, the stunning hostess looked at him as if he was stupid.

"We don't take reservations and we have eight rooms."

We set out on the hunt, finally spotted him at a smallish table near the center of the sixth room surrounded by hordes engrossed in their food. No one paying attention to the white-haired, mustachioed man in the black shadow-stripe suit, white silk tab-collar shirt, gray-yellow-scarlet Leonard tie that screamed *more is more*.

He saw us when we were thirty feet away, looked up from chop-sticking noodles into his mouth, wiped his mouth and drank from a glass of dark beer.

I looked around for his bodyguards, spotted a pair of cold-eyed burlies four tables over, pretending to concentrate on a platter of some-thing brown.

"Sit down. I ordered spareribs, pepper steak, shrimp-fried rice, and some sort of deep-fried chicken thing, hopefully they won't include the damn feet." Glancing at Milo. "You I know will eat anything." To me: "That sound suitable for your constitution?"

"Sure."

"Easy to please today, Doc? Strange phase of the moon?"

He'd been trying to hire me full-time for years, had never accepted failure with anything approaching good nature.

He returned to eating, chopsticks whirling like darning needles. Ex-cellent fine-motor coordination motivated a huge load of noodles under the mustache. He chewed, had more beer, looked around. "Damn barn."

One of the old waiters brought tea and beer and sped away.

The chief said, "You stirred up a hornets' nest, Doctor."

"Keeps life interesting."

"Maybe yours. Okay, give me a brief summary. And I mean brief. You, not Sturgis. He already went over the basics when he called and made my life complicated."

I said, "At least three people who lived at Premadonny's compound have been murdered."

"Three?" he said. "I've got the nanny and the guy—Wedd."

"The baby found in the park."

"That," he said. "All right, go on. Why do you suspect dark events at Xanadu?"

"A couple of years ago, I received a call from a man I believe to be Donny Rader, requesting help—"

"Why do you think it was him?"

"The way he spoke."

"Like a moron."

"Indistinctly," I said.

"Okay, he needed a shrink for a brat, he's an actor, big surprise. What else?"

"I set up an appointment that was canceled. I didn't think much of it. But the death of one, maybe two child-care workers got me wondering about the family situation and I tried to learn as much as I could. That turned out to be next to nothing because the family's basically gone underground. Moon and Rader used to be ultra-public figures. They peddled their fame. Now they've disappeared. No venturing out in public, no chatter on the Web, and right around the time I got that call they abruptly canceled a major film project due to 'family issues.'"

"Maybe they didn't like the script."

The waiter returned. Platters were slammed down unceremoniously. The chief said, "So they're miserable maladjusts. So what?"

"My experience is that extremely isolated families are often breeding grounds for psychopathology. Three people with connections to them are dead. Something's going on there."

"Sounds like you've got nothing, Doc."

"Until recently, I would've agreed with you. Then I learned that Prema Moon purchased flesh-eating beetles and surgical tools. Right around the time the baby was born."

"Show me the proof."

I produced the form from JayMar, began explaining the purchasing process.

He cut me off. "They've got peons to wipe their asses for them, another big shock." He put on glasses, read, frowned, slid the form into an inner jacket pocket.

Milo said, "Only thing missing, sir, is beeswax. If we can get access to the rest of their—"

The chief waved him quiet. "Beetles. Crazy bitch. How exactly did you get hold of the form, Doctor?"

"I called supply houses pretending to be someone from Apex, said I wanted to renew the order. Eventually, I found the right one."

"Planning on billing the department for your time?"

"Hadn't thought about it."

"You just do this for fun, huh?"

"I'm a curious guy."

"How long did it take you to find the right company?"

"A few hours."

"You're a persistent bastard, aren't you?"

"I can be."

"Deceptive, too . . . no telling how that'll play into the hands of some nuclear-powered lawyer. If you're deemed a police agent, it could open up claims of insufficient grounds, hence illegal search. Which is probably bullshit but with judges you never know. If you're deemed to be a civilian, it could open *you* up to some ball-squeezing cross-examination, not to mention an invasion-of-privacy suit by people who can buy and sell you a thousand times over. That happens, forget any chance of a quiet life for the foreseeable future. These people are like governments, they go to war. You willing to take that risk?"

I said, "Sounds like you're trying to discourage me."

He put his chopsticks down. "I think long-term, Alex." First time he'd used my name. "That separates me from ninety-nine percent of the population. Even at Harvard."

He loved putting down the Ivy League, rarely missed the opportunity to bring up his graduate degree from the iviest of all.

I said, "You think I was wrong to dig up the information."

"I *think* this could get nasty."

"What happened to that baby was beyond nasty."

He glared. "I got a white knight here." Lifting a sparerib with his fingers, he chewed down to the bone, ingesting meat, gristle, and fat. "Take one, Sturgis. You not stuffing your face scares me. It's like the sun stopping mid-orbit."

Milo spooned some fried rice onto his plate.

The chief said, "Not into ribs, today, Lieutenant?"

"This is fine, sir."

The chief smirked. "Establishing your independence? That makes you feel like a grown-up, be my guest." To me: "This is a mess."

He reached for the plate. Another rib got gnawed to the bone.

I said, "Another thing I did—"

"Another thing? Jesus Almighty, you figure you're running your own investigation?" His eyes shifted to Milo. Milo's head was down as he shoveled rice into his maw.

The chief turned back to me. *"What?"*

I told him about the morning's hike. "None of the principals entered or exited the compound but I did learn that it's a pretty busy place. In the space of three hours, I saw a seven-man groundskeeping crew, a grocery delivery, a repairman from a home-theater outfit, and a plumber. I copied down the tags—"

"Why?"

"I figured it might offer a possible way to get in—"

"Sturgis pretends to be a gardener or a plumber? *Habla español,* Sturgis? Know how to unclog a sink? *I* do, my *father* was a plumber, I spent my summers elbow-deep in rich people's muck. You ever do that, Sturgis? Wade in rich folk shit?"

Milo said, "Frequently, sir."

"Don't like the job?"

"Love it, sir. It is what it is."

The chief looked ready to spit. "Don Quixote and Sancho Panza . . . so, being a psychologist, Doc, you figure a crafty way to gain entry would be to hitch a ride with one of the peasants who services the castle, once you're inside, you just mosey around at random in the hope of stumbling across definitive evidence?"

"I was hoping to catch Moon, Rader, or any of the kids leaving. But when I saw the volume of traffic, it occurred to me there might be an opening."

"If Moon or Rader had left, you figured to tail them."

"Discreetly."

His face darkened. "Dr. Do-A-Lot. You talk to animals, as well?"

"If I've overstepped, I'm sorry."

"Overstepped?" He laughed. "More like you've invented new dance moves. What day does the garbage get taken out at that place?"

Milo said, "I'll find out." He walked to the dining room doorway, talked on his cell.

The chief returned to his ribs, tried some pepper steak. Pincer-grasped a plump little pink shrimp out of the fried rice. "Not hungry, Doc?"

"Actually, I am." I tried a rib. Greasy and delicious.

"Just like you," said the chief.

"Pardon?"

"You're like the damn ribs. Unhealthy but satisfying. Congratulations, Sturgis plodded along but you're the one who learned something."

"He—"

"No need to defend him, I know what he is, he's good at what he does, as good as I'm gonna get. You, on the other hand, are a different animal. You piss me off without trying. You also make me wonder what the department would be like if everyone was super-smart and psychotically driven. Don't tell Sturgis I said that, you'll hurt his feelings."

He and I ate in silence until Milo returned.

"Garbage collection's in two days, sir."

"Be there before the trucks arrive, Sturgis. Wear comfortable clothes and bring enough empty barrels to haul away every bit of trash. Don't be noticed. Separate anything with DNA potential and run a match to the baby bones. Maybe this Qeesha character is still alive and shedding cells, we find an eyebrow pencil, a tampon, whatever, that links her to the bones, we're a step forward. We also get an accurate victim count, two not three, and think of her as a homicidal bitch who killed her own kid."

Milo said, "DNA analysis could take a while."

"I'll speed it through to the max."

"Until then—"

"Until then you and your geniuses try to do what the doctor, an allegedly untrained civilian, was apparently able to accomplish: Watch the goddamn place without being seen. Prema or Donny or Qeesha appear, they get tailed. With finesse. Seduction, not rape, Sturgis."

"Got it, sir." Milo started to rise.

"Where do you think you're going?"

"Getting back to work."

"This *is* work, Sturgis. Amusing the boss. Now don't let me down, I want to see some calorie consumption."

Amusing the boss translated to a quarter hour of near-silent scarfing. The chief was a lean man but he had a staggering capacity for intake. We watched him polish off the ribs and pick all the shrimp out of the rice before he shot a French cuff and smiled at his Patek Philippe. On cue, the burly duo got up and headed toward us. The chief got to his feet, buttoned his jacket.

He looked down at Milo. "Who's paying for this repast?"

Milo said, "If you'd like—"

"Just kidding, Sturgis, I don't exploit the workingman. Or in your case, Doc, the theorizing man."

He threw bills on the table. "Stay as long as you like. Just be gone in ten minutes so you can resume what the city pays you for, Sturgis."

Before his minions could reach him, he race-walked out of the room.

Milo looked at the picked-over rice. "Would your Hollywood buddies call that a good meeting?"

"My buddies?"

"Contacts, whatever."

"Well," I said, "depends on whether the picture gets made."

We left the restaurant, headed to a parking lot across Hill Street.

Milo said, "He talked a good case but what I got out of it was 'let's stall.'"

"Why'd you call him?"

"I didn't, I called Maria. She listened, hung up, two minutes later his secretary informs me where to go for lunch."

I said, "He's got to know he can't forestall the inevitable."

"Maybe, but he'll sure try. So with Prema getting the bugs and the tools, what's our theory?"

"Maybe competitive culling."

"Meaning?"

"One female eliminates another's offspring in order to maintain dominance and eliminate competition for the desirable male. Big cats and primates do it all the time, and where polygamy exists, humans do it, too."

"Donny's the baby's daddy?"

"Movie star, attractive younger woman with a penchant for manipulation?"

"Yeah, that's a recipe. So what, Donny was big-time naughty with Qeesha—Simone, whatever—but Prema wants to hold on to him anyway?"

"Prema wants to avoid public humiliation."

"Manipulation," he said. "If it's true, think Qeesha planned to get pregnant?"

"Could be. A baby with Donny Rader could kick up her lifestyle."

"If she held on to her life."

I said, "Maybe Qeesha wanted more than generous child support. Maybe she thought she could actually replace the Queen Bee. Unfortunately for her, the Queen figured it out and took care of business. That could explain why the bones were treated so cruelly: deconstructing the competition, reducing the problem to a lab specimen in a coldly efficient way. It would also serve as a warning to Donny. Look what I'm capable of when I'm threatened."

"Where does Wedd fit in?"

"To me he still looks good as Adriana's killer, because even with doping her up, I don't see Prema managing to physically restrain another woman, drive her to the park, shoot her. Plus, Wedd's car was spotted near the scene. Wedd could've also dispatched Qeesha—talk about your efficient estate manager. But at some point he turned expendable."

"Queen Bee tying up loose ends."

"She's a tall woman," I said, "might fit the seat position on the Explorer. Getting Wedd to drive her somewhere wouldn't be a problem. Attending to her needs was his job. And the spot where he got shot isn't that far from the compound. Laurel up to Mulholland, hook west to Coldwater, drive a few miles. For someone in good shape, no challenge walking back."

"Shoot a guy, mosey on home, do Pilates," he said.

"And maybe ditch the gun along the way."

He phoned Sean Binchy, ordered him to search Mulholland Drive between Laurel and Coldwater for a .45.

I said, "Qeesha was an experienced con. Had enough street smarts to pick up on any growing tension at the compound. She called in Adriana for support because she was unwilling to give up her dream. Figured if she could hold out until the baby was born, Donny would bond with his child and protect her."

He said, "Buzz buzz buzz goes the Queen Bee and the Drone wimps out."

We reached the Seville. He pointed to his unmarked, several vehicles up the row. "Off to garbage patrol."

"When will you start the surveillance?"

"After the trash reap. Why?"

"I'm kind of into hiking," I said. "For the exercise."

He looked at me. "Free country. Hope you get good weather."

◆

I was back on Coldwater by nine the following morning, had added a small backpack. Inside was a pair of miniature binoculars, two bottles of water, a few snacks.

Being noticed wouldn't be a problem, just the opposite, but that was good: I was now that guy who parked his Cadillac on the turnoff and was foolish enough to brave oncoming traffic in the name of aerobics.

I'd also brought a companion: Blanche trotted along happily at the end of the short, pink leash she favors when making personal appearances. I made sure to keep her away from the road and she picked up the drill quickly, heeling and adjusting herself to my pace, breathing audibly but easily.

Nothing like a dog to make you look harmless. Especially a small cute dog and there's nothing cuter than a French bulldog.

And no Frenchie is more appealing than Blanche.

Still, she's not a setter or a retriever and even with cool weather and ample hydration, I knew my time would be limited by her stubby legs and her flat face.

My first sighting of the compound entrance was at nine eighteen. Sixteen minutes later, I used my phone to record a delivery from an organic market on Melrose. Eight minutes passed before the truck exited.

Just before ten a.m., a dry cleaner from Beverly Hills completed a similar circuit, then nothing for the next half hour. Blanche and I settled in a shady, safe spot up the road. Water for both of us. I ate a PowerBar and she made short but dainty work of a Milk-Bone, burped happily, and grew entranced by flowers, flies, butterflies, bees, potato bugs. A small plane that circled overhead for a few seconds.

We were back at ten forty-eight, watching the entrance to the compound. Seconds later an unmarked white Econoline van with blackened windows passed us, rolling down from the east. No livery number that I could see, so not hired transport. No I.D. of any sort. As it turned up the compound road, I got my binocs out.

An arm shot out and punched the call button. As the van idled, I managed to make out the lettering around the license-plate frame.

There was a 323 phone number on the top slat.

Home Sweet Home Schooling on the bottom.

The gate swung open, the van drove in. I called Home Sweet Home's number, got voice mail for Oxford Educational Services followed by a brief description of the mission statement:

Specialized instruction and on-site learning experience provided by alumni of top universities, designed to augment and enrich the educational experiences of homeschooled children.

Did that include anatomy and forensic anthropology?

Nine minutes after the Oxford van had entered, it drove back out, headed south on Coldwater. One of the windows was half open. I caught a flash of juvenile face before the glass slid back up.

On-site learning.

A field trip?

Scooping Blanche into my arms, I ran back to the Seville.

46

I caught sight of the van descending Coldwater. A Jaguar and a Porsche traveled between us. Perfect cover as we crossed into Beverly Hills.

The cars kept going as the van turned right at Beverly Drive, edging Coldwater Park and cruising slowly.

The park was small but well equipped, with a shallow rock-stream, a playground, and barbered grass. Toddlers frolicked. Mothers nurtured. Nice place for the youngest of the Premadonny brood—the little blond girl—to recreate. The older kids would probably be bored. Then again, these were children who rarely got out. Maybe swings and slides would be a big thrill.

The van made that moot by rolling past the park. Mansions gave way to small charming houses on narrow lots, as the road grew dim under canopies of shaggy old trees. Potholes appeared. The ambience was more funk than luxe, not unlike the slice of Beverly Glen where I lived.

Fifteen mph signs and speed bumps began to appear every few seconds. No problem for the van; it had been crawling at ten miles an hour, came to a full stop at each bump. I hung as far back as I could without losing visual contact, allowed a gardener's truck to sandwich in. The new convoy continued for another mile before the van veered right and the truck stayed on Beverly Drive.

Now I knew our destination. Good clean fun for all ages.

Franklin Canyon Park is a hidden slice of wilderness minutes from the self-conscious posing and the hypertensive drive of the city. Six-hundred-plus acres of untamed chaparral, skyscraper cedars, pines, and California oaks surround miles of hiking trails and a central hub bejeweled by a sun-mirror lake. A smaller pond is chock full with ducks and turtles and sunfish and minnows.

I knew Franklin because I used to take my previous Frenchie there when he grew restless. A bully, black-brindle heathen named Spike, he loved to explore. Though his affinity for poultry made the duck pond a challenge.

Packs of feral dogs were rumored to prowl the park's upper reaches but we'd never seen them. We did spot chipmunks, squirrels, the occasional late-rising skunk, lizards, and snakes, including a rattler or two that Spike dismissed as unworthy of his attention. A couple of times our presence provoked a chorus of ululation from distant coyotes. It was all I could do to restrain Spike from hunting down the uncouth intruders.

I'd never brought Blanche to Franklin Canyon, probably because she's so content with short strolls, hanging with Robin, and consulting on clinical cases.

As I drove up the mile and a half of sinuous mountain road that led to the park's entrance, she was sitting up, alert, head cocked quizzically.

"First time for everything, gorgeous."

Space for cars was limited and once the van entered, I could afford to hang back. Pulling over at the next turnoff, I retrieved additional supplies from the Seville's backseat, slipped them into my pack.

I rolled into the main lot, a rectangle of dirt bordered by post-and-beam fencing and surrounded by waist-high native grasses. No other vehicles in sight.

Leashing Blanche, I put my pack on and began walking down an oak-lined road. One curve and there was the van, right where I'd guessed.

Just above the fenced hollow that contained the lake. Several yards above the pond.

At this hour, not a lot of people around. Which, I supposed, was the point. An attendant helped an old woman trudge along the pathway. A few other dog-walkers strolled. Everyone smiled at Blanche and a woman with a longhaired dachshund stopped to chat, asking the usual canine-related questions.

Pleasant woman but the wiener dog wasn't nearly as amiable and it began to growl and chuff. The woman said, "Easy, Hansel."

Blanche looked up at me with *what's-his-problem* curiosity.

Hansel lunged.

"Bad boy," said the woman with obvious insincerity. The dachshund barked. The woman smiled, said, "My, yours is quiet," and walked on, the perfect enabler.

My attention shifted to a spot up the road. Two people exiting the front of the van.

The first was the driver, a soft-looking, fuzz-bearded guy in his twenties wearing a blue shirt, jeans, and sneakers. He placed a wheeled suitcase on the ground.

From the passenger side came a bespectacled, curly-haired woman around the same age, garbed identically. She carried a multicolored paisley bag heavy enough to require both hands.

The man slid open the van's rear door and extended his hand. A doll-like Asian girl accepted his help and descended, truing the straps of her own pink backpack. She wore a yellow T-shirt, lavender shorts, bubblegum-colored running shoes topped by frilly socks. Long black hair was held in place by a silver band.

She began laughing as a younger Asian boy leaped out, landed on his feet, and punched air. His hair was spiked, his backpack, black dotted with white specks that were probably skulls. A white T-shirt billowed over green shorts worn long and baggy, skater-dude-style.

Next came an older boy, skinny, smallish, with skin the color of coal. I knew he was thirteen, but puberty hadn't arrived and his limbs were licorice sticks. His purple shirt and yellow satin basketball shorts sported the Lakers logo. On his feet were black athletic shoes with silver trim.

Kembara.

Kyle-Jacques.

Kion.

The youngest boy tried to get Kion sparring. Kion mussed his brother's hair, waved his hands, feinted back, refused to take the bait.

Kyle-Jacques shouted, "Aaaah—you die!"

Kion hooked thumbs to his chest, flashed a *who-me?* grin.

Kyle-Jacques bounced, turned to his sister, began to harass her the same way. She looked at him the way compassionate gods regard sinners. He appeared to settle down. Then he leaped in the air and let out what the non-initiated would consider a martial arts yell. Landing off-balance, he flailed, stumbled back comically, managed to stay on his feet.

The bearded man said, "Good save, K.J."

Kion and Kembara laughed uncontrollably.

Kyle-Jacques scrunched his face, jumped around, stood still as if abruptly sedated.

The bearded man said, "Okay, tribe, time to learn some science—Julie, we doing the full tribe or is Bunny-Boo still reluctant?"

"I'll check." Julie disappeared around the van, appeared seconds later holding the hand of a little towheaded girl.

Four-year-old Kristina wore a white blouse, a pink chiffon tutu, and sparkly sandals that said she'd picked her own outfit. She rubbed her eyes, yawned.

Julie said, "Still sleepy, Boo? Want me to carry you?"

She began lifting Kristina. The child resisted. Julie backed off. Kristina whimpered.

Julie said, "It'll be okay, Boo, you just woke up—wanna see the turtles?"

Head shake.

"How about the ducks—remember the ones with the funny red heads?"

Silence.

Kristina sat down on the dirt.

Kion said, "Here we go again. Drama."

Kembara said, "*Always* drama with Boo."

Kyle-Jacques resumed shadowboxing.

Julie said, "Sam?"

Sam shrugged. "If she needs to rest . . ."

Julie said, "Okay, Boo, you can rest in the van, I'll take you back."

Kristina began toeing the dirt.

Sam said, "Okay, remainder-of-tribe, Julie will deal with Boo and we will proceed to learn about protozoans and other good stuff."

Julie kneeled by Kristina. The little girl ignored her. Let out an abdominal grunt of protest.

A woman appeared from around the van. Tall, thin, in roomy gray sweats and a broad-brimmed straw hat that shielded her face, she walked over to Kristina, bent her knees, held out her hand.

Kristina shook her head. The woman in the hat swooped her up. Kristina molded to her. The woman said something. Kristina didn't respond. Then she giggled. The woman tickled her chin lightly. Kissed her cheek. Turned Kristina's face gently and kissed the other cheek, the tops of the child's eyelids.

She rocked the child. Said something else. Kristina nodded.

Kembara sang out, "*Draaa*-maaa!"

Still carrying Kristina, the woman in the hat walked to the older girl, kissed her the same way.

Kembara said, "Ugh," but she looked pleased.

The woman in the hat had tilted her face so I could see her jawline.

Clean and defined to begin with, tightened by a broad smile.
She placed Kristina down on the ground, took the girl's hand.
"Time for you to learn, too, Boo. You'll love it."
Kristina considered her options. Nodded.
The procession began.

I'd eavesdropped half turning from the van and its occupants, outwardly focused on canine toilet behavior.

Blanche obliged by taking care of business in her usual dainty manner, sniffing the dirt to find a perfect spot upon which to bestow her natural resources. Upon finishing, she kicked up some dust. One of the strategic implements I'd retrieved from the backseat was a plastic poop bag and I used it to good effect. The nearest trash basket was right on the way. Karma.

Swinging the bag conspicuously, I sped up and passed the group. The woman in the hat was carrying Kristina again. Julie wheeled the suitcase, Sam toted the plastic bag.

As I got several paces ahead, one of the boys, probably Kyle-Jacques, said, "Cool dog."

Kembara said, "Looks like a gremlin."

"It's a bulldog," said Sam. "They were bred to fight bulls but that was a long time ago, now they're just pets."

Kyle-Jacques said, "That one couldn't fight nothing."

"Anything," said a new voice, adult, female.

Familiar. In another context, sultry. What I heard now was gentle, maternal instruction.

Kyle-Jacques said, "Yeah, whatever."

Blanche and I reached the pond with time to spare.

A couple dozen ducks swam and splashed. Concentric rings on the surface of the water betrayed the presence of fish. Turtles the size of dinner plates lazed on the banks. An old pittosporum tree in the process of dying, it roots decaying slowly, leaned precariously toward the water. A queue of turtles lined its wizened trunk. Half a dozen glossy shells stationed as precisely as marines at roll call, heads and limbs retracted. Arrayed that way, the reptiles looked like exotic pods sprouting from the wood.

Two benches at the far end of the pond were shaded by sycamores and oak. I selected one, placed my backpack at my feet, lifted Blanche and set her down next to me. Checking out the world beyond the Seville's passenger window, walking, and pooping had pretty much exhausted her. She snuggled up tight against my thigh, placed her knobby little head in my lap, fluttered her eyes, and began to snore.

I stroked her neck until her breathing grew rhythmic and slow. *Sweet dreams, Gorgeous.*

The group arrived at the pond just as I retrieved the other strategic object I'd stashed in the pack: the current issue of *The International Journal of Child Psychology and Psychiatry.* The lead article was a survey of pediatric responses to hospitalization. An area I'd studied years ago. I'd been meaning to get to it.

As I alternated between reading and peeking above the top of the magazine, the party of seven stopped at the turtle-clad tree branch. Sam pointed and lectured, motioned to Julie, who did the same. The kids—including little Kristina—paid attention. Kion and Kembara stood still. Kyle-Jacques was a little jumpier and he moved toward the old tree to reach for a turtle.

Julie held him off with a hand on his arm.

He asked her something. Julie drew him closer to the amphibians, pointed to some detail of the turtle's shell.

Kyle-Jacque nodded, backed off.

Sam opened the wheeled suitcase, removed a blanket, and spread it on the dirt. Extricating a stereoscopic microscope, he carefully placed the instrument in the center of the fabric. The scope was joined, in turn, by a fishnet, a ladle, and a plastic vial. Then a small wooden box whose contents glinted when Sam popped the lid. He held something up to the light.

Glass specimen slides.

Julie said something. The older three kids removed their backpacks, laid them down, began unzipping. Kristina held on to the hand of the tall woman in the hat.

I thought: Time for the latest whiz-bang e-tablets.

Out came three spiral notebooks and marker pens.

Wrong, Smart Guy.

About so much.

As Julie lectured and pointed, Kion, Kembara, and Kyle-Jacques sat cross-legged on the bank, sketching and jotting notes. Sam walked to the pond's edge, steered clear of the inert turtles, and ladled water. Transferring the green liquid to the vial, he capped it and brought it back to the microscope on the blanket.

It took several attempts to set up a slide bearing a water bubble. By the time Sam was finished, Kristina's interest had been piqued and she'd pulled free from the tall woman in the hat, stood next to the teacher. Sam focused the microscope, narrowed the eyepieces to fit the little girl's face.

She peered. Looked up beaming. Peered some more.

The woman in the hat said something. Kristina joined her sibs. Julie gave her a pad and a green crayon.

The woman walked a few paces away, stopped, called out, "You okay, now, Boo?"

Kristina ignored her.

"Boo, I'm going to sit down over there." Pointing to the free bench.

"Go, Mommy!"

I continued reading as the woman sat down a few feet away. Out of her purse came a book. *Happiest Toddler on the Block.*

She read. I read. She snuck a few peeks at Blanche, now awake and serene.

I'd canted the journal cover to offer a clear view of the title.

The woman had another go at her book. Looked at Blanche, again.

I pretended to focus on the magazine. Read some of the lead article, began skimming. Nothing had changed much since I'd worked in a hospital.

Blanche stretched, jumped from the bench onto the dirt, stretched some more.

I said, "Morning, Sleeping Beauty." Blanche licked my hand, rubbed her head against my fingers.

The woman said, "Are you just the cutest?"

Blanche grinned.

"Excuse me, but I have to ask. Did she just smile at me?"

"She does that with people she likes."

"Totally adorable. With some dogs it seems like they're smiling but they're putting out a different energy—more of a warning? This one . . . she really *is* something."

"Thanks."

The brim of the hat rose, offering me a full view of the face below.

No makeup. No need. Classic, symmetrical bone structure the camera adored. Fine strands of hair escaped the confines of the hat but most remained tucked in. Mousy brown, now, blow-away fine. Filaments clouded the back of a long, graceful neck.

Impossible not to know who she was.

Today, I was playing the most clueless man in L.A. Offering her the merest of smiles, I returned to my magazine.

◆

Footsteps caused me to lower the pages.

Kristina, running toward her mother.

"Easy, Boo, don't trip."

"Mommy, Mommy, it's a smail!"

Holding out a brown, cochlear shell.

"Is there actually a snail in there, Boo, or is it empty?"

"It's empty."

"So the snail left its home."

"Huh?"

"The shell is the snail's home, Boo. Maybe this one left to find an-other one."

"Huh?"

The woman kissed the child's cheek. "It's a beautiful shell, Boo."

"It's a smail—aaahh wanna see the doggy!"

"We don't bother doggies, Boo—"

"Wanna *see!*"

I closed the magazine. "It's okay."

"You're sure? I really don't want to bother you."

"Of course. Her name is Blanche and she loves kids."

Hand in hand, the two of them approached. On cue, Blanche as-sumed the sit-stay. Kristina reached to pet the top of her head.

I said, "Actually, she likes it better when you do it this way." Placing my hand low, in tongue range. Kristina imitated me. I said, "Perfect." Blanche licked. Kristina giggled and moved in for another tongue-bath.

Her mother said, "Okay, that's fine. Thank the nice man, Boo."

Kristina began petting Blanche. Her strokes quickened. Veered on slaps. Her mother took hold of her wrist, guided the tiny hand down.

Blanche licked pudgy fingers.

Kristina squealed.

The woman said, "Blanche. Like in *Streetcar.*"

I smiled. "She likes the company of strangers."

The woman laughed. "I can see that. Great disposition. It's a bless-ing."

Kristina showed the shell to Blanche and shouted, "Smail!"

Blanche smiled.

Kristina ran off laughing.

The woman said, "Sorry for interrupting your reading."

I said, "Talk about adorable."

Her eyes drifted to the magazine. "You're a psychologist?"

"I am."

"I'm reading something kind of related—hold on."

Her walk to her bench was languid, graceful. She returned with the toddler book.

"I know it's pop stuff," she said. "Would you mind telling me if it's worth anything?"

"It is," I said. "I know the author."

"Really."

"We trained at the same time. At Western Pediatric Medical Center. Your little one's a bit past toddler."

"I know," she said. "I just like to learn." The book dropped to her side. "That hospital, I actually did a— I spent some time there. Not with my kids, thank God. Just . . . I helped out. Years ago, before I had kids."

"It's a good place."

"You bet . . . anyway, thanks for sharing Blanche with Kristina."

She offered her hand. Long graceful fingers, clean nails, no polish.

I said, "Blanche lives to socialize."

Taking a cue with the panache of Streep, Blanche wiggled her hindquarters.

The woman laughed. "I see that—um, do you happen to have a card?"

I gave her one.

She read it. Her eyes saucered.

I said, "Everything okay?"

"Oh, sure . . . it's just . . . I almost . . . this is going to sound totally weird but a few years back someone actually referred me to you."

"Small world," I said.

"I'm sorry, this is kind of awkward . . . the appointment got canceled. I listened to someone else who gave me another name. It wasn't very helpful."

"Sometimes," I said, "it's a matter of fit."

"This was a bad fit—listen, this is going to sound pushy but would you be willing to give it another try? An appointment, I mean."

"Sure."

"Wow," she said, "that's gracious of you. Um, could it be relatively soon?"

I pulled my appointment book out of my pack, knitted my brow.

She said, "You're booked solid. Of course."

I closed the book. "Got a cancellation tomorrow, but it's early. Eight thirty if you can make it."

"I can. Sure, that'll be fine." She looked at the card. "There's no address here."

"I work from home. I'll give it to you."

She produced an iPhone, punched in the info. "Eight thirty it is, thank you so much, Dr. Alexander Delaware—I guess I'd better be getting back to my tribe."

We shook hands. Her skin was cool, dry, thrumming with the faintest tremor.

She said, "I'm Preem, by the way."

"Nice to meet you."

Flashing a million bucks' worth of smile, she hurried to her brood.

I pretended to read another article, slipped Blanche a Milk-Bone. "You earned caviar but this is all I've got."

When she was finished nibbling, we left, passing the kids and the teachers and Prema Moon, everyone busy with an assortment of vials, slides, leaves, illustrated books.

Prema Moon gave me a small wave and held a leaf up to Kembara. "Look at this, honey. Tri-lobar."

The girl said, "Great, Mom," in a voice ripe with boredom.

"Pretty, no?"

"Uh-huh."

"That means it has three lobes—three of these little roundy things."

"*Mo*-om, I need to *draw.*"

48

H ang around L.A. long enough and you're going to spot actresses. I've probably seen more than the average citizen because a few famous butts have warmed the battered leather couch in my office and once in a while I tag along with Robin at the type of party most people imagine to be fascinating but typically turns out to be mind-numbing.

I've learned that cinematic beauty is a funny thing. Sometimes it's limited to the screen and real life offers up a plain face that closes up like a frightened sea anemone when the camera's not whirring. Other times, physical perfection transcends time and place.

Prema Moon sat on the couch wearing *couldn't-care-less* clothes: loose jeans, brown sneakers, a shapeless V-necked sweater that had begun life as sad beige and had faded to tragic gray. Her macramé bag was one shade sootier, fraying where the fabric gathered into bamboo handles.

Like yesterday, she wore no makeup. Indoor lighting turned her hair mousier than it had been at the park. The ends were blunt and

uneven, barely reached her shoulders. Homemade hack job or an exor-
bitant styling meant to look that way.

If she indulged in Botox, she was overdue. Fine lines scored her
brow, the space between her eyes, the sides of her mouth. The skin
beneath her eyes was puffy. The indigo of her irises was lovely but oddly
low-watt. Warm but sad.

She was gorgeous.

She'd arrived precisely on time, driving a small gray Mercedes with
black windows and squeaky brakes. Blanche and I greeted her at the
door. Prema stooped to pet. "Hello again, Princess." She did the usual
quick-check of the living room, offered the comment I get all the time:

"Nice place, Dr. Delaware. Kind of hidden away."

"Thanks. This way."

When we arrived in the office, Blanche waddled to Prema's feet and sat
down.

"Is she a therapy dog?"

"She can be," I said. "But she has no problem waiting outdoors."

"Oh, no, I couldn't do that to her—c'mon, baby, you join us."

She sank into the couch, turned small, the way skinny, high-waisted
people do. Leaning to scratch behind Blanche's ear, she said, "I don't
want to break any rules, here, but is it okay if she sits up here with me?"

I clicked my tongue. Blanche jumped up on the couch, settled in
close.

Prema Moon said, "Well, that was pretty nimble."

I sat back and waited, the calm, patient therapist. Wondered if
someone with her training would see through the act.

I'd had a restless night, waking up four times with a pounding head
and a racing mind. Wondering if I could trust my own judgment.

Had I dragged Milo's case into a bog destined to sink it?

How would I tell Prema I'd stalked her without scaring her out of
the office?

At five a.m., I'd crawled out of bed, padded to my office, scrawled notes.

I returned an hour later. Gobbledygook.

However it shook out, Prema passing through my doorway bought her insurance: From now on I was bound by confidentiality, maybe useless to Milo.

A logistical mess; I hadn't expected it to turn out this way. Had been aiming for a chance to observe the kids. Hadn't counted on Prema being in the van.

Not completely true.

The slim chance the putative Evil Queen might materialize had led me to bring Blanche and the psych journal, a pair of perfect lures.

Even with that, I'd expected small talk at best. Some kind of observational insight I could bring back to Milo.

My clever little plan had worked too well.

I'd been wrong about so much.

Prema Moon kept massaging Blanche. Checked out the prints on the wall. Put on dorky glasses and squinted at my diplomas, returned the specs to her macramé bag.

"Nice," she said. "The feeling, here. What you imagine a therapist office is like. *Should* be like. The other one—the doctor I went to instead of you—that was a cold space. Just screamed *I don't care about people.* Cold and expensive—what's your fee, by the way?"

"Three hundred dollars for forty-five minutes."

"Compared with her, you're a bargain." She counted out cash, placed the bills on a side table. "This place talks softly. Earnestly."

She fooled with her hair. A strand broke off and floated to her knee. She tweezed it between thumb and forefinger, tried to deposit it in the wastebasket. The hair adhered to her fingertip. She rubbed until it dropped. That took a while.

"As you can see, I'm a little compulsive."

I smiled.

She smiled back. Hard to read the emotion behind it. By comparison, Mona Lisa was blatant.

"Okay," she said, "the thing with therapy is to be utterly honest, right?"

"As honest as you feel you can be."

"There are degrees of honesty?"

"There are degrees of revelation," I said. "It's a matter of what you're comfortable with."

"Ah," she said. "Yes, I suppose you're right. In the end, we're all strangers except to ourselves, that's why your job is so interesting, you try to . . . span the gap." Head shake. "That probably didn't make sense."

"It made perfect sense."

Her eyes drifted back to the paper on my wall. Blanche snuggled closer. "Never had a pet. Don't know exactly why."

"Four kids," I said, "I'd imagine you're pretty busy."

"I mean even as a child. I could've had a pet if I asked. I could've had anything. But I never asked."

She blinked. "Okay, time for that honesty: The reason the appointment was canceled wasn't because I was urged to see someone else. It was because of you specifically. The other work you do. Do you understand what I'm saying?"

"Police cases."

"Exactly. Someone thought it would be a bad idea for someone like me to get involved with a doctor who did that. No one close to me, just a suit—a person paid to be careful."

A beat. "But here I am, after all. Which leads me to a second bit of honesty, Dr. Delaware. I suspected you were following us the moment you turned off Coldwater onto Beverly."

I took a second to digest that. "You suspected but you didn't sound an alarm."

"If it was me alone, I'd probably have turned around and gotten the heck out of there. But with the tribe, a trip that had been planned for a long time? I suspected but I didn't know for sure, so no sense scaring them, ruining their day. So I waited to see what you did once you entered the park and you just walked your dog and ignored us and I figured I was wrong, you were just a guy with a dog. Then we met up by the pond and you cleverly ignored me but made sure I'd see that magazine. Even then, I didn't think much of it. Then I read your card and I remembered your name. Remembered that other work you do and started to wonder."

She twisted a thicker clump of hair. Several more strands fell to her lap. She made no attempt to clear them.

"And yet," she said, "I'm here."

I said, "I'd like to help you."

She said, "With what?"

Thinking of Holly Ruche, I said, "Owning your life. Finally."

"Really?" she said, as if finding that humorous.

Then she cried.

I supplied a box of tissues and a bottle of water. She dabbed, drank. I waited for her questions.

The first one she asked surprised me. "What do you think of my tribe?"

"They seem like a great bunch."

"Four gems, Dr. Delaware. Four flawless diamonds. I'm not taking credit but at least I didn't screw them up."

"Prema, a friend of mine says happiness comes from taking all the credit and none of the blame."

She clapped her hands. "I love that . . . but sometimes it's hard to separate blame from credit, isn't it? To know what's real and what isn't. Back when I was a public person, people who'd never met me had opinions about everything I did. One day I was a goddess, the next I was evil incarnate."

"Celebrity's all about love–hate," I said, thinking, as I had a hundred times over the last few days, of the venomous contempt expressed by Brent Dorf, Kevin Dubinsky. Len Coates, who should have known better, because he'd been trained to analyze facts not rumors, had never laid eyes on her.

None of them had.

She said, "I'm not complaining, it's part of the game. But I used to wonder where all that crap was coming from. People so *sure*. Alleged *experts* accusing me of swooping into orphanages at random, bribing officials so I could walk away with the cutest babies. As if building a family was as simple as choosing strays at the pound. Or, worse, I raided Third World villages with a private army and stole infants from poor people."

Speaking in the singular.

She hugged herself. "*True* reality is I went through channels, got screened. Had the kids screened, too, because I'm not that selfless, forget all that sainthood crap they've also tried to lay on me—stupid diplomats at the U.N. making like I'm Mother Teresa. I'm a mother, small 'm.' Didn't *want* an incurably sick baby or a mentally challenged baby. Didn't want to be surprised by bad news. Does that offend you?"

"Not at all."

"I mean I was willing to deal with whatever came up naturally, but why make life harder than it needs to be?"

"Makes sense."

"I mean there's no reason not to make your life as good as it can be, right? To feel *worthy* of happiness."

She crumpled a tissue. "I was clueless. About creating a family. It's a challenge under the best of circumstances. If you do it right, it's daunting, you have to put in time, personal investment, doubting yourself. Educating yourself. You can't just read books or dial it in, you can't just delegate it to other people. So I decided to do it right and changed my life."

She swiveled toward me. "Big insight to a psychologist, huh? But what did I know? Not that I'm some Suzy Housewife baking cookies. Keep me away from kitchens, keep me *far* away if you value your intestinal tract. And I know I'm lucky, I can pay people to do things I don't want to do. But actually raising my children? The real stuff? That's *my* job."

She smiled. "Listen, I'm not some martyr, claiming I gave it all up for them. I lost nothing, gained everything. They bring me meaning every day, the other stuff never did. Now the thought of blabbing someone else's lines makes me want to throw up."

I kept silent.

"You think I'm a burned-out weirdo?"

"I think you've moved on."

"Well," she said, "whether you mean it or not, you say the right things—sorry, I tend to be a little cynical." More hair fluffing, more ciliary rain. "So they seemed well adjusted to you?"

"They did."

"Did you expect spoiled monsters?"

"I didn't know what to expect, Prema."

"Aw c'mon, 'fess up, Dr. Delaware, you had to have a little bit of expectation, no? Crazy Hollywood mom, crazy kids? But trust me, no way that was going to happen. No way they were going to have a childhood like mine. I don't believe—I *refuse* to believe that we're condemned to repeat our own crap."

My personal mantra. When things got low I congratulated myself for not ending up like Harry Delaware.

I said, "If I didn't agree, I wouldn't do this job."

Prema Moon's eyes watered up again. The tissue had wadded so tightly it disappeared in her fist. "I don't know why I'm getting into this. Why I feel the need to justify myself to you."

I said, "It's normal to feel judged in a situation like this."

"You followed us. That was based on a judgment. What's going on?"

"I've been trying to learn about you and your family. Haven't been very successful because you've dropped off the grid. When families isolate themselves, it's often because of serious problems and that's what I suspected. I know now that you've been trying to take control of your life, are focused on protecting the kids. For good reason. You know that better than anyone."

She bit her lip. "Great monologue, Doctor. You could've made a living in my old business. But you still haven't answered my question."

"You need help, Prema. You know that. That's why you're here."

She opened her palm, watched the tissue expand like a time-lapse flower. Crushed it again. "Maybe you're being sincere, I hope you are. But with the good ones—the *performers*—you can never be sure. Meryl, Jack, Judi. Larry Olivier—I knew Larry when I was a kid, he was always sweet to me. But when he chose to be someone else? Good luck. Maybe that's you, Dr. Alexander Delaware."

"You're the performer, Prema."

"Me? I'm a hack. I made a ridiculous fortune doing crap."

"I think you're selling yourself short."

"Not in the least, Dr. Delaware. I know what I am and I'm okay with it." Her knuckles were white and shiny as ivory. "How long have you been *learning* about us?"

"I did a bit of digging right after that first appointment was made. Because the circumstances were odd: The person who called was evasive, wouldn't even tell me who the patient was. I assumed I'd be seeing one of the kids, looked for anything I could find about them. Which wasn't much but I did come across a photo. You and the kids, a theater lobby in New York. They seemed unhappy. Ill at ease. You stood behind them. You came across detached. Not exactly a happy family portrait."

Her eyes flashed. "Detestable picture, you have no idea how much time and money it took to get it offline."

"I'm glad I saw it before you succeeded. Now I understand."

"Understand what?"

"I'd missed the emotional content. You were scared—all of you."

She flinched. "Why would I be scared?"

I said, "Not why. Of who."

She shook her head. Closed her eyes. Sat lower and got even smaller.

I said, "My guess is you—all of you—were scared of the person who set up the shot. Someone who doesn't care about kids, but didn't mind using them."

The eyes opened. New shade of indigo, deep, hot. "You're frightening."

"Am I wrong?"

Silence was my answer.

I said, "You talk about your children in the singular. 'I,' not 'we.' You're doing it alone. For good reason."

She crossed her arms. Blanche licked her hand. Prema remained unmoved. Her lips set. Angry. I wondered if I'd lost her.

I said, "No matter what you do, he rejects them completely. It must be tough, living with that degree of callousness. Your kids are your world. Why can't he see how wonderful they are? Understand the joy of being a parent. But he doesn't. And now there's a new level of fear and that's why you're here. Because of the other work I do."

Shooting to her feet, she stormed out of the office, made it halfway up the hall where she stopped short, swung the big bag as if working up momentum to use it as a battering ram.

I had a clear view, stayed in my chair.

The bag grew still. Her shoulders heaved. She returned, stood in the doorway, leaning against the jamb for support.

"My God," she said. "The things that come out of your mouth."

Then she returned to the couch.

49

Another head shake. More hair fell. A woman coming apart strand by strand. She hugged herself. Shuddered. Ten fingers began working like Rubinstein on Rachmaninoff.

I said, "If you're feeling cooped up, we can talk outside."

"How did you know I felt that?"

Because you look like a caged animal.

I said, "Lucky guess."

I told Blanche to stay in the office, paid her with a Milk-Bone.

Prema Moon said, "She can come with us."

"She needs to nap." The real reason: Time to minimize distraction. And comfort.

I walked her through the house, out through the kitchen and down the rear steps to the garden, stopping by the pond's rock rim. The waterfall burbled. The sky was clear.

"Very mellow," she said. "To encourage confession?"

"I'm not a priest."

"Isn't this the new religion?"

"God doesn't talk to me."

"Only Freud does, huh?"

"Haven't heard from him in a while, either." I sat down on the teak bench that faces the water. The fish swarmed.

Prema Moon said, "What are they, Japanese koi? Pretty."

She took in the garden. Robin's studio, softened by trees and shrubs. A whine cut through the waterfall. The band saw.

"What's that noise?"

"The woman I live with builds musical instruments."

"She's going to come out here and see me?"

"No."

"You've trained her to stay inside when a patient's here?"

"Once she's in there, it's for hours."

"What if she does come out?"

"She'll go right back in."

"What's her name?"

I shook my head.

"Sorry," she said. "I'm just . . . I'm jumping out of my skin, this is . . . I don't *know* what it is. Don't know what to *do.*"

I uncapped the canister of fish food, scooped a handful of pellets, tossed.

She watched the koi eat. Said, "Well, yummy for them."

Not a word out of her for a long time. When that didn't look as if it was going to change, I said, "Tell me what frightens you."

"Why should I?"

"You're here."

She reached for the koi food. "May I?" Tweezing again, she threw in one pellet at a time. "I like the silver one. Elegant."

I said, "Okay, I'll start. People who work for you seem to die unnaturally."

Her arm shot out. She hurled the rest of the food. The fish feasted. "People? All I know is Adriana. And I only know about her because I heard it on TV and it freaked me out completely."

"Did you contact the police?"

Long pause. "You know the answer. I didn't. Because I couldn't see what I could possibly offer. She worked for me only for a short time. I really didn't know her."

I said nothing.

She said, "What did you mean 'people'? You're freaking me out."

"First Adriana, then Melvin Jaron Wedd."

Her hand flew to her face. *What! Mel? No! When?*

"A few days ago."

"Oh, God, no—what are you *telling* me?"

"He was murdered a few days ago. Was he a good employee?"

"What?"

I repeated the question.

"Sure, fine, he was great. Murder? What happened—"

"Reliable? Skilled at organizing?"

"Yes, yes, all that, what does it matter?"

I said, "In addition to all that, he had a special talent. Vocal impressions."

"What? Oh, that, sure, yes, he'd do cartoon characters for the kids. So?"

"He did a pretty good imitation of Donny. When he called me for that appointment on your behalf."

"What!"

"I thought it was Donny. But it was Mel, wasn't it?"

She said, "Mel called for me but—I never told him to do that."

"Guess he improvised."

"Why would he?"

"I thought you might be able to tell me."

"Well, I *can't,* I have no *idea* why."

"Then I'll take a guess, Prema. Subtle hostility. He didn't much care for Donny, because he'd learned what Donny is like. He knew that Donny wouldn't be happy about your consulting a child psychologist. So he mimicked Donny. Mel's little bit of nasty irony."

She stared at the water.

I said, "Mel refused to tell me which kid I'd be seeing because the answer was none of them. The kids didn't need help, they were doing fine. All things considered."

She looked at me. Her eyes were wet. "I'm doing my best."

"I believe that you are. So the question remains: Why did you want to see me? I'm a child psychologist so it wasn't about therapy for you. That leaves some kind of family issue."

She didn't answer.

I said, "Maybe a marriage that's unraveling? A concerned parent wanting to learn about the impact on the children? And how to minimize it?"

She covered her face with both hands.

I said, "You care about everyone and everything. Donny couldn't care less. You always wanted kids, he never did. You convinced yourself his attitude would change once he saw how cute they could be. It didn't, he cut them off completely. And they know it. That's why that picture in the lobby was so stressful. It was his idea, the first time he'd shown any interest in family life, so there had to be an ulterior motive. What was he planning to do with the shot? Use it for publicity?"

She raised her arms, punched air clumsily. "Damn him! For a stupid movie! Big lead role for him, he was going to play a *dad*."

"Typecasting."

Her laugh was bitter. "Caring, bumbling, lovable *dad*. Can you believe the morons who thought of that?"

"Not exactly *Citizen Kane*."

"Not exactly *Citizen* Sane. Piece-of-crap script, piece-of-crap casting, *his* big comedy debut, it was going to open a whole new world for him."

She got up, walked several steps away, returned.

"His *plan* was to sell the photo to *People* for big bucks. He never asked me, knew what I'd say. Instead he sprang it on me as we drove from the airport into the city. He'd instructed the driver to go straight to the theater, his agent had paid to rent the lobby. The whole purpose of the trip was educational. Show the kids the Metropolitan Museum of

Art, the planetarium. I was surprised when he offered to come along. Allowed myself to be hopeful, maybe he'd seen the light. Then he pulled that! Expecting them to pose for hours of pictures. Him with the tribe, both of us with the tribe. He wanted them to jump in the air and laugh and hug him and kiss him! *Disgusting!* I killed it. The rule from the beginning was always they *never* got used. For his crap or mine. He knew that and now he's trying to *change* it? Because someone's paying him to be a *dad*? He tried to force the issue, I stood my ground. It got ugly, I told the kids to wait in the limo. By the time I got back to the lobby, he was gone. He drove straight back to Teterboro, chartered a plane to Vegas, stayed there for weeks, doing his Vegas thing. The tribe and I tried to make the best of it. I'd rented a big quiet apartment on Sutton Place, doorman, security, off the beaten path. I managed to take them a few places without attracting attention. They wanted to know where he'd gone. I said he wasn't feeling well but they knew I was lying. I tried to reach out to him, maybe we could talk, work something out. He wouldn't take my calls. Then he texted me a picture of himself and some . . . girls. Let me know quite graphically that he didn't miss me."

Her face tightened. "After that, we moved even further apart."

"Lovable dad," I said. "Don't recall that film."

"Never got made."

"How come?"

"Maybe someone realized how bad he sucks as an actor?" Shrug. "That's the way the business works, mostly it's air sandwiches." Her toe nudged the rock rim.

Time for me to nudge her. "Have you told the kids about Adriana's death?"

"Of course not!"

"How did you explain her absence?"

"I said she went away on vacation. It would only matter to Boo, Adriana was Boo's person, the others don't need anything like that."

"A nanny."

"Not even a nanny, just someone to watch Boo when I'm tied up."

"Four kids," I said. "Sometimes you can get spread pretty thin."

"I manage." She sniffed. "There's nothing else I'd rather be doing."

Out of my pant pocket came a piece of paper. I unfolded, pretended to read.

She pretended to ignore me. But it had been a long time since she'd performed and she struggled with her curiosity. "What is that?"

I handed it over. Fumbling in her bag, she produced her glasses. Scanned the receipt from JayMar Laboratory. The copy I'd kept for myself. "Beetles? Scalpels? What is this?"

"Check the name of the recipient, Prema."

"Who's that?"

"Someone who buys stuff for you through Apex Management. For you only."

Her mouth dropped. "What? That's ridiculous. I've never heard of this place! Beetles? Scalpels—a *bone* saw? What the hell's going on?"

She tried to return the receipt. I kept my hands in my lap. "Kevin Dubinsky ordered all that stuff for you."

"Mel handles my purchases."

"You wanted something, you'd tell Mel, he'd pass it along to Kevin?"

"Who's Kevin? I don't know any Kevin. Everything's done by email, anyway."

"You'd email Mel and he'd pass it along to—"

"This is crazy." She re-read. "Der-mestid—sounds gross. Why would I want bugs in my house? We pay a pest service to get rid of bugs, last year it took two days to clear a wasp nest. Kyle-Jacques is allergic to bees and wasps."

"Dermestid beetles aren't household pests, they're specialists, Prema."

"At what?"

"They consume flesh. Quickly and cleanly. Scientists use them to clean bones."

"That's disgusting! Why would I want something like that?"

Her hands shook. The paper rattled.

I'd given her the perfect opening but she'd made no attempt to weasel out by offering a plausible explanation.

Oh, those beetles. I forgot, they were part of the kids' science project. I'm big on teaching them science, you saw that yesterday.

She said, "Beetles? Scalpels?" She turned white. "You're saying someone cleaned *Mel's* bones? Or Adriana's—omigod—"

"Mel was shot and left intact. Same for Adriana. Is anyone else authorized to contact Kevin Dubinsky on your behalf?"

"I keep telling you, I don't know any Kevin Dubinsky. My life— you delegate, things get . . . away from you."

"Who has access to your email account?"

"No one has access to my personal account. I don't use it much, anyway, try to stay off the computer because the Internet's nothing but mental pollution. I'm into reading. Books. Never had much school, I need to catch up. So I can be smart for the tribe, already they know stuff I don't. Especially K.J., he knows so much math."

"Are there other email accounts at your home?"

"Of course, for the household," she said. "I can't tell you how many or who uses them—I sure don't. We have a computer company, they set it up. For day-to-day things."

"Would those household accounts be used for shopping?"

"For food, toilet paper. Not bugs!"

"Who's on your staff?"

"Total? If you mean people coming in and out, like gardeners, pool service—those pest-control people—I couldn't even tell you, there's always someone around fixing something."

"Who lives on the premises, like Mel?"

"It used to be crazy, we used to have an army," she said. "After I stopped working I began to pare down. Mel is—was the overall manager. I used to have a personal assistant but I let her go a few years back, the only reason most people have P.A.s is they're afraid of being alone. I *relish* being alone."

"Does Donny have an assistant?"

"Always," she said. "They come and go. Girls, always girls. The latest one I couldn't even tell you her name, we live . . . Other than that there's just the housekeepers. Imelda, Lupe, Maria, I need three to keep the place clean, it's a big undertaking, they're lovely. Religious ladies, cousins. That's it. Oh, yeah, a cook. For healthy food."

"Plus Adriana."

Tears filled her eyes. "Plus her. She was also religious. I could tell because she kept a Bible by her bed and sometimes I'd see her praying. Personally, I'm not into that but I respect it. Are you saying the same person who killed her killed Mel?"

"Too early to tell," I said. "Have you moved to replace Adriana?"

"I'm not sure I need to, Boo's growing more independent. More interactive, hanging out with the tribe more."

"Do you have chauffeurs?"

"We used to have two, one for him, one for the rest of us, but that was a waste, we don't go out much, I switched to a car service."

"Did Donny keep his driver?"

"No . . . I don't think so."

"You don't know?"

She exhaled. "We don't exactly live together."

"Where does he live?"

"Next door. The adjoining property. I mean it's one property, I bought it years ago, but it's three separate parcels. I was going to develop it as one big estate but then . . . things changed. The tribe and I use the big lot. Seven acres, a main house, some outbuildings, tennis court, pool, stuff."

"And Donny?"

"He took the middle one, around three acres. The smallest one is a little less than an acre. No buildings on it, no one goes there."

She thrust the JayMar form at me. "Take this back, it's freaking me out."

I pocketed the paper. "When you heard about Adriana, did you talk about it to anyone?"

"No."

"Not Mel?"

"Why would I discuss it with him?"

"People work together, they talk to each other."

"Mel and I weren't like that," she said.

"No socializing."

"We talked when there was something to talk about. Don't get the wrong picture, I didn't snob him out but it's not like—wasn't like we were friends, a friend is someone who likes you for yourself. Mel wouldn't have stuck around for a second if I didn't pay him."

Her smile was grim. "I don't have friends, Dr. Delaware. I have people I pay."

Thinking of all the women Robert Sommers had spotted parading in and out of Wedd's apartment, I said, "How was Mel's love life?"

"He had none that I knew about."

"No girlfriend?"

She smiled. "Mel was gay."

"You know that because—"

"He told me. Like I said, when there was something to talk about, we talked. One time Mel was looking upset and I asked him what was wrong and he told me. I have to admit, I had no idea, he never gave off any gay vibe. What was bothering him was he has—had a brother, some macho cowboy-type, and they hadn't seen each other in a long time because Mel had run from who he was. Now Mel wanted to . . . what's the word he used—*resurrect,* he wanted to resurrect the relationship, was worried once the brother found out it would screw things up permanently. Why is his love life important?"

"Someone gets murdered, it's good to know about their relationships."

"Mel may have had some but I'm unaware of them. Why did you show me that beetle thing?"

"The night Adriana was killed, something else was found in the park. The skeleton of a two-month-old. The bones had been cleaned by dermestid beetles."

She gasped, made a retching sound, bent low. "I'm supposed to be connected to *that*? That's *insane*." She clawed her hair. "This *can't* be *happening*!"

"Who'd want to set you up, Prema?"

"No one."

I said, "One more thing. After the bones were cleaned they were coated with beeswax."

She clutched my arms. Looked me full in the face. Shrieked.

Springing to her feet, she backed away from me as if I were diseased. Ran toward the house, made it to the kitchen steps but didn't climb them.

Instead, she began pacing the yard. Fast, robotic, tearing at her hair. Great workout companion for Milo.

On her ninth circuit, she sped to the rear of the yard where tall trees blacken the grass. Leaning against the trunk of my oldest coast redwood, she sobbed convulsively.

Just as I'd decided to approach her, she straightened her shoulders, sucked in breath, and returned to the teak bench.

"The park where she—where they were both found. If they mentioned it on the TV, I didn't hear, I really wasn't paying attention until I heard Adriana's name. Was it Cheviot?"

"How'd you know that, Prema?"

"Oh, I know." Gripping her knees with both hands, she put herself in an awkward crouch. As if prepping for a leap off a cliff.

Nowhere to fly. She remained frozen. Moaned. "I know all *sorts* of things."

Milo was at his desk. "You did *what*?"

"It started out as surveillance," I said. "Things progressed."

"You told her everything?"

"I told her enough to get through to her."

"She's your new pal."

"She's not the offender."

"You know that."

"I'll put money on it."

Silence.

I said, "You need her and at this point she thinks she needs you."

"Needs me for what?"

"Keeping her kids safe."

"All of a sudden Devil Princess is a saint?"

"Think of it this way," I said. "You may get out of garbage detail."

"She came to your house alone? No paparazzi in the bushes?"

"Not her style, anymore," I said.

"Just a simple gal. Your new best friend."

"Love to chat, Big Guy, but you need to get over here."

He grumbled. I heard a door slam. "On my way."

"Good man."

"So few of us left."

Back in the office, I poured Prema herb tea, gave her some playtime with Blanche, allowed her to drift into abstract discussions on child-rearing. Then I got back to the questions.

She offered no resistance, was answering freely when the bell rang. She blinked. "That's him? We really need to do this?"

"We do."

"Only time I've ever dealt with the police was in London, a bunch of us got busted for smoking hash in a park. Rich little twits, everyone had connections, we got off with a warning."

"You've got connections, again."

"Do I . . . ?"

"Prema, there's a reason you decided to come here." I got to my feet. "Ready?"

Standing slowly, she teetered for a second, hooked her arm in mine.

"No red carpet," she whispered. "But here we go."

Introductions were brief. Both of them were wary. When they shook hands, Prema used both of hers, as if wanting to prolong contact. Milo offered only his fingers, pulled away soon.

I led Prema to the living room sofa, sat down next to her. Milo settled in a facing chair. His suit was one I'd seen for years, a baggy green-brown hopsack worn over a white shirt and a muddy blue tie that Prozac couldn't fix.

One thing was different: He'd slicked down his hair. Two-hundred-forty-pound kid waiting for communion.

Prema said, "You look just like a cop should."

Milo said, "You look just like a movie star should."

"I meant that as a compliment, Lieutenant. I find it reassuring."

"So taken." His expression was unreadable. "What can I do for you, Ms. Moon?"

She turned to me.

I said, "Just go for it."

She inhaled. "Okay . . . all right . . . Donny Rader smokes meerschaum pipes."

"Does he."

"Do you know what meerschaum is?"

"Some kind of carved stone."

"It's a mineral, Lieutenant. It washes up on the beach and people carve it into smoking pipes. Donny Rader has lots of carved meerschaum smoking pipes, I don't know how many. He smokes weed in them, not tobacco. He's a compulsive collector, loves *things*. To my mind, it's just greed. Like cars: He's got a dozen, maybe more, even though he hardly ever drives them. He has more clothing than I do." One hand kneaded the other. "He collects women. But we don't need to go there."

"Sounds like your husband leads a busy life, Ms. Moon."

She flinched.

I said, "There's another collection."

"Yes," she said. "There is. He has a closet full of guns. When we were living together I made him lock them up in a big safe. That I paid for. For the children's safety."

"Where are the guns now, Ms. Moon?"

"At his place."

"You don't live together?"

"He lives in the adjoining property. I bought all of it years ago but I only use part of it."

"You know about his gun closet because—"

"I saw it. Not recently, we don't have much . . . I stay at my place, he's at his."

"When did you see the gun closet?"

Her chest heaved. "Maybe half a year, I really can't be sure."

"You went to visit—"

"Not a visit, an obligation. He needed to sign a tax form from our accountant. Our life is complicated, you can delegate a lot of things but at some point you still need to sign your name to papers. All the financial forms come to me because he'd neglect them."

"So around six months ago—"

"Could be seven months, eight, five, I don't know. What I do recall is he was still in bed, the place was a mess, as usual. There was a woman. I asked her to leave for a moment. So he could sign the tax form. The safe's in a closet in his bedroom. The closet door was open, there were also loose guns. On shelves. And big ones—rifles—propped up on the floor of the closet. I got out of there."

"Has he ever threatened you with a firearm?"

"Not yet."

"You think he might."

"At this point, Lieutenant, I don't know what to think."

I said, "About the meerschaums . . ."

Milo's eyebrows rose.

Prema said, "Yes, of course. The meerschaums. The lovely meerschaums . . . when you collect them, the big deal is to get them to color gradually as you smoke them. From white to amber. For that to happen, the pipes are coated after they're carved. Then the owner recoats them from time to time."

Her hands clenched. "What's used for the coating, Lieutenant, is beeswax."

Milo's lips pursed. "Really."

"Specifically, confectioner's beeswax, Lieutenant. With all those pipes, Donny Rader must go through the stuff like crazy because he buys pots of confectioner's beeswax. Back when we were living together, I saw it in his workshop. He builds things. Birdhouses, ashtrays. Not very well."

"You've seen him work with beeswax."

Nod. "One time he called me in to watch him work on a pipe. Showing off. He heated up the beeswax, brushed it on, waited for it to cool, then buffed it shiny. About a month ago, he ordered six fresh pots of beeswax. I know *that* because instead of going through his purchasing assistant—a gopher at Apex, our management firm, we each have one—he ordered it online himself. Using *my* personal credit card, the package ended up on my desk. It came from a baking supplies outfit, my first thought was the cook had bought it, someone had screwed up and used my personal card instead of one of the household cards. Then I opened it and realized what was inside and called him to take it. We met at the gate to his place. I asked him why he'd bought it using my name. He didn't really have an answer, was pretty much loaded on weed or whatever. As usual."

"He say anything at all?"

"He mumbled something about not being able to find his own card. Which made sense, he's always losing things. It didn't explain why he hadn't gone through Apex, but I didn't push it, this was wax, no big deal, and frankly the less contact we have with each other the better. I forgot about the whole incident until I learned today that he'd bought something else saying it was for me. Only this time he *had* contacted my purchasing assistant at Apex, probably using one of my email addresses, and bought . . . those terrible things."

"You know the order came from him because—"

"Because *I* didn't buy them, Lieutenant. He's obviously trying to cover his tracks. By casting suspicion on me."

Milo studied her.

She said, "I know it sounds crazy, but, Lieutenant, I will take any lie-detector test you want me to take. I have never once in my life bought beetles or surgical tools. *Or* beeswax. Nor have I ever asked anyone to buy those things for me. Check out every single computer in my house including my personal computer. I'm sure you've got specialists who can do that."

"Do you know for a fact that he bought the wax online?"

"How else?"

"Maybe he got on the phone and ordered."

She thought. "Okay, good point, maybe—so examine our phone records, we've got I don't know how many lines between us, go ahead and trace them all. Then do the same thing for his phones and see what you learn."

Milo rolled his tie up to his collar, let it drop. "Any idea why your husband would need beetles and surgical tools?"

Her hands clenched. "Do I have to say it?"

She turned to me.

I gave her my best therapist smile.

She said, "Fine, I'm afraid—I'm terrified that it had something to do with that poor baby in the park. And that's another thing. The park. Like I told Dr. Delaware just before you got here, Donny Rader has a connection to that place. He used to work as a caddie at the golf course right next door. Back when he was a nothing."

Milo's bulk inched forward. "This is all very interesting, Ms. Moon. Thanks for coming forward."

"What's my choice, Lieutenant? He's obviously trying to ruin me."

"So you believe your husband is—"

"Could I ask a favor, Lieutenant? Please don't call him that, he's my husband in name only."

"You believe Mr. Rader had something to do with the baby in the park."

"I don't know what else to think, Lieutenant. Those bones were treated just like he treats his stupid pipes. After he sicced those horrible bugs on them."

"Any idea why he'd do such a thing?"

"No," she said. "I mean he's not a caring person, quite the opposite. But I never imagined . . . not until Dr. Delaware told me about the beeswax."

"No idea at all what Mr. Rader's motive might be?"

The question I hadn't gotten to when the bell rang.

Her eyes filled with tears. "I have an idea. But not one that makes sense."

"What's that, ma'am?"

"It's not rational. Not in terms of normal people, anyway," she said. "I mean how can you ever explain things like that?"

"Explain what, ma'am?"

She pulled at her hair. "This is . . . even for him it's—let me ask you one thing, Lieutenant. Was the baby in the park black?"

Milo looked at me. "Why would the baby be black, Ms. Moon?"

"Because the only baby I can think of who lived at my house since Boo—my youngest—was born was black. The mother was someone who worked for us. She went into labor early, actually delivered in her room in the staff house. Needless to say I was shocked. One day she's pregnant, the next she's got a baby. She said she delivered it herself. Her, a little girl. I wanted to get her to the hospital, she said no, she was fine. I thought that was absolutely crazy but she insisted and she *seemed* fine. Even though the baby was small. Not abnormal small, not a preemie. Everything seemed okay. Except for the blood and crud on her bed."

She frowned. "My home, her delivery."

"How long ago was this?"

"Maybe . . . four months ago?"

"What happened after that?"

"The baby was adorable—lovely little thing, great disposition. Cordelia. That's the name the mother gave her. I gave the mother time off to care for her. Gave her some of Boo's old baby clothes. Had Boo's crib set up in her room. She repaid me by leaving without giving notice. That's what I assumed—a flake-out. But now . . ."

"You think something worse happened."

She didn't reply.

Milo said, "Ms. Moon, why would Mr. Rader harm this particular baby?"

Long silence.

Prema said, "Maybe you can do DNA?"

"For what?"

"To find out who the father was."

"You think it could've been Mr. Rader."

Her eyes narrowed. "I know what he is. I *didn't* know he could be that stupid."

"What is he?"

"Anything with a vagina gravitates toward him. He doesn't exactly play hard-to-get."

"You suspect the mother of the child and Mr. Rader had an—"

"I don't suspect, I know. Once, after her workday was over, I saw her go over to his place. After dark. Wearing a minidress. There was no reason for that, she worked for *me.* Watching *my* children."

"Did you mention it to her?"

Head shake. "No big deal, everyone has sex with *him,* it's about as meaningful as taking a drink of water."

"His promiscuity didn't bother you."

"In the beginning—when we started out—it sure as hell did. But later? Just the opposite. Kept him out of my hair. But did I suspect he'd knocked her up? Never, because that had never happened before. And she never got that look *they* always get."

"Expectant mothers."

"No, no," she snapped. "Freelance vaginas thinking they've snagged him. When that happens they get a certain smile, a smug smile. I've fired assistants, cooks, maids. Not because I'm jealous. But don't think you can collect a paycheck from me and give me that smile."

Milo said, "The baby's mother didn't have the smile."

"She had a nice smile, the way a woman gets when she's productive. It's a special thing for women, Lieutenant."

Her hand grazed her belly. Tears filled her eyes. "Or so I've been told—no, no, scratch that, no playing the pity card, I've got my tribe, they're gems, just as precious as if I'd carried them myself."

She bounded up, hurried to the door, flung it open, ran out.

No footsteps from the terrace.

Milo glanced at me. I held up a restraining palm.

A minute later, she returned. Positioned herself between us.

Center stage.

Milo said, "Please," and pointed to the sofa.

She said, "I know you guys are just doing your job but this is cutting the *guts* out of me."

CHAPTER

51

The police detective strode to the movie star's side, placed his arm around her, guided her back to the sofa.

"I'm sorry, Ms. Moon, I really am. If it makes you feel any better, you're helping achieve justice. For that baby and others."

Prema didn't answer. Milo relocated to a closer chair. Pulled it even nearer.

She said, "Mr. Fuck-everything-that-moves. *Another* collection. That's why my estate manager is—was a man. That's why the maids I have are Church Ladies in their sixties."

"You think Donny Rader killed the baby."

"I never would have thought him capable. I mean I know he couldn't care less about kids. But . . . I guess he's capable of anything if it's in his best interests. She probably became an inconvenience—pressured him."

"For money?"

"Money or emotional commitment—wanting him to step up to the plate. I will tell you one thing: Giving her serious money would defi-

nitely be a problem for him. Because he has no control over the finances. Gets an allowance because he's an idiot."

"What's serious money?"

"Anything more than ten thousand dollars a month. If he needed to
come up with something like that, he'd have to ask me. Or else start
selling his crap."

She turned to Milo. "That's probably the motive, Lieutenant. She
got greedy, put him in a bind." She sagged. "But that poor baby. How
did it die?"

"That's unclear."

"What do you mean?"

"The skeleton bore no evidence of trauma."

"The skeleton," she said. "Why would he do that?" She turned to
me. "What kind of insanity is that, Dr. Delaware?"

I shook my head.

Milo said, "This woman, what was her—"

"Simone. Simone Chambord."

He showed her Qeesha D'Embo's mug shot. In this photo, no con-
cealment of the booking numbers around her neck.

Her mouth formed an oval. "She's a criminal?"

"She had a police record."

"Oh, God, what a sucker I am. She told me she was a teacher's aide,
had preschool experience. That's what the agency told me, because of
that I hired her to watch over Boo, Boo was just a toddler."

Another stare at the arrest form. "You're telling me I entrusted my
Boo to a criminal?"

"Sorry to say, Ms. Moon."

"I must be the biggest fool in the universe."

"Anyone can get taken, ma'am."

"There wasn't a hint of anything off. She was kind to Boo, Boo
liked her, and Boo doesn't take to everyone. I liked her. That's why
when she got pregnant and her energy flagged, I took pity on her and
helped her out by hiring another person."

"Adriana Betts."

"You're going to tell me *that* one was an ax murderer?"

"No, ma'am. Clean-living church-girl. How'd she and Simone get along?"

"Fine," she said. "Why?" She shuddered. "Oh, of course. He killed her, too, so *she* was connected." She rubbed her face. That plus the pacing; Milo's spiritual sister. "What was *her* story?"

"I was wondering if you knew."

"Well, I don't. Adriana was . . . there seemed nothing complicated about her. Then again, I liked Simone." She laughed. "To think I helped her with her pregnancy—gave her clothes, books, encouraged her to take it easy."

"Adriana came on to relieve Simone."

"Yes."

"Your suggestion or Simone's?"

"Mine. I used the same agency and once Simone was gone Adriana took over completely, did a great job. Then she walked out on me, too. Or so I thought."

"Did you try to find out why she left?"

She threw up her hands. "My life is hectic, people come and go, you have no idea how hard it is to find dependable help."

"Like Mel Wedd," said Milo. "Did he work for Mr. Rader as well as for you?"

"He was the estate manager and, technically, all three properties are the estate. But his day-to-day job was under my supervision."

"How did he and Mr. Rader get along?"

"He didn't respect Donny. Or so he told me."

"Why?"

"Because of Donny's behavior."

"Promiscuity."

She ticked her fingers. "Promiscuity, being constantly stoned, never taking responsibility. Mostly, not caring about the kids. Mel thought that was unconscionable."

Milo said, "Mr. Rader shut the kids out of his life."

"To shut them out, he'd have to be aware of them, Lieutenant. He acted as if they didn't exist. How do you explain that to a child?"

Her hand touched her mouth. "I guess with that attitude, doing things to a baby isn't so big a stretch."

Milo said, "Back to Mel Wedd for a moment. Any idea why Mr. Rader would kill him? Assuming he did."

Another easy opening, if she was manipulating. Once again, she didn't take it. "No. I can't imagine."

Milo looked at me again.

I shrugged. *Still your play, Big Guy.*

He said, "Was Mr. Wedd involved in any of Mr. Rader's activities with women?"

"Mel? Why would you ask that?"

"Wedd's been spotted in the company of several attractive women. Streaming in and out of his apartment. Including Simone Chambord."

"You're saying Mel *pimped* for that bastard?"

"Or he might have been in charge of the finances."

"What finances?"

"Paying women off when Mr. Rader was through with them. In Simone Chambord's case, that may have included getting a car for her. A red BMW. It once belonged to Mr. Wedd but he reported it stolen and Simone Chambord was seen driving it."

"Oh, this is all too much. What else do you want to drop on me, Lieutenant?"

"That's it."

"Insanity," she said. "Okay, now what do we do about it?"

52

The plan was logical, meticulous, elegant in its simplicity.

Even in the chief's grudging appraisal. "Assuming you're lucky, Sturgis."

At eight thirty a.m., two days after my session with Prema Moon, the tutors from Oxford Educational Services drove through the stout wooden gate of her estate.

Newly scheduled all-day trip to SeaWorld, in San Diego, the kids had visited last year, begged to return. Prema had punted with the classic parental "Soon, one day."

At seven thirty she announced, "Surprise!" to a quartet of sleepy young faces.

"How come, Mom?"

"Because Sam and Julie say you've all been great with your studies."

"Oh."

"Whoa. Cool."

"When are we going?"

"Right now, everyone get dressed. Afterward, Sam and Julie will take you to a great Mexican restaurant and you can all stay up late."

Mumbled thanks. Big smile from Boo.

At ten fourteen a.m. a brown, dust-caked, kidney-punishing Dodge van rolled through that same gate. Entering Prema's spread required a thousand feet of climbing past the wrought-iron barrier that blocked access to the tree-shrouded private road. At the top were three identical barriers of weathered oak inlaid with oversized black nail-heads, each equipped with a call box.

Per directions, Milo drove up to the left-hand box. As we waited to enter, I spotted a black glass eye peering from the boughs of a pine. Closed-circuit lens focused on Prema's gate. Then another, aimed at Donny Rader's. Maybe he'd installed his own security system. Or Prema cared more about his comings and goings than she'd let on.

I pointed the cameras out to Milo. His placid nod said he'd already seen them.

Four beeps from the call box, the gate swung open smoothly, we rattled through. The brown van had been borrowed from the Westside LAPD impound yard. Cheap stick-on signs on each flank read *Adaptive Plumbers.* The 213 number below was printed in numerals too small to read from a distance. If someone actually called it, they'd get a disconnect.

I sat up front in the shotgun seat. Behind me was a tech sergeant named Morry Burns who occupied himself playing Sudoku online. The slew of equipment he'd brought, including a portable dolly, occupied the van's rear storage area. Behind Burns sat K-9 specialist Tyler O'Shea and a panting retriever mix named Sally.

Milo said, "Pooch okay?"

O'Shea said, "She's awesome. Lives to do the job."

"All-American work ethic."

"El Tee, I'll take her any day over your garden-variety so-called human."

◆

Prema Moon was waiting for us in the parking lot west of her mansion. The area was an easy acre, paved beautifully, ringed by river rock, cordoned by low privet hedges. Space for dozens of cars but only four today, all compact sedans. Three bore the bumper sticker of a Spanish-language Christian station. The fourth had customized plates reading *TRFFLES.*

The mansion hovered in the distance, a frothy, pink-beige Mediterranean that almost succeeded in looking old, perched assertively on the property's highest knoll. Windows gleamed like zircons. Red bougainvillea climbed the walls like gravity-defying rivulets of blood. The hue of the stucco was a perfect foil for an uncommonly blue sky.

Several smaller outbuildings dotted the property, same color, same genre, as if the mansion had dropped pups. North of the structures, walls of cypress surrounded something unseen. To the rear of the property was a black-green cloud of untamed conifer, sycamore, eucalyptus, and oak.

As we got out of the van, Prema strode toward us, holding a sheaf of papers. She wore form-fitted black jeans, a black mock turtle, red suede flats. Her hair was combed out and shiny, held in place by a thin black band. She'd put on lipstick and eye shadow and mascara.

New take on gorgeous.

Milo said, "Morning."

"Morning, Lieutenant. I just called the tribe, they're halfway to San Diego, should be gone until eight or even nine. Is that enough time?"

Milo said, "We'll do our best." He introduced her to Morry Burns.

She said, "Pleased to meet you."

Without answering, Burns laid down a pair of metal carrying cases, returned to the van, brought out the dolly. A third trip produced the flat sides of several unassembled cardboard boxes. He walked up to Prema. "Is there some hub where all your computers feed?"

"Like command central? I don't think so."

"You don't think or you don't know?"

Prema blinked. "No, there's nothing like that."

"How many computers on the premises?"

"Don't know that, either. Sorry."

"You have a smart-house setup? Crestron running the lights, the utilities, your home theater, all your toys?"

"We do have a system, but I'm not sure the computers go through it."

"Show me your personal machine. We'll work backward from there."

"Right now?"

"You got something better to do?" Burns began stacking his dolly.

Milo pointed to the papers in Prema's hand.

She said, "I pulled phone records for the last six months. Every line that goes through this property."

Without looking back, Burns said, "Landlines and cells?"

"Yes."

"Your employees have personal cell accounts?"

"I'm sure they do—"

"Then that's not every line." He made another trip to the van.

"Well . . . yes," said Prema. "I just wanted to help."

Tyler O'Shea appeared with Sally in tow.

Prema said, "A dog?"

Milo said, "While you work with Detective Burns on the hardware, Officer O'Shea will be exploring the property with Sally."

O'Shea, young, virile, muscular, gawked at Prema. When he managed to engage eye contact, he beamed.

She smiled back. O'Shea blushed.

"Hi, Sally, aren't you a pretty girl?" She reached to pet the dog. O'Shea blocked her with his arm. "Sorry, ma'am, she needs to concentrate."

"Oh, of course—concentrate on what?"

Milo said, "Finding anything interesting."

"You think you'll find evidence *here*?"

"We need to be thorough, Ms. Moon."

Sally's leash strained as she oriented herself toward the forest. Her nose twitched. She panted faster.

Prema said, "Sally's one of those . . . dogs that look for bodies?"

O'Shea said, "That's part of her repertoire, ma'am."

"Oh, my." Head shake.

"What's back there in the trees, ma'am?"

"Just trees. Honestly, you're not going to find anything."

"Hope you're right, ma'am." O'Shea clicked his tongue twice. He and Sally headed out at a quick trot.

Morry Burns returned. Tapped his foot. Checked his watch.

Milo said, "Who's working on the premises today, ma'am?"

"Just the core staff," she said. "The maids and the cook. Do you need to talk to them?"

"Eventually. Meanwhile, go with Detective Burns. Dr. Delaware and I will stroll around a bit."

Prema forced a half smile. "Of course. He's a psychologist, anything can be interesting."

First stop: the four walls of cypress. An opening on the east side led us into a flat area the size of two football fields. One corner was devoted to a safety-fenced half-Olympic pool with a padlocked, alarmed gate. The opposing corner housed a sunken tennis court. Diagonal to that were a regulation basketball court, a rubber-matted area set up with four trampolines, a moon-bounce, a tetherball pole, two Ping-Pong tables, and a sand pit that hosted a plastic slide, a swing-set, a seesaw, and a yellow vinyl tunnel-maze.

Milo said, "Kid-Heaven, courtesy Super Mom. What's that, making up for her own shitty childhood?"

"Could be, if you're in an analytical mood."

"You're not?"

"Let's find the maids and the cook."

The interior of the house was what you'd expect: the requisite vaulted rooms, quarry-emptying expanses of marble, enough polished wood to threaten a rain forest. The art on the walls was professionally spaced, perfectly framed and lit: oil paintings biased toward women and children as subjects and the kind of pastel landscape that combats insomnia.

The maids were easy to find. Imelda Rojas polished silver in the dining room, Lupe Soto folded laundry in a white-tiled utility room the size of some New York apartments, Maria Elena Miramonte tidied up a playroom that would thrill a preschool class. All three women were in their sixties, solidly built and well groomed, wearing impeccable powder-blue uniforms.

Milo spoke to them individually.

Easy consensus: Senora Prema was wonderful.

Senor Donny was never here.

Despite that, Rader's name elicited tension but when Milo asked Imelda Rojas what she thought of him she insisted she didn't know. He kept up the questioning but stepped aside early on and punted to me. My doctorate wasn't any help, at first; Maria and Imelda were unable, or unwilling, to articulate their feelings about Rader. Then Lupe Soto opined that he was "a sinner," and when pressed, specified the nature of Rader's iniquities.

"*Putas,* always."

"Lots of girls."

"No girls, senor, *putas.* Is good he no live here. Better for the chillin they no see that."

"He used to bring *putas* here?"

Lupe said, "You kidding? Always there."

"His place."

"Yeah, but we know."

"How?"

"The TV in the kitchen."

"Could you show me, please?"

She led us down a double staircase too grand for Tara through a succession of big bright sitting rooms and into a tin-ceilinged, maple-and-steel kitchen easily forty feet long. Mounted on the far wall were a dozen small screens.

Lupe Soto pointed to one. The image was inert. One of the wooden gates.

"See?"

I said, "He didn't try to hide what he was doing."

"Nah."

I showed her the well-worn mug shot of Charlene Chambers aka Qeesha D'Embo aka Simone Chambord.

"La negra?" said Lupe Soto. "Yeah, she, too."

"She went over to Senor Donny's place?"

"All the time. But I don tell Senora Prema."

"Why not?"

"Not my business." She placed a hand over her heart.

"No one wanted to hurt her feelings."

"Yeh."

"What's Simone—this woman—like?"

"Who she like? Him." She sneered. *"Puta."*

"What kind of person is she?"

"Smile a lot, move a lot hoo hoo hoo." Illustrating with a brief shake of ample hips. "Then she have the baby and she go way."

"When did she have a baby?"

"Mebbe . . . four, fie month ago?"

"And when did she leave?"

"I don remember, senor."

"Where'd she go after she left?"

"Dunno. Now, I gotta work."

We revisited the other two maids, repeated the same questions. More of the original reticence. But Imelda Rojas's eyes were jumpy.

I said, "You're sure you have no idea where Simone went?"

"Nup."

"What kind of car did she drive?"

"Car? Red." Giggle. *"Rojo.* Like *mi nombre*—my name." More amusement. *"My* car is white."

"Thought the red car was Mel Wedd's."

"Him? No."

"You never saw him drive the red car?"

"Nup, I see a black one. Big." She shaped a circle with her hands. "Like Senor Donny car."

"Mel and Senor Donny drove the same type of car?"

"Zactly the same," she said. "Senor Donny got a lot of cars." She thought. "Mebbe he give one to Senor Mel."

"He likes Senor Mel?"

"Dunno." No objection to my usage of present tense. No idea Wedd had been murdered.

"Is Senor Mel a nice person?"

"I gue-ess."

"He treats you well?"

"I don work with him."

"Was he friendly with Simone Chambord?"

"Everyone here friendly. Senora Prema the more friendly."

"More than—"

"All peoples. She for the kids."

"Senor Donny—"

Head shake. "I gotta work."

"What about Adriana?"

Sudden flash of smile. "She nice. Read the Bible."

"Have you seen her recently?"

"No."

"Any idea where she is?"

"You know?"

I shook my head.

She said, "Nice lady. She go away?"

"Looks like it."

She shrugged.

I said, "People come and go, all the time?"

"Not me."

"You like it here."

"I like to work."

"Could you show us where Senor Mel lives?"

"Building Two, we all there."

"Could you show us?"

Prolonged sigh. "Then I got to *work*."

Building Two was a pleasantly landscaped single-story structure due north of the mansion. An eight-by-eight lobby set up with dried flowers in big copper vases opened to hallways on two sides. Like a nice boutique hotel. Four doors lined each corridor. Lupe Soto said, "Okay?" and started to leave.

Evoking additional sighs, I got her to show us her quarters, a spotless, daylit bedroom with a small sitting area and an en-suite bathroom. Imelda and Maria slept in the flanking rooms.

"Same as me. Zactly."

The farthest room was occupied by the cook, a stick-like woman in her late twenties wearing mini-check chef's pants and a white smock. She answered our knock, filing her nails.

The layout behind her was identical to Lupe's, but festooned with rock posters and oversized illustrations of food. The bed was unmade. The smell of gym sweat and perfume blew out into the hallway.

"Yeah, what's going on?" Her hair was short, yellow, textured like fleece. Bruise-colored tattoos coiled up the side of her neck. I wondered if avoiding the carotid and the jugular had been a challenge.

Milo's badge caused the skin around the illustration to pale. She lowered the nail file. "Police? What's going on?"

"Nothing serious, we're just here to check a few things out at Ms. Moon's request."

"About what?"

"An employee who worked here seems to have gone missing."

"Who's that?"

"Simone Chambord."

"Sorry," she said. "Must be before my time."

"How long have you been working here, Ms. . . . ?"

"Georgie," she said. "Georgette Weiss. How long? Like a month.

Make that thirty . . . eight days. She okay? That woman? I mean did something happen to her?"

"Don't know yet, Ms. Weiss. You like working here?"

"Like it? You kidding?" said Georgie Weiss. "This is like a dream gig."

"Easy."

"Cook healthy for her and the kids? No maniac E.C.—executive chef—going nuclear on me, no asshole customers trying to prove they're important by sending perfectly good plates back? Yeah, it's easy. Plus she pays me great. More than I made working twice as hard at restaurants."

"She's a nice lady."

"You bet. Especially," said Georgie Weiss.

"Especially, what?"

"Especially considering."

"Who she is."

"I mean face it, she could get away with anything, right? But she's like a real person."

"What about him?"

"Who?"

"Donny Rader?"

"Never seen him, actually." She looked to the side. "They don't live together—don't quote me, I need to be whatyacallit—discreet."

"Of course. They live separately?"

"He's like next door so I'm not sure what that is. I mean, it's not far, there's like an empty property and then his place." She shrugged.

"You ever cook for him?"

"Never. That's all I know, don't quote me, okay?"

"No prob," said Milo. "What about Mel Wedd?"

"What about him *what*?"

"He easy to work for?"

"I work for Prema, he does his thing, we really don't interact." Another sideward glance. "Can I tell you something but really please I mean it don't quote me."

"Sure."

"Seriously," said Georgie Weiss.

"Seriously."

She scratched her head. "Mel. He's not the friendliest guy but that's not what I'm talking about. Officially, I think he works for Prema. At least he seems to, he's like here all the time. But . . . I think he could also be hanging with *him*. Donny, I mean. Because I've seen him drive over there. At night."

"After hours."

Nod. "That's another thing. About Prema. When the day's over, it's over. Some of them, they think they own you, it's like slavery, you know? Do for me twenty-four-seven?"

"Not Prema."

"Prema makes the rules and you're expected to keep them but *she* keeps them, too."

"She doesn't exploit the help."

"Trust me, that's rare," said Georgie Weiss. She rattled off the names of two other actresses and a male star. "Spent some time P.C.ing—private chefing—for them. *Slavery.*"

"Nice to know someone's different."

"You bet. Maybe it's 'cause she has kids. She's totally into them."

"Eating healthy?"

"She's like . . . an involved mom. But not crazy-healthy like every anorexic Westside bitch, they see a glass of juice they have a seizure. It's reasonable stuff, just watch out for too much sugar and fat. That's my food, anyway."

"Good deal."

"The best. I *love* it. Hope you find that woman." She began to close the door.

Milo didn't try to stop her physically. His voice was enough. "So you think Mel Wedd is going behind Prema's back after hours?"

She studied him. "You're trying to say *he* did something to that woman?"

"Not at all," said Milo. "Just checking everyone out."

"I just thought it was weird, Mel going over there. Because he works for Prema and obviously they're not—it's not like they're a couple—so what could he be doing over there?"

"Mel's the estate manager," I said. "Maybe the entire property's considered the estate."

"Hmm," she said. "Guess so." Nervous smile. "Whatever, keep me out of it, okay? I just want to cook my food."

The second hallway contained three rooms, instead of four. A utility closet at the rear housed the water heater and the A.C. unit.

The first door was unlocked. Bare mattress, empty nightstand and dresser. A portable crib stood folded in the corner.

Milo gloved up, had me wait as he went in, emerged shaking his head. "Nothing and it's obviously been cleaned. But I'll have it processed, anyway."

The second room was locked. He said, "Stay here, make sure no one goes into Simone's," and left the building. Ten minutes later, he returned with a large ring of keys.

"Stored in the laundry room but none of the maids would tell me that, so I had to bring Prema down."

"She inspires loyalty," I said. "How's it going with the computers?"

"Hard to tell with Burns, he's so damn grumpy."

"How come?"

"You're the shrink." Selecting a key, he unlocked the second room.

Tightly made bed, Bible on the nightstand. Framed pictures on the dresser.

Regloving, he ran through the same solo search. Opened a closet door wide enough for me to view the contents from the corridor.

Sparse supply of bland-looking garments.

He went into the bathroom, called out, "Nothing sexy here, either."

Returning to the dresser, he opened drawers, inspected the framed pictures. Stepped closer and held them out for my inspection.

Adriana and her church group, including the woman she'd known

as Qeesha D'Embo but had come to accept as Simone Chambord because friends in need did what was expected of them.

The two women stood heads together, beaming.

Qeesha cradled a tiny brown infant.

The baby had a round face, inquisitive black eyes, a sweet mouth,
graceful, long-fingered hands, a full head of dark hair.

Beautiful child.

Finally, the bones had a face.

Cordelia.

My throat clogged.

Milo raced out of the room.

Melvin Jaron Wedd's quarters veered toward messy but smelled okay.
Probably the Armani cologne in his medicine cabinet.

The fragrance shared space with Viagra for fun, Lunesta for sleep,
five varieties of caffeine pills for energy. Tube of lube in the top nightstand drawer. In the second, a short stack of gay porn.

Nothing interesting in the dresser until Milo kneeled low and pulled
a small blue leatherette spiral notebook out of the bottom, right-hand
drawer. Stashed under a stack of beefy sweaters too warm for L.A.

The book bore the gold-imprinted legend of an insurance broker
with an office in Beverly Hills. Probably one of those Christmas give-
aways.

Inside was an appointment calendar, complete with holiday notations, dated the previous year. Wedd hadn't used it to organize his
schedule; the pages were unmarked.

Milo leafed through. Toward the end, several blank pages headed
Notes contained just that.

Mel Wedd's penmanship was impressive. Nice straight columns,
too. Two side by side per page.

Cheryl, Jan 3–7: 1000.00
Melissa, Jan 6–7: 750.00
Shayanne Jan 23: 750.00

Forty-nine women's names, fifteen of them occurring twice or more. Monthly totals approached ten thousand dollars but always fell slightly short.

"Simone" showed up sixteen times over a two-year period.

First payment: three hundred dollars. An increase to six hundred, then six notations of eight fifty.

Milo said, "Merit raise—whoa, look at this."

Sudden boost on the eighth payment: $4,999.99. Seven more of those, each dated the first of the month.

Milo said, "She takes up a whole bunch of the ten-grand limit, leaving less for other girls. Guy's a superstar, would have to come begging for dough, talk about demeaning."

I said, "He's Prema's bad child."

He looked at me. "Been carrying around that insight for a while?"

"Just thought of it."

"She couldn't raise him properly, moved on to real kids?"

"She's invented her own world." I took a longer look at the log. "Eight big payments conforms to the final months of Qeesha's pregnancy. Up to that point, she was figuring out what to do, by the fourth month she couldn't hide it any longer, decided to take action. Donny told her to abort, she strung him along, kept delaying as he kept paying. Then it was too late and she had the baby and her hold over him was telling Prema. She continued to live here, got Prema to hire Adriana for backup. To serve as an insurance policy if things got ugly."

"Adriana didn't turn out to be much insurance."

"When Qeesha and the baby disappeared, Adriana suspected the worst. But going to the police wasn't an option. Child-care aide makes accusations against mega-celebs, no evidence to back it up, how far would that get? So Adriana decided to stick around and snoop. Then the baby skeleton showed up under Holly Ruche's tree and it made the news and someone heard about it and thought it would be a grand idea to ditch a second set of bones not far from there so the police would think some sort of serial ghoul was at work."

"Fifty years between dumps is a serial?"

"Not well thought out," I said.

"Not a genius," he said. "Aka Donny."

"He's the one with the wax and the knives and the bugs. And the guns."

"According to Prema."

"All verifiable accusations."

"And I'm the verifier."

We left Wedd's room. Milo carried the appointment book away from his body. "Gotta get an evidence bag for this . . . Here's something else to chew on, Alex: Donny dumping his own kid's bones and doing Adriana the same night seems like a challenge for someone supposedly that dumb."

I said, "Agreed. Had to be a two-person job. Donny and Wedd. That way there'd be no need to schlep Adriana across the park. Wedd was Prema's guy by day, but Donny's pimp and paymaster and who-knows-what-else by night. The maids knew about it, everyone knew about it except Prema. Wedd was a wannabe actor, wanted to emulate the star—drove the same kind of car as the star. He wasn't ridiculing Donny when he imitated him over the phone. He was pretending to *be* him."

"Hell, Alex, maybe it was more than that: What if Wedd had a crush on Donny? So when Donny asks him to take care of nasty business, he's fine with it. Unfortunately, Donny grew uncomfortable with his knowing too much and took care of *him*."

I said, "Nighttime drive, weed and a bong. Sure, it fits. Wedd probably figured he'd be partying with his idol."

"Power of celebrity," he said.

"It even got the best of a wily, manipulative woman like Qeesha. If her head had been clear, she'd have known from the way Donny shut out four kids that he wouldn't take well to fatherhood. To being pressured."

"Playing her usual game," he said. "But out of her league."

Footsteps at the mouth of the corridor made us turn.

Tyler O'Shea held a tired-looking Sally at the end of a slack leash.

Milo said, "Anything?"

O'Shea gave a thumbs-down. "Only dead thing in that forest was a really gross, rotting squirrel way at the back, that's what was attracting her. Sorry, El Tee."

"No big deal," said Milo.

"You knew already?"

"I never know, kid. That's what makes the job fun."

"Oh. Okay. So we're finished?"

"Not even close."

53

We came upon Morry Burns and Prema leaving the big house. Burns walked ahead of her, wheeling his dolly, now piled high with boxes. When he saw us, he picked up speed. Prema stopped, stood there for a second, walked back through her front door.

When Burns reached us, Milo said, "You're really starstruck, Morry."

Burns said, "Huh?"

"What'd you learn?"

"Her system stinks." Burns cocked a head at the mansion. "All that dough, the kids have rooms like a Broadway production, and she cheaps out on crap hardware. I could get technical but it wouldn't mean anything to you, so leave it at crap. Nothing's linked, real pain to go through each machine."

"Same question."

"Huh?"

"Learn anything?"

Burns tapped a metal case. "Nah. But I took her hard drive, will dig deeper. Also drives from other machines they use—get this—to buy groceries. Or-gah-nic arugula. No need to encrypt that."

"What about the kids' computers?"

"Two desktops for four of them." Burns cackled. "Maybe they're learning how to share. She's got them on every parental lock known to mankind, they're lucky to get the weather. Maybe that's why they hardly ever go online."

I said, "Could be they like to read."

Burns stared at me as if I'd talked in tongues. To Milo: "We through here?"

"Not even close."

O'Shea and Burns took a lunch break near the pool. Take-out Mexican Milo had brought along.

We found Prema in her cavernous kitchen, sitting at a granite-topped counter drinking tea. No maid in sight. The CCTV screens remained inert.

Milo said, "Do you have those real estate documents?"

"You need to actually see them?"

"We do."

She left, returned a few minutes later. "Here's the trust deed on the entire property."

Milo read carefully, per Deputy D.A. John Nguyen's instructions.

"As you can see, I'm the sole owner," she said. "I bought it before I knew him."

A divorce lawyer would laugh at that but for Milo's purposes, the deed was sufficient.

He produced a form of his own: Prema's consent to search the entire property. She scrawled her name without reading.

"Okay?" she said, drumming granite.

"You're sure he's over there."

"He drove in late, like one thirty in the morning, hasn't left since. I saw it right there." Pointing to the bank of screens.

"It records twenty-four-seven?"

"It sure does. Everything feeds into a computer and before you got here, I scrolled through. He has *not* left."

"Does Detective Burns have the hard drive for that computer?"

Prema's perfect mouth formed an O. "Sorry, forgot to tell him about it. But all it does is record feed from the security system and most of that's blank."

"Where's the computer?"

She slid open a drawer beneath the screens, pulled out a small laptop.

"How far back do you keep recordings?"

"Hmm. I really don't know."

Burns's grumpiness turned to outright hostility. "I told you to give me everything. You didn't think to mention this?"

Prema said, "I—it slipped my mind."

He began pushing buttons, muttered, " 'Nother piece of crap."

Prema looked to me for support. I gave her a *who-knows?* smile. She returned to her tea as Burns fiddled with the laptop.

"What date do you want, Lieutenant?"

Milo told him.

"Hmmph. Here you go."

Nothing the night of the murders until one thirty-three a.m., when a vehicle passed through Donny Rader's gate.

Big, dark SUV.

"No front plate," said Burns. "Tough luck for you, Lieutenant, the camera angle could pick it up."

From across the kitchen, Prema said, "That's got to be his. He's piled up a bunch of tickets for not putting on a front plate."

Burns mumbled, "Ooh, major scofflaw."

Blocking Prema's view with his own bulk, Milo placed his hand on Burns's shoulder. Burns looked up at Milo. Milo's wolf-grin lowered his head. A naughty child finally disciplined.

Milo pulled out the pages he'd received from DMV: regs on Donny

Rader's sixteen vehicles. Four Ferraris, three Porsches, a Lamborghini, a Maserati, a Stryker, a pair of Mercedeses, an Aston Martin Rapide, a vintage Jaguar E-type.

Two SUVs, both black: a Range Rover and Ford Explorer. "Go back, let's see if we can figure out which it is."

Three rewinds later, the bet was on the Explorer.

Milo said, "Now go forward."

"Sure, Lieutenant."

We didn't need to wait long.

Forty-nine seconds after the first SUV had exited, an identical set of wheels rolled through Rader's gate.

Front plates on this one. Milo said, "Freeze that," and checked the tags against his notes. "Yup, Wedd's."

Prema said, "Mel was there?"

"Any reason he would be?"

She shook her head. Rested her chin in her hand and stared at nothing.

Milo said, "Why don't you relax somewhere, Ms. Moon."

"It's okay, I've got nowhere to go."

Low, morose tone. Burns looked at her as if for the first time. Bland curiosity, no sympathy.

Milo prodded Burns's shoulder with a fingertip. "Keep going."

Twenty-nine seconds after Wedd's exit, a third vehicle, smaller, shaped like a car, zipped through Prema's gate.

Pinpointing the make and registration was easy: brand-new Hyundai Accent, Banner Rental. It took several calls but Milo finally reached a supervisor at the company's corporate headquarters in Lodi and obtained the details.

Adriana Betts had rented the car three days prior from the Banner office on Santa Monica Boulevard in West L.A. Taking advantage of special weeklong rates.

Poor deluded woman playing amateur detective.

Milo took the laptop from Burns, fast-forwarded through another ten minutes. Twenty. Nothing. He handed the machine back to Burns, said, "Let's go."

Prema said, "It's happening?"

"In a bit, Ms. Moon."

"Why the delay?"

"We're organizing, ma'am. Now I suggest you go and find a place where you can—"

"Just as long as you do it before the tribe returns. I can't have them exposed to bad things."

I thought: *If it were only that simple.*

CHAPTER

54

We headed for Prema's acre of parking lot.

Burns said, "Fresh air. Finally."

I said, "You don't like actors."

"Don't try to shrink me, Doc."

Milo said, "It's a reasonable question, Morry. Whatever your bullshit is, it came close to obstructing."

Burns turned pale. "I—"

"It's still a good question, Morry."

"Whatever," said Burns. He began to walk ahead of us, thought better of it, stopped, threw his hands up. "My sister was an actor. Did some crap off-Broadway, nothing serious. She killed herself five years ago. Completely ruined my parents' lives."

"Sorry," I said. "The business was too much for her?"

"How would I know about the business?" said Burns. "She ruined their lives by killing herself because she was a narcissistic drama queen, always had been."

Milo said, "Morry, stay in the van, see if you can do anything else with the machines."

"Yeah, sure. I'll get nothing but I'll try."

◆

As Burns loaded his equipment, Tyler O'Shea emerged with Sally. He rubbed Sally's scruff. The dog looked rejuvenated.

Milo said, "We're a go, Ty, let's do it on foot. I'm gonna start with the soft approach, nothing SWAT-ty, because this joker's no genius, he has drug issues and a closetful of guns, I'm hoping the element of surprise will be enough."

"Plus he's famous," said O'Shea.

"What does that have to do with it?"

"More of a surprise, El Tee. Probably no one ever bugs him."

"Famous," said Milo. "If everything works out, that'll change to infamous."

The walk from Prema's property to Rader's took six minutes. Sally would've preferred to run it in two. Milo had the gate code, courtesy Prema Moon: 10001.

"Had to keep it simple, Lieutenant, because he can't remember anything."

He pushed the buttons, the gate cooperated, we continued along asphalt in need of resurfacing. Longer, steeper access than to Prema's estate, an easy quarter mile with nothing visible other than greenery. At some points the trees grew so thick that the sky disappeared and day turned to imposed dusk.

O'Shea said, "Man likes his privacy."

Milo lengthened his stride. O'Shea took that as the *shut up* it was meant to be.

As we kept climbing, Sally's fur rippled in the breeze. Soft but acute eyes analyzed the world at hand. Her posture was erect, her trot rich with pride. Work-dog heaven.

Then she stopped.

O'Shea said, "Would you look at that."

The road ended abruptly at a mesa filled with cars. Enough parking space for a dozen vehicles positioned properly but I counted seventeen sets of wheels stacked within inches of one another, some extending to the surrounding brown grass.

Donny Rader's black Explorer was positioned nearest to the road, slightly apart from the automotive clog. Easy exit for the daily driver. Milo photographed the SUV from several angles, scribbled in his pad.

The other cars, exemplars of high-ticket Italian, German, and British coachwork, were caked with dust, splotched by bird-dirt, fuzzed by leaves. A few tilted on deflated tires.

Sixteen matches to the DMV list. The addition was a red convertible sandwiched in the center of the stack.

Milo squeezed his way over to the BMW, took more pictures, made more notes.

O'Shea said, "Can I ask why that one, El Tee?"

"Victim's wheels."

"He kept it? What an idiot."

"Let's hope he stays that way. Onward."

The house was a low, long box that had been stylish in the fifties. My guess was an expat architect from Europe—Schindler or Neutra or someone trying to be Schindler or Neutra. The kind of site-conscious, minimalist design that ages well if it's kept up.

This one hadn't been. A roof meant to be flat sagged and dipped. Stress cracks wrinkled white stucco grimed to gray. Windows were pocked with birdshit. Rain streaks and pits blemished the flat façade. Like Prema's property, Rader's acreage was backed by forest. But everything else was hard-pack.

We approached the house. Internal shutters blocked off the view the architect had intended. The door was a slab of ash in need of varnish. Solid, though. Milo's knock barely sounded.

He pushed the doorbell. No chime or buzzer that I could hear.

Louder knock.

The door opened on a girl-woman in a thong bikini. Her hair was a riot of white and black and flamingo-pink. Late teens or early twenties.

She stared at us with bleary, heavy-lidded eyes. White powder smudged the space between her perfect nose and her perfect lips. The bikini was white, barely qualified as a garment with the bra not much more than pasties on a string and the bottom a nylon triangle not up to the job of pelvic protection. Breasts the size of grapefruits heaved a split second after the rest of her chest moved, the mammary equivalent of digital delay. Her feet were bare and grubby, her nails blood-red talons.

She rubbed her eyes. "Huh?"

"Police, ma'am. Is Mr. Rader here?"

She swiped at the white granules above her mouth.

Milo said, "Don't worry about your breakfast, we just want to talk to Donny Rader."

The girl's mouth opened. A frog-croak emerged. Then a squeak. Then: "Don-*nee*!"

No need to shout, Rader was already behind her, materializing from the left, wearing a red silk robe. The robe was loosely belted, exposing a hard, tan body. The pockets bulged. A bottle of something with a booze-tax seal around the neck poked from one. The contents of the other were out of view. Maybe a bag of white powder. Or just a glass. If he bothered with a glass.

He pushed the girl out of the way, did the same eye rub. "Whus happening?"

Big man, larger and more muscular than he came across on the screen. Coarser, with a near-Neanderthal brow shelf, grainy skin, thickened nostrils that flared like a bull's.

Long, shaggy, ink-black hair flew everywhere. His eyes fought to remain open. Described in the fan mags as black, they were actually deep brown. Just enough contrast to see the pupils. Widely dilated despite the bright afternoon light.

White powder on his face, too, a thick smear on his lips and chin. Snowy dust littered the red robe's shawl collar. The top seam of the other robe pocket.

Milo said, "Police, Mr. Rader."

"Whu the fuh!" Throaty growl. The iconic slur.

"Police—"

"Fuh!" Donny Rader backed away.

Milo said, "Hold on, we'd just like to talk—"

"About whu?"

"We'd like to come in, Mr. Rader."

"Whu the fu—hey! You ain't cops, you're some shit from her, trying to mess with my mind—"

"Sir, I can assure—"

"Assure my asshole, get the fuh outta here!"

"Mr. Rader, we really are the police and we—"

Donny Rader shook himself off hard, hair billowing, a hyena clearing its maws of blood. The girl in the bikini had remained behind him, clutching her face and hyperventilating.

Milo stepped forward, aiming to get his toe in the door.

Howling, Rader jammed his hand into the robe pocket that didn't hold the bottle, yanked out something metallic and shiny.

He faded back, began to straighten his arm.

The last time Milo had faced madness, he'd been caught off-guard and I'd saved his life. That didn't fit the script of seasoned cop and shrink and despite his acknowledgment, it would scar him.

Maybe that's why this time he was ready.

One of his hands clamped like a bear-trap on the wrist of Donny Rader's gun-arm, pushing down and twisting sharply as his foot shot between Rader's bare legs and kicked laterally to the left. As Rader lost balance, Milo's other arm spun him around and by the time Tyler O'Shea was ready with cuffs and a now snarling Sally, Rader was down on the ground and the .22 lay safely out of reach.

Rader foamed at the mouth, turned dirt to chocolate soda.

The girl in the bikini whimpered.

Milo said, "Ty, take care of her."

O'Shea checked out the tight, tan body. "You're a pal, El Tee."

He cuffed the girl displaying no particular reverence. Something to the left caught his eye. "El Tee, you better look at this." Something new in his voice. Fear.

Milo hauled a struggling, howling Donny Rader to his feet. "Hold still and shut it."

"Fuh you."

O'Shea walked the girl out of the house. He looked stunned. "You got to see this."

Milo said, "Check it out, Alex."

The house was a sty. Piles of trash blanketed the floor and the furniture. The air was putrid with rotted food, body odor, weed, a medicinal smell that might've been poorly cut cocaine.

A cat-urine stench that might've been cats or crystal meth.

O'Shea had seen and smelled worse, so that wasn't it.

Not wanting to disturb potential evidence, I stepped carefully over the garbage. Then I saw it. Hanging from a low rafter, the feet dangling a few inches from the floor.

A human skeleton, wired and braced by a steel rod running parallel to the spine.

Stripped and clean but for hair left on the head. Long hair. Dark, curly.

Full-sized skeleton. I guessed it shorter than me by at least six inches.

The pelvic arch left no doubt: female.

The jaws had been positioned to create a gaping cartoonish grin. Exaggerated glee that was the essence of horror.

I made my way through the slop-heap, got right up to the skeleton. Sniffed.

New smell.

Pleasant, sweet. Herbaceous.

Honeybees buzzing in the hive.

55

Milo plastic-tied Rader's ankles and belted him into the brown van's second row. Tyler O'Shea positioned Sally up front as a sentry. She enjoyed snapping and growling at the now cringing, weeping actor.

Allowing himself the luxury of an unlit cigar clenched between tight jaws, Milo played the phone, calling in jail transport, crime scene techs, the coroners.

The chief's office, almost as an afterthought. The boss was out; Milo declined to leave a message.

Tyler O'Shea continued to guard the girl in the bikini.

Barbara "Brandi" Podesky, self-described as a "performer and dancer," had no wants but a warrant did pop out of the database: failure to show up for community service on a first-offense marijuana bust. She'd be heading to West L.A. lockup. The news stunned her and she began whining that she was cold.

O'Shea checked out her body, said, "We'll get you something soon." Not a trace of sincerity.

Milo went to look at the skeleton, emerged seconds later and positioned himself in the doorway. Chewing his lip and wiping his face, he got back on the phone. As he waited for a connection, his facial muscles relaxed and something aspiring to be a smile stretched his lips.

"Ms. LeMasters? Milo Sturgis . . . yeah, I know it has been, but not to fret, how're your ace-reporter chops this beautiful day? And are you still in love with your husband? . . . Why? Because trust me, Kelly, you're gonna dig *me* more than *him,* do *I* have a scoop for *you.*"

Just as he clicked off, the chief beeped in. Milo began to supply details I already knew so I left him there, figuring to walk off some excess energy.

I circled right of the car-crush. Came face-to-face with Prema Moon.

Milo had instructed her to stay behind. Some leading women didn't take well to direction.

"Where is he?" she said.

"In the van, but you need to stay away."

"Why wouldn't I stay away? So. It's over."

For the justice system, it was just beginning.

I said, "Yes."

No response for a second. Then she winked at me. Turned her back and tossed her hair and offered a frisky shake of her perfect rear.

Laughing—a giddy, knowing, brittle sound—she walked off the set.

CHAPTER

56

On TV, it would have been a cinch.

The female skeleton's DNA tracked to Qeesha D'Embo, that of the baby in the park was linked to both Qeesha and Donny Rader. Bloodstains, bone fragments, skin flakes, and hair found in the double garage that Rader had set up as his taxidermic workshop belonged to mother and child.

Several of the women located through Mel Wedd's little blue book confirmed that Rader had often retired to the dark, dingy, space after partying, demanding to be left alone with his "projects."

The bullet pulled from Mel Wedd's brain matched a .45 in Rader's firearms closet. Rader's collection consisted of thirty-seven poorly maintained weapons included an Uzi and a Russian assault rifle.

Milo had hoped that the .22 bullet pulled from Adriana Betts would match the gun he'd taken from Rader. But it didn't, couldn't be traced to any of Rader's armaments. That lent credence to the notion that someone else, most probably Melvin Jaron Wedd, had murdered her.

Most probably at Rader's request, but good luck proving that.

The more I thought about Rader's and Wedd's identical SUVs, the stronger the hero-worship scenario got. But Deputy D.A. John Nguyen didn't like it, was intent upon finding something more ominous and premeditated.

"I need creepy psycho stuff, Alex. Give me Manson, bloodlust, a folie à deux, the works."

Milo said, "Seems creepy enough as is, John."

"Never enough." Nguyen grinned. "Maybe I'll get a book deal out of it."

Reality was, the case would stretch on for months, maybe years. Donny Rader, despite being buttressed by an army of high-priced legal talent, had failed in his request for bail. But the special cell he occupied at the men's jail put him safely away from the gangbangers and the lunatics and the trophy-hunters, and stories had begun to circulate about special privileges for the star, mailbags overflowing with love letters sent by severely disturbed women all over the world, female deputies charmed by the artfully slurring actor.

Kelly LeMasters got a serious book deal from a New York publisher and quit the *Times*. Tough luck, John N.

The smart money had Rader avoiding trial via diminished capacity, serving some time in a cushy mental hospital, maybe eventually getting out.

I wasn't so sure. Then again, I'd been wrong about so much.

At this point, I could live with that.

One month and five days after Rader's arrest, I drove to Western Pediatric Medical Center, looked for Salome Greiner, found her again in the doctors' dining room. Late in the day for lunch. Just her and her Jell-O, cottage cheese, and tea. As if she never left the place.

I sat down across from her.

She said, "The prodigal psychologist returns."

I said, "Jimmy Asherwood was a wonderful man who led a tragic life. I can see why you'd want to protect him. I have no desire to smear his memory. He did nothing to deserve that. Quite the contrary."

She sighed. For all her vitality, an old woman. I felt like a troublesome son. Continued, anyway.

"I know about his war injury, know that any relationship you and he had wasn't sexual."

Anger caused her mandible to jut. "From you," she said, softly, "I'd expect a bit more imagination."

That threw me.

She said, "What exactly do you want?"

Rather than answer, I said, "Jimmy respected the right of a woman to control her own body but he was aware that sometimes women—girls—could be pushed into decisions they really didn't want. Girls from a certain social caste who'd created an inconvenience for their families. Enter, Swedish Hospital."

"Goods and services for cash, darling. What could be more patriotic?"

"When the girls decided to terminate, Jimmy went along with it. But unlike the other physicians, he tried to find out what they really wanted. Stepped in when he felt they were being steamrolled. How'd he convince the parents?"

"You're the expert on human nature."

"My guess is he told them the procedure could endanger their daughter's life. And I'll bet some parents didn't care and found themselves another doctor because for a certain genre of alleged human being, stigma trumps everything."

Her response was to saw a cube of Jell-O.

I said, "When the babies were born, Jimmy's involvement didn't end. Just the opposite, he took care of everything. With the help of Eleanor Green, a compassionate soul who loved kids. Exactly the type of person who should become a nurse."

"Ellie," she said. A liver-spotted hand rose to her breast.

I said, "Ellie and you. Maybe others."

"Army of the just," she said. "We were a little battalion of . . . idealistic meddlers." She put down her fork. "After Dachau, I felt I needed to."

I touched her hand. She pulled away. "Are you satisfied, Alex?"

"Sometimes Jimmy delivered the babies, sometimes you did. When the infants were up to the journey, they were transferred to Ellie's care. In a big house in a nice neighborhood that Jimmy rented for that purpose. After being medically screened for a few months, they were given to families who wanted them. People who'd been screened. Not official adoptions, everything had to be off the record."

"Thirty-three," she said. "That's how many we placed. People all over the country. Thirty-three adults who have no idea."

"Thirty-three minus one," I said. "What happened?"

Shaking her head, she got up. I expected her to leave but she walked to the hot-water urn, filled a fresh cup, unwrapped a tea bag, watched it dangle.

When she returned to the table, I said, "Salome, I'm sorry if—"

"Crib death. That's what we called it then, later we got fancy, the way we always do, and it became sudden infant death syndrome. That didn't explain what caused it but it sounded more scientific, no? Nowadays we have our theories but we still don't really understand it. We do know how to prevent a significant amount of it."

"Sleeping on the back, never the stomach."

She smiled. "All those babies with flat heads, parents get all exercised, thinking their little gift's going to grow up looking funny and not get into Harvard. I tell them relax, stop worrying about stupid things."

She shook her head. "No sleeping on the tummy, so simple. That's how she—how Ellie found him. On his belly, not moving. A boy, boy babies are more vulnerable than girl babies. Maybe that never changes, eh, Alex?"

I said, "You live longer than we do, that's why we get to postpone our maturity."

Now her hand rested on mine. "You were always a witty one."

I got myself some coffee. The two of us drank for a while before she said, "Ellie thought it was her fault. Jimmy and I found her rocking the baby, he'd been dead for a full day, she'd sat with him all that time, didn't want to let go of his body." Shivering. "I had to pry it from her."

"So you allowed her to bury him in the backyard."

She gripped both my hands, exerted astonishing pressure. "Why not, Alex? Her grief was monumental and we couldn't exactly report it to the health department."

"Of course not," I said.

"We had a little ceremony. At night. Nondenominational. Each of us offered a prayer. Whispering to avoid alerting the neighbors. Jimmy dug the hole. I planted a little sycamore tree I'd purchased at the nursery. And flowers. Clivia. Around the base. They're beautiful orange, love the shade. We wanted Sam—we gave him a name, so he'd be someone—we wanted to place him in a miniature coffin, but we couldn't figure out where to find one without arousing suspicion. So we used . . . something else."

"Metal box from the hospital. Used to bring money to the bank."

"It's what we had, the alternative was, what, an orange crate?"

"I assumed there was symbolism, Salome."

"What?"

"He was seen as having great value."

She stared at me. Smiled. "I like that. I will adjust my memories to include that. Now if you'll excuse me—"

"Did Jimmy and the rest of you continue placing babies?"

"Of course," she said.

"But Ellie stopped."

Nod.

"What happened to her?"

"She moved to another city, I will not tell you where. Married a man who loved her, I will not tell you his name. Had a baby of her own. Died. That's all you need to know, Alex."

I stood. "Thank you."

"You will tell the policeman?"

"No reason to."

"Then why—ah, of course. You were always driven. A little obsessive, maybe?"

I smiled. "It happens."

CHAPTER

57

Ninety days after Donny Rader's arrest, Milo emailed me a link from *Daily Variety*.

His scrawled comment: *No comment.*

Prema's Aura Shines Gallically

Mega-star Prema Moon has emerged from self-imposed retirement to ink a deal with the Feinstein Group for an action-adventure pic featuring a superhero mother struggling to raise her children while combating cosmic evil forces. The mega-budget production, still untitled, will film in Croatia and France, enabling Prema to travel easily to her newly purchased chateau-cum-organic-farm in the Loire Valley. When asked about the parallels between the story line and her real-life situation in which ex Donny Rader was arrested for multiple murders while she was forced to shield her four-tot brood from his nefarious behavior, Prema's representative declined comment. Chad Zaleen penned the script with Garvey Feinstein producing through his Lighthouse shingle, along with Andrew Bronson, Bill Kander and Dan Elhiani. Ethan White, Barry Urbanovitch and Prema, herself, will exec produce. Filming is slated to begin . . .

◆

Five months later, the mail included a silver-edged pink card in a matching envelope.

We are so joyful
And thankful
To the Earth Aura
And the Goodness all around
As we proudly welcome:

Aimee Destiny

Born beautiful and healthy and brilliant
at a whopping 8 lb. 4 oz!

Holly and Matt Ruche

In lieu of baby gifts please donate to Western Pediatric Medical Center

---

ABOUT THE AUTHOR

JONATHAN KELLERMAN is the #1 *New York Times* bestselling author of more than thirty bestselling crime novels, including the Alex Delaware series, *The Butcher's Theater, Billy Straight, The Conspiracy Club, Twisted,* and *True Detectives*. With his wife, bestselling novelist Faye Kellerman, he co-authored *Double Homicide* and *Capital Crimes*. He is also the author of two children's books and numerous nonfiction works, including *Savage Spawn: Reflections on Violent Children* and *With Strings Attached: The Art and Beauty of Vintage Guitars*. He has won the Goldwyn, Edgar, and Anthony awards and has been nominated for a Shamus Award. Jonathan and Faye Kellerman live in California, New Mexico, and New York.

jonathankellerman.com
www.Facebook.com/JonathanKellerman

ABOUT THE TYPE

This book was set in Simoncini Garamond, a typeface designed by Francesco Simoncini based on the style of Garamond that was created by the French printer Jean Jannon after the original models of Claude Garamond.

HEALTHY PERSONALITY

HEALTHY PERSONALITY

An Approach from the Viewpoint of
Humanistic Psychology

SIDNEY M. JOURARD

Macmillan Publishing Co., Inc.
NEW YORK
Collier Macmillan Publishers
LONDON

Earlier editions, entitled *Personal Adjustment: An Approach Through the Study of Healthy Personality,* © 1958 and 1963 by Macmillan Publishing Co., Inc.

MACMILLAN PUBLISHING CO., INC.
866 Third Avenue, New York, New York 10022

COLLIER-MACMILLAN CANADA, LTD.

Library of Congress Cataloging in Publication Data
Jourard, Sidney M.
  Healthy personality.

  Published in 1958 and 1963 under title: Personal adjustment: an approach through the study of healthy personality.
  Includes bibliographies.
  1. Personality   2. Mental hygiene.   3. Humanistic psychology.   I. Title. [DNLM: 1. Adaptation, Psychological.   2. Mental Hygiene.
3. Personality BF698 J86p 1974]
BF698.J63 1974   155.2   73-8587
ISBN 0-02-361410-2

Printing: 1 2 3 4 5 6 7 8   Year: 4 5 6 7 8 9 0

PREFACE

Some ways of behaving in the world are life-giving to the person and not destructive to other people, to animals, or to the environment which supports us all. These are the ways I call healthy personality.

Not only do these ways enhance life and health for the person, they also stimulate, or at least do not impede, the growth and actualization of his more desirable possibilities. Healthy personality fosters personal growth and sustains health and well-being.

In this book, I have presented what we have learned in psychology—through clinical experience and through research in laboratories and natural settings—about healthy personality.

The point of view from which this book is written is that of humanistic psychology.

Humanistic psychology is the study of man based on the assumption that, as a human being, he is free and hence responsible for his actions and their consequences to his well-being and growth. The humanistic orientation in psychology has flourished in the past decade, and I have sought to incorporate some of the vigor of that approach into my efforts to discuss healthy personality.

The two previous editions of this book were entitled *Personal Adjustment: An Approach Through the Study of Healthy Personality*. In this third effort of mine to portray man at his human best, I have made enough changes and have added enough new material to justify changing the title to the one I have now employed.

I have added four new chapters. The first of these, on consciousness, brings to the students' attention the more recent efforts to study human experiencing in its own right. I have tried to provide a point of view from which a student can make sense out of the contributions that phenomenology has made to psychology, and to comprehend the bewildering array of material on "altered states of consciousness."

Work and play are parts of life that I neglected in the previous editions; I have corrected that omission in this volume and have related these themes to man's need for meaning as well as security in his life.

The third new chapter is on religion. I have seen the strength which good religion gives, and I have seen the destruction wrought in people's lives by misguided piety. I have attempted to show the reader ways to distinguish between true, life-enhancing religion and mere church attendance and literal belief in unexamined scripture.

Each of the other chapters has much new material. In the first, I have added the contributions to the concept of healthy personality made by F. Perls, W. Reich, A. Lowen, A. Ellis, A. Assagioli, B. F. Skinner, E. Berne, V. Frankl, and J. Wolpe. I have discussed recent work in the study of body experience and techniques of re-embodiment and psychotherapeutic advances. I have added a chapter which seeks to clarify the humanistic approach to the study and practice of psychology as a profession.

This book was written for undergraduate courses in personality development and as a humanistic introduction to psychology in those colleges where only one course may be available, or where such an approach is of interest, to supplement the more standard introductory course. I believe, however, that what I have written will be useful to students and practitioners of any of the "helping professions" at undergraduate and graduate levels of instruction. Certainly, counselors and psychotherapists, nurses, social workers, and clergymen would find some guidance for their work in these pages.

In 1955 the late Abraham Maslow read the first draft of *Personal Adjustment* and dictated a forty-page, line-by-line critique which helped me immeasurably and which confirmed me as a beginning author. I gained much from the example of his courage and persistence in pursuit of truth about man and his possibilities. I dedicate *Healthy Personality* to his memory. SIDNEY M. JOURARD

CONTENTS

HEALTHY PERSONALITY

1

WHAT IS HEALTHY PERSONALITY?

INTRODUCTION

Men have sought to perfect themselves throughout history. Early Jews sought to redeem themselves and their world from unbridled nature. The Christians sought salvation. The Buddhists and Hindus were seekers of liberation, and the Sufis underwent training for rebirth in love and enlightenment. In all these cases it was recognized that man is capable of states of being which far surpass the average in beauty and goodness.

The term healthy personality *is used here to describe those ways of being which surpass the average, and it is about those ways that this book is written.*

Man can be studied as a natural phenomenon, with methods appropriate to the study of zoology or ethology. But man has the capacities for speech, and for self-consciousness. This makes him unique. He alone gives meaning to his world and is capable of communicating his meanings to other persons. If we wish to understand human behavior, we must not view it as we would an animal's responses, in terms of its contribution to survival in a given environment; we must regard behavior as action, as a kind of speech. Man "says" something to the world and his fellows by his actions, even with his physiology. If we wish to understand man in his existence as a human being, we must find out what he means to say, to whom he is speaking, and how he says it in words, action, and even his physiological responding. Of course, we find out what he means by asking him to tell us.

The study of healthy personality could be undertaken from a behavioristic standpoint, and some parts of our discussion show a behavioristic influence. However, we shall try to illumine man in his uniquely human characteristics, basing our discussion on a view of man as a conscious, meaning-pursuing being capable of freedom and responsibility in the conduct of his life.[1]

Images of Man: Their Significance for Healthy Personality

Another unique trait of man is that he has no innate ways to experience the world or to act. More than any other creature, he is an imitator of the examples that are available to him and an inventor of new ways to be in the world. This means that the way someone believes man is, and is capable of becoming, influences all who are aware of that image. A person tends to live according to what he takes his "nature" and his possibilities to be. His view of his nature will be influenced by the views held by his parents and peers. Their view of his nature and possibilities, in turn, is influenced by the writers and teachers whose view of man is deemed authoritative for an age. In this chapter some images of man at his *best* are presented, each of which is grounded upon some assumptions about what is most fundamental about man—what functions and needs most nearly define man as the singular creature he is or which place him where he "belongs" in the animal kingdom.

Descriptions of man do not merely describe, they *prescribe*. A person acts in the world as a being with the limits, strengths, and weaknesses he believes are his "nature." Someone persuaded him that that is how he *is*. We will see in later chapters how this peculiarity about man, his vulnerability to persuasion and influence, can at once be the basis for his growth and transcendence (of apparent limits), and for sickness and death.

I have come to see sickness, for example, as an outcome of not changing when the time for change has come. People sicken when they persist in ways of being after those ways have ceased to be meaningful and life-giving. If a person *believes* he cannot live in any way other than the way he has, he will persist in it until stress or despair sicken him.[2] A person will persevere in a difficult project so long as he has hope, and *believes* he has the capacity to succeed. As soon as he begins to doubt that it is within his capacity, he gives up, and "natural sequences" take over. A man's thrust toward consummation of his goals inserts another force— man's action toward his goals—into nature itself. If the action is persistent and versatile enough, then nature is conquered and man prevails. Thus, the Antarctic Sea and the freezing elements nearly destroyed Sir Ernest Shackleton in 1916, when he made a three-week voyage in an open boat with several companions. Shackleton refused to yield to the elements. He *believed* that he could overcome the dangers. He did. He completed his voyage and saved his men. A man's views of his capacities to cope, to survive, to grow, are decisive influences upon the course of his life. Because men are always surpassing what once were believed to be ultimate limits, it clearly matters what people believe to be true about man's potentialities.[3] The next section deals with views of man as a *fully grown being* that have been presented by a variety of psychiatrists, psychologists, and philosophers.

We begin with Freud.

Some Concepts of Healthy Personality

A PSYCHOANALYTIC VIEW OF HEALTHY PERSONALITY

What Is Healthy Personality?

Freud,[4] the founder of psychoanalysis, did not make a serious effort at describing healthy personality, because he was primarily interested in neurosis. He contented himself by stating that health consisted in the ability to love and to do productive work. His theory of personality structure, however, points to factors that permit fulfillment of the capacities to love and to work.

Healthy personality (ability to love and work), in psychoanalytic terms, is an outcome of *harmony among id, ego, and superego*. Another trait of healthy personality is implied by a statement Freud made about the goal of psychoanalytic therapy, "Where id was, there shall ego be."

According to the psychoanalysts, personality is divided into three substructures—the *id*, the *ego*, and the *superego*. Id is the term used to refer to instincts. Ego refers to the active, controlling, perceiving, learning functions of personality. Superego refers to the moral ideals and taboos a person acquires as he grows up. It is the task of the ego to scan external reality and inner experience, and then choose action which will gratify needs without violating moral taboos. In unhealthy personalities, such as neurotic patients, the ego is weak, and hence unable to appraise outer and inner reality and to reconcile conflicts among impulses, morals, and reality. Neurotic patients handle conflicts between impulses (such as sex or aggression) and morality by *repression*, that is, by blotting them from awareness. Repression is the initial cause of the neurotic symptoms.

If a person's upbringing had been adequate (the psychoanalysts did not fully explain such adequacy), his ego would be strong enough to resolve conflicts between needs, or between impulses and morals. A healthier personality would be able to gratify his needs and yet remain free of guilt or of social blame. Because he would be less prone to repress many of his feelings (repression consumes energy), his energy would be available for productive work. Because he would not be ashamed of his feelings and emotions (because of a reasonable conscience), he could be freer in expressing himself in loving relationships. Hence, the relationship between ability to love and work, and the concept of harmony among id, ego, and superego, can assume greater meaning. The phrase "Where id was, there shall ego be" can be translated to mean "where a person behaved compulsively or impulsively, he can, if healthy, substitute rational choice and control." That is, healthy personalities can *choose* between expressing feelings and withholding such expression; between gratifying needs and postponing gratification.

The theory is plausible and has some explanatory power.

It is difficult, however, to specify signs of a strong ego and to describe a humane superego. Later in this book (pp. 64–70, 160) we shall attempt to overcome these deficiencies. The psychoanalytic concept of health, however, has been mentioned for historical reasons, and also because it has had a profound effect on later workers, as we shall see below.

ADLER'S VIEW: SOCIAL FEELING

Alfred Adler [5] was one of the few psychiatrists in the early 1900's who were drawn to Freud's ideas. He soon disagreed with Freud, however, about the role of sex in the development of healthy personality and of neurosis. Adler asserted that inferiority feelings and compensatory strivings for superiority played the most crucial roles in neurotic illness and interfered with the capacity to love and to work. He saw *gemeinschaftsgefühl* as the most important goal of personal growth and of therapy. The German word *gemeinschaftsgefühl* has been translated as "social interest" or "social feeling." It refers to a feeling of oneness, a brotherly feeling toward one's fellow man. People who have achieved *gemeinschaftsgefühl* no longer compete irrationally with others, nor do they strive to be "one-up" on them. They see their fellow men as worthy beings to be regarded as ends in themselves, not as threats or as mere tools to be used for self-advancement.

Adler thus introduced and emphasized an explicitly *interpersonal* dimension to theories of healthy personality. His writings have been influential in psychiatry and in education, though perhaps less widely recognized than those of Freud. The concept of social feeling accords with the highest precepts of ethics and religion and represents a wholesome corrective to the more pathology-oriented psychoanalytic writing.

OTTO RANK: CREATIVITY, INDIVIDUALITY, AND AFFIRMATION OF ONE'S OWN WILL

What Is Healthy Personality?

Otto Rank [6] was another of Freud's early followers who, like Adler and Jung, later went his own way. The points in his numerous writings which bear on healthy personality have to do with "willing" and with "creativity." Rank regarded the creative artist as a pinnacle of human growth. The artist was seen as one with the courage to assert his differences from the mass of men, and who dared to shape reality as he wished it to be, rather than passively "adjusting" to a fixed, frozen reality. Rank saw neurotics as persons with strong wills and strong creative urges, but who lacked the final courage to reveal their individual perspectives to the world. Instead, they "shaped" their own personalities (as a sculptor shapes his clay) *in order to please others.* Healthy personality, for Rank, implied the courage to become a separate, distinct person, the courage to express and celebrate one's difference from others, and the courage to be inventive and creative in various spheres of existence.

Rank's emphasis on willing, creativity, individuality, and emancipation from dependency upon others has had an influence on many contemporary workers. Certainly, we would have to agree that healthy personality must imply some ability to assert oneself and to behave not in slavishly conforming ways, but in more autonomous fashion. I have come to appreciate Rank's view of man-as-artist more in recent years; I now regard healthy personality as the ability to respond to the human situation in inventive, creative ways.

JUNG: THE ATTAINMENT OF SELF-REALIZATION

Carl Gustav Jung developed an extraordinarily complex theory of personality which has gained increased attention in the past ten years. Although Jung was at one time a student and colleague of Freud, he too parted with the latter's theories. He came to call his developing system of thought *analytical psychology.*[7]

Of special interest to us is his view of the structure of personality. Jung viewed man as having a conscious aspect of his psyche and a covert, "shadow" side, which remains unconscious to him and invisible to others. Personal growth was seen as a gradual unfolding and expression of the unconscious, shadow side, and the integration of these unfolding aspects of personality into a coherent, meaningful way of life.

Jung stated that each person has a masculine, assertive aspect to his personality, called *animus,* and a passive, soft, yielding dimension, which he designated *anima.* In males, the animus is most salient, and the anima remains part of

Healthy Personality: An Approach from the Viewpoint of Humanistic Psychology

6

the "shadow" self; among women, the anima is most fully expressed, and the animus is repressed.

Humans experience the world in various ways; Jung recognized a basic polarity of attention which he called *extraversion-introversion*. The extraverted person is most attentive to the happenings of the external world. The introvert is more given to reflection and introspection, attending to his own experience as it is affected by the external world. Through upbringing, and perhaps hereditary and congenital influences, persons grow to emphasize one of these fundamental attitudes, while the opposing attitude remains undeveloped.

Although "extraversion-introversion" defines direction of interest, the ways of contacting the world are also diverse, as Jung saw them. He recognized four fundamental ways of experiencing the world, which he designated, respectively, *sensing, intuition, feeling,* and *thinking.* Sensing refers to the act of receiving the disclosure of the world by way of one's several sensory systems. Intuition refers to a kind of imaginative knowing; it consists of rapid guessing about what lies behind obvious sensory inputs. Feeling refers to the emotional quality of experience—its pleasant or unpleasant, frightening, or ugly qualities. Thinking, of course, refers to man's capacity for reasoning, conceptualizing, and abstract thought. According to Jung, people differ in the degree of emphasis they accord to each way of knowing. Some seem to observe much and think little, whereas others are more emotionally reactive, and given to intuitive leaps into the unknown. The Myers-Briggs Personality Type Indicator, a widely used personality test, provides researchers and individuals with a picture of how a person emphasizes the different ways. For example, I am defined by this test (which I took a year or so ago) as an "extraverted, intuitive, feeling, perceptive" type. The Myers-Briggs Instruction manual describes such persons as follows: [8]

The extraverted intuitive is the enthusiastic innovator. . . . He has a lot of imagination and initiative for originating projects . . . wholly confident of the worth of his inspirations, tireless with the problems involved, and

7

ingenious with the difficulties. . . . He gets other people interested too. Being a perceptive type, he aims to understand people rather than judge them . . . achieves an uncanny knowledge of what makes them tick, and uses this to win support. . . . His faith in his intuition makes him too independent to be a conformist. . . . At its best, his insight, tempered by judgment, may amount to wisdom. His trouble is that he hates uninspired routine. . . . Worse yet, even his projects begin to seem routine and lose their attraction as soon as he has solved the problems. . . . He may discipline himself to carry through, but he is happiest and most effective in jobs that permit of one project after another, with somebody else taking over as soon as the situation is well in hand. . . . May be an inspired and inspiring teacher, scientist, artist, advertising man, salesman, or almost anything it interests him to be. [p. 12].

I can recognize myself in this rather flattering description. The only problem is that I can also recognize myself in most other descriptions of types. For example, I was born January 21; this places me under the astrological sun sign of Aquarius. A recent book on astrology [9] describes Aquarian men as follows:

An Aquarian man doesn't want to reveal his true feelings, in spite of his favorite pastime of penetrating the feelings of others. His own reactions and motives are complex, and he intends to keep them that way for the pure pleasure of fooling you . . . [p. 404]. . . . Aquarius understands the fair play rules of sports as if he had invented them, and he carries these rules into his personal relationships. His interests are scattered all over the place. . . . Aquarians can't stand to be called narrow-minded. He responds to unusually high ideals, thanks to his rigid moral code (though you'd better understand that it's his own code, which may not necessarily reflect or correspond to the one accepted by society in general). He'll almost surely lead a life of change, controversy, and unexpected events. . . . When he senses something is hidden, he just won't sleep at night until he's unravelled the mystery and penetrated the veil. . . . [p. 405].

Healthy Personality: An Approach from the Viewpoint of Humanistic Psychology

There's always an excellent possibility that an Aquarian will achieve some sort of prestige during his lifetime.

. . . Aquarians don't take to marriage like a baby takes to candy . . . [p. 407]. He will rarely, if ever, be physically unfaithful himself, mostly because the whole subject of sex, though it's interesting, doesn't consume him. . . . There may be times when you don't know where he is. . . . Don't be hurt when he's in one of his solitary moods and prefers to be alone with his silent dreams. . . . His idea of a good wife and mother is quite simple: a woman who keeps at it almost constantly. . . . He's so full of interesting surprises himself you won't need soap operas, or women's magazines . . . to keep your mind and emotions challenged. . . .

Strangely, since he's so realistic about most things, the Aquarian will never forget his first love [p. 412].

The Myer-Briggs classification is based upon a person's agreement and disagreement with a substantial number of self-descriptive statements on a questionnaire. His responses are then categorized according to the kind of experiencing which they illustrate. It is not clear to me how such knowledge is useful. Indeed, I can see some harm arising if a person takes his type too seriously, and believes he is an "essence," a mechanism fated to function in some limited way.

The astrological typing grows out of a centuries-old tradition which maintains that one's character structure is somehow "set" by the constellation of the stars and planets at the moment of exit from the maternal womb. It would make more sense to me if the typing of character was based on the position of the stars at the instant the paternal sperm united with the mother's ovum. Although I do not know the ultimate validity of a horoscope, I do read the astrology columns in newspapers and magazines, and frequently find my life situation presented with what seems like uncanny accuracy. I do not, however, base any decisions on such astrological advice, preferring to take my chances with my own appraisal of the situation.

I mentioned the astrological system of typing to show the temptations, and the problems of placing credence in *any* system of personality types, including Jung's.

In any case, I have presented a glimpse of Jung's views of the structure of the human personality. The most singular and important characteristic about man, asserted Jung, was his capacity to *symbolize* his experience in dreams, myths, art, and folklore. Freud too noted man's capacity for symbolizing his existence through dreams, but Freud was more interested in the sexual content of the unconscious than was Jung. Jung saw the content of dreams as symbolic expressions of universal human themes—called archetypes—which represent possibilities of experience for the dreamer. Jung believed he saw the hints in dreams for the next stages of a person's growth toward fuller *self-realization.*

Self-realization, becoming an "individuated" person, required that a person become aware of repressed, "shadow" sides in his personality, and struggle to express these in his way of life. The motive for such self-discovery was suffering. Jung treated many people who sought his help because their lives had become stale. They didn't want help in overcoming childhood "hang-ups," which Freud's therapy seemed to focus on. Jung helped them to resume their growth. For Jung, healthy personality entails the endless struggle to transcend one's initial "socialization" (training to become a *socius,* a citizen) in order to discover and express one's own repressed possibilities of functioning. Integration of the capacities to think, feel, intuit, and sense is fostered by commitment to new purposes for existence. Thus, persons whose growth was adequate to enable them to marry, raise families, and achieve vocational success would arrive at an impasse in their growth, and suffer from it. Their attainment of healthier personality—self-realization —was fostered by relinquishing projects that had animated their youthful years and choosing new aims. The "human potentialities" movement in the United States owes a great deal to Jung's writing, whether the debt is acknowledged or not.

AN "UNARMORED" BODY AND HEALTHY PERSONALITY

Wilhelm Reich, originally a psychoanalyst, became more and more convinced that healthy personality was impossible so long as a person defended himself from the experience of vitality, sexuality, and other emotions by repression. Such repression produces muscular tension. He gave the name *muscular armor* to those groups of muscles which a person kept in chronic tension so as not to feel unwanted dimensions of his experience. One indication that a person was not living a chronically "armored" life was the capacity to experience a complete sexual climax in love-making. Reich referred to this as *orgastic potency,* and he regarded it as an important indicator of the attainment of maturity and healthy personality. One of the techniques of therapy Reich invented was called *vegetotherapy;* this involved physical handling of the patient's body in a diagnostic and therapeutic manner, instruction in breathing, and bodily stretching exercises designed to heighten a person's awareness of his muscular tensions—to help him be in his body in a less "armored" way.[10]

Alexander Lowen [11] adapted some of Reich's ideas and techniques and founded a school of therapy which he calls *bioenergetic analysis.* He observes a person's body, noting peculiarities of chronic tension and posture which are the outcome of the way he lives his life. For example, a person with chronically hunched shoulders, who breathes shallowly, may reveal thereby a sense of personal helplessness in a hostile world. Lowen uses many of Reich's techniques, and developed new ones which overcome devitalizing repression. He too has his patients do certain stretching exercises to identify areas of tension; but he also encourages them to yell, and to beat a pillow or mattress with a tennis racquet, or fists and feet, to release tension. Lowen believes that healthy personality calls for the ability to breathe fully, to move freely, and to express one's emotions adequately. "Unarmoring" a person frees him from the repressions that protect him from pain but also destroy his capacity for pleasure.

EXPERIENCING THE HERE AND NOW:
THE PERSPECTIVE OF GESTALT THERAPY

Fritz Perls [12] was a German-born psychiatrist who was prescient enough to leave Germany before the Nazi takeover. He settled in the United States after a sojourn of several years in South Africa. He developed a theory of man in wellness and neurosis—called Gestalt therapy—which combined diverse traditions. He had a firm grounding in psychoanalysis and also in Gestalt psychology (the study of the meaningful patterns in man's experience). Beyond this, he had an interest in theater, in existential and phenomenological philosophy, and in Zen Buddhism. His view was that the average man comes to fear living and experiencing the "here-and-now." Rather, he tends to live mainly in the past, through obsessive remembering, and in the future, through anxious expectations of catastrophe. He is chronically self-conscious and dreads spontaneous action. The average person experiences himself as dependent and helpless; he turns to others for support, and becomes angry when they do not live up to expectations. The healthier personality struggles to emancipate himself from morbidly dependent relationships with others, and is capable of direct awareness of his perceptions and feelings rather than engaging chronically in abstract thinking, in recall, or in wishful or anxious imagination. He can trust himself to be spontaneous in action. Perls summed up the aim of his therapy in the "Gestalt prayer":

I do my thing, and you do your thing.
I am not in this world to live up to your expectations.
And you are not in this world to live up to mine.
You are you and I am I.
And if by chance we find each other, it's beautiful.
If not, it can't be helped.

Like Freud and Jung, Perls devoted much attention to his patients' dreams. He would ask them to act out all the parts of the dream during the therapy session; the idea was that every aspect of a dream represents some dimensions of a person's experience, much of which is disowned by him. By identifying with the different parts of the dream, the person could broaden his self-awareness, which, in turn, would increase his sense of vitality and foster continuing personal growth.

Perls' emphasis on the importance of immediate perceptual and emotional experience as factors in healthy personality growth is a wholesome corrective to views of healthy personality which emphasize the past and the future. His attention to the importance of self-sufficiency, of standing on one's own two feet rather than relying on others for

Healthy Personality: An Approach from the Viewpoint of Humanistic Psychology

one's security is reminiscent of Blatz's views (see p. 16), though these two men did not know one another.

ERIC BERNE: TRANSACTIONAL ANALYSIS AND THE GAMES PEOPLE PLAY

The late Eric Berne [13] wrote a book which became a best-seller, called *The Games People Play*. Like most of the other men whose work is discussed in this chapter, Berne was a psychiatrist. He developed an approach to psychotherapy which he called *transactional analysis*. According to Berne, people suffer in adult life because they will not grow to adulthood, but insist upon struggling, sometimes with ingenious cunning and subterfuge, to get other people to cater to their needs and wishes the way they wanted their parents to serve them during infancy. The sneaky ways in which persons strive to thus exploit others were documented in sometimes hilarious ways in the *Games* book. Thus, an adult might play the game of "wooden leg"—asking for deference from others, and seeking to justify failures, by calling attention to real or imagined handicaps: "I could have been more successful in my career if my stomach hadn't been hurting me all those years."

Berne was influenced by Alfred Adler and also by Stephen Potter, the English humorist who wrote those delightful books *Gamesmanship—The Art of Winning Games Without Cheating* and *Lifemanship, or How to Be a Success in Life Though Mediocre*. Berne believed that healthy personality consisted of affirming one's personal worth ("I'm OK"), making reasonable demands upon others as befits an adult, and simple honesty in one's dealings with others—living a relatively "game-free" existence.

HEALTHY PERSONALITY: AN EXISTENTIAL VIEW [14]

The existential philosophers—Kierkegaard and Nietzsche in the nineteenth century and Heidegger, Marcel, Sartre, Tillich, and Buber in the twentieth, to name the more important among them—wrote about the implications of freedom for the human condition; their writings have commanded increased attention from psychologists and psychiatrists.

According to existential writers, man alone has the capacity to choose his behavior and hence to shape his "essence,"

What Is Healthy Personality?

13

that is, his observable characteristics, at any point in time. The healthy adult personality takes responsibility for his actions, makes decisions, and seeks to transcend the determining, limiting effects on his behavior of handicaps, social pressures to conformity, extreme stress, and biological impulses and feelings. He becomes aware of the pressures these impersonal forces impose on his action, but he *chooses* whether or not he will yield to them or oppose them. Only man can thus choose, and hence make himself.

The healthy personality displays "courage to be." This term implies knowing and disclosing one's feelings and beliefs, and taking the consequences which follow from such assertion. It implies freedom to choose between hiding or faking one's real self and letting others know one as one is.

Healthy personality means regarding oneself as a *person,* as free and responsible, not as a will-less instrument of impulses or the expectations of other people. In dealing with other people, a healthy personality treats them as persons too, like himself, rather than as objects or tools. As Buber puts it, he lives in dialogue with his fellow men in a relationship of "I and thou" rather than between I and "it," "him," or "her."

The healthy personality becomes aware of his finitude and sees his life and what he makes of it as *his own responsibility,* not the responsibility of others. A person becomes most keenly aware of his time-bound existence when he squarely faces the fact that he will die someday.

From the existential point of view, average people and the mentally ill both suffer some degree of estrangement from their own being, from nature, and from their fellow men. They find the responsibility of freedom too frightening, and so they let their lives be lived for them by impulses or by social pressures to conformity. In the process, they lose their selves.

Viktor Frankl,[15] an existentially oriented psychiatrist, shows many of these themes in his writings about logotherapy, a term he uses to emphasize man's basic need for *meaning* in his life. Frankl sees man as free and as responsible for the fulfillment of values and meaning in existence. Life is to be lived, and each man is called upon to fulfill *creative* values, through productive work; *experiential* values, through enjoying the beauties and pleasures that can

Healthy Personality: An Approach from the Viewpoint of Humanistic Psychology

be sought and found in life; and, finally, when creative and experiential values are not to be found—when a person is lying in his death bed, or he has been condemned to live and die in a concentration camp—*attitudinal* values. He is responsible at these times for giving his unique meaning to his suffering and death. Frankl forged his existential psychiatry during more than seven years in Hitler's death camps during World War II, and is himself living testimony to the life-giving importance of a firm sense of meaning in life. He coined the term *noögenic neurosis* to describe neurotic suffering arising from a loss in the sense of meaning in life (akin in meaning to dispiritedness and to Kierkegaard's concept of despair). Logotherapy is a kind of psychotherapy which aims to help a person find enlivening meanings when older meanings have lost their validity.

ALBERT ELLIS AND RATIONAL THINKING

Albert Ellis [16] developed an approach to psychotherapy which he calls *rational–emotive therapy,* to highlight the fact that he is concerned with feelings, but no less concerned with sensible *thinking* about life problems. He regards neurotically disturbed people as individuals who talk nonsense to themselves, who refrain from vital living because they dread catastrophic consequences for ordinary self-assertiveness. They do not think clearly, and they do not check the validity of their thinking. For example, a painfully shy and lonely person may be saying to himself, "I would like to ask that girl for a date, but she might refuse me, and that would be awful." Dr. Ellis might reply to this patient, "Well, suppose she does refuse you, what's so terrible about that? You are 'awful-izing,' and that interferes with life." By virtue of such arguments with a patient's excuses for diminished living, and for not changing self-defeating patterns, Ellis is often able to convince him to try ways to live that generate satisfaction and growth. Ellis provides a wholesome reminder that, although excessive thinking can paralyze a life of feeling and action, wrong thinking can paralyze life itself.

JURGEN RUESCH: EFFECTIVE COMMUNICATION

Ruesch,[17] a contemporary psychiatrist, proposed that competence at communication is an indicator of the health of personality. He regards the mentally ill as persons who are deficient in some of the skills essential to full communication with others, for example, ability to transmit "messages" (thoughts and feelings), perceive messages, or decode (i.e., understand the meaning of) them. Healthy personality, from this point of view, entails mastery of the many problems involved in communication with others.

Ruesch's emphasis on the importance of communication for health represents a valuable synthesis of psychiatric concepts with concepts derived from communication-engineering theory and practice. By calling attention to the crucial role played by communication in the attainment and maintenance of healthy personality, Ruesch opened the way to numerous important researches. Moreover, as we shall see later (pp. 222–225), his work shows how dread of communicating certain aspects of one's experience to others can seriously impair health, whereas frank and free communication makes possible the fulfillment of love and growth.

BLATZ: INDEPENDENT SECURITY

The late Professor William Blatz [18] founded the Institute of Child Study at the University of Toronto. He developed a theory of security which illumines the study of healthy personality. The theory grew out of his observation of the way children grow, and the way adults hinder or help the process. According to Blatz, human beings are born with basic needs which he called "appetites." These include hunger, thirst, elimination, rest, change, and sex. When any of these appetites are deprived, or when a child encounters some problem, he is said to be in a state of *insecurity*. Such insecurity is natural for a man; it cannot be avoided. When confronted by insecurity, a person can seek to overcome it in a dependent way, by appealing to others to intervene in his behalf. *Dependent security* is achieved when a person has been able to assure himself that the persons upon whom he relies to gratify his needs and to make his decisions are always available, and willing to act in his service.

More desirable, from the standpoint of growth toward maturity, is the quest for *independent security*. This entails learning a new skill, in order to gratify the need or to

Healthy Personality: An Approach from the Viewpoint of Humanistic Psychology

solve the problem by oneself. Independent security is a person's growing edge—as he encounters dilemmas throughout life, he augments his independent security if he attacks his problems by learning a new skill.

Blatz did not make a fetish out of self-reliance, however. He recognized that no human being can face life without help and affection from other people. He emphasized independent security as a goal, to guide the efforts of parents and teachers as they strove to influence a child's growth in wholesome ways. He drew a distinction between *immature* dependent security, which is shown by persons who retain infantile patterns of dependency upon parents, or parent substitutes and authority figures, throughout life. *Mature* dependent security is shown in relationships of mutual love, where each person relies upon the other to provide for those needs which can never be gratified in solitude or without help, for example, sexual love and satisfying companionship.

A person can deal with the pain of insecurity by resorting to defense mechanisms such as repression and rationalization. These ways of coping with distress do not promote growth, because they do nothing to enhance a person's competence, and they insure he will be vulnerable to the same problems indefinitely.

These patterns, of independent security, mature and immature dependent security, and the false security based on defense mechanisms, are manifested in the major realms of life. These realms include vocational life, one's avocations or leisure pursuits, one's relationships with other people, inside and outside the family, and one's philosophy of life. Thus, a person might display independent security in connection with his work, mature dependent security in his relationships with members of his family, immature dependent security in his use of leisure time, and insecurity with regard to his religion or philosophy of life.

To Blatz, independent security means,

. . . the state of consciousness which accompanies a willingness to accept the consequences of one's own decisions and actions. . . . (It) can be attained in only one way— by the acquisition of skill through learning. Whenever an individual is presented with a situation for which he is inadequately prepared . . . he must make one of two choices—he must either retreat or attack. . . . The individual must, if he is to attack, emerge from the state of dependent security and accept the state of insecurity. This attack will, of course, result in learning. . . . The individual learns that satisfaction results from overcoming the apprehension and anxiety experienced when insecure, and that he may thus reach a state of independent security through learning. [pp. 165–168.]

The continuous acquisition of skills that leads to independent security also builds the self-confidence which makes a person willing to face the unknown, and to face conflicts in a decisive way. Willingness to make decisions and to act upon them is the subjective side of independent security.

Blatz' emphasis on the importance of skills is a valid reminder of a increasing threat to healthy personality—that posed by technology. The more that people rely on machinery, electronic devices, and other apparatus, the more dependent they come to be on that very machinery. In fact, Marshall McLuhan [19] has pointed out that reliance on media, "the extensions of man," robs man of the very powers that are embodied in the gadgets. Periodic excursions to the wilderness, with training in survival skills, is a wholesome corrective to the skill-depleting way of life that is the lot of most people who live in cities. Fritz Perls' emphasis upon self-reliance is also foreshadowed in Blatz' work. Blatz' ideas are drawn upon in our discussion of work and play, and religion (see Chapters 13, 14).

LIBERATION: THE ZEN BUDDHIST VERSION
OF HEALTHY PERSONALITY

The quest for health and happiness has existed as long as man has been able to reflect upon his condition. In the East, Hindu, Buddhist, and Taoist monks and philosophers concerned themselves many centuries ago with the problem of how man could liberate himself from cramping habits to attain a happier, freer existence. Some of those who attained liberation and enlightenment became teachers, seeking to help others attain the same degree of emancipation from stifling life styles. Alan Watts,[20] a present-day philosopher, devoted years to the study of Eastern philoso-

Healthy Personality: An Approach from the Viewpoint of Humanistic Psychology

phies and religions; in a series of readable books, he interpreted the major teachings of ancient Eastern philosophers to Western audiences. He saw a parallel between the goal of liberation, which Buddhist monks offer their disciples, and the goal of healthy personality, which psychotherapists offer their disturbed patients. Further, he saw parallels between the various techniques employed by Eastern *gurus* (spiritual teachers) to elicit "enlightenment" and modern techniques of therapy practiced by present-day psychiatrists and psychologists. Finally, he noticed parallels between the state of enlightenment and the state of healthy personality.

According to Watts, the Zen Buddhists explain neurotic suffering as an outcome of separating oneself too radically from nature, one's fellow man, and one's own organism. The average person equates his very identity with a concept of himself *instead of with his whole being.* In the process of so separating himself from nature, his fellows, and his organism, he loses contact with the "flow" or "process" of life, which is essentially spontaneous. Man replaces spontaneity in his experience, thinking, and behavior with efforts to *make* them happen. Liberation (and, by implication, healthy personality) occurs when a person is able to adopt the attitude of "letting be," or "letting happen." That is, he "lets go" his conscious, controlling ego, or self, and experiences life in somewhat the following fashion: Instead of experiencing vision as "I am looking at the tree," he experiences it as "looking at the tree is happening." Instead of a person's "trying" to swim, "liberated" swimming is experienced as "Swimming is permitted to happen" or "Swimming is going on." When a person *stops trying* to make things happen, when he stops trying to *make* himself behave in some desired way, it is argued that the desired events or behavior will spontaneously happen.

In the Zen Buddhist view, healthy personality entails liberation from effortful constraint on, and control over, spontaneous thinking, feeling, and action; it entails attainment of an attitude of "letting oneself be" and letting others and nature "be."

A BEHAVIORISTIC VIEW OF HEALTHY PERSONALITY

Behaviorism has enjoyed a renaissance in the past decade, largely through the influence of B. F. Skinner,[21] the Harvard psychologist, and Joseph Wolpe,[22] a South African psychiatrist now residing in the United States. Skinner developed his views of man as an organism subject to laws of "operant conditioning" over a period of nearly forty years. He began his work with studies of rats in "Skinner boxes," and extended it to research in the "shaping" of pigeon's behavior. At present, he and his fellow behaviorists have developed sophisticated techniques for influencing behavior of persons as well as animals.

The behaviorists try to explain human activity without recourse to terms referring to consciousness, such as *reward* or *satisfaction*. Instead, they invoke a circular argument, stating that behavior is "shaped" (into skills, or patterned habits) by "reinforcers." A "reinforcer" is any consequence to action which "strengthens," that is, increases the probability of the recurrence of, a response. To an observer who is not a behaviorist, the "reinforcing stimulus" may look suspiciously like a reward or a pleasant experience; the behaviorist prefers to eschew such subjectivistic terms.

Skinner and his followers have been consulted by officials concerned with the management of prisoners' behavior in prisons and the behavior of patients in mental hospitals, and by administrators of school systems who wish to make teaching and learning more efficient. There is considerable controversy between humanistic and behavioristic psychologists about the issue of behavior control, and the student should become familiar with the points of debate.

Skinner described a utopia, *Walden Two,* organized along lines growing out of his view of man. It is a society where the "reinforcers"—the good things in life—are sensibly made contingent upon action that is socially useful or harmless.

Healthy personality according to a behavioristic view calls for competence and self-control—the ability to suppress action which no longer yields "positive reinforcers," and to learn action that is successful in attaining the good things. Such rapid adaptability is mediated by the ability to discern the "contingencies," or rules implicit in nature or in society, according to which needs are gratified and dangers averted.

I have always been uneasy about the behavioristic approach to man, because it appeals to the power motive in

Healthy Personality: An Approach from the Viewpoint of Humanistic Psychology

the behavior scientist. Moreover, research in behaviorism is frequently funded by agencies interested in controlling the behavior and experience of others, not necessarily with their knowledge or consent nor always with the best interest of the controllees at heart (see Chapter 16).

PSYCHOSYNTHESIS AND HEALTHY PERSONALITY

Roberto Assagioli,[23] an Italian psychiatrist, developed a theory of healthy personality and a set of techniques for fostering this goal, which he named *psychosynthesis*. He combined contributions to the study of man that were made in psychosomatic medicine, psychology of religion, study of higher modes of consciousness, parapsychology, Eastern philosophy, personality theory, anthropology, and, finally, active techniques for fostering personality growth.

His theory of personality structure states that man's being comprises seven levels, or modes, of functioning:

1. The *lower unconscious*, which includes drives and urges, repressed feelings, and the like (similar in meaning to the id, in Freud's writing).

2. The *middle unconscious*, which comprises the background of our ordinary waking consciousness—similar to Freud's preconscious, or to the "background" of awareness described by Gestalt psychologists.

3. The *superconscious*, which Assagioli states is the source of "higher" feelings, such as altruistic love, and higher inspirations and intuitions, which give rise to truly creative works.

4. The *field of consciousness*, which designates our ordinary awareness of perceptions, memories, feelings, and urges.

5. The *conscious self*, or "I," designates a "point of pure self-awareness" independent of the content of one's awareness. The self, or "I," he claims, is an enduring center in our consciousness, similar to a light illuminating the objects that are seen.

6. The *higher self*, of which we are generally unconscious, which transcends the "I," our conscious self. This higher self seems to stand for the possibility of more fully developed experiencing and acting.

7. The *collective unconscious*, a term which Assagioli

borrowed from Jung, refers to the beliefs, assumptions, traditions, myths, and symbols which form a source for and background to a person's ordinary consciousness, a source he shares with the other members of his society.

Assagioli's conception of personality structure is illustrated by a diagram:

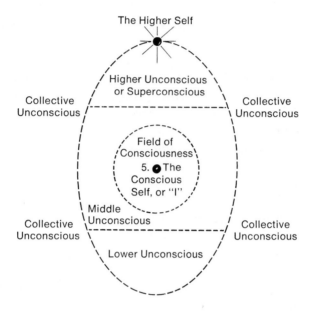

Assagioli views ordinary men as

limited and bound in a thousand ways—the prey of illusions and phantasms, the slaves of unrecognized complexes, tossed hither and thither by external influences, blinded and hypnotized by deceiving appearances. No wonder, then, that man, in such a state, is often disconcerted, insecure, and changeable in his moods, thoughts, and actions. Feeling intuitively that he is "one," and yet finding that he is "divided unto himself," he is bewildered, and fails to understand either himself or others [p. 20].

The task for man, says Assagioli, is to free himself from enslavement by ignorance and unconsciousness, to attain a "harmonious inner integration, true Self-realization, and right relationships with others." The goal of such integration—true psychosynthesis—is achieved in four stages:

Healthy Personality: An Approach from the Viewpoint of Humanistic Psychology

1. Thorough knowledge of one's personality, as can be achieved through self-study or, better, through a relationship with a teacher or therapist.

2. Control of the various elements of personality. This is achieved by a technique called disidentification. Assagioli states, "We are dominated by everything with which our self becomes identified. We can dominate and control everything from which we dis-identify" (p. 22). Thus, a person who might say "I am depressed" is saying, in effect, that depression identifies him.

If he views the mood of depression as an invitation to stay depressed, or as an attack, he disidentifies his self from the force of feeling, and he can decline the invitation and fight off his depression.

New energies are released by discovery of one's make-up and freedom from control by urges and feelings. Progress toward psychosynthesis is furthered by the next stage:

3. Realization of one's true self, the discovery or creation of a unifying center. This stage entails the quest for the best, most fully functioning person that one can be through commitment to a worthwhile mission.

4. Psychosynthesis, the formation or reconstruction of the personality around the new center. This phase calls for commitment, study, struggle, and action to actualize the mission and, thereby, the image of the best possible self.

A. H. MASLOW: SELF-ACTUALIZING PEOPLE

A. H. Maslow [24] devoted his life to studying the conditions under which man develops his human capacities to their fullest degree. He believed the key to such development was gratification of basic needs. These needs exist in a hierarchical sequence. Man must meet the demands of his lower needs before those of the higher levels can emerge. This hierarchy, from lowest to highest, includes *physical* needs, such as the need for food and water; *safety* needs, illustrated by the quest for a milieu relatively free from threats to life and fostering a sense of security; *belonging and love* needs, illustrated by the hunger for affectionate, accepting relationships with other persons; *esteem* needs, manifested in the desire to be respected by others for one's accomplishments and in the quest for recognition and prestige. Once a person has successfully learned to cope with

What
Is
Healthy
Personality?

these needs as they arise, his energies will then be more readily freed for *self-actualization*. Actualization of self cannot be sought as a goal in its own right, however; rather, it is a by-product of active commitment of one's talents to causes outside the self, such as the quest for beauty, truth, or justice. Without some such mission in life, a person is likely to experience boredom and a sense of stultification. Once he finds a purpose (or purposes), he can then dedicate his energies and talents to its fulfillment. As he meets the challenges he will encounter, his growth or actualization will be fostered as a by-product of his quest. The task awakens the person's dormant capacities; without the mission, the person would never discover his hidden resources.

Maslow developed his ideas through the study of people who met his criteria for being well along in the process of actualizing themselves. Some of the traits that appeared consistently in his self-actualizing (S-A) cases were the following:

1. *A more adequate perception of reality and more comfortable relations with reality than occur in average people.* His S-A cases seemed to detect the spurious, the fake, and the dishonest in interpersonal relationship and to be attuned to truth and reality in all spheres of life. They eschewed the illusory and preferred to cope with even unpleasant reality rather than retreat to pleasant fantasies.

2. *A high degree of acceptance of themselves, of others, and of the realities of human nature.* They were not ashamed of being what they were, and they were not shocked or dismayed to find shortcomings in themselves or in others.

3. *Spontaneity.* The S-A people displayed spontaneity in their thinking, emotions, and behavior to a greater extent than average people.

4. *Problem-centeredness.* Maslow's subjects seemed all to be focused on problems *outside* themselves. They were not overly self-conscious; they were not problems *to* themselves, and could hence devote their attention to a task, duty, or mission that seemed peculiarly cut out for them.

5. *A need for privacy.* The S-A people could enjoy solitude; indeed, they would even seek it on occasion, needing it for periods of intense concentration on subjects of interest to them, and for meditation.

6. *A high degree of autonomy.* The S-A people seemed

able to remain true to themselves in the face of rejection or unpopularity; they were able to pursue their interests and projects and maintain their integrity even when it hurt to do so.

7. *A continued freshness of appreciation.* The S-A people showed the capacity to "appreciate again and again, freshly and naively, the basic goods of life . . . a sunset, a flower, a baby, a person"; it was as if they avoided merely lumping experiences into categories and then dismissing them. Rather, they could see the unique in many commonplace experiences.

8. *Frequent "mystic experiences."* The S-A people seemed subject to periodic experiences that are often called "mystic" or "oceanic"—feelings that one's boundaries as a person have suddenly evaporated and one has truly become a part of all mankind and even of all nature.

9. *Gemeinschaftsgefühl.* The German word *gemeinschaftsgefühl* means brotherly feeling, the feeling of belonging to all mankind (related to the mystic experiences above); the attitude was found to be characteristic of S-A people. They felt a sense of identification with mankind as a whole, such that they could become concerned not only with the lot of members of their immediate family, but also with the situation of persons from different cultures.

10. *Close relationships with a few friends or loved ones.* Maslow found that his S-A subjects, although not necessarily very popular, did have the capacity to establish truly close, loving relationships with at least one or two other people.

11. *Democratic character structures.* The S-A people tended to judge people and be friendly with them not on the basis of race, status, religion, or other group membership traits, but as individual persons.

12. *A strong ethical sense.* The S-A subjects were found to have a highly developed sense of ethics. Though their notions of right and wrong were not wholly conventional, their behavior was always chosen with reference to its ethical meaning.

13. *Unhostile senses of humor.* The S-A people had senses of humor which made common human foibles, pretensions, and foolishness the subject of laughter, rather than sadism, smut, or rebellion against authority.

14. *Creativeness.* The S-A people were creative and inventive in some areas of their existence, not followers of the usual ways of doing or thinking.

15. *Resistance to enculturation.* The S-A subjects could detach themselves somewhat from complete brainwashing or imprinting by their cultures, permitting them to adopt critical attitudes toward cultural inconsistencies or unfairness within their own society.

Truly, this is a most impressive collection of attributes. One would like to meet or to become such a person. Maslow's portrait of self-actualization is presented last because it clearly shows the influence of several of the earlier portrayals. Maslow continuously pondered what man might become, in the hope of learning how more of us might grow toward those seemingly Utopian levels of being. In a sense, this book is devoted to further exploration of paths to self-actualization.

Lethal Personality: The Generation of Death

Throughout this chapter we have explored some views of man at his best, in his most life-giving possibilities. That is what healthy personality has to be; it must enhance life, not only in the person himself, but also in other persons, and in the animals, plants, and fishes in the midst of which he lives. Look at the living beings which surround a person. Do these beings flourish as a consequence of contact with him? Or does the person leave a swath of diminished functioning and death in his wake?

Because man is human and the embodiment of untold possibilities, we must consider his capacity for murder and genocide. He also can destroy the conditions of life for the generations that follow. The Nazi regime in Germany produced specialists at murder by the hundred thousands. The S.S. men, for example, ran concentration camps within which millions of human beings were gassed and then cremated. The Nazis showed extraordinary talent for resocializing the people of a country thought to be civilized. The student may try to imagine how he would go about training someone to repress his feelings of brotherliness toward fellow human beings so that he could dispatch them with less emotional concern than he would feel gassing cockroaches.

Rudolf Hoess' autobiography, *Commandant of Auschwitz,* shows that training for evil can masquerade as patriotic duty.[25]

The Concepts of Healthy Personality: An Overview and Prospectus

The student may experience himself as "average," or even "sick," in the light of the preceding discussion. There seems little doubt that it is worthwhile to be self-actualizing, a rational thinker, living in the here and how, capable of effective communication, creative, an integrated self living in dialogue with others, with an unarmored body, and so on. How does one go about changing in such splendid ways?

All these views illustrate man's conviction that he can grow beyond mere conformity to the social roles to which he is trained. New institutions of learning and healing have emerged in the past decade which aim to promote a person's education and training beyond the point where a typical upbringing has brought him. There are now "growth centers" where people can go to learn greater autonomy, creativity, and authenticity. The first of these—Esalen Institute —was founded in 1962 at Big Sur in California. Since then more than two hundred have sprung up in the United States and the rest of the world.[26]

What, then, might healthy personality be? How can we recognize it in ourselves and in others? Do the characteristics of healthy personality differ at various age levels? Between the sexes? In different social classes and different cultures? Is healthy personality more than "adjustment" to the norms of one's society? Are there criteria for healthy personality that transcend conformity to the status quo? How can we ascertain whether a family, a work setting, a religious ideology, or an entire society with its culture is good for human beings and other forms of life? [27]

These questions are not merely rhetorical or academic. We are living in an age where the population is increasing to the point where the earth may not support life. Human beings have destroyed each other by the hundreds of millions, sometimes praying to the same God, through the same clergy, for guidance as to more effective ways to do this. White men of the West have, in the name of economic de-

What Is Healthy Personality?

27

velopment, destroyed entire civilizations, animal species, and the soil, water, and air, making life an uncertainty for the generations that follow, and of dubious quality for those now living.

It is difficult, if not impossible, to give a succinct definition of healthy personality. This entire book is given over to the effort at such definition. Nevertheless, for purposes of orientation I offer this as a preliminary effort: Healthy personality is a way for a person to act, guided by intelligence and respect for life, so that his needs are satisfied and he will grow in awareness, competence, and the capacity for love.

Some Existential Suggestions

A useful exercise at this point is for the reader to ask, "What do I think my best possibilities are? To what extent do I approximate these conceptions of healthy personality? What changes might I make in my life in order to grow more in the direction of my better possibilities? What do I believe is preventing me from further growth?"

I suggest this because it is now apparent that what a person believes to be his strengths, weaknesses, and limits are self-fulfilling prophecies. If someone is convinced that he has reached his limits, then he will struggle no more. If he believes there is no end to his limits, he may keep struggling.

At the end of each of the following chapters, a number of questions will be posed to help the reader apply the content of this book in ways that are conducive to growth toward healthier personality.

SUMMARY

Man has always striven for personal perfection. Throughout history, this quest has been religious in nature; the goal has been named salvation, redemption, liberation, enlightenment, and rebirth. Man only pursues what he believes is a possibility for him. Images of man do not merely describe man, they persuade him of what his possibilities for life and growth are.

In contemporary times, psychologists and psychiatrists have offered the authoritative views of man at his best, as guides to growth, to education, and to psychotherapy. Conceptions of healthy personality are abstracted from the work of Sigmund Freud; Alfred Adler; Otto Rank; Carl Jung; Wilhelm Reich and Alexander Lowen; Fritz Perls; Eric Berne; an existentialist view adapted from the writings of Kierkegaard, Nietzsche, Marcel, Sartre, Tillich, Buber, and Viktor Frankl; Albert Ellis; Jurgen Ruesch; William Blatz; Zen Buddhist writings; writings of B. F. Skinner and Joseph Wolpe; Roberto Assagioli; and Abraham H. Maslow. These conceptions of man at his best all embody a different theory of the growth of personality, and of the factors responsible for unhealthy and healthy personal development.

Man may also become more expert at producing death as well as life, and the human capacity for murder, genocide, exploitation of his fellows, and the annihilation of the environment is discussed.

Growth centers have been founded where people who are not sick can go to explore further dimensions of their growth.

A preliminary definition portrayed healthy personality as a way for a person to act, guided by intelligence and respect for life, so that as his needs are satisfied he grows in awareness, competence, and the capacity for love.

NOTES AND REFERENCES

1. The study of man from the standpoint of humanistic psychology has gained momentum since 1962. This volume is written from that perspective. A good introduction to this point of view is provided by J. F. T. BUGENTAL (ED.), *Challenges of Humanistic Psychology* (New York: McGraw-Hill, 1967).

2. I presented this approach to illness in S. M. JOURARD, *The Transparent Self*, 2nd ed. (New York: Van Nostrand Reinhold, 1971), especially pp. 75–102.

3. A psychology of transcendence is presented in S. M. JOURARD, *Disclosing Man to Himself* (New York: Van Nostrand Reinhold, 1968), pp. 204–228.

4. Freud's view of personality development is summarized in S. FREUD, *An Outline of Psychoanalysis* (New York: Norton, 1949). The psychoanalytic conception of the "genital character" —the mature, healthy personality—is well presented in W. REICH, *Character Analysis* (New York: Orgone Institute Press, 1948), pp. 158–199, 254–280.

What Is Healthy Personality?

29

5. Adler's writings are well presented in H. L. Ansbacher, and Rowena R. Ansbacher (Eds.), *The Individual Psychology of Alfred Adler* (New York: Basic Books, 1956).

6. See O. Rank, *Art and the Artist* (New York: Agathon, 1932). A good exposition of Rank's ideas is in Fay B. Karpf, *The Psychology and Psychotherapy of Otto Rank* (New York: Philosophical Library, 1953).

7. Jung was a prodigious writer. A useful introduction to him is provided in Jolande Jacobi (Ed.), *Psychological Reflections: An Anthology from the Writings of C. G. Jung* (New York: Pantheon, 1953) and Violet de Laszlo (Ed.), *The Basic Writings of C. G. Jung* (New York: Random House, 1959). One should read his autobiography, C. G. Jung, *Memories, Dreams, Reflections* (New York: Pantheon, 1961).

8. Isabell Briggs-Myers, *Manual: The Myers-Briggs Type Indicator* (Princeton, N.J.: Educational Testing Service, 1962).

9. L. Goodman, *Linda Goodman's Sun Signs* (New York: Taplinger, 1971).

10. W. Reich, op. cit., especially Chapter 15.

11. A. Lowen, *The Betrayal of the Body* (New York: Macmillan, 1969), especially Chapter 12.

12. Perls presents his own ideas in most readable form in F. Perls, *Gestalt Therapy Verbatim* (Lafayette, Calif.: Real People Press, 1969). The prayer is from p. 4 of this volume.

13. E. Berne, *Games People Play* (New York: Grove, 1964). A popular account of the perspective of transactional analysis is given in T. A. Harris, *I'm Ok, You're Ok* (New York: Harper & Row, 1969).

14. For a review of the impact of existential philosophy on psychology, see R. May (Ed.), *Existential Psychology* (New York: Random House, 1961); see also P. Tillich, *The Courage to Be* (New Haven: Yale, 1959), and M. Buber, *Between Man and Man* (Boston: Beacon Press, 1955), pp. 19–24.

15. V. E. Frankl, *Man's Search for Meaning*, rev. ed. (Boston: Beacon Press, 1963).

16. A. Ellis, and R. A. Harper, *Guide to Rational Living* (Englewood Cliffs, N.J.: Prentice-Hall, 1961).

17. J. Ruesch, *Therapeutic Communication* (New York: Norton, 1961).

18. W. E. Blatz, *Understanding the Young Child* (New York: Morrow, 1944); also his posthumous book, *Human Security: Some Reflections* (Toronto: University of Toronto Press, 1966).

19. M. McLuhan, *Understanding Media: The Extensions of Man* (New York: McGraw-Hill, 1965), especially Chapter 4.

*Healthy
Personality:
An Approach
from the
Viewpoint of
Humanistic
Psychology*

20. See A. W. Watts, *Way of Zen* (New York: Pantheon, 1957); *Nature, Man and Woman* (New York: Pantheon, 1958), and *Psychotherapy East and West* (New York: Pantheon, 1961). See also E. Herrigel, *Zen* (New York: McGraw-Hill, 1964). Eastern psychologists have recently sought to integrate the wisdom of the East with Western psychology. The relation between Sufism and healthy personality is explored in A. R. Aresteh. *Final Integration in the Adult Personality* (Leiden, Netherlands: Brill, 1965).

21. B. F. Skinner, *Science and Human Behavior* (New York: Macmillan, 1953); *Beyond Freedom and Dignity* (New York: Knopf, 1971); *Walden Two* (New York: Macmillan, 1948). A sensible critique of behaviorism is given in P. London, *Behavior Control* (New York: Harper & Row, 1969). See also the classic debate C. R. Rogers and B. F. Skinner, *"Some Issues Concerning the Control of Human Behavior: A Symposium," Science*, 1956, Vol. 124, pp. 1037–1066.

22. J. Wolpe, *The Practice of Behavior Therapy* (New York: Pergamon, 1966).

23. R. Assagioli, *Psychosynthesis: A Manual of Principles and Techniques* (New York: Hobbs, Dorman, 1965).

24. A. H. Maslow, *Toward a Psychology of Being*, 2nd ed. (New York: Van Nostrand Reinhold, 1968).

25. R. Hoess, *Commandant of Auschwitz* (London: Weidenfeld & Nicolson, 1959). See also H. Hohne, *The Order of the Death's Head: The Story of Hitler's SS.* (New York: Coward-McCann & Geoghegan, 1970); and P. Neumann, *The Black March: The Personal Story of an SS Man* (New York: Bantam, 1960). For a perspective on the victims of Nazi "order" see J. Glatstein, I. Knox, and S. Margoshes, *Anthology of Holocaust Literature* (Philadelphia: Jewish Publication Society of America, 1969). Read the series of books by Elie Wiesel: E. Wiesel, *Night* (New York: Hill and Wang, 1960); E. Wiesel, *Dawn* (New York: Hill and Wang, 1961); E. Wiesel, *Legends of Our Times* (New York: Holt, Rinehart and Winston, 1968); E. Wiesel, *Accident* (New York: Hill and Wang, 1962). Wiesel tried to make human sense out of the experience of the "holocaust."

26. Jane Howard, *Please Touch* (New York: McGraw-Hill, 1970), gives a personal account of experiences at a growth center.

27. Marie Jahoda published a technical book representing an effort to define the important dimensions of "positive mental health." See Marie Jahoda, *Current Concepts of Positive Mental Health* (New York: Basic Books, 1958).

2

CONSCIOUSNESS AND HEALTHY PERSONALITY

INTRODUCTION

The capacity to experience the world in its richness, and in all available modes of consciousness, gives life its personal meaning. When a person's experiencing is diminished by any factor whatsoever, his life is thereby diminished. Healthy personality is dependent upon continuously expanding consciousness of self, other persons, and the world.

Some Properties of Human Consciousness

CONSCIOUSNESS IS "REFLECTIVE"

Several terms are used interchangeably in the following discussion: consciousness, experiencing, and awareness.[1] They all mean the same—man's unique capacity, not only to perceive, remember, think about, and imagine the world, in its many possibilities, but also to *reflect* upon his immediate way of being aware. Thus, you can engage in remembering the past; if someone asks, "What are you doing right now?" you can reply, "I am trying to remember something." You can tell the difference, through such reflection, between perceiving, remembering, and imagining. Indeed, loss of the capacity for such discriminating reflection, confusion of seeing with imagining, is one of the signs by which students of abnormal personality identify psychosis. The first property of human consciousness to which we call attention, then, is that it can be reflected on. Man is capable of being self-conscious as well as conscious of the world beyond himself.

CONSCIOUSNESS IS OF MEANINGFUL CONTENT

Philosophers who have studied human consciousness have spoken of the *intentionality* of human experiencing. This term does not refer to, for example, the intention to go to the theater or read a book. Rather, it refers to the assertion that human consciousness is always awareness *of something*. If we are not conscious of anything, then we are unconscious. If we are conscious, we are aware of something, and this something *has meaning for us*. We name it, think about it, remember it, imagine some of its possibilities, attribute reality to it, and have feelings about it.

CONSCIOUSNESS IS ORGANIZED INTO FIGURE AND BACKGROUND

The work of the Gestalt psychologists taught us that perception is organized into the focus of interest, which they designated as *figure,* and the *ground*—a term which describes the rest of the field of awareness and which affords a context or background for the figure. Although figure and ground are most clearly relevant to visual perception, the terms apply metaphorically to the other sensory fields of experience too. Thus, the meaningful words you hear someone utter are *figure* in the auditory field, whereas the sound of passing cars and shuffling feet are present as the *ground*.

THE AFFECTIVE QUALITY OF EXPERIENCING

Consciousness and Healthy Personality

Our experiencing is always of some meaningful content, such as a person's face, or the sound of his voice, or the recollection of his acts. This content stands forth as figure in one's

33

field of awareness. Another basic characteristic of experiencing is that it always has some emotional quality. Thus, my memory of my father is accompanied by feelings of warmth, nostalgia, and sometimes laughter as I recall some of his conversations. My perception of a lovely woman is accompanied by aesthetic and sensual feelings. "Unemotional" experiencing is an outcome of the repression of affect, and represents an effort on the part of the unemotional person to imitate a camera or tape recorder. (In Chapter 5, emotional experience is discussed in relation to emotional behavior.)

THE ATTRIBUTION OF REALITY TO OUR EXPERIENCING

One of the most fundamental distinctions we make about the content of our experiencing has to do with whether it is *really there*, whether we are perceiving something or only imagining it. Each person, and for that matter each society, is committed to a set of assumptions about what is real (what can be perceived) and what is unreal. Reality is what a person or group of persons take to be real.[2] In the last analysis, reality is an attribution, that is, an act or judgment performed by a person, imbuing some experience with the quality of a reality that must be reckoned with. By the same token, we can withdraw our attribution of reality from some experience, and view it as not real. Thus, a person may awaken from deep sleep with the conviction that someone is trying to harm him. Upon awakening he reflects upon this experience and says, with relief, "It is not real—no one is trying to harm me, I was only dreaming." On the other hand, he may experience himself as trapped in the coils of a dominating mother and believe she has more power to control his destiny than he has strength to oppose. He lives his life, then, according to her wishes, or what he believes her wishes would be. To an outsider, his estimate of his own strength in relation to hers seems unrealistic. But he lives according to what he takes to be the case, what he experiences as real. He attributes reality to his estimates of his strength in comparison with his experience of his mother's power.

People in some societies attribute reality to experiences of ghosts and spirits, and they experience plants, animals, and all of nature as having souls and personalities. The "real world," the world that is real for them, differs from that ex-

Healthy Personality: An Approach from the Viewpoint of Humanistic Psychology

perienced by the modern Westerner. He regards that world view as mere animism—the ghosts, spirits, and souls with which the "primitive" person lives in his daily life are figments of imagination to the sophisticated person of the modern world. For him, only what can be recorded upon instruments, such as cameras and sound recorders, are taken to be real.

CONSCIOUSNESS IS PERSPECTIVAL

No two persons occupy the same space, and so each has a different place from which to view the world. It follows that, if there are three billion human beings in the world, there are three billion ways for this world to be experienced, none more real or valid than another. If each person embodies a unique perspective, then it is a momentous thing indeed to invalidate or destroy it. This is one cruel feature of colonial exploitation, which destroyed the perspectives of black Africans, Australian aborigines, and American Indians. Women and blacks around the world have complained, legitimately, that their perspectives are currently ignored or invalidated by the dominant white male populations. With the advent of the various liberation movements, the neglected perspectives are revealed to the world, and an enriched existence accrues to all concerned. The growing interest of young people in the religion and the life styles of traditional peoples such as the American Indians and Africans, and in Hinduism and Zen Buddhism, is a quest for perspectives upon self and world which are experienced as more life-giving than the perspective of white, male, middle-class America.

Ronald Laing, whose writings will be noted in many places throughout this book, has a gift for felicitous expression. About perspectives, he says,[3]

> The human race is a myriad of refractive surfaces staining the white radiance of eternity. Each surface refracts the refractions of refractions of refractions. Each self refracts the refractions of others' refractions of self's refractions of others' refractions. . . . Here is glory and wonder and mystery, yet too often we wish to ignore or destroy those points of view that refract the light differently from our own [p. 3].

Laing published a provocative volume called *The Politics of Experience*,[4] the content of which is germane to the theme of this book. The politics of experience implies a contest to see whose perspectives will be recognized and confirmed as right, sane, and true, and whose will be invalidated. Thus, the mass media are devoted to establishing views of people, concepts of value, and ways to construe events that will serve the interests of some political or economic group. The censoring of literature and movies, the selection of which kinds of films and television productions will be shown, all illustrate the politics of experiencing in action. These mass media not only serve an informative and educational function, but function as a kind of rhetoric which persuades audiences how things *should* be seen. Laing points out how members of the psychotherapeutic professions can function as representatives of prevailing views of truth and reality; they are not agents for enlightenment and growth, but agents of social control, dismissing dissenting perspectives as "insane."

There is a sense in which even a conversation is a contest between the participants over the question of whose perspective will prevail. Views of what is real, what is important, and what is possible can be infectious. A person's perspective is vulnerable to being so altered, through contact with others, that his action no longer serves his own needs, but those of the other person. When this happens, he is said to be *mystified*.

DIVIDED AND UNIFIED EXPERIENCE: SELF-CONSCIOUSNESS AND SPONTANEITY

Eastern philosophers are fond of pointing out how Western man lives with a "divided" consciousness, experiencing a gulf between mind and body, between self and nature.

Divided consciousness is a chronic *self*-consciousness, such that the person is aware of himself at all times. Whether he is watching a sunset, making love, or playing a game of tennis, he is always aware of himself as the "subject" whereas that which he is noticing is experienced as the "object," as "out there," distant from the self. Even our language, with its grammatical structure, encourages us to enter a chronic

Healthy Personality: An Approach from the Viewpoint of Humanistic Psychology

state of self-consciousness, of reflection upon our experiencing. A child, before he has taken on language, apparently has the capacity to perceive in selfless fashion. Eventually, he learns to monitor his experience and action, because he knows he will be called on to give an account of what he has been thinking and doing. He is to become a spy or witness of his own action, and is to give a report to his parents, upon request.

As the child grows older, such self-vigilance becomes habitual, and the rift in consciousness which hinders spontaneity has been permanently inserted. When a happening fully absorbs his attention, the person may re-experience the long-lost mode of unreflective, unself-conscious perception. One of the attractions of alcohol and marijuana is that both drugs make one unself-conscious, so that one can speak, act, listen, see, remember, and feel, without the experience of being a witness at the same time one is the agent.

This is a terrible way to live—always to be watching oneself. The capacity to be self-conscious is unique to man, because of the relative size of his cerebral cortex. Doubtless, the ability to observe the flow of one's experiencing has some adaptive and adjustive value. However, chronic self-consciousness is agonizing, and it destroys enjoyment of living; in extreme instances, self-consciousness can so handicap a person that he becomes unable to act at all, until he has first checked and rechecked his proposed action or communication. When self-consciousness is carried to this extreme, the individual may become nearly paralyzed by doubt and indecision, as in a pattern of neurosis called doubting compulsion.

Zen and Yoga were developed as means of healing the breach in consciousness. The purposes of Zen "sitting," of the disciplines of Hatha Yoga and transcendental meditation, are to help a person "transcend" his ego and experience a unification of himself with all that exists. When such enlightenment and unification occur, the person becomes more capable of effortless action, grace of movement, and power of reason, because he is not doing two things at once, that is, doing something and reflecting upon what he is doing. As the Zen aphorism puts it, "Sit when you sit, stand when you stand, don't wobble."

Thus, there is a similarity between the experiences of

samadhi among followers of Yoga, *satori* among Zen disciples, "rebirth" among followers of the Sufi way, and the "peak experiences" of which Maslow has written so extensively.[5] The experience of overcoming chronic fixation upon a self-conscious, reflective state of awareness, so that one begins to smell and taste, and remember and imagine with greater vividness, can easily be described as "an enlargment of the world," a rebirth, or a self-unification.

Reflection, or self-witnessing, helps a person learn skills. But once he has learned, he does not need to watch his performance any more. If a novice swimmer, or novice piano player, or psychotherapist in training continues to watch his technique, he will never reach heights of spontaneous, inspired action. Self-consciousness robs action of its spontaneity and of its joy. The aim of healthy personality is to be able to reflect upon experience when it is appropriate to do so, and to engage unself-consciously like a child in action, and in personal relationships, when there is no need to reflect.

Action is one way to obtain temporary respite from self-consciousness. Warm-up exercises, followed by intense involvement in a game of tennis or basketball, or in dance, enable a person to be engaged without reflection. Other means for temporarily suppressing the act of reflection include listening to music, engaging in hobbies, and absorption in a book or a drama. Dialogue with another person which fully engages one's attention is also a means of overcoming self-consciousness. When such dialogue is going on, each person is responding to the other without premeditated efforts to produce a particular impression of himself in the experience of the other.

Modes of Experiencing

We experience the world in a variety of ways, or modes, all of which are essential for the fullest personal functioning.[6] The most fundamental mode of experiencing is *perception*.

PERCEIVING THE WORLD

Our sense organs, like the radio with many stations, permit us to receive a many-faceted disclosure of the world.

With our eyes, we receive the impressions of things that are transmitted by light refraction. Our ears receive the sound of things, brought about by vibration. With our olfactory and taste receptors, we receive the scents and flavors emitted by things, and our touch receptors receive impressions produced by direct physical contact—texture, pressure, and pain. The state of our muscles and joints and the location of our arms, hands, legs, and feet are communicated to our reflective awareness by means of kinesthetic sense organs. Our position in relation to vertical posture is mediated by receptors located in the semicircular canal of our ears (equilibratory senses). Finally, the condition of our body—its comfort and discomfort, our fullness and emptiness, the need to eliminate—is detected and received by visceral receptors located in our stomach, intestines, and other hollow organs of the body.

What we perceive, and the sensory modalities by means of which we receive disclosure, depends on what is there, what we have been told is there, and also on our needs and projects of the moment. Generally speaking, the salient figure in our field of perception is always related to our immediate needs and goals. Everything else is blurred into the background of experiencing.

When we perceive, that is, receive the disclosure of, something, we always give it *meaning*. We name the objects and persons in the world, and make inferences about what the world is "promising" or "threatening" to do to us. We experience the world "inviting" us to do some things and not others, and to be in some way. Perception, whether visual, tactual, auditory, or visceral, is a kind of hearing. All our sense organs function in a way analogous to the hearing of speech. In a profound sense, we do not merely see the world, we read the world as we read a sign or a letter. Just as writing is a form of speech, so seeing something and calling it a car is analogous to the car saying, "I am a car, drive me." If all our sense organs are variable ways of hearing, then there is a sense in which our entire body functions as a voice, speaking our replies to the "voices" of the things and beings heard in the world. Our acts, seen by ourselves or by others, have meanings equivalent to speech. To kiss someone can be another way of saying, "I am fond of you," and it can mean "Hello" or "Good-bye."

The act of giving meaning to the perceived beings in our world is called *construing*.[7] As indicated earlier, construing is a kind of listening. We give the meanings to things in the world which our parents and teachers have given them. If mice are dangerous to our mothers, then we will hear mice say "Beware," metaphorically speaking, every time we see them. There is a sense, more than metaphorical, in which the world speaks with a voice, with warnings and invitations, that it was given by the significant teachers and exemplars in our lives. We live in the world as it was experienced and described to us by others. This fact makes it possible to speak of the world as a chorus of voices which threaten and promise, seduce and persuade; the world for man is not an environment which stimulates him to respond. Rather, the world speaks, invites, tempts, and threatens. Our action is our answer, and our action is thus more akin to speech than it is, say, to the conditioned responses of a dog or monkey. When Don Juan sought to "stop the world" for anthropologist Carlos Castañeda,[8] he was seeking to introduce him to another way for the world to be experienced than the conventional way to which he had been trained.

CONCEPTUALIZING: CONCEPTS, METAPHORS, AND ANALOGY

To conceptualize something is to fit it into a class. Such abstracting and classifying is essential in human existence, because it frees a person to act in service of his needs once he has classified what he has just perceived. If I classify that person over there as a woman, and a married woman at that, I act differently toward her than if I classify her as a spinster. When we conceptualize, however, we "close down" our perception, and no longer notice the continuing disclosure of the being in question. Once I identify someone as "Mother," I assume I know her, know what to expect of mothers in general and of mine in particular. In fact, concepts of persons and things inevitably get out of date, because every person and every thing is more than we presently believe to be the case; and everything changes in time. My mother today is not identical with my mother yesterday.

Poets and writers make use of metaphors, analogies, and symbols to express truths of experience that cannot be ex-

Healthy Personality: An Approach from the Viewpoint of Humanistic Psychology

pressed in more prosaic terms.[9] For example, how else can one describe the experience of being in the company of a very dependent person except to say, "He is a leech who sucks my blood every time he comes near." To say, "He is a leech," is not to classify him as would a zoologist, but it does point to a characteristic of his which is real. The ability to see such similarities between things, people, or actions and other phenomena that seem remote aids a person to enrich his understanding of the world. Metaphor and analogy are ways to foster insight in a person who is having difficulties in living; psychotherapists frequently interpret a patient's dilemmas in metaphoric and analogical ways, in the hope that the patient will be aided, thereby, to see his situation more clearly or in a new perspective. Thus, a patient might complain that he cannot give up his girl friend, even though she no longer wishes to see him; he suffers the tortures of the damned when he is not in her company, yet he only fights with her when they are together. The therapist might say, "You are addicted to her company the way an addict is to heroin. You have withdrawal symptoms." The patient might then discover that he can "kick" the habit of seeing his girl, and get on with a livable life.[10]

Metaphor is a way to make sense out of something new that appears within one's horizon. Novel phenomena may be frightening. To use metaphors, analogies, or symbols to describe them is to "tame" them, to note the similarity between something novel and something old and familiar. Metaphoric thinking is also a way to bring about "breakthroughs" in scientific fields of inquiry.[11] For example, the behaviorists say that man is an organism, like a dog or a beetle. They then proceed to study man with methods proven useful in the study and control of dogs. Actually, such description is a case of subtle use of metaphor, or more precisely, *analogy*. To say man is an animal conceals the fact that man is like an animal, but not entirely like one; he has some capacities which differ from those found in animals. To say that man is a machine is likewise to conceal the analogy that has been seen by the discerning inquirer. Man is not a machine, but he functions in ways which resemble machines, so that to understand a machine is to understand something about man. Scientists who have the capacity to employ new metaphors, similes, and analogies are frequently more creative in their fields of research and theory than those confined to only one model or metaphor.

REMEMBERING

Remembering past perceptions of the world is another way to experience it. As with conceptualizing, we close down the "gates of perception" when we experience the world recollectively. The capacity for vivid and relevant recall of the past is essential for effective action. Anything which hinders our ability to recall jeopardizes our access to healthy personality. We tend to recall schematically in the rush of a busy existence, searching the storehouse of our memory for ways to solve problems of living and to discern the meanings of things; but memory also serves a function of enriching the experience of life itself. When the immediate world of perception is grim and joyless, and there is nothing to be done to ameliorate it, vivid recollection of a happier past may enable a person to endure his present until circumstances change. Such eidetic recalling can, of course, also serve an escape function. Reminiscences of the past can prevent a person from addressing problems of the present with passion and energy.

THINKING

The act of disciplined thinking about one's world, in order to make sense of what has been going on and to solve problems, is another way of experiencing the world with the doors of perception temporarily shut. In fact, when people want to reason and argue with themselves in order to arrive at some conclusion, they seek quiet surroundings. Thinking in a disciplined way, according to rules of logic, is a skill which contributes to effective action. But we can think wishfully, and fearfully, too, when our needs and passions are aroused. Such *autistic* thinking may lead us to conclusions which conform to our feelings but misinform us about the way the world really is. Autistic thinking calls for reality testing—a way to review the argument the thinking embodies and to check the conclusions by means of fresh perception (see Chapter 3).

Compulsive thinking interferes with living; it blocks perception and inhibits effective action. Indeed, one of the

Healthy Personality: An Approach from the Viewpoint of Humanistic Psychology

42

functions of meditation is to "still" one's chattering mind. Such "stilling" is akin to learning how to discipline the act of speaking. Compulsive thinking is like compulsive talking; it does the person no good.

Disciplined thinking to solve a problem is illustrated as follows: the person speaks silently to himself, saying, "If I act in this way, it is likely to produce these consequences, whereas if I don't, the problem will persist." Whether or not this type of thinking will lead to effective action can then be tested. Autistic thinking is a kind of reverie where the person's talk to himself is deliberately allowed to proceed unchecked by the discipline of reason, and merges into imagination; for example, "I wish I had ten women in love with me at once, wouldn't that be grand?" and so on. Alienated thinking, or chatter, is very akin to being in the companying of a boring chatterbox who will not allow you to see, hear, or think as you wish because of his constant din of talk.

IMAGINING

When we imagine, we are envisioning possible ways for the world to be. Imagination is play with the possibilities of transforming the world from the way it is now perceived to be to some new form. Of course, it takes action to transform an image of a possible self in a possible world into an actuality which can be perceived by others and oneself. Imagination is a way of "traveling," of overcoming one's present situation, so as to envision possibilities which might make life more livable, more fulfilling. The free play of imagination, then, is the way in which we experience new possibilities for the world. It is one of man's most precious gifts of evolution, because it is only through such vision that man can save himself when his situation has become unlivable.

Anything which diminishes or banalizes our imagination chains us more tightly to a here-and-now which may not be viable. Every compelling goal and project, whether projected for five minutes or five years into the future, rests upon man's capacity to imagine another way for the world *Consciousness* to be, with him in it. Such a vision, of a transitional utopia, *and* may function as an irresistible temptation or invitation *Healthy* which the person may accept, showing his acceptance by his *Personality* action.

43

Just as imagination can enliven a person, ordering and directing his life, so it can demoralize him, even kill him. If a person imagines himself to be weak or helpless, it is but a short step from imagination to belief that such is the case. Healthy personality calls for the ability to discriminate among modes of experiencing. Under conditions of intense need or emotion, a person may confuse imagination with perception, and with confirmed truth. There is another aspect of imagining, or, literally, "image-ing," which when misunderstood can affect a person's body and his action in deleterious ways but which, appreciated, can serve the person's well-being and growth. When a person engages in imagining, he is doing so not just with his mind, but with his entire body. Indeed, the art of acting on the stage is a deliberate, imaginative imitation of some other person. One "becomes" the imagined person, acting and experiencing the world as the role requires. Being hypnotized is another kind of embodied imagination. The hypnotist tells his subject that he *is* tired, or strong, or that he can remember the past so well he will become three years old again, and the compliant subject "yields." He fulfills the hypnotist's suggestions by being as he imagines a tired or strong person is, and he acts as he imagines or remembers what it was like to be three years old.[12] One's body image is the way in which one chronically imagines his body to be, whether weak or strong, energetic or exhausted, vulnerable to disease or resistant. Fisher and Cleveland[13] were able to show that an image of one's own body as only weakly "bounded" was related to increased susceptibility to diseases and malfunction of the internal organs, such as stomach ulcers; an image of one's body as rigidly armored against the world—excessively so—was related to diseases of the skin, bones, and muscles, for example, arthritis.

I have been so impressed by the influence of imagination upon one's body and one's capacities to act that I say to my patients, "Be careful how you imagine yourself to be, because you might become that way." So-called psychocybernetics and positive thinking work in this way, as a kind of self-hypnosis or intense argument with oneself, by saying, "I can do this, I can survive, I can succeed," and believing the statement. This self-persuasion can affect a person in beneficial ways, just as imagining oneself as dead, or as failed, can bring the image of doom to reality.

Freud called dreams "the royal road to the unconscious." Recent research has shown that everyone dreams several times during each night. When people say they never dream, the probability is that they do not *recall* their dreams. We tend to recall dreams only when they have been especially intense or dramatic and when we have some special interest in recalling them.[14] Busy, extraverted people seldom pay attention to their dreams, and would find it a waste of time to write them down. Yet, increasingly, it is being found that recording one's dreams and thinking about them, seeking hints of new possibilities for personal growth, is an enterprise rewarded by new insight.

Dreaming is a way of being aware of the world, although, paradoxically enough, it is a kind of consciousness which "happens" when we are asleep, when our waking consciousness is suppressed. Laing believes that the dreaming consciousness is active, as a kind of underground or background to our waking consciousness.[15] He calls this underground mode of experiencing *fantasy*. Fantasy is a form of perception, a way to perceive the world by noting the effect one's situation is having upon one's body. Our vocabulary for describing bodily states is scant, and so we employ metaphors, symbols, and analogies to describe the way our situation and the people in it are affecting us. Thus, when a person says, "I have just been stabbed in the back," he is speaking metaphorically, but he is also talking about a real experience. If one says of another, "You turn me on," he may be speaking of an enlivening effect that the other person is inducing. These somatic metaphors are efforts to describe one's real condition as a human being. They are attempts to assess whether a relationship or a situation are enlivening, or whether they are devitalizing and debilitating. Fantasy and dreaming are, in a sense, guardians of one's existence, because the content of dreams and of somatic experiencing is always found to be related to one's survival, well-being, and growth. Gestalt therapists and followers of Jung and Freud have been able to help persons overcome

Consciousness and Healthy Personality

45

impasses in their lives through serious consideration of dreams.

Careful attention to the way one's body feels as one lives his life can also be useful for growth and well-being. One's body can function as did the canaries that miners used to take into the depths of a mine, where oxygen depletion was a grave danger to life. If the canary stopped singing, the miners would know that the air was becoming unfit for humans, and they would improve ventilation or get out. Vague feelings of being "shafted," "sucked dry," "turned on," "ripped apart," tell a person something about his situation that should be explored by more direct perception. Fantasy, that waking dream which lurks behind our ordinary consciousness as vague feelings metaphorically described, is a way of knowing. So is dreaming.

Characteristic Ways of Experiencing the World

Now that we have explored some of the ways in which the world *can* be experienced by everyone, we turn to the problem of how persons actually *do* experience their world, as a function of their culture and individual upbringing. Both Rorschach and Jung called attention to *erlebnistypus* (literally, "experience type"). Rorschach made inferences about the ways people habitually experience the world from their responses to his famous ink-blot test, whereas Jung inferred "type" on the basis of his psychotherapeutic interviews. The widely used Myers-Briggs Personality Type Indicator uses Jung's analysis of consciousness to describe such types. Persons who emphasize thinking and judging, in their usual waking consciousness, as opposed to persons who are more emotional and intuitive in their approach to the world, are examples of types.

People become specialists at some kinds of experiencing. For example, creative writers are specialists at imagining and at remembering. Many college professors become specialists at thinking, with diminished or repressed ability to pay perceptual attention to what is going on around them. Eliade [16] points out that shamans, in primitive tribes, are specialists at the self-induction of ecstatic states of consciousness, during which time they are capable of "seeing" the

Healthy Personality: An Approach from the Viewpoint of Humanistic Psychology

future, healing illnesses, walking on coals, and other such feats. It may be that such capacities lie within everyone's possibilities, but upbringing and the need to adjust to the specialized environments within which we live prevent us from discovering and cultivating such ecstatic states.

IS EXTRASENSORY PERCEPTION POSSIBLE?

There continues to be much dispute over man's ability to transmit messages to others by thinking about what he wants to say with great intensity of concentration, and to receive such messages transmitted by others. Disciplined scientific research into ESP is being done under J. B. Rhine, at Duke University Parapsychology Laboratory; by workers at the Menninger Clinic, in Kansas; at Maimonides Dream Laboratory in Brooklyn; and in several European countries.[17] I have not been in any of these laboratories, or seen any demonstrations, but I cannot neglect the reports of findings which I take to be true, written by reputable and competent scientists. I regard it as a reasonable hypothesis that some such capacity for extrasensory communication is an innate human capacity which is but rarely developed because few people believe that it is possible, and perhaps, too, because it is not valued. Indeed, if persons were capable of "tuning in" on everyone's thoughts, or of intruding into the thoughts of others, everyday life would be impossible because of the constant inundation with messages. From the perspective of this hypothesis, the known adepts at sending and receiving messages must have been persons who were not trained for it, but who retained the ability in spite of their socialization. In short, they could conduct extrasensory communication because nobody in their culture told them that it was impossible.

POSITIVE EXPERIENCE

Maslow proposed the term *peak experiences* to describe occasions of great joy, moments of intense happiness and satisfaction that may be occasioned by knowing one is loved, by a fulfilling sexual climax, by the completion of a long and difficult project, or even by eating simple fare after a period of long privation. An intensely contested game of golf, tennis, or handball can be a "high." Maslow argued that the

Consciousness and Healthy Personality

47

world is seen in its essence, as it really is, during and after such occasions of peaking. He further asserted that such moments are times when a person "has it together," is more integrated, less self-conscious; indeed, is more fully functioning and less armored against the world.[18]

Although Maslow chose the term *peak experiences* (current slang uses the terms *highs,* or *ups* as opposed to *downs*), I would like to extend its meaning and use Ted Landman's term *positive experiencing.*[19] Positive experience refers to all occasions of pleasure, fun, satisfaction, completion of projects, fulfillment of hopes—the good moments of life. Of course, positive experience can also include pain and suffering, when these are undergone in order to bring about some meaningful and hoped-for outcome.

Positive experience, then, is what life is *lived for*. This statement is not a return to a hedonistic theory of human life, because meaningful positive experience goes beyond, though it includes, sensuous pleasure. Positive experience includes the experience of the fulfillment of meaning.[20]

When a person lives a life that does not yield its due measure of positive experiencing, he begins to lose morale. He becomes increasingly dispirited and hopeless, and under these circumstances he may even attempt suicide. Certainly, sudden reductions in customary positive experience, and long intervals without positive experiences, and with no apparent hope of amelioration, are likely factors in reduced resistance to infectious ills. Positive experiencing is good for physical, psychological, and spiritual health.[21] Indeed, one definition of love for another is concern that positive experiencing will come his way more often. Healthy personality entails the ability to act in ways that produce positive experiencing for the self and for others.

Altered States of Consciousness

We have mentioned the experiences of ecstasy [22] and of unification (pp. 36–38); these states are in contrast with the usual ways in which man experiences himself and his world in the usual conduct of daily life. When man goes about the regular business of living in his usual roles with others (see Chapter 9), he experiences the world under the influence

48

of deficiency motivation. Many people never have the opportunity to experience the world in other than this everyday way, or even a conception of the possibility of such experience.

Yet it is now being shown that "B-cognition" is only one of myriad possible ways to experience the world. B-cognition, or experiencing self and world as they are, unrelated to our immediate needs, usual roles, and projects, is a possibility for everyone.[23] When one is under the influence of some need, goal, or social role, the world is experienced in only one of countless possible ways. This way of awareness is also a way of being *unaware* of other possibilities thought to be irrelevant to need, project, or role. When one is induced to suspend his effort, to surrender, experience is indeed "altered." [24] One becomes more open and experiences the world in nonordinary ways.

SUSPENSION OF STRIVING AND ALTERED STATES OF CONSCIOUSNESS

After considerable experimentation with ways to alter my usual ways of being conscious of my world, I have arrived at a hypothesis which makes such alterations intelligible to me. I believe that anything which ends a searching, striving attitude toward the world triggers off an alteration in all modes of experiencing, even when the objective state of the world has not changed. Thus, the psychedelic drugs, such as marijuana and LSD,[25] seem to work by rapidly disengaging a person from commitment to his usual projects and roles. Once this disengagement happens, there is no reason for the person to repress hitherto distracting modes of being conscious; so he will then smell, taste, touch, and hear more than he ordinarily did, his recall will be more concrete and eidetic, and his imagination more playful.

The revelatory power of prayer perhaps stems from a similar cause; a person may pray for divine guidance when his struggles have come to naught. If he authentically "surrenders" and begins to pray, this disengagement from the struggle may enable him to see solutions that always were there, although he could not see them. Meditative disciplines alter and enlarge a person's perceptual and other experiential modes by way of disengagement. One cannot

Consciousness and Healthy Personality

truly "get into" the various Hatha Yoga postures until one disengages from one's customary modes of experiencing and striving.

Hypnosis appears to work in similar fashion. When one is being persuaded by the hypnotist's suggestions, one is actually being seduced into suspending usual ways of being conscious of the world. If one yields, one's consciousness is indeed altered.

The "outsiders"—a theme Colin Wilson [26] addressed with such insight—were people "who saw too much" for their time and place. They were not wholly in the clutch of the norms, goals, and standards of their place, and so their consciousness of the world within which they were living was radically "altered," different from that of the typical person. Thus, such characters as Meurseault, in Camus' *The Stranger*, and such real persons as William Blake, Nijinsky (the great ballet dancer), and Lawrence of Arabia were all outsiders, and as Wilson pointed out, their "vision" wrecked them because they did not understand why their vision was different or how to protect themselves.

R. D. Laing has said that what has hitherto been regarded as the madness of schizophrenics is likewise an authentic but different way of experiencing the world which happens when a person gives up an identity no longer viable for him. The act of surrender triggers off such alterations of consciousness as hallucinations, visions, and the like.[27] Of course, any deviations from ordinary consciousness give rise to action which appears strange to the average person. This is why "altered consciousness" can be troublesome unless a person learns how to use his richer experience to guide him to action more effective than that of his fellows.

SOLITUDE, ABSTINENCE, AND "HIGHER" CONSCIOUSNESS

Shamans and men in search of their god have for millennia pursued a path of disengagement, and not only from the worldly pursuit of wealth, power and fame; they have also renounced sex, food, drink, drugs, and the company of other persons.

I have experimented with many of these routes to altered and enlarged awareness, short of total commitment to the way of a holy man. I am persuaded that my hypothesis about the relation between disengagement from one's situa-

Healthy Personality: An Approach from the Viewpoint of Humanistic Psychology

tion and the enlargement of consciousness retains high explanatory power. Food, sex, alcohol, and narcotic drugs appear to shrink consciousness. The sensuous pleasure and anesthetic effects "fix" a person into only one of his many possible ways to experience the world; pleasant, but confining. Perhaps this was why Odysseus had his men tie him to the mast as their ship passed the island of the Sirens, whose seductive songs might have diverted him from his mission.

The reason for solitude is apparent. We all are readily influenced by others' perspectives, which they transmit as they talk to us. Disengagement from others enables a person to reflect in silence, to discern what his own perspective might be. It should not be forgotten, however, that another basic way to alter and enlarge consciousness is through listening to a person speak who is more aware of the world's possibilities than oneself.

EXPERIENCING THE UNEXPECTED

Kurt Goldstein described a condition among brain-damaged patients which he called the "catastrophic reaction." Treating German soldiers during World War I who suffered gunshot and shrapnel wounds in the brain, he noted that such patients, after some time for recovery, were able to function reasonably well if their world was kept tidy and unchanging, and if their time was ordered in rigidly scheduled ways. For example, they needed to know where their clothes were located and when to expect meals. If some sudden alteration was introduced in the way their time and space was arranged, they would not welcome it as a respite from boredom; rather, it was experienced more as a disaster, a catastrophe with which they could not cope. They would become furious, panicky, and might even faint.[28]

This reaction to the unexpected is but an exaggeration of a similar reaction which occurs in average people. Everyone is socialized so that he acquires a set of assumptions about the world which enables him to live his customary life. If something new, different, and unexpected enters his world, the average person may react with panic or with violence. It is as if the unexpected reality that has just been experienced calls upon inadequate capacities to respond. Accordingly, the person may try to deny that anything new has appeared,

Consciousness and Healthy Personality

51

saying, "Why, it's nothing but something old, in new clothes"; or he may try to destroy that which is new or different. Many young men who were among the first to appear with long hair in America experienced varying degrees of violence from people who felt that men were supposed to have short hair. If a man experiences tender, or even sexual, feelings for another man, he may undergo panic, even though he does not express the feeling.

For healthy personalities, the experience of the unexpected serves as an occasion for new learning and growth. To be surprised, or to encounter something which challenges one's assumptions about oneself and the world, functions for healthy personalities as a motive for reality testing (see Chapter 3), as well as an opportunity for the enlargement of one's awareness of the world.

On Recognizing a Consciousness Larger than One's Own: An Hypothesis

A person's experience of the world is invisible to others. All that anyone can perceive directly of another person is his action, his body, and his speech. The gulf between one consciousness and another cannot be crossed, except through acts of intuition, empathy, and imagination. If the other person experiences the world in more dimensions, in greater depth, and with more breadth of vision than oneself, one cannot even imagine what that experience might be, because one can imagine only within limits set by one's own experience. How, then, can a person recognize when he is in the presense of a teacher, a *guru*, or a "sorcerer" as Don Juan, the Yaqui teacher, viewed himself? [29]

The key to an answer lies in surprise and unpredictability. If the other person presents ideas which come as a surprise to the listener, if his actions are of surprising skill and grace, or if he achieves feats which seem unthinkable to the average person, the possibility arises that the other person is an enlarged consciousness. To feel that the other person can predict one's own actions and counteract them with his own is another sign that one's level of awareness has been transcended. Thus, a child may feel that his parents can read his mind, because they can anticipate some of his actions. A general who finds his army outflanked and outmaneuvered realizes he is opposed by a larger, better-informed consciousness than his own. Boris Spassky, the Russian chess master, may have had a moment of suspicion that Bobby Fischer was a larger awareness, when finally he yielded the championship to him.

A person with a larger awareness faces a problem in communicating with those of lesser awareness. In all the traditions of enlightenment, different paths are recommended by the teacher, to bring the seeker to the desired "light." Socrates followed the path of dialogue, questioning his student until the latter suddenly achieved an understanding. The Zen master assigns *koans,* impossible problems to solve, such as, "What is the sound of one hand clapping?" The seeker would be obliged to ponder this paradox until, after enough struggle, the enlightenment would occur. Moses enjoined the Hebrews to live in a very particular way that he could see would lead to an enriched life. If they would follow in the disciplined way, they would live more fruitfully and experience more. The yogis guide their followers toward a larger awareness of the world by assigning them the disciplines of Hatha Yoga, meditation, good works, and simple living. The Sufi masters assigned disciplines, and employed wine, stories, and ecstatic dancing to lead their pupils to a larger awareness of their possibilities. In all such instances, the "disciplines" were ways provided by a master to invite a person to detach himself from the commitments and projects which locked his consciousness at its ordinary level; new dimensions of awareness of the world would then present themselves. The teacher was sought by the pupil because the latter was suffering, or because he was enthralled by feats which appeared superhuman, so surprising were they to the pupil.

It is an interesting hypothesis, then, that great religious teachers, such as Buddha, Christ, Moses, and Patanjali, were men of very high awareness, whose teachings constituted instruction to followers who might, if they were strongly enough committed, arrive at comparable levels of awareness.

Consciousness and Healthy Personality

Indeed, we cannot help but realize that all training schemes, even those devised by "behavior modification" experts, are ways to alter and enlarge consciousness. The art instructor does not teach the skill of drawing so much as he

53

invites a student to persist in making marks on paper, while really looking and really seeing what he looks at. Artists teach a way of being aware as much as they teach a manual skill.

Enlarged consciousness is infectious. Thus dictators of authoritarian nations seek to censor writers and artists, to avoid having their awareness of tyranny and control transmitted to the masses, who, then, would be less manipulable.

Awareness is *power,* the power to affect others for their betterment or to their detriment. Perhaps this is why, in all the mystical and religious traditions, the "mysteries and secrets" are never revealed to novices until they have proven to their elders that they will employ the knowledge that is revealed to them for the good of men, not to exploit them.

Carlos Castañeda was subjected to many tests by Don Juan, his teacher of the "Yaqui way of Knowledge," before true knowledge and seeing became possible for him.[30] And in the traditions of primitive peoples, young people must undergo tests of their manhood and virtue before they are initiated into the knowledge and responsibilities of adulthood.[31]

Enlarged Consciousness and Healthy Personality

Whether or not the enlargement of consciousness is conducive to healthier personality depends upon several factors, including the projects to which a person is committed and his ability to acquire skills commensurate with the enlarged awareness he has attained. Healthy personality rests upon *competence,* the ability to act effectively in pursuit of the gratifications and meanings which make life possible and worth living. If a person has become excessively aware of himself and the world, as sometimes happens with unwise users of psychedelic drugs, he cannot deal effectively with everything of which he has become aware. Maslow [32] was aware of this when he wrote of the "dangers of Being-cognition." The hyperconscious individual may arrive at a sense that all things are of equal importance and value. Such a stance is equivalent to valuelessness, and it results in paralysis of action. Old men prepared to die may have such enlightenment, but it is not of much use to younger persons with a life yet to be lived. There is some optimum harmony among the magnitude of a person's awareness of his world, the goals and projects to which he commits his life, and his skills and capacities for effective action. If enlarged and altered consciousness enriches one's sense of meaning and is accompanied by increased effectiveness at living a life-engendering existence, then such alteration is conducive to healthy personality; otherwise, it might be pernicious.

Some Existential Suggestions

It is good to be able to reflect upon one's own experiencing, but excessive reflection makes action difficult, if not impossible. Nevertheless, there is value in examining the structure of one's field of consciousness, especially in the light of a quest for further self-development.

What modes are predominant in your consciousness? Is there some one sensory modality which is not functioning? When was the last time you really looked at something, smelled it, tasted it, fondled and touched it? There are "sensory awakening" exercises that are fun to do and that enrich the quality of experience. Bernard Gunther's books [33] are good as guides to this.

Dreams offer a person glimpses of other ways for him to live, as well as flashes of truth about himself and his situation. Ann Faraday's book *Dream Power* [34] offers a useful guide to recording and making existential sense out of one's dreams.

The reader might examine his ways of meditating or of reaching "higher" levels of awareness. Is he dependent upon mind-expanding drugs, or can he detach himself from his usual consciousness through meditation, fasting, or other "natural" means?

SUMMARY

Consciousness and Healthy Personality

Consciousness is man's unique and supreme gift. It is difficult to define and talk about, because one can only do so in terms of consciousness itself. Some basic properties of consciousness are that it is reflective; it is always intentional, that is, of some meaningful content; it is organized

55

into figure and ground; it always has some affective, or emotional, quality; the quality of reality or unreality is attributed by a person to his experiencing; each perspective upon the world is unique; there is a "politics" of experiencing, that is, competition between people to see whose definition of the common situation is held to be authoritative; it may be divided and unified; and finally, it always occurs in some mode.

The modes of consciousness include perception, conceptualizing, remembering, thinking, imagining, and dreaming and fantasy. Each person develops a characteristic way of experiencing his world (in German, an erlebnistypus), where some sensory modality, such as vision or touching, is highly developed and some experiential mode is predominant, for example, imagination or thinking.

Extrasensory perception, positive experience, and altered states of consciousness, as well as the effect of experiencing the unexpected, were discussed. The problems of recognizing a consciouness more developed than one's own and the relationship between enlargement of consciousness and healthy personality were explored.

NOTES AND REFERENCES

1. The content of this chapter is based upon the philosophical position known as existential phenomenology. *Phenomenology* refers to the science of "phenomena"—the way the world appears to human beings. *Existentialism* is a philosophical position which concerns itself with the study of what it means to be in the world as a human being. Edmund Husserl is viewed as the founder of phenomenology as a modern philosophical school; existentialism is associated with Kierkegaard, Nietzsche, Heidegger, Jaspers, Sartre, Berdyaev, and Buber. An introduction to existential phenomenology is provided in W. LUIJPEN, *Existential Phenomenology*, 2nd ed. (Pittsburgh: Duquesne, 1971). Humanistic psychology draws heavily upon this discipline in its concern with the study of man as a human, rather than an animal or mechanical, being. Two recent books by psychologists that illustrate this approach are E. KEEN, *Psychology and the New Consciousness* (Monterey, Calif.: Brooks-Cole, 1972), and A. GIORGI, *Psychology as a Human Science: A Phenomenologically Based Approach* (New York:

Healthy Personality: An Approach from the Viewpoint of Humanistic Psychology

Harper and Row, 1970).

2. The phenomenon of attribution has been studied most thoroughly by FRITZ HEIDER in his book *The Psychology of Interpersonal Relations* (New York: Wiley, 1958). Laing applies Heider's concepts to the study of disturbed human relationships. See R. D. LAING, *Self and Others* (New York: Pantheon, 1970), especially Chapter 10, and *The Politics of Experience* (New York: Pantheon, 1967), Chapter 1.

3. R. D. LAING, H. PHILLIPSON, and A. R. LEE, *Interpersonal Perception, A Theory and a Method of Research* (New York: Springer, 1966).

4. LAING, *The Politics of Experience*, op. cit.

5. A fine introduction to the ideas presented in this section or a source for further study, is C. NARANJO and R. E. ORNSTEIN, *On the Psychology of Meditation* (New York: Viking, 1971). A further source is D. GOLEMAN "The Buddha on Meditation and States of Consciousness. Part I: The Teachings," Part II: "A Typology of Meditation Techniques," *Journal of Transpersonal Psychology*, 1972, Vol. 4, pp. 1–44, 151–210.

6. This analysis of consciousness is adapted from Laing. See R. D. LAING, *The Divided Self* (New York: Pantheon, 1969), also the references cited in notes 2 and 3. See also S. M. JOURARD, *Disclosing Man to Himself* (New York: Van Nostrand Reinhold, 1968), especially Chapters 13 and 14.

7. See G. KELLY, *The Psychology of Personal Constructs*, Vol. I (New York: Norton, 1955) for a thorough analysis of the act of construing and a development of the point of view Kelly called "constructive alternativism."

8. C. CASTAÑEDA, *Journey to Ixtlan* (New York: Simon & Schuster, 1972), pp. 291–315.

9. See W. A. SHIBLES, *Metaphor: An Annotated Bibliography and History* (Whitewater, Wis.: The Language Press, 1971). Also C. M. TURBAYNE, *The Myth of Metaphor*, 2nd ed. (Columbia: University of South Carolina Press, 1970).

10. H. R. POLLIO, "The Whys and Hows of Metaphor and Their Measurement." Paper presented at Southeastern Psychological Association, 1972. J. R. BARLOW, "Metaphor and Insight." Paper presented at Southeastern Psychological Association, 1972.

11. T. S. KUHN, *The Structure of Scientific Revolutions*, 2nd ed. (Chicago: University of Chicago Press, 1970).

12. For a review of theories of hypnosis, see T. X. BARBER, *Hypnosis: A Scientific Approach* (New York: Van Nostrand Reinhold, 1969); and E. HILGARD, *The Experience of Hypnosis* (New York: Harcourt Brace Jovanovich, 1968).

13. S. Fisher and S. Cleveland, *Body Image and Personality* (New York: Dover, 1968); see also S. Fisher, *Body Consciousness: You Are What You Feel* (Englewood Cliffs, N.J.: Prentice-Hall, 1973), especially Chapter 2.

14. A splendid, most readable review of scientific studies of sleeping and theories of dreaming is Ann Faraday, *Dream Power* (New York: Coward, McCann, 1972). She presents the approaches of Freud, Jung, Perls, and Calvin Hall to the interpretation of dreams, and then shows the reader how to make sense of his own dreams. But everyone should read primary sources: S. Freud, *The Interpretation of Dreams* (New York: Basic Books, 1955); C. G. Jung, *Memories, Dreams, Reflections* (New York: Vintage, 1961); F. Perls, *Gestalt Therapy Verbatim* (Lafayette, Calif.: The Real People Press, 1969); C. Hall, *The Meaning of Dreams* (New York: McGraw-Hill, 1966). I have always liked E. Fromm, *The Forgotten Language: An Introduction to the Understanding of Dreams, Fairytales and Myths* (New York: Holt, 1970).

15. Laing, *Self and Others*, op. cit., Chapters 1 and 2; *Politics of Experience*, op. cit., pp. 30–32.

16. M. Eliade, *Rites and Symbols of Initiation* (New York: Harper & Row, 1958), pp. 94–96.

17. Articles on ESP appear frequently in the *Journal of Transpersonal Psychology;* there is also a journal devoted exclusively to "parapsychological" phenomena. A useful book with which to begin study in this area is Sheila Ostrander and Lynn Schroeder, *Psychic Discoveries Behind the Iron Curtain* (New York: Bantam Books, 1970).

18. A. H. Maslow, *Toward a Psychology of Being,* 2nd ed. (New York: Van Nostrand Reinhold, 1968), Chapters 6 and 7.

19. T. Landsman, unpublished manuscript, University of Florida, 1973.

20. V. E. Frankl, *Man's Search for Meaning,* rev. ed. (Boston: Beacon Press, 1963).

21. S. M. Jourard, *The Transparent Self,* 2nd ed. (New York: Van Nostrand Reinhold, 1971), Chapters 9 and 10.

22. Besides Eliade (note 16), Marghanita Laski has investigated the experience of ecstasy. See Marghanita Laski, *Ecstasy: A Study of Some Secular and Religious Experiences* (London: Cresset Press, 1961).

23. Maslow, op. cit.

24. This is an area of intense study at the present time. A good introduction is C. Tart (Ed.), *Altered States of Consciousness* (New York: Wiley, 1969). It has papers by authorities on dreaming, "hypnogogic" states, meditation, hypnosis, psychedelic

drugs, and the psychophysiology of altered states of consciousness. Nondrug approaches to "higher" consciousness are discussed by R. S. De Ropp, *The Master Game* (New York: Delacorte, 1968).

25. D. Solomon (Ed.), *LSD: The Consciousness Expanding Drug* (New York: Putnam, 1964); see also A. Hoffer and H. Osmond, *The Hallucinogens* (New York: Academic Press, 1967).

26. C. Wilson, *The Outsider* (Boston: Houghton Mifflin, 1960).

27. R. D. Laing, *Politics of Experience*, op. cit., Chapters 5 and 6. See also the account by Mary Barnes of her experience of surrender to a wish to regress to infancy in order to re-enter the world in a more authentic and life-giving way. Cf. Mary Barnes and J. Berke, *Mary Barnes: Two Accounts of a Journey Through Madness* (New York: Harcourt Brace Jovanovich, 1971).

28. K. Goldstein, *Human Nature from the Point of View of Psychopathology* (Cambridge, Mass.: Harvard University Press, 1940); K. Goldstein and M. Scheerer, "Abstract and Concrete Behavior," *Psychological Monographs*, 1941, Vol. 53.

29. C. Castañeda, *Teachings of Don Juan: A Yaqui Way of Knowledge* (New York: Ballantine Books, 1968); *A Separate Reality: Further Conversations with Don Juan* (New York: Simon and Schuster, 1971); *Journey to Ixtlan* (New York: Simon and Schuster, 1972).

30. Castañeda, op. cit.

31. Eliade, op. cit.; A. Van Gennep, *The Rites of Passage* (Chicago: University of Chicago Press, 1960).

32. Maslow, op. cit., Chapter 8.

33. B. Gunther, *Sense Awakening* (New York: Macmillan, 1968); *What to Do Till the Messiah Comes* (New York: Macmillan, 1971).

34. Faraday, op. cit.

Consciousness and Healthy Personality

3

REALITY CONTACT AND HEALTHY PERSONALITY

INTRODUCTION

Healthy personality depends upon acting in ways that foster well-being and growth. Effective action is impossible without accurate perception of the world and valid beliefs about it.

Reality testing is the term many psychologists use to describe the procedure for determining whether some perception or belief is warranted by evidence and logical reasoning or whether it is illusory.

Our behavior is always undertaken with reference to the world as we believe it to be. We can hardly make sense out of anybody's behavior unless we somehow learn from him how the world appears to him—what he is paying attention to, how he interprets the things he sees and hears, and what his expectations are regarding the world about him.[1] We will be puzzled if we see a man run in terror from a kitten, because to us the kitten looks cute and harmless. An interview with the terrified man may reveal that he believes the kitten is rabid. Once we learn what the kitten means to him, his behavior becomes intelligible. However, we can always raise the question, "How efficient is this man's contact with reality?"

A person's perceptions and beliefs will be inaccurate or distorted unless he takes steps to verify them. Reality contact is not a given, it is an achievement! Efficient contact with reality must be worked for, because there are powerful forces at work at all times tending to distort perception, thinking, and recall.

Some Influences on Consciousness of the World

In the first place, the content of our field of consciousness is necessarily selective; it cannot include all inner and outer reality that exists at a given moment. Only part of the ongoing flow of feelings, thoughts, and external events is detected by our sense organs and represented in our field of awareness. Our sense organs resemble TV or radio receivers in that they are differentially sensitive to stimuli of different intensities and qualities. But even within the receptive range of our senses, we still notice only a fraction of all the sensory information reaching our brain. One of the important determiners of *figure,* that is, of our interested attention, is emotion and unfulfilled needs.

Our feelings and our needs direct our perception, thinking, remembering, and fantasy, so that the figure will be that percept, thought, or memory most relevant to our needs of the moment. Our cognitive processes are thus servants of our needs. When we are hungry, we think and dream about food, we search for it, and we tend to ignore everything in the world which is inedible or which will not help us to get food. If we are sexually deprived, we tend to have fantasies with erotic themes, we find it difficult to think about other things, and we look at the world from the standpoint of the sexual gratification and frustrations it is likely to afford. If a person is anxious because of some threat to his security, he is unlikely to notice the beauties of nature; he is too busy seeking the source of danger so that he might escape from it. There have been many experiments conducted to demonstrate how needs determine our attention and the content of our consciousness and so we need not dwell further upon this point. More germane to our discussion is the manner in which emotions and unfulfilled needs operate so as to

*Reality
Contact
and
Healthy
Personality*

61

distort our perceptions and beliefs. The theory of autism will serve as a framework for our discussion.[2]

Autism refers to the tendency of persons to perceive, remember, imagine, and believe in ways that are determined more by needs and emotions than by evidence or logic. Freud referred to this tendency as the "pleasure principle," and he saw it as a factor which constantly opposed the reality principle. Freud's hypothesis of the pleasure principle is not so general as the theory of autism, because it proposes only that we perceive and believe what will yield pleasure, and deny painful aspects of reality. The theory of autism makes allowance for beliefs which are unpleasant and at the same time untrue.[3]

Autism is evident whenever we jump to some conclusion without checking its congruence with available data or other, tested truths. A thirst-ridden prospector on a desert may conclude that the shimmering he sees in the distance is an oasis where he will be able to drink, and he exhausts himself running toward it, only to find it recedes into the distance. A woman starved for affection may conclude that a man who places a hand on her shoulder is expressing thereby his undying love. In fact, he may only be leaning to avoid stumbling. A student, unsure of his ability to complete his studies, gets a note from his professor that reads, "Please come to see me." He feels certain his professor is going to fail him. In fact, the teacher may be intending to invite the student to his house for dinner.

The probability of forming autistic beliefs is highest when needs or emotions are most intense, and when the available information is ambiguous.

The passenger with little faith in the safety of airplanes will conclude that the engines are on fire if he should look out the window on a night flight; actually, he is noticing only normal exhaust flames. His anxiety is strong, and the amount of information available to him is limited. Consequently, he jumps to a conclusion based upon his emotions, rather than postponing his judgment until he has considered other hypotheses.

Our needs and emotions not only make us believe things

Healthy Personality: An Approach from the Viewpoint of Humanistic Psychology

that are untrue, they also blind us to truth. If a perception gives rise to devastating depression or hopelessness, there is a tendency for people simply to ignore the disquieting truth. Anyone who has suffered the death of a loved one will know how difficult it is to realize that the deceased will not be seen anymore. People tend to forget, or more accurately, to repress the memory of painful or humiliating events.

Many needs can be gratified only through relationships with other people. This means that strong emotions are mobilized in our interpersonal relationships. Reliable information about another person is difficult to obtain, because much of his behavior goes on at times when we cannot see it. Furthermore, his consciousness of the world is not accessible to our direct vision. We can only learn the subjective side of another person if he confides in us, and he may not be willing to entrust us with personal information.[4] Often, we are obliged to form our concept of another person on the basis of his overt behavior alone. Hence, it should be no surprise that our concepts of other people are frequently inaccurate.

OTHER PEOPLE'S INFLUENCE ON OUR
SENSE OF REALITY

Reality is what we take to be real. This, in turn, is powerfully influenced by what significant other people have told us is true, real, and important in the world. We are continuously told by newspapers, comics, friends and family members, movies and television programs about the way things are. Sometimes, this influence is subtle; someone merely describes some aspect of the world to us, and we find that this description impels us to see the world as we were told it is. One teacher played a classroom game; he asked the children to pretend that blonde, blue-eyed children were evil. In time, the black-haired children came to loathe the blondes, who in turn felt inferior.

Reality
Contact
and
Healthy
Personality

Other people, then, can so influence one's ways of perceiving, and attaching meaning and value, that one loses his own, autonomous perspective. If other people are strong, with high status, they may invalidate one's own perspective on reality; the weaker person accepts the perspective of the stronger.

A person may need to disengage from other people, and go into solitude, in order to separate his parents' perspective on reality from one that is more truly his own.[5]

Ontic projection is Thomas Hanna's[6] term to describe what a person takes to be real—his attributions of reality. Each language provides words which sensitize a person to those aspects of the world that are most important for survival in that place. Thus, we have only one word for snow, whereas Eskimos have many, corresponding with different qualities of snow that indicate whether hunting or igloo building are possible.[7] We do not see the world; rather we "read" the meanings of what we see, just as we read the words in a book. These meanings are provided for us as we grow up by the person who teaches us to speak our "mother tongue." It is our mothers who give the first meanings to our world, who give the world the "voices" with which it tells us of dangers and gratifications. In developing countries like Indonesia, or India, each child learns three languages, each of which highlights some aspects of the world more than others, and which gives different meanings and emotional qualities to the perceived world. Thus, a child will learn the language of his village from his mother; in India, or Indonesia, it will be one of the several hundred local languages which differ so much that people fifty miles apart cannot understand one another's mother tongues. At school an Indonesian child will learn Malay, and an Indian child will learn Hindi—both languages are the national tongue, which facilitates communication throughout the country. Finally, both Indonesians and Indians may learn English, which makes communication beyond national boundaries possible.

In each case, the language that is spoken affects perception. In order really to perceive what is there in the world, a person will have to suspend language, and really look and listen, to discern the reality *beyond* language (pp. 67–69).

Reality Testing

Our chances of behaving effectively are increased if we perceive the world accurately and form valid beliefs about

Healthy Personality: An Approach from the Viewpoint of Humanistic Psychology

it. But we know that unfulfilled needs and strong emotions can so shape our experience that we misinterpret facts, arrive at erroneous conclusions, and, indeed, frequently fail to see and hear what is there. How does a person go about increasing the efficiency of his perception and thinking? How does a person carry out reality testing? Indeed, why would a person seek the truth when unreality is often more pleasant in the short run?

Reality testing means applying the rules of logic and scientific inquiry to everyday life. When we engage in reality testing, we are systematically doubting our own initial perceptions and beliefs until we have scrutinized them more carefully and checked them against further evidence. We do this when we have learned that truth, ultimately, is the best servant of our needs, and is a value in itself.

AN EXAMPLE OF REALITY TESTING

A nineteen-year-old girl once consulted me, seeking help with a problem that was bothering her. She believed her roommate was stealing her money, jewelry, and even stationery. She noticed various items missing from her dresser from time to time, and she concluded her roommate was guilty. However, she dared not confront the girl with her suspicion. Instead, she felt distrust and resentment and struggled to conceal these feelings from her. Their relationship gradually deteriorated to one of formality, forced politeness, and false expressions of friendship.

I asked the girl why she didn't bring the whole issue out into the open. She stated that if she did this, the other girl would hate her, and she couldn't stand this. I asked if there was any other possible way of interpreting the loss of her money and jewelry. She replied that she hadn't thought of any. Rather, she had concluded that if her things were missing, they must have been stolen by the person closest to her. When I suggested that her roommate might be saddened at the way their friendship had deteriorated and that she might welcome some frank talk to settle things, the girl admitted that this might be possible, but she was afraid to talk about the problem. However, she agreed to broach the subject.

Next time I saw the girl, she was happy to report that she had discussed the whole affair. She learned that her

Reality
Contact
and
Healthy
Personality

roommate was puzzled by the way their relationship had changed. Moreover, she was glad to discuss the loss of the articles with her and she was able to clear herself of any blame. In fact, the roommate too had been missing some money, and investigation by the dormitory counselor brought forth the fact that other girls had been robbed and that the guilty party was a cleaning woman, who was promptly discharged.

The example illustrates how some initial, untested beliefs that one person forms about some aspect of the world—in this case, about another person—can lead to misunderstanding in interpersonal relationships and to considerable unhappiness.[8] At first, the girl was afraid to carry out any efforts at reality testing to see if her assumption of the guilt of her roommate was warranted. This illustrates another aspect of reality testing; frequently, people may be reluctant to go after the information which is crucial to the formation of accurate beliefs. Yet if a person gives in to his fear of getting at the truth, he is almost sure to become increasingly out of touch with reality.

RULES FOR REALITY TESTING

Everyone can learn to become more effective at reality testing if he will follow these rules:

1. State the belief clearly.
2. Ask, "What evidence is there to support this belief?"
3. Ask, "Is there any other way of interpreting this evidence?"
4. Try to determine how consistent the belief is with other beliefs that are known to be valid.

Now we shall illustrate. A student believes his teacher dislikes him. Let us put words in his mouth and arrange an imaginery monologue.

My teacher hates me. What evidence do I have for this belief? Why, the fact that he gave me a very low grade, plus the fact that yesterday when I greeted him in the hall, he didn't turn my way to acknowledge the greeting. But let me see. Is there any other way of interpreting this evidence? Well, what factors can produce low grades? One of them is insufficient study and faulty understanding of the course. As it happens, I haven't

Healthy Personality: An Approach from the Viewpoint of Humanistic Psychology

glanced at a book all quarter, and I cut half my lectures to smoke dope and listen to music. Maybe that's why I flunked. But what about the fact that I greeted the professor and he didn't even nod? Well, maybe he didn't hear me. I must admit I spoke very low, and the hall was noisy. Finally, this professor is widely believed to be fair in his dealings with students, and so my belief about his hating me isn't consistent with his reputation.

Systematic application of these rules will help the reader to insure his beliefs come closer to accuracy than would be the case if he ignored reality testing.

Living in the "Raw World": The Return to Experience

It is probably the lot of a person that once he has learned speech, his perception of reality is always filtered through, and guided by, his *concepts* of reality. For example, if you learn the concept gun and then look at a gun, you probably see something entirely different from what a primitive savage might: guns have no place, nor even a word to describe them, in his culture.[9]

Words limit what a person will actually experience in a concrete situation. Once a concept has been learned, a person will look at a given object long enough to place it in its proper category or to assign an appropriate name to it. He may then ignore much of what is actually there before him. We are all familiar with the bigoted person who, once he has determined that a person is a Jew or a Negro, never looks further at the person. He "knows" the properties of all members who fall into those classes. In reality, the bigot fails to observe the enormous amount of variation among members of a class of any sort.[10]

The ability to break down categories and discern uniqueness is as essential for healthy personality as the ability to classify. But the ability to see what is there, to transcend labels and classes and apprehend the thing before one's view, is a means of enriching one's knowledge of the world and of deepening one's contact with reality. Fritz Perls [11] would have his patients in Gestalt therapy go through exercises of simply looking at something or somebody, in order

Reality Contact and Healthy Personality

67

to discern the reality beyond the concept. To be able to sense the "raw world" involves the ability to abandon presently held concepts and categories. This ability is possessed by the productive scientist who deliberately ignores the orthodoxies, and looks ever afresh at the raw data which prompted the formation of present-day concepts and categories. The artist probably possesses to a marked degree the ability to apprehend the unique, the individual object.

The ability to set conventional categories and concepts aside and to look fully at the world with minimal preconceptions seems to be a trait which facilitates scientific discovery, art, human relations, and, more generally, an enrichment of the sensory experiences of living.

The capacity to let oneself see or perceive what is there seems to entail the *temporary cessation of an active, searching, or critical attitude*. Need-directed perception is a highly focused searchlight darting here and there, seeking the objects which will satisfy needs, ignoring everything irrelevant to the need. "Being-cognition," as Maslow has called it, refers to a more passive mode of perceiving. It involves letting oneself be reached, touched, or affected by what is there so that the perception is richer. In Maslow's own words,[12]

> The most efficient way to perceive the intrinsic nature of the world is to be more passive than active, determined as much as possible by the intrinsic organization of that which is perceived and as little as possible by the nature of the perceiver. This kind of detached, Taoist, passive, non-interfering awareness of all the simultaneously existing aspects of the concrete, has much in common with some descriptions of the aesthetic experience and of the mystic experience. The stress is the same. Do we see the real, concrete world, or do we see our own system of rubrics, motives, expectations and abstractions which we have projected onto the real world? Or, to put it very bluntly, do we see or are we blind?

This mode of cognition, however, seems to be possible only at those times when a person has adequately fulfilled his basic needs. When a person is anxious, sexually deprived, or hungry, it is as if his organs of perceiving and of

Healthy Personality: An Approach from the Viewpoint of Humanistic Psychology

68

knowing have been "commandeered" to find the means of gratification. Our consciousness seems most free to play, to be most receptive to new impressions, when the urgency of needs is diminished. The implication is clear—if a person wants to know hitherto unnoticed features of the world which confronts him, his chances of so doing are increased when his basic needs are satisfied.

The direction of our cognition by needs has adaptive value, because it increases our chances of finding the things that will satisfy our needs and it permits us to avoid dangers in our environment. However, if persons are *always* perceiving the world under the direction of their needs, they will simply not perceive much that exists. The aesthetic, appreciative contemplation of reality, with no purpose other than the delight of looking at it, or experiencing it, lends a dimension of richness to an existence that is ordinarily characterized by the search for satisfaction. Competence at gratifying one's needs frees one from time to time of the necessity to be forever struggling, and permits one the luxury of aesthetic sensing.

Some Existential Suggestions

When was the last time that you *really looked* at your mother or closest friend of either sex? What do you believe is true about her or him? When did you last check your beliefs by observing these people or asking them questions?

One of the exercises Gestalt therapists ask their patients to engage in is really looking at someone familiar. This is a way to break up one's concepts so that one really sees what is there, not what is *said* to be there.

Really look at yourself, or someone else in your life.

Be careful what you believe to be true, because so long as you believe it, then for you it is true. But your beliefs about reality, your "attributions of reality" or your "ontic projections," profoundly influence your life. Of especial importance for healthy personality are those beliefs about limits, about your weaknesses and lack of aptitude. If you believe you cannot learn a musical instrument because you lack talent, get a musical instrument and learn it. If you believe you cannot do without food for three days, go on a five-day fast. Challenge your own beliefs, especially about yourself

*Reality
Contact
and
Healthy
Personality*

and others, because what you believe to be true about self and others functions more as persuasion than as description.

SUMMARY

Healthy personality depends upon accurate perception of and knowledge about the world. Our perception and our thinking is subject to influence by needs and emotions (autism), and we are vulnerable to confusion of perception with imagination. Consequently, our perception may be very selective and distorted, and our beliefs unfounded. Reality testing is the technique of verifying our perceptions and beliefs by seeking further information, and engaging in rational thinking about the implications of our perceptions. Other people can influence our perspective, even to the point of replacing it with their own. Reality testing entails disengaging from action and querying one's views of a situation, to discern whether they are compatible with fresh perceptions and with reason.

The "return to experience" involves viewing the world afresh, uninfluenced by language and ongoing needs and projects. This basic perception is what Maslow described as "B-cognition," and appears to be the aim of the enlightening disciplines, such as Zen, Taoism, Sufism, and as the Yaqui sorcerer Don Juan called it, "stopping the (speech of) the world," so that one can really see it.

NOTES AND REFERENCES

1. For a discussion of the "assumptive world" see H. CANTRIL, *The Why of Man's Experience* (New York: Macmillan, 1950), pp. 87–104. The relationship between "assumptive worlds" and effectiveness of action is given in J. D. FRANK, *Persuasion and Healing*, 2nd ed. (Baltimore: Johns Hopkins Press, 1973).

2. The theory of autism is presented in G. MURPHY, *Personality: A Biosocial Approach to Origins and Structure* (New York: Harper & Row, 1947), Chapters 14 and 15.

3. S. FREUD, "Formulations Regarding the Two Principles in Mental Functioning," in S. FREUD, *Collected Papers*, IV (London: Hogarth, 1953), Chapter 1. See also A. H. MASLOW, *Toward a Psychology of Being* (New York: Van Nostrand

Reinhold, 1962), Chapter 5, "The Need to Know and the Fear of Knowing."

4. S. M. JOURARD, *Self-disclosure: An Experimental Analysis of the Transparent Self* (New York: Wiley-Interscience, 1971) provides a review of my research into factors in self-disclosure.

5. See R. D. LAING and A. ESTERSON, *Sanity, Madness and the Family* (London: Tavistock, 1964) for dramatic illustrations of the way the perspective of one member of a family is invalidated by others.

6. T. HANNA, *The Other "Is"* (University of Florida, unpublished manuscript, 1973).

7. B. L. WHORF, *Language, Thought and Reality,* J. B. CARROLL (ED.) (Cambridge, Mass.: M.I.T. Press, 1956). Also see S. HAYAKAWA, *Language in Action* (New York: Harcourt Brace Jovanovich, 1941). See also H. WERNER, *Comparative Psychology of Mental Development* (Chicago: Follett, 1948), Chapters 9 and 12; R. BROWN, *Words and Things* (New York: Free Press, 1958).

8. G. ICHHEISER, *Appearances and Realities: Misunderstandings in Human Relations* (San Francisco: Jossey-Bass, 1970), pp. 1–120.

9. See note 7.

10. G. W. ALLPORT, *The Nature of Prejudice* (Reading, Mass.: Addison-Wesley, 1954), especially Chapter 2.

11. See F. PERLS, P. GOODMAN, and R. HEFFERLINE, *Gestalt Therapy: Excitement and Growth in the Human Personality* (New York: Dell, 1951), Chapters 2–4, for examples of these exercises.

12. MASLOW, op. cit., pp. 67–96. The quote is from p. 38. See also E. SCHACHTEL, *Metamorphosis: On the Development of Affect, Perception, Attention and Memory* (New York: Basic Books, 1959), pp. 220 ff.

4

BASIC NEEDS AND
HEALTHY PERSONALITY

INTRODUCTION

Healthy personality calls for competence at gratifying basic needs. One is then free to pursue goals beyond personal security. It is difficult to be concerned with truth, justice, or beauty when starved for love, or when life itself is endangered. First things come first. A person must be able to take care of himself before he can assume responsibility for the care of others and be free to do the creative work of the world.

The person who can meet his needs through his own skill is independently secure. The child relies upon grown-ups to devote their time and skill to his needs; to the extent that they do this, the child is dependently secure. An adult who remains dependent upon others to meet his basic needs (except for love and companionship) may pay dearly for their intervention; he may be obliged to conform to restrictive demands which call for unhealthy suppression of action and repression of experience. Immature dependent security is costly.

To be deprived of basic need gratification is painful. There is no denying the hurt of starvation, loneliness, or political tyranny. Some people try to deal with this pain by denying it exists or by anesthetizing themselves to their suffering with drugs, alcohol, or immature religion, but these responses only postpone the inevitable recognition that problems and pain do not go away until one has acted.

Definition of Basic Needs

NEEDS, WANTS, AND "REINFORCERS"

It is often difficult to distinguish between a need and a want. Wants are infinite in number, and they change moment by moment. I want a yacht, but I don't need one to survive. I may, however, need a yacht to achieve the status which is essential to me. Wants are a person's interpretation of what he needs in order to achieve happiness or well-being. Needs are what scientists agree a person requires to sustain life and to foster growth of desirable human potentialities.

Incentives, rewards, and reinforcers are what other people believe will move you. A man needs food. His wife knows he really likes rare roast beef. She may reward (or reinforce) his attention to her wishes by cooking it for him. Whoever possesses the means of gratifying needs and wants has power to influence action. This makes a person vulnerable to being controlled by others in ways that can undermine his freedom and his dignity. He is vulnerable in this way, however, only when others know what he needs or wants—what it takes to "buy" him.[1] Competence at gratifying one's basic needs can protect one from being controlled by others. There are situations in which self-concealment may be required in order to elude control.

On the other hand, if a person wishes the love of others, he must "open" himself, and disclose his needs and wants to his beloved, who can then act in his behalf. It takes trust to accept the love of another. The other must earn this trust by being trustworthy.

Basic Needs and Healthy Personality

What does a person need for a healthy personality? What does he need for himself so he can be free to give to the world as well as take from it?

73

Maslow presents an authoritative analysis of needs. He stated a need can be adjudged basic if

1. Its deprivation breeds illness (mental or physical).

2. Gratification of the need prevents illness.

3. Identification and gratification of the need restores health in a person who is presently ill.

4. The deprived person prefers gratification of this need over any other, under conditions of free choice.

5. The need is not in a state of tension or privation in healthy persons.

6. A subjective feeling of yearning, lack, or desire prevails when the need is not fulfilled.

7. Gratification of the need feels good; gratification produces a subjective sense of healthy well-being.[2]

There is further implied the idea that when the need is met, the person does not think about it until the next time it arises; he is free for other pursuits.

Opinions among biologists and psychologists vary about the precise number of basic needs in man. Agreement can be reached on what is required for sheer physical survival, but not on what man needs to fulfill his unfathomed human potentialities. The following section offers a hypothesis about such needs, the test of the hypothesis being a judgment of the quality of life with and without the gratification of these needs.

Some Basic Needs in Man

TO VALUE LIFE ITSELF

Most basic of all human needs is the affirmation of life, the desire to continue living. When his life is under threat, a man will do almost anything, break laws, kill others, and sacrifice wealth, to eliminate the threat and preserve his existence. Such occasions are rare. It will suffice merely to remind the reader that the wish to live is the most powerful determiner of action that man can know. A man may, however, decide to sacrifice his life for love of another or for his country.

Paradoxically enough, a person can be persuaded that further existence is neither meaningful nor possible. A long period of suffering or joylessness may so dispirit him that he

Healthy Personality: An Approach from the Viewpoint of Humanistic Psychology

resigns from life. He may commit suicide, or yield to a sickness which would not be lethal had he retained his desire to live. Anyone who reduces zest for life in another, or who convinces him that life is impossible, is akin to a murderer.

PHYSICAL NEEDS

By physical needs is meant food, drink, relief from pain and discomfort, and adequate shelter. Modern society does a better job of satisfying these needs than was true in earlier times, and so the quests for food, shelter, and comfort are less powerful determiners of everyday action than they used to be. However, when a person experiences a threat to his supplies, or his access to supplies, of food and shelter he may be forced to take desperate measures to secure these vital things.

LOVE

A child needs parental love to survive and grow.[3] If he has been sufficiently loved as a child, and has learned acceptable ways of behaving, the probability is high that some other person will choose him to love when he is an adult. One of the most powerful determiners of one's lovability is the willingness to love first, or at least reciprocally. When a person feels insufficiently loved, the quest for love from others may become a lifelong mission.

STATUS, SUCCESS, AND SELF-ESTEEM

Man needs to feel recognized and approved by other members of the groups within which he lives. Without such recognition he tends to feel inferior. The quest for power and prestige is universal, though the means of attaining status differ from society to society.[4] A man may work to the point of exhaustion, neglecting his health and the needs of his family, in order to purchase a Rolls Royce motor car. The status symbolized by the Rolls seems worth the cost. He may not enjoy his work, he may not enjoy seeing his family suffer from neglect, the limousine may not transport him any better than a less costly vehicle, but so urgent is his quest for status he is willing to pay the price.

Let us not underrate the strength of the status drive in modern man. The puzzling thing is, how does it become so powerful? One hypothesis is that the fanatic quest for status

Basic
Needs
and
Healthy
Personality

is in compensation for lack of love or for physical deprivations associated with poverty. It is as if the "success-starved"
person is trying to make up in adult years for childhood
privations, and he can never get enough.

FREEDOM AND SPACE

Man needs varying degrees of freedom to conduct his life
according to his own wishes and plans. Many wars have
been fought in the name of freedom. We can distinguish
between *objective* freedom, which refers to the relative absence of real restrictions on one's behavior, and the *feeling*
of freedom. The latter refers to a person's estimate of how
free he is to express himself. Healthy personalities find an
environment within which there is the greatest possible
amount of objective freedom. Unhealthy personalities may
dread both objective freedom and the feeling of freedom.
They find it anxiety-producing. They can only carry on as
long as they feel under compulsion or restraint from laws
or orders.[5]

Man not only needs room to move and to express his
unique ways, he needs private space for solitude and for
uninterrupted intimacy with others. In the absence of such
assured space, people tend to become irritable and chronically defensive. As we enter an age of vastly increased population, and the concentration of this population in crowded
cities, the need for more space becomes increasingly urgent.[6]

CHALLENGE

Deprivation of challenge is experienced as boredom, or
as emptiness in existence.[7] The need for challenge manifests
itself most keenly when a person has made a "sucessful
adjustment" to his life, when he has been able to fulfill his
material needs, and cannot then find anything to do. Without challenging goals, people eat or drink to excess, or pass
the time getting intoxicated with marijuana. Our affluent
societies continue to need nondestructive equivalents of war.

MEDITATION AND DISENGAGEMENT

Just as man needs intense involvement to foster full functioning and growth, he also needs disengagement. He needs
to get away from his customary consciousness of himself
and his world. The "getting away" can be literal, as in the

*Healthy
Personality:
An Approach
from the
Viewpoint of
Humanistic
Psychology*

form of travel; but it can also take the form of what are now called *altered states of consciousness.* [8] There are two ways to alter one's consciousness of his situation. One of these is literally to change situations. The other is to suspend the customary way of experiencing a situation, to allow new modes of consciousness to appear. One's situation functions hypnotically, influencing a person to perceive, recall, think and even imagine in stereotyped ways. One way to break the quasihypnotic spell is to engage in meditation. Za-zen, or sitting-Zen meditation, is one such method. It entails sitting cross-legged, or in any comfortable position, letting one's stream of consciousness simply "happen." Another technique is that of transcendental meditation, which also calls for the attainment of a state of quiescence, where one's "chattering" mind is stilled. Hatha Yoga, together with deep, slow breathing, is yet another method through which a person can disengage from his usual situation. The significant aspect of these meditative disciplines is not the state itself, but rather the effect they have on a person's awareness of his situation when he returns to it. New aspects of the situation are perceived, and the person can imagine, think, and remember in more flexible ways.

Psychedelic drugs, such as lysergic acid diethylamide (LSD), cannabis derivatives (marijuana and hashish), mescaline, psylocybin, and peyote, are all pharmacological means by which a person can leave his situation (in a metaphorical sense). Indeed, in current jargon persons who ingest LSD or mescaline are said to be "tripping." Although these drugs often produce an absorbing and sometimes pleasant change in experience, they can have deleterious effects upon the capacity to cope effectively with problems, and so caution is advisable in their use.

COGNITIVE CLARITY

Man cannot endure ambiguity or contradiction in his knowledge. In the face of uncertainty, he seems impelled to construct answers, because he can act only when he has made a satisfactory interpretation of the situation. His interpretation may not be valid, but it seems true that man prefers a false interpretation to none. Thus, a person may hear noises in the sky which he cannot at first identify. The experience of not knowing may fill him with anxiety. He may be virtually paralyzed until he knows what the noise means. For example, he may interpret the sound as that made by a jet aircraft which has just crashed through the sound barrier. This satisfies him, and he gets on with whatever he was doing. Or he may construe the noise in some bizarre way—perhaps he regards it as the sound of a missile carrying an atomic warhead and he promptly runs to find shelter. He may be wrong, of course, but at least his interpretation permits him *to do* something.

In addition to the need for some interpretation of situations, man needs consistency among his presently held beliefs. When new cognitions—perceptions and beliefs—are not compatible with those already held, the state of *cognitive dissonance* is said to exist. Cognitive dissonance influences behavior like any other basic need.[9] When there is a conflict between present knowledge and new information, people may deny and distort truth to eliminate dissonance. Healthier personalities can tolerate ambiguity better than unhealthy personalities; they resolve cognitive dissonance in ways that do the most justice to logic and evidence (see Chapter 3).

MEANING AND PURPOSE

To ask about the purpose of human life is to raise an existential question, rather than one answerable through experiment or logic. Existential questions are answered by the way one lives his life. Every man's life, and the daily actions and decisions which comprise it, represent his answer to the question, "How, then, shall I live?"

These answers are almost by definition the embodiment of a person's religion. The chief function of religion is to provide ultimate answers to the questions that existence poses (see Chapter 14). In the absence of credible and life-giving answers to the questions, "How shall I live, and why?" a person enters the state Frankl calls noögenic neurosis—a kind of despair or cynicism.[10] Much depression and neurotic suffering stem from a failure to find meaning in life, or to find new meaning when old goals have been consummated or have lost their inspiriting power.

Fromm regards "a frame of orientation and devotion" to be as essential to healthy personality as food. The process of self-actualizing, of which Maslow wrote, and the achieve-

Healthy Personality: An Approach from the Viewpoint of Humanistic Psychology

ment of selfhood (in Jung's sense) appear to be impossible without such a religious orientation. Of course, it does not matter whether the religion is theistic, and it is possible to judge whether or not a person's objects and ways of worshiping are life-giving. But life for man is impossible without something to live *for*.

VARIED EXPERIENCE

Man needs varied stimulation, not just to avoid boredom but actually to preserve his ability to perceive and to act adequately. When a person is radically deprived of the customary variety of sights, sounds, smells, conversation, and so on—as happens in solitary confinement—he begins to feel strange, and he may show signs of deteriorating as a person. "Sensory deprivation" experiments show that when volunteer subjects are placed in a special room that is soundless, with their vision closed off by special goggles, and immersed in warm water kept at body temperature (to reduce the experience of tactile stimulation), some begin to hallucinate and go through other psychoticlike experiences. I have been in such an isolation chamber, and I found it tranquil and conducive to meditation.

Variety in "stimulus input," then, may be regarded as a basic need, even though deprivation as extreme as that produced in the laboratory seldom occurs in everyday life.[11]

CONTACT WITH NATURE AND ONE'S BODY

A substantial proportion of the world's population lives in cities where trees and grass are never seen, where the sounds of birds and babbling streams are never heard. The air they breathe is either filtered through air-conditioning units or heavily polluted with smog. Such persons adapt to the milieu within which they live, but it is an unnatural environment. Contact with nature, with the seaside, forests, and parks, with fields and animals gives man a sense of rhythm which contrasts with the rhythms of industrialized urban life. These experiences remind man that he does not simply have a body, but he *is* a body, an embodied being who is in and of nature. Chronic physical and muscular tension, accelerated rhythms of speech and movement are common to people who live apart from their own nature and the nature around us all.

Basic Needs and Healthy Personality

Just as man suffers from estrangement from the rest of nature, he also suffers a kind of alienation and distance from his own body (see Chapter 6). From infancy, man needs physical contact with other human beings and with the world. Infants and grown-ups alike need caressing, sensuous massage, enjoyable exercise and dance in order to feel the vitality of their bodies. As Reich, Lowen, and Rolf have pointed out, growing up leaves a person with many muscular systems chronically tensed, as part of an overall defense against danger and pain. This "muscular armor" interferes with fullest respiration, with proper posture, with sleep and rest; it often requires specialized massage and manipulation before the muscular system is restored to the pliability most compatible with a health-giving life. Reich especially pointed out that a chronically defensive attitude reduces a person's capacity for the fullest sexual climaxes. According to Reich, sexual orgasm serves a biological function of energy discharge; it restores optimum muscle tonus, respiration, and the capacity for restful sleep. Of course, orgasm is also an exquisite experience.[12]

Our culture, with its puritan heritage, has encouraged people to repress sensuality, perhaps because it interferes with compulsive work. Recent counterculture developments have introduced a variety of approaches to a re-engagement with nature and with one's own body that seem compatible with healthier personality.

Frustration

Satisfaction of needs seldom can be attained without some measure of struggle and delay. When delay and interference are prolonged, and when the need is of some urgency, psychological tension increases. When the tension mounts to an extreme degree (the precise amount will vary from person to person, and in the same person at different times), disorganization of behavior occurs.

Frustration is the level of tension which produces irrational, disorganized conduct. This meaning of the word corresponds roughly to the usage adopted by Maier.[13] Maier distinguished between motivated behavior and frustration-instigated behavior. The former refers to flexible, voluntary behavior in pursuit of some goal. Frustration-produced behavior has as its sole aim the reduction of frustration tension. Consequently, it may not be adapted to the requirements of the environment. A frustrated person is one who cannot reason and who cannot behave in effective ways. All he can do is "blow off steam."

Frustration of this degree is undesirable from the standpoint of healthy personality growth. Delay in gratification is not a bad thing, however. As long as the level of tension permits effective action, delay can actually promote personal growth, for it assures a person will feel his tensions acutely enough to get into action. In addition, experience with delay helps to build up frustration resistance, or ego strength—a desirable consequence for healthy personality.

SOME FACTORS INFLUENCING
FRUSTRATION THRESHOLDS

There is a level of tension below which the person can think rationally and act effectively. When tension increases above this point, efficiency breaks down, and irrational thinking and expressive behavior take the place of rational thinking and effective action. This point on the tension continuum is called the *frustration threshold*. It varies from person to person, and within the same person at different times.

A mother wants her house to be clean and orderly. In the forenoon, her three-year-old son might spill a glass of milk, leave his toys in disarray, and scatter magazines all over the newly cleaned living room. Her reaction at the time is one of mild anger, followed by efficient attempts to set things straight. At five-thirty in the afternoon, the child repeats his efforts at messing up the house. This time the mother "explodes"—she spanks the child, hurls some chinaware herself, and is unable to prepare supper until she has vented her tension.

Health. It can easily be demonstrated that optimum physical health produces a high frustration threshold. A sick or exhausted person is more easily frustrated than one who is fit.

Competence. A broad repertoire of skills will decrease the frequency of frustrating experiences, even if it does not affect the frustration threshold, because a skilled person is not blocked so often in his quest for satisfaction.

*Basic
Needs
and
Healthy
Personality*

A Strong Sense of Meaning and Purpose in Life.   People who managed to survive the extremely stressing conditions of wartime concentration camps in Germany—so-called death camps—have pointed out that a strong commitment to life and a sense of a mission to fulfill were definite factors in survival. Individuals with such a sense of mission were less readily frustrated by the deprivations, stresses, and pressure of extremely hostile environments.

Opportunities for Release.   When Zorba the Greek was unable to express his grief following the death of his beloved son, he danced a Cretan dance until he dropped from exhaustion. On another occasion, when he felt he had at last found the solution to a problem of bringing logs down a mountainside, again he danced. Finally, when the plan to bring logs down the mountain failed, and his boss's investment was dismally lost, the boss asked Zorba to show him how to dance, and the two men danced and laughed like madmen.

When a person has access to such means of self-expression, as in dance, violent exercise, painting, or song, he can release the inevitable frustration of life without recourse to mindless, destructive outlets of tension. As Reich pointed out,[14] sexual orgasm also provides a natural means for the dissipation of tension. In fact, prolonged sexual privation is a common cause of frustration, with its attendant disorganization of rational thinking (emotional plague) and accompanying tendencies to uncontrolled destructive expression.

Conflict

It is common for a person to experience conflict between his wishes. He may want to study, and also to go to the movies. He may want to marry one girl, and at the same time love another. He may want to have fun but also to be "good."

The healthy thing to do with conflict is to admit its existence, study all the alternatives as rationally as one can in the light of one's value system, make a decision, act on it, and accept all the consequences. Among the consequences to be accepted are regrets over what one has lost in connec-

Healthy Personality: An Approach from the Viewpoint of Humanistic Psychology

tion with the abandoned alternatives. No decision can ever be made without some fear that it is the wrong decision. There is nothing inconsistent with healthy personality in the idea that a decision once made will still leave the person uncertain that it is the best or "rightest" one.

Existential conflicts frequently arise where each choice has positive values and negative implications associated with it. Any alternative, if chosen, will affect one's life profoundly. To make decisions, such as whether to marry or not, to take this job or that, calls for courage. The ability to decide such conflicts is an attribute of healthy personality. Such courage seems to grow out of past experiences at decision-making, experience which fosters independent security.

Need Privation and Sickness

People may sicken in consequences of excessive life stress or from infection ensuing from lowered resistance. An inability to gratify needs by effective action contributes to physical sickness in direct ways. If a person is obliged to persist in ways of acting that are required by his familial, occupational, or age roles, when these ways fail to produce basic need gratification, the person will gradually become *dispirited*. Dispiritation refers to a state of lowered morale, diminished zest in living, and a sense of hopelessness which lowers one's resistance to infection by germs, bacteria, and viruses. A student may develop the flu after being rejected by his girlfriend. A mother may be deprived of fulfilling sexual love, of affection, and appreciation and yet persist in living the joyless life because she can envision no other; her chances of contracting various illnesses are increased. Any prolonged need deprivation dispirits a person and reduces his commitment to life. This reduced commitment to living appears to be responsible (in ways not fully understood) for alterations in the efficiency of the immunity mechanisms of the body.

Everyday life itself is stressing, and persons rest in order to regain strength to cope with the challenges of existence. If a person is living a joyless existence, and cannot alter it, he necessarily forces himself to fight his impulse to flee the

Basic
Needs
and
Healthy
Personality

83

scene. This unremitting struggle to *remain* in a thwarting situation imposes even more stress and can contribute to cardiovascular diseases and respiratory and eliminative disorders.[15]

The Unconscious

To be aware of a need means to experience and identify some lack. Thus, a person may be sexually deprived, admit it, and set about the task of obtaining sexual gratification. But suppose he regards sexual wishes as forbidden? Under these conditions, acknowledgment of his real feelings might give rise to powerful guilt or anxiety. The guilt or anxiety will then motivate him to rid his mind of the offending thoughts. This effort is called repression. Repression of wishes and feelings does not annihilate them; it renders them unconscious. One of Freud's greatest contributions to human understanding was his effort to decipher unconscious motivation through the study of dreams, slips of the tongue, and accidents.[16]

THE INFERENCE OF MOTIVES—
CONSCIOUS AND UNCONSCIOUS

We continuously try to "read" our own and others' motives. The most common bases employed for inferring the intentions, feelings, and needs of the other person are (1) observation of his facial expression, tone of voice, and gestures, which generally disclose what the person is feeling; and (2) observation of the person's action and its consequences, from which we try to infer what he is up to. Ordinarily, we can check our inferences about the other person's motives by asking him.

When are we justified in assuming that our own or another person's motives are unconscious? We can never be absolutely certain, but we can entertain the hypothesis of unconscious motivation (1) when the person acts in ways that produce consequences he denies intending to produce; (2) when he shows many signs of emotion without admitting he is experiencing strong feeling; and (3) when there are obvious inconsistencies in action at different times, for example, kindness and brutality, intelligent and stupid behavior.

Healthy Personality: An Approach from the Viewpoint of Humanistic Psychology

In addition to these general signs of unconscious motivation, there are other more subtle indicators that a person is not conscious of real influences upon his behavior. These include:

1. Dream content that seems bizarre and incomprehensible to the dreamer.
2. Daydreams that surprise the daydreamer.
3. Errors and "slips" in speech and writing.
4. Body postures and evidence of bodily tensions.
5. The forgetting of intentions, and the names of people and places.
6. Accidents of all kinds.
7. Performance on certain projective tests of personality.

ILLUSTRATIONS OF LIKELY INSTANCES
OF UNCONSCIOUS MOTIVATION

During my training I was influenced by Freud's monumental books *The Psychopathology of Everyday Life* and *The Interpretation of Dreams,* which are full of examples of unconscious motives. Here are some collected out of my experience as a psychologist:

An Example from Dreams. A nine-year-old child was judged by all who knew him to be very "good." He was "respectful" to his parents and affirmed his love for his father in almost every conversation. He related this dream to me: "I dreamed that I was a soldier, and we had a very mean captain. One day, when nobody was around, he was beating up a very nice lady. I took my machine gun and shot him a million times. He fell into a lot of little pieces when I was finished."

One does not have to be a professional interpreter of dreams to suspect that the officer was a symbolic version of his father, toward whom the boy had a strong but repressed hostility, and the "nice lady" his mother, to whom he was very attached.

An Example from Daydreaming. A student preparing for the ministry related to me with much embarrassment and guilt that he was afraid to be alone or without some busywork to perform. As soon as he was idle, his mind filled with the most "sinful and voluptuous images of sex." He couldn't understand why this should be, as he was ordinarily an upright, "clean-thinking" young man.

Slips of the Tongue and Pen. The following item came from a local newspaper: A minister had spent some time in Hollywood, and was interviewed by a local reporter with respect to his impressions. The article related how the minister deplored the moral turpitude of many movie stars. The article ended with this sentence (the italics are mine): "It is a shame the way our nation's best entertainers, in their lives offstage, are forever making *pubic* spectacles of themselves."

Examples from Body Posturing and Tensions. Variations in the muscle tonus of parts of a person's body may reflect repressed emotions and need tensions.[17] A flaccid handshake may disclose a lack of sincerity. A soft, suckling mouth may reveal unconscious wishes to be passive and dependent.[18] A female student complained that men were forever "making passes" at her, yet she denied any erotic interest in males. Observation revealed her bodily movements were very provocative. She wiggled her hips when walking and pushed her chest high. When talking with a man, she glued her eyes, alternately opened and narrowed, to his. Repressed hostility may be manifested by excessive muscular tension in the forehead, neck, or shoulders, often resulting in headaches, a "pain in the neck," and back pain.[19]

Forgetting of Intentions, Names. I once forgot to write a letter of recommendation for a graduate student whom I disliked for personal reasons that had nothing to do with his ability. Fortunately the student received the position without the benefit of my letter.

Accidents. Accidents may result in disadvantage either to the person himself or to others, depending upon the unconscious motivation, guilt in the former case, hostility in the latter. A colleague's wife spilled ink on a manuscript her husband was working on (neglecting her as he did the work) as she cleaned his study. A student broke his hand shortly before he had to take an examination for which he felt unqualified.

Examples from Projective Tests. A twenty-two-year-old undergraduate student once consulted me for help with vague guilt feelings, inability to study, and fierce headaches which occurred whenever he went home or was obliged to spend any time with the Dean, one of his professors, or his boss at a part-time job. He appeared to be extremely polite. (He used the word *sir* in almost every sentence when talking to me.) In the Thematic Apperception Test, many of his stories included some expression of violence and hatred toward authority figures. The student told this story about Card 12M, which shows an old man stretching his hand toward the reclining figure of a younger man:

> This boy is having a nap. The old man, his father, is coming in to get him out of bed so he'll get back to his studies. His father has been nagging him for ages about how lazy he is. The boy has been putting up with this for a long time. This is the last straw. When he wakes up, he'll be so mad he'll start beating up on his father. He'll grab a chair and start mashing in his head. When he finishes, his old man will be a bloody pulp. The boy will get the electric chair, but he won't care, it was worth it.

It is not too farfetched to infer at least some unconscious hostility toward authority figures in this young man.

There is no discovered way, as yet, to prove that an inference of unconscious motivation is warranted. Nevertheless, it can be shown that the motives a person will consider as possible influences upon his action will change under special circumstances. A patient entering psychotherapy may act in ways that humiliate his wife; yet at the outset he may vigorously deny having hostile feelings toward her. Finally he can admit having hostile feelings, without guilt or anxiety. In addition, his hostility, if rational and warranted, may come to be expressed much more openly than it was before. It often happens that recognition and understanding of irrational hostility will reduce or eliminate it.

Repression, obviously, is not an effective way to deal with problems of existence. People sometimes repress experience because they have a strict conscience; it is often healthier to attempt to change the conscience or to accept the fact that one is not as "good" as one would like to believe. Repression is a way to ward off anxiety, but there are more effective and healthier ways. Repression may ward off painful frustration, but there are healthier ways to avoid frustration, such as learning skills. Only where repression is temporary and permits important action to be completed, or where it forestalls psychosis, can it be regarded as good for healthy personality.

HEALTHY FEATURES OF THE UNCONSCIOUS

Creativity.   Healthier personalities have been more successful than average people in gratifying their needs. Consequently, their unconscious is not a dreaded source of evil, but a fount of innovation, self-integration, and creativity. Creative individuals show less fear of the free play of fantasy, and so they can "unrepress" to a greater degree than the average. In freeing their unconscious from its customary bonds, they experience the welcome admission to consciousness of new ideas, solutions to problems, insights into themselves, and other valued creations.

Health-Giving Morality.   Sexuality or unacceptable drives such as aggression are not the only aspects of personality that are typically repressed. Mowrer has shown that individuals repress their consciences, and hence are unconscious of the guilt that would arise if the conscience were not repressed. If a man has acquired a conscience that could guide him in the direction of his fullest growth and personal integration, then its repression could thwart his healthiest potentials. The individual said to have a "hardened heart," like Scrooge in Dickens' classic *Christmas Carol,* is one who has likely repressed his conscience and the guilt to which it might give rise. The unrepression of conscience in such individuals will produce acute guilt. The guilt, if acknowledged, could motivate the person to change his usual ways of behavior from self-centered pursuit of satisfaction to more loving concern for others.[20]

Glimpses of Growing Possibilities.   While Freud showed how people repressed undesirable dimensions of their experience, Jung called attention to the fact that we remain unconscious of our "higher," more fully humanized possibilities.[21] The unconscious is not only a repository of our psychological "sewage"; it is also the source of our most sublime possibilities.

Just as dreams reveal morally repugnant wishes for tabooed sexuality or murder, so they can reveal, albeit in metaphoric language, possible ways for a person to rise above barriers to his growth. In dreams, many persons discover the solutions to vexing personal problems.

Our usual waking consciousness is limited by our chronic preoccupation with daily needs and projects. Other possible ways to experience ourselves and the world remain unconscious, or potentially conscious, and may be revealed to us in our dreams.

Goals Beyond Basic Need Fulfillment: Self-actualization

If a person is coping with his basic needs, his energy and thoughts are freed for other interests. The exact nature of these interests will differ from person to person, but the diversity and intensity of involvement in matters outside the self is a good indicator of healthy personality. When a man ceases to be a problem to himself, because he has fulfilled his needs for security, love, and status, he will begin to see the world in a manner which differs from the way "deficiency-motivated" persons see it.[22] He can forget himself and become involved in play, or in another person's problems, and perhaps with the well-being of mankind as a whole. It is difficult to become concerned about the hunger or enslavement of another person when one is in the midst of such privation oneself. When a person has experienced and transcended these conditions, he can empathize with (i.e., imagine with vividness) the experience of others and devote himself to serving them.

Many interests and values grow out of a person's earlier quest for the means of gratifying basic needs. Thus, a man may become a physician as a means of assuring his economic security. However, once he is earning the money he was seeking, he may (indeed, he *should*) find intrinsic fascination in the challenges posed by illness. His motivation for the practice of medicine changes then from a quest for money to a quest for knowledge of new ways to relieve suffering. Whenever an interest in some activity comes into being as a means of satisfying basic needs, and then changes into a spontaneous fascination, the motive is said to be *functionally autonomous* [23] of its more basic origins. We do not fully understand the mechanisms by which functional autonomy of motives occurs; it appears to be a matter of commitment.

Man needs meaningful activity to give direction and value to his existence. We have little difficulty understanding much human action, because it clearly serves the most basic needs. But when a person has assured his access to his basic requirements, the question arises, What shall he do now with the time and energy that has become available? What is worth doing? One can consume only so much food, he can only be loved a certain amount, he can only be safe to some degree. What will he next do with his time and resources?

We are dealing fundamentally with the question of persuasion. Some challenges, tasks, hobbies, and vocations which have little to do with one's basic needs are "invested" with value and worth by our observation of someone else. We see him doing something with his time which seems to give him much satisfaction. Either by invitation or by self-initiative, persons explore ways to spend their time, and commit themselves to such activity. The billions of interests which absorb persons attest to the fact that man can give value to anything from collecting seedpods to scaling mountains at great risk to life and limb, because they are there. The capacity to commit oneself to activities and projects beyond basic need fulfillment is a further defining characteristic of healthier personality.[24]

Some Existential Suggestions

What has been lacking in your life at times at which you have found yourself bored, miserable, or even sick? What can you do about these lacks? Upon whom do you depend to gratify these needs? What does your dependency "cost" you in the way of submission to the wishes of the person upon whom you are dependent? What do you believe you cannot do without? Viktor Frankl showed that it is possible not only to survive, but moreover to transcend lethal circumstances; he wrote most of a book while he struggled to survive for eight years in a Nazi death camp.

Healthy Personality: An Approach from the Viewpoint of Humanistic Psychology

Can you identify what you need to enhance your life, and learn the skills that will enable you to gratify these needs? This is what Blatz has described as overcoming insecurity through action—the way of independent security.

Whenever you become sick—with a cold, flu, mononucleosis, or other illness—reflect upon your life, and see if you can identify an episode of dispiritedness brought on by loss of someone's love, an abrupt change in way of life (such as moving to another residence), or some failure. Or consider whether your style of life or family role are preventing you from gratifying certain basic needs; prolonged deprivation may have stressed or dispirited you. Sickness is a splendid opportunity to reflect upon your way of living, so that when you have recovered, you can make changes that will reduce the likelihood of becoming sick again. Sickness is often an indication that one's habitual way of life has not yielded those basic need gratifications that sustain health and keep a person growing in vital ways.

When all is not well in your life, it is good to record dreams for hints as to possible changes you could make to revitalize yourself. Getting back to nature—a walk in the woods or by the sea, away from machinery and work—can provide an opportunity to meditate and gain perspective upon an unsatisfying life style. I strongly suspect that, if a person could apply the contents of this chapter to his life, he would seldom get sick; if he did sicken, and used that time to explore ways to change his life, he would radically reduce the probability of future bouts of illness.

SUMMARY

Basic
Needs
and
Healthy
Personality

Nobody knows, ultimately, what man needs in order not merely to survive, but to prevail and to develop his full possibilities. Man's most basic needs include the need to affirm life itself, physical gratifications, love, status and self-esteem, freedom and space, challenge, meditation, cognitive clarity, meaning, variety and change, and contact with nature. There may be more basic needs, and some of those mentioned may not be essential to life itself, but they certainly make for a richer existence if they have been met.

Prolonged deprivation may bring about a state of frustra-

tion, when a person loses contact with reality and may engage in destructive tension-reducing action.

Frustration thresholds are heightened by good health, competence, meaning in life, and opportunities for release. Prolonged deprivation of basic needs can sicken a person through diminished resistance to infection which is brought about by stress or dispiritedness.

Needs and emotions that threaten a person's self-esteem and sense of security may be repressed, and operate as unconscious influences upon action and experience. Such unconscious motives may appear in the content of dreams, in accidents and errors, in body postures, in the forgetting of intentions and promises, and in certain projective tests of personality. The unconscious harbors one's possibilities for achievement and growth as well as for action that is personally or socially reprehensible.

Once a person has gratified his basic needs, his energies and experience are liberated so that he can turn to projects beyond basic need satisfaction, such as the pursuit of freedom, justice, beauty, or truth. The problem is to find goals and projects that are challenging and fascinating.

NOTES AND REFERENCES

1. This analysis of needs and wants comes from Blatz's thirty-year-old book dealing with children. Blatz was one of my first teachers at the University of Toronto, and this book still is valid. See W. E. BLATZ, *Understanding the Young Child* (New York: Morrow, 1944), pp. 80–82 and also Chapter 9, on security. Man's vulnerability to control by other people—not only by the physical environment which "selects" the "right" behavior—is shown in B. F. SKINNER, *Beyond Freedom and Dignity* (New York: Knopf, 1971).

2. A. H. MASLOW, *Motivation and Personality,* 2nd ed. (New York: Harper & Row, 1970).

3. Cf. J. BOWLBY, *Child Care and the Growth of Love* (London: Pelican, 1953); M. RIBBLE, *The Rights of Infants* (New York: Columbia University Press, 1943); R. SPITZ, "Hospitalism," in *Psychoanalytic Study of the Child, I* (New York: International Universities Press, 1945).

4. D. C. McCLELLAND, *The Achieving Society* (New York: Free Press, 1967). Also see V. PACKARD, *The Status Seekers* (New York: McKay, 1959).

Healthy Personality: An Approach from the Viewpoint of Humanistic Psychology

5. See the article by Frank Barron, which analyzes freedom as a feeling, like affection or anxiety: F. BARRON, "Freedom as Feeling," *Journal of Humanistic Psychology,* 1961, Vol. 1, pp. 91–100; Erich Fromm's classic *Escape from Freedom* (New York: Holt, 1941) should be read in this context. In the English edition, this book is entitled *Fear of Freedom.*

6. D. MORRIS, *The Human Zoo* (New York: McGraw-Hill, 1969); R. ARDREY, *The Territorial Imperative* (New York: Atheneum, 1966); R. WESTIN, *Privacy and Freedom* (New York: Atheneum, 1967); R. SOMMER, *Personal Space: The Behavioral Basis of Design* (Englewood Cliffs, N.J.: Prentice-Hall, 1969); S. M. JOURARD, *The Transparent Self,* 2nd ed. (New York: Van Nostrand Reinhold, 1971), Chapter 8, "The Need for Privacy."

7. Shaw wrote effectively upon the need for challenge. See F. J. SHAW, *Reconciliation: A Theory of Man Transcending* (New York: Van Nostrand Reinhold, 1966), posthumously edited by S. M. JOURARD and D. OVERLADE.

8. C. TART (ED.), *Altered States of Consciousness* (New York: Wiley, 1969).

9. See ELSE FRENKEL-BRUNSWIK, "Intolerance of Ambiguity as an Emotional and Perceptual Personality Variable," *Journal of Personality,* 1949, Vol. 18, pp. 108–143; L. FESTINGER, *A Theory of Cognitive Dissonance* (New York: Harper & Row, 1957); G. A. KELLY, *The Psychology of Personal Constructs,* I: *A Theory of Personality* (New York: Norton, 1955), Chapter 2; M. ROKEACH, *The Open and Closed Mind* (New York: Basic Books, 1960).

10. V. E. FRANKL, *Man's Search for Meaning,* rev. ed. (Boston: Beacon, 1963); E. FROMM, *The Sane Society* (New York: Holt, 1955).

11. D. W. FISKE and S. R. MADDI, *Functions of Varied Experience* (Homewood, Ill.: Dorsey, 1961), Chapter 5; J. P. ZUBEK (ED.), *Sensory Deprivation: Fifteen Years of Research* (New York: Appleton-Century-Crofts, 1969); J. C. LILLY, *The Center of the Cyclone* (Garden City, N.Y.: Doubleday, 1971).

12. W. REICH, *The Discovery of the Orgone: The Function of the Orgasm* (New York: Noonday, 1961), Chapters 2 and 8. See A. MONTAGU, *Touching: The Human Significance of the Skin* (New York: Harper & Row, 1972), for a fine review of evidence on the need for physical contact.

13. N. R. MAIER, *Frustration: The Study of Behavior Without a Goal* (New York: McGraw-Hill, 1949); R. LAWSON, *Frustration: The Development of a Scientific Concept* (New York: Macmillan, 1965).

14. W. Reich, *Character Analysis* (New York: Orgone Institute Press, 1949), Chapter 12.

15. H. Selye, *The Physiology and Pathology of Exposure to Stress* (Montreal: Acta, 1950), or his less technical book *The Stress of Life* (New York: McGraw-Hill, 1956). See also Jourard, *The Transparent Self*, op. cit., pp. 75–102; D. Bakan, *The Duality of Human Existence* (Chicago: Rand McNally, 1966); and D. Bakan, *Pain, Disease, and Sacrifice: Toward a Psychology of Suffering* (Chicago: University of Chicago Press, 1968).

16. S. Freud, *The Interpretation of Dreams* (New York: Basic Books, 1955); S. Freud, *The Psychopathology of Everyday Life* (New York: Norton, 1971). These are classics that every student should read, as part of a liberal education.

17. Reich, op. cit.

18. E. Fromm, *Man for Himself* (New York: Holt, 1947).

19. See J. C. Moloney, *The Magic Cloak: A Contribution to the Psychology of Authoritarianism* (Wakefield, Mass.: Montrose Press, 1949), pp. 99–101; also Chapter 13, for a discussion of diverse psychosomatic symptoms which Moloney found associated with repressed hostility among people who work in authoritarian settings. Hemorrhoids, back pain, and high blood pressure are not uncommon in persons who daily are provoked to anger but dare not express their feelings. For experimental demonstrations of muscular tension, see R. B. Malmo, C. Shagass, and J. F. Davis, "Electromyographic Studies of Muscular Tension in Psychiatric Patients Under Stress," *Journal of Clinical and Experimental Psychopathology*, 1951, Vol. 12, pp. 45–66.

20. O. H. Mowrer, *The Crisis in Psychiatry and Religion* (New York: Van Nostrand Reinhold, 1961); C. G. Jung, *Two Essays on Analytic Psychology* (New York: Meridian, 1956), pp. 182–197.

21. A. H. Maslow, *Toward a Psychology of Being*, 2nd ed. (New York: Van Nostrand Reinhold, 1968), Chapter 3.

22. Commitment is a case of attribution of importance to some possible future. See my essay "Some Notes on the Experience of Commitment" in Humanitas, *Journal of the Institute of Man,* 1972, Vol. 8, pp. 5–8. The entire issue of the journal was devoted to papers on commitment. Commitment illustrates the "functional autonomy" of motives from their origins. See G. W. Allport, *Pattern and Growth in Personality* (New York: Holt, 1961), pp. 226–229.

5

EMOTION AND HEALTHY PERSONALITY

INTRODUCTION

Emotion gives life its intensity and meaning. We are amused and we laugh; someone insults us and we become angry. A young woman has just received a proposal of marriage from the man she loves; her excitement and joy are dramatically evident. Emotion is not only a quality of experience; when we feel anything, there is more going on than consciousness itself. An angry person knows that he is angry. An observer will be able to infer that the person is angry by noting his facial expression, his action, and signs of altered physiological activity—flushing, tremor, and increased heart rate.[1]

Emotion is a quality of experience and an expressive quality of action. We can speak thus of emotional experience and emotional expression. The former is emotion viewed from a phenomenological perspective, that is, from the standpoint of the person himself, whereas emotional expression is the way emotional experience appears to an observer.

There is no authoritative catalogue of emotional experience. Furthermore, there is no precise differentiation of the physiological expression of emotion. Physiological psychologists have difficulty naming the emotional experience that a person is undergoing when their only data are markings on a polygraph which depict alterations in autonomic nervous system activity. Each society and subculture has stereotyped ways in which persons express, and hence communicate, their feelings to one another. The behavioral, gestural, and facial expressions can be faked—one can pretend to experience feelings he does not actually have. Perhaps the only person who knows with certainty what feelings he is experiencing is the person himself, and even he may be unaware that he is in an emotional state; it is a human possibility to repress the affective quality of experience.

In spite of these qualifications, we can identify some common feelings and emotions and recognize them in ourselves and others. From the standpoint of healthy personality, it is desirable to be free to experience the fullest gamut of emotion, because of the enrichment it affords to the quality of life. Not to know emotion is to be like a robot or zombie. Further, it is vital that a person's feelings be authentic rather than pretended. Pretended emotion falsifies relationships with other people; such inauthenticity undermines health and distorts personal growth.

THE INTELLIGIBILITY OF EMOTION

Emotional expression is an aspect of communication. If we share a common upbringing and cultural heritage, we will not have difficulty in understanding the subtleties and nuances of emotion that are conveyed by the flare of a nostril, the narrowing of eyelids, or the ripple of muscle along the jawline as a person suppresses rage. When we enter another culture, however, such as happens when an American from New York visits a Southern state, or another English-speaking country, we frequently do not recognize when our speech and actions are angering or amusing the local people. Indeed, it may take years to learn the perspective, expectations, and evaluative norms of the natives, and until that happens, a visitor may feel lonely and out of

Healthy Personality: An Approach from the Viewpoint of Humanistic Psychology

touch. Many students have had the experience of joy and relief at encountering someone from their home when they were abroad.

Understanding one another's feelings is usually immediate between people who know one another. There are occasions, however, when the emotional disclosure of someone well known becomes unintelligible; we cannot comprehend why a friend is terrified, angry, or sexually aroused. This is the case with so-called schizophrenic [2] and neurotic people; their emotionality does not appear to make sense, even to members of their families. Yet, because they are human, it must be assumed that the emotional experience of such sufferers makes sense to them, in the light of their perspective upon the world. If someone is terrified, it is because he experiences imminent danger; if he is enraged, it is because someone has violated his space and his integrity. All emotion makes sense when we have imaginatively grasped the perspective of the person who is feeling it. It is such empathy, and the willingness to encounter and enter into dialogue with someone with a different perspective, which is so important for therapists, teachers of children, parents, and those who seek to live and work in another country.

Some Common Forms of Emotional Experience

PLEASURE

It feels good to eat when one is hungry, to drink when one is thirsty, to urinate and to empty one's bowels when the time to do so has come. Physical massage and the sheer sensuality of being caressed yield pleasure not overshadowed by sexual orgasm, which is viewed by most humans as the acme of human pleasures. Although pleasure as such cannot serve as the chief purpose of life—the reality principle discussed by Freud tells us that the quest for pleasure can endanger life itself—a life without pleasure is hardly worth living. Gratification of basic needs is pleasurable in and for itself, and the capacity to feel such pleasure is one of the rewards of healthy personality. Although it may seem surprising, many persons actually dread the experience of pleasure, and repress it. Such repression is most likely in

Emotion and Healthy Personality

97

persons reared under puritanical regimes in which "self-indulgence" is regarded as a sin.[3]

Pleasure comes not only from the act of satisfying basic needs, however. There is joy to be found in contemplation of beauty in music, art, and nature, in the sound of birds, the sight of a child taking his first steps, the smell of new-mown hay. Another source of pleasure is to be found in the zest accompanying action. Zest is engendered when a person engages in activities which will challenge, but not overwhelm him. Thus, a game of tennis or handball, surfing along the perfect wave, skiing down a fast slope, yield pleasure no less than that afforded by a sensuous, passive massage. Similar zest arises in those who love their work, whether it be that of an artist in his studio, a scientist in his laboratory, or a businessman planning a sales campaign. People who experience pleasure in living do not develop the "up-tight," armored bodies and grim facial expressions of those whose life has been hard and joyless or whose religious orientation proscribes pleasure as a sin. And those who find zest in their work and play appear "childlike" or ageless—they do not grow old.

Pleasure engulfs the experience of persons who have just had their hopes fulfilled, or who have just completed a valued project. The delights of winning a prize or receiving an unexpected gift are among the "highs" in life, as are the joys of finishing a difficult mountain climb or writing a book.

Pleasure—whether occasioned by sensuality, physical activity, or the consummation of projects—is a goal and reward of healthy personality.

DEPRESSION

A person typically becomes depressed when his life has lost delight, and any sense of meaning or hope. Occasions for depression include the death of a loved person, prolonged failure of one's projects, the loss of beauty or one's health and vitality. When a person is depressed, he experiences life as hellish—time slows down, nothing is happening, he may feel worthless, guilty, and beneath contempt. Clearly, when a person is depressed, his life is not yielding what is needed for vital, enlivening existence. Depressed people frequently make suicidal attempts, and they sometimes succeed—which is a shame, because a person can dis-

Healthy Personality: An Approach from the Viewpoint of Humanistic Psychology

engage from a hopeless way of being, and, with a little imaginative help from his friends or a psychotherapist, reinvent himself and his situation in ways that engender more positive experience. Although depression is hellish, it can and perhaps should serve as a motive to the sufferer to change his situation to a more life-giving one.

ANXIETY AND DREAD

Anxiety or dread are experienced when one believes his way of life is in jeopardy, and there is no possibility of further existence. Anxiety differs from fear in that with the latter, one can see the source of the danger, and can, perhaps, cope with it by combat or flight. Anxiety is more likely to arise when one has violated a personal or a religious taboo, and experiences the imminence of annihilation while helpless to do anything about it. It is also triggered by signals that do not appear to make sense, such as a horror of high places, panic over insects, or a dread of dirt. A simple onslaught of such anxiety or dread is enough to traumatize a person for a lifetime, if he survives it. Indeed, some of the most rigid character traits and so-called defense mechanisms are developed as desperate means of ensuring the horror will never again be experienced. Many compulsive habits, like primitive religious taboos and injunctions, persist throughout a person's life, interfering with his personal relations and with the spontaneous enjoyment of life, in order to prevent the dreaded anxiety. When a person cannot avert the experience of anxiety by regulating his life or his environment, he may develop any of the life styles that are described by psychiatrists as neurotic or psychotic. These ways of being are themselves devoid of joy, because they are so hemmed in by inhibitions; but the diminished life is preferred by the patient to facing, unaided and alone, that annihilation of his world and his identity which is called anxiety.

It is impossible, however, to live without some encounter with anxiety. The posture most compatible with healthy personality, in an encounter with dread, is the posture of courage, the "courage to be" of which Paul Tillich wrote so beautifully. The person with courage to face the unknown with resolve and fortitude discovers his unplumbed capacities to grow and to cope with life. As paradoxical as it

Emotion and Healthy Personality

may sound, the experience of anxiety is essential for growth. Courage is most likely to appear, however, in those persons fortunate enough to have an "encourager" in their lives, whether it be a friend, family member, counselor, or their deity.[4]

ANGER, HOSTILITY, RAGE

The capacity to experience anger, like the ability to become afraid, is a biological endowment; presumably, it served the interests of man's survival as a species. The problem, however, is how to regulate anger, for it can lead to violence between people. Open violence makes family and community life impossible. Chronically suppressed anger is a factor in the development of many psychosomatic illnesses, including peptic ulcers, high blood pressure, asthma, colitis, and so on. Anger typically arises when someone or something enters one's "territory" unbidden; and it arises when people get in the way of one's projects. Finally, it arises, in the form of moral indignation, when one sees people acting in ways which one profoundly feels are evil. Anger energizes a person for attack, just as fear energizes for flight. When a person is at war, his rage will serve him well, enabling him to fight without reserve. In everyday life, however, the recurrent provocation to anger or irritation, without the possibility of full expression of anger or escape from the provokers, undermines health and well-being.

A person needs to find respite from nagging irritation, and to find socially and personally acceptable ways to express accumulated anger. Violent exercise, such as in handball or tennis, is frequently helpful as a harmless way to express anger that cannot be expressed in other ways. Of course, the attainment of a more positive attitude toward life may reduce the frequency with which a person becomes angered. Very conservative people often become enraged at the appearance and actions of so-called hippies, even to the point of wishing them to be imprisoned or killed; a broader perspective upon what is regarded as acceptable ways to be human certainly diminishes the anger of such persons.

The problem with anger is to learn how to accept it as natural in oneself and to express it in nondestructive ways.

Healthy Personality: An Approach from the Viewpoint of Humanistic Psychology

One author, Israel Charney, regards marriage and family life, not as a haven of peace and happiness, though it can be that; rather he sees the relationship between man and wife, and between parent and child, as a place to learn ways to reconcile differences, and to deal with anger without destroying the persons toward whom one is angry. George Bach has actually provided instructions to married people on ways to fight fairly and nondestructively with one another.[5]

GUILT

We are not capable of experiencing guilt until we have formed a conscience. Young children, prior to the internalization of their parents' moral expectations, may experience fear of punishment for misdeeds, but this is not guilt.

Guilt is the experience of self-loathing that arises when a person transgresses his own moral principles. It can be so powerful an emotion that a guilt-ridden person may kill himself rather than endure the onslaught of self-hatred. Common occasions for guilt include hurting another person, stealing, violating one's own sexual morality, or cheating in examinations.

A distinction can be drawn between guilt which arises from the violation of moral taboos one truly has outgrown, and existential or humanistic guilt, which arises when a person has diminished the quality and possibility of life for himself and others. Maslow calls the former, "silly guilt," as in instances when an adult engages in masturbation and feels a catastrophic loss of self-esteem for what is properly viewed as a harmless solitary sport. Existential guilt is illustrated by the failure to respond to a call for help, or the failure to fulfill one's own possibilities through lack of nerve. The capacity for existential guilt is an achievement; of course, the most life-giving response to such guilt is to make restitution, and to seek then to live in conformity with one's ideals.[6]

WEEPING

In our society at least, only women and young children can weep without self-consciousness and embarrassment. Grown men are generally regarded as weak if they cry when sad or hurt. Perhaps the only exceptions are instances where a man has lost someone close to him through death. Then tears are grudgingly accepted in a man, or at least regarded as understandable.

The ability to cry—in men as well as in women and children—is desirable for healthy personality. It is deemed desirable when it does not preclude more active ways of coping with problems, and when it is effective in releasing feelings of despair, joy, anger, or a sense of loss. Such emotional "catharsis," or release of feelings, frees the person to resume his life once more on an active basis. Psychotherapists find that when their patients are finally able to weep during therapy sessions, the course of therapy proceeds more satisfactorily. This is especially true of male patients who find weeping a drastic threat to their self-esteem and their masculine identities. Therapy calls for the fullest disclosure of experience on the part of the patient, and if he will not permit himself to cry when he wants to, it indicates a lack of trust in his therapist.

The inhibition of weeping which characterizes the average male in our society seems to be but part of a more generalized suppression of many other kinds of feelings, including tenderness and sentimentality. Such suppression, if carried to extremes, can have unhealthy consequences for the body and can also render men's relationships with others empty and lifeless.

HUMOR AND LAUGHTER

The capacity to see humor in situations and to respond with laughter is an indication of being well. Loss of the ability to laugh at oneself and at comic situations is one of the early symptoms of more serious personality disorders. When a person can laugh even in potentially grim situations, it implies some degree of freedom from the press of fate and circumstances. Prisoners in Nazi concentration camps during World War II could find something to laugh at, though they lived but a hairbreadth from torture and death.

One psychologist, Franklin J. Shaw, regarded laughter as one of the purest examples of characteristically human behavior. Laughter is a response that can be made only by persons who have transcended their animal heritage as well as the conformity-producing pressures of society. Laughter

Healthy Personality: An Approach from the Viewpoint of Humanistic Psychology

is defiance of brute necessity, a proclamation of freedom, and the ability to transcend the limits of otherwise grim circumstances.

Of course, there are rough norms defining the appropriateness or inappropriateness of laughter. Schizophrenics will often laugh in situations where a more intact person might weep or become angry. But a good sense of humor, the ability to find something ludicrous in situations, is not only a social asset; it is an indication that a person is able to do more than just struggle to exist.

Frivolity as a Defense. Some persons will joke about things which probably should be taken seriously. People who are afraid to admit their righteous and justified anger, or who are afraid to be taken seriously, may cloak matters of genuine concern in laughter. When they do this chronically, they permit situations to be perpetuated which could be changed for the better if they dropped the humorous façade.

Jokes. A clever and even off-color story can add zest to a gathering, but it takes a certain savoir-faire to be able to distinguish between those times when a joke will contribute enjoyable laughter to a situation and when it will bring agonizing embarrassment to the listeners.

Healthier personalities are able to find humor in situations, they are able to laugh at themselves as well as at others who might strut or huff and puff in phony pretense, but they will not be addicted to jokes which inflict harm or express malice. It should not be forgotten, however, that there are some situations, as in dictatorships, where overt hostility against the leaders of a regime might bring death or imprisonment to the rebels. Under conditions of this sort, satire, jokes, and cartoons which cleverly deride the ruling regime may be the only available outlet for feelings. Furthermore, such humor may serve a valuable function in sustaining morale.[7]

THE FEELING OF FREEDOM

In an important theoretical paper Frank Barron proposed that freedom be defined not only as the repertoire of adaptive responses available to a person in a given situation, but also as a *feeling*. The implication of this view of freedom— seeing it as a feeling in the sense that anger, sex, or guilt are feelings—is that one can study how persons cope with it. Thus, the feeling of freedom can be repressed, projected, and have reaction formations constructed against it, and it can be responsibly acknowledged.

"In what situations, with what other persons, does a given individual feel free?" This question can be used as a guide for the student to survey his own life situation. The opposite of the feeling of freedom is the feeling of compulsion, or the feeling of being driven. Maximization of the feeling of freedom is a desirable quality for healthy personality. However, little direct study has yet been made of the conditions upon which the feeling of freedom is dependent. Tentatively, we may propose that persons feel most free when they perceive their environment as safe, when they perceive other people as accepting, trustworthy, and loving, and when they perceive themselves as competent and fundamentally good. This latter point is made because it seems likely that the man who regards himself as good does not have to watch his own behavior carefully in order to make certain that no evil or dangerous behavior will emerge. Instead, he can permit himself to be spontaneous. Spontaneity in expression and behavior is one of the forms in which the feeling of freedom manifests itself.[8]

BOREDOM

Boredom arises from doing repetitive, unchallenging work. It arises as a consequence of relationships with persons who lack spontaneity and who do not relate to us in ways that meet our needs for affection, understanding, or intellectual stimulation. Boredom arises when people do not actively choose what they will do, but instead permit their lives to be lived for them by social pressures to conform with rigid roles and concepts of respectability. Boredom is inevitable in human life, but there are healthy and unhealthy methods of coping with it. The unhealthy patterns include (1) permitting it to continue for indefinite periods of time without making an effort to understand its causes, and (2) impulsively seeking excitement or diversion without striving to understand the causes. For example, some people may drive automobiles at breakneck speeds simply to interrupt monotony. Others flee ennui by attending many movies, drinking too much liquor, staying "stoned" on marijuana or other drugs, watching television for long

Healthy Personality: An Approach from the Viewpoint of Humanistic Psychology

hours, or reading "escape" literature. Any of these is harm-less as a temporary palliative, but they endanger one's health when they are the sole reaction. The healthier approach to boredom is to reflect upon one's life, to ascertain what one truly wants and the ways in which existence is failing to provide legitimate satisfaction. If a person is unable to diagnose his own needs, he is serving the interests of healthy personality by discussing his situation and his personality with a friend, or by seeking counseling from a psychologist or psychiatrist.

AFFECTION AND TENDERNESS

Well-loved children feel and express affection for parents, siblings, friends, and animals. As they grow and become socialized to their sex roles, and ultimately their occupa-tional and community roles, they frequently lose the ca-pacity to feel affection and tender concern for others. Men of our culture especially appear to be subject to a "tender-ness taboo." [9]

Their relationships with other men frequently are limited to reserved expressions of friendship or competition in work or in games. The male role, as socially defined, impels many men to regard affection and tender solicitude between men as evidence of homosexuality or effeminacy. Women are en-couraged, by contrast, to be more open in experiencing and expressing their affection. There is evidence that such rigid differentiation between the sexes is breaking down in Amer-ica and other Western countries, so that men can be softer, less aggressive, and more affectionate in their relationships with others, regardless of age or sex. From the perspective of healthy personality, such liberation from rigid sex roles is good for men, women, and children alike, and may even add years to the typical male life expectancy. Affection is life-giving, both for the object of the affection and the one who is feeling and bestowing it.

The Origins of Emotional Habits

Thus far, we have regarded emotion as a quality of per-sonal experience, adding flavor and tone to our perception, memory, imagination, and thinking. But emotional experi-ence can also be regarded as a kind of *habit*, that is, as a re-curring association between the perception of some happening and a recognizable quality of experience. Thus, a person displays an emotional habit when he experiences fear every time he is called upon to speak before an audience; anger when someone criticizes his appearance; erotic feeling when he looks at nude pictures; and so on. To the extent that emotional experience does become patterned, it is appropriate to explain it in terms provided by the psychology of learning. We learn our emotional habits. There are wide individual and cultural differences in emotional habits; within a given society, however, many emotional habits are shared. Our emotional habits are acquired through *conditioning,* through *learning expectancies,* and through a kind of mimicry, or imitation, of the emotional reactions of other people called *identification.*[10]

CONDITIONING AND EMOTIONAL RESPONSES

The reader is no doubt familiar with the experimental procedure named *conditioning* discovered by Pavlov. In brief, the laboratory procedure of conditioning involves:

1. Discovering some response or reflex which can regularly be elicited by some stimulus, called the unconditioned stimulus. Examples of such reflexes and the unconditioned stimuli which evoke them are the eyeblink, a puff of air; knee jerk, a blow on the patellar tendon; salivation, the presence of food or acid in the mouth. The response itself, when considered together with its relevant unconditioned stimulus, is described as an unconditioned response.

2. Presenting a neutral stimulus along with the unconditioned stimulus for a number of trials. After a suitable number of pairings of the neutral stimulus with the unconditioned stimulus, the former will come to elicit the response ordinarily evoked by the unconditioned stimulus. When this has occurred, the previously neutral stimulus is given the name conditioned stimulus, and the response is now called a conditioned response.

As a laboratory procedure, conditioning has been used by scientists to study brain functions and to discover some of the laws of learning. Animal trainers use conditioning principles in order to train animals to perform all manner of tasks. But aside from being the name for a laboratory procedure, conditioning has come to be given a much more generalized meaning; it refers now to any occasion that a neutral stimulus is presented along with an effective stimulus, such

Healthy Personality: An Approach from the Viewpoint of Humanistic Psychology

that the former comes to elicit the response regularly evoked by the latter.

The manner in which emotional habits are acquired is analogous with (if not identical to) the laboratory procedure for establishing a conditioned response. Fear, for example, appears to be a by-product of experience with pain. A painful unconditioned stimulus produces activity of the autonomic nervous system. Other stimuli, such as the sight, sound, or smell of the painful stimulus, become conditioned stimuli for these autonomic responses. Thus, the person comes to respond with fear to conditioned stimuli that were associated with the pain-producing, unconditioned stimulus. In a sense, the conditioned stimuli become signals that pain, the unconditioned stimulus, is close by. The conditioned stimulus thus evokes an experience of expectation.

A person perceives some stimulus. Past experience has led him to expect some other stimulus will be forthcoming, one which will affect him in a pleasurable or painful way. He sees his girl friend frown, and he becomes anxious—he expects rejection. He sees her smile, and he feels good—he expects to get a kiss. Emotional responses thus are determined by the interpretation of the stimulus, by the expectancy which past experience has built up in the person.

EXPECTANCY AND EMOTION

An expectancy is a prediction that B will follow A, where A is an event that has been followed by another event B which has had an impact upon the person's life. Expectancies are acquired through observation and generalizing from observation. Because generalization is a tricky activity, even for the professional logician or scientist, it follows that a layman may overgeneralize from his observations, or generalize without an adequate sample of observations. We have all observed night following day with absolute regularity, and so we have accurate expectancies with regard to this occurrence. We have all heard thunder following lightning with absolute regularity, and so our expectancies will be quite accurate when we predict that soon after we see lightning we will hear a thunderclap.

Emotion and Healthy Personality

But we may have been bitten by one dog—the bite produces pain. On the basis of that one occurrence, a person may generalize and expect that all dogs will bite him. He sees another dog and expects to be bitten. He becomes afraid.

If we know that the dog which he fears has never bitten anyone, that in fact the dog has no teeth, we say his expectancy is inaccurate and his emotional response inappropriate. But appropriate or inappropriate, a person's emotional responses will be predicated on his expectancies, and his expectancies are grounded in his own experiences with paired stimuli, conditioned and unconditioned. When he observes the conditioned stimulus, he expects the unconditioned stimulus to be near, and he responds emotionally. When someone responds with fear or hostility to some object which does not evoke those responses in us, we can assume that our expectancies with respect to the object differ from his. If we interpreted the stimulus as he does, and if we had had similar experiences with stimuli of that sort, then we too might display a similar emotional response.

From all of this we may conclude that conditioning, the pairing of neutral stimuli with events that affect us pleasurably or painfully, goes on unremittingly from birth until death; that we continually acquire, revise, and abandon expectancies; and that our emotional responses are elicited by (conditioned) stimuli interpreted in such a way that they acquire signal or predictive properties.

IDENTIFICATION AND EMOTIONAL RESPONSES

Anyone can observe similarities in emotional habits within a family or between two close friends or spouses. A father and his sons all display similar emotional responses to politicians, salesmen, women, and animals. A woman, before she became married, responded emotionally after the fashion of her mother and siblings; after several years of marriage, her parents and siblings notice she no longer feels about things the way she used to—she has changed. She has come to share some of the emotional habits of her husband, and he in turn has acquired many of hers, so that his former bachelor friends notice striking differences in him. He is no longer amused by the same things, angered or afraid of the same things, as when he was "one of the boys."

The mechanism responsible for the acquisition of emotional responses which resemble those of someone else is identification. Identification is a learning process by means of which one person models himself after another. It may be a deliberate attempt to imitate the other person, or it may be an unconsciously purposeful emulation. It is not known

Healthy Personality: An Approach from the Viewpoint of Humanistic Psychology

whether emotional habits are acquired through direct identification or whether the similarity in emotional habits between two persons derives from identification with each other's values, expectancies, and attitudes. Nevertheless, it can be asserted that either directly or indirectly, persons acquire certain of their emotional habits by means of identification.[11]

SOCIALIZATION AND EMOTIONAL RESPONSES

A sociologist or anthropologist observes that most members of a given social class or society share many emotional habits. These emotional responses differ, however, from typical emotional responses of people in other classes or societies. For example, the exposure of women's breasts arouses no erotic interest in an African tribesman, whereas it may excite a middle-class American man.

Part of the total socialization process—the efforts of parents, teachers, and others to mold and shape the typical personality for that society—is devoted to insuring that the growing children acquire the appropriate emotional habits. It is desired by the society that most members of a group perceive and interpret aspects of the world in a uniform way, and react with similar emotional responses. This uniformity is achieved in part through formal education—the child knows that pain and fear are associated with danger, and so his elders and instructors teach him to interpret many things as dangerous. It may also be achieved less formally through experiences within the family which have the effect of training most members of the society to react in a uniform way to certain classes of stimuli.

Expression and Control of Emotion

What does a person do when he has been provoked to emotional arousal? The alternative reactions of a person to emotional arousal are (1) immediate uncontrolled expression and release, (2) suppression of emotional behavior, and (3) repression of the emotional quality of experience.

IMMEDIATE EXPRESSION OF EMOTION

Immediate expression is the characteristic pattern among young children when they experience emotional tension. They laugh, cry, strike out, jump up and down, throw tan-

Emotion and Healthy Personality

109

trums—in short, they appear to be almost out of control. It is as if their cerebral cortex has been dethroned from rational control over behavior and their entire organism is directed by "explosions" of subcortical brain structures, such as the hypothalamus.

On the positive side, immediate expression of emotional tension in this uncontrolled manner is effective in getting rid of the tension. Once it is given expression, the person is able to proceed in a more controlled and less tense way. On the negative side, immediate expression is undesirable, especially in an adult, because:

1. Society condemns uncontrolled expression of emotion in an adult on a purely normative and moral basis. The adult who throws tantrums or who cannot control his emotions is viewed as immature, as one who cannot be trusted with important responsibilities.

2. While expressing uncontrolled emotion, the person is out of touch with external reality. A person out of touch with reality does not perceive the world with accuracy— indeed, he is not interested in the external world during his tantrum. Further, he does not protect other important values while in the throes of an "affective storm." He may break things which he values; he may say or do things which cost him his job, his marriage, his reputation.

SUPPRESSION OF EMOTIONAL BEHAVIOR

Emotional control is made possible through the gradually acquired ability of a person to choose responses to a situation (emotion-provoking or otherwise) that are compatible with the largest number of important values. This choosing in turn is predicated on the ability to postpone immediate responsiveness, to delay responding in order to allow time to reason, plan, or think. A young child cannot do this because he has not yet learned how, and because his nervous system has not yet matured to the point where it is physically possible for him to tolerate tension and inhibit motor expression.

When the nervous system has matured to the point where delay and purposeful planning are possible, then suppression of emotional behavior becomes possible. There are no precise norms available for the age at which such control becomes possible, and for the quantity of tension a person

Healthy Personality: An Approach from the Viewpoint of Humanistic Psychology

can be expected to tolerate without exploding into expressive behavior; however, it can be expected that the ability increases from infancy to maturity, and then probably declines with approaching senescence.

Let us now examine some of the implications of emotion suppression for personality and physical health.

Physical Consequences of Emotion Suppression. When a person is provoked to emotional tension, widespread changes occur throughout his body, in consequence of heightened autonomic nervous system activity. If expression is possible in the form of muscular activity, weeping, laughing, sexual behavior, then the physiological processes will shortly be restored to normal.

If no release is possible, if the person suppresses emotion for a long period of time, then the physical events which constitute part of the emotional response will be prolonged. If the prolongation is marked, it is possible that the functions and even the structure of inner organs may be permanently impaired. The field of psychosomatic medicine is devoted to study of the effects of emotionality on health.[12]

Psychological Consequences of Emotion Suppression. Suppressed emotional excitement interferes with rational activity. Reich coined the term *emotional plague* to describe the far-reaching impairments of logical reasoning and accurate perception produced by prolonged suppression of sexual and emotional tension. A paranoid dread of communists or a chronic belief that one is going to be sexually assaulted illustrate forms of emotional plague.[13]

In addition to the effects on rational thinking, emotion suppression appears to interfere with the efficiency of skilled behavior. One cannot play the piano, repair machinery, or knit with efficient speed and dispatch when one is full of unexpressed fear, hostility, grief, or laughter.

Finally, it may happen that the cumulative effects of suppression may eventuate in such powerful tension that control becomes impossible; the person then explodes with more violent expression than would have been the case had he reacted much earlier. Many persons have committed acts of destruction when they could no longer suppress conscious hostility.

Healthy Emotion Suppression. The capacity to suppress emotional expression and to delay immediate responsiveness is valued by moralists and also by personality hygienists. But the personality hygienist may differ from the moralist in that he affirms the value of the capacity to express emotional tensions just as much as the capacity to suppress them. The healthy personality displays neither immediate expression nor chronic suppression of emotion exclusively. Rather, he displays a capacity to *choose* between the alternatives of suppression and expression. When it will not jeopardize important values, he will express his feelings freely, laughing with gusto, crying without restraint, or expressing anger with vigor. If other values would be endangered by such emotionality, he is capable of suppressing his feelings and carrying on with whatever behavior was in process at the time of emotional arousal. In the long run, however, this regime of selective suppression and release insures that the person's body and his ability to perform will not suffer the effects of prolonged emotion suppression; and he will not needlessly endanger his job, his reputation, his self-respect, and other important values by heedless emotional explosions. He can suppress when he chooses, and he can let go when he chooses—and it is he who does the choosing.

Unhealthy Emotion Suppression. Emotion suppression becomes unhealthy when it is prolonged for any reason. When a person chronically suppresses his emotions, he generally does so because he fears the consequences of his emotional expression. Fear of emotional expression is often irrational, based on overgeneralization from unpleasant occurrences in the past. Perhaps he was severely punished, or lost his job, because of an emotional outburst. From this one event, he may have generalized that all emotional expression is dangerous, or bad. Thus he comes to suppress his feelings—though he is fully aware of them—without discrimination.

The longer-range consequences of chronic suppression may be psychosomatic illnesses (provided other necessary and sufficient causes are present), such as elevated blood pressure, mucous colitis, asthma, peptic ulcers; or chronic fatigue (it consumes energy to suppress hostility and other strong feelings), muscular aches and pains, migrainelike headaches; or impaired work and study efficiency, inability to concentrate, impaired reality contact, and impaired relationships with people, who want their friends and loved

Healthy Personality: An Approach from the Viewpoint of Humanistic Psychology

ones to be able to express feeling. The chronic suppressor is often derogated as a "stick," "stone-face," or "iceberg"—someone who is "less than human."

REPRESSION OF EMOTIONAL TENSIONS

A person is said to repress his emotions when he takes active steps to avoid experiencing certain affects, and when, confronted by a stimulus adequate to induce an emotional response, he denies (and believes his own denial) he is experiencing emotion. Repression in the first instance is achieved by regulating one's life so that one will never encounter the objects known to induce feelings, and also by refusing to think about objects or events which might induce unwanted feelings. Repression in the second instance appears to be achieved by means of some form of self-deception or denial—as if the person says to himself, and believes, "I am not angry [afraid, sexy, amused]." In order to rid his awareness of the unwanted emotional tensions, he may think about things and perform tasks that induce feelings incompatible with the unwanted emotional tension. Thus, a small child, confronted by a fear-inspiring dog, might say, "Nice puppy"—puppies evoke tender feelings, not fear in the child. The nervous and timid speaker at a banquet, who is afraid he will be ridiculed, may address the audience as "My friends." If he believes that they are his friends, his fear will evaporate.

Repression occurs automatically and unconsciously, because the emotional tensions trigger off strong anxiety over the anticipated consequences of expressing them; too, the emotional tensions conflict strongly with the person's conscience and self-ideal—if he admitted he had these feelings, he might have to change his concept of himself, with accompanying losses in self-esteem.

In most, if not all, instances, a personality hygienist condemns repression of emotional tensions as unhealthy. The main reason for this condemnation lies in the fact that in spite of repression, the feelings exist—or at least the capacity to experience these feelings remains present and unchanged. When feelings have been provoked but are not recognized by the person, they produce both physical and psychological effects. In Chapter 4 we discussed some of the ways in which unconscious feelings (and needs) manifest themselves in thinking and behavior. In addition to the psychological consequences, repressed affects produce the same effects on the body as do consciously suppressed feelings, only the person is not aware that he has these feelings.

When feelings have been repressed more or less successfully, it is not only the person himself who is unaware of their presence. Other persons as well will not know how the person really feels. Thus, a husband may irritate his wife for years by certain of his habits. She, however, may have repressed her annoyance and hostility. Then, at some future date, she leaves him or becomes overwhelmed with uncontrollable rage at some trivial annoyance. Naturally, the husband is surprised and shocked. If she had openly vented her feelings, he might have altered his behavior easily, and without complaint.

One of the most important tasks in psychotherapy and in the treatment of so-called psychosomatic illnesses is aiding the patient to recognize his own feelings—to "unrepress" them, to experience and express them fully. This uncovering process generally is met with strong resistance on the part of the patient, however, for the experience of these feelings is threatening to security and to self-esteem.

FACTORS WHICH PROMOTE CHRONIC
SUPPRESSION AND REPRESSION OF EMOTION

In view of the fact that chronic suppression and repression of affect produce such unhealthy consequences, we shall inquire into some of the factors responsible for the adoption of these unhealthy patterns.

Dependency upon Others. When a person must depend upon others for the solution of his problems and the satisfaction of his needs, he is thrust into a situation which can promote unhealthy suppression and repression. So long as he is in the dependent role, and needs the other person's good will, he must express nothing which will incur the displeasure of the other person. Thus, a child, an employee, or an inadequate person may have to withhold honest expression of feelings and express (or pretend to feel) only those which will improve his status in the eyes of the dominant one. Most of us have had the fantasy at one time or another of telling someone with whom we have been closely associated in a dependent role just how we really feel toward them. Some people, on achieving autonomy, wealth, or cour-

Healthy Personality: An Approach from the Viewpoint of Humanistic Psychology

age, come right out and express long-withheld feelings. Sometimes, the dissolution of a dependency relationship will remove only the motives for suppression, so that the person vents feelings he has long been aware of. Sometimes, however, with the break-up of the dependency relationship, long-standing repressions will be undone, and the person will himself be shocked and surprised at the feelings which well up for expression.

Excessively Strict Conscience and Self-ideal. A person may chronically suppress or repress certain emotions not only for external reasons, such as avoiding rejection or criticism, but also to conform with demands of conscience. A person may have acquired values which make his self-esteem contingent on the exclusion of certain feelings and emotions not only from behavior, but even from consciousness. He can accept himself only as kind, pure, and strong, and so he must repress all those feelings which would produce guilt if they were recognized.

Rigid Role Definitions. Everyone learns a variety of social roles in order to live acceptably in his society. Examples of roles include those associated with age, sex, occupation, and one's family position. Each role has strong social norms governing the experience and expression of emotion. For example, a physician is expected to appear calm in situations of illness and crisis, whereas a layman or a patient can experience and express panic without social blame. Similarly, men in our culture are expected to appear stronger, more competent, and more in control of their emotions than are women (although these roles are changing through the influence of women's liberation advocates). Thus, men commonly feel ashamed if they experience tenderness, weakness and dependency, or the impulse to weep. The necessity to appear before others in conformity with conventional role definitions thus fosters suppression and repression of emotion. If a person cannot find opportunities to be "out" of his roles, in order to experience and express the feelings engendered by life happenings, then his roles are endangering his health.[13]

Healthy Personality and Emotion: An Overview

The dimensions of healthy personality are interrelated. The capacity to experience a broad range of emotion, and to control its expression, is most likely to be found in persons who have been competent at satisfying their basic needs, who have retained a firm grasp on reality, who have achieved a healthy "self-structure" (see Chapter 7), and whose relationships with other people are secure and authentic (Chapter 10). This suggests that if a person represses his emotions or experiences troubling emotional responses (such as irrational fears and manias), he should endeavor to improve his competence, his relationships with others, or his view of himself. On the other hand, the work of behavior therapists has shown that people who complain of excessive anxiety or a specific phobia can be aided to live more fully by a direct attack upon the symptom itself. The techniques of "extinguishing" unwanted emotional responses do work, and they can make life more livable for a person who has been thwarted by hitherto uncontrollable fear or rage. I have helped patients of mine to overcome a fear of the opposite sex, of public speaking, of authority figures, by methods of classical conditioning and behavior modification, as well as through interviews aimed at encouraging the patient to learn new skills, alter his self-concept or self-ideal, and change his relationships with others in the direction of greater authenticity. Patients who have been helped in these ways attest that there is great joy and enlivenment in overcoming the repression of feelings, so that one is free to feel and to express such feelings; and there is comparable joy in being free of a hitherto uncontrolled emotional response that rendered life unendurable.

Some Existential Suggestions

Hardly anyone experiences the fullest range of emotion of which man is capable. Not only does one's culture impose limits upon the experience and expression of emotion; one's own family will also influence which emotions are aroused, and which will be expressed.

Because the expression of emotion is so important to both the quality of life and to health, it is important to reflect upon your own emotional habits. What situations provoke you to anger, for example? And to fear or anxiety? Both fear and anger can enrich life and foster growth, but irrational fears and rage can destroy the quality of existence.

If you are chronically in a fury about everything—if everyone's behavior seems imperfect, if their appearance angers you, if the slightest deviation from your view of perfection puts you into an ill-concealed rage—then your life might be enhanced if you could alter your expectations in reasonable ways.

If you are "running scared," it is possible that you view yourself as weaker and more helpless than is warranted; you might be able to challenge yourself to face those situations you dread, and discover that you can cope.

Can you express your emotions without guilt or anxiety, and without being destructive to self and others? One of the most wholesome guarantors of health and *joie de vivre* is the freedom to express your feelings. If you are chronically suppressed and emotionally inhibited, it may be worthwhile to "let go" a little, to test whether it is really so dangerous to laugh, cry, become angry or tender and affectionate. Encounter groups, if available and properly led, can provide a person with the opportunity to explore his possibilities for experiencing and expressing his genuine feelings.

Falsifying emotion can be a pernicious influence upon your life. Let the other people in your life know your authentic feelings toward them, especially those with whom you have a personal relationship (as opposed to a more formal role relationship; see Chapters 9 and 10 for the distinction). To be emotionally dishonest is to set the stage for estrangement from others and for self-alienation.

SUMMARY

Emotion is a quality of experience and an expressive quality of action. When a person is provoked to emotion, his awareness, his behavior, and his physiological functioning all change.

There is no complete catalogue of emotional experience, but emotional expression is a kind of communication, and some "states" of emotion are identifiable by a person himself and by those who associate with him: pleasure, depression, anxiety and dread, anger, weeping, humor, the experience of freedom, boredom, and affection and tenderness. The capacity to experience a broad range of emotion is an indication of healthy personality.

Emotion
and
Healthy
Personality

Our emotional habits are acquired through conditioning, through the learning of expectancies, and through identification with significant others in our lives.

Immediate uncontrolled expression of emotion and chronic suppression and repression are incompatible with healthy personality. The ability to suppress and express emotion selectively is the pattern of emotional control most compatible with healthy personality.

NOTES AND REFERENCES

1. I am limiting my discussion of emotion to those aspects relevant to understanding healthy personality. The student may benefit more from the discussion in this chapter if he reviews the chapter on feelings and emotions in any recent textbook on introductory psychology. See, for example, R. ISAACSON and M. HUTT, *Psychology: The Science of Behavior*, rev. ed. (New York: Harper & Row, 1971).

2. R. D. LAING and A. ESTERSON, *Sanity, Madness and the Family* (London: Tavistock, 1964).

3. A. LOWEN, *Pleasure* (New York: Lancer, 1970); T. SZASZ, *Pain and Pleasure: A Study of Bodily Feelings* (New York: Basic Books, 1957); A. MONTAGU, *Touching: The Human Significance of the Skin* (New York: Harper & Row, 1972); W. REICH, *The Discovery of the Orgone: The Function of the Orgasm* (New York: Noonday, 1961), pp. 184–220; W. SCHUTZ, *Joy* (New York: Grove, 1967). A discussion of zest is given in E. SCHACHTEL, *Metamorphosis: On the Development of Affect, Perception, Attention, and Memory* (New York: Basic Books, 1959), Chapters 2 and 3.

4. See S. FREUD, *The Problem of Anxiety* (New York: Norton, 1936); R. MAY, *The Meaning of Anxiety* (New York: Ronald, 1950); P. TILLICH, *The Courage to Be* (New Haven: Yale University Press, 1952).

5. See J. DOLLARD, N. E. MILLER, L. W. DOOB, O. H. MOWRER, and R. R. SEARS, *Frustration and Aggression* (New Haven: Yale, 1939); H. CASON, "Common Annoyances: A Psychological Study of Everyday Aversions and Irritations," *Psychological Monographs*, 1930, Vol. 40, No. 2 (Whole No. 132); I. CHARNEY, *Marital Love and Hate* (New York: Macmillan, 1972); G. R. BACH and P. WYDEN, *Intimate Enemy: How to Fight Fair in Love and Marriage* (New York: Morrow, 1969).

6. This is the view of guilt held by Mowrer; see O. H. MOWRER, *The Crisis in Psychiatry and Religion* (New York:

Van Nostrand Reinhold, 1960), Chapter 8. See also M. Buber, *The Knowledge of Man* (New York: Harper & Row, 1965), Chapter 6, "Guilt and Guilt Feelings."

7. S. Freud, "Wit and Its Relation to the Unconscious," in A. Brill (Ed.), *The Basic Writings of Sigmund Freud* (New York: Modern Library, 1938); F. J. Shaw, *Transcendence: A Theory of Man Transcending* (New York: Van Nostrand Reinhold, 1966), Chapter 3; G. W. Allport, *Pattern and Growth in Personality* (New York: Holt, 1961), pp. 292–294; J. H. Goldstein and P. E. McGhee (Eds.), *The Psychology of Humor* (New York: Academic Press, 1972).

8. F. Barron, "Freedom as Feeling," *Journal of Humanistic Psychology*, 1961, Vol. 1, pp. 91–100. E. Fromm, *Escape from Freedom* (New York: Holt, 1941).

9. I. Suttie, *The Origins of Love and Hate* (London: Peregrine Books, 1963), pp. 86–100; J. Bowlby, *Maternal Care and the Growth of Love* (London: Penguin, 1953); Montagu, op. cit.

10. A review of psychological and physiological aspects of emotion is given in Magda B. Arnold, *Emotion and Personality* (New York: Columbia University Press, 1960), 2 vols.; a good analysis of expectancies is in J. B. Rotter, *Social Learning and Clinical Psychology* (Englewood Cliffs, N.J.: Prentice-Hall, 1954), pp. 165–183.

11. O. H. Mowrer, *Learning Theory and Personality Dynamics* (New York: Ronald, 1950), Chapter 21; I. Hendrick, "Early Development of the Ego," *Psychoanalytic Quarterly*, 1951, Vol. 20, pp. 44–61.

12. Considerable evidence shows that many illnesses arise following some "dispiriting" or demoralizing experiences, such as loss of a loved one. See S. M. Jourard, *The Transparent Self* (New York: Van Nostrand Reinhold, 1971), Chapter 10; any medical textbook on "psychosomatic medicine," such as F. Alexander, *Psychosomatic Medicine* (New York: Norton, 1950), reviews the evidence on the influence of emotion on health.

13. W. Reich, *Character Analysis*, op. cit., Chapter 12; Jourard, op. cit., Chapter 4, "Some Lethal Aspects of the Male Role."

6

THE BODY AND HEALTHY PERSONALITY

People of the Western world have thought of man in dualistic terms, as a nonmaterial mind dwelling within a fleshly body subject to mechanical and biological laws. This tendency to split one's thinking about man has led to thinking about man as actually split. Moreover, there has been a tendency in the West to depreciate the experience of body, as a distraction from salvation and from compulsive work. Many devout people believe the body is a beast to be subdued, and that a person should eliminate feelings, appetites, and emotions from his life through assorted disciplines. This peculiar perspective upon our actual embodiment has led to a state of being which R. D. Laing calls unembodiment. In its extreme form, as in schizophrenic sufferers, unembodiment is experienced as being not "in" one's body.[1] Many people appear insensitive to the way their bodies feel and function. Such somatic repression is a factor in physical as well as psychological illnesses.

Some Manifestations of Unembodiment

One way for a person to rid himself of his body is to pretend to be somebody else. In so doing, he is "in" neither his acts nor his body.[2] This pretense is abetted if he can obliterate the experience of his body. Such obliteration is carried out through repression of unwelcome somatic experience.

A person will repress any dimensions of his experience which terrify him, or which have led to unbearable pain. Thus, when parents observe a child masturbating, they may punish him severely. To avoid future pain, the child may repress all pleasurable body experience. It is as if he has divested himself of his genitalia to avoid rejection by parents who cannot love a child with sexual urges.

Chronic repression of body experience must manifest itself in some way. Subjectively, repression of bodily experience is experienced as no experience, as a "hole" or an absence in the person's experience of being.[3] Thus, one person complained, "I feel numb, like a robot." Objectively, somatic repression manifests itself as character structure, or muscular armor—a peculiar configuration of muscular tonus and flaccidity, which results in a person's characteristic bodily posture, style of movement, and tone of voice. Somatic repression has profound effects upon autonomic functions of the body, such as breathing, elimination, circulation, and rest. Wilhelm Reich was adept at looking at a naked body and "reading" from it what impulses a person was repressing, and what kinds of conflicts he likely had with his parents.[4] There is no magic in this. If a person has been obliged to live a dutiful, unpleasurable life, and dares not experience, much less express his rage and resentment, then he must hold the rage in. If the reader will clench his teeth, tighten his neck, pinch his buttocks tightly together, and then look in the mirror, he will improve his ability to empathize with others who are repressed.

DEVITALIZING EFFECT UPON OTHERS

A person who has repressed his sense of vitality may inhibit the vitality of another person who, before the encoun-

*The Body
and
Healthy
Personality*

ter, felt "full of beans and juices," very much alive. On making contact with the unembodied one, he notices himself feeling diminished in vitality and zest for life.

I once had a colleague who affected me in this way. I would arrive at work in the morning, full of plans and projects, literally dancing with excitement. The colleague would simply appear in my room to discuss his work for the day, and I would notice my zest oozing away. This man affected me the way witches must have affected their victims. In fact, I became so fascinated with this man's effect on me that I began to observe my bodily states whenever I was involved in conversation or shared activity with all kinds of people. I noted that, when I was with my favorite people, I burst with vitality, I laughed, my life and actions had meaning and worth. When I was with certain others, my sense of life would flow out, leaving me drained, flaccid, and empty. I suspect that when this happens, I am in the presence of someone who wishes I were dead, or at least, less alive.

I believe we have enough technology available so that a physiologist could take various measurements of activation, using GSR, EEG, pulse and blood pressure measurements, and so on, and record the enlivening, calming, or deadening effects of one person upon another, below the threshold of immediate awareness.

The discipline known as kinesics enables a person to read bodies through characteristic gestures and postures. Thus, Birdwhistell [5] has been able to demonstrate how people's bodily posture may contradict as well as be congruent with their words. A person may say, "I'm open to your suggestions," while holding his body "closed," with arms folded, legs crossed, buttocks pinched—nothing could budge such a person from his pledge to sameness. He may not be aware that his body is saying something which contradicts his words.

AUTISTIC BODY IMAGES

The way in which a person perceives, thinks about, and imagines his body to be (body image) is another way in which unembodiment, or peculiar ways of being embodied, may be revealed. Seymour Fisher and Sidney Cleveland [6] were able to show that persons who saw many things in the

Healthy Personality: An Approach from the Viewpoint of Humanistic Psychology

Rorschach ink-blot test that had shells, walls, or definite boundaries (high "barrier" scores) differed from persons who saw objects with blurry or shattered boundaries (high "penetration" scores), in styles of behavior and sickness. Thus, patients with cancer of internal organs had higher "penetration of boundary" scores and lower "barrier" scores than persons with skin cancers. Fischer and Cleveland propose that the responses to the ink-blot test reveal the way in which a person unconsciously imagines his body to be. However warranted their hypothesis, it does appear that what a person *believes* to be the case about his body becomes a self-fulfilling prophesy. I believe that we have been grossly unimaginative in our ways of thinking and theorizing about the body. The way physicians, anatomists, and physiologists see the body, from the outside, has become the way in which schoolchildren and finally adults experience their bodies. We do not yet have a phenomenological anatomy and physiology which would heighten our consciousness of our body from the living inside.

Another person, such as one's mother, can take over the function of detecting one's own bodily states and estimating one's strengths and weaknesses. The child who is told that he is weak, hungry, or sleepy by his loving, overprotective mother may lose the ability to construe his bodily states and possibilities. Consequently, he may eat when his mother says he is hungry, and not be allowed to stop eating until that human gauge of his capacity, his mother, says "You have eaten enough." Such a child may become very fat indeed, if his mother's estimate of his food needs do not coincide with what his body actually needs to maintain itself.

If a person underestimates the capacity of his body to endure stress and hardship, he may sicken or die long before it becomes a physiological necessity. "Outward Bound" training, for example, teaches young people that they can endure and survive well beyond limits they had been taught to believe were inflexible.

In short, one's body is very plastic indeed—it does what one expects of it. One should be careful what one expects of one's body, because that, likely, is what one will get. Clearly, the Olympic records of endurance and speed, which change annually, show that we seldom expect enough of our bodies, but instead overestimate their fragility. Actually, our potential toughness and endurance have yet to be put to the ultimate test.[7]

If a person believes with utter certainty that he is going to die—for example, if he learns he has "terminal and inoperable cancer" or a fatal heart condition—then he is likely to *imagine,* even *wish himself dead,* thereby hastening the advent of his physical demise. "Spiritual" death or imagined nonexistence become prophesies to which the organs and cells of the body respond. There is no way of estimating how many people die, as it were, through being hypnotized or persuaded by symbols and other people's nonverbal expressions that signify, "Your life is finished." I have even argued that cultural expectations about the "right" age to die function in the same way, as hypnotic suggestions or invitations to die; when a person reaches eighty or ninety-five years of age, there is nothing for him to do, and he is expected to view each day as his last, thereby hastening his end.[8] If he remained involved with the pleasures and challenges of life, then death would take him by surprise. Kazantzakis tells of the nonagenarian who would goose and fondle young girls at the village well. When asked, "Grandfather, tell us of life," he replied, "It is a glass of cool water." "Are you still thirsty, then?" "Of course," said the old man, "I want to drink to bursting."

A challenge confronting scientists is to explore how "inspirited" states of being—being engaged in meaningful tasks and projects—are reflected in bodily states, such that immunity mechanisms are most efficient; the nuclei of cells do not release cancerous growth; and the mechanisms of wound-healing and recovery from fatigue are most rapid and efficient.

SOMATIC PERCEPTION

Thus far, I have proposed that conventional upbringing in the Western world produces a partial sense of unembodiment in the majority of persons so socialized. This unembodiment manifests itself in interpersonal duplicity (play-acting, pretense, role-playing, pseudo-self-disclosure) and in diminished awareness of one's own bodily being. I presented the hypothesis that unembodiment is the outcome of the repression of the early experience of pleasure and pain that young children undergo in the process of growing up,

*Healthy
Personality:
An Approach
from the
Viewpoint of
Humanistic
Psychology*

and that such repression produces a loss of a very important dimension of consciousness I call somatic perception.

Somatic perception refers to a person's awareness of the response of his body to the situation in which he finds himself. He perceives the world somatically by "tuning in" on his bodily states as he goes through life situations. Thus, his eyes see a person smiling; his ears hear that person say "I love you"; yet he continues to feel tense and on guard. He does not feel loved. Somatically, the person is perceiving that all is not well; more information is called for, before a less defensive posture will be taken. Reduction of the capacity for somatic perception appears to be a factor in the development of physical and psychological breakdown. If a person cannot discern how his relationships with others and his physical regimen are affecting him, he will continue to live in a way that generates harmful stress. He will be anesthetic to the pain and dispiritedness which are being generated, and hence will not change what he is doing in some life- and health-saving way. Consequently, the unembodied person *behaves* his way into situations of stress and entrapment so overpowering that physical and psychological collapse are his only ways out. Medical care which does not seek to "re-embody" a person, and sensitize his somatic perception, is, at best, only first aid. Any sedating or tranquilizing medical care which further destroys the capacity for somatic perception is ultimately a menace to health, according to this perspective.

If it is true that conventional socialization results in unembodiment in varying degrees, then the salutary functions of certain embodying disciplines and techniques become understandable. These techniques will be discussed later in this chapter. Next let us look at the body from some technical perspectives.

The Body and Personality

THE BODY AND THE EGO

The Body and Healthy Personality

The *ego* is a term psychoanalysts use to designate the functions of coordinating and controlling the movements of one's body. One of the first signs that the ego has developed is the infant's capacity voluntarily to control his movements.[9]

Mastery of the outer environment and mastery of one's body appear to be correlated. Before such mastery has been achieved, body movements are global, undifferentiated, and not subject to voluntary control. Once such mastery has been achieved, the infant or child is able to suppress undifferentiated responses to events, and respond in a discrete, skillful manner. The ability to coordinate eyes, hands, and mouth is probably among the first signs that the ego is developing.

As physical maturation proceeds, the child acquires increasing mastery over his body and is able to perform according to his wishes. By the time he reaches adulthood the person, if suitably trained, may be able to achieve such levels of bodily control as are found among athletes and dancers.

The loss of control of body functions and performances is experienced as catastrophic by most persons. Not to be the master of one's body—its movements, needs, and functions—is a loss of the most basic level of control. An adult who cannot control his appetite, or his bowel and bladder sphincters, will feel deep shame, and will lose confidence in himself.

Embodiment and the Self

THE BODY AND SECURITY

The unattractive person generally has a more difficult time winning friends, and in being popular with the opposite sex, than the person with a pleasing appearance. One of my students demonstrated that a man judged attractive in appearance from his photographs was overwhelmingly preferred as a prospective date by a group of college girls over two men judged less good-looking.[10]

Several studies have demonstrated that a person's appearance may be a source of anxiety for him. Paul Secord and I showed that measures of the degree to which people liked their bodies were negatively correlated with measures of anxious body preoccupation and security. In other words, the more a person accepted his body, the more secure and free from anxiety he felt. Persons with a high measured degree of anxiety tended to be dissatisfied with their bodies.[11]

Anxious overconcern with the body is called *hypochondriasis*. The hypochondriac is an individual who is continu-

Healthy Personality: An Approach from the Viewpoint of Humanistic Psychology

126

ally preoccupied with his health. He makes the rounds of doctors' offices and doses himself regularly with laxatives, vitamin pills, and sedatives. Hypochondriacal anxiety is a substitute for, or a displacement of, anxiety that derives from other sources: repressed hostility, sexuality, or achievement problems. The hypochondriac evidently finds it less threatening to worry about his health than to think realistically about other problems.

A person may become excessively concerned about his appearance. This is most likely to occur among persons who use their appearance to gain acceptance from others, to enhance their social status, or to attract attention. The name *narcissistic overconcern* seems appropriate to describe this pattern. Such a person will become panic-stricken if a wrinkle, gray hair, or change in weight appears.

Hypochondriasis and narcissistic overconcern both may be viewed as unhealthy responses to the appearance and functions of the body. They are unhealthy for a variety of reasons: They fail to solve the problems basically responsible for the anxiety in the first place. Furthermore, while the person concentrates so much attention on himself and his body, he neglects other concerns of importance to healthy personality, for instance, productive work and healthy relationships with other people.

Reasonable concern for one's health and appearance is compatible with healthy personality, but reasonable concern does not place other values in jeopardy. If the individual with a healthy personality becomes physically ill, he will take the steps necessary to restore or improve health, but then he will turn his attention to other matters. Furthermore, he will live in accordance with a habitual health regime—adequate diet, rest, and exercise—which maintains his health without requiring too much conscious attention. He will take whatever steps are necessary for him to look his best, and then he will take his appearance for granted. He does not rely totally on his appearance for successful living.

THE BODY AND SELF-ESTEEM

A high degree of self-esteem means that a person accepts himself as worthy. A number of studies have shown that self-esteem is highly correlated with a positive attitude toward one's body. In other words, persons who accept their bodies are more likely to manifest high self-esteem than persons who dislike their bodies.

One reason for this correlation lies in the fact that the self-ideal includes a set of ideals pertaining to the appearance of the body, the so-called *body-ideal*. Each person has a more or less clear concept of how he wants to look. If his body conforms in dimensions and appearance with his concept of an ideal body, he will then like his body. If his body deviates from his body-ideal, he will tend to reject and dislike his body.

In one study of college women, it was found that the ideal body proportions (which all girls in the sample shared) were 5 feet, 5 inches tall; weighing about 120 pounds; and 35 inches, 24 inches, and 35 inches for bust, waist, and hips, respectively. The girls liked their dimensions if they coincided with these ideals and disliked them increasingly as they deviated from them. The actual measurements of the girls were slightly larger than these ideals, on the average—except for bust size, where the average size was slightly smaller than the ideal.

A comparable study of college males showed that acceptance of the body was related to *large size*. The women all wanted to be slightly smaller in dimensions than they actually were, but the men mostly aimed at larger size; they wanted to be taller, with broader shoulders and chests.[12]

It is evident that the body-ideals of the subjects in these studies are closely related to the cultural concept of an *ideal body*.

THE BODY-IDEAL AND THE IDEAL BODY

Each society has its idiosyncratic standards of personal beauty.[13] The Bushman of the Kalahari Desert, for example, esteems enormous hips and buttocks on a woman, whereas in America the desired hip measurements are much slimmer. The American woman wants to have large (but firm) breasts, a small waist, and narrow hips, and she wants to be relatively tall. In days gone by, the American glamor girl was considerably heftier than our present beauties. Old pictures of burlesque queens look to the modern eye like advertisements for a reducing salon.

The cultural concept of an ideal body has consequences

Healthy Personality: An Approach from the Viewpoint of Humanistic Psychology

128

for healthy personality, because the cultural ideal influences the personal body-ideal and congruence of the actual body with the body-ideal helps to determine self-esteem. If a person in our society is not able to conform with prevailing ideal body concepts, he may face problems growing out of diminished self-esteem. If the ideal body concepts in the society are highly restrictive and difficult for many people to conform with, the implication is that *many* people will suffer loss of self-esteem.

The widespread dread that many people have of aging may be an outgrowth of both the rigid concept of an ideal body and the role of bodily appearance in gaining recognition. Although a rational degree of concern for appearance is compatible with personality health, too much concern indicates that the individual's self-esteem is founded on *too narrow a base*. Under optimum conditions, an individual will predicate his self-esteem on a variety of grounds, for example, achievement, social status, ethical behavior. Attractive appearance is thus only one of many determiners of self-esteem. The healthy personality can face the inevitable changes in appearance associated with aging without a loss of self-esteem. He (or she) does not feel that when youthful beauty is gone, so goes personal worth. He believes, in the words of a homely twelve-year-old girl at a summer camp, "After all, beauty is only skin. Be a beautiful *person,* and don't worry so much about how you look."

SOME PROBLEMS RELATED TO THE CULTURAL
CONCEPT OF THE IDEAL BODY

The prevailing concept of the ideal body is adopted by most people as their personal body-ideal. This is the source of many somatic concerns.

Obesity. The most common difficulty people have with their appearance in America is obesity. This is also a health problem, for overweight people are more susceptible to disease than thinner people. But the cosmetic aspects of obesity are just as acutely worried about as the physical health aspects. America is one of the few countries in the world where overweight is a public health problem; where food is abundant, but a slender body is a cultural value.

Obesity is, of course, the result of eating too much. Overweight people seem unable to maintain their food intake at a

The Body and Healthy Personality

level that will enable them to lose weight. When a person wants to stop some behavior pattern but finds that will power is ineffective, it is evidence that unconscious motives of great strength lie behind the behavior. The overweight person is overeating for reasons other than hunger.

Clinical studies of chronically overweight people have shown that they have unhealthy personalities. They may, for example, be unable to derive satisfaction from their work. They may be starved for love. Rather than live with no "highs," they resort to a very primitive type of satisfaction—that provided by a rich meal.

An obese person is not unlike a chronic alcoholic in that he is addicted to a practice which harms him at the same time that it relieves anxiety and provides immediate gratification. Like an alcoholic, the obese person might make daily, renewed vows to "taper off," but he never seems to achieve this end. In some cities, groups of obese people—Weight Watchers—organize as do the members of Alcoholics Anonymous; they are all dedicated to the aim of reducing, and they lend each other moral support in adhering to reducing diets. Such groups are probably the most effective means for achieving and maintaining a weight loss. However, unless the conditions, medical or psychological, responsible for the excessive appetite are removed, the person will be obliged to remain dependent upon his group membership in order to preserve his weight loss once it has been achieved.[14] This is not an unhealthy dependency.

Skinniness. Just as we deplore fatness in our society, so do we pity the "skinny" person. Chronic underweight due to undernourishment is a fairly simple malady to remedy if suitable food is available. But many persons are thin in spite of a sizable caloric intake. There are usually reasons for inability to put on weight, for example, overactive thyroid glands or a finicky appetite; but these may derive from more basic psychological causes. An intensive personality diagnosis may disclose many unhealthy personality traits in the chronically thin person. In such instances, psychotherapy may produce as a side effect a desirable increase in weight. Sometimes simply changing the amount of exercise that the person takes will suffice to stimulate appetite and promote a desirable gain in weight.

Breast Cultivation. Men in our society are highly breast-conscious, and many men equate sexual attractiveness in a woman with a prominent bosom. Because most women want to be attractive to men, they consider a flat bust to be a handicap. The reasons for this cultural emphasis on the breasts are not readily determined. Some anthropologists and psychoanalysts believe it is a derivative of painful weaning experiences undergone by male children in our society. Probably, however, the reasons are more complex.

Nevertheless, many women want to have prominent breasts, and if they have not been naturally endowed with them, they may strive to cultivate them by assorted exercises such as are advertised by health clubs, or they will wear brassiere padding of one kind or another.

There is nothing intrinsically unhealthy in a woman who wears "falsies" in order to appear buxom. Personality health is assessed in terms of a number of different criteria, including what the person does to, with, or for her body. So long as males deem breasts to be an index of attractiveness, then women who wish to attract male attention are justified in doing all that is practicable to gain that end.

Noses. We even have rigid cultural ideals pertaining to noses. The ideal nose is not the majestic protuberance of a Cyrano de Bergerac nor the proud, delicately curved sweep of an aquiline "beak." Instead, it must, at least in the woman, be a short, medium-width, uptilted "snub" so that an onlooker can see the nostrils. This, obviously, is a Caucasian ideal which does not grant beauty to black Americans. Many women feel their facial beauty is marred because their nose differs from this stereotype, and so they undergo plastic surgery to achieve the valued snub. Whether or not "nose-bobbing" is a healthy thing to do depends on its consequences for the total personality. Some persons may undergo a healthy personality change following the operation, whereas others may go through life after such an operation feeling they are fakes.

Facial Wrinkles. The appearance of wrinkles in the facial skin and on the neck is an inevitable part of aging. Yet many women, especially, become panic-stricken at the first appearance of a wrinkle. This panic derives from a dread of being old and from the cultural overemphasis on the importance of appearance as a basis for security and self-esteem.

The person who panics at wrinkles, and goes to any length to regain, at age forty, the complexion of a sixteen-year-old, is an unhealthy person. Such an individual might well seek to find more stable sources of self-esteem than facial appearance.

Genitalia. People have all kinds of problems in connection with their sexual organs. Some men feel they are inferior if they have what seem to be small genital organs. There are cases on record where an entire neurotic personality structure began from the belief that the sex organs were smaller than those of other men. There is no connection between "manliness" and the size of the genitalia.

Many people in our society are prudish about, almost ashamed of, the reproductive and eliminative functions of their bodies. They become panic-stricken at the prospect of being seen nude. Some may actually avoid a medical examination if it requires that the genitalia be exposed. Indeed their concept of their own genitalia and those of the opposite sex may be autistic. These unreal concepts may involve notions that the female organs are dangerous and castrating or that penises are destructive weapons. Some women may acquire attitudes of resentment and shame over their menstrual functions and needlessly isolate themselves through the duration of their periods—as is done in some primitive societies.

Muscle Cultivation. In response to the cultural ideal of a muscular male, many sedentarily occupied men undergo strenuous weight-lifting and body-building courses to become visibly muscular. There is nothing inherently healthy or unhealthy in such efforts. They are healthy if they result in an improvement of appearance, vigor, and health without loss of other values. They are unhealthy if they are expressions of unnecessary compensation or overcompensation for other kinds of deficiencies and inferiorities.

Body Image and Healthy Personality

A HEALTHY BODY-IDEAL

The body image comprises a person's body-ideal and his body concept. Each of these will be discussed in relation to healthy personality.

A person's body-ideal can be assessed with respect to its healthy or unhealthy implications. An unhealthy body-ideal is one that is rigid and unchanging and that includes dimensions impossible for the individual to conform with. Thus, we observe an unhealthy body-ideal in a woman who, at age forty, feels she is ugly and unattractive because she no longer looks the way she did when she was nineteen. If she devotes extreme attention to her appearance to the neglect of other values, her body-ideal is unhealthy. Similarly, a young man with a slender physique who rejects his body appearance because he is not heavily muscled and proportioned like a football hero may be said to have an unhealthy body-ideal.

A healthy body-ideal is one which is not too discrepant from the cultural concept of an ideal body but which is *revised by the person himself, so as to make allowances for his own, idiosyncratic dimensions and features.* With increasing age, a healthy personality will modify his body-ideal, so that he can continue to regard himself as reasonably attractive at each stage of life. He does not aspire after an impossible (for him) degree of beauty. Rather, at each stage of life, he strives to look his best and then lets the matter drop so as to attend to other important concerns.

THE BODY CONCEPT AND HEALTHY PERSONALITY

A person's body concept includes everything he believes about the structure, capabilities, and limits of his body. As with any other concept—one's concept of self, of other people, of animals—the body concept may be accurate or inaccurate, complete or incomplete. An accurate body concept is important for achieving healthy personality.

Accuracy of the body concept is achieved by all of the means employed to arrive at reality-tested knowledge in general: through observation, through continual verification of conclusions, and through contact with reliable authorities and sources of knowledge. But many persons have been taught erroneous beliefs about diet, health requirements, and the like. Further, a person may become so alienated from his body (as part of the more general process of self-alienation) that he loses the capacity to "listen" to his body, the capacity for somatic perception.

Thus, some people may fail to recognize that inadequate

The Body and Healthy Personality

diet, lack of exercise, insufficient rest, and excessive self-indulgence are gradually weakening their bodies. To the extent that a person has knowledge of the effects of various things on his health, then to that extent his body's welfare is his own responsibility. In societies where medical knowledge is not available, people may have erroneous beliefs about the causes of health and of illness. Consequently, one may observe that entire sectors of a population suffer from some chronic ailment which they all accept as "natural," as part of the scheme of living, for instance, rickets or TB. It is only from the standpoint of the contemporary scientific concept of the body that it becomes possible to make judgments about how healthy (or sick) an entire society might be.

Some overprotected people grow up ignorant of the process of reproduction; a nineteen-year-old student of mine believed that menstruation only occurred in virgins; once a girl engaged in sexual relationships, she stopped menstruating. She couldn't discuss sexual questions with her mother, and she was too embarrassed to talk about sex with her less prudish girl friends.

An aging person with false pride may misjudge his strength and endanger his health through overexercise. But just as a person may overestimate his body's capacity, so may he underestimate it. We are all tougher than we have been led to believe.

PERSONALITY, THE BODY, AND HEALTH

Personality refers to the characteristic ways in which an individual experiences and acts in life situations. Action affects not only the external environment, but also the health of the body.

A Physical-Health-Promoting Personality. The meaningful question to ask is, "What regimen, what ways of behaving in the world will promote health?" The most obvious answer to this question relates to such matters as diet, rest, and sensible exercise. People who have been adequately educated in general hygiene will follow a diet that maintains health, energy, and weight; they will care for their teeth; they will sleep enough to restore their energy; and they will exercise enough to keep fit.

Healthy Personality: An Approach from the Viewpoint of Humanistic Psychology

A more subtle factor in the production and maintenance of physical health is morale, or "spirit." Increasing evidence indicates that if a person finds his life challenging and satisfying, his body works better and he resists infectious illness better. Meaningful work, enjoyable leisure, love and friendship are inexpensive health insurance.

An Illness-Yielding Personality. A minority of the population is afflicted with the vast majority of illnesses that come to the attention of physicians. Defective heredity or a weak constitution only partly explain this high incidence of recurrent illness. We must look as well into the ways of life of these people with a talent for sickening.

Studies of the frequently ill show they share many traits. Among other things, it is found that they may simply not take care of themselves; that is, they do not eat, sleep, or exercise sensibly. Another, less obvious factor in frequent illness is stress. Many people encounter more stress in everyday life than is objectively necessary. They find everyday interpersonal relationships lacking in satisfaction, and, indeed, positively stressing. Demanding roles are a source of such stress. If a person must present himself to others as something which he is not—if he is obliged to seem friendly when he is unfriendly, or if he is obliged to hide his real feelings and wants from others—then every moment spent in the presence of others is stressing. It is as if he is traveling incognito, with his true identity hidden. He feels that if he is "found out" by others, terrible harm will befall him. Consequently he trusts no one, and keeps his guard up. Other people by their very existence then function as stressors, adding to the stress of daily life.

Another factor in frequent illness is an overdeveloped sense of duty. Persons who feel obliged by their consciences to keep working at unsatisfactory jobs or to keep involved in unrewarding relationships are actively creating the conditions for their own illness. Periods of being sick may thus function as periods of respite from a dispiriting way of life. If they could change their work or their ways of relating even slightly, they would become ill less often. A brief vacation from work or family is usually less expensive than a stay of equal length at a hospital—and the vacation may forestall the illness.

The Body and Healthy Personality

Transcending "Handicap"

A person may become "handicapped" by accident or by disease. He may lose a limb, his sight, or his strength. Whatever the impairment, the person's capacity to come to terms with his environment has not been eliminated completely. A blind person can still be sensitive to all the properties of his physical environment save those mediated by vision. The single amputee can still locomote in his environment, though he may have to hop on one leg or limp with a prosthesis. The double amputee could, if necessary, drag his body along by means of movements with his arms and hands.

HEALTHY REACTIONS TO HANDICAP

When a person suffers some affliction which results in a handicap, there may be, quite naturally, some rather devastating emotional reactions. These include a sense of hopelessness, anxiety about the future, and losses in self-esteem.

Once the fact of handicap has been accepted by the individual, however, the healthy thing to do is to make an assessment of the residual capacities of the body and the person's goals in life. If the person's goals remain fixed, then he must experiment until he can find ways of reaching his goals in new ways. Thus, a professional dancer, following the amputation of a leg, may wish to continue in his profession. He will be obliged to acquire an artificial leg and practice until he once again can move with skill and grace.

It is probably easier for a person to retain his goals and seek new ways of achieving them than for him to change his goals. It is common for the handicapped person to feel hopeless and sorry for himself; but with resolve, courage, and encouragement, he can find new ways to re-engage in active life. The most helpful people in rehabilitation work are those who have themselves been handicapped, and have found the strength to overcome passive dependency and self-pity.

UNHEALTHY REACTIONS TO HANDICAP

Once blindness, crippling, or debilitating disease have afflicted a person, it is natural that his life will be thrown into chaos. Plans for the future will have been disrupted.

Healthy Personality: An Approach from the Viewpoint of Humanistic Psychology

It becomes a physical impossibility for the person to exploit former sources of satisfaction. If his security and self-esteem have been dependent upon certain kinds of activity which are now precluded, then his life will seem empty and futile indeed. An athlete may become very depressed when a heart ailment makes it necessary for him to give up active sports. A woman whose self-esteem is predicated primarily on her physical beauty will see little point in living, following an accident which leaves her with unsightly scars.

The reactions of depression and self-pity are inevitable when handicap occurs. What we are interested in here is the person's reactions to the emotional responses. The healthy reactions already have been described. The most common unhealthy reaction is resignation. Resignation to handicap means giving up, or "digging in" for a life devoid of satisfaction. When resignation occurs, and lasts for more than some period of time, say six months to a year, the resigner may be deriving some kind of enjoyment from his affliction and the power it gives him. He may make claims on intact people, in accordance with the idea, "Since the world has handed me such a dirty deal, I am entitled to a lot of support and consideration from others." [15]

One way to lift a resigner out of his rut is to "blast" him out—with scolding, anger, even contempt. Naturally, this blasting should be viewed as a last resort, when other means, such as inspiration and encouragement have failed. The best person to do the blasting is another handicapped individual. He knows all the advantages accruing to resignation, and all the devious resistances to full rehabilitation and self-reliance.

A man began to have "epileptic" seizures some years ago. They were intense, grand-mal convulsions, such that he frequently broke his hands as he thrashed about during the period of unconsciousness. Over a period of years, the medications to control the seizures elevated his blood pressure and damaged his kidneys. It appeared he was going to die from kidney failure or from circulatory failure.

Two psychologists undertook to train this man, through correspondence, to recognize his "auras" and to engage in actions that might forestall his seizures. The frequency of his losses of consciousness with convulsions was dramatically reduced, as was his need for sedating, anticonvulsant medications. Their hypothesis was that, once the man had his first seizure, and showed the characteristic "spikes" on his EEG tracing, he became the subject of a hypnotic, brainwashing onslaught of suggestion, as if his doctors were saying,

Why, you lost consciousness and had a seizure. You are a sufferer from epilepsy. Never mind, there is no shame connected with this. Julius Caesar was an epileptic, Shakespeare and Jesus probably were, and of course Dostoievsky was. But you are lucky. Advances in medical science have made it possible for us to control seizures with some powerful drugs. Trust us, and put yourself in our hands. Of course, you may feel sleepy, and your gums may get puffy, but if you are careful to take your medicine regularly, you can live a normal life.

It is difficult to resist such a powerfully seductive invitation to view oneself as helpless, with no power to prevent the loss of consciousness and the seizure; in short, to become dependent upon drugs, to become passive in order to let outside agencies control bodily happenings. There is reason to suspect that many people deemed "epileptic" are leading drugged lives, rather than being helped to find ways of mobilizing their strength and wits so as to stay conscious and nonconvulsing.

Some Approaches to Re-embodiment

At the beginning of this chapter various manifestations of "unembodiment," of the loss of a keen awareness of one's body were spoken of. Clearly a health-giving way of living in and with one's body calls for such awareness. Next we will discuss ways that have been employed by teachers of body awareness and control to "re-embody" their pupils.

PHYSICAL CONTACT

We have had a puritanical attitude toward physical contact in the United States and northern Europe. Touching, embracing, and holding hands all appear to be restricted to relationships between parents and young children, or between lovers and spouses. In Latin countries, such as France or Italy, and in Asiatic and African countries, it is more common to see men holding hands as they walk down a street, or embracing upon greeting one another. Physical contact is given more meanings there than as a prelude to sexual arousal or an expression of parental concern, as has been the case in our culture. We appear to observe strong taboos relating to touching, yet touching and massage are direct ways to awaken a dormant sense of embodiment.

I conducted a study of touching among college students, their parents, and their friends. Several hundred students were asked to show, on a questionnaire, the areas of their bodies on which touches had been exchanged with their mothers, fathers, closest same-sex friend, and closest friend of the opposite sex. The data, shown in Figure 1, indicate that not a great deal of touching went on between these students and their parents and their same-sex friends. With the opposite-sex friend, considerably more touching was exchanged, presumably an expression of affection and erotic caressing. But our data showed that many of the students tested did not have a lover, and were virtually "out of touch"

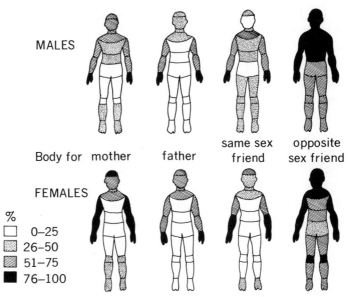

MALES

Body for mother   father   same sex   opposite
friend   sex friend

FEMALES

%
☐ 0–25
▦ 26–50
▨ 51–75
■ 76–100

The Body and Healthy Personality

FIG. 1. The Ss' "Body-for-Others," as experienced through amount of touching received from others. Percentages are based on N = 168 males and 140 females. The darkest portions signify that from 76–100 per cent of the Ss reported being touched by the target person in question on the body region indicated.

with the people in their lives. These findings suggest that many Americans may be starved for sensual physical contact without being aware of what they are missing.

The experience of total body massage (not just a back rub) slowly and sensuously conducted can produce extreme relaxation, and a softening of the tense "muscular armor" from which many people suffer. Esalen Institute, the growth center at Big Sur, California, pioneered in introducing such massage to a larger public. Bernard Gunther's books *Sense Relaxation* and *What to Do Till the Messiah Comes* are readable accounts of ways to relax another person through massage, and to heighten one's capacities to sense the world through touch as well as taste and smell. Physical contact is coming gradually to be incorporated into the helping repertoires of psychotherapists, in both the psychiatric and psychological professions, in recognition of the fact that problems of a psychological nature occur to an embodied person, and hence have somatic concomitants that can be treated directly.[16]

ROLFING

Ida Rolf, an extraordinary physical therapist, developed a technique for altering posture by means of deep manipulation of the entire body musculature, muscle by muscle. The purpose is to soften the fascia, those membranes which sheathe each muscle fiber in the body. The fascia become tightened, and constrict muscles into chronic tension, as a consequence of blows, emotional stress, and occupation-linked postural defects, such as the forward droop of the head found in many scholars. The configuration of muscle spasm and flaccidity which defines a person's characteristic posture pulls the skeleton out of alignment, so that excessive energy is consumed in standing, sitting, or walking. Ida Rolf and her trainees (called 'Rolfers') believe that the change in posture brought about by this "structural integration" technique will improve sleep, energy level, elimination, sexuality, and overall health.

I received a course of Rolfing treatments and found that the pressure of knuckles and elbows upon muscles (in order to stretch the fascia) is painful, but not unbearable. My posture was improved by the realignment of the musculature of my thighs, back, and abdomen, but since my posture and

Healthy Personality: An Approach from the Viewpoint of Humanistic Psychology

overall health were good before Rolfing, I cannot notice any dramatic changes; however, in some colleagues and friends with bad posture and health, the alterations in appearance have been quite noticeable. They stand taller and are more energetic and more coordinated in their movements.[17]

DIET AND FASTING

People typically eat without consideration of what they need for optimum nourishment or for full consciousness of body and world. Excessive eating is a sedative, insuring that a person will not feel the impact of his life style upon him. Fasting has played a crucial role in every religious tradition and every discipline which aims at enlightenment. Avoiding food for periods ranging from a day to a month or longer will result not only in some loss of weight, but also in heightened somatic perception and keener senses of touch, taste, and smell. In my own experiences at fasting, I have gone no longer than six days without food; I completed a partial fast of forty days, however, limiting my nourishment to vegetable and fruit juices. The fasting was not unlike a trip to another culture—it gave me a changed perspective upon the situation within which I had been enmeshed.

Many persons in recent years have begun to experiment with vegetarian diets, with organically grown foods, with foods that have not been preserved with chemicals. Such intelligent concern with one's nourishment is quite compatible with healthy personality, and it certainly contributes to the experience of re-embodiment.

HATHA YOGA

In the West, physical bulkiness, with large, prominent musculature, has long been a masculine ideal, and similar robustness among women has been praised in popular magazines and sought by women. Heavy musculature has been cultivated by violent exercise, vigorous calisthenics, and comparable feats of endurance. One function of such heaviness (not obesity, just heavy musculature) is to decrease sensitivity to pain and to enhance endurance. In the East, perhaps because patterns of nourishment have been different, slenderness is more the rule. The disciplines of Hatha Yoga have been employed in India for several thousand years as a way to bring the body under more control, so that

The Body and Healthy Personality

meditation and contemplation will not be obstructed by an insensitive or a tense, uncomfortable body.

Hatha Yoga is one part of the Hindu religion, and is one of the means of achieving the experience of "union of inner and outer," of dissolving the ego and unifying awareness. In the West, Hatha Yoga has been undertaken by many, not for religious purposes so much as for exercise to stretch and relax the musculature and produce vigor by releasing energy contained in chronic body postures. Hatha Yoga comprises several hundred positions into which one gently folds or stretches his body to the accompaniment of slow, regular breathing. As in all things, a person can only enter fully into one of the Yoga postures by "letting go" his muscular commitment to the chronic postures of the body generated by his life style. Thus, one position entails bending over, clasping the calves or ankles, to place one's face against one's knees. In the beginning, a person may only be able to clasp the backs of his knees, and bend half over. In time, with gentle pressure at the limit of his bend, the person may enter more fully into the position. When an entire repertoire of postures is practiced daily, the person does indeed despecialize his body so that it becomes more limber and better able to sustain diverse forms of effective action.

Body inflexibility and insensitivity is a kind of overspecialization of one's body in adjustment to a chronic life style. Techniques like Hatha Yoga foster a letting go, a metaphoric "erasure" of the muscular and postural configuration that makes up one's character, wiping out the traces of one's way of living, the effects of one's usual roles and projects upon one's body and ways of experiencing the world. Old yogis have surprisingly unlined faces and pliable bodies because of assiduous practice of the postures, with the attendant despecialization of the body.[18] Hatha Yoga appears to be a means of producing the effects which Rolfing does, but the Yoga student is despecializing himself, rather than giving himself into the hands of the Rolfer.

KARATE, TAI CHI CHUAN, AND OTHER MARTIAL ARTS

The martial arts of attack and defense that originated in China, Korea, and Japan call for a rigorous program of discipline and exercise. The beginner must learn to control his breathing, remain calm and balanced, and concentrate his power in sudden blows, kicks, and slashes with the side of the hand. Although one may wonder why a person would want to learn arts of killing or maiming others through the use of hands and feet, the learner is more fully embodied after the training than he was before it. In fairness, it must be said that teachers of these arts are always concerned to teach their pupils never to attack, only to defend, to use their power to conserve, not to destroy life.

BIOENERGETIC ANALYSIS

As noted in Chapter 1, Alexander Lowen and his associates have developed a set of exercises designed to identify muscle groups in the body which are chronically tense—the so-called muscular armor which Wilhelm Reich described. Lowen is a practicing psychiatrist, and he developed his physical techniques as adjuncts to the traditional conversational methods of conducting psychotherapy. He had studied with Reich, who, as we now know, was a genius, and adept at seeing how life-depleting ways of existing were revealed in stereotyped ways of acting and in rigid musculature.

Lowen puts his patient into various physical postures that stress the body, and asks him to hold the position until a tremor comes. Often a patient will spontaneously begin weeping, or become angry, or recall some painful or humiliating event from the past, as he enters the diagnostic postures. The purpose of the techniques is to release taut muscles and long-repressed patterns of emotional expression. For example, Lowen may ask a patient to scream, "No, No, No" very loudly, kicking the bed on which he is lying with great vigor. Or he may ask an inhibited person to strike a mattress with a tennis racquet. These procedures, together with the diagnostic postures, aim at bringing a person's consciousness of his body into a more unified state, so that the bodyless self and an unconscious body are unified in action and in experience.[19]

The Body and Healthy Personality

Somatic Specialization and Despecialization

Man's peculiar genius among living forms, the trait which enabled him to prevail while dinosaurs and other creatures became extinct, is his peculiar lack of specialization. When

·

environments change, inflexible organisms die off. Conventional upbringing and life style encourage a person to become overly adapted to some fixed range of environmental challenges. A person living a sedentary, scholarly life, for example, may become fat, with his head jutting forward; someone who works at a machine calling for a strong right arm may develop monstrous biceps in that arm, whereas the left remains of usual size.

Sickness, both physical and psychological, can stem from overadaptation to an environment or culture. Besides so-called occupational diseases, produced by the stresses peculiar to given occupations, there are the symptoms brought about by change in environment. When a person's resources have been committed to coping with one set of demands and challenges, he may not readily uncommit them to respond to challenges coming from another sector of life. Thus, many persons become sick when they change jobs, neighborhoods, and even family status. The neurotics whom Freud treated were persons overly specialized to survive within the structure of their family of origin. When they were asked to leave home, to start another family, they were unable to despecialize themselves from the role of son and daughter in order to take on new roles of husband or wife.

There is a real sense, then, in which various psychotherapies and the techniques for re-embodiment are despecializing procedures, making it possible for the person to let go his somatic "recall" of his past—to forget his past *somatically* —in order to learn how to act effectively in the present. Memory resides in the muscles, joints, and viscera as much as in the brain cells. Thus, the methods of Yoga, Rolfing, fasting, and meditation all are approaches to the erasure of the past, as it is recorded in the musculature and habitual patterns of physiological functioning.

These techniques also function as means to alter one's usual way of being aware of self and the world. We are usually involved in various life projects, such as the pursuit of our profession; and in various interpersonal roles, for example, the role of son to parents, student to teacher, and man to woman. These are commitments of our "embodied" consciousness which influence the way the world appears to us and the way we experience ourselves. Our projects and our roles represent the specialized way in which we appear

Healthy Personality: An Approach from the Viewpoint of Humanistic Psychology

to ourselves and others in the world. When the somatic aspect of this specialization is "wiped out" so that one truly becomes *no one,* it is possible to re-enter one's old ways with more vigor and with new perspectives, and it is also possible to begin disengaging from chronic roles and projects so that growth of self can occur.

Athletes and dancers would never think of beginning their contest or performance without a series of "warm-up" exercises. Although they are specialists, dancers and athletes have had to train hard to liberate their musculature so that their bodies become versatile instruments, capable of flexibility unavailable to the average person. But when these people engage in routine daily pursuits, their musculature follows suit. For a performance they must disengage their thinking and their bodies from these mundane involvements. Hence, warming up is a way of disengaging from one way of being in order to re-engage in another. In current slang, "psyching oneself up" to undertake some task or feat is a variety of disengagement and warming up.

The Experience and Somatic Manifestations of Enlivenment

Religion is concerned with life itself, with ways to live that are the most viable. The question is, "What are the experiential and objective signs of being most fully alive?" How can a person tell when his actions, his life style, his relationships with other people, his diet, are conducive to life itself, and when they diminish life? Sensitive somatic perception clearly is essential to discern when one's way of life is enlivening. To experience one's appetites keenly, to enjoy one's senses, to feel emotion, to breathe deeply, to sleep well, to eliminate adequately—all these vital signs may show a person that his life style is good for him. The experience of zest, vitality, and rich meaning in life are further manifestations of enlivenment.

The Body and Healthy Personality

A useful exercise for a student to undertake is to list all the people with whom he has regular dealings, such as parents, friends, teachers, and all the activities in which he regularly engages, such as studies, sports, hobbies, and rate himself in each of these situations for the degree to which he experiences himself as most fully alive. He may find that some relationships, as with his mother, or with some one friend, induce in him a sense of being deadened, a loss of enthusiasm for living, and loss of a sense of being oneself. Such a discovery may enable a person to make vitalizing changes in his life situation.

A problem for physiological psychologists is to develop ways to measure how alive a person is at any time. One could envision, for example, taking a series of continuous measurements of blood pressure, pulse, skin conductivity, EEG, and so on. As these readings are obtained, they may be fed into a computer which relates the indices to estimates of reduction of life or proneness to disease. These readings in turn could be transformed into electrical charges and fed into a source of light such that when a person is most fully alive, his light would shine most brightly. Decrements in enlivenment would cause the light to diminish in brilliance. Just as the simplified electroencephalograph made it possible for persons to train themselves to enter a tranquil, meditative state by observing when the alpha waves appear,[20] so a person might train himself to heightened sensitivity to his own degree of being alive through such equipment. He could then note when his life was dispiriting him before he collapsed in illness.

Some Existential Suggestions

How many, if any, of the manifestations of unembodiment apply to you? Do you repress much of your somatic experiencing, or is your somatic perception keen and sensitive? You can use your body as a test of others' embodiment; if you feel devitalized in one person's presence, but not in another's, then there is something that is not well going on with that other person or with your relationship to that person. As a psychotherapist, I pay keen attention to the way I feel—enlivened or devitalized—when I am with a patient, because this tells me something about *his* state of being.

What do you believe is beautiful about your body and what ugly (to you)? Stand in front of a mirror and ask yourself, "What do I feel about my hair, my eyes, nose, teeth, and so on." This exercise will reveal a great deal to you about your own body-ideal, in terms of which you come to like or to scorn your own appearance.

Especially if you are handicapped, it is good to challenge your own beliefs, including your medical beliefs, about what you are capable of doing despite the incapacity. I have suggested to people who run an "Outward Bound" program that they take amputees, blind people, aging people, drug addicts, and grossly overweight people out to the wilderness, to scale mountains and cross deserts and to learn how their concepts of what they can or cannot do are extremely self-limiting.

Learn to give and to receive a massage. An hour of mutual massage each day, between spouses, friends, or strangers, would not solve the problems of the world, but it would certainly improve the quality of daily life.

Experimenting with dieting and fasting is also a good thing to do, to learn how self-limiting and habitual we have become in regard to our eating.

SUMMARY

Partial repression of somatic experience is common among people of the West. "Unembodiment" manifests itself as pretense, as a devitalizing effect upon others, and in autistic body images. Somatic perception sensitizes a person to the effect his life style is having upon his health.

The capacity for control over bodily functions and over the movement of the body is a sign of ego development.

Physical appearance is an important basis for a sense of security and self-esteem. The cultural concept of the ideal body condemns many people who adhere to this ideal to diminished self-esteem, because the ideal is very restrictive. Thus, many people dislike their appearance because they are too fat or thin, or have facial wrinkles or a nose which seems to them to be ugly.

Valid knowledge about the structure, functions, and limits of one's body is essential for healthy personality. Some ways of life associated with culture, occupation, or role are destructive to health.

"Handicap" typically leads to depression and helplessness. Healthy reactions to handicap include assessing remaining capacities and readdressing life with vigor.

The Body and Healthy Personality

Some techniques for "re-embodying" oneself, and heightening somatic perception include massage, Rolfing, special diets and fasting, Hatha Yoga, various martial arts, and bioenergetic analysis. These techniques all appear to work by despecializing an overly specialized body. A proposal was made to explore ways to measure degrees of somatic enlivenment.

NOTES AND REFERENCES

1. The antisomatic bias appears to have begun with St. Paul. "Unembodiment" is discussed in R. D. LAING, *The Divided Self* (London: Tavistock, 1960), pp. 67–81.

2. Again Laing has made a fine analysis of the way in which people elude direct experience of themselves in their bodies and acts. See R. LAING, *Self and Others* (New York: Pantheon, 1969), Chapter 3, "Pretense and Elusion," and Chapter 4, "The Counterpoint of Experience."

3. R. D. LAING, Politics of Experience (New York: Pantheon, 1967).

4. W. REICH, *The Discovery of the Orgone: The Function of the Orgasm* (New York: Noonday, 1961), Chapter 8.

5. R. BIRWHISTELL, *Kinesics and Context* (Philadelphia: University of Pennsylvania Press, 1970).

6. S. FISHER and S. E. CLEVELAND, *Body-Image and Personality* (New York: Dover, 1968); also S. FISHER, *Body Experience in Fantasy and Behavior* (New York: Appleton-Century-Crofts, 1970).

7. E. JOKL and P. JOKL, *Physiological Basis of Athletic Records* (Springfield, Ill.: Thomas, 1968).

8. S. M. JOURARD, *The Transparent Self* (New York: Van Nostrand Reinhold, 1971), Chapter 11, "The Invitation to Die." (See also the article on the cultures where it is normal to live past 100 years: Alexander Leaf, "Every Day Is a Gift When You're Over 100," *National Geographic*, 1973, Vol. 143, pp. 93–119.)

9. W. HOFFER, "The Development of the Body Ego," *Psychoanalytic Study of the Child*, V (New York: International Universities Press, 1950), pp. 18–23.

10. Mark Lefkowitz did his Master's thesis on this problem. I narrated his study in S. M. JOURARD, *Self-disclosure: An Experimental Analysis of the Transparent Self* (New York: Wiley-Interscience, 1971), Chapter 12.

11. P. SECORD and S. M. JOURARD, "The Appraisal of Body-Cathexis: Body-Cathexis and the Self," *Journal of Consulting Psychology*, 1953, Vol. 17, pp. 343–347.

Healthy Personality: An Approach from the Viewpoint of Humanistic Psychology

12. S. M. Jourard and P. Secord, "Body-Cathexis and the Ideal Female Figure," *Journal of Abnormal and Social Psychology*, 1955, Vol. 50, pp. 243–246; "Body-Size and Body-Cathexis," *Journal of Consulting Psychology*, 1954, Vol. 18, p. 184.

13. Margaret Mead, *Male and Female* (New York: Morrow, 1949), pp. 138–142.

14. See H. Bruch, *The Importance of Overweight* (New York: Norton, 1957).

15. See Horney's discussion of "neurotic claims" in *Neurosis and Human Growth* (New York: Norton, 1950), Chapter 2; also E. Berne, *Games People Play* (New York: Grove, 1964).

16. A. Montagu, *Touching: The Human Significance of the Skin* (New York: Harper & Row, 1972). My study is reported in *Disclosing Man to Himself* (New York: Van Nostrand Reinhold, 1968), Chapter 12; a follow-up study appears in *Self-disclosure: An Experimental Analysis of the Transparent Self*, op. cit., Chapter 11; B. Gunther, *Sense Relaxation: Below Your Mind* (New York: Macmillan, 1968) and *What to Do Till the Messiah Comes* (New York: Macmillan, 1971).

17. Ida Rolf currently is writing an authoritative book on the subject (1973); an earlier article by her is "Structural Integration," available from Esalen Books, Big Sur, California 93920. A brief discussion of several re-embodying techniques, including Rolfing, is found in W. Schutz, *Here Comes Everybody* (New York: Harper & Row, 1972), pp. 202–223.

18. There are hundreds of books available on Yoga. I have found R. Mishra, *Fundamentals of Yoga* (New York: Lancer, 1959) reasonable. K. Behanan, *Yoga: A Scientific Evaluation* (New York: Dover, 1937) offers a Western scientific perspective on Yoga. See also A. S. Dalal and T. Barber, "Yoga and Hypnotism" in T. X. Barber, *LSD, Marijuana, Yoga, and Hypnosis* (Chicago: Aldine, 1970), Chapter 3. I have just read a book in which the author, a professor at the University of Bombay, shows how the ancient Indian scriptures, called the Upanishads, and the early writings about Yoga anticipate current findings in neurophysiology and in the psychology of perception. See T. Kulkarni, *Upanishads and Yoga: An Empirical Approach to the Understanding* (Bombay: Bharatiya Vidya Bhavan, 1972).

19. See A. Lowen, *Betrayal of the Body* (New York: Macmillan, 1967); also S. Keleman, *Sexuality, Self and Survival* (San Francisco: Lodestar Press, 1971).

20. See J. Kamiya, "Operant Control of the EEG Alpha Rhythm and Some of Its Reported Effects on Consciousness," in C. T. Tart (Ed.), *Altered States of Consciousness* (New York: Wiley, 1969), Chapter 33.

7

THE SELF AND HEALTHY PERSONALITY

INTRODUCTION

Everyone experiences his identity differently, but everyone experiences who he is. A person acts in the world and interacts with other people as the person he believes himself to be. Our very names designate our personal, as well as family, identities, and we act in the ways expected of the person so named. I am a Jourard, and of all the Jourards, I am that one named Sidney. People from my home town had little difficulty recognizing me as a Jourard when I was growing up; there was a physical resemblance among us and we all took pride in being hard-working, friendly, and independent. But I am that Jourard named Sidney, and I do not behave in ways identical with my brothers and sisters, nor do I experience the world in the ways they do. My identity is my own. My first name and my surname come to stand for some limits on the ways in which I will act—there are many things I will not do because I am a Jourard, named Sidney, and there are many things which I demand of myself, and which others expect of me, because I am that very person. I am that Jourard named Sidney; but I am called Professor by my students, Doctor Jourard by my psychotherapy clients, Sid by my friends, Daddy by my children, and Dear, at times, by my wife. These are the names for each aspect of my identity and for the social roles (see Chapter 10) which guide my relationships with others. The names prescribe and proscribe what I disclose to and what I conceal from others; and they define what action is appropriate in my relationships with the people who address me in those terms.[1] If a student addressed me thus: "Professor Jourard, darling . . ." I would be confused over which of my possibilities are being summoned.

Identity and the Self-structure

Some psychologists describe a person's sense of his identity with the term *self-structure*. This term implies that the individual is somebody in particular (a self), and it also signifies that he can experience his being in several perspectives, or modes, e.g., the modes of perception, of conceptualizing, and of imagination.

When a person perceives his own being, when he becomes aware of the "flow" of his consciousness and knows that it is his own, it is appropriate to designate this stream of awareness as his *real self*, or *actual self*. A person comes to know his real self by reflecting upon his experience, and naming what he is perceiving, feeling, or wishing with honesty.

The repertoire of beliefs a person has acquired regarding who he is is termed his *self-concept*. My self-concept is the set of beliefs and assumptions I have affirmed, relating to the ways in which I typically experience and act. But I also acquired a set of ideals and moral taboos as I grew up; these functioned as goads to "good" action and barriers to "bad." These ideals and taboos represent an idealized image of myself—the way I ought to be. This optimum way for me to be, and to become, is called the *self-ideal*, or *ideal self*. It is the basis for conscience, the moral judgments we make of our own conduct.

The other aspect of the self-structure is the way a person wishes to be seen and known by others. Everyone monitors his speech and actions before other people, taking care that

The Self and Healthy Personality

151

he says or does nothing to destroy the impression he is seeking to produce, nor to transgress the limits of behavior appropriate to his social role. Indeed, the "management of impressions" is an important activity for people to learn; Goffman has written with lucidity and wit about the myriad ways in which people seek to induce in other people a view of themselves which will be approved.[2] The name for this dimension of the self-structure is *public self*. It is the subjective side of one's social roles.

A person's self-structure functions as a regulator of his experience and action, so that from day to day, and year to year, he will sense continuity in his existence, and will recognize himself with a sense of familiarity. Lest the student believe that this sense of familiarity is unimportant, I will point to the sheer terror which arises when a person does not know who he is, when he acts and experiences in ways he feels are not his own. Loss of a sense of identity is tantamount to dying; *schizophrenia* is the name psychiatrists use to describe the confusion, horror, and estrangement which follow a total loss of self.

Healthy personality calls for action which achieves satisfaction of a person's basic needs, and which fulfills the projects he undertakes to give meaning and direction to his life. A person's sense of his identity has a decisive influence upon what action he feels free to engage in, and what is taboo for him. Thus, a person can so define himself that the very action which is essential for his well-being and growth is not compatible with his self-concept, his self-ideal, or his public self. Accordingly, he refrains from the activity and lives out his identity, even though it may be sickening him. We will be interested in exploring how a person acquires his self-structure, how each dimension of it influences his experience and action, and the conditions under which the self changes in sickening and in health-engendering ways.

The Self-concept

A person's self-concept comprises all his beliefs about his own nature. It includes his assumptions about his strength and weakness, his possibilities for growth, and it includes his explicit descriptions of his customary patterns of behavior and experiencing. Thus, a person may say of himself, "I am lazy; I always give up when the task becomes difficult. I usually feel happy. I am warm and friendly; however, I need a great deal of help to make it through life." These self-descriptions resemble statistical formulations, in the sense that the individual believes there have been many occasions when he acted in the ways he just mentioned.[3]

People describe themselves as if they were describing a fixed essence, or a class of objects of which they are a specimen. When a person says he is lazy, or sincere, it is as if he is saying, "It is my nature to be lazy, or sincere, just as it is the nature of a wolf to be fierce." But human beings do not have fixed natures; neither do wolves. Under most circumstances of life, humans have the freedom to choose how they will be and how they will act. Thus, when a person forms a self-concept, thereby defining himself, he is not so much describing his nature as he is making a pledge that he will continue to be the kind of person he believes he now is and has been. One's self-concept is not so much descriptive of experience and action as it is *prescriptive*. The self-concept is a commitment. Because our self-concepts are such powerful influences upon our experience and action, it follows that anything or any person who influences what we believe to be true or possible for ourselves will have a powerful influence upon our lives.

If I can convince you that you are strong, when hitherto you believed you were weak, you may then begin to act in ways that befit a strong person. What you believe to be true of yourself *is* your "nature"; what should never be forgotten is that one's beliefs about self are just that—beliefs—and they can be changed. One's self-concept is open to change, just as one's beliefs about God, one's parents, or the world are open to change.

The Influence of Other People upon One's Self-concept. A person's self-concept is open to influence by views other people have of him. Beliefs about oneself are not based on conclusions arrived at through independent self-study, but rather are derived by listening to what other people have said about one's nature.[4] Other people define us to ourselves, if we listen to them. Thus, one's mother may say, "You are lazy, like your father." The child didn't know he was lazy until he was told. Once he believes that this is his essential nature, he will act as a lazy person is expected to. When other people attribute traits to a person, their descriptions function like hypnotic suggestions, inducing or persuading the individual to conform with the other's view of him. This vulnerability to others' influence is a liability, if the others define him as weak or bad; it is also an asset, because one can attribute strength and goodness to a person, who then will discover he can be strong and good. Psychotherapists exert a beneficial influence upon their patients by seeing them as potentially strong and self-reliant when all others, including the patients themselves, see them as weak, dependent, and worthless.

I always talk to patients who consult with me as if they embodied astonishing strength and unquestioned ability to cope with life. I don't have to say this in so many words; I just assume it, and hold the assumption relentlessly. Such attribution of strength comes as a surprise to the patient, who may say after several interviews, "Why, you treat me as if I had the ability to cope with my life." I might then reply, "Of course."

People constantly define one another, thereby confirming one another's self-concepts, for better or for worse. Listen to everyday conversations between parents and their children, between close friends, or between spouses: "John, put your coat and hat on; you know you are weak and will catch cold." (John is being led to believe that his body will not tolerate temperature changes without risk of pneumonia.) "Mary, you are such an obliging and generous girl—you could never refuse anyone, or say an unkind word." (Mary is being condemned to a life in which she cannot lose her temper, or do anything to please herself; her nature has just been defined for her.) A husband may define his wife as follows: "Here, dear, let me balance the checkbook; you know you could never add two numbers together." (She is confirmed in a view of herself as silly, helpless, and impractical).[5]

We Instruct Others on How We Wish Them to See Us. People attribute to the "other" the traits and qualities that they believe define him. Thus, the parents of a student who consulted me told him, many times: "You are such a nice, obedient boy. You always do what you are told. Ever since you were a baby, you wanted to please us." Under such a hypnotic and persuasive regime, he came to believe he was nice and obedient, eager to please others. Once he formed his concept of himself, his way of relating to others functioned as an invitation to *them* to view him as he had come to view himself.

It seems strange, but a person's self-concept represents an answer to the question, "Who am I?" which his parents first answered. If he accepts their answer, he transmits it to others who want to know who he is. He tells others who he is, in every relationship that he enters. How odd if you and I are no more than carriers of a view of ourselves which our mothers gave us as a kind of legacy. We define ourselves in terms provided by our mothers, say, and confirm that definition by our action, which invites and persuades others to believe we are that way.

The student I saw in psychotherapy told me that for years his father had been saying, "You take after your Uncle Billy. He started many things, but always gave up half way through." His father was defining him as essentially a failure, and he believed that is how he was. He tried to persuade me that he was, essentially, a failure, and there was little anyone could do about it. Of course, I refused to see him that way. Instead I attributed strength to him and the capacity to overcome self-doubt and the difficulties of study. The student did change his concept of himself under this continuous "invitation" to change it. After having had competence attributed to him, the student not only changed his self-concept, but invited others, including his father, to change their view of him.

This cycle of having one's identity defined by others, believing it, and then persuading others to view oneself in the same way, is continuous throughout life. It is the basis for personal growth, and it is also the basis for endless confirmation of a sense of identity which is self-defeating.

THE SELF-CONCEPT AND THE SENSE OF IDENTITY

People act in ways that confirm their self-concepts. When a person acts "out of character," as in the case of a person who thinks of himself as kind but then flies into a violent rage, he experiences threat to his sense of his identity. He may say, "I was not myself when I was so enraged." Such a threat is extremely painful, and people go to great lengths to

The Self and Healthy Personality

retain a continuous experience of their preferred identity. One's sense of being who he believes he is can be threatened, not only by action that is out of character, but also by thoughts, feelings, and memories. A person may engage in daydreaming that produces thoughts and feelings of an outrageous nature; for example, a loving mother may find herself entertaining fantasies of strangling her children. People repress many of their possibilities of experiencing so as to affirm their present concepts of themselves.

It is intolerable to lose one's sense of identity, even if it is a "spoiled" identity. For example, obese people and alcoholics may believe they remain addicted to sweets or to alcohol because they "have no will power." This belief may be the basis of their sense of who they are; if they act decisively, they do not recognize themselves; paradoxically, this is so frightening that they revert to the ways that are destructive to their well-being. People find it difficult to change their behavior, even when it is destructive to growth and to health, because their self-concepts have not altered.

Conscience

Conscience is the act of judging one's experience and action, comparing them to the standards of an idealized self. Conscience has been likened to a "still small voice," and it has been described as a person's imaginative view of how he would like to be, and how he believes he ought to be. The standards of conscience, in terms of which a person condemns or approves his conduct, are usually based upon the laws and customs of the society within which he has been reared. Seen from a sociological viewpoint, conscience—man's capacity to make moral judgments of his own conduct—is one of the "agencies" for social control. The necessity for controlling behavior through social pressure, or through threats of imprisonment or violence, is decreased when people have acquired a conscience.

Conscience plays an important role in the development of neurotic and psychotic illness. Moreover, conformity to some moral standards can sometimes force a person to live in ways that are joyless and which endanger his physical health.

Healthy Personality: An Approach from the Viewpoint of Humanistic Psychology

Psychological Health. Freud believed that neurosis was partly caused by an overly severe, mainly unconscious, infantile conscience. (He called it the superego.) According to his view, a neurotic sufferer was obliged to avoid sexual behavior, and even sexual fantasies, in order to be free of guilt. One aim of psychoanalytic therapy was to help the patient modify his conscience so that its taboos were less restrictive and more in keeping with adult life.

Mowrer disagreed with the psychoanalytic views. According to Mowrer, a neurotic is a person who persists beyond childhood in the pursuit of irresponsible pleasures, including sexuality, and who represses his conscience to avoid guilt. Neurotic symptoms arise as defenses against guilt, not against infantile sexuality, as the Freudians might maintain. Consequently, Mowrer claims, the aim in therapy is not to render the conscience more lenient, but to make it conscious, so that a person will feel guilt more acutely and seek in future to obey his conscience rather than repress it.

Clinical experience shows that neither Freud nor Mowrer is wholly correct or wholly incorrect. Some neurotic patients do indeed have a conscience that is too strict; in order to remain guilt-free, they must refrain from all pleasurable activities, including those which society condones. Other patients have the make-up Mowrer has regarded as nuclear to all neurosis—they repress conscience so they can break social taboos without conscious guilt. In still others both patterns of unhealthy conscience may be found.[6]

Conscience and Physical Illness. If a person's conscience is based on a cruel and punitive morality, he will have an exaggerated sense of duty which makes him deny himself legitimate pleasures. Thus, a parent may deny himself or herself all fun in life, insisting upon a spartan existence, in order to provide for the children. The necessity to repress anger, resentment, and temptation to enjoyment can impose excessive stress upon the person, and demoralize him such that his resistance to infectious illnesses is diminished. Conscience can kill a person, if it is inhumanely demanding and restrictive. Such conscience is often found in persons with various forms of stress-induced disease, such as high blood pressure, cancer, and heart disease.

The Self and Healthy Personality

Conscience is acquired gradually through *identification*. Identification is the process of adopting traits of some valued model. It is through identification that intrafamilial resemblances in behavior, values, gesture, attitudes, and morals are acquired.

The child comes into the world only with the capacity to develop a conscience. He acts in accordance with his momentary needs and feelings, and his parents are usually watching him closely, making moral judgments about his behavior. If he acts in ways which violate the parents' concepts of what is right, they will punish him for behaving in that way. The parents appear huge, powerful, and admirable from the child's standpoint; he wants to become like them. In order to avoid punishment, to retain the parents' love, and to acquire their wonderful attributes, the child strives to become like them in many ways. He identifies with their demands and expectations of him; these gradually become his expectations of himself. In short, he comes to forbid in himself what his parents forbade. He comes to demand of himself what his parents demanded. He comes to expect of himself what his parents expected. In this manner his conscience commences.[7]

UNHEALTHY CONSCIENCES

Excessively Strict Conscience. This pattern of unhealthy conscience limits behavior more drastically than do law and custom. The unfortunate bearer of such a conscience allows himself fewer satisfactions than other members of his social group; he expects more of himself, more difficult achievements, and a sterner morality than his peers. Thus, many persons may have been taught that sexy or hostile fantasies and thoughts are equivalent in sinful significance to sexual and hostile action, and so they dare not even think such thoughts.

Authoritarian Conscience. An "authoritarian" person is one who believes authority figures are omnipotent and must be obeyed without question. Indeed, to disobey or to question authority is synonymous with sin for the authoritarian character; he becomes overwhelmed with guilt at even the thought of challenging vested authority. A person may

Healthy Personality: An Approach from the Viewpoint of Humanistic Psychology

experience his conscience in the same way; it is to be obeyed blindly, without question, hesitation, or criticism. Its commands have the feeling of certainty and unquestionable rightness. Fromm has named a conscience with such characteristics an authoritarian conscience.[8]

Repressed and Projected Conscience. To repress is to refuse to think about something, or to refrain from engaging in some mental operation, such as thinking, remembering, daydreaming, or evaluating. Conscience functions by means of the comparison of one's own behavior, feelings, or motives with relevant taboos and "shoulds." A person may have learned to refrain from making value judgments about aspects of his own behavior so as to avoid the painful experience of guilt. This avoidance of value judgments concerning one's own behavior is what we mean when we speak of the repression of conscience. Laymen speak, in this connection, of the "hardened heart." Scrooge, in Dickens' classic *Christmas Carol,* had such a hardened heart until he was overcome with guilt.[9]

A person can project his conscience as well as repress it. Concretely, this involves repression of self-evaluation and ascribing evaluations of the self to others. Thus, a person might engage in some act, but deny it is wrong for him to do this. However, he may impute condemnation of himself to some other person, and feel without warrant that the other person is criticizing and condemning him. In extreme cases of disturbed personality—for example, paranoid schizophrenia—the patient projects all of his self-criticism to others, and believes that everyone is criticizing and persecuting him.

Consciences in Conflict. In conflicted conscience, the values, ideals, and taboos contradict one another. Thus, conformity with one value requires violation of another, with consequent guilt. A common source of conflicted conscience is parents who have different standards for judging the behavior of their children. The mother may value gentleness, submissiveness, obedience, and "womanly things," whereas the father affirms self-assertion, aggressiveness, muscular strength. In pleasing his father, the child displeases his mother, and vice versa.

Some people attempt to resolve value conflicts by compartmentalizing their lives. They follow one set of values at work, another set in the home, another set when they are among their peers, and so on. More desirable from the viewpoint of personality hygiene is the attempt to reconcile one's values with one another so they constitute a harmonious and hierarchically arranged system.

CHARACTERISTICS OF HEALTHY CONSCIENCE

A person with a healthy conscience will foster healthy personality if he strives to conform with it. Such conformity will have a number of consequences. It will enable the person to obtain enough basic need gratifications to make life worth living, but in a guilt-free manner. The person will enjoy relatively high self-esteem. His behavior may be approved by other members of his social group—at least to the extent that his conscience is congruent with the group's value system. A healthy conscience will be compatible with continual personality growth; indeed, it may be a strong motivating force toward personal growth. Let us now list some of the more salient attributes of a healthy conscience.

Accessibility to Consciousness. A healthy conscience is one which can be reflected upon. The person is able to formulate its component taboos, ideals, and ethical precepts in words. This accessibility to consciousness is important for resolution of moral conflicts. If a person is faced with a decision that he must make, he can make his decision along moral lines much more readily when his ideals can be clearly stated.

When I say that a healthy conscience is conscious, I do not mean the person is always thinking about his moral standards. Most of the time, the healthy conscience will be unconscious; the person will conform with his conscience automatically. But when he does feel guilt, he will be able to determine what aspects of his conscience he has violated; and when he has to resolve some conflict, he will make the relevant moral aspects explicit, so that his decision will be made after due consideration of the moral issues at stake.

Self-affirmation. A healthy conscience is not experienced as an "alien power" within the total personality structure, a power compulsively obeyed out of dread. Rather, it is composed of a set of ideals and taboos, each of which has been examined by the person and affirmed by him so that it becomes a true part of his real self. A self-affirmed conscience is one to which the person conforms because he

Healthy Personality: An Approach from the Viewpoint of Humanistic Psychology

160

wants to, not because he is afraid of disobeying. Another way of saying this is to assert that the person feels he owns his conscience; it is his. He has had a voice in determining the rules by which he will live. He is like the citizen in a democracy who does not mind conforming with rules he has helped formulate.

Receptivity to Questioning and Change. A healthy conscience is based upon general values and ideals which remain fixed throughout life. But the specific behavior which these values call for is not rigidly defined. The person can challenge his self-demands when they are no longer relevant to his present life circumstances. For example, a student may have been trained to believe that premarital sex relationships are evil, and destructive of love. In his college career, he may live with a girl and enjoy sexual intimacies within the context of a loving relationship. He discovers that no harm befalls the girl or himself. He may change one of the taboos that are at the root of his conscience. This openness to change is most possible if the conscience is not authoritarian.

Some Degree of Congruence with the Social Value System. The person with a healthy conscience is living among other people and so he will be obliged to share at least some of their ideals and taboos. This is not to say that his conscience must be absolutely congruent with the social mores. It may happen that the person finds his values *more ethical* than the prevailing mores, and so he will follow his conscience rather than the moral expectations of his peers. It may be necessary for the person with a healthy conscience to resist the efforts of others to make him conform with their moral precepts. He may even have to leave home because of moral–ethical differences and seek a group more congenial to his outlook.

It is not implied that a healthy conscience will be highly lenient, permitting any antisocial behavior. Indeed, it may be difficult to conform with the precepts of a healthy conscience. Fromm has stated that the voice of a humanistic conscience may be only dimly heard, because it is readily masked by the authoritarian elements of the conscience. As Fromm puts it, conscience "is the voice of our true 'selves' which summons us back to ourselves, to live productively, to develop fully and harmoniously—that is, to become what we potentially are." He points out further that guilt arising from violation of a healthy conscience may be difficult to identify; we might feel guilt arising from our authoritarian conscience when we ignore its demands, in order to pursue the requirements of a healthy conscience.[10]

The Public Self

A person's self-concept represents what he believes to be true about his own personality. His conscience grows out of an idealized view of how he ought to be. Next, we will explore the identity a person wishes to have in others' experience of him—his *public self*. Man has the capacity to select his action and his speech, in order to influence the experience others will have of him. Typically, a person wishes to believe that he is law-abiding, highly moral, and with other traits that evoke a favorable impression.

The layman's term for the public self is *wanted reputation*. Everyone strives to construct a reputation with respect to his typical behavior; i.e., he chooses his behavior before other persons so they will form the beliefs that he wants them to form. Almost everyone draws a distinction between his "public" life and his "private" life. Ordinarily, only those persons an individual trusts are allowed to observe the full range of his behavior repertoire. Outsiders are permitted to observe only the "expurgated" edition of his behavior. Goffman speaks in this connection of "on-stage" behavior, as opposed to backstage or off-stage behavior.[11]

The most important reason for constructing public selves of various sorts is *expedience*. It is only when others believe certain things to be true of you that they will like you, marry you, give you jobs, refrain from imprisoning you, appoint you to public office, buy things at your store, or consult you professionally. If for any reason other people believe undesirable things to be true of you, they will ostracize you, jail you, and so on.

A person may construct highly diversified public selves, depending upon his goals. The young man seeking a spouse strives to behave in ways that the girl will be likely to value and approve. He does not allow her to see the rest of his behavior, which may vary tremendously from the censored version of him she does see.

Healthy Personality: An Approach from the Viewpoint of Humanistic Psychology

The construction of public selves resembles the art of sculpture. A sculptor manipulates clay, then steps back to see whether the statue he is creating resembles the image he has in mind. If it doesn't, he continues to work at it, until by successive approximations he has brought into reality something which hitherto existed only as a preferred idea or image.

By the same token, a person may hold an image of his own personality that he wants to construct in the mind of another person. Instead of clay, he employs his own carefully selected behavior and conversation. From time to time, his audience will offer feedback, indicating how he has been seen. If the way he is being seen does not yet coincide with the preferred image, the individual engages in more behavior and talking, until he is assured by the other's responses that he is now seen as he wishes to be seen.

A person may "slip" during the process of constructing, or living up to, a given public self. He may want his audience to believe one thing about him, say, that he is morally scrupulous, yet he may forget himself and use obscene language, and destroy the image he was seeking to create. Such experiences produce embarrassment, to say the least. The reading public has an insatiable curiosity for details which conflict with the public selves of newsworthy people.

SELF-DISCLOSURE AND THE PUBLIC SELF

Self-disclosure refers to the act of communicating one's experience to others through words and actions. If a person wishes others to know him the way he knows himself, he will disclose himself in truth. If he wishes to present a false public self, he will lie, pretending to be someone else, as it were. Authentic self-disclosure is not merely a way to make oneself known to others; it is a way to develop relationships with others which are themselves conducive to healthy personality (see Chapter 10).

If a person feels it necessary to mislead others about the kind of person he is, he will engage in false disclosure, as if he were an actor trying to convince his audience of his authenticity. But such chronic misrepresentation of self leads to serious consequences. If a person lies chronically to others about his real feelings, wishes, memories, and plans, he will eventually lose touch with his authentic experienc-

The Self and Healthy Personality

ing. He will not know who he really is, so lost is he in the assumed identity he was enacting. This loss of self, or self-alienation, results from repression of one's real experiencing, as one pretends to be the person projected as his public self. Self-alienation is the source of most psychological illness (neurosis and psychosis), and it also is a factor in the development of physical illness. Persons with high degrees of self-alienation are out of touch with reality, especially the reality of their own bodies and needs. Consequently, their action does not serve their well-being and growth; it only protects their public selves.[12]

Self-alienation

Through chronic lying to others and himself, a person may develop a self-structure radically estranged from the reality of his spontaneous experiencing. He may believe that he is a devoted husband (self-concept), he may approve of his attitude toward his wife (conscience), and he strives to get his wife to see him as a devoted spouse by the way he speaks to her (public self). Yet his wife may act in ways that infuriate him, and he may be carrying on an affair. If he acknowledged the anger that his wife's actions engendered in him, it might threaten his sense of identity and undermine his self-esteem. If he evaluated the moral significance of his infidelity, it might make him feel guilty. He may avoid the guilt and embarrassment by repressing the unpleasant dimensions of his experience. To the extent that a person represses aspects of his experience, we can assert that he is *alienated from his real self*. He is pretending to be someone other than his real self; he can believe his own pretense only because he continuously represses his experience.

SOME SIGNS OF SELF-ALIENATION

Horney listed a number of indicators of self-alienation which a person can look for in self or in others:

1. The general capacity for conscious experience is impaired. The person is living "as if in a fog. Nothing is clear to them. Not only their own thoughts and feelings but also other people, and the implications of a situation, are hazy."

2. There may be a decrease in awareness or concern for

Healthy Personality: An Approach from the Viewpoint of Humanistic Psychology

the body, for its needs and feelings, or for material possessions such as a house, car, or clothing.

3. There is a loss of the feeling of being an active, determining force in one's own life.

The factors which Horney sees as responsible for the process of self-alienation include:

1. The development of compulsive solutions to neurotic conflicts, such as striving for affection, detachment from others, or chronic hostility to others.

2. Active moves away from the real self, such as the drive for glory, and striving to live up to an impossible self-ideal.

3. Active moves against the real self, as in self-hate or self-destruction.

The consequence of alienation from the self, Horney says, is that the person's "relation to himself has become *impersonal*." More specifically, in the self-alienated person pride governs feelings—the individual does not react with spontaneous emotion. Instead, he feels what he should feel. Further, the self-alienated person does not feel in possession of his own energies; his powers are not his own. Another consequence of self-alienation which Horney describes is an impairment in the ability to assume responsibility for the self. The self-alienated person is lacking in plain, simple honesty about himself and his life. The lack of honesty manifests itself, she states, as (1) an inability to recognize oneself as one really is, without minimizing or exaggerating, (2) an unwillingness to accept the consequences of one's actions and decisions, and (3) an unwillingness to realize it is up to oneself to do something about one's difficulties. The person who is self-alienated insists that others, fate, or time will solve these difficulties for him.[13]

Self-alienation means, basically, that a person is not choosing his action by consulting all components of his real self, e.g., his needs, his values; instead, he serves some *part* of his real self. But if the total self is not the source of direction for the individual's behavior, what is? Let us distinguish among the following partial sources of behavior direction, namely, pride, conscience, authority, peers, impulses, and finally real-self direction.

Pride and Conscience Direction. Riesman's [14] concept of the "inner-directed character" is an excellent illustration of the person whose behavior expresses the dictates of conscience and self-ideal rather than the real self. When choices for action arise, such a person experiences a conflict between what he really wants to do and what he believes he ought to do. In this connection, Horney has written of the "tyranny of the should." [15] Implicitly, such a person believes his real self is an unreliable guide to conduct, and so he represses it. The consequence of ignoring the real self in favor of a rigid conscience is that the person may behave in a moral and exemplary fashion, but his real needs are ignored, and he will be perpetually thwarted.

Authority Direction. The "authoritarian character" is a person who seeks some authority figure to direct his conduct. He strives to discern what behavior the authority figure expects of him, and he hastens to comply. If there is any conflict between his own wishes and the demands of authority, he habitually suppresses his own and compulsively complies with the authority's wishes. Indeed, he experiences his real self as evil or weak, not worth considering. Fromm interprets the manner in which authoritarian characters perceive authority as a by-product of real-self repression, followed by a projection to the authority figure of all of one's own repressed "powers." Hence, the authoritarian character perceives himself as weak and the leader as all-powerful and possessing unusual strength and wisdom—the "charismatic" leader.[16]

Peer Direction. Riesman's concept, the "other-directed" character, describes an individual who allows the wishes and expectations of his social peers to direct his actions. The other-directed character becomes sensitized to others' wishes and actively seeks to comply with them. The result may be popularity and acceptance, but it is purchased at the cost of knowledge of the real self and of thwarting many basic needs.[17]

Impulse Direction. Impulse and emotions are a part of the real self, just as are will and ideals. Everyone has to struggle to reconcile the conflicting demands of impulses, ideals, and the expectations of other people. An impulse-directed person is one who habitually ignores all demands upon his behavior save those imposed by his impulses and feelings. He ignores his conscience, the rights of other people, even his own long-range welfare and growth. All is subordinated to the immediate gratification of his needs

Healthy Personality: An Approach from the Viewpoint of Humanistic Psychology

and impulses and the immediate expression of his feelings. Psychoanalysts refer to such individuals as "instinct-ridden" characters; they idealize and rationalize their drives and emotions because they cannot voluntarily control them. They are like adult children who have evaded growth.

The Real Self and Authentic Being

In all the preceding instances, the person was acting without taking responsibility for *choosing* his action. Instead, it was as if the question "How shall I act?" had been asked once and an answer chosen for all life, no matter what the personal cost. Life was then lived automatically. Thus, the conscience-directed person evades conflict and the necessity to make decisions by following an inflexible moral code. The authoritarian character never chooses; he seeks his leader's wishes and expectations, and conforms with them, like a soldier getting his orders from a superior officer. The other-directed person likewise does not choose his action, but instead acts as he believes his peers would wish him to. In none of these cases does the person realize that *he is free to choose his action in every situation he encounters.* He can change his action at will, though at times it may be difficult. Man is free, and hence responsible for his actions and their consequences. But as the existential philosophers point out, awareness of such freedom and its accompanying responsibility may be terrifying: it is certainly common for people to wish to "escape from freedom." Erich Fromm's book with that title is a classic, and should be read for the insight into the human situation that it affords. I recommend to my students that they should also read some of the writings of Kierkegaard, Sartre, Buber, and Kazantzakis for the same reason. All these authors remind their readers relentlessly that human beings are condemned to freedom, and they must (and do, with or without awareness) choose their responses to life situations, and they are responsible for their choices.

Authentic being, or being one's real self, means that the person explores the opportunities and challenges afforded by each situation, and then chooses a response which expresses his true values, needs, feelings and commitments. An authentic person is less predictable than an inauthentic, self-alienated person, because each life situation, each problem, each encounter with a person is experienced as *new,* with different invitations and demands issuing from it. But such authenticity is only possible when the person has not repressed entire dimensions of his experiencing, but is, instead, in steady contact with his real self. It takes courage to be real in this sense, because one's own experiencing often gives rise to fright and sometimes disgust. Moreover, such authenticity requires a person to face decisions time and time again, with the awareness that the outcomes of his life are his responsibility, not the responsibility of his parents, his superior officers, or public pressure. Authentic deciding of this nature is most likely to be started by a person after he has somehow realized, with intensity, the fact that he will die someday. An encounter with death functions as an invitation for many people to live more decisively, more intensively, and more authentically.[18]

Authentic being is a sign of healthy personality, and it is the means of achieving healthy personality growth.

SELF-DISCLOSURE AND AUTHENTIC BEING

When a person is authentic he not only acknowledges the truth of his feelings, needs, and wishes but he is capable of revealing his true being to the other people with whom he has personal relationships. We humans can lie to one another, aiming to be seen by others as a person we know we are not. We also have the capacity for entering into true dialogue with our fellows, disclosing what we think, feel, and are planning, without reserve. Obviously, such transparency exposes a person to real danger, because to be that open with others means to be without defenses. The interests of healthy personality are served if a person can disclose himself honestly and spontaneously to others. People are more likely to be cautious than excessively open, with the result that they are relatively safe, but lonely and misunderstood by others.

It may seem paradoxical, but a person comes to know his real self, and becomes able to introspect honestly, as a consequence of spontaneous disclosure of self to another person. The individual who has a trusted friend or relative to whom he can express his thoughts, feelings, and opinions honestly is in a better position to learn his real self than the one who has never undergone this experience, because as he reveals himself to another, *he is also revealing himself to himself.* The act of stating one's experience to another, making oneself known to him, permits one to "get outside oneself" and see oneself. This process of self-discovery through making oneself known to another is facilitated if the other person reflects back what he has heard you say. His reflection or restatement, like a mirror, then permits you to compare your words with your experience as you feel it directly and immediately. The capacity to be a transparent self in one's personal relationships is a sign of healthy personality.

Some Existential Suggestions

The only suggestion I have to make with regard to the self-concept is to invite you to ask yourself a question, "Just *who* do I think I am?" Once you have answered this question, raise another: "*Why* do I believe those things about myself? Who told me that is who, and how, I am?" Answers to this question may make it possible to ask another, "Who, and how, can I *become?*"

As I said in this chapter, I see the self-concept as a self-fulfilling prophecy; as a commitment rather than as a self-description. Thus, if you do not like the way you find yourself just now, it is possible to envision another way to be, and then struggle to be that way.

One's self-ideal can be demonic, capable of destroying the quality of life and even life itself. Consequently, it is urgent that a person examine the ideals and taboos that guide his conduct. Episodes of guilt should be occasions for examining the ideal that is being faulted rather than the occasion for unthinkingly changing action. It is only good to conform to a humanistic conscience; unreflective obedience to an authoritarian conscience infantilizes a person and blocks his ability to change in ways that enhance life.

Our public selves are among our chief idolatries. The wish to be seen in some special way can so cramp our spontaneity as to make a self-conscious ordeal of social existence. The main suggestion I have to offer in this connection is to experiment with authentic self-disclosure cautiously or boldly, but with tact and a loving heart. Authentic self-disclosure to others keeps one's self-concept from becoming congealed, and others' views of oneself from being traps.

SUMMARY

The term self-structure *refers to a person's sense of his own identity, of who he is. The self-structure includes the self-concept (the person's beliefs about himself), the self-ideal (his view of how he ought to be), and his public selves (the way in which he wishes to be experienced by others). A person's self-concept is a powerful influence upon his action, because each person acts as the person he believes he is and can be. People's views of themselves are strongly influenced by other's definitions of them. Furthermore, we continually instruct others as to how they should perceive us.*

Our self-ideal is the basis for conscience, the act of making moral judgments about ourselves. We acquire our consciences by taking over the moral views of those who raised us. Our conscience, as given, may be too strict, too authoritarian, and incompatible with healthy personality. The interests of healthy personality are served if a person examines and periodically reformulates his self-ideal so that conformity with it is compatible with a health-engendering way of life.

A person's public selves—how he wishes to be seen by others—influence his action and his self-disclosure before others. A person acts as the person he wishes others to believe he is. If his public selves are radically different from his self-concept and his real self, the person will become increasingly self-alienated. Authentic being and authentic self-disclosure are factors in the attainment of healthy personality.

NOTES AND REFERENCES

1. See R. BROWN and MARGUERITE FORD, "Address in American English," *Journal of Abnormal and Social Psychology,* 1961, Vol. 62, pp. 375–385; also R. BROWN, *Social Psychology* (New York: Free Press, 1965), pp. 51–71.

2. E. GOFFMAN, *The Presentation of Self in Everyday Life* (Garden City, N.Y.: Doubleday, 1960).

Healthy Personality: An Approach from the Viewpoint of Humanistic Psychology

3. Reviews of theory and research on the self-concept may be found in Ruth Wylie, *The Self-concept: A Critical Review of Pertinent Literature* (Lincoln: University of Nebraska Press, 1961); and C. S. Hall, and G. Lindzey, *Theories of Personality,* 2nd ed. (New York: Wiley, 1970).

4. Sullivan was most explicit in stating that the self consisted in "reflections of the appraisals of 'significant others.'" See H. S. Sullivan, *Conceptions of Modern Psychiatry* (Washington, D.C.: William Alanson White Psychiatric Foundation, 1947).

5. See R. D. Laing, *Politics of the Family* (New York: Pantheon, 1969), pp. 78–82, for a superb discussion of the way in which a parent's attributions to, and assumptions about, a child function to induce the child to be in that way. Chapter 10, "Attributions and Injunctions," in his *Self and Others* (New York: Pantheon, 1969) is an earlier formulation.

6. The Freudian view of neurosis is presented in O. Fenichel, *The Psychoanalytic Theory of Neurosis* (New York: Norton, 1945); Mowrer's arguments against it, and his alternate view, are presented in O. H. Mowrer, *The Crisis in Psychiatry* and *Religion* (New York: Van Nostrand Reinhold, 1961), Chapters 2 and 13.

7. Fenichel, op. cit., Chapter 6; and O. H. Mowrer, *Learning Theory and Personality Dynamics* (New York: Ronald, 1950) offer accounts of the origins of conscience through identification. J. C. Flugel, *Man, Morals and Society* (New York: International Universities Press, 1945), Chapters 4, 9, 11, and 12, offers an explanation for the strictness of conscience.

8. E. Fromm, *Man for Himself* (New York: Holt, 1947), pp. 143–175.

9. Mowrer, op. cit.

10. Fromm, op. cit., pp. 159 ff.

11. Goffman, op. cit.; also his later volumes *Stigma: Notes on the Management of Spoiled Identity* (Englewood Cliffs, N.J.: Prentice-Hall, 1963).

12. See S. M. Jourard, *The Transparent Self,* 2nd ed. (New York: Van Nostrand Reinhold, 1971), Chapters 3 and 4.

13. Karen Horney, *Neurosis and Human Growth* (New York: Norton, 1950), Chapter 6.

14. D. Riesman, *The Lonely Crowd* (New Haven: Yale University Press, 1950).

15. Horney, op. cit., Chapter 3.

16. E. Fromm, *Escape from Freedom* (New York: Holt, 1941); T. W. Adorno, Else Frenkel-Brunswik, D. J. Levinson, and R. N. Sanford, *The Authoritarian Character* (New York: Harper & Row, 1950); W. Reich, *The Mass-Psychology of Fascism* (New York: Noonday, 1970).

17. RIESMAN, op. cit.

18. M. HEIDEGGER, *Being and Time* (New York: Harper & Row, 1962). Bradley Fisher demonstrated that an encounter with death intensified a person's subsequent experience of his life. See B. FISHER, "Self-Exploration Experience in Death Encounter" (unpublished doctoral dissertation, University of Florida College of Education, 1968); Sharon Graham showed that students who believed in the finality of death were more open and self-disclosing in their personal relations than people who believed in heaven. Her thesis is summarized in my book *Self-disclosure: An Experimental Analysis of the Transparent Self* (New York: Wiley-Interscience, 1971). The discussion in this section is influenced by A. W. WATTS, *The Way of Zen* (New York: Pantheon, 1957).

Healthy Personality: An Approach from the Viewpoint of Humanistic Psychology

8

DEFENSE VERSUS GROWTH

A person discovers who he is and what he must do to live effectively, and then something changes. His needs vary moment by moment, sometimes subtly, occasionally in obvious ways. Other people with whom he lives change their habits, and their attitude toward him. The machines, the environment, the domestic and foreign policies of the government, even one's own taste in music alter in time. It is man's task, no less than it was the task of the dinosaurs, to come to terms with this change. Dinosaurs were endowed with small brains and very specialized bodies. When their world changed too abruptly, they could not change, and so they became extinct. Human beings have vast brains, and untapped potential for new ways of experiencing and coping. Our bodies are relatively unspecialized. We can live under fantastically diverse circumstances, ranging from the Australian desert to the concrete of New York. We must specialize in order to survive. The Australian aborigine who wanders the desert carrying nothing but a spear or two is a superb specialist at desert survival; as was the polar Eskimo who needed nothing more than warm clothes and a harpoon. Aborigines, Eskimos, and city dwellers alike retain the capacity to despecialize when circumstances change, in order to respecialize for living effectively in new circumstances. Anything which blocks a person's awareness of his capacity to suspend an ineffective way of being (so he can learn another way) is a threat to life itself, or to the quality of his existence. He may even choose to die rather than live in ways out of keeping with his identity. It is not easy to be human, because there are so many ways to be, and no guidelines for choosing the identity that is most viable. This is one aspect of the "dreadful freedom" of which the existentialist philosophers speak. We must live with it.

The capacity to experience threat is man's margin of safety. Anxiety and guilt are early warning signals. They indicate that unless the person changes something, his life, his self-esteem, or his very identity may be taken from him. It is good to be able to experience threat.

But threat opens options. It can spur defensive maneuvers that are themselves barriers to life, and it can promote enlarged awareness and greater competence. If every time a person was threatened, he put on a heavier suit of armor, then in time he would be immobile—safe but out of touch. If he could postpone defensive maneuvers long enough, he could act in ways that further his growth.

Threats to the Self

Threats to the self originate from external as well as internal sources. We are not concerned here with danger to one's sheer survival, such as war or the destruction of the environment. We are considering threats to the way a person feels he *is*, to his sense of his own identity.

EXTERNAL THREAT TO IDENTITY

Buber points out that human beings need confirmation from one another: "Man wishes to be confirmed in his being by man. . . . The human person needs confirmation because man as man needs it." [1] Without such confirmation from one's fellow human beings, a person can doubt he exists at all. Few people are that "ontologically secure," so firmly grounded in their sense of self that they can withstand a barrage of disconfirmation, or a life in which their perspective is ignored.

Disconfirmation. A person may experience himself being treated like a thing or an animal, for example, by his father. If he says, "You are not treating me right—I feel like a machine or an animal when I'm with you," the father might say, "You're crazy, son. Your mother and I love you, and we are doing what's best for you." The father is disconfirming his son's perspective, and threatening his sense of identity. If the son says, "I don't like the Republican party because its policies seem too reactionary," the father may disconfirm him by saying, "You hippies don't know what you are talking about." Such disconfirmation is common, unfortunately, in family life. People who disconfirm one another's perspectives in this way certainly do not contribute to each other's senses of identity, except to help one another feel worthless.

Invalidation. A threat to one's identity related to disconfirmation is invalidation. This is most commonly seen in the behavior of grown-ups with children, and in members of some dominant group in the presence of those over whom they are dominant. Thus, parents may talk about their child *in his presence,* as if he were a doll or a robot: "He never seems to be happy; he doesn't dress properly, messes up his room, and will not work hard enough at his studies." Physicians may discuss a patient with each other and with students while the patient is present; thus, a psychiatrist may say, "Notice, with this patient, how rigidly he sits, the blank expression in his eyes, and how angry he becomes if I pinch him." The patient's perspective here is not even acknowledged, much less consulted. His sense of being a worthwhile human being is threatened by such experiences. Women are frequently invalidated in similar fashion by insensitive men: "The little woman cooks well, but she doesn't say anything worth listening to about business or politics."

Disconfirmation and invalidation do not threaten a person's life, but they certainly undermine his sense of being a person, of existing as that very person. Laing and Esterson showed how an upbringing marked by continuous invalida-

Defense Versus Growth

tion and disconfirmation was a factor in the development of schizophrenia. The anger of blacks, women, and colonized peoples, all of whom have felt thus treated, is testimony that no one wishes to be invalidated or disconfirmed.[2]

INTERNAL THREATS TO IDENTITY

A person's sense of being who he believes he is, and wishes to be, is assaulted by some aspects of his own experiencing. Thus, a mother who wishes to be seen as kind and loving toward her children will be threatened by the experience of rage toward them. A student who believes he is bright and competent will be terribly threatened by the realization that he does not know enough to pass an exam. A person who believes he is morally pure (whatever that means to him) may be terribly threatened by erotic daydreams involving his brother or sister. Men especially are threatened by the experience of helplessness and dependency. If a man feels unable to cope with some problem, he may accept total failure rather than admit he feels the need for help from others.

What Are Defense Mechanisms?

Defense mechanisms are automatic, reflexlike ways in which a person reacts to threatening perceptions so that his self-structure will remain unchallenged and unchanged. Whenever anything of value is threatened, the person will naturally strive to defend it. But there are realistic and rational ways of defending something of value, and there are shortsighted ways to defend values. If we value our body, and our body is threatened by disease, the rational means of defense is to study the disease, determine its cure, and administer it. The unrealistic means for defense is to ignore the pain, or anesthetize ourselves against the pain, and pretend there is no threat to life and health.

If we value some theory, we can defend it unrealistically by distorting and ignoring conflicting evidence. The earlier discussion of autism (Chapter 4) illustrates this kind of autistic cognition.

The defense mechanisms are autistic means of defending the self-structure. They make it possible for a person to continue believing he is the kind of person he wants to believe he is when there is much evidence (from the real self) to refute these beliefs.

DEFENSE MECHANISMS ARE INSTANCES OF UNCONSCIOUS ACTION

Defense mechanisms may be viewed as "preconscious" or unconscious. The defensive individual is not aware he is defending himself against threat. As a matter of fact, once a defensive person recognizes he is being defensive against some threatening impulse or feeling, he may achieve voluntary control over his defensive behavior.

HOW DEFENSE MECHANISMS MILITATE AGAINST GROWTH

Growth is change in a valued direction. One of the goals of personal growth is a healthy self-structure, i.e., a state where the real self, the self-concept, the self-ideal, and the public selves are all mutually congruent. Whenever such a state of affairs exists, it can be only temporary—an unstable equilibrium. Any change in the real self will disrupt this equilibrium, and such changes are always occurring. The self-structure grows when the necessary adjustments are made following real-self changes. But if the person defends his self-structure, then he will ignore or distort the messages of his real self, thus preserving his present self-structure despite its increasing alienation from the real self.

The person who defends his self-structure against change is like the aging matron who keeps wearing the clothing of an eighteen-year-old beauty queen, in spite of increasing girth. Her girdle might be so tight that she nearly faints, but she will not admit her clothing does not fit. Such is the case with a defended self-structure; the underlying real self may have become so discrepant from the self-concept, self-ideal, and public selves that the individual is really two distinct persons: the one he believes he is and the one he really is.

The real self inevitably finds its way to expression. A real self which has been excluded by defense mechanisms manifests itself through boredom, frustration, vague anxiety and guilt, depression, unconscious motivation, and the symptoms of alienation from the self—in short, the whole repertoire of clinical psychopathology with which psychiatrists are familiar in their daily practice. Clinical symptoms of neurosis

Defense Versus Growth

and of psychosis may be regarded as a by-product of the conflict between the real self and the attempt to preserve a self-structure markedly discrepant with it.

Some Common Defense Mechanisms

The mechanisms of defense might just as legitimately be called mechanisms for increasing self-alienation or methods of evading growth, for such are their consequences. They are modes of behavior undertaken by a person with a relatively weak ego when threat to the self-structure arises. If they are effective, they reduce anxiety and guilt; but whenever the defenses are themselves weakened, threat is again experienced, for its causes continue to be operative. A defense is like a drug; it must be kept operative if it is to reduce discomfort. But a defense, like a drug, does not remove the conditions responsible for the pain and discomfort.

What are the major patterns of defensive behavior and how may they be recognized? The person himself can seldom recognize his own defensiveness, except under special conditions. The observer may be able to infer, from certain signs, the nature of the defense, the consequences of the defense, and the aspects of the real self that are being defended against.

REPRESSION

Repression is the most basic defense.[3] It consists in actively excluding from awareness any thought, feeling, memory, or wish that would threaten the self-structure. Freud introduced the concept of repression to explain some phenomena that he regularly observed in his efforts to treat neurotic patients. He found that his patients displayed resistance to the injunction that they say everything which came to mind. He used the term *resistance* to describe any deviation from unselected, uncensored talking. The term *repression* was invoked to explain the efforts of the person to avoid not merely speaking about embarrassing topics, but even thinking about these topics.

Repression manifests itself by the omission in the person's speech, emotion, and behavior repertoire of responses which might ordinarily be expected under given circumstances.

Healthy Personality: An Approach from the Viewpoint of Humanistic Psychology

For example, if a person has been deeply insulted by someone, and he displays no overt signs of hostility, the hypothesis can be entertained that he has repressed these feelings.

It should not be assumed that because some thought, feeling, or need has been repressed, it simply fades out of existence altogether. Rather, what appears to occur is that the repressed feelings and tensions continue to operate as unconscious determiners of behavior (see Chapter 4), because the causes of these feelings persist in life itself. The represser may betray many signs of his repressed feelings to a keen observer—in his dreams, accidents, slips of the tongue, and so on.

Repression also manifests itself as chronic tensing of various muscle groupings. If a person has repressed rage, yet lives continuously among the people who provoke it, he may chronically display tension in the muscles of the jaw, the neck, and the shoulders. This muscular "armor" is what Wilhelm Reich, Alexander Lowen, and Ida Rolfe all addressed directly, through exercises and massage (see Chapter 6). It often happened to patients of these practitioners that, when a set of muscles had relaxed, in response to the therapist's manipulations, the patient would express rage, or tears and convulsive sobbing; moreover, the patient might then recall with vividness some childhood events related to the original repression.

An important indicator of repression is a refusal by the person to examine and consider any other motives for a given action than the one he presently admits. Thus, a person may spank his children quite severely, he may forget their birthdays, he may never spend time with them at enjoyable activity, and he may continually scold them. An observer may gather the impression that such behavior expresses hatred and dislike for the children. He asks the father why he treats his children so. The father says, "Because I love them, and I am trying not to spoil them. I am trying to raise them right." If the observer asks him, "Could it be that you don't like your children?" the father might become quite indignant, and refuse to explore the possibility that this might be true. He is repressing his hostility to his children. To admit that he dislikes his children might threaten his self-structure to a profound degree.

Another important indicator of repression is selective recall of the past. In relating aspects of the past, much may be omitted from the account. If the observer knows what has been omitted, he may confront the person with these details, only to have him deny that the events occurred. It is as if he had a vested interest in forgetting these details, so as to preserve his present concept of self. Many experimental studies have shown how our recall and our forgetting are determined to a high degree by the need to maintain self-esteem and to preserve the present self-concept.[4]

In principle, a person can repress any aspect of his real self, whether it is socially desirable or socially reprehensible. Thus, a person may repress antisocial sexual urges and hostility, but he may also repress his feelings of attraction, his own intellect, and his own strength and resources, if these aspects of his real self imply some threat to his self-structure. The authoritarian character who exaggerates his own weakness and the strength of his hero or boss is repressing his own powers, and ascribing them (projecting them) to the authority figure in question. Fromm has detailed this point in his discussion of authoritarianism in everyday life and even in religion; he has suggested that the image of an all-powerful god, in contrast with weak, powerless man, rests on man's repression of his own powers, and the ascription of these very powers to the deity.[5]

Repression is quite an unstable mechanism, calling as it does for unremitting (but unconscious) effort from the person. Whenever there is any reduction in the energy devoted to repression, there is likely to be a breakthrough of the repressed aspects of the real self. When this occurs, the person may be incredibly threatened by feelings and impulses that he did not know he possessed. It may happen that the feelings are so intense that he explodes into uncontrolled activity—for instance, sexual or hostile violence. Probably many of the sex and homicide crimes which one reads about in the papers ("Nobody would have expected him to do that, he was always so nice, so moral") illustrate the breakthrough of repressed feelings and impulses. When a person is fatigued, or ill, he may be overwhelmed with fantasies, feelings, and impulses that are shocking to him and to those who know him.[6]

Although repression is usually involuntary and unconscious, it can be conscious and deliberate. Every reader will recall occasions when he has had thoughts which were fully conscious, but quite repugnant. On those occasions, he may have striven to get rid of the unwanted mental contents by just putting them out of mind or by trying to change the subject of thinking, in order to think of more pleasant things. Such efforts, if successful, may be called voluntary and conscious repression. They are analogous with the conversation between two persons; when an unpleasant subject comes up, the person who finds it is unpleasant will ask that the subject be changed, or else he may skillfully guide the conversation so that the dangerous topics are avoided.

RATIONALIZATION

It is striking that whenever a person is asked why he did anything, his motives usually appear exemplary, to him and to the observer. A person will seldom admit intentions of an immoral or antisocial sort. Yet the consequences of many actions are often discrepant with the admitted motive. Thus, a person intends to help his friend and actually interferes drastically with his friend's success. A man loves his wife, yet his behavior toward her may produce grief and discomfort for her.

For any action that a person undertakes, it can be assumed its consequences were desired by the person. If the aim is denied, or if the consequences appear at variance with the aim, then the observer may assume the intent has been repressed. The motive that the person admits may be called a rationalization. It is an explanation for an action and its consequences which is compatible with the individual's self-structure. The motive behind rationalization is not to give a factual account of authentic intent; rather, it is to do justice to the need to explain conduct and at the same time protect the self-structure.

A rationalization, then, is an explanation of one's conduct which has been selected from many possible explanations because it enhances and defends the individual's self-structure.

Defense Versus Growth

A theology student had asked a girl for a date. She was known to be quite proud of her sexually "liberated" attitudes. He said he wanted to persuade her to change her ways and denied any sexual interest in her. He was quite possibly rationalizing.

VERBAL REFORMULATION

There is a subtle defense mechanism often employed by well-educated persons. Psychoanalysts originally called it isolation, but I prefer the more general term *verbal reformulation*. What verbal reformulation amounts to, in the last analysis, is selecting words to describe one's feelings, motives, perceptions, and behavior on the basis of the feelings which they induce in the self. Thus, a perception described one way may invoke threatening feelings and meanings; if stated another way, with different language, these meanings and feelings are avoided. Let us illustrate with euphemisms. A euphemism is a "nice" way to talk about something threatening. Thus, some people are made uncomfortable by frank discussions about biological functions; they refer to pregnancy with the term *infanticipating* or with the French word *enceinte*. Menstruation may be referred to as "falling off the roof" or "a visit from Aunt Nellie." Most of us have been trained to avoid obscene words; only nasty, evil people swear. And some of the words to describe excreta are regarded as obscene; children who employ four-letter Anglo-Saxon words in reference to bodily wastes are severely punished. Even to think these words is enough to induce anxiety and threat. And so euphemisms or technical terms may be learned as substitutes.

Verbal reformulation was discovered by psychotherapists. They found their patients avoided emotions by choosing their language on the basis of its "feel." Thus, a patient who might break into tears if he admitted he hated his father, might relate to the therapist, "You know, I do have some antipathy against my father." If the therapist reflected back, "You mean you hated him," the patient might become severely upset. A patient from a lower-class background was striving to elevate her socioeconomic status. She spoke of her sexual affairs not in the four-letter language of her partners, but rather in pseudotechnical terms: "Well, I had an intercourse with him, and then I had an intercourse with that other fellow, and an intercourse with still another man."

Words are powerful conditioned stimuli; they carry emotional, as well as cognitive significance. Jung regarded certain words as "complex-indicators"—stimuli for strong but repressed emotional responses.[7]

It is in order to avoid the unwanted emotional tensions some words produce that verbal reformulation is adopted as a defense. Verbal reformulation takes many different forms besides euphemisms. Understatement may illustrate this defense; a person, after narrowly escaping death from drowning, might say, "You know that could have been dangerous."

Intellectualizing and the use of technical language to describe events, behavior, and motives often reflect defensive verbal reformulation. If the person were to use other language to describe the same things, the feelings which might be provoked would be overly threatening. One patient could not even think, much less say, the common vulgar word for flatus. The four-letter word, when spoken or even thought, would bring back the memory of a painful episode which occurred early in childhood involving flatulence in a social situation.[8]

Obscenity itself may be an instance of verbal reformulation for purposes of defense; a person may be able to accept himself only if he is rough and tough and virile, and he believes that swearing is synonymous with masculinity or emancipation from parents. Thus, an educated person who compulsively uses profane words may be employing them to keep dependency feelings and "sissy" feelings in a repressed status.

REACTION FORMATION

A person may defend himself against unwanted thoughts, feelings, and wishes, first by repressing them and then by compulsively thinking and striving to feel the opposite. It is as if it were not sufficient for the person to free himself of threat by merely eliminating the unwanted thoughts and feelings from his mind. He can only convince himself (and others?) that he is not that kind of a person if, and only if, he displays the opposite kinds of behavior in extreme degree. Reaction formation reveals itself through the compulsive and exaggerated nature of the behavior and attitudes that the person manifests; yet the repressed aspects of the real self may still leak out. Thus, a compulsively generous person may betray his repressed egocentricity and selfishness by giving gifts which the receiver does not like or cannot use; he gives expensive cigarette lighters to nonsmokers and bottles of expensive Scotch whiskey to teetotalers. The person who is compulsively kind to animals betrays underlying sadism by the brutality with which invective is leveled against those who experiment with animals. ("I think people who are cruel to dogs should be shot, and ground up as hamburger.") The devoted, overprotective mother keeps her child from growing by exaggerated overconcern with his health and safety. The guilty, philandering husband showers his wife with lavish gifts and with surprising and unusual tenderness and solicitude. The man with repressed dependency strivings displays exaggerated self-reliance, until he gets sick, when he becomes a virtual baby.

PROJECTION

The ability to perceive the world accurately is a relatively difficult achievement. The probability is high that persons will perceive the world autistically unless they take active steps to "reality-test" their perceptions. Autistic perception is animistic and "physiognomic." The young child, the regressed psychotic, and, to some extent, primitive people all manifest such "primitive" perception. Primitive perception is characterized by the tendency for the individual to personalize animals, trees, water, and nature—assuming they have motives, feelings, and wishes just as the perceiver has.[9] The defense mechanism of projection is a special case of primitive perception. Projection is the name given to the tendency to assume that another person has motives, feelings, wishes, values, or, more generally, traits that the individual himself has.

Assimilative Projection. If a person assumes that someone else is similar to himself, the term *assimilative projection* is used to describe such an assumption.

Projection as such is not a defense mechanism; rather, it might be called misperception of another person. Or it may be regarded as a sort of logical fallacy—the act of formulating beliefs about another person's motives and feelings without adequate evidence. Thus, I may notice that some man resembles me in age, sex, educational level, and so I assume he is responding to some situation in a manner identical

Healthy Personality: An Approach from the Viewpoint of Humanistic Psychology

with my own. Both of us look at a pretty girl; I notice I am pleasantly affected by the girl, and I assume that the other person is similarly affected. Further questioning of the other person may prove my assumption is wrong; my assumption itself illustrates assimilative projection.

Disowning Projection. Suppose I have repressed interest in pretty girls; to admit such interest would threaten my self-structure. I may assume the other fellow is very interested in the pretty girl, but I would myself vehemently deny any such interest. I would be displaying disowning projection. This unwarranted assumption about the other person's motives would be a defense mechanism. I would be protecting my self-concept by repressing certain feelings in myself and assuming without warrant that other people, not I, are motivated by such unacceptable drives.[10]

The evidence which prompts the observer to suspect disowning projection is to be found in the beliefs that a person holds concerning his own motivation and that of others. One suspects disowning projection if (1) the motives imputed to others are derogatory and immoral, (2) such motives are vigorously denied in the self, (3) there is not much evidence to support the belief that the other person has the motives imputed to him, and (4) the person himself gives evidence of these imputed motives, but at an unconscious level.

Not only can a person disown and project unsavory aspects of his real self, he can also repress and project his own positive potentialities. Where this occurs, the person perceives himself as imperfect, weak, and base, whereas the object of his projection is perceived as perfect, strong, and ideal. Authoritarian characters often appear to do this. Many a romantic lover, too, has seen himself as worthless and evil and has projected his own moral potential onto his beloved, perceiving her as the embodiment of all that is clean, wonderful, and morally perfect. He may become disillusioned in the face of reality.

DENIAL

Repression is really an instance of refusing to see or hear aspects of inner reality, the real self. But one can defend one's self-structure by refusing to see or hear aspects of outer reality if such perception would result in threat to the self-structure. The psychoanalysts coined the term *denial* to describe this tendency to ignore aspects of outer reality which induced anxiety and losses in self-esteem. Experimental psychologists use the term *perceptual defense* to describe the same phenomena. Sullivan spoke of "selective inattention" in this connection.

Humans tend to ignore or reconstruct reality when it is painful. It is such a stubborn tendency that Freud spoke of it as one of the "principles" of mental functioning—the pleasure principle in contrast with the reality principle.[11] When there are two possible meanings which might be assigned to some perception, one pleasant but untrue and the other true but painful, we must actually fight the pleasure principle in order to arrive at accurate cognition. Thus, we do not hear derogatory remarks uttered by someone about us even though our hearing is quite adequate to notice whispered praise. We do not see the blemishes in our loved ones if our self-esteem rests on the premise that we have made a wise choice of a perfect mate. In extreme forms, among persons with weak egos, we may actually see something quite clearly but then deny we saw it and believe the denial. For some persons the death of a loved one is so catastrophic, calling as it does for much reorganization of behavior and the self-structure, that they will not believe the person is dead.

PSYCHIC CONTACTLESSNESS

The term *psychic contactlessness,* coined by Wilhelm Reich,[12] refers to an inability, or a refusal, to communicate with or get emotionally involved with another person. If one has been deeply hurt in relationships with people, one may protect oneself against further hurt and losses in self-esteem by walling the self off from people. One is *among* people without being really *with* them. Avoidance of close contact and emotional involvement with others serves many defensive functions, not the least of which is the fact that others will never come to know you. Because others are never given the opportunity to observe his real self, the contactless person can entertain all manner of grandiose fantasies about himself; these are never known or criticized by others.

If an individual does not allow himself to think of others as human beings with feelings and hopes, he protects himself in many ways. He may be afraid to become personally involved, and so he stubbornly refuses to pay attention to the other person as a feeling, sensitive human being. Instead, other people are seen only as the embodiment of their social role; they are workers, or wives, or doctors, not persons. The act of depersonalizing others may thus protect the person against guilt feelings he might experience if he knew he was hurting others. Or if he suffers from an inability to love, he might protect himself against such a disquieting insight through depersonalizing others. Physicians, nurses, and dentists often depersonalize their patients or clients, adopting a "bedside manner" or a "chair-side manner," when dealing with them. The adoption of such contrived patterns of interaction permits them to treat their patient without being disturbed by the latter's suffering. Further, it permits them to hide their true feelings of like or dislike behind a professional mask.[13] Depersonalizing makes it possible for acts of extreme violence to be performed. The Nazis were able to slaughter millions of Jews because they had convinced themselves Jews were not human beings.

Defense of the Public Self

A person's various public selves are important to him. He can feel assured others will like him only when he believes *they* believe he is the kind of person they can like. And, as Willie Loman pointed out in "Death of a Salesman," it is important to be well liked. Consequently, it is not enough simply to construct public selves; a person usually feels obliged to defend them.

The most general means of defending the public self is by means of selective suppression of behavior which is inconsistent with the public self, replacing authentic with false self-disclosure. A mother may have heard reports about her son's behavior which conflict with her concept of him. She confronts him with the report, and he denies it flatly.

*Defense
Versus
Growth*

187

He does not want her to believe that he behaves in such a way. Secrecy is more common than lying as a means of defending our public selves. We can do almost anything without fear (though not necessarily without guilt) if no one discovers what we have done. The secret activities may be incredibly disparate with the public selves of the individual. Men at conventions sometimes display behavior markedly different from their usual home-town behavior and are quite disconcerted if their family and neighbors hear reports of their conduct.[14]

A really intelligent person can construct public selves with ingenuity and finesse—sometimes fantastically diverse and contradictory selves. The more diverse they are, however, the greater the difficulty in maintaining them; persons who hold contrasting concepts of the individual may meet him simultaneously, and he is at a loss to know how to behave.

Persistence of the Self-ideal

Once a self-ideal has been constructed, the person finds it difficult to change it. Why is this so, especially when the conscience is inhumane and impossibly strict. Consider an individual with incredibly high standards of performance; he never attains them, and believes he is a failure. If only his self-ideal could be altered, he could experience self-esteem, perhaps for the first time in his life. Yet when he is urged to relax his standards, he will refuse, saying, "I wish I could, but I can't."

The reason why a person finds it difficult to alter his self-ideal is because it came from sources *he dares not question*—his parents, teachers, God, or the Bible. His values have been acquired in the context of an authoritarian relationship, and he is in dread of horrible consequences should he question the "commands." [15] Freud said, "As the child was once compelled to obey its parents, so the ego submits to the categorical imperative pronounced by its superego." [16]

This fear of obscure consequences if one should change his conscience presents a powerful conserving force in the personality. A person may anesthetize his conscience with alcohol, he may lull it with self-deceptive arguments and rationalizations, he may even repress it; but he rarely changes it. This refusal has disastrous consequences for one's well-being and maturity.

Growth of the Self

Thus far, we have discussed the myriad ways in which a person maintains a stable identity in the face of experiencing which threatens it. Such stability is not pathology-producing in its own right; everything depends upon the availability of action which serves the person's needs and fulfills his projects. If the different aspects of the self are in reasonable harmony, and the person can cope with the challenges of work, leisure, and personal relationships, a stable self-structure is compatible with healthy personality. But there are times when healthy personality can be achieved only by changes in the self. I shall discuss these occasions now.

THE TIME FOR CHANGE

There are various indicators of the time for change. These include boredom, sickness, chronic anxiety and guilt, failure in work, and failure in personal relationships. In all these instances, the person's self-structure may have gotten out of touch with his real self, and he is out of touch with external reality. Something has changed, and he has not acknowledged or recognized it.

Boredom. The experience of boredom signifies the person's action is not serving his true needs and interests. Boredom also arises from prolonged exposure to monotonous surroundings, unchanging relationships, and repetitive work and leisure activity. Boredom is evidence of unperceived change in the self; the person whom one takes himself to be, *used* to be satisfied by those ways of being. Boredom means that one *no longer is that person,* and it is time to discover new dimensions of the self.

Sickness. Illness may signify that the person was not living in health-engendering ways. If a person is recurrently sick, it means, among other things, that he does not know what he needs to do, or to stop doing, to achieve buoyant health; he must do something besides take medicines. So-called nervous breakdowns—a radical inability to cope with conflict and responsibility in life—likewise indicate that a change in the structure of the self is overdue. Physical and

*Defense
Versus
Growth*

psychological breakdown are the ultimate price one pays for resisting change in the self when life calls for it. If a person "worships" his present self-concept, his public image, or his present self-ideal and is willing to sicken rather than change, then he truly is guilty of the sin of idolatry so strongly condemned in the Old Testament. Self-idolatry in this sense is sickening.[17]

Chronic Anxiety and Guilt. An existence plagued by anxiety is hellish. The anxious person feels doom lurking everywhere, that the end of his world is at hand, and that he is helpless to avert it. He may take tranquilizing drugs or engage in compulsive busywork so as never to have "idle thoughts," but the terror is there, appearing in nightmares and obsessional worry about health or imminent failure. Clinical experience with neurotic persons shows that such anxiety arises when life engenders feelings and impulses which the neurotic person dares not acknowledge. The anxiety "replaces" the rage, the sexuality, or the affection which is being provoked in life, but which would devastate the person's sense of identity if he acknowledged and expressed them. Such anxiety is a sign of the time to face personal reality and change the self.

Chronic guilt and diminished self-esteem likewise show that the person is violating his self-ideal and is condemning himself for failing to live up to this vainglorious image. Such guilt indicates that it is time for the person to "straighten up" and live up to his ideals—which is a form of growth; or it may rather be a time to change the self-ideal so that it falls more in the realm of human possibility.

Dread of Being "Unmasked." If a person has been disclosing himself falsely, thereby showing other people a false self, then it is as if he has been living as a spy in hostile territory, or playing an ungenuine role on the stage of his life. Under these circumstances he will be obliged to repress all spontaneity in his relationships with others and will remain chronically self-conscious. Such cramped and cramping self-scrutiny makes life hardly worth living, yet the person continues, because he dreads the reaction of others should they ever come to know him as he really is. Such a false public self, with the suffering it produces, likewise indicates that it is time for authenticating change—that is, for growth.

Failure in Work. Success at one's work or one's studies

Healthy Personality: An Approach from the Viewpoint of Humanistic Psychology

is essential for self-esteem and for securing one's livelihood. If a person fails dismally at his work and does so repeatedly, it may signify that he is not "putting himself" whole-heartedly into it. This may happen when the person has not chosen his vocation by himself, so that the activities that it calls for fail to arouse and sustain interest. Especially for students, academic failure signifies self-alienation rather than dullness. The failing student is out of touch with his real goals and his potential strength and ability. Failure is the time for an encounter with one's real self, to make some growth-fostering changes in the self.

Unexpected Failure in Personal Relationships. If a person is rejected by friends or divorced by a spouse without wishing it, it signifies a fundamental incompetence. Inter-personal competence—the ability to be with others in ways that engender their affection and interest—is essential for healthy personality. If one cannot relate lovingly to others, one will indeed suffer a lonely existence. Inability to love others and to be loved by them signifies that one's self-structure is alienated, that one is repressing many of his possi-bilities. Such failure points to the time for self-study and change.

The Process of Personal Growth

Growth of the self is not the same as physical growth, although both dimensions of growing are simultaneous in children. Growth of the self is a change in the way of ex-periencing the world and one's own being.[18] Not all change in experiencing is growth, however. One can speak of growth only when the changes enhance the person's ability to cope with challenges in his existence. Some alterations in experience, as occur in psychosis, make effective action im-possible; they may be described as regression rather than growth. Yet the experience of growing is almost always con-fusing, and occasionally frightening. It does not have to be terrifying, however; growing to a larger perspective and a more authentic identity can be exhilarating, perhaps be-cause of the excitement and uncertainty that almost always are involved. Personal growth is often likened to the experi-ence of a voyage,[19] leaving home (one's present iden-tity, or view of self), traveling to strange places (openness

Defense Versus Growth

to new dimensions of experience of self and world), and a return, to enlarge home in ways that befit the "larger" person one has become. We outgrow our self-structures just as we outgrow our clothing, cramping family roles, and the way of life accepted in a small town.

Growing entails "leaving home," a letting go of one's clutch upon his present way of being involved with other people and with one's projects. As I pointed out earlier (Chapter 2) our projects and commitments impose structure upon the way we experience the world and our own identities. As soon as a person abandons his projects and usual relationships, the world "opens up." To suspend one's usual ways of being involved gives rise to an experience akin to opening a door to a hidden room or to a new world. "Letting go" releases all modes of experiencing from repression. When the person was living his prior identity (which he is now in process of enlarging), his work and his relationships with others required that he be inattentive to all perceptions, memories, and imaginative productions, save those relevant to that identity. Suspension of this identity opens the person to an enlarged experience of his own possibilities, and the possibilities of the world.

The means of letting go, of suspending one's present identity, are myriad—as numerous as the means of clinging to one's identity (defense mechanisms) which we have discussed. Earlier (Chapter 2) we discussed some of them. It will be appropriate to review some of them here.

All the meditative disciplines, such as Zen "sitting," "transcendental meditation," and various yogas (Hatha Yoga, Raja Yoga, Tantra Yoga, and so on) function as means of disengaging a person from his ways of experiencing, and they release new dimensions of consciousness. The several "psychedelic" substances, such as marijuana, lysergic acid, mescaline, peyote, and psylocybin mushrooms also disengage a person from his projects and his accustomed experience of self and world. Under these circumstances, as in meditation, the person is "leaving home," and opening himself to the free play of perception, thinking, remembering, imagination, and feeling.

Exposure to a perspective larger than one's own can also

Healthy Personality: An Approach from the Viewpoint of Humanistic Psychology

disengage a person from his commitment to his present view of self and world. Thus, dialogue with a wise person (so that one realizes there are "higher" consciousnesses) can explode a person's view of his own possibilities. The same can happen through reading books written by authors who have achieved larger perspectives. Certain authors have always challenged me in this way, for example, Kazantzakis, Henry Miller, Martin Buber, and Sartre.[20] An encounter with death, either through a near escape or the loss of a loved one, can persuade a person to suspend his present identity and the way of life that accompany it, in order to review new possibilities. The realization that one will inevitably die can liberate a person from attachment to unimportant activities, relationships, and confining places.

In other civilizations and times, a variety of techniques for letting go were employed in religious ceremonies and rites; in a sense, they were deemed ways of encountering the gods in the quest for guidance in life. Thus, fasting, chanting, dancing, solitude in the desert or upon a mountain, all have been employed to disengage a person from the reminders of who he has been, so that he might become a different, more viable self.

I regard Homer's account of the Odyssey and the story of Moses leading the children of Israel out of the land of bondage (which provided them with security as much as tyranny) as allegories about growth, from a limited view of the possibilities in living to a boundless vision.

Literally to leave home, of course, is a way to commence an episode of growing. But it takes vast energy and courage sometimes, to put one's body into an automobile or an airplane, to go elsewhere. People one is leaving behind may impose astonishing pressure to keep one there, in that place, in that way of being oneself. They may try to make the voyager guilty by suffering in his presence, or by reminding him of the duty he has to his "loved ones." Growth, even the initiation of the growth episode, presents the challenge of change to the other people in one's life.[21] They do not always welcome this change.

Defense Versus Growth

OPENNESS TO EXPERIENCING

The world is always "disclosing" itself to people, but each person "receives"—that is, pays attention to—only a tiny fraction of all there is to be perceived. Each person perceives, remembers, thinks, and imagines only what is relevant for his needs and projects, and what is "appropriate" for a person with that identity to be conscious of. The rest of the world of possible experiencing is closed off. This possible world is the "unconscious" mentioned by Freud, the "shadow" side of existence of which Jung wrote; it is the "ground," as opposed to "figure," which Fritz Perls and the earlier Gestalt psychologists spoke of. The myth of Pandora's box, the knowing that came from eating of the "tree of knowledge," the Medusa myth, and the myth of Oedipus who knew too much, all attest the awareness of men throughout history that there is more possibility for experiencing than we customarily are aware of. All the mystical traditions, such as Sufism, alchemy, kabbala, and shamanism, are recognitions of larger realms of awareness, and ways to achieve contact with them. Dreams—the "hidden language," the "royal road to the unconscious"—have always been consulted as paths to a larger awareness of self and world. All point to the "world beyond" our present consciousness, and a self that is "beyond" our present awareness.

When a person lets go, in any of the ways mentioned, he does open himself to sights, sounds, smells, feelings, and contact which always were there but to which previously he was inattentive. Laing believes that the realm of psychotic experience—and of hallucinations, delusions and illusions, cherubs, angels, demons—is a normal, health-giving event that can occur to anyone during the transition from an identity that was destructive to life to another as yet unchosen and undiscovered identity more compatible with healthy personality. In other words, schizophrenia is not a disease; rather, it is an intensification of the *experience of transition* from one self-structure that has been outgrown to one that is more authentic and life-giving. Laing believes that such transitional experiences are not diseases to be "treated" by psychotherapy, drugs, and hospitalization; rather they are experiences of growing that are to be understood, protected, and encouraged by persons who have themselves frequently gone through such growing episodes.

A Peyote "Trip." The descriptions of "psychedelic trips" provide one with a more dramatic portrayal of the openness

Healthy Personality: An Approach from the Viewpoint of Humanistic Psychology

to experiencing which occurs with "letting go." On one occasion, I ate a fist-sized peyote button. Its taste was absolutely hideous, and the effort to keep it in my stomach after swallowing each bite was heroic. The content of this cactus is an alkaloid poison, and so as fast as I was eating it, my stomach was reflexly attempting to expel it. Nevertheless, I held it down for about two hours before I finally yielded to the need to regurgitate. I was in Mexico at the time, and a trusted friend was sitting with me on the roof of his house. About an hour after I vomited, I began to shiver from an experience of cold. I huddled in my chair. This ended after a short time, and I felt energized to an extraordinary degree. I began to dance with rhythms which my friend said were African or Indian. I looked at lights from the street, and they had intense blue auras. The heavens appeared to me as they might if one were living inside a volcano, with only the cone open to the skies. I believed I could see the Aztec serpent god *Quetzlcoatl* flying through the air. During the plant-induced surges of energizing, my perceptions of distance were altered; the street appeared only a footstep away, whereas the actual distance from the roof was more than 25 feet. I recall telling my friend, "Peyote is definitely not for children, or unstable people; I can see how someone would believe he could fly, or step from a building to the ground, and then go ahead and do it, only to die. I at least know that my experience is from the peyote."

During the period of strength and energy I broke a piece of tile about an inch thick with my bare hands, and I pulled a foot-long metal spike from out of a brick wall and bent it. (Next morning I could neither break the tile nor bend the spike.) I believed then that I could get into the "rhythm" of bricks and metal, and by such contact, perform what looked like superhuman feats.

After perhaps two hours of such goings on, I became exhausted and lay on a cot; the period of quiet began a voyage in time to my early childhood, perhaps the years between two and four. I re-experienced some of the vivid visual and auditory memories from that time, which I also had done some five years earlier, when I took lysergic acid (LSD) under the guidance of a physician experienced in those matters. I also could recognize myself again as various animals, for example, a lion, an eagle, a snake, and a dog. After

Defense
Versus
Growth

another two hours or so, I slept. On awakening next morning I discussed the experience with my friend, and found it enlightening.

I do not believe such drug-induced experiences are growth-enhancing for everyone. If a person is of narrow perspective, immature and incompetent, and not responsibly engaged in work and personal relationships, I believe that powerful disengagement from his customary identity can be disturbing, even destructive to his capacity to cope with the world. The other "natural" ways of disengaging are more self-regulating, in that the person can get no further "out" of his identity and his customary experience of the world than he authentically "earns."

THE RETURN

Growth, according to the present metaphor, entails a return to the place one had left, in order to make it suitable for living, and moreover, living as a person of enlarged perspective.

A growth cycle is completed when a person affirms his larger experience of self and world and modifies his concept of self, his public self, and his self-ideal in the light of the enlarged awareness. He now knows he *is* more, and *can be more*, and different, than he hitherto believed possible. This alteration and enlargement of one's sense of self is desirable and conducive to a healthy personality. The process of integrating the larger consciousness of self and world is helped immeasurably by re-engagement in life projects and personal relationships. Indeed, it is the demands, challenges, and rewards of work, play, and personal relationships which provide the incentive to grow, and the rewards of such growth. Without such ways of being engaged in the world, I believe efforts to let go and to open oneself to new experiencing have destructive and regressive consequences. Chronic users of psychedelic drugs, like fanatics at yoga or meditation, confuse means with ends; they spend their time "in their experience," but out of action.

The return is often difficult, because the people with whom one has been engaged may not have changed; further, they may resent the changes which the growing person has introduced into their world. They may impose considerable pressure upon the individual to revert to the way he was

Healthy Personality: An Approach from the Viewpoint of Humanistic Psychology

196

prior to the episode of growing. To yield to such pressure is disastrous, for it makes a nonevent out of the person's growth.

OUTCOMES OF GROWTH

Growth is change, but change in the direction of greater awareness, competence, and authenticity. With each episode of growing through which a person passes, his knowledge of the world increases and his ability to be more aware of what is going on likewise is enlarged. Growth reveals itself publicly, in the person's action, but the more important dimensions of growing are secret and invisible.

Growth in consciousness makes it possible for a person to see connections between ways of behaving and their consequences for well-being.

Typically, a person's growth in awareness and competence occurs imperceptibly, in small increments. Occasionally, however, a person is so well defended against change that it takes an episode of illness or some more dramatic tragedy to dislodge him from his bastion of immobility. We are often so heavily "reinforced," or rewarded for remaining the same, that it takes powerful pain to make us willing to give up our more familiar ways in order to risk change.

Growing will go on throughout a person's life span, even into his seventies and nineties, if he has the courage (and the encouragement) to accept threat, and not respond reflexively with mechanisms of defense. Properly understood, the experiences of anxiety and dread will evoke the "courage to be" and they will be harbingers of growth to richer existence. Improperly understood, or encountered in a spirit of timidity, they lead a person to make of his identity an impregnable bastion. He then leads a safe but often unproductive and joyless life. Courage and encouragers assist one to grow.

The courage to grow can sometimes be generated in psychotherapy and in a properly conducted encounter group. In Chapter 15, psychotherapy as a means for stimulating personal growth is discussed.

Defense
Versus
Growth

AN EXAMPLE OF A GROWING SELF

A woman student, age twenty, consulted me for help with some problems which were so painful that she had been considering suicide. She was attractive, intelligent, and obtained good grades. Our first meeting was dramatic; she had phoned me for a session after spending most of the previous night debating whether to end her life with sleeping pills or with a razor blade applied to her wrists.

The crisis that brought her to this point was the feeling that she did not know who she was. She had found herself involved in an affair with another student, yet she did not love him. He wanted her to share an apartment with him, as many of their classmates had been doing. On the one hand, she was tempted to set up housekeeping, because she had never lived with anyone but her own family and her present roommate, who was a girl. On the other hand, she did not like the fellow anymore. Yet she could not end the affair, because she was convinced her boyfriend would kill himself. He had convinced her that he found his life possible only if she were his woman. Sometimes subtly, sometimes openly, he controlled her by making her feel guilty over not yielding to his wishes and needs.

To make matters worse, she had been reared by conventional parents who neither smoked nor drank, who went regularly to church, and whom she loved dearly. She lived in the dread they would find out about her affair. When she reflected upon her situation, it seemed hopeless; she could not displease her lover, nor could she turn to her parents for emotional support. She was convinced that if her mother discovered she had been intimate with a man outside marriage, it would break her heart. Furthermore, like many of her classmates, she smoked marijuana, and this too was opposed to her parents' wishes and their beliefs about her. She was no longer a virgin, obviously, but her parents assumed she was. On her visits home she concealed her birth-control pills.

She described her situation in these terms:

> I feel trapped. I don't know my real feelings. I am such a jellyfish. I please everyone, but I don't know what I want for myself. I feel guilty for my deceptions, and yet I can't be the person my parents thought I was either—I've changed. I really feel terrible. I can't leave John because he'll kill himself, if not right away, then by drinking, and smoking too much dope. He has gone to pieces

Healthy Personality: An Approach from the Viewpoint of Humanistic Psychology

every time I get selfish. I love my parents, but I can't tell them what I've been up to. They think I'm still their sweet, unspoiled daughter.

We met for therapeutic interviews over a period of a month—about seven sessions in all. During this time, she spoke at length about her background, and the way she had been living, and how she thought about herself. Because I didn't think she was as despicable as she felt she was, she began to feel she belonged within the human race. She examined her conscience, and came to the conclusion that she was not living a life that warranted such intensities of self-hate. She had loved, or at least liked, her lover at one time, and their intimacies grew out of what she regarded as mutual love. She stopped condemning herself for entering the affair. But as she talked about herself, she gradually came to see that she had been trying to live out a false self-concept. "It's not like me to act selfishly, to do what *I* want rather than what *others* want. My parents raised me to be unselfish." She recognized the resentment she felt about being controlled by both her parents' wishes and her lover's, and came to feel that it was all right to experience anger and to express it in appropriate ways.

As she acknowledged more and more of her real feelings, and came to accept herself in the light of this enlarged awareness, she felt that her entrapment was at an end. She ended her affair with John, who did get very drunk when she told him it was over, but he did not kill himself. In fact, he moved in immediately with an older and more motherly student.

She recognized that she had outgrown the perspectives of her parents, and could no longer pretend to be a virginal model of propriety. However, she believed that if she confided fully in her mother, as she had when she was a high school student, her mother would be shocked. And so she let her parents know that she was growing and learning a lot at the university, but she kept her private life to herself. She confided in her closest girl friend, with whom she had a relationship of total honesty.

Defense Versus Growth

We ended the sessions when she felt that she had a much larger perspective on her life. She liked herself better, and she felt more honest. In technical terms, she enlarged her self-concept, modified her conscience in humane and mature ways, and presented a public self more in keeping with the realities of her own personality and the demands of the situation. My involvement, as a therapist, was mostly limited to listening to her talk about her situation, and confirming her as a worthwhile human being in spite of (or because of) the fact that she had allowed herself to be trapped in a destructive relationship. She began to live in conformity with her own true feelings and values, rather than others' expectations, and she found this authentic way more life-giving and freeing.

Some Existential Suggestions

The most common sign of excessive defensiveness is frequent experiences of threat. If other people have to be careful about what they say or do in your presence, it can signify that they sense your grasp of your identity is frail indeed. If you are easily upset by criticism or frightened by your anger or sensuality, it may signify that you are trying to live up to some glorified image.

The time to grow—to begin to let go of one's present self-concept—is evidenced by boredom, failure, and anxiety. These experiences signify that you and your real self have changed but that your self-structure has not. You are *impersonating* an identity that up to yesterday may have been authentic and life-giving. Now, however, it is not. To start a growth episode is frightening, but it need not be terrifying. All it means is that you may have to suspend your usual activities and relationships in order to get a fresh perspective upon your own possibilities, and the possibilities of changing some aspects of your life.

If you meditate or retreat to a quiet place from time to time, the chances are that you change aspects of your activity and your self-structure more or less frequently. If, however, you are "locked into" various roles, and a fixed way of being yourself, the experience of threat may be more acute when it happens, and the prospect of change more frightening.

If your present identity is not sustaining a rewarding and health-engendering life and you do not see ways to grow and change, then it might be valuable to find a personal

Healthy Personality: An Approach from the Viewpoint of Humanistic Psychology

counselor or psychotherapist. Conversations with a professional person can frequently lead to growth-producing changes that are neither drastic nor destructive.

SUMMARY

The self-structure, described in the last chapter, keeps a person from changing. People dread the experience of threat to their sense of themselves. The threat arises from aspects of experience that are not compatible with a person's self-concept, his self-ideal, or his public selves. One can react to such threat defensively, by resorting to one of a myriad of defense "mechanisms"; and one can acknowledge the threatening experience and alter one's self-structure in the direction of greater authenticity.

Mechanisms for defense of the self-concept include repression, rationalization, verbal reformulation, reaction formation, projection, denial, psychic contactlessness, depersonalizing others, fixation, and regression. All these operations which a person performs upon his own experience and behavior enable him to maintain his present belief in his own identity. More to the point, they insure that a person's self-concept becomes increasingly estranged from his real self.

A person maintains his public selves by selective self-disclosure and by inhibition of all action that would adversely affect the way others see him. The self-ideal resists change, usually, because a person has acquired it in an authoritarian fashion, and is encouraged to regard challenging his present moral precepts as a sin.

Threat can lead to growth, however. A person can recognize when his self-structure has become estranged from his real self through the experience of boredom, sickness, chronic anxiety and guilt, dread of being unmasked, and failure in work and in personal relationships.

Growth, as a response to threat, is likened to a voyage. It entails leaving home—letting go of one's present sense of his identity; opening oneself to all the new dimensions of experiencing that hitherto had been repressed, in order to defend the past sense of identity; and then "returning home," reforming one's sense of identity in the light of the enlarged experiencing, and disclosing to others the person

*Defense
Versus
Growth*

one has newly become. Of course, growth as a response to threat is most compatible with the development of healthy personality.

NOTES AND REFERENCES

1. The quote comes from M. BUBER, *The Knowledge of Man* (New York: Harper & Row, 1965), p. 71.

2. See R. D. LAING and A. ESTERSON, *Sanity, Madness and the Family* (London: Tavistock, 1964), for illustrations of disconfirmation and invalidation of experience.

3. See O. FENICHEL, *The Psychoanalytic Theory of Neurosis* (New York: Norton, 1945), pp. 148–151.

4. S. ROSENZWEIG, "An Experimental Study of Repression, with Special Reference to Need-Persistive and Ego-Defensive Reactions to Frustration," *Journal of Experimental Psychology*, 1943, Vol. 32, pp. 64–74; THELMA ALPER, "Memory for Completed and Incompleted Tasks as a Function of Personality: An Analysis of Group Data," *Journal of Abnormal and Social Psychology*, 1946, Vol. 41, pp. 403–420; C. W. Ericksen, "Psychological Defenses and Ego Strength in the Recall of Completed and Incompleted Tasks," *Journal of Abnormal and Social Psychology*, 1954, Vol. 49, pp. 51–58.

5. E. FROMM, *Psychoanalysis and Religion* (New Haven: Yale University Press, 1950).

6. Bettelheim discusses the difficulty encountered by emotionally disturbed children in establishing "ego controls" upon awakening from sleep. See B. BETTELHEIM, *Love Is Not Enough* (New York: The Free Press, 1950), Chapter 4.

7. C. JUNG, *Studies in Word Association* (New York: Moffat, Yard, 1919).

8. M. FELDMAN, "The Use of Obscene Words in Psychotherapy," *American Journal of Psychoanalysis*, 1955, Vol. 15, pp. 45–48.

9. H. WERNER, *The Comparative Psychology of Mental Development* (Chicago: Follett, 1948).

10. The distinction between assimilative and disowning projection is taken from N. CAMERON and ANN MARGARET, *Behavior Pathology* (Boston: Houghton Mifflin, 1951).

11. S. FREUD, "Formulations Regarding the Two Principles in Mental Functioning," in S. FREUD, *Collected Papers, IV* (London: Hogarth, 1953), Chapter 1.

12. W. REICH, *Character Analysis* (New York: Orgone Institute Press, 1948).

Healthy Personality: An Approach from the Viewpoint of Humanistic Psychology

13. S. M. Jourard, *The Transparent Self* (New York: Van Nostrand Reinhold, 1971), Chapter 20, "The Bedside Manner."

14. E. Goffman, *The Presentation of Self in Everyday Life* (Garden City, N.Y.: Doubleday, 1954), Chapter 4.

15. Fromm, op. cit.

16. S. Freud, *The Ego and the Id* (London: Hogarth, 1927), p. 69.

17. E. Fromm, *You Shall Be as Gods: A Radical Interpretation of the Old Testament and Its Tradition* (New York: Holt, 1966).

18. See S. M. Jourard, *Disclosing Man to Himself* (New York: Van Nostrand Reinhold, 1968), Chapter 13, "Growing Experience and the Experience of Growth," for elaboration of this view. Also F. J. Shaw, *Reconciliation: A Theory of Man Transcending* (New York: Van Nostrand Reinhold, 1966); and his paper "Transitional Experiences and Psychological Growth," *ETC, Review of General Semantics*, 1957, Vol. 15, pp. 39–45; K. Dabrowski, *Mental Growth Through Positive Disintegration* (London: Gryf Publications, 1960).

19. See the account of a "ten-day voyage" in R. D. Laing, *The Politics of Experience* (New York: Pantheon, 1968), Chapter 7.

20. See Jourard, *The Transparent Self*, op. cit., Chapter 7, "Self-disclosure, the Writer and His Reader."

21. H. Otto and J. Mann, *Ways of Growth* (New York: Viking, 1969).

9

SOCIAL ROLES AND
HEALTHY PERSONALITY

INTRODUCTION

We spend much of our lives with people whom we know only superficially; our main interest in them is whether or not they live up to our expectations. In contrast, we spend a significant part in personal relationships with others, where our feelings and needs and idiosyncrasies are cherished and confirmed. Healthy personality is impossible without the ability to enter into a variety of nonintimate social roles, and the complementary ability to enter close personal relationships, where mutual self-disclosure and intimate knowing are of the essence. In this chapter I will explore social roles in their relevance to healthy personality. In the following two chapters I will discuss friendship and love.

Roles and the Social System

Social roles make life with others possible, yet they are a hidden source of stress and demoralization which can make people sick. Roles are invisible to us, for they are at the heart of our identities, and we simply *live* them. A sociologist, studying a group like a family, or an entire society, is able to see that people's behavior with others displays recurring patterns. Interpersonal relationships do not occur in random fashion, but instead are seen to follow rules, like a script for a play. Thus, the older male in a family group typically earns the living, and protects the woman and the children. The woman nurtures young children, is affectionate and loving to the older man, and is careful to avoid intimacy with other males.

When seen from the perspective of a sociologist, roles are prescribed ways for people to divide the labor of a society and to interact with others. They keep the social system going, and prevent it from changing.

Because the stability of a society is so important, people are carefully trained to live within the limits defined by their roles, and strong penalties await those who violate role definitions. The task of training people to their roles is assigned to the agencies and agents of *socialization*, whereas that of keeping people in conformity with their roles is the responsibility of agents and agencies of *social control*. Agencies of socialization include the family, schools, and the mass media such as television and radio; these are all institutions within society which train people in the "right" ways to act. The *agents* of socialization are the actual persons who shape the behavior of a growing and learning person so that it will fit the definition of the roles he is to assume. Thus, one's parents, siblings, and peers are all socializing agents, as are the teachers one encounters in school.

Agents of social control are the persons who provide punishment for violation of the rules, laws, and customs. The police are clearly agents of social control. The institutions of the law—the legal system, the courts, prisons and the police force—are all social control agencies. Parents, peers, and neighbors are social control agents who control our behavior by threatening to withdraw love and friendship, and through criticism and shaming. A more subtle agent of social control is the person's conscience, which functions like an invisible parent or police officer, inflicting guilt and self-hatred at each lapse from the behavior that is deemed right and proper for him.

Each of us defines his identity to himself and to others

Social
Roles
and
Healthy
Personality

in terms of the roles he has had assigned to him, and those he has sought to assume because of the status and privilege associated with them. Thus, I define myself as a man (my sex role), in my forties (age role), father of my children and husband to my wife; son of my parents and brother of my siblings (family roles); and psychotherapist, teacher of my students, researcher, and writer (occupational roles). I had to be trained for some of these roles, whereas I seemed just to "grow" into others. There are norms and rules governing the ways in which I act my age, my sex, my family roles, and my occupational roles. People come to depend upon me to act in stable and predictable ways, and I come to expect such stability of myself.[1]

Each social role a person embodies serves as a kind of badge entitling him to participate in life with others in prescribed ways, and each role sets limits on his freedom and his access to material goods. Roles, in short, entitle the person to the privileges associated with high status in a group, or they condemn him to the dregs reserved for those of low status. A white person need only stain his skin to discover that the role of "colored person" has a status lower than that of a white person. And women have become keenly aware that the female role in most societies condemns girls to inferior education, lower occupational status, and usually the exclusive responsibility of rearing children, unless they resist this definition. And people in their sixties or seventies find themselves treated by younger people as if they were fragile, stupid, and lacking in fundamental human traits such as the needs for companionship, love, and ennobling work.[2]

Even sickness is governed by social norms. When a person feels unwell, he enters the role of patient, which entitles him to interact with physicians and nurses, or with psychotherapists, if he is diagnosed as "mentally ill." [3] Recent research has shown that people are trained to act like a "good patient" in hospitals, and this training has nothing to do with the treatment of illness. Moreover, the hospital itself is a complex web of professions, uniforms, titles, and badges which define status, authority, and responsibility. I worked for several years with a college of nursing; the hospital where the nursing students trained had as employees the graduates of four-year colleges of nursing, who earned a B.A. degree as well as the Registered Nurse (R.N.)

Healthy Personality: An Approach from the Viewpoint of Humanistic Psychology

206

diploma; R.N.'s with a degree from a community junior college; licensed practical nurses who had had no college training; and nursing assistants. This bewildering array of backgrounds puzzled the nurses and the physicians as much as it did the patients; the nurses with each type of training felt somehow different from the others, and felt entitled to more or less responsibility, salary, and so on.

The patients in hospitals were often made to feel like the least important, lowest caste members of the hospital community. They were treated as children about to be disobedient, and they were often kept in the dark about the nature of their illness, and the precise nature of the medicines or operations which were prescribed for or conducted upon them.[4]

In mental hospitals I visited, even to *be there* as a patient insured that the staff would not treat the patient as a free, responsible human being; rather, he was seen and talked about—sometimes in his presence—as the embodiment of his mental illness. He was required to participate in the therapeutic processes, to take medicine, and so on.

Recently a group of psychologists were admitted to mental hospitals as patients, in order to study the career of mental patient firsthand. They found that they could not convince the attendants and professional staff that they were "sane," though the authentic patients knew they were.

Role Versatility and Healthy Personality

Roles and the badges, titles, and uniforms which identify them enable others to predict how we will act in social situations. The ability to master a variety of roles throughout life is a decided asset for healthy personality, because it facilitates the interactions with others that bring satisfaction of many basic needs. Not to be able to enter roles because of an unhealthy self-structure or irrational fears thus impedes healthy personality development. If a young man cannot make a career choice, because he lacks confidence in his ability to master the training, he may face a life of low economic status. A woman with sexual inhibitions may avoid intimate relationships with men and live a life that is safe but devoid of loving relationships.

Although role conformity implies some limitations on

Social Roles and Healthy Personality

one's freedom of expression and action, there is a sense in which the ability to act in ways appropriate to one's family position, age, sex, and profession is *liberating*. Not to adhere to reasonable definitions of appropriate behavior is to invite social censure, which can interfere radically with effective living and the attainment of satisfactions. It sometimes appears hypocritical to students that older people may display politeness and feign delight at being with people they dislike. Actually, the ability to conform to the "niceties" in a variety of situations can be life-giving and liberating, because it clearly separates personal relationships (where spontaneity is expected) from the more formal relationships between strangers. In some cultures, like the English, the French, and the Spanish, much time is spent in ceremonious interaction with others, yet there is room in those cultures for great freedom in the privacy of personal relationships. Europeans often complain that Americans seem friendly in impersonal situations, as in business, but that in private they avoid deepening relationships.

How We Learn Roles

We learn our roles by being trained into them, and by imitating, or identifying with, the role models available to us.[5] Thus, as children, our behavior is rewarded by our parents when it conforms to *their* image of the way a little boy or girl should act. At each age level, our behavior is "shaped" by the consequences of approval and of punishment which they provide to our action.

As we get older, we are encouraged to emulate the behavior of people who function as exemplars or role models. This is the way we begin to learn how to be a husband or a father when the time comes, and it is the way we learn our occupational roles. Each person thus serves as a model to be emulated by others.

People encounter difficulties in fulfilling their sex roles and family roles when they have grown up without regular contact with role models or when the role models differ from the norms of their group. Some male homosexuals, for example, have grown up without a father in the home or with a father who was so hateful that the boy would not identify with him. When divorce is common, many chil-

Healthy Personality: An Approach from the Viewpoint of Humanistic Psychology

208

dren grow up without a father, because they usually are raised by the mother. Under these conditions, the girls may not learn what adult man–woman or husband–wife behavior can be expected, nor will the little boys. Consequently, they do not learn reasonable family role expectations for self and for others; they may acquire idealized notions of what to expect from their spouses and children when they marry, expectations which their spouses and future children cannot fulfill.

In professional and vocational training, the learner is both "shaped" by his teachers and encouraged by them to copy his ways of performing his skills. I served as consultant to a nursing college and found that the faculty and the staff nurses were not serving as authentic exemplars of the kind of nursing practice they wished the students to learn. They wanted the students to be very open, to be responsive to and empathic with patients, doctors, and colleagues. However, they were *not* functioning in those ways themselves. Many of the nursing faculty had left bedside nursing because they did not like regular contact with the ill. Many floor nurses were afraid of close, communicative relationships with patients, doctors, and each other. My task was to help the faculty and staff *become* the kind of nursing exemplars that the students could emulate. We attempted to do this, first, by encouraging the nursing college faculty to return to regular bedside nursing and, second, by conducting regular faculty meetings where the purpose was to practice open, personal communication with each other. There is some evidence that the strained, formal, and impersonal atmosphere of the college was replaced by one that encouraged greater openness of communication and that the students did become better at relating empathically and warmly with their patients.[6]

Some Common Roles

FAMILY ROLES

The experience of being "in" and "of" a family is essential to a vital sense of identity and fulfills the needs for security and intimacy. It is within the family that most people find their most fulfilling personal relationships, first as sons, daughters, brothers, and sisters; then as spouses, mothers and fathers, uncles and aunts; and later as grandparents. Even when the family breaks down, people seek a "primary group"—a small group of intimate friends with whom life may be lived communally, with or without sexual intimacies. Thus, many young people explore the possibilities of living communally as an "alternate life style" to traditional family life.

Traditional family roles are socially defined, and each person must learn those ways of being a family member which are acceptable within his family. The behavior and experience expected of a person because of his family position may be detrimental to healthy personal growth. Laing and Esterson [7] showed how being a daughter in ways deemed acceptable to the parents contributed to the development of schizophrenic behavior in the patients they studied.

The mother role as well has been found to require behavior from the mother which can easily contribute to her personal and physical breakdown. The father's role, in contemporary culture, calls for being a "good provider" and upward social mobility; it frequently imposes a dull or stressing life upon the father. Indeed, the divorce rates attest to the fact that husbands and wives, and mothers and fathers often find traditional ways of being in these roles unrewarding, and they look to new partners for the satisfactions that were missing in their prior marriage.[8]

David Cooper,[9] a British psychiatrist, wrote a book entitled *Death of the Family*, in which he pointed out the destructive possibilities of family roles as we have known them. He argued in behalf of alternative ways for men, women, and children to live together which would avoid such destructiveness. The family, in some form, however, is likely to be with us forever; the challenge and opportunity facing each person is how might he invent or adapt his way of being in various family roles so as to do justice to his needs for security and for freedom, without stifling the growth and well-being of those in the complementary roles. Traditional family roles are "givens," and each person has the freedom and responsibility to do something with what is given him—conform to the roles, refuse to enter them, or fulfill them in creative ways.

Healthy Personality: An Approach from the Viewpoint of Humanistic Psychology

Each society differs in its concept of masculine and feminine behavior. Mead showed that in three New Guinea tribes, there was considerable difference from tribe to tribe in the typical male and female roles. In one group, the Arapesh, men and women alike were passive, "maternal," cooperative, and nonaggressive. In the Mundugamor, a tribe geographically close to the Arapesh, men and women alike were fierce, cruel, aggressive, and self-assertive. A third tribe, the Tchambuli, showed a different pattern of sextyping. The men were passive individuals who spent their time cultivating the arts, whereas the women were assertive and had to cultivate the gardens and make a living.

In America, rigid definition of sex roles has broken down. Thus, many middle-class men take an active role in child care and housekeeping, and their wives do many things once deemed to be a male prerogative: they keep the budget, spend the money, and work at occupations that formerly were strictly male. In some European countries, male and female behavior contrasts in certain ways with the American concept of masculinity and femininity. Thus, in Latin countries, a man can comfortably kiss another man, and he can cry openly without shame. But these men might look askance at the American woman who likes to wear trousers. For them, women belong in dresses.

In order to "wear" one's sex role comfortably, a person has to be trained into it. Yet some men have been reared in ways that promote the development of traits ordinarily regarded as effeminate; they may also have acquired, in the process of growing up, the cultural concepts of the male role. Therefore, they find it a strain to "be a man." In acting in manly ways, they are going against their (acquired) "nature." But if they were to act in the ways which were most natural for them, they might experience a considerable threat to their sense of identity as a man and expose themselves to much ridicule. The same considerations apply to women. Some individuals are so insecure about their sexual identity that they must "overprotest." Instead of being content to be manly, they must be "supermanly." They exaggerate their manly traits as if to convince themselves and others that they are indeed men. If anyone questions the

*Social
Roles
and
Healthy
Personality*

211

masculinity of such a person, he may become dangerously aggressive. His life involves a continual quest for reassurances of his own masculinity.

Because sex roles are relatively fixed by society, each person, man and woman, must find ways of fitting himself to his sex role, of coming to terms with it. Some men and women find their sex role too constraining, and they adopt many of the patterns of the opposite sex, both sexually and behaviorally.

The healthy personality is able to redefine his own personal sex role in ways that dovetail better with his needs. Consequently, he has greater freedom to express and act out his real self and is much less easily threatened. Thus, a healthy man can do many things that might be deemed effeminate by other men, yet he will not experience any threat to his masculinity. He may wash dishes, change babies, and perform jobs such as hairdressing or ballet, yet still feel manly.

To the extent that women have assented to traditional, male-dominated views of what their "true" roles and function might be, to that extent they have realized only a fraction of their potentialities as fully functioning human beings. Healthy personality for the individual and a life-giving culture for a society are no longer possible so long as half the world's population, women, consents unknowingly to continue breeding and raising children, and to reflect male perspectives, rather than develop a more truly educated and enlightened womanhood about the world. There seems little doubt that if all women received an enlightening education, then the more enlightened population resulting from such a program would contribute to the solution of problems of untrammeled population increase, destruction of the environment which supports life, and war. Women are too important an influence upon healthy personality growth to remain less well educated than men and to limit their involvement in society to maternal roles and subordinate professional and occupational roles.

It is disconcerting to realize that the first influence upon a child's education is his mother—a person who, for millennia, has been denied access to higher education and professional opportunity. I am a champion of women's liberation because I see in that movement a force that contributes to

Healthy Personality: An Approach from the Viewpoint of Humanistic Psychology

healthier personality for all human beings. Of course, I present the same argument in behalf of political movements which aim toward the liberation of all peoples who are being exploited by colonizing nations.[10]

AGE ROLES

Each society expects a progression of behavior in its members, a progression that will keep pace with the person's chronological age. If a person is keeping pace with his age roles, he is said to be mature. If he is behind other people his age, he is said to be immature or fixated. If he reverts to behavior characteristic of a younger age, he is said to display regression, and if he shows a premature development of traits expected from older persons, he is said to display precocity. As with sex roles, age roles may conflict sharply with the person's needs. He may not be ready to progress to the next age role when the time for it comes. Or he may enforce conformity with his age role on himself, at considerable cost in satisfactions.

By the time an individual has become an adult, as this is defined in his culture, he acquires a vested interest in regarding himself as mature. Yet need gratification may be possible only if he behaves in ways deemed immature in his social group.

The healthy personality can regress when he wants to or when he feels like it, without threat to self-esteem or to his sense of identity. A person who is insecure about his maturity may strive to convince himself and others that he is mature and avoid regressive behavior like the plague. Thus, some men may not allow themselves to be taken care of even when they are gravely sick because it would imply that they had regressed. Some women may refuse tenderness and solicitude from a man because of the implication that they are not independent adults. Some adults cannot play because frolicsomeness feels childish to them and threatens their self-esteem.

Social Roles and Healthy Personality

As with family and sex roles, age roles are part of the "facticity"—the "givens"—with which each person must come to terms. The behavior expected of each person by others (because of his chronological age) can be irrelevant to his authentic needs and capacities. Older people are often virtually invited by those younger to be feeble and helpless

213

when they have great reserves of vitality latent within them. The fact is, that so long as a person has vitalizing, challenging work and projects, and confirming personal relationships, he can be fit and active into his eighties and nineties or older. Bodies respond to life style and to people's expectations. I have suspected that people die of "old age" not because their bodies had no more strength, but because they were bored or lonely, with no incentives to stay alive.

Authenticity and Inauthenticity in Roles

It is a human peculiarity that people can *be* in roles, and they can *act* in roles. To be a student, for example, is to commit oneself to the aims of being a student—to pursue learning with seriousness. When one is *being* a student, in unself-conscious pursuit of knowledge, he is not aware of being in a role. But a student can impersonate a serious learner when he is himself not remotely interested in learning. When someone pretends to be in some role but is committed to objectives other than those appropriate to that role, he is said to be in bad faith, or to be inauthentic. Thus, a salesman who pretends to be interested in your welfare is being inauthentic, and in bad faith to you, because he may be trying to impersonate someone in the role of friend. In fact, he may be authentic in his commitment to making a sale and inauthentic in his relationship to you. Man's capacity for semblance, for acting and impersonating, is at once the means whereby he learns and grows to take on new roles, and also the basis for beginning the process of self-alienation. We begin to learn how to become doctors and lawyers, wives and mothers, by first mimicking those parts at play or in school. But if a woman continues to play act the part of wife and mother after marriage, without serious commitment to the tasks of a wife and mother, then she has commenced a career of inauthenticity which will lead to painful consequences.

In order to be inauthentic in a role, a person is obliged to imitate authentic action, and to repress his authentic experience. A son who is unhappy in the career his father chose for him may try to persuade himself and his father that he is contented with the courses he is taking for the career. If the choice is inauthentic, and he is in fact miserable, then

Healthy Personality: An Approach from the Humanistic Viewpoint of Psychology

each day becomes an ordeal, of forcing himself to seem happy and consuming energy to suppress his spontaneous urges to get away from the scene of his discontent. The student may then find himself becoming very tired, disinterested in his studies, even frequently sick, because of the stress and demoralization engendered by remaining in the inauthentic role. To be authentic in a role, a person must be honest with himself and with others about what he truly is up to, and how he feels about the roles he is committed to. Chronic inauthenticity in one's roles is a factor in physical and personality breakdown. Authenticity, by contrast, although it may lead to personal and interpersonal conflict, is a factor in personal growth to healthier personality.

Authenticity in roles calls for honest self-disclosure to the others with whom one is involved. Faking and dissembling is commonly chosen by many people, who dread the reactions of others, and the problems they would encounter if they revealed the truth of their feelings about the roles they are living.

Roles and Sickness

The person who is living with others within the limits of his roles goes through changes. The way of being son or daughter, parent, student, or teacher which up to yesterday was rewarding becomes boring or meaningless today. To continue being in those roles in the same way gradually becomes stifling and depressing. The person finds himself dreading each day, because it means being the same person, enacting the same roles, eliciting the same reactions from others, with no hope of respite from the increased irritation and boredom. A theory of illness has been developed which traces the connection between prolonged involvement in unrewarding roles and physical diseases of all kinds. A person acts in order to meet his needs. If his action does not meet his needs but only maintains the stability of a family or work arrangement, then he is truly neglecting his own well-being. A prolonged regime of action which neglects one's own needs for love, esteem, full emotional expression, or excitement will generate stress and dispiration—both factors in physical illness.[11] If a person feels truly trapped in unrewarding roles, he may develop psychiatric illnesses,

Social Roles and Healthy Personality

exchanging, thereby, an unrewarding existence as a wife and mother, for example, for a career as a patient in a mental hospital.

Everyone begins to feel locked into his assorted roles at various times in his life. Other people's expectations provide a powerful force restraining a person from changing his roles, or from changing his ways of being in those roles. It is astonishing to see how surprised, even outraged, other people become when a person decides to drop out of a role or change his role behavior even in trifling ways. For example, a simple change in appearance, such as growing a mustache or shaving one off, will evoke a barrage of commentary, some critical, some complimentary, from the others with whom one is involved. For a woman hitherto docile and dependent upon men to become involved in Women's Liberation activities may infuriate the men in her life. The obedient son or daughter, after a year at school, begins to act in ways that outrage the parents, who feel that their child is "out of his mind." In all these cases a person finds that to remain as he was has become intolerable, yet sometimes immense courage and energy are called for to stop being in roles in the customary ways, in order to act in more life-giving ways.

A strong sense of duty, stemming from an authoritarian conscience, will often keep a person in sickening roles. A mother may feel that her husband will collapse and her children will be neglected if she devotes less time to their needs and more to herself. Accordingly, she may neglect her health, her appearance, and the cultivation of her intellect in order to meet her family's needs. The consequence may be that she suffers and that her spouse and children all feel vaguely guilty. Mrs. Portnoy, the mother in *Portnoy's Complaint,* was expert at inducing guilt in her son and husband by excessive care at the expense of her own pleasures.

Opportunities for solitude and meditation help one to disengage from roles in order to discover or invent more life-giving ways of re-entering them. Personal growth calls for creative use of imagination, to ponder ways of reconciling commitments to others with one's personal needs. Such creativity is encouraged by periods of quiet, uninterrupted solitude.

Once a person has discovered a more self-expressive and

Healthy Personality: An Approach from the Viewpoint of Humanistic Psychology

enlivening way to be himself in relation to others, he faces a problem: will the other people in his life confirm the changes he is now inserting into *their* world? Or will they resist the change, refusing to accept or recognize him unless he reverts to the ways in which they knew him? It is a poignant choice which a growing person often has to face: if he remains as is, as the person locked in roles that were recognized by others, he becomes increasingly angry and dispirited. When he changes in the ways that are most vitalizing, his parents, friends, and associates no longer like him. Growth frequently calls for the sad necessity of "leaving home," in search of people who will accept and confirm a person as the one he has just become.

Some Existential Suggestions

I have been exploring the hypothesis that rigid roles and conformity to them are the main source of physical as well as psychological breakdown in our culture, at least for middle-class people. If the hypothesis is sound, then it means a person can do much to foster his own health by examining the ways in which he is living out his various social roles. One piece of existential research anyone can carry out is to itemize the various roles that he is committed to, and then do a self-rating as to the degree of *enlivenment* he feels in each role (in relation to the others with whom he regularly deals while he is in that role—for example, son to mother, son to father, employee to boss, colleague to colleague, husband to wife, and so on). Thus, I could list the following roles for myself: husband, father to each of three sons; son of my mother; brother to each of five siblings; friend to each of several people that I see regularly; and so on. I could compare how alive I feel in each of these relationships; how authentic I can be in each; how free I feel to disclose myself in each relationship. Moreover, I could try to alter my ways in each role that I found oppressive.

I have found that when I am serving as someone's psychotherapist, I spend a great deal of time exploring the patient's ways of being in his roles, in the quest for more authentic and vitalizing ways. Certainly a person can, with a bit of imagination, begin to experiment with more life-giving ways of being in his age, his sex, his assorted family and occupa-

*Social
Roles
and
Healthy
Personality*

tional roles, without waiting until he has gotten sick. It is not easy but it is necessary and possible to redefine one's roles. If the other person will not confirm one's changed ways of being in the role, it may be necessary, for one's well-being, to withdraw from that relationship altogether.

SUMMARY

Social roles lie at the heart of our identities. We are trained early to live according to social definitions of behavior that is appropriate to our age, sex, family status, and occupation. Agents of socialization train us to our roles, and agents of social control keep us in them, even when they become stressful and dispiriting. The ability to fulfill the requirements of a variety of roles is essential for healthy personality.

Family and sex roles can so limit a person's degree of freedom that his health and growth are undermined. Women's Liberation was presented as a valuable contribution to the possibilities of healthier personality for women. Age roles were seen to be challenges to grow, and also invitations to act "old," even to die at the age deemed appropriate by society.

The ability to disengage from social roles and to interact with others as persons, in a personal relationship, is an essential complement to living one's life in roles.

NOTES AND REFERENCES

1. For a discussion of socialization and social control, from the perspective of a sociologist, see T. PARSONS, *The Social System* (New York: The Free Press, 1951), pp. 297–321; T. PARSONS and R. F. BALES, *Family, Socialization and Interaction Process* (New York: The Free Press, 1955), Chapter 2.

2. A good discussion of caste, class, and status is given in R. BROWN, *Social Psychology* (New York: The Free Press, 1965), Chapter 3.

3. See T. SCHEFF, *Being Mentally Ill: A Sociological Theory* (Chicago: Aldine, 1966); E. GOFFMAN, *Asylums* (Garden City, N.Y.: Doubleday, 1961).

4. See CAROLE TAYLOR, *In Horizontal Orbit: Hospitals and the Cult of Efficiency* (New York: Holt, 1970) for an anthropologist's account, sometimes hilarious, about roles and status

in a major university hospital. Also, T. PARSONS, op. cit., Chapter 10.

5. A good discussion of roles is given in T. SARBIN, "Role Theory," in G. LINDZEY (ED.), *Handbook of Social Psychology,* I (Reading, Mass.: Addison-Wesley, 1954).

6. The chapters on nursing in S. M. JOURARD, *The Transparent Self,* 2nd ed. (New York: Van Nostrand Reinhold, 1971) came out of this experience.

7. R. D. LAING and A. ESTERSON, *Sanity, Madness and the Family* (London: Tavistock, 1964); see also A. ESTERSON, *The Leaves of Spring: Schizophrenia, Family and Sacrifice* (London: Tavistock, 1970). See also the very moving account of Mary Barnes' struggle to transcend her family's definition of her, in MARY BARNES and J. BERKE, *Mary Barnes: Two Accounts of a Journey Through Madness* (New York: Harcourt Brace Jovanovich, 1971).

8. PARSONS and BALES, op. cit.

9. D. COOPER, *Death of the Family* (New York: Random House, 1971).

10. See T. PARSONS, "Age and Sex in the Social Structure of the United States," in his *Essays in Sociological Theory* (New York: The Free Press, 1954); MARGARET MEAD, *Male and Female* (New York: Morrow, 1949); BETTY FRIEDAN, *The Feminine Mystique* (New York: Norton, 1963).

11. JOURARD, op. cit., Chapters 4, 9, 10.

10

PERSONAL RELATIONS AND
HEALTHY PERSONALITY

INTRODUCTION

Next to the death penalty, the gravest punishment that can be inflicted upon a person is to deprive him of intimate human company. Not to have someone to talk to, to share life with, is to be dehumanized. Enforced solitude can lead a person to madness, unless he has a strong ego and can discipline himself to retain his identity and his values. People need one another simply to be human.

In some families the relationships among the members are those of strangers among strangers. Everyone plays his part. The father is paternal, the mother does motherly things, and the children do their filial duties; not one knows the experience of the other. Their relationships with each other are impersonal. In my research in self-disclosure, I found many instances where the members of a family were completely ignorant of one another's hopes and fears, likes and dislikes, problems and joys. They simply did not discuss "personal" things among themselves.

The experience of feeling at a standstill in one's relation-

ships with friends, where the relationship does not seem to be "going anywhere," is likewise common. "Where" can a relationship with another person "go" anyway?

It is in the intimacy of personal relationships that an individual's upbringing receives its most rigorous test. The ability to stay in growing relationships with a few others, without diminishing one another's existence, is what healthy personality is about.

In this chapter, I provide a set of criteria in the light of which a person can evaluate his friendships and relationships with family members, to discern the extent to which these are life-giving to the self and the other, and the degree to which they diminish health and block personal growth. These same criteria provide goals for assessing whether or not one's relationships are "moving," and the direction of such movement.

Characteristics of Healthy Personal Relationships

The following characteristics describe relationships between two persons which engender growth and well-being in both parties:

1. The two people communicate authentically with one another and stay in touch with each other's perspectives.

2. Their demands and claims upon one another are reasonable.

3. They are actively concerned with one another's growth and happiness.

4. Each treasures the freedom of the other to be himself and does not try to control the other.

No relationship begins this way, neither within the family, nor outside it. People make contact with each other as persons in many ways—through sheer physical nearness, as at home; through shared hobbies and interests; and through accidental meeting. According to one investigator, the first four minutes of any acquaintance are decisive for the fate of that relationship—whether it will move in the direction of greater intimacy or will remain distant and superficial.[1]

Once people have met, however, a period of mutual exploration begins. The desire to know the other as the person he *is*, rather than as he seems to be, motivates the mutual "interviewing" which goes on between persons in relation.

Getting to know one another is like unveiling a mystery which may further bind the two people in friendship, or it may serve to terminate the acquaintance.

Authentic Communication

There is only one way for people to come to know one another, and that is through mutual self-disclosure. This is what differentiates personal relationships of love and friendship from formal role relations—the participants seek to make their subjective worlds known to one another, in an ongoing dialogue.[2]

The experience of freedom to tell another person of one's hopes and fears, joys and sorrows, plans for the future, and memories of the past is the essence of relief from loneliness. But such freedom appears to be rare. More common is the fear of disclosure, limiting self-revelation to topics that are "safe" and superficial.

I devised a simple exercise to provide people with a feel for the pleasure and anxieties of mutual self-revelation. My students and I have used the technique in our experimental research, and I have also employed it in conducting encounter groups. The game calls for two people—a pair of roommates, friends, or people going together—to take turns telling each other all they feel comfortable in telling about the following topics. (These are sample topics; the two people can choose other topics of interest to them.)

1. My hobbies and interests.
2. My likes and dislikes in food and drink.
3. What I like and dislike about my parents and siblings.
4. What I like and dislike about my appearance.
5. My chief personal problems and concerns.
6. My experience with the opposite sex.
7. My personal religious views or philosophy of life.
8. My past problems with health and present concerns about health.
9. How I feel about you (the present partner).

I have found that people sometimes feel awkward at the artificiality of beginning a conversation in such a structured way, but once the partners begin actually to disclose themselves, they find the experience rewarding.

Healthy Personality: An Approach from the Viewpoint of Humanistic Psychology

Under what conditions will persons disclose themselves fully and authentically to others? One factor is the perception of the other person as trustworthy. This places the onus upon the other individual to be trustworthy.

Another factor seems to be a considerable measure of security and self-esteem. Individuals who are relatively unafraid of others and who regard themselves as acceptable will be readier to let themselves be known than will insecure, dependent individuals.

Curiously enough, some individuals feel freest to disclose themselves to strangers, such as a casual companion on a plane, a hairdresser, or bartender. This freedom to disclose the self to strangers probably stems from the conviction that it does not matter what the other person thinks, because one is unlikely to encounter him in one's everyday life.

One of the most powerful factors in self-disclosure is the willingness of the other person to disclose himself. My research has shown that people tend to disclose themselves to one another at a mutually regulated pace and depth. If one person volunteers a great deal of intimate disclosure, the other person is likely to reciprocate. If the other person is a "low discloser," one is less likely to confide in him, because there is no reward for disclosures of comparable intimacy.

BARRIERS TO SELF-DISCLOSURE

Social Norms. Although honest communication is valued in our society, there is another value that is often more strongly affirmed than honesty. "If you can't say something nice about another person, don't say anything." In personal relationships, such as friendship or the relations between a mother and son, the recipient of "nice" evaluations can never know how his behavior really affects the other person. Further, the "nice" appraisals of him made by significant others will contribute to the formation of an inaccurate self-concept.

Personal Relations and Healthy Personality

Another socially derived precept holds that people should not be demanding or complaining. A wife who would lose self-esteem if she made demands on her husband may refrain from so doing. Because he has no sign that he is thwarting or depriving her of legitimate satisfactions, he will continue blithely to behave in his accustomed ways. The upshot will be that the wife will preserve her self-esteem, true enough, but the cost may be a life of suffering and repressed resentment. The same holds for complaints. Complaints are to an interpersonal relationship what pain is to the body—a sign that something is wrong, a sign that something must be done in order to restore the valued state of affairs. Vigorous complaints will at least create an impasse, which is the first step in the direction of adjustments. In my therapeutic and counseling work, I have advised quietly martyred spouses to learn the art of complaining. It may happen that a person complains on the basis of irrational and unrealistic needs and demands. In such cases it is to the other's advantage to rebut the complaints with as much vigor as they have been presented. This reaction insures that all sides of the issue are brought into the open where they can be more effectively resolved.

Dependency. A helpless person may avoid full disclosure of self to the one upon whom he is dependent, because he fears the other will withdraw his support. The dependent employee doesn't tell his boss how he feels about him out of dread he will be discharged from a job he needs. The dependent wife doesn't tell her husband all her feelings, needs, thoughts, and opinions, because she fears he will leave her. The dependent friend doesn't tell his buddy what he thinks and feels, because he fears he will be abandoned. Any factor which promotes dependency and interferes with the attainment of independent security is a factor which interferes with full communication.

It should not be assumed that the sheer amount of self-disclosure between participants in a relationship is an index of the health of the relationship or of the persons. There are such factors as timing, interest of the other person, appropriateness, and effect of disclosures on either participant which must be considered in any such judgment. In one research study, it was found that of the two least liked and most maladjusted members of a work setting, one was found to be the most secretive and undisclosing, and the other was the highest discloser in the group. If a relationship exists between self-disclosure and factors of health, it is likely curvilinear, not linear; that is, too much disclosure and too little disclosure may be associated with unhealthy personality, whereas some intermediate amount, under appropriate conditions and settings, is indicative of healthier personality. However, as a general principle, it may be proposed that persons who feel obliged to lie to others about their inner being are making themselves sick. Honesty may yet prove to be the best policy—in this case, the best health insurance policy. And we may find that those who become sick most frequently, physically and mentally, have long been downright liars to others and to themselves.[3]

Realistic Demands on the Other Person

In a healthy personal relationship, the demands that each partner imposes on the other as conditions for the continuation of the relationship are realistic, mutually agreed upon, and consistent with the values and happiness of the other. What does this prescription imply? What is a realistic demand?

As we have seen, people enter into personal relations to enrich their existences. Each partner needs the other to act in certain ways in order to attain those ends. In most friendships, the participants are willing to accede to the requests, demands, and needs of the other. But it can happen that one of the partners has unusual needs—needs deriving from an atypical life history. That person needs the other to act in atypical or perhaps impossible ways in order to produce satisfactions. Where one partner has unusual needs, or where each has an inaccurate concept of what the other is capable of doing, the demands may be unrealistic and impossible of fulfillment.

There is a distinction between a demand that is difficult to conform with and one that is impossible for the other to fulfill. In the case of difficult demands or challenges, efforts to fulfill these may well contribute to growth. In fact, challenges made by one person to the other may serve to motivate new efforts and creative achievements that would not have materialized without the challenge. In the case of impossible demands, they may be physically impossible to fulfill, or they may cost so much that other values would have to be sacrificed, thus making it not worthwhile.

A sweetheart may demand of her lover that he abandon

Personal Relations and Healthy Personality

225

his work in order to spend all his time with her. Or a mother may demand a straight A average from a child of below-average intelligence. In these instances, the demands cannot be met. Growth would not consist in one person conforming with the other's demands; rather, growth would be promoted if the individual refused to conform and strove instead to show that the demands were unrealistic. If these attempts were successful, and the demanding one accordingly adjusted his demands, to bring them into reasonable limits, then we could assert that the one who modified his demands had grown.

As two persons interact over a period of time, revealing their thoughts, feelings, and needs to one another, they will of course come to know one another better. But beyond mutual knowledge, honest disclosure of demands and wishes inevitably will produce an impasse in the relationship. It is in the resolution of these impasses that growth can be fostered.

IMPASSES AND THEIR RESOLUTION

An impasse between two persons exists when one has a need or expectation which, if fulfilled by the other, would promote satisfaction. The other person, however, either will not or cannot comply with this wish. Impasses may be open or covert. Only open impasses can be resolved in growth-promoting ways. Covert or hidden impasses are likely to result in a gradual deterioration of the relationship.[4]

The most obvious sign that an impasse has arisen in a relationship is open conflict. However, many impasses occur before they are recognized as such: they manifest themselves as boredom, irritation, restlessness, dissatisfaction with the other, nagging, recurrent criticism, or anger. These symptoms indicate that one of the partners is being thwarted in the relationship but is unable or unwilling to specify in what precise ways the other person is failing to satisfy. A girl found herself getting increasingly bored with her fiance and overcritical of his appearance, eating habits, hobbies, and other minor matters. When he changed his grooming, eating habits, and abandoned his hobbies for the time, she still remained bored and irritated. She had not yet put her finger on the precise way in which he was thwarting her needs. It was only when he spontaneously lavished affection upon her that the impasse was resolved. She did not realize that this was what she had wanted.

The simplest case of an interpersonal impasse consists in one person disclosing his wish or demand that the other person do something, or stop doing something; the other person refuses openly. The simplest case of impasse resolution consists in either (1) the person withdrawing the demand, (2) the other person complying with the demand, or (3) some compromise between (1) and (2). The resolution of an impasse fosters growth if it results in changes in either partner such that

1. Each displays the behavior that is appropriate to his age.

2. His self-structure changes correspondingly, so that his self-concept remains accurate, his self-ideal remains congruent with social mores and with actual behavior, and his various public selves remain accurate and mutually compatible.

3. The growing person becomes increasingly capable, through learning, of a broader repertoire of skills.

4. His action and his self-disclosure become increasingly authentic.

Everyone is involved within his family and outside it in a number of personal relationships. Some of these relationships may be neutral with respect to growth; others may produce regression, others may prevent growth, and still others may promote growth.

Personal Relationships and Growth

RELATIONSHIPS WHICH ARE NEUTRAL WITH RESPECT TO GROWTH

Any relationship with another person which does not produce change in his personality is neutral with respect to growth. In this category of "growth-neutral" relationships we would include all brief encounters with other people for specific purposes: the brief contact with a garage mechanic fixing your car; a person sitting beside you on a train, with whom you converse about assorted subjects, perhaps sharing a drink, but that is all; it could also be a relationship with a brother, sister, or roommate. We should not assume, how-

Personal Relations and Healthy Personality

ever, that brevity is the sole characteristic which defines a "growth-neutral" relationship. Some relationships with others last for years, but neither partner changes his reaction patterns or his values one whit. Other relationships may last five minutes, but the partners may have been radically changed. Thus, a stranger may say something to you which produces a marked change in your self-concept, a marked change in your values, or a marked change in behavior.

RELATIONSHIPS WHICH INDUCE REGRESSION

Students of personality development have developed crude norms which describe the range of reaction patterns "normal" for each of several age levels. Thus, we can divide a total life history into infancy, early childhood, late childhood, adolescence, early adulthood, middle adulthood, late adulthood, old age, and senility. Different behavior patterns are expected in each society from persons falling into each age bracket. Sociologists speak of this kind of categorizing as age-grading. Whereas growth means progressive change in behavior consistent with age norms, regression means growth in reverse.

Experimental psychologists have formulated the general proposition that frustration or, more generally, stress are factors which promote regression. A stressor is any factor which interferes with the ongoing course of activity. Thus, physical danger, illness, frustration, interference are all stressing agents and as such can induce regression, or growth in reverse. Adult persons will usually display childish behavior when they are ill, thwarted, or in danger.

There are some relationships which produce stresses resulting in permanent regression in one of the partners. Thus, one of the participants in a friendship or marriage may act in such a way that it literally "childifies" the other person who otherwise can act in ways appropriate to his age. The wife may impose such impossible demands on her husband that in attempting to implement them he is forced by stress to act in childish ways. Bettelheim described the regressive behavior of concentration camp inmates, behavior which derived from the physical stresses of prison camp life as well as from the arbitrary behavior of the guards.[5] Many of the prisoners were reduced to childlike levels of behavior.

Healthy Personality: An Approach from the Viewpoint of Humanistic Psychology

228

Dependency relationships promote regression in the dependent person.

We must distinguish between situational regression and more generalized, or stabilized, regression. A person may display regressive behavior only in one kind of relationship whereas in all others he can act his age. A husband may behave in a childish manner with his wife (not much differently than the way he behaved as a child toward his mother), but toward other women he may act in mature fashion. Or an employee may act like a grudgingly obedient child toward his boss and other authority figures, but toward his peers he may act his age.

A truly regression-producing relationship is one which produces permanent regression in the participant—regression which carries over to other relationships, so that other people are impressed by the juvenile or childish behavior of the individual. Such relationships reverse a slogan adopted by many schools: "Send us the boy, and we'll return a man." Instead, some people, by virtue of their demands and their power over anyone with whom they get involved, seem to say, "Send me a man, and I'll return a boy."

In this discussion we have overlooked the very important fact that in a healthy relationship, the participants can allow each other to regress; they do not necessarily demand perpetual adultness from each other. This is an entirely different state of affairs from what we have been discussing. There is a difference between a relationship which enforces regression and one which permits both regressive behavior and growthful behavior to occur. There is even reason to believe that genuine personal growth is not possible unless the individual is able to abandon his present modes of behaving, regressing for some time to a more infantile level of behaving and experiencing, and then progressing to an even more adult level.

RELATIONSHIPS WHICH PREVENT GROWTH

Personal
Relations
and
Healthy
Personality

There are some relationships which continue on the unspoken condition that neither partner will grow. Thus, a man and woman marry. Each holds a certain concept of the other that each has deliberately constructed in the mind of the other. At the time of the marriage his concept of her personality was inaccurate and incomplete. She did not know him as he "really" was. However, he believed she had all the traits of an ideal wife. If either behaved contrary to expectations, then the other would be disappointed, would feel let down and deceived: "You are not the person I married or the kind of person I want to stay married to." In order to preserve their marriage (for whatever satisfactions it does provide), each partner would strive to remain unchanged; each partner might believe that a change in personality would result in the dissolution of the marriage—a consequence which is dreaded. Such a marriage prevents growth.

A bachelor, living with his parents long after his peers have been married, does not grow. His present behavior repertoire may be acceptable to his parents; they are willing to support him, cook his meals, and do his laundry; they make no demands on him he cannot readily fulfill. For him growth is contingent upon moving away, exposing himself to new challenges and to new people who make new demands upon him.

Some parents actively prevent growth in their children, either through ignorance, because they do not place a value on their children attaining maturity, or because their own self-esteem is dependent upon playing the parental role. So long as their child is getting satisfactions out of the child role, he will not break away and expose himself to growth-promoting influences.

RELATIONSHIPS WHICH MAKE ONE SICK

When one is thrust into prolonged, intimate contact with other persons of a certain kind, the chances of illness—physical or personality illness—are increased. For example, if an individual is obliged to remain in close contact with someone on whom he is dependent for any reason, and this other person is obnoxious, depressing, overdemanding, or irritating, it can literally give rise to a "pain in the neck," headache, digestive upsets, and other by-products of suppressed emotion. The experience of psychotherapists has amply shown that when parents make excessive or contradictory demands on their children, when they will not let their children be themselves, the children are likely to develop neurotic or psychotic disorders.[6]

Healthy Personality: An Approach from the Viewpoint of Humanistic Psychology

Many physicians who have become alert to interpersonal sources of stress have been able to prove that for given patients, their symptoms of asthma, hemorrhoids, skin eruptions, hypertension, diarrhea, and so on, arose and lasted as long as the patient was inescapably involved with another person, and disappeared as soon as the relationship was ended.

Probably there exist some few people with a special talent for spreading misery, who always depress or sicken, disorganize, and undermine the self-confidence of all they come in contact with. It is meaningful to regard such individuals as today's witches. The comic character Joe Btflsk, in Al Capp's strip "Li'l Abner," is a fictional representative of the modern witch. In the comic strip, Joe always walks with a rain cloud over his head, and whenever he appears, expert workmen hit their thumbs with their hammers, hens do not lay, and the most robust people feel miserable. There is need for further study of those persons like Joe Btflsk who affect others in a deleterious fashion.

HOW DOES SELF-DISCLOSURE PROMOTE GROWTH?

Growth in personality occurs as a consequence of meeting conflicts and impasses head on, and reconciling them. Interpersonal conflicts and impasses constitute problems which require solution so that a satisfying relationship may be maintained. Whenever a person encounters a problem in his everyday living, he is obliged to vary his behavior until he discovers some mode of responding which is successful in achieving a solution. With no conflicts, with no impasses, there would be no instigation to change—one would, in short, not learn. If a person had no need to keep afloat and move in water, he would never learn to swim. If he had no occasion to keep records or to communicate by letters, he would not learn to write. If nobody made demands upon him, he would never learn ways of behaving which would please the other person.

Personal Relations and Healthy Personality

In interpersonal relationships, it is only when there is open conflict between the participants that an occasion is provided for growth. Interpersonal relationships, besides being a rich source of satisfactions for the participants, also provides a rich source of problems.

Mutual Respect for Freedom and Individuality

Ours is a democratic society in which personal liberty is treasured. This emphasis upon the autonomy of the single person contrasts with concepts of the ideal man that are held in other societies. Thus, it could be said that in Nazi Germany, the ideal man was the "obedient man," obedient to the leaders of the state. Nazi parents raised their children toward this goal of obedience; Nazi wives admired husbands who showed unflinching obedience to superiors and condemned those who were so "weak" and "selfish" as to put private interests above those of duty.

In a healthy personal relationship, each partner will value the autonomy of the other, and, further, will value the goal of growth toward self-actualization of the other. When these values are clearly stated, it becomes apparent that many other values can readily conflict with them. In a marriage, for example, a husband may refuse his wife's wishes to resume her education, because he is afraid of her freedom; he wants her to be dependent and compliant. A parent may force unwilling compliance from the child so as to maintain his own self-esteem. In each case, we observe a lack of respect for the individual needs of the other person. This is a subtle point but one which warrants elucidation because of its importance.

In a healthy relationship, each partner wants the other partner to do what he wants to do. Certainly friends or spouses choose one another because of similarities in values, i.e., similarities in what each wants to do. In our society, because of the high value placed on free will, few spouses would want the other to remain married unwillingly. What we are here saying is that a sign of a healthy relationship is present when each participant shows an active concern for the preservation of the integrity and autonomy of the other, even when this involves at some time the dissolution of the relationship. If a divorce, break-up of a friendship, departure from the parent's home, or resignation from a job is an important means of promoting growth and increasing autonomy, then in a healthy relationship, the other person will want this to occur.

Very often a concern and respect for the other person's

Healthy Personality: An Approach from the Viewpoint of Humanistic Psychology

232

right to integrity and autonomy involves some pain. For that matter, to be concerned with one's own freedom may often involve a good deal of social pressure—especially in those instances where one's wishes differ from those of the majority of people. The "nerve of failure," as Riesman and others have called it, is rare. By this is meant the courage to continue to assert one's difference from the mass of other people, despite economic and social pressure to conform.

INDIVIDUALITY

To respect and to value another's individuality means that one sees his unique qualities as priceless and irreplaceable. His individuality includes not only those characteristics that are considered socially valuable, but also traits that might be called faults. Yet in a healthy interpersonal relationship, the participants seek to learn one another's distinctly idiosyncratic qualities, and to affirm them.

Martin Buber [7] stated this appreciative view of the other person's idiosyncrasies in elegant terms:

> The basis of man's life with man is twofold, and it is one —the wish of every man to be confirmed as what he is, even as what he can become, by men; and the innate capacity in man to confirm his fellow-men in this way. . . . Genuine conversation . . . means acceptance of otherness. [Everything] depends, so far as human life is concerned, on whether each thinks of the other as the one he is (and) unreservedly accepts and confirms him in his being this man and in his being made in this particular way [p. 102].
>
> Man wishes to be confirmed in his being by man, and wishes to have a presence in the being of the other [p. 104].

The concept of confirmation, as employed by Buber in these passages, has a precise meaning, one which amplifies our assertion that respect for individuality of the other characterizes healthy interpersonal relationships. To "confirm another man in his being" means that one acknowledges he is what he is. One may not necessarily like all that he is, but at least one acknowledges and respects the fact that he is that very person, with those very characteristics, and not someone

Personal Relations and Healthy Personality

233

else. This is the direct means of respecting another's individuality. I feel confirmed by the other person when I recognize myself as the person he addresses. I can tell by his words and actions directed to me if his concept of me is valid, that is, matches my experience of myself.

Rogers referred to it as "unconditional positive regard," and he sees it as a necessary condition for helping others fulfill their individuality. Perls expressed this ideal in his Gestalt "prayer": "You do your thing, and I do mine. . . ." [8]

Concern for the Welfare and Growth of the Other

In a healthy personal relationship each partner is actively concerned for the welfare of the other. What is meant by concern? Out of what conditions does it emerge? What do we mean by active concern?

Concern for the other person means that his well-being *matters*. The first person wants the other to be well, happy, and growing.

When we say active concern, we mean that the happiness of the other is not passively longed for; rather, we mean that the concerned person *acts*. He engages in action, the aim of which is to provide the conditions for happiness and growth of the other person.

We become concerned about the other person because our life would be diminished without him sharing it. He will enrich our life most if he is himself satisfied. Thus, we acquire a vested interest in his welfare, happiness, and growth. Concern for the happiness of the other person is insurance for one's own satisfactions. A workhorse cannot work for us when he is ill treated. We use the horse's energy as a means for the attainment of our own goals. Thus, we have a vested interest in tending the horse's needs very carefully.

It may offend the reader thus to be compared to a horse, yet the analogy is not farfetched. The other person, like the horse (though in different ways), embodies qualities and powers that we need to enrich our lives. His affection is important to us for security and self-esteem. His very company serves as entertainment and relief from loneliness. In order for him to continue to satisfy us, it is important that he be happy. Therefore, each dissatisfaction of his promises

Healthy Personality: An Approach from the Viewpoint of Humanistic Psychology

a withdrawal of satisfactions from us. In order to avoid this eventuality, we learn to anticipate his wants and fulfill them. We help him when he asks for help. We help him to grow, because a mature partner is more satisfying than one who is immature.

Parents are concerned for the happiness and growth of their children for a number of reasons. Happy children are signs of success in child rearing, and this is an important condition for the parents' self-esteem. This also provides satisfactions for the parents—even security, for it is possible that the parents may need the future economic support of their children in old age.

A wife is concerned for the happiness and growth of her husband, because a happy and mature husband is a much richer source of satisfactions for her than a miserable, thwarted, and childish husband.

It should not be construed that all concern for others is an outgrowth of the calculated view that "if I take care of that person, then he will take care of me." A healthy personality is capable of *disinterested* concern for others; it gives a feeling of fulfillment, or of abundance, to be able actively to care for another person. Thus, grandparents may delight in the growth of their grandchildren, whom they indulge and nurture, yet they get no reward other than the experience of pleasure from watching the children's antics.

A further determiner of concern which must not be overlooked is the fact of identification with the other person. In a healthy interpersonal relationship—say, one between spouses—one partner identifies very closely with the feelings and needs of the other. Where this has occurred, the satisfactions of the other person are felt as deeply as satisfactions for the self.

It appears, then, that concern for the other person is a kind of devious concern for one's own happiness and growth. This may appear offensive and selfish. Yet, with Fromm, we shall ask this question, "Why should we not be concerned about our own happiness and growth?" There is growing evidence that one can love another only if one loves oneself; that love and concern for the self and the other person are not mutually exclusive. Rather, they are correlated, and derive from something else, a common factor which, for want of a better name, we shall call the "power to love." [9]

235

In other words, only if one can be concerned for the self can one be concerned for the other.

People who appear to be totally unconcerned for themselves, and who instead make all manner of "sacrifices" in order to help another person (they are called "unselfish"), usually demand a terrible price in return and usually get this price—absolute conformity with their wishes. We are all familiar with the "unselfish" mother who sacrifices a great deal to help her son get through school. Would it not be ungracious if the son then, against his mother's "reasonable wishes," married a girl of his choice but not his mother's?

THE WISH TO CHANGE THE OTHER

Psychologists know that human nature is not fixed, that behavior and personality structure are quite subject to change within broad biological limits. Psychologists even have acquired some rudimentary knowledge of the conditions under which behavior and personality will change, and they stand in a position where they can influence the rate and direction of changes in behavior and personality structure. Teachers, psychotherapists, social workers, military training personnel, all seek to influence the process of change in other people, with or without their knowledge and consent.

A person may get into difficulty in his relationships because of an inaccurate estimate of the changeability of the other person. He may overestimate or underestimate the changeability, or fail to identify the conditions under which personal change is most likely to occur.

The Effects of Underestimating Changeability. A person may believe that the other's behavior is unyielding and immutable. In consequence, he may develop fixed modes of relating to the other which perpetuate the undesirable behavior of the other person by evoking it. For example, a man may believe that human nature is basically evil, that people are "just no damn good"; no matter what is done for them, they will remain untrustworthy, dishonest, selfish, animal-like, lustful, and everything else that is bad. If a person with this belief has children, his child-rearing behavior will necessarily be influenced. It makes a difference to a parent whether he is dealing with a child who he believes will turn into a savage beast unless curbed or whether he is dealing

Healthy Personality: An Approach from the Viewpoint of Humanistic Psychology

with a malleable piece of "clay" who will become, roughly, what he is expected to become. In the former instance, child rearing will consist primarily of a tense battle between the parent and the forces of evil that are assumed to be inherent in the child; one false step, one weak moment of unwatchfulness, and catastrophe will result.

Probably many marriages have been terminated, or endured with resignation and martyrdom, because one spouse has incorrectly diagnosed the changeability of his partner. The husband may assume his wife cannot be changed, and the wife has tried unsuccessfully to change her man. The couple then "digs in" for a life of dissatisfaction, or they institute divorce proceedings. Many a spouse, following a bitter divorce, has been dumbfounded to observe that, like magic, the discarded partner became everything which was desired during the marriage. The husband about whom the wife forever complained, "He is such a stodgy, unimaginative, unromantic man," becomes attentive to his appearance, more considerate of women, more romantic after she divorces him. This is certainly evidence that he was capable of change, but more than this, it is evidence he did not *want* to change for her, and that she did not know how to behave so he would want to change for her.

The Effects of Overestimating Potential for Change. Although behavior is mutable, there are powerful forces which militate against change. These factors include the need to feel safe, the need to maintain self-esteem, the need to maintain a sense of identity, and other people's expectations. Each time a person alters some accustomed mode of response, he may feel anxious about disapproving responses of others; he may lose self-esteem if his present value system opposes the new behavior; he may fear that other people will no longer recognize him. These factors thus operate to restrict behavior to a fixed range. But a man may choose a friend, or a spouse, with a view to transforming this person, like Pygmalion, into something new and different. The person "as is" is not acceptable. A sort of silent wager is laid down that the chooser will in time be able to change the other person. Thus, a woman may displace her zeal as a sculptress from clay to people. She chooses a bum or a criminal as husband, not because he is attractive the way he is, but because she believes she can change him into a new

Personal Relations and Healthy Personality

man. In theory, it is possible to arrange conditions so that a man will change his reaction patterns, but few laymen are so skilled that they can manipulate conditions in precisely the ways which will promote behavioral change. For that matter, trained psychotherapists, criminologists, and other professional personality changers have a difficult time doing their job, because knowledge about personality change is as yet incomplete and incompletely tested. Therefore, the layman is advised not to choose friends and lovers with the aim of changing them. If the other is not acceptable the way he is, do not accept him. The major consequence of overestimating changeability of the other person is disappointment and failure in effecting the changes.

How to Change the Other Person. The most effective and the most healthy way to produce change in the other person is to ask him to change. People choose their action, and they can choose to change it. If a person's behavior is unsatisfactory to himself, he can usually modify it. If his behavior is unsatisfactory to another person, he can alter the behavior so it will satisfy the other person, if he wishes. Naturally, it may not always be easy, but it is possible.

If the relationship is one which provides satisfactions for both participants, then each will want to please the other.

But there is a difference between a cold, calculated attempt to *bribe* another person into conformity with one's wishes, and a spontaneous wish that the other person, who is loved, will change. In the former instance, the one being bribed will eventually discover he is being manipulated. In the latter, the relationship is more likely to be one of mutual requests to change and mutual compliance with the other's wishes.

It should not be overlooked that we can change another person by force, by threats, or by "brainwashing" procedures. Although change induced by threat, manipulation, or sanction may be effective in the short run, it will usually be achieved at the cost of resentment and hostility toward the person dictating the terms. The overbearing parent or teacher seldom takes into consideration the other person's needs and values. As these are violated and thwarted, hostility is provoked. Whenever the subject becomes less dependent upon the other, he will rebel, and either terminate the relationship or inflict violence upon the would-be manipulator of his behavior.[10]

Manipulation of Others' Experience and Behavior.   Some people dream of being able to manipulate other people into doing what they want them to do. The average student is fascinated with accounts of the effects of propaganda in shaping the attitudes of the populace; of the shrewdness of advertisers at molding the buying habits of people; at the skill of the college Romeo who can boast of his conquest with the opposite sex by virtue of a "smooth line." The extreme case of manipulation of others is provided by hypnosis, in which the subject will comply with the wishes of the hypnotist. The aim of such control is to destroy the other person's freedom.

When manipulation becomes the usual mode of interacting with others, it is a serious sign of impaired personality health. It implies, among other things, a profound distrust of the other person, even a contempt for him. Furthermore, the habitual manipulator of others must repress his spontaneous feelings, thereby promoting further self-alienation.

The contriving, manipulative, insincere individual, often without conscious awareness, places popularity and "success" at the peak of his value hierarchy. He sells his soul (his real self) to achieve it. He strives to determine what kind of behavior the other person likes and then pretends to be the kind of person who habitually behaves that way.

The major factor responsible for habitually contrived interpersonal behavior is the belief, conscious or implicit, that to be one's real self is dangerous; that exposure of real feelings and motives will result in rejection or ridicule. Such a belief stems from experiences of punishment and rejection at the hands of parents and other significant persons. In order to avoid punishment in the future, the child represses his real self in interpersonal situations and learns to become a contriver, an "other-directed" character. Of course, more serious outcomes are possible too: neurosis, psychopathic personality, and psychosis.

Scientific students of the learning process, following the lead of Pavlov, Watson, and Skinner, have been able to demonstrate that people's behavior can be manipulated without their awareness.[11] A psychologist was able to get subjects in an experiment to increase the frequency with which they uttered plural nouns simply by murmuring "Mm-hmm" whenever the subject spontaneously uttered the desired class of words. Many other experimenters have demonstrated that the content of another's conversation can subtly be controlled by properly timed "reinforcing" stimuli, such as saying, "That's good." There seems little doubt that, with a little training, anyone could improve the efficiency with which he could thus influence the behavior of others without their awareness that they had been so manipulated. All it calls for is study of the other person, to discern what things will function as reinforcers to his behavior, and then supplying these things whenever the desired behavior occurs. However, most people resent being manipulated, and they become properly angry when they discover that they have been treated like puppets or animals.[12]

A nineteen-year-old male student once consulted with me, seeking help in improving his relations with people. He stated that he had studied Dale Carnegie's book *How to Win Friends and Influence People* and found the advice given there extremely helpful to him in "conning" others, especially girls. He was successful as a campus lover and had six of the most attractive coeds in love with him at the time of seeking help. The help he sought was any suggestions that psychology might offer to him in his campaign to win over the affections of the campus queen, who rejected him, telling him he was a "phony." This rejection upset him. He wondered if there were some new gimmicks he might learn in order to seem authentic. Parenthetically, he mentioned that, once he won a girl's affections, he rapidly became bored by her, stating, "Once you've won a girl, it's like a book you've just read; you don't want to have anything more to do with her." I refused to help him learn new manipulative methods. In a number of interviews, I helped him gain insight into his motives and background, and he became more authentic and less the unscrupulous user of other people.

Friendship and Love Between the Sexes

In the preceding discussion I did not specify whether I was talking about friendship between partners of the same or opposite sex, between members of the same family, or between spouses. Different norms and expectations guide each of these relationships, and there are differing degrees of commitment and of self-disclosure in each type of dyad. However, most of what has been said applies in some degree to any personal relationship. My concern was to show some dimensions along which any personal relationship can grow. In the next chapter I explore love relationships, mostly between the sexes, but not exclusively so. Love occurs between friends, and, of course, among family members other than a husband and wife. But the ability to love is a criterion of healthy personality, and I have devoted a chapter to its exploration.

Some Existential Suggestions

As Buber sees it (and I concur), personal relations call both for "distance" and "relation." This means being able to disengage from dialogue with the other, and to enter into relationships of authentic revealing with the other. It is useful, then, to see the extent to which one can sustain dialogue with each of the "significant others" in your life. You probably will find that with each person, there is a point of mutual knowing at which you have arrived, and where you may be content to rest. If any of your relationships have become unrewarding, it might be worthwhile to renew disclosure and see if the bases of discontent can be brought into the open.

A review of the demands one makes upon others will sometimes be shocking. You may find you have been depending upon others in almost infantile ways, to entertain you, to guide you, to govern *their* lives in the light of *your* hopes and anxieties. The other person "is not in the world to live up to your expectations." See the extent to which you can enlarge your sphere of independent security by learning new skills.

The most difficult thing to discover in oneself is one's efforts to manipulate and control other persons rather than stay in dialogue with them, inviting them truly to be free agents. Study your relations with parents, friends, and siblings to see if you can identify the "games" you play with them, subtly to induce them to conform to your wishes.

Personal Relations and Healthy Personality

241

SUMMARY

Personal relationships call for mutual knowing through authentic self-disclosure. Self-disclosure is inhibited by social norms and by dependency upon others, which makes a person fear he will be rejected if he is truly known. The most powerful factor in one person's self-disclosure is the other person's willingness to disclose information of comparable intimacy.

In healthy personal relationships, the participants make realistic and feasible demands upon one another. Relationships become frozen into impasses when one partner makes demands that are not being met by the other. Impasses are vital for fostering both personal growth and the growth of the relationship, but they must be brought out in the open and resolved in ways that enhance the maturity and self-reliance of the participants. Some relationships actually inhibit or reverse personal growth, and some foster sickness.

Self-disclosure between persons fosters growth because it reveals the impasses which inevitably arise in an honest personal relationship.

Mutual respect and confirmation of one another's individuality are essential in personal relationships. The participants are concerned about one another's well-being and growth, and they strive to act in ways that foster these goals. They do not try to change one another through devious manipulations, but openly express any desires for change in the other.

NOTES AND REFERENCES

1. L. ZUNIN, *Contact: The First Four Minutes* (Los Angeles: Nash, 1972).

2. For the classic exposition on dialogue, see M. BUBER, *I and Thou* (New York: Scribner, 1970); and *Between Man and Man* (Boston: Beacon, 1955), pp. 1–39.

3. See S. M. JOURARD, *Self-disclosure: An Experimental Analysis of the Transparent Self* (New York: Wiley-Interscience, 1971) for a review of our scientific studies; the significance of self-disclosure in everyday life is explored in *The Transparent Self*, 2nd ed. (New York: Van Nostrand Reinhold, 1971).

4. For further discussion of expectations, impasses, and their resolution, see C. WHITAKER and T. MALONE, *The Roots of*

Healthy Personality: An Approach from the Viewpoint of Humanistic Psychology

Psychotherapy (New York: Blakiston, 1953); C. Whitaker, J. Warkentin, and Nan Johnson, "The Psychotherapeutic Impasse," *American Journal of Orthopsychiatry*, 1950, Vol. 20, pp. 641–647; F. Perls, *Gestalt Therapy Verbatim* (Lafayette, Calif.: Real People Press, 1969), pp. 28–40.

5. B. Bettelheim, *The Informed Heart* (New York: The Free Press, 1961).

6. R. D. Laing and A. Esterson, *Sanity, Madness and the Family* (London: Tavistock, 1964) gives a strong argument for this point. See also J. P. Spiegel and N. W. Bell, "The Family of the Psychiatric Patient," in S. Arieti (Ed.), *American Handbook of Psychiatry*, I (New York: Basic Books, 1959).

7. Buber, op. cit.; the quotes come from his book *The Knowledge of Man* (New York: Harper & Row, 1965).

8. C. R. Rogers, "The Necessary and Sufficient Conditions of Therapeutic Personality Change," *Journal of Consulting Psychology*, 1957, Vol. 21, pp. 95–103; Perls, op. cit.

9. This discussion is based on E. Fromm, *Man for Himself* (New York: Holt, 1947), pp. 96–141.

10. Contrasting theories and methods for promoting change of personality and behavior are given in C. B. Truax and R. P. Carkhuff, *Toward Effective Counseling and Psychotherapy: Training and Practice* (Chicago: Aldine, 1967), Chapter 2; and L. Krasner and L. P. Ullman (Eds.), *Case Studies in Behavior Modification* (New York: Holt, 1965); and their more recent volume, *Behavior Influence and Personality: The Social Matrix of Human Action* (New York: Holt, 1973). An effort to reconcile "humanistic" and "behavioristic" approaches to behavior change is given by F. J. Shaw, *Reconciliation: A Theory of Man Transcending* (New York: Van Nostrand Reinhold, 1966); and A. Lazarus, *Behavior Therapy and Beyond* (New York: McGraw-Hill, 1971).

11. See my critique of "behavioristic" methods of influence in *The Transparent Self*, op. cit., Chapter 16, "Dialogue Versus Manipulation in Counseling and Psychotherapy."

12. When she discovered that she had been thus "manipulated," the heroine in Koestler's novel shot her lover. See A. Koestler, *The Age of Longing* (New York: Macmillan, 1951).

*Personal
Relations
and
Healthy
Personality*

11

LOVE AND HEALTHY PERSONALITY

INTRODUCTION

Freud once remarked that lieben und arbeiten, *loving and working, were the crucial signs of maturity and healthy personality. Loss of the capacity to love or failure to develop it are now universally agreed-upon signs that health of personality is impaired. Yet love is among the least understood of all human phenomena.*[1]

One reason for difficulty in understanding love is the ambiguity of the word itself. A woman loves her fiancé, her mother and father, her country, fudge, swimming, bone chinaware, and many other things besides. She "falls" in love, she longs for love, she gives love, she makes love, she feels love, and so on.

Fromm [2] *has been almost singular among writers on the subject by defining love in terms of action as well as experience. In his work, love is not exclusively a passion or emotion; rather, it is partly action. A love relationship exists when a person behaves toward the object of his love in ways that show the lover knows, cares for, respects, and feels re-*

sponsibility for the other. Unless there is knowledge, care, respect, and responsibility, there is no love.

The Definition of Loving Behavior

I will modify Fromm's definition, and speak of loving behavior. Loving behavior is distinguished from other kinds of action by its motives and by its consequences. We can speak, with Fromm, of the "power" or capacity to love. It should be possible to determine whether loving behavior is effective in achieving its aims, and it should be possible to study the relationships between loving behavior and the health of personality.

Loving behavior refers to all action which a person undertakes to promote happiness and growth in the being he loves.

It is not enough, however, that the lover wants to promote happiness and growth; he must want to promote these values in his object for their own sake, as ends in themselves. We make this point because it is possible for a person to act in ways which look like loving behavior, although his reasons are ulterior—he wants to impress the other favorably or to use him. Loving behavior cannot be defined as such unless the lover does freely whatever he is doing to make his loved one happy. A near synonym for *loving* is *giving*.

Probably love begins as a feeling or a commitment—both subjective reactions. But if these feelings or the commitment to another's well-being are real, they will inevitably become manifest in loving behavior.

Emotions, Motives, and Loving Behavior

When love is defined as behavior, we can inquire into its motives. As we have seen, the motive basic to love is a desire to give, to do whatever will be effective in promoting happiness and growth in the loved one. The act of giving is free from ulterior motives. It is giving for the sake of the loved one. There is no compulsion in love. Loving behavior cannot be commanded or ordered; the lover is not doing his duty to his loved one under threat of punishment or guilt. He is, above all, doing what he wants to do when he loves. The loving act is the acme of free choice.

But we think immediately of powerful emotions when we

*Love
and
Healthy
Personality*

speak of love: affection, lust, longing, tenderness, romance. What is the relationship between such emotional responses and love?

EMOTIONAL EXPERIENCE AND LOVING BEHAVIOR

When somebody loves another person (or an animal, or our country), he identifies with him. Because the lover is concerned with the happiness and growth of the other, he will feel the pleasures and pains, the dangers to and the happinesses of his loved one as if they were his own. It is as if he had extended the contact surface of his organs for feelings and experiencing. He reacts emotionally to the events which affect his loved one, just as he does to the events which affect him personally.

Just as the lover becomes angry when someone hurts or insults him, so he becomes angry when something hurts the being he loves. Just as he is happy at his own successes, so is he affected by the successes and gratifications of his loved one. Just as he is concerned about his own growth, so is he concerned for the growth of the other. Identification, empathy, and sympathy are all involved in loving. Empathy involves the correct interpretation of cues which reflect the feelings and wishes of the other person.[3] Identification— becoming like the other, in imagination, for longer or shorter intervals of time—makes sympathy (literally, feeling *with* the other) possible.

Experiences which affect the loved one provoke emotions in the lover. These in turn serve as important motives for loving behavior. Under the impetus of emotion provoked by whatever has affected the loved one, the lover strives to do those things which will promote happiness and reduce unhappiness in the one he loves.

SEX IN LOVE

Sex is a rich source of happiness for the self as well as for the other. There are many love relationships, of course, where sex is out of place: in the love of parents for their children or in the love of a woman for her close girl friend. But in a love relation where sexuality is socially and personally sanctioned, for instance in marriage, sexual behavior can be regarded as one of the patterns of loving behavior— it is indeed behavior which makes the other person (and the

Healthy Personality: An Approach from the Viewpoint of Humanistic Psychology

246

self) happy. Sociologists interpret the sexual act as a ritual not unlike religious behavior; it has the function and consequences of cementing the "solidarity" of a small group—the married couple.[4]

It should be pointed out that there can be sexuality without love, and there can be love without sexuality. We would not call sexual intercourse which was desired by one partner but not by the other an expression of loving behavior. And we could call it a love relationship between a man and his friend, male or female, when there was active concern for happiness and growth, but no sexuality. We will discuss sex more fully in the next chapter.

Choice in Love

We have seen of what loving behavior consists; we can assume that any human has the capacity to love someone or something if he is capable of behaving at all. But there remains the question of the choice of someone upon whom a person will bestow his power to love, i.e., his power to satisfy, make happy, and help grow.

In principle, a person can choose anything or anyone to love, if he wants to love at all. But it is well known that when choices are made from among a variety of possible alternatives, the motivations may be complex. As the psychoanalysts say, choices are "overdetermined."

A person may choose someone on the basis of certain estimable characteristics. Or he may choose someone he thinks will give him much love. Let us explore some of the more common bases for choice in love.

SOME COMMON CRITERIA FOR LOVING

Helplessness and Need. One may be moved to love another because the other seems to be helpless and in need of loving behavior. Thus, most people find it easy to love small children or helpless animals, without necessarily expecting anything in return.

Conformity with the Lover's Ideals. A potential lover may have ideals of appearance, personality, and behavior with which the other must conform before love will be offered. The concepts of the "ideal wife" and "ideal husband" may be decisive factors in determining whom a young man

Love and Healthy Personality

or woman will select to fall in love with. The young adult observes someone who accords with his ideals; he may then pursue this person as the one he will love. There is considerable cultural stereotyping in the characteristics which define the beautiful and/or ideal person whom a person seeks, but there may be much individual variability as well. Langhorne and Secord, in one study, showed that unmarried college males sought a pleasing personality, tenderness and consideration, moral uprightness, and a complex trait which included health, emotional maturity, stability, and intelligence. Freud described a class of men who were most attracted to women who were the "property" of another man, or whose fidelity and sexual propriety were questionable. I know of men who can only love women much older or younger than themselves. A sociologist gathered evidence to show that people select mates on the basis of complementary needs, for example, dominant men choose passive women. Some men may choose women who will not make them feel inferior, for example, someone less intelligent or from a lower socioeconomic status. The range of possible variability in choosing someone to love is remarkable.

Ability of the Loved One to Reciprocate Love.   A person may not experience the desire to love another person until and unless the other person shows clear signs of a desire to love first. In other words, the person can be moved to love if and only if he has been first assured that he is loved. It is almost as if the would-be lover is afraid to risk rejection of his love, or is not willing to love, unless there is some guarantee that the love will be returned.[5]

RATIONAL CHOICE OF SOMEONE TO LOVE

The following discussion applies mainly to marriage, where mutuality of love is almost a *sine qua non* of a successful and happy marriage. In our culture, it is the custom that would-be spouses must first "fall in love" with each other before they consider marriage. The process of falling in love is itself a nonrational phenomenon, probably based on deprivation of sex and on loneliness. When a person in our culture is "in love," he (or she) displays most of the characteristics associated with deprivation: preoccupation with the need object, "overestimation" of the value of the object, a desire to possess and "consume" the object so as to

Healthy Personality: An Approach from the Viewpoint of Humanistic Psychology

appease the hunger, and so on. In fact, what is called romantic love sometimes resembles narcotic addiction. The lover will do anything to experience his loved one's company and embraces. If there is separation, he will do anything to be reunited. If the lover is rejected, he shows the withdrawal symptoms of a heroin addict.

Romantic love becomes active loving when the lovers actually behave in ways which will produce mutual happiness and which promote growth in each other. The hunger to "be loved" may serve as a factor which brings people together. But whether or not love can emerge from romantic love depends on the actual loving capacity of each partner, and the actual suitability of each person's traits for promoting happiness and growth in the other.

The person who would choose wisely for marriage should soberly ask himself the question, at some time prior to marriage, "Can I make this person happy, and can I help her to grow?" Obviously the more reality based the answers are to these questions, the more likely it is that a rational choice will be made.

Whether or not a given choice of a spouse has been suitable can be determined only by observation of the subsequent relationship through time; time will tell. It is possible, however, to make a choice of a spouse in ways that will increase the *probability* of the relationship moving in a healthy direction. The guiding philosophy of choice would be to state, as clearly as possible, (1) the needs and values of the choosing person and (2) the traits of the person being chosen in as detailed a fashion as is practicable. If choices are predicated on such a broad base, the chances are greater that they will be fortunate choices. Naturally, though, there are many purely technical problems involved in specifying the needs and values of the chooser. Because these are psychological problems, or problems within the professional realm of the psychologist, one can sometimes obtain professional help in making a judicious choice of a partner in such important interpersonal relationships. Thus, to an increasing degree, engaged couples consult professional marriage counselors to assist them in clearing up misconceptions about each other and about marriage. This is not a very romantic practice, but it can be helpful.

One's family and friends frequently serve as an investigating committee to examine and pass judgment on a lover's choice of a spouse. "Lovers are blind," it is assumed with some validity; and so the well-intentioned family and friends try to examine all the fiancée's traits which have been ignored as unimportant by the love-blinded youth. He may have fallen in love because of some one need-related trait and may ignore all the rest of her characteristics. The uninvolved others look the girl over from many other standpoints, looking at such things as her health, her income, her religion, her attitudes and values, her tastes, and so on. If these judges know the over-all needs and value hierarchy of the young lover, they may be able to see she has attributes which make her unsuited to him. He may not pay attention to their advice.

FACTORS WHICH PROMOTE UNWISE CHOICES IN LOVE

Let us consider some of the factors which will impair the capacity of a person to make a suitable choice of someone to love.

Chronic Needs.　An individual with strong, unsatisfied needs will be likely to perceive other persons in autistic fashion. He will seek satisfaction of his immediate needs, and ignore other traits in a person that are important to his growth and over-all happiness. In consequence, he might choose a person who can gratify these needs. He doesn't realize he has other needs and values that will become important when the present needs have been satisfied.

Thus, the inadequate man who needs to be taken care of and to have decisions made for him may fall in love with a dominant woman. Eventually, he may outgrow his need to be dominated and require other modes of behavior from her. If she cannot change her ways of behaving toward him, an impasse may arise which will result in termination of the relationship. Or a man may be attracted only to women who are "owned" by another man—the fact of being the "property" of another man constitutes their appeal. And so he pursues and wins such a woman. Once he has won her, he might look her over and find that she doesn't have what it takes to make him happy. His need, if it can be called such, is to prove himself a better man than others—and if the psychoanalysts are correct, it may be an outgrowth of an unresolved "Oedipus complex."

Healthy Personality: An Approach from the Viewpoint of Humanistic Psychology

250

Lack of Self-knowledge. The person who is alienated from his real self will not know what he needs to make him happy or to help him grow. Because his choice is not based upon consideration of these important factors, it will be based on other criteria that are irrelevant to growth and happiness. Thus, he might choose a possible wife just on the basis of appearance alone, because other people regard the woman as desirable. He doesn't know if he really desires the woman; rather, he wants her because he believes he ought to. This would be the case with the other-directed character described by Riesman. Or he may choose a woman as a possible mate because his parents, or his conscience, demand he make that choice. Again he is ignoring his own needs and wants. It is not rare for a person to fall in love, court, and marry someone, and then, much later, come face to face with his real self and wonder, "How did I ever get joined to this person?"

Lack of Knowledge of the Loved One. I pointed out earlier that there is only one way to know another person: that is, to observe, to come to tentative conclusions, and then continuously to modify these conclusions as more observations are made. This calls for time to make many observations of the other person's behavior in a wide range of situations.

When this procedure has not been adopted by the would-be lover, then it follows that his concept of stable traits of the other will be autistic, or inaccurate. That is, it will be based on need-selective observation, attribution, disowning or assimilative projection, hearsay, or other mechanisms which guarantee inaccurate concepts of the other (see Chapter 3).

Optimally, of course, in anything so intimate as marriage, the couple should explore each other, perhaps for a long time, so that each will come to know the other's stable traits before they become legally committed to one another. This is unromantic, however, and seldom done; the longer-range consequence is either divorce or a long life of boredom or martyrdom. But even more, each person may strive to *hide* many of his characteristics from the other because he needs the other person. He is afraid he will be rejected should the other person discover these traits. And so a courtship, instead of being a period of mutual self-disclosure and study, becomes a period of mutual deception, and the construction of false public selves. Many a person has experienced tragic disillusionment with his spouse once the ceremony has been completed and the marriage begun. Even more tragic, however, is a longer-run consequence—that of striving to conform with a false public self that has been constructed during the courtship. The "perfect lovers" in "The Chocolate Soldier" found their relationship too idealistic, too perfect. It was a strain, and so the nobleman married the maid, with whom he could be himself, and the girl of high degree married the bourgeois chocolate soldier-innkeeper for the same reason.

The Need to Love and to Be Loved

We are born helpless, and so we need to be loved by our parents if we are to survive. Good physical care is not enough to insure healthy personality growth. Unless the child has received loving care, including emotional displays of affection and attention to his idiosyncratic needs, he is likely to grow in deviant ways. Spitz showed that children raised from birth in a foundling home, with adequate physical care but no personalized attention from a mother figure, were retarded in physical growth, were less resistant to disease, and were retarded in their over-all "development quotients," compared to infants raised by their own mothers. Goldfarb showed that institution-raised children, by the time they reached adolescence, were severely handicapped in their ability to relate to others on an emotional and loving basis. Ribble saw lack of adequate mothering as a causal factor in the development of infantile marasmus, a rare disease in which the infant literally wastes away. And Spitz showed that depression in infants was the by-product of separation from the mother. It is a definitely established fact that loving is needed to foster a child's physical growth and the growth of healthy personality.[6]

Harry Harlow, the gifted psychologist, was able to demonstrate that even infant monkeys who were denied access to a mother during their earliest days and were instead reared with a "mother" constructed out of terry cloth or wire reached maturity with impaired ability to mate.[7]

It is doubtful if anyone ever completely loses the need to be loved. The strength of conscious longings for love,

Healthy Personality: An Approach from the Viewpoint of Humanistic Psychology

however, is probably related to the amount of love a person has experienced. If from early infancy, a child has had no love, he may grow into a psychopath who is incapable of active loving and who experiences no conscious longings for love. If the child has had a "taste" of love, just enough to learn that it feels good, but not enough to satisfy, then he may develop what Levy called "primary affect hunger" and pursue love for the rest of his life, at any cost.[8]

The ability to love actively is an outgrowth of having one's love needs gratified earlier in life. There is logical basis for such a statement, as well as empirical grounding. A person whose needs are thwarted is a "hungry" person, seeking to be filled. When one is empty, one can hardly give. Active love seems to rest on the economics of plenty rather than of scarcity. The healthy lover is as one who is "filled" and who gives freely to his loved ones not only because of their need, but because of his abundance. He gives out of the joys of giving with no preconceived notion of getting something in return.[9]

No one, however, is so "full" that he can love endlessly without receiving love in return. In relationships of mutual love, where the partners have chosen wisely, each can give freely what the other needs, and each receives in return, freely given, what is needed for happiness and growth. Thus, it is doubtful if a parent could actively love young children without receiving love from the spouse, or from the children, or from some source. It is doubtful if a psychotherapist could meet the needs of his patients if he was not receiving love from his spouse or friends.

But once a person has approached mature years, society expects him or her to have the capacity and the desire to become an active lover. If the person has been sufficiently loved in the past, the likelihood will be increased that he will be able to establish a mutual loving relationship with another person, rather than a relationship of continued passivity and dependency.

FACTORS WHICH ENLARGE A PERSON'S
CAPACITY FOR ACTIVE LOVE

*Love
and
Healthy
Personality*

Gratification of Basic Needs. As a general rule, a person who has experienced rich need gratification will be in a position to become an active lover. He is not obliged to devote all his energies to personal need satisfaction. He can afford to use some of his time, skills, and energies for other people's happiness and growth.

Affirmation of the Value of Love. If a person has acquired a strong sense of the worth and value of love in and for itself, he will undoubtedly seek opportunities to love. His self-esteem will be based, at least in part, on his ability to love actively. In other words, unless he is involved in an active loving relationship, he may feel less than whole and fully "actualized"—less than a whole person.

High Frustration Tolerance. Loving another person often involves deprivation of one's own needs. The more fully the lover's ability to tolerate periods of privation is developed, the better able will he be to love.

Self-love. Fromm has pointed out, in an important essay, that love of self and love of some other person are not mutually exclusive, as was long believed. He states emphatically that one can love another only if one loves himself. The rationale behind this precept may be stated in these terms: To love oneself means that one is concerned with his own growth and happiness and will behave in ways which implement these values. Self-loving, in a real sense, gives one actual practice in loving; to the extent that others are similar to the self, then these ways of acting which constitute self-love will make another person happy if they are directed to that person. Self-love makes one attentive to one's own needs and probably increases one's sensitivity to the needs of others; if one has experienced needs and gratifications, one can visualize more vividly what the partner's needs and gratifications feel like.

It should also be pointed out that healthy self-love is an outgrowth of having been loved by parents and other significant persons; and we have shown that the experience of having been loved enlarges one's capacity for active love.

When a person ignores or hates himself, he is less able to love others. The self-hater cannot love others, because he usually claims total obedience from those for whom he has "sacrificed" so much. The mother described by Philip Roth in *Portnoy's Complaint* was such a martyr, who "loved" her son more than she did herself; she sacrificed her happiness on his (unasked) behalf. All she wanted in return was complete conformity with her wishes and demands, which is incompatible with genuine love. Mrs. Portnoy was a tyrant, whose love for her son nearly destroyed him.

Psychoanalysts regard excessive unselfishness as a neurotic trait, and personality hygienists such as Maslow and Fromm place a positive value on "healthy" selfishness. This is no more than a recognition on the basis of clinical experience that the person who is concerned for his own growth and happiness will have acted so as to promote it; in consequence, he is a better person and better able to give.[10]

Competence.   The more skills a lover has, the more diversified will be the needs he can gratify through his loving behavior. This presumes, of course, that the individual has few inner barriers, such as an unhealthy self-structure, to the full use of his entire behavior repertoire. If he has, then he will experience threat whenever he is about to behave in a loving manner, and so he will suppress the loving behavior.

Healthy Self-structure.   If the lover has a self-concept, a self-ideal, and public selves which permit him to function freely and fully, then his capacity for loving will be promoted. In other words, the lover will have access to all his behavior potential. He will not be obliged to exclude some ways of behaving in his love relationships because of the need to defend an unrealistic self-concept or to conform with a false public self or an excessively strict conscience.

Thus, if the loved one wants tenderness, affection, or domination, the healthy lover will be able to sense these needs and behave in a gratifying way without a sense of forcing, faking, or threatening himself.

In principle, the more diversified the personality structure of an individual and the healthier his self-structure, the broader the range of persons he can effectively love. Practically, however, the healthy lover probably prefers to seek someone who has an equally diversified personality and healthy self-structure, because his needs may require just such a person to love him. Anyone with a less complex personality would be less able to meet his needs.

Reality Contact.   It takes knowledge of the loved one to be able to love effectively; the person with autistic other-concepts will be unable to act in ways which meet the loved one's needs.

Reasonable Ideals. A person may construct such impossible ideals and expectations as conditions for expressing his own love, that no human could ever hope to qualify. He may then engage in an endless and fruitless quest for the "worthy" and "perfect" recipient of his love. Of course, he will never find this paragon, or else he will experience perpetual disillusionment. If it happens that a person has married on grounds other than love, he may place such stringent conditions on his love that it is never given. The spouse doesn't "deserve" his love and must meet his impossible demands for perfection before it will be given. Sometimes a person who has only limited capacity to bestow affection will show remarkable skill in finding out what his mate *cannot* do; once he discovers these inadequacies, he uses them as the reason for not loving the other.

Reasonable demands and ideals apropos of the other are likely to be held by a person who holds reasonable demands and expectations of himself.

Emancipation from Parents. A person who is not alienated from his real self will be better able to govern his loving behavior in accordance with the needs and wishes of his loved one, and with his own real feelings and wishes. But if the person behaves only to please his parents, his capacity to love may be reduced. The reason for this lies in the fact that much of the behavior which might be necessary to promote happiness in the spouse may be tabooed or condemned by the parents, and the individual does not dare to displease his parents. The psychoanalysts have shown that sexual difficulty in marriage, such as impotence and frigidity, stems from failure to emancipate the self from parental control, and failure to withdraw unconscious sexual interest in the parents. It is as if the spouse cannot devote love and sex to the partner because unconsciously, love and sex "belong" to the opposite-sexed parent.

SOME DETERMINERS OF ABILITY TO ACCEPT LOVE

Some persons cannot accept the deepest expressions of the real self of another person who loves them. They find such expression cloying, threatening, or embarrassing. When someone loves them, they become suspicious of the lover—the lover may be just pretending to love in order to disarm him and make him vulnerable. Or the lover may be trying to get the individual to do something. The person who cannot accept love may believe that the need for love means one is weak, and such an admission may diminish his self-esteem.

We may generalize and suggest that the factors which might prevent a person from accepting authentic love from others include (1) fear of being hurt and (2) repression of the need to be loved.

Fear of Being Hurt. Because of past experiences with people, the individual may project or attribute motives to others which they do not possess. He may assume they do not, or cannot, love him. If he believes this, then he will probably misinterpret loving behavior from others; he will believe their behavior toward him is motivated by sentiments other than concern for his welfare.

Repression of the Need to Be Loved. In the past the individual's longings for love may have been thwarted, or he may have been hurt in his quest for love. He may then repress his wish for love; he may, indeed, develop reaction formations against his love needs and make loud protestations of his independence from others: "I don't need anybody for anything." Such a person may strive to *prevent* others from loving him, with considerable success in such efforts.

The healthy personality is able to accept freely given love just as he is able to give love freely. He does not demand love from his lover as a duty for his partner to fulfill. Rather, he assumes that if he is loved, the lover is giving out of free will, with no strings attached, and so he can accept it without guilt or fear. "Love is never having to say you're sorry."

LOVE AND DEPENDENCY

Self-sufficiency—independent security—is important for healthy personality, but this is relative. In the first place, it is impossible for a person to be completely self-sufficient; indeed, attempts directed toward complete independence may be regarded as pathological, because they are likely to be predicated on a profound distrust of all people.

In the second place, it is undesirable for a person not to need people for some things. People *want* to feel needed by those to whom they feel close. There are occasions where dependency upon another person is an expression of active

Love
and
Healthy
Personality

257

loving, for it implies trust and accords dignity to the one who is needed.

A healthy love relationship involves two persons who are relatively self-sufficient in most ways but who are mutually dependent for important gratifications. The love relationship involves mutual giving and mutual taking, mutual needing and mutual willingness to provide what is needed.

HOW MANY PEOPLE CAN AN INDIVIDUAL LOVE?

Love is action, and there are limits upon how many things a person can do. If one devotes more time and attention to one sphere of activity, then other spheres of activity will suffer relative neglect. A farmer has numerous fields, livestock, and buildings to maintain, and a family to look after. If he spends all of his time and skill at cultivating his corn fields, then his wheat fields and vegetable plots will become overrun with weeds; his farm buildings will begin to deteriorate from neglect, and his livestock may fall victim to diseases. He has to apportion his time so that everything is attended to according to its requirements.

Now an adult has many things to attend to, not the least in importance being the needs of the people whom he loves. Thus, the husband must earn a living and satisfy his own urges toward productivity and status, but he also wants to promote growth and happiness in his wife and children. How much of himself should he give to his work and how much to his wife and children? His friends? His parents? Is there room in his life for other loves in addition to his wife and children?

There is no simple answer to these questions. The needs of the lover, and the needs of the other persons have to be taken into consideration. In addition, there will be broad individual differences from love relationship to love relationship, with respect to the "amount of self" that must be invested.

In some marriages, for example, the wife is quite happy with only occasional contacts with the husband, who may be immersed in a career or traveling at his occupation. In others, the wife may receive the loving attention of her spouse for all of his time away from his work, and yet it is not enough to make her happy.

Because there is a limit on how many things a person can

Healthy Personality: An Approach from the Viewpoint of Humanistic Psychology

do, there is thus a limit on the number of people a person can love.

Many a wife has complained her husband loves his work or his hobbies more than he loves her. If he devotes more of his undivided attention to these than he does to her needs, then to that extent she is correct.

The healthy personality is able, like the good farmer, to apportion his time and his care so that he is able to harmonize his own needs with the growth and happiness of his loved ones. This is not a simple task but one which requires continuous reassessment, readjustment, and vigilance. A healthy personality actively loves as many people as he can, without doing violence to his own growth and happiness, and the growth and happiness of his loved ones.

ATTRACTING LOVE FROM OTHERS

A person may assume he is unlovable and that he is powerless to induce someone to love him. This belief may stem from a childhood that was devoid of parental love and an adolescence devoid of friendship.

How does one induce others to love him? Ignoring for the time being such factors as attractive appearance, we can assert that love begets love. Active concern for the needs of another individual will, in general, tend to motivate the other person to become actively concerned for the growth and happiness of the giver. Unfortunately, a vicious circle often appears. The unhappy person who believes no one can love him is usually in such a chronic condition of need deprivation that he cannot give freely to others. Hence, although he may be pitied by others, he is unlikely to be loved. How can one break this vicious circle? How can one arrange it so that the person who "hath not" love will be given love? The Biblical precept "To him that hath shall be given" seems to hold true for love.

In our society the love-deprived individual may be able to love only through effective therapy. The professional psychotherapist is, in a sense, a source of love for the deprived individual. The therapist behaves toward his patient in ways which will promote his growth and happiness—and this is love, albeit without romance. Through successful therapy, an individual may acquire the capacity to love others and thus make it possible to induce others to love him.

Love and Healthy Personality

Love and Self-disclosure

When two people love one another, they open themselves to one another's gaze; they become transparent to each other. Such openness makes it possible for each to know the other's needs, and to know what the other is up to. There is no room for duplicity or inauthenticity in loving relationships.

Love *is* self-disclosure. When one person loves another, he reveals his love by his actions as well as his words. A loving act is a nonverbal way of saying, "I love you." Love cannot be faked for long, because when it is authentic, it enlivens the loved one as well as expresses the vitality of the lover. If a person pretends to love, but instead is indifferent or even hostile, then in time the "loved" person will notice that he does not feel loved in the company of the other. Instead, he may feel trapped, smothered, or even drained of energy.

Because love and self-disclosure are related, each person in a loving relationship knows the other, and knows that the other knows him. However, because love implies respect, lovers respect one another's right to privacy when it is requested. I do not have to be chronically open and transparent to the people who love me, nor do I wish for them to be that open, always, with me. Sometimes the most loving thing a person can do for another is to withhold self-disclosure, so that the loved one will not have additional burdens to cope with.

Love, Marriage, and Divorce

When and whom should a person marry? When should a divorce occur? In this age, one marriage in three terminates in divorce, and persons who remain married often feel trapped or unhappy in the relationship.

The reasons for undertaking marriage in the first place are varied. Young couples enter marriage for companionship, for an opportunity to raise a family, for sexual gratifications, to change their status in the eyes of the community, or, in a more general sense, to find greater happiness in the married state than in the single state. Although many achieve these desirable outcomes, others do not.

In Chapter 10 I provided some criteria for assessing

Healthy Personality: An Approach from the Viewpoint of Humanistic Psychology

whether a relationship such as marriage is healthy. When a marriage relationship deviates strikingly from these criteria, the participants experience the marriage as flat, dead, devoid of meaning or satisfactions; more emphatically, they may experience the marriage as positively agonizing, stifling to the self and partner. When there are children in the family, an additional problem is presented, because the children will require some care that will help them attain maturity and a healthy personality.[11]

If the partners are unable to work through interpersonal impasses themselves, in a growth-productive manner, then ideally each should consult a psychotherapist or marriage counselor. With expert assistance, each partner can often be helped to grow, so that an autonomous, responsible, and mutually agreed-upon reconciliation or divorce can be arrived at. When the partners will not avail themselves of such help, or seek it out, then the probability is high that whatever decision they make will be incompatible with their own well-being and that of the children. It is an open question whether children are better off, from a personality-hygiene point of view, living with two unhealthy parents enmeshed in an unhealthy marital relationship. A strong case could be constructed to show that children raised by one parent who is divorced from the other, where the divorce was a healthy one, have a greater chance of attaining personality health than the children raised in a miserable marriage.

When Is a Divorce Healthy?　A divorce is healthy when it becomes apparent that the changes necessary to improve the marriage are just not practicable. There are limits to how much a person can change his personality to meet the other's needs; often the changes required to keep a marriage going would be personality changes in a direction away from health. Thus, one partner may need the other to be a paragon of moral perfection in order to be happy. No amount of feasible change could make the partner attain those ideals. Further, no amount of therapy is successful in altering the needs of the spouse who demands perfection. They may be too deeply rooted. Perhaps, in such an impasse, the best that can happen is divorce, in the fervent hope that each will be better able to grow when separated from the other (something which happens quite often) or that if they don't

Love
and
Healthy
Personality

grow, and still want to marry, they will find a spouse with a personality which complements their own.

I know several marriages which went stale, and where insurmountable impasses existed between the partners. Each needed the other to be different, but neither partner could comply, or wanted to comply, with the other's demands and needs. When a divorce finally occurred, each partner became, almost like magic, the embodiment of the desires of the former spouse (perhaps out of unconscious or conscious hostility). It seemed, then, that their prior relationship blocked growth, rather than promoted it. The traits which drew the couple together into marriage in the beginning later became obstacles to growth.

In one marriage, the man fell in love with his wife because of her cute, childish innocence, dependency, lisping manner of speech, and so on. He evidently needed to enact a fatherlike role for assorted reasons, and she needed to be fathered. As time proceeded, he began to feel the need of an adult peer, and he made this need known to his wife. She reacted always with tears and the assertion, "You don't love me any more." She could not, or would not change. He divorced her and remarried. She suffered considerably through the divorce, sought therapeutic help, and eventually achieved an understanding of the reasons for her infantile characteristics; she was assisted in growing to a healthier level. She remarried, and the new marriage appeared to be healthier.

The Power to Love and Healthy Personality

In the last analysis, love is a gift, freely and spontaneously given by the lover to his loved one. The being who is loved may be the self, a spouse, a child, a friend, and so on. The gift which is proffered to the loved one is the real self of the lover. He gives himself—he focuses his powers so that the loved one may be happier and may better actualize his potentialities. The criterion of the success of loving behavior is evidence of happiness and growth in the loved one.

The individual who is alienated from his real self cannot love. He cannot even love himself, because he does not know what he needs. The individual with a personality ill-

Healthy Personality: An Approach from the Viewpoint of Humanistic Psychology

ness—neurosis, psychosis, or character disorder—is a person who cannot love. Many patients who have undergone psychotherapy report they have acquired, for the first time in their lives, the power to love themselves and others. Probably what the psychoanalysts refer to as "genitality" or as "orgastic potency" refers to more than sexual adequacy; it may be interpreted as the power to love in the broader sense in which we have interpreted the word *love*. The neurotic who does not "command" his sexual functions, who is "alienated" from control of his own sexuality, is a person in whom sexuality is symbolic of all that is summed up by the term *real self*. Just as he cannot give sexuality to his loved one, so he cannot give his real self.

Some Existential Suggestions

The line between love and possessiveness is thin. It is likewise difficult to distinguish between needing another person and loving him.

I do not have any existential suggestions about loving. I don't think one should place his loved ones, with whom he relates in the second person, as "you," into the third person—"he," "she," or "it"—unless it is to wonder what will surprise him with some new delight.

SUMMARY

Love is a commitment to another's well-being. Loving behavior is motivated by knowledge and concern for the well-being of the loved one. This concern is an outcome of identification, empathy, and sympathy with the loved one's condition. Sexuality is a factor in heterosexual love, but there can be love without sex, and sex without love.

People choose someone to love on the basis of the other's helplessness; in conformity with the lover's needs and ideals; and in return for being loved. Strong needs, lack of self-knowledge, and lack of knowledge of the loved one are factors in unwise choices of someone to love.

Healthy personality is fostered by both giving and receiving love. The capacity for loving is fostered by basic need gratification, affirmation of the value of love, frustration tolerance, competence, a healthy self-structure, reality contact,

Love
and
Healthy
Personality

self-love, reasonable ideals, and emancipation from parents.

People reject love out of fear of being hurt and repression of the need to be loved. It is compatible with healthy personality to love as many people as one can without jeopardizing other values. Love from others is attracted by offering love first. A healthy self-structure liberates a person to act in loving ways. Impasses arise in marriage. Struggle with these may enrich the relationship; if the impasse cannot be resolved alone, or with help from a marriage counselor, divorce may be essential.

The power to love is a crucial sign of healthy personality.

NOTES AND REFERENCES

1. See, however, Rollo May's magisterial treatise *Love and Will* (New York: Norton, 1970).

2. E. FROMM, *Man for Himself* (New York: Holt, 1947), pp. 96–101; *The Art of Loving* (New York: Harper & Row, 1956). For an account of love as experience, see S. M. JOURARD, *The Transparent Self* (New York: Van Nostrand Reinhold, 1971), Chapter 6, "The Experience and Disclosure of Love." See also H. OTTO (ED.), *Love Today* (New York: Association Press, 1972).

3. D. A. STEWART, *Preface to Empathy* (New York: Philosophical Library, 1956); R. KATZ, *Empathy* (New York: The Free Press, 1963); R. D. LAING, H. PHILLIPSON, and A. R. LEE, *Interpersonal Perception: A Theory and a Method of Research* (New York: Harper & Row, 1972); M. BUBER, *The Knowledge of Man* (New York: Harper & Row, 1965), pp. 78–85.

4. T. PARSONS and R. F. BALES, *Family, Socialization and Interaction Process* (New York: The Free Press, 1958), p. 21: ". . . genital sexuality (is) . . . the primary 'ritual' of marital solidarity."

5. S. FREUD, "On Narcissism: An Introduction," in S. FREUD, *Collected Papers*, IV (London: Hogarth, 1953); M. C. LANGHORNE and P. F. SECORD, "Variations in Marital Needs with Age, Sex, Marital Status, and Regional Location," *Journal of Social Psychology*, 1955, Vol. 41, pp. 19–37; S. FREUD, "Contributions to the Psychology of Love: A Special Type of Choice of Object Made by Men," in FREUD, op. cit., Chapter 11; R. F. WINCH, *Mate-Selection* (New York: Harper & Row, 1958).

6. R. A. SPITZ, "Hospitalism: An Inquiry into the Genesis of Psychiatric Conditions in Early Childhood," *Psychoanalytic Study of the Child*, I (New York: International Universities

Press, 1945); W. GOLDFARB, "Emotional and Intellectual Consequences of Psychological Deprivation in Infancy: A Revaluation," in P. HOCH and J. ZUBIN (EDS.), *Psychopathology of Childhood* (New York: Grune and Stratton, 1955), pp. 105–119; MARGARET RIBBLE, *The Rights of Infants* (New York: Columbia University Press, 1943).

7. H. HARLOW, "The Heterosexual Affection System in Monkeys," *American Psychologist*, 1962, Vol. 17, pp. 1–9.

8. D. M. LEVY, "Primary Affect-Hunger," *American Journal of Orthopsychiatry*, 1937, Vol. 94, pp. 643–652.

9. A. H. MASLOW, "Love in Self-actualizing People," in A. H. MASLOW, *Motivation and Personality* (New York: Harper & Row, 1954).

10. FROMM, *Man for Himself*, op. cit., pp. 119–140; P. ROTH, *Portnoy's Complaint* (New York: Random House, 1969).

11. There are numerous books dealing with love, marriage, and divorce which offer different perspectives on this most difficult of institutions. See, for example, I. CHARNEY, *Marital Love and Hate* (New York: Macmillan, 1972), which I regard as most instructive; NENA O'NEILL and GEORGE O'NEILL, *Open Marriage: A New Life Style for Couples* (New York: M. Evans, 1972); H. OTTO (ED.), *The Family in Search of a Future* (New York: Appleton-Century-Crofts, 1970).

12

SEX AND HEALTHY PERSONALITY

Sex is a source of boundless delight, and a means to express the profundity of love between man and woman, yet sex is a problem to many people in our society. The problem stems, in part, from the obvious fact that children are conceived through the sexual relationship. Every society restricts sexual behavior to insure that when children are born, they will be born to parents who are willing to assume responsibility for their upbringing. Our society, perhaps, has been overzealous in seeking to instill a sense of caution and responsibility regarding sex; as a result, many people grow to adult years regarding sex as dangerous and immoral. Healthy personality is difficult to achieve unless the individual is able to reconcile his sexual needs with such other values as the integrity of others, some measure of conformity with prevailing morality, and a sense of self-esteem. Persons unable to integrate sexuality with other values will suffer.

266

A Sexual Revolution

A sweeping revolution in sexual morality has occurred in the Western world in the past decade, stemming in part from the accessibility of contraceptive pills. The pill has made it possible for women to engage in sexual relationships without dread of unwanted pregnancy, and without having to interrupt the spontaneity of love-making to use more complicated contraceptive procedures, such as a diaphragm or contraceptive jellies or foams.

To an extent hitherto unknown in the United States, young people are living together without being formally married, and are engaging in sexual relationships as part of the living arrangement. Although such living arrangements are an approximation to conventional monogamous marriage, there are groups of people around the country who have changed the traditional meaning of sex, as an expression of love for a particular person, to a game or sport. Thus, there are organizations of "swingers," who meet for shared sexuality—an approximation to ancient orgies; and there are "swapping" networks, where people change partners for the fun of it. "Adult" (pornographic) films are available in most cities around the country, displaying sexual intercourse and other erotic activities on the screen. Finally, sexual themes in popular literature have been presented with total explicitness, and frequently without artistic merit.

This liberalization of popular attitudes toward sexuality has opened an aspect of life that hitherto was viewed as sacred, mysterious, illicit, and even dirty, into the realm of open discussion. It opens options for people that were not available to earlier generations. The ideal norm up to a decade ago was for young people to be asexual until they married, at which time they were to learn how to make sexual love with their spouse. Of course, this ideal was violated by most people, as Kinsey's classic study showed. Masturbation, premarital intercourse, extramarital sex relations, and homosexuality were all viewed as sins, sicknesses, or crimes. Now growing numbers of people who were raised with those moral convictions have the opportunity to act differently, without having to face social shaming.[1]

The liberalization of attitudes toward sex does not eliminate problems, however. In my psychotherapeutic work, I have found that people, however "emancipated" from the morality of their parents, or practiced in the varieties of sexual conduct, still experience jealousy, possessiveness, impotence, frigidity, and false expectations about what sex will and will not do for them. Before the sexual revolution gathered momentum in the United States, it had been completed in Sweden. In that country, young unmarried girls would invite their lovers to spend the night in bed with them in their parents' home. Yet Sweden is not without problems, as evidenced by a relatively high incidence of suicide and alcoholism among its citizenry. In America, our sexual mores are in continuing transition, and so people are obliged to grope for a solution to the conflict between their sexual needs and their wishes to be free of guilt and shame.

Before examining sex in relation to healthy personality, I will review the psychoanalysts' contribution to our understanding of this important topic. Freud was the first of the modern psychologists to attempt to trace the changing patterns of sexuality all the way from infancy to adulthood.

Psychoanalytic View of Sexual Development

Freud [2] devoted considerable attention to the sexual side of his patients' lives, correctly recognizing that in his time, people were especially prudish about sexual matters. Such excessive prudery played some part in the development of neurotic disorders. He postulated that early in infancy sensual gratification centered around the child's mouth, in sucking behavior especially. He termed this period the *oral* stage of "psychosexual development," and it was considered to last into the second year of life. During the second year and up until about the third or fourth year, Freud claimed, the most important bodily focus of sensory pleasure shifted from the mouth to the excretory organs, especially the organs of defecation. He termed this phase the *anal* stage. Readers of his writings at the time were disgusted at this acknowledgment that pleasure might be associated with bowel evacuation. Many contemporary readers may share this disgust. That Freud had some empirical warrant for his assertions can be readily attested by candid observation of small children or upon frank self-examination.

By about the fourth or fifth years of a child's life, the

Healthy Personality: An Approach from the Viewpoint of Humanistic Psychology

zone of the body directly concerned with pleasure appeared to shift to the genital organs. Freud termed this phase the *phallic* stage, applying the term to girls as well as to boys. The main source of pleasure for children in this stage, he claimed, was direct manipulation of the genital organs, as in masturbation. During this stage, too, the child of either sex typically becomes involved in the so-called Oedipus complex. Freud used the term *Oedipus complex* to describe a common infantile fantasy. The little boy wishes, in his imagination, to possess his mother and to exclude the father from her attentions and affection. The little girl wants to own or marry her daddy and be done with mother. Yet each child has positive feelings toward the rejected parent, and to make matters more complicated each child fears retaliation from the rejected parent—retaliation for secret wishes that the rival parent would die. It may be seen that the period of the Oedipus complex is fraught with acute conflicts. Freud claimed that the conflicts were commonly resolved in the following manner: The child would give up his wish for exclusive possession of the parent of the opposite sex. Further, he would strive to become like the parent of the same sex. This solution, if successful, would permit growth to resume. The child was then said to enter the *latency* period.

The latency period was said to last from about the age of five to twelve or thirteen, when puberty brings it to a close. Sex play during this time is not united with romantic or Oedipal fantasies; instead it is pursued out of curiosity, or for the excitement and pleasure it yields. As the child enters adolescence, however, he has begun the process of rapid physiological maturation, with its attendant strong sexual urges. The adolescent may participate in solitary or in shared sexual play, but by this time, the real or imagined partners become increasingly suitable as possible marriage partners. That is, they are of appropriate age and sex as contrasted with the fantasied partners of the Oedipal period. Unless earlier conflicts have prevented growth, the adolescent gradually enters what Freud called the *genital* stage of psychosexual development. By the time he reaches his adult years, he is ready to integrate his quest for sexual pleasure with other values, such as love and respect for the partner. He is increasingly ready for marriage.

Persons who have successfully passed through the "pre-genital" stages become "genital characters." Again, this term may seem somewhat outrageous to the thoughtful student, but it is a term that derives its meaning from the complex theory of development that has been sketched out above.

For the psychoanalysts, the *genital character* is the healthy personality.[3] Adults who have successfully become genital characters have been described as follows: They are able to love and work effectively. They are not hampered by unresolved conflicts with their parents, conflicts arising from earlier childhood. They are not obligated, by guilt or anxiety, to repress their imaginations or their feelings. They can reconcile their sexual feelings toward a partner with feelings of tenderness and esteem. Hence, they can be affectionate, spontaneous, creative, playful, able to work productively, and able to love other people.

Some Factors in Sexual Behavior

Freud showed that experiences in childhood can have a decisive effect upon the sexual life of the adult. Frightening experiences relating to sex and prudish attitudes learned from parents can make it difficult to achieve a healthy pattern of sexual behavior. Let us now discuss sex in its relation to healthy personality.

MOTIVES FOR SEXUAL BEHAVIOR

Healthy Motives. The main purpose for which sexual behavior is commonly undertaken is pleasure. This holds true for children and adults alike. The sexual climax, or orgasm, is probably among the most intense pleasures that humans can experience, and so it is no wonder that it is sought even into advanced years as long as persons are in reasonably good health. Contrary to common expectation, not only do very young children have a rudimentary sex life but people in their eighties and nineties are known to maintain their sexual activity at a level compatible with their physical health.[4]

Pleasure, however, is not the sole motive for which healthy personalities will engage in sex. Sex is heavily freighted with symbolic meaning, and in our society it is generally regarded as a symbol of love. In fact, it is probably only within the context of an authentic loving relationship, where both partners feel free to express themselves fully, that sexual experience is the source of the richest pleasure.

Married couples will engage in the sexual relationship not only for love and for pleasure but also to conceive children. We live in an age when the means of preventing conception have been developed to a high degree so that, in principle, married couples can have more freedom to choose the time of conception as well as the size of their families. It should be recognized, however, that interference with conception is forbidden among some religious groups, such as the Catholics.

Thus, the attainment of pleasure, expression of love, and conception of children are all motives for sexual behavior which fall within the healthy range. Now let us explore some motives which are less healthy.

SOME UNHEALTHY MOTIVES FOR SEXUAL BEHAVIOR

We shall select for discussion the following: (1) sexual behavior as reassurance, (2) sexual behavior as an opiate, and (3) sexual behavior as an exchange commodity.

Sex as Reassurance. It is not uncommon for males in our society to have grave doubts concerning their adequacy, sexual potency, or general competence as men. Sexual behavior is a primitive proof of one's masculinity, and so a man might seek numerous sexual experiences to demonstrate his prowess to himself. So long as he continues his "conquests" he can maintain his self-esteem; if any factor, such as illness or enforced abstinence, prevents him from maintaining a certain level of sexual activity, he is likely to undergo feelings of depression, inferiority, or anxiety.

A woman might have grave doubts concerning her attractiveness to males and her "womanliness." Where this is the case, she might become sexually promiscuous, to reassure herself that she is indeed desirable.

The use of sex as reassurance is deemed unhealthy in these cases because it does not get to the root of inadequacy which motivate the need for reassurance.

Sex as an Opiate. Sexual gratification is a fundamental pleasure. For many persons, everyday life may be quite "gray" and devoid of satisfactions. Their work may be boring and their relationships with people superficial and unsatisfying. Under such conditions, a person might engage in very frequent sexual relations or masturbation as compensation for the emptiness of his life. Again, such a use of sexual behavior is unhealthy because it does not get to the root of the difficulty. Instead, the sexual pleasures may so "tranquilize" the person that he loses some of the impetus for efforts that could change his circumstances. If there is no other recourse, however, sex is at least a pleasant way to pass the time.

Sex as Exchange Commodity. A person might engage in sexual behavior as a means of getting things he believes cannot be gotten in any other way. The most obvious example of sex as an exchange commodity is provided by the practice of prostitution. The prostitute sells sex for money.

Less obvious examples, but apparently quite common, occur in some marriages. A wife "starved" for affection may engage in sexual relationships with her husband when she does not really want to; she feels it is only through such submission that she can gain her husband's affection.

In one case (mentioned later in this chapter) a frigid wife would abstain from sexual intercourse with her husband whenever she wanted to force him to comply with her wishes for a major household purchase or a trip. She would "submit" only after her husband came around to her point of view. She was employing sex as a reinforcer, to "shape" his behavior according to principles of operant conditioning.

The use of sex as an exchange commodity runs counter to our social mores. More important, it implies that the "vendor" is treating himself or herself as a commodity. This is degrading and dehumanizing to the "buyer" and the "seller."

HEALTHY CONDITIONS FOR SEXUAL AROUSAL

A man in our culture is likely to become sexually interested when he looks at an attractive, shapely woman clad, partially clothed, or nude. Part of the reason for his arousal may stem from the fact that women *seek* to dress, speak, and move in ways that are subtly inviting. For the man to respond with interest probably signifies that he is "getting the message"; that is, he is in good health and in contact with reality.

Women, typically, can be aroused by expressions of love, tenderness, and caresses. By their manner of dress, their gait,

Healthy Personality: An Approach from the Viewpoint of Humanistic Psychology

272

and glances, they may give off signals meaning they would welcome advances from a man, but whether they will respond to these advances depends upon many other conditions being met. These conditions include reassurances of the love and esteem in which they are held by the other, safety, and the degree to which ethical precepts are being observed.

In a socially sanctioned relationship like marriage, many of the barriers which ordinarily might block full sexual arousal will be absent. If the couple truly love one another, they will learn the idiosyncratic conditions for full mutual arousal, and they will find little difficulty in providing these for one another, for example, tenderness, expressions of endearment, caressing, and the like. Now let us consider some of the unhealthy conditions for arousal.

UNHEALTHY CONDITIONS FOR SEXUAL AROUSAL

A failure to respond sexually to the usual forms of sexual stimulation is called *frigidity* in a woman and *impotence* in a male. The most common cause of these conditions is emotion that is incompatible with sex, such as guilt, anxiety, or disgust. Thus, a woman may have many irrational fears associated with sex. The signals which would arouse a healthy person serve only to induce anxiety and disgust in this woman. Likewise, a male may have various fears pertaining to sex which preclude his becoming aroused even under conditions where there is no rational basis for these fears. Such fears usually stem from early training, and traumatic experiences with sex. For such persons to become capable of sexual responsiveness, it is necessary that the incompatible emotional responses to sexual stimuli be removed.

Some persons will respond sexually to stimuli not generally regarded as sexual symbols in our society. The homosexual, for example, is a person who fears, is repelled by, or is indifferent to persons of the opposite sex; he can only be aroused by members of the same sex. The fetishist is aroused by the objects of his fetish and not by a receptive partner of the opposite sex. The sources of these deviations are to be found in an intensive study of the life history of the persons who suffer from them. There is no evidence that deviant sexuality is innate, or caused by endocrine disturbances.

Sex and Healthy Personality

273

Sacred and Profane Love

Many persons, because of strict sexual training, are unable to fuse the tender and sexual aspects of love. They cannot respect and care for the same person toward whom they experience sexual feelings. Thus, a man may marry a woman because she has admirable traits, but finds he cannot become sexually aroused by her. He may be quite potent with other women whom he does not respect. Similarly, a woman may admire and respect her husband but not be able to respond sexually to him; with a lover (who is quite unsuitable as a marriage partner), she may find herself sexually responsive.

This state of affairs is common. Freud thought it was a derivation of an unresolved Oedipus complex. That is, a man might choose as a spouse some woman who resembles his mother. Sexual feelings are tabooed toward the mother; it is as if the man transferred many of the same feelings and attitudes from his mother to his wife. The woman might likewise transfer many of her attitudes and feelings from her father to her husband.

Healthy Sexual Behavior

Sexual behavior is compatible with healthy personality when it produces satisfactions without transgressing the limits of good taste and integrity of the participants. If the aim is to achieve a climax for the self and the partner, the healthy personality will display the capacity to achieve these ends. If the aim is to express love and esteem for the partner, the healthy personality will behave in ways which convey these sentiments. Among healthy personalities, sex is a source of satisfaction and enjoyment with considerable freedom in the choice of modes of sexual behavior.[5]

Among some persons, the conscience may impose certain restrictions on the variety of sexual behavior. Thus, certain modes of sexual stimulation, caressing, and sexual intercourse may be deemed desirable by one partner and distasteful by another. Such incompatibilities in values and ideals may produce dissatisfaction with the sexual relationship between the spouses. Sexual behavior cannot be discussed without attention to the person's self-structure. Healthy sexual behavior presumes a healthy self-structure in the individual and, of course, a loving relationship between the partners.

Some partners find their sexual relations become boring, but fear if they change their mode of intercourse, they will be doing something perverse. This is absurd. Variety in styles of intercourse is good, because it keeps interest high.

Freedom and spontaneity in sexual love-making is most possible when the couple have established a loving relationship within which they have learned to know, respect, and trust one another. In the love-making of such couples, "anything goes." [6]

Other Patterns of Sexual Behavior

Let us discuss some patterns of sexual behavior which deviate from conventional ideals. These patterns are neither healthy nor unhealthy in themselves. Whether they influence the health of personality for better or worse can only be ascertained after careful study.

MASTURBATION

The practice of masturbation is well-nigh universal among members of our society, yet it runs counter to official social mores. This implies many persons undergo acute moral conflicts at some time during their lives because they masturbate.

Many parents instill erroneous beliefs into their children concerning the supposed effects of masturbation. The child may be told that this practice will weaken him, will destroy his mind, make him insane, or render him impotent later in life. There is no evidence to support these beliefs. Some parents even make dire personal threats to their children in connection with "self-abuse." [7]

Children with strict training in regard to masturbation will have severe guilt feelings because they cannot withstand the impulse to masturbate. These guilt feelings often produce feelings of inferiority and worthlessness. Some children become so threatened by the supposed consequences of masturbation that they completely repress sexuality. Such a means of handling sexual feelings can lead to serious personality illnesses.

The sternness with which masturbation is condemned

has gradually diminished. More and more parents regard masturbation as a natural part of growing up; they may attempt to discourage their children from masturbation, but they no longer punish it with severity. Some parents overlook it completely, or regard it as a harmless solitary sport.

PREMARITAL INTERCOURSE

Strict taboos used to be directed toward premarital sexual behavior. The reasons behind the taboo were partly moral and partly practical, for example, the possibility of pregnancy, venereal disease, and so on. Almost everyone in our culture has been raised to regard premarital sexual relations as morally wrong. Now the taboo is bypassed by a growing number of young people. Among teen-agers, the fact of virginity is sometimes regarded as a sign of inferiority.

Many of the practical reasons for avoiding premarital relationships are less pressing than they were at an earlier stage in history. Methods of avoiding conception have improved, and are more available to married and unmarried persons. These methods do not guarantee 100 per cent effectiveness, but they reduce the probability of conception. Methods for preventing and curing venereal diseases are easily available, and so this reason for premarital continence is less urgent than it once was.

These observations mean that spokesmen for premarital chastity have primarily religious grounds to support their arguments; practical reasons for avoiding premarital intercourse have been solved by technology and better sex education.

HOMOSEXUALITY

Throughout this chapter I have been speaking only of heterosexual love. There are, however, some whose love and sexuality are expressed to a person of the same sex. It used to be believed that homosexuality was a mental disease. With greater enlightenment has come the realization that, if someone has been "bent"in a homosexual direction by his upbringing, this does not mean he is criminal or sick. Many states regard homosexuality as a criminal offense; this is an unenlightened policy.

It is true that some "gay" persons (as homosexuals sometimes describe themselves) are unhealthy personalities, but there is no evidence that they are more neurotic or psychot-

Healthy Personality: An Approach from the Viewpoint of Humanistic Psychology

ically incapacitated, as a group, than any other group in the general population. Of course, if homosexual people live in a "straight" society with conventional sexual morality, they run the risk of ostracism, or of being fired from their jobs. I agree with the aims of the Gay Liberation Society, and hold the view that, among consenting adults, any way of expressing sexuality is a private matter.

I have served as a psychotherapist to numerous people who were homosexual, and in some of these cases, their avoidance of the opposite sex was grounded in irrational fears. Through the therapeutic interviews, it was possible for them to overcome their fear of the opposite sex and to establish heterosexual relationships. Other patients learned how to live nondestructively with their homosexuality, when it became apparent that the homosexual way was deeply established. Some patients learned to "swing both ways."

Various Responses to Sexual Arousal

Let us examine some of the ways in which a person can respond to sexual feelings once they have arisen. First, let us discuss the healthy pattern and then comment upon some of the less healthy responses.

THE HEALTHY PATTERN: SELECTIVE SUPPRESSION AND RELEASE

The healthy personality will have formed a set of ethical and perhaps aesthetic conditions under which he will feel free to express his sexual feelings. He will be aware of sexual feelings whenever they arise, even under conditions that for him are inappropriate. He does not feel threatened by his own feelings, and hence does not need to deny their existence through repression. When the preceding conditions have not been met, however, he will suppress (not repress) his sexual feelings and refrain from sexual behavior. The reason for such suppression, fundamentally, is that sexual intercourse is not satisfying when the conditions are not right. We may call this pattern *selective suppression and release.*

Sex and Healthy Personality

SOME UNHEALTHY PATTERNS

Immediate Release of Sexual Tensions. A person may find it impossible to delay sexual gratification, so intense or urgent are his tensions and desires. Consequently, he may seek release in any way immediately available to him. The quest for immediate release reflects an inability on the part of the person to control his impulses. This inability to impose control is likely to result in sexual behavior that jeopardizes many values. If the person seeks sexual release with a partner, he may choose that partner only on the basis of immediate availability, ignoring other important criteria for the choice of a sex partner. Thus, the person chosen may be unsuitable because of age differences, ill health, intelligence level, or social class. Probably many unwanted pregnancies, instances of venereal disease, hasty marriages, rapes, and other undesirable occurrences derive from the inability to tolerate delay in the attainment of sexual gratification.

If the person seeks relief from urgent sexual tensions through masturbation, and if he has strong taboos with respect to this practice, he will probably experience intense guilt and feelings of inferiority. His life becomes a vicious circle of sexual arousal, masturbation, self-hate, dissatisfaction with his everyday life and relationships with people, compensatory sexual desire, and so on.

Repression. Repression of sexual feelings is likely to occur in persons who have rigid sexual morality, and who fear sexuality in general. Repression of sex manifests itself in (1) an absence of conscious sexual wishes or desires or (2) a denial of any sexual intent. All of us repress sexuality at various times because we have been trained to observe certain taboos, for example, the incest taboo. Most of us would become upset if we became sexually aroused by members of our immediate family. Yet psychoanalysts have shown that such feelings occur at one time or another in our lives; however, we found this so threatening to self-esteem and security that we repressed sex within the family circle.

Repression of sexual desire in the right times and places is compatible with personality health, provided the repression is not too general. Social living would be impossible if persons were chronically aroused sexually. Imagine being sexually aroused all day, every day, every year. It would interfere with other pursuits, to say the least. But if sexuality has been totally repressed, many unhealthy consequences ensue. The represser carries a virtual "well" of unconscious sexual desire, manifested in unpredictable and

Healthy Personality: An Approach from the Viewpoint of Humanistic Psychology

278

uncontrollable ways, in accidents, gestures, and unwitting sexualization of interpersonal relationships. Chronic unconscious sexuality disturbs the person's capacity to work effectively, and it disturbs his relationships with people by making him unduly defensive or autistic. The psychoanalysts assert that repressed sexuality contributes to the development of neurosis and to other patterns of unhealthy personality.

The worst danger associated with a total repression of sexuality is the fact that from time to time the repression may be overcome in explosive fashion. This may occur when the sexual tensions become too strong or when the energy required to maintain the repression is decreased, for example, in fatigue or intoxication. On such occasions, the represser may engage in impulsive sexual behavior or he may become overwhelmed with guilt and anxiety without really understanding why.

Chronic Suppression. A person can be fully aware of his sexual tensions but suppress sexual behavior for a number of reasons: fear of disease, fear of pregnancy, guilt, ideals, and so on. Chronic suppression sets the stage for unremitting sexual tension.

Chronic sexual tension will produce many undesirable effects. The most obvious is unhappiness and a sense of frustration. In addition, the suppresser will be plagued with chronic sexual fantasies so that he cannot concentrate on his work. His relationships with people will be impaired for a number of reasons; for example, he may not be able to appraise the feelings of others with accuracy, or he may be irritable and short-tempered.

Suppression of sexual behavior is unhealthy when the consequences to which it leads are unhealthy, and when the reasons for the suppression are unrealistic and unwarranted. The ability to suppress, however, is a desirable ability, as we shall see in the next section.

Some Factors in Healthy Sexuality

Healthy sexuality in an adult is no accident, nor is it a natural phenomenon. Some of the factors which foster a health-engendering sex life include (1) sensible sexual instruction, (2) early nontraumatic sexual experiences, (3) availability of suitable sex partners, (4) a wide repertoire of other satisfactions, and (5) the capacity to establish love relationships.

Sensible Sex Instruction.   Humans have to learn how to behave sexually, and they have to learn when it is socially appropriate to become sexually aroused. Some of this learning results from deliberate parental instruction of children. Much of this instruction in our society is negative; it consists in admonishments about what is taboo. Children are told not to masturbate, not to display thier bodies; in fact, from an early age many children are actively trained to be ashamed and afraid of things pertaining to sex. Because many parents are embarrassed or tense about sexual matters, their children may be afraid to ask questions about their sex organs or about reproduction. The children may then acquire false beliefs concerning these matters.

Healthy sexuality is most likely to be promoted if the sexual instruction that the children receive is matter of fact, accurate, and in response to the children's spontaneous curiosity.

Nature of Early Experiences with Sex.   Healthy adult sexuality is most likely to be achieved against a background relatively free of fears and guilts pertaining to sex. Many children have undergone severe punishments for childhood masturbation or sexual experimentation. These punishments have made sexual situations a stimulus for emotions incompatible with sex. The severely punished child may, if other contributing factors are present, develop impotence, frigidity, various perversions, and other unhealthy patterns. Healthy sexuality will be promoted if the parents handle the children's deviations from their own sexual ethics with kindness, understanding, and explanations the child can understand.

Thus, if a child is observed to be masturbating, the parents should let the child know why they do not want him to continue this activity if they don't like it. They should not tell lies about the results of masturbation; if need be, they can just say that it is not nice, and they would like him to stop. If the relationship between the parents and the child is a healthy one, the child will gradually acquire the standards and ideals which the parents would like him to have. Failures to accord with these ideals should be viewed as

Healthy Personality: An Approach from the Viewpoint of Humanistic Psychology

signs of immaturity in the child or as evidence of an unsatisfactory relationship between parent and child, not as signs of moral turpitude and worthlessness.

Availability of Suitable Partners. It is not uncommon for homosexuality to occur among students in all-male or all-female schools; among prisoners in jails, camps, and penitentiaries; and among sailors. In rural areas, where the population is scanty and the opportunities for marriage are limited, sexual contacts with animals may occur.

The incidence of such deviant patterns could be reduced if appropriate partners were made available to persons living under these conditions. The policy of denying prisoners any access to spouses or lovers is particularly brutalizing.

A Generally Satisfying Life. The probability of attaining and maintaining healthy sexuality is increased if a person is gaining satisfactions in other realms of life. Adequate sexual relationships will promote a person's ability to function satisfactorily in his work, his leisure, and his nonsexual relationships with people. The reverse also appears to be true: If a person is able to derive satisfaction from his work, his leisure, and his relationships with people, he is likely to be better able to achieve healthy sexuality. A person filled with unresolved tensions arising from other areas of his life may try to compensate by means of sexual activity. He may demand more of sex than it can deliver. And further, the burden of nonsexual tensions that he is carrying may prevent him from performing adequately in a sexual situation. A tense, thwarted person can't be a relaxed, effective sexual lover.

Love for the Partner. Many barriers to healthy sexuality will not arise in a healthy love relationship. If a person has the capacity to love another person, he will doubtless have the capacity to develop a satisfying sex life within that relationship. Loving involves knowing the loved one, caring for him, behaving in ways which will promote the other's growth and happiness, and making the self known to him. If a couple has been able to establish such a relationship, then neither will be afraid or ashamed to make needs and desires known to the other. Each wants to please the other and to promote the happiness of the other. At the outset of a marriage, a loving couple may not achieve full harmony and mutual satisfaction in sexual relationships, but in time they should be able to accommodate each others' changing needs and wishes. The richest sexual satisfactions occur in the context of a love relationship, where the communication barriers between the partners are reduced to a minimum.

Therapy for Unhealthy Sexual Patterns

The individual with an unsatisfactory sex life suffers. The sexual represser is afflicted with prolonged sexual privation. The person with deviant sexual behavior may suffer from fear of punishment, and possibly losses of self-esteem. The impotent husband and the frigid wife suffer from disturbances in the over-all relationships with the spouse.

Such persons may seek psychotherapy. Although assistance cannot always be guaranteed, often guidance, instruction, or more intensive therapy may be effective in removing some of the obstacles to healthy sexuality.

A woman undertook therapy because of marked difficulties in her relationship with one of her children. During the course of therapy, it was discovered she was not sexually responsive to her husband. She merely endured the sexual aspects of marriage. Indeed, she used her sexual compliance as a way to control her husband. It was soon discovered her lack of responsiveness derived largely from attitudes acquired from her mother. Her mother had instructed the patient to view sex as dirty. The patient, when she became aware of the origins of her attitudes, came to see them as silly. Her lack of responsiveness vanished, and with it vanished also the lack of zest in the marriage, a lot of tension, and finally, the difficulties in her relationship with her child.

Although counseling is often sufficient to help a person overcome difficulties with sex, other approaches have been employed by psychologists and psychiatrists. Masters and Johnson,[8] the pioneer researchers of orgasm in women, developed sophisticated methods for supervising the sexual behavior of married couples who have not been successful in bringing each other to a sexual climax. Classical aversive conditioning techniques have been employed to help men overcome impulses to engage in fetishistic or homosexual activities. For example, a man who found himself unable to resist the impulse to fondle young boys might have elec-

Healthy Personality: An Approach from the Viewpoint of Humanistic Psychology

trodes attached to some part of his body; each time he is shown a picture of a young boy, or thinks of a young boy, a shock is administered to him. The rationale is that he will then experience anxiety, rather than sexual arousal, each time he is confronted by the "forbidden" sex stimulus.

In my opinion, such a direct attack upon the symptoms of unhealthy sexuality should occur only within the context of a counseling relationship where the person's over-all life style is explored; the aim would be to seek ways of changing other aspects of life that have contributed to the development of the sexual difficulties.

Some Existential Suggestions

I have no suggestions to make regarding sex. It does no harm, and some good, to read books about sex, in order to become better informed. There is no excuse nowadays not to know about methods of contraception, about diverse ways of engaging in sexual love-making, and ways of overcoming sexual difficulties. If a person's sex life is not rewarding, then it would be more than worthwhile to consult a professional psychotherapist or marriage counselor, to seek counseling to overcome the barriers to enjoyable sex. There still is no better aphrodisiac, however, than authentic love for the partner.

SUMMARY

Sexual mores have changed in the past decade in a revolutionary way. Premarital sexual relationships are more common, and there is more widespread interest in ways to make sexual love more fulfilling.

The psychoanalytic theory of sexual development, with its division of sexuality into the oral, anal, phallic, and genital stages was presented.

Some unhealthy motives for engaging in sexuality include using sex as a quest for reassurance, as an opiate, and as an exchange commodity.

Sex and Healthy Personality

Inability to become aroused sexually is termed frigidity *in the female,* impotence *in the male. Such unresponsiveness may signify unhealthy personality.*

Among loving partners, great freedom in the expression

of sexuality is an expression of healthy personality and enlightened attitudes. Some patterns of sexual expression, once regarded as evil or dangerous, are now viewed less critically, for example, masturbation, premarital intercourse, and homosexuality. The ability to control one's sexuality is important for healthy personality; repression and uncontrolled expression of sexuality are destructive. Some factors in healthy sexuality are proper early instruction, nontraumatic early sexual experiences, availability of suitable sex partners, a generally satisfying life, and the capacity to love. Psychotherapy is available for persons with sexual difficulties.

NOTES AND REFERENCES

1. See W. REICH, *The Sexual Revolution* (New York: Farrar, Straus and Giroux, 1969); R. RIMMER, *The Harrad Experiment: Letters to R. H. Rimmer* (New York: Signet, 1971); A. ELLIS, *Sex Without Guilt* (New York: Lyle Stuart, 1958).

2. S. FREUD, *Three Essays on the Theory of Sexuality* (New York: Basic Books, 1962).

3. See W. REICH, *Character Analysis* (New York: Orgone Institute Press, 1948), for discussion of the genital character.

4. G. NEWMAN and C. R. NICHOLS, "Sexual Activities and Attitudes in Older Persons," *Journal of the American Medical Association,* 1960, Vol. 173, pp. 33–35.

5. See my treatment of this subject in S. M. JOURARD, *The Transparent Self* (New York: Van Nostrand Reinhold, 1971), Chapter 5, "Sex and Self-disclosure in Marriage."

6. There are many "how-to" books available on sexual love. One that I find aesthetically pleasing and that is presented in a spirit of joy is A. COMFORT (ED.), *The Joy of Sex: A Gourmet Guide to Love Making* (New York: Crown, 1972).

7. See the list of parental reactions to children's masturbation—some brutally sadistic—compiled in M. HUSCHKA, "The Incidence and Character of Masturbation Threats in a Group of Problem Children," *Psychoanalytic Quarterly,* 1938, Vol. 7, pp. 338–355.

8. W. H. MASTERS and VIRGINIA E. JOHNSON, *Human Sexual Inadequacy* (Boston: Little, Brown, 1970).

Healthy Personality: An Approach from the Viewpoint of Humanistic Psychology

284

13

WORK, PLAY, AND HEALTHY PERSONALITY

INTRODUCTION

Everyone must work, even if the work consists only in persuading someone else to put forth effort for one's own benefit. From a sociological perspective, work is the activity which persons undertake to keep the social system going. The total labor necessary to sustain life in common is divided among the participants in the society, and each person thus fulfills his occupational role, just as he fulfills his various social roles. In most societies, work is age graded, caste and class graded, and sex graded. There is men's and women's work, and there is the work for the children and for the aged. There is high-status work and menial work for those of low degree. In our society, with increasing sophistication of technology, many of these distinctions are breaking down; machinery has come, more and more, to do the work hitherto done by persons. This increasing replacement of humans by machines in the world of work poses challenges for healthy personality. It becomes increasingly difficult for young people to find vocations which are meaningful to enter. Conse-

quently, they suffer boredom which is unknown in societies where adolescents have essential work to do. Unemployment is an additional stress that is common in industrialized societies. In agricultural, hunting, and fishing societies, everyone's work is needed at all times; no one is without essential and meaningful work to do. In industrialized societies, especially those organized on capitalistic bases, overproduction of goods results in periodic stoppages of production, with workers being laid off to fend for themselves, until such time as their labor is again needed. Discussion of ways to insure optimum employment of people is beyond the scope of this book; here we will limit ourselves to exploring the challenge of finding meaning in work, and the relationship between work and healthy personality.

Because most people are obliged to work more than one third of their waking adult lives, it is obvious that one's work is a decisive influence upon one's sense of identity and one's health.[1] There is a relationship between various trades and professions, and assorted kinds of disease. Ulcers of the stomach and intestine are more common among upwardly mobile executives in corporations than among secretaries employed in the same firms. Moreover, if a person is obliged to work at menial or monotonous tasks, the sheer boredom of daily existence can undermine morale and contribute to physical and psychological breakdown.

Man needs meaningful leisure pursuits as a balance to his work. The contrast to work is not play, but leisure, or avocational activities. One can work playfully, and one can put forth vast effort in his play. Healthy personality calls for hobbies, interests, for leisure-time activities which provide enjoyment and which sustain joie de vivre. Leisure is actually becoming a threat to healthy personality as the necessity for forty or more hours of work is altered by increased automation of the labor process. Unless people are trained or learn early how to use leisure time in rewarding ways, they find such time oppressive.[2] We will discuss the role of avocation in healthy personality later in this chapter.

Choice of Vocation

The *Dictionary of Occupation Titles* lists thousands of occupations at which people can earn a livelihood in the

286

American society. As new technology is developed for space travel, computers, and behavior management, new trades and professions are generated as possibilities for young people to consider. The same technological changes make some vocations obsolete, thus making many highly trained people "redundant" in the economy—but not redundant to themselves and their families. Computerized techniques of production have eliminated many jobs hitherto filled by persons.

This raises the question of what a young person should choose to prepare himself for? Is there anything which can be said by psychologists to increase the likelihood of a satisfying choice of profession? In past times, vocation was determined for a person by tradition; a male, typically, adopted the vocational specialty of his father, and a girl mastered the arts and skills associated with being a wife and mother. Now the world of vocation is open to all who can get the training. Men enter professions hitherto almost exclusively female—for example, nursing, kindergarten teaching, and secretarial work—and women now drive trucks, do police work, and, of course, enter scientific and medical careers in increased numbers.

When the number of options open to a person was slight, the problem people faced was vocational *adjustment*—how to make life bearable in the vocational slot to which one was fated. As in all realms where freedom is encountered, for some the freedom is terrifying and paralyzing, but for others, it is exhilarating. Many college freshmen and high school seniors face a career choice in a state of total confusion, and with a feeling of desperate urgency, that a choice must be made now, and it must be the right one, or disaster will be forthcoming.

The profession of vocational counseling developed to help young persons choose a vocation which would utilize their talents and aptitudes and fulfill their economic aspirations. Sophisticated batteries of aptitude tests are available to give a person a view of how he compares with others in intelligence, patterns of interest, and specialized skills. Although such testing and interviewing can be a valuable experience for a person seeking guidance, I have found that many young people have allowed a vocational choice *to be made for them,* rather than take the risk of committing themselves to a career. In short, the quest for guidance may express a more generalized dread to make decisions and commitments.

SOME BASES FOR VOCATIONAL CHOICE

Parental Choice. Some young men and women are guided into a vocation which their mother or father now occupies, or which either parent *wishes* he had entered. In such cases, the child is seen as an extension of the parent, or a family representative whose task it is to fulfill dreams and goals of someone other than himself. There is nothing intrinsically healthy or unhealthy in such a basis for a choice; everything depends upon the personal characteristics of the child. I have known many students who were contented and productive in a career path which simply seemed ready and waiting for them as soon as they finished high school. One person enters the family business because it was always expected of him, and another starts training to become a lawyer or physician with as little conflict.

Difficulty arises in such cases when there is conflict with the parents over goals in life, or where the student is struggling to achieve some measure of emancipation from parental control. Parents often equate obedience with their wishes with love for them—a fallacy which produces agonies of guilt for students who find themselves unhappily enrolled, say, as a student of dentistry when they would prefer to study art. Any expression of discontent is encountered with a barrage of criticism: "You must be out of your mind to want to study art. You can't make a living at it. You know you'll be happy as a dentist. You never did know your own mind. Besides, do you know how much money we've invested in your training so far . . . etc., etc." A student has to have courage to follow his choice under such onslaughts of disconfirmation.

There are students who find training for *any* vocation meaningless, and the experience of being in junior or senior college absurd. This is true during times of cultural change in our society, where a "generation gap" seems to prevail. Such a student may drop out of college for a time and travel, take an unskilled job, or enter a skilled trade for training. Although parents might become alarmed to find their children thus dropping out, I have on occasion en-

Healthy Personality: An Approach from the Viewpoint of Humanistic Psychology

288

couraged students to withdraw from college when it seemed meaningless for them to be there. The period of being out has enabled such persons to find their own aims in life and to pursue them with more mature resolve than they experienced when they merely went automatically into a career under family prompting, without a responsible commitment.

Psychological Tests. In many high schools students have taken aptitude tests and have met with a guidance counselor to review their strengths and weaknesses. This facility is made available to the students on the assumption that it will reduce the period of indecisive floundering about choice of a career. If a student already has committed himself to a career plan, aptitude tests can provide a fair estimate of his ability to complete the training he will have to undergo to reach his aim. If he doesn't know what he would like to train himself for, certain tests like the Strong Interest Inventory or the Kuder Preference Test compare the student's array of likes and dislikes with those of people already engaged at various careers. Thus, a student may find that his ways of spending his time, his hobbies, reading interests, preference for friends, resemble those expressed by physical scientists and engineers rather than businessmen, or social workers. If a student can make a career decision on the basis of such data, well and good. Such test results, however, do not relieve anyone of the necessity to live with the decision they have made. As with parental guidance in the choice of career, so with counselor guidance—the aim is to help a youngster achieve greater independent security and confidence in making his own decisions in life. It is good for a person to flounder in indecision, even to delay commitments for months, or years, rather than commit himself halfheartedly to a career plan. In Blatz's [3] terms, a person who allows his decisions to be made for him by others shows *immature dependent security*; responsibility for "right" or "wrong" decisions is attributed to these agents, rather than to the person himself.

Independent Security in Vocational Choice. As I noted earlier (Chapter 1), Blatz saw independent security as the goal of child-rearing and personal growth. According to this view, *insecurity* is inevitable and desirable in the course of life. It is the state of being which a person undergoes when some need is unmet, or some challenge or problem confronts a person, requiring decision and action. A person can evade the problem or need, and employ various defense mechanisms in order to avoid the necessity to do anything different. This solution to insecurity is deemed unhealthy. The person can turn to someone to solve the problem for him, or to act in his behalf. This solution is called the way of *dependent* security; it is deemed immature if the person assigns responsibility to the other for failure to solve the problem. It is regarded as *mature* dependent security if the person takes the responsibility for the other's intervention in his life. Thus, mature dependent security is displayed if a student asks his parent to advise him on some problem but accepts as his own responsibility the consequences of following the parental advice. The greatest contribution to personal growth is provided by the way of *independent security*—the person encounters insecurity in the conduct of his life, accepts it, and addresses it with the resolve to master it by learning a skill and by gathering information in order to make an autonomous decision.

A person achieves independent security in the vocational sphere of his life if he has made a choice—*any* choice, for *any* reason—and has then pursued it with commitment, accepting the difficulties as well as the satisfactions as part of his lot.

When I finished high school, I had no idea what I wished to do for a career. I knew I wanted further education, but I didn't know in what area. I did not think I would like to be a businessman, a lawyer, a dentist, a doctor, or a worker, skilled or unskilled, in a factory. My parents left me alone with my dilemma; my father told me he would back me in any career plan I chose, but that I would have to make the decision. One option he offered was to enter the retail clothing business which was our family livelihood, but he put no pressure on me to do so. I chose to enter college in an unspecialized liberal arts program. As it happened, my psychology teacher, Dr. Mary Northway, was a fine lecturer; I read a great deal of psychology under her influence. We had to choose a "major" in our sophomore year, and for want of any other inspiration, I chose psychology. I had no idea about careers in psychology. I had no information about the ways of life open to people with undergraduate or graduate degrees in this discipline; I made the choice because we had

Healthy Personality: An Approach from the Viewpoint of Humanistic Psychology

to make some decision. Once in, however, I began to find interest and challenge. I retained a lively interest in many other areas, such as sociology, anthropology, literature, and languages, but I have stuck to the profession of psychology and have found challenge, boredom, excitement, financial reward—in short, satisfaction with the career which I chose with about as much foresight as one displays if he sees a body of water, closes his eyes, holds his breath, and jumps in to see if he can swim in it. Once in, however, one has to swim.

The point of this personal anecdote is that choice of a vocation can be made upon *any* basis; once the choice is made, it contributes to healthy personality if the person remains the responsible agent of his existence, and lives with the consequences of his decision until these become untoward, when he will again have to make a decision.

Being in a Profession

There are many ways to be at, and in, one's work. A person can view his vocation as something miserable he has to do, and endure, in order to earn enough money to "really live." If such is the case, his career choice has been unfortunate indeed, because he is spending over a third of his adult life in stress-producing activity. However, there are times of economic hardship when people are forced to take employment which is boring, even humiliating, in order to eat and to provide for their dependents. Thus, many people work at physical labor, as waiters and waitresses, or unskilled trades, to put themselves through school or to support children. There is nothing incompatible with healthy personality in having to work for one's livelihood. Unrewarding work, however, can drain a person of vitality and morale, rendering the rest of his life unlivable. The interests of healthy personality and self-actualization are served by changing vocations when one's present work has lost zest and meaning. This is not always easy, and it frequently is costly, but if the change offers hope of more challenging and rewarding work, then the period of transitional seeking and training, with its expense, is worth it. Unrewarding work is one of the sources of the stress and dispiritedness which undermine physical health. Changes in voca-

Work,
Play,
and
Healthy
Personality

tion, after long periods of stress and boredom, can be rejuvenating.

Meanings of Work. One can work to earn a livelihood, to avoid boredom in life, or to fulfill the meaning of one's life. There are many meanings which a person's work can have for him. A common basis of meaning, especially within some of the professions, is to test oneself in comparison with others—the *achievement motive,* as McClelland called it.[4] The striving for excellence, for conquest, for being the best, is a powerful motive in American society, and, of course, in other societies around the world. The pursuit of high excellence, or recognition, is one of the basic human needs. High achievement is the basis for enhancing one's status in the eyes of contemporaries, and it is at the heart of self-esteem. While work is not the only source of such enhanced status and self-esteem, for many it is the most important. Each profession and trade offers its challenges and rewards for high achievement, and these rewards reinforce the persistence and the creativity of the workers. A person is fortunate, and has chosen his vocation wisely, if he finds challenge and reward in the daily activities which define his work.

A person may work "religiously"; that is, he sees his work as a "calling," whether from God or from the world, which he feels needs him, and only him, to do some essential tasks. Thus, a person may enter the ministry in response to the experience of a "call," or he may enter politics, or the profession of teaching, because he feels that he can make a unique contribution which is needed. People often enter and remain in helping professions, such as medicine, psychology, social work, and teaching, because they feel uniquely called upon to help solve problems in the world or to relieve ubiquitous suffering. I feel some of this motivation in my work.

Meaningful work is essential for healthy personality. It doesn't matter if the work is salaried; it need only be participation in the work of the world which needs to be done and which yields the reward of meaning. Thus, housewives do not receive a salary, but they often experience the work of family care and housekeeping as meaningful. When work becomes meaningless, or when a person has no work at hand—as occurs with older, retired persons—they may begin to sicken, even to die. It is common for men to deteriorate,

Healthy Personality: An Approach from the Viewpoint of Humanistic Psychology

292

sicken, and die within a few years of retirement from some lifetime career of work. It is also unfortunately common for people in their vigorous years to develop illnesses related to stress and dissatisfaction in their work. Heart attacks, peptic and gastric ulcers, heightened susceptibility to infectious ills are all common occurrences among people whose daily activity generates more stress and meaninglessness than satisfaction. Boredom and sickness are powerful indicators that it is time to introduce change into one's world of work.

Change of Vocation

In my opinion, Marx was correct when he stated that a person's "relation to the means of production" imposed a powerful influence upon all aspects of his life—his beliefs and attitudes, his future, his family life, his health, even his life expectancy. Work uses one's time and energy, and these are all that anyone truly "has." In return, work yields money or a product. If it also yields boredom and sickness, then a change is essential for healthy personality. But as in changes in personal relationships and in one's own personality, powerful barriers often oppose such change.

BARRIERS TO CHANGE

Fear. A person who is unhappy in his vocation may remain in it, nonetheless, because he simply fears change. Although his present situation is miserable, he remains in it because at least it is familiar misery; he dreads the unknown challenges he would face if he were to drop out to seek a career which *might* (no guarantees) be more life-giving.

Present Sense of Identity. A person may base his sense of personal identity upon his present vocational activity, so that to withdraw from that work, or place of work, is tantamount to a dreaded loss of identity. Although such a narrow basis to identity and self-esteem is incompatible with healthy personality, that may be a person's present status. Under such circumstances he may remain at unrewarding work because he cannot envision himself at any other. His imagination and confidence in his powers of rejuvenation are repressed.

Others' Expectations. The expectations of others, that a person will remain as they have known him, can keep that

*Work,
Play,
and
Healthy
Personality*

person in unrewarding social roles and in stressing work, long past the time it was good for him. Frequently a person's family may; with the best of intentions, keep a person "at" his present work, even if it is sapping his morale and vitality, because the *other* family members dread change. I have counseled several people at times when they were in despair over the meaninglessness of their work, and they have told me that whenever they would discuss changing jobs or careers, their spouses or friends met the suggestion with barrages of disconfirmation. "You'd be a fool to give up this job. You are well-liked, you earn a good living, you can handle the responsibilities . . . etc." Such persuasion often sufficed to keep a person in sickening (for him) work. It takes courage and encouragement to make such changes, in face of fear, limited senses of personal identity, and others' disconfirmation.

CHANGE IN VOCATION AND
HEALTHY PERSONALITY

Meaningful work is essential for healthy personality, throughout the life span; and, of course, a social system keeps going only if the work "gets done." As automation proceeds, the amount of physical presence at working places diminishes and so the number of people who are displaced from their jobs by machines increases annually. Moreover, in the course of a career which has been rewarding, a person may find that, gradually, the meaning and joy in his work has gradually oozed away, and he finds himself depressed and bored at what hitherto were tasks encountered with zest. Creating new work for the technologically unemployed is a new challenge facing the government and private industry; each person has, as well, the personal responsibility to create or to find useful and meaningful work.

Many men and women are making drastic career changes in mid-life and finding such change invigorating. It takes self-assurance and some confirmation from significant others to make such major changes, but I have witnessed many of them, and I've been impressed with the liberating effects of the decision. For example, one person sold a small business which he had struggled to develop for fifteen years. He had found that the life of a storekeeper had become absurd for him. He bought a trailer, traveled with his family until he

Healthy Personality: An Approach from the Viewpoint of Humanistic Psychology

found another city in which he thought they would like to live, and returned to college as a forty-year-old student. His wife worked to help support him, and his children likewise worked at after-school jobs. In another case, a woman in her early fifties, who found the life of a middle-class housewife enervating, went across the country to resume graduate work for a doctorate in counseling psychology. She lost 30 pounds as a student, and looked much more alive. Her husband and children, across the continent, discovered they could run the household without her, and found new interests in common.

As a psychotherapist, I have often seen connections between stresses in work and the suffering which led my patient to seek help. This has been especially true among the people in mid-life. Often they have entertained fantasies of "chucking it all," and running off to the sea-side, or to a hippie commune with a teen-aged mistress. Some have checked out of their dispiriting family and occupational roles. Others have explored the possibility of resigning from their present work to start on a new vocation, even if it called for a return to school or university. Change is good for you, when it is responsible change. Impulsive change can be disastrous; but even if it is, at least a person has moved from stultifying places, and he can then pick himself out of the disaster to explore more life-giving possibilities for vocational change.

As women become increasingly conscious of former "sexist" limitations upon career possibilities, they pursue a broader range of careers than was hitherto the case. A good society makes careers available to anyone, of any age, sex, religion or race, on the basis of ability. While being a housewife and mother continues to be rewarding to many women, many more are choosing to enter other careers. And, once children are grown, women resume occupational aspirations which might have animated them prior to marriage and motherhood.

Older people, especially those faced with enforced retirement, face a dilemma not encountered in other, nonindustrialized societies. There is nothing for them to do, and they often die of boredom. In our society, retirement communities and old-people's homes have flourished, yet some older people regard them as ghettos and storage depots for obsolete flesh. Many retired people have prepared themselves for meaningful lives of leisure after retirement, for example, by travel, return to school and community college, pursuit of hobbies such as woodwork, art, music, and sailing. (Chichester sailed around the world in his sixties, with only one lung functioning.) Until education insures that more people will reach retirement age with inspiriting activity to engage in, there will be need for counselors of the aged, to help them find rewarding work and avocational pursuits.

THE IMPORTANCE OF SABBATICAL LEAVE

Some universities offer their faculty the opportunity to spend one year in seven away from usual teaching and scholarly duties. The purpose of such sabbatical leave is to provide the teacher with an opportunity for self-renewal, so that he will not stagnate in his work. Everyone is susceptible to becoming "efficient," stereotyped, boring, and bored in his way of being a professional person. Sabbatical leave, when needed, is invaluable. A person's situation imposes a hypnotic spell upon him, so that he may not be able to envision other, more creative ways to work at his calling. A prolonged absence from home base, with opportunity for leisure and study, "dehypnotizes" the person, such that on his return, he can work in more enlivening ways. A person might leave a profession because he found it unrewarding, yet he could have remained in it in productive ways, if he had had sabbatical leave when it was needed. As our nation becomes sufficiently affluent, I believe that it would be a contribution to the quality of existence to make it *mandatory* for people in all vocations to take sabbatical leave each year, or every few years, in order to renew themselves. I suspect that the cost of such leave would be made up by savings in medical costs incurred by bored, miserable, uncreative working men and women.[5]

Play and Healthy Personality

If work is activity which produces a product, play is activity or inactivity which yields the reward of fun. Work can be playful, and yet be work; play is undertaken out of exuberance, out of interest, out of the opportunities that life provides when work to sustain itself has been completed.

Everyone needs meaningful avocational pursuits to make the quality of his life worth living.

People who are engaged in meaningful work, who have rewarding personal relationships, and a vital leisure life seldom become addicts to overeating or excessive alcohol consumption, or users to excess of such intoxicants as marijuana, LSD, or various sedative and antidepressant drugs. These indulgences for instant consciousness change are the refuge of the bored, the uninvolved, and the unimaginative. Although intoxicants and overeating have always been part of every culture, their chronicity is usually destructive of health and life itself.

The trouble with and the attraction of food and drugs is that they afford the experience of instant, unmistakable pleasure. When a person's life is dull or stressing, he will seek to enrich it in any way that he can—seeking to produce a "high." There are periods of unproductivity, stress, and monotony in everyone's existence, but healthy personality is fostered by countering them with the bases for natural highs, that is, with challenging work and play, enjoyment of beauty, and authentic loving and friendly relationships with others. As a psychotherapist, I have observed that indulgence in drugs and overeating has carried a person through some difficult times, harmlessly enough, but such indulgence becomes destructive when it becomes a life style. Many people get drunk or stoned on marijuana when life has dealt them a hard blow, and then they regain strength and perspective, and return soberly to their tasks, none the worse for the blow or the intoxication.

As the length of the work week diminishes (futurists state that in a few decades, no one will work longer than ten or twenty hours weekly, to keep the economy going), the need for "nonproductive" avocational activity will become more apparent.[6] At the present time, it has been noted that among many factory workers, much leisure time is spent watching television and drinking beer; when the work-week has been shortened, the response has been to watch more television and drink more beer.

Undemanding, entertaining literature, movies, televi-

Work, Play, and Healthy Personality

sion, and radio programing serve the same function as drugs and overeating; they offer the experience of pleasure without personal effort. They prevent personal growth and the enlargement of awareness of one's possibilities. Thus, blatant pornography, violent, blood-spattering films, and commercial advertising against a background of popular rock music all insure that the audience will not engage in serious thinking about the human condition, including their own.

Healthy personality is not fostered by any of the sources of instant pleasure, although they may make life endurable for a time. Healthy personality *is* fostered by seeking to cultivate meaningful and absorbing ways to spend time apart from work. Independent security in the avocational sphere of existence is displayed by the person who encounters boredom and the opportunity presented by leisure with efforts to learn new skills, new dimensions of appreciation of beauty, both man-made and natural, and new, challenging games and sports to play.

Some Avocational Pursuits

Play is truly a uniquely human characteristic, although there is reason to suspect that animals also engage in play for the sheer hell of it. Not all animal life is spent in the struggle for survival. Anyone who has seen dogs wrestle to get possession of a stick, or otters slide down a bank,[7] or cats chase a ball of string can hardly doubt that they get bored and are looking for fun. But man can obtain more respite from brute necessity than animals, and, paradoxically enough, he needs to find fun or he will sicken. In our society, with the heavy emphasis that has been placed on upward mobility and professional achievement, many people have spent so much time at their careers that they have not *taken time* to learn how leisure can be spent. In the following pages, I will offer an overview of some kinds of avocational pursuits.

Sports. The value of competitive sports is that they provide a way to obtain physical exercise in an absorbing way. Most city people lack the opportunity for regular use of their bodies in strenuous ways, and unless they take exercise, they become flabby. It is enriching to master a variety of games, as one grows up, so that one can play throughout the life span. Thus, winter and water sports, like skiing, skating, swimming, diving, and sailing can provide solitary and shared play from infancy into old age. An advantage of the more physically active sports is that they afford intellectuals with an opportunity to "still their chattering minds" with involving activity. (I have always found it difficult to stop thinking about aspects of my work, so absorbing has it been. A challenging game of handball never fails to turn off obsessive thinking.)

There are so many sports available to anyone, including those which call for expensive equipment, that no one need be without several, to turn to in various seasons, or when one becomes bored.

Hobbies and Arts. The world of hobbies is inexhaustible. Collecting things, ranging from stones to match covers, has always been rewarding for people. The cultivation of an art—painting, drawing, sculpture, gardening, mastering a musical instrument—develops dimensions of man's possibilities for creating beauty which *should* be developed if man is to broaden his awareness of the possibilities in the world. Jung pointed out how man overdevelops some of his possibilities as he grows up, earns a living, and raises a family. Hobbies and involvement in some of the arts insures that other, dormant possibilities will be awakened, to enrich the person's experience of his life and his contribution to the lives of his friends. No one is more boring as a companion than a person without interests outside his work.

Sedentary Games. There is an entire world of games to be played alone and with others. Chess and checkers, bridge and rummy, Monopoly, Careers, and Scrabble—all challenge one's wits and afford an opportunity to do something with others besides engage in conversation that may not be challenging, or drink. One outcome of commercial television is that it diverted many youngsters from learning games that could be enjoyed with others.

Nature. Nature can balance a person's way of life. In Chapter 3, I noted that contact with nature is a basic human need. It provides rich recreational and life-giving experience to persons in their leisure time. Back packing, camping,

Work,
Play,
and
Healthy
Personality

299

skiing, bird watching, fishing, and hunting (though animal lovers and conservationists rightly protest) are all ways to be in nature in ways that lift one out of the mechanizing influence and rhythms of customary work.

Being with People.   Just being with friends or family to laugh, reminisce, plan, listen to music, walk is one of the most rewarding avocations. The challenge, of course, is to find friends and to establish the kind of mutually confirming personal relationships that makes being with others a source of joy rather than stress (see Chapter 10). Ted Landsman spoke of the "magnification effect" that is produced when one listen to music or watches a sunset with a loved person. Without a loving and confirming relationship, the presence of another person can make one so defensive and "up tight," that the beauties of nature and art cannot be savored. One has to be *open* to appreciate beauty, and a defensive attitude protects one from danger and anesthetizes one to the experience of beauty.

Meditation.   Leisure affords an excellent opportunity for meditation. Meditation is a way of leaving or transcending one's everyday situation, in order to get perspective upon one's life, and to see new possibilities in stagnant situations. In recent years, eastern techniques of meditation have been taught in colleges and at growth centers and institutes around the country. Meditation of any kind—Transcendental Meditation, Raja Yoga, Hatha Yoga, and so on—is a valid approach to personal growth and a meaningful way to spend leisure time.[8]

Personal Growth.   The growth centers (see Chapter 15) have become a community resource for meaningful use of leisure time. As people come to spend less time earning their living, they experience boredom more readily and become increasingly aware that they have other possibilities than the ones they have cultivated. Growth "guides" or counselors may advise a person to take part in encounter groups or other programs that have been developed to evoke new potentialities in persons. Some centers for personal growth offer weekend, or longer, programs, during which people explore themselves and each other, seeking to awaken and confirm new ways to relate to others and to involve themselves in work and play.[9]

Adventure and Excitement.   There are many who find

meaning in adventurous hobbies, such as ocean racing, mountain climbing, automobile racing, motorcycle racing, sky diving, underwater exploration, and the like. Everyone needs some measure of excitement in his life or it palls with boredom. The element of risk to life and to health must be taken into account when a person chooses a more adventurous avocation. Energetic people, however, find that they must take part in such absorbing activities or they cannot take their mind off regular pursuits.

Helping Others. A rich arena for avocational activity is the realm of helping others, either individually or through some kind of community participation. Volunteer activity at boys' and girls' clubs, at crisis centers, old people's homes, hospitals, all afford the person an opportunity to extend himself, to know the lot of others, and to devote some time and resources to their betterment. There are some who see such involvement in helping to improve others' lives, and the quality of the community, as their civic and religious duty.

Being an Amateur "Professional." For every profession there are amateurs who work at it for the fun of it. There are amateur astronomers, pilots, mechanics, sculptors, biologists, zoologists, physicists, and psychologists. An amateur is someone who does what he is doing for the love of it, not for gainful employment. Some great discoveries and contributions to knowledge have been made by amateurs who never made their livelihood at the activity they love. Darwin, for example, was not a professional biologist, in the sense of being salaried by a university or commercial research laboratory, and his contribution to knowledge can hardly be seen as trivial.

Learning and Study As leisure increases, the importance of schools and community colleges increases. Some observers have estimated that before the twenty-first century is reached, continuing education will be the most important activity for the world's population—assuming problems of poverty, war, and destruction of the environment have been solved. Perhaps a ceaseless life of learning is the means whereby everyone can renew himself, find new ways to appreciate the world, and enrich his quality as a companion to others. So long as a person has life, he can always learn a new language, a new art, a new body of knowledge.

Healthy Personality and Leisure

A rich avocational life yields many benefits of value for healthy personality. Most obvious, it lends balance to life, especially when one's vocation calls for specialized use of the self. My work calls for me to be sedentary, and in the experiential mode of thinking (see Chapter 3). I find that competitive games (handball, tennis, water sports) are effective at lending balance to my life, affording an opportunity for release of tensions engendered at work.

Another benefit lies in the fact, noted above, that the demands, challenges, and companionship found in one's leisure pursuits foster personal growth in enriching ways. One's regular occupational and household duties call for the development of some human possibilities, but these are in the realm of practical functioning. The beauty of one's hobbies is that they call for the development of aesthetic, athletic, emotional, and intellectual powers which otherwise would remain dormant.

Some Existential Suggestions

If you are not fascinated with or passionate about the vocation you are in (or training for), it is valuable to go on a retreat, to seek some perspective, and perhaps some new aspects or opportunities in one's work. I find that if I can get completely away from my work for periods of time, I re-enter it renewed.

It is enriching, as well, to find leisure activity that is diametrically opposed to one's work in as many ways as possible. When I was a student, I sought part-time jobs at heavy physical labor, I worked on a carnival, in stores, and at a children's camp. The experience these jobs afforded was enriching, and it counterbalanced the heavy emphasis upon the intellect in college. Sedentary people might well balance their existences with hobbies of a more physical sort.

Solitary leisure pursuits are invaluable. One cannot always have company, and so reading, playing a musical instrument, painting, or engaging in some craft are all enriching avocations.

A twenty-year-old student who had attempted suicide was consulting me as a patient. The occasion for his attempt at self-destruction was his rejection by his girl friend. During our conversation I discovered that he had never extended himself in his studies, and during the time of his relationship with this girl (three years), he had done nothing but "be" with her and do minimal school work. I challenged him to pick up the sports and hobbies he had neglected during his orgy of dependency. He accepted the challenge, and it was good for him.

SUMMARY

Work and leisure both play important roles in healthy personality. Choice of a vocation especially is important, because it is the means of making a livelihood, and one spends nearly a third of one's life at work. People choose their work on the basis of parental influence, psychological tests, and sometimes on impulse. Whatever the basis for the initial choice, the person serves the interest of healthy personality if he faces the consequences of his choice realistically. If there is little satisfaction in his work, he will change it. However, many factors make vocational change difficult, for example, one's sense of identity and other people's expectations.

Absorbing avocational pursuits contribute to the enjoyment of life and provide balance to one's working activities. The quest for instant pleasure through drugs, alcohol, or television usually signifies a deficient avocational life. Challenging sports and hobbies, games, relaxation with nature, meditation, pursuit of growth, adventure, company of friends, learning, and study all serve valuable avocational purposes.

NOTES AND REFERENCES

1. Meaningful work is essential for a firm sense of identity. Erikson calls work the "sense of industry." See E. H. ERIKSON, *Identity, Youth and Crisis* (New York: Norton, 1968), pp. 122–128.

2. Blatz recognized this problem before the age of automation and increased leisure. He insisted that training for "avocation" was as important as vocational training. See W. E. BLATZ, *Understanding the Young Child* (New York: Morrow, 1944).

Work, Play, and Healthy Personality

3. BLATZ, op. cit.

4. D. McCLELLAND, *The Achieving Society* (New York: The Free Press, 1967). The Greeks called it *areté*, which means, roughly, "courage in battle," or more generally, "prowess"; it was the goal of classical education in ancient Greece. See W. JAEGER, *Paideia: The Ideals of Greek Culture*, Vol. I: *Archaic Greece: The Mind of Athens* (New York: Oxford University Press, 1965).

5. See W. HARMON, *"Humanistic Capitalism: Another Alternative"* (mimeographed manuscript, Stanford Research Institute, Menlo Park, Calif., 1972).

6. For a perspective on life in the future, see J. C. BROWN, *The Troika Incident* (Garden City, N.Y.: Doubleday, 1970). Brown has explored work, play, family life, and other aspects of human existence as it can be in less than 100 years. His utopian vision seems more feasible, and more fit for human beings than Skinner's *Walden Two*.

7. The late Gavin Maxwell knew the fun and mischief of others. See G. MAXWELL, *Ring of Bright Water* (New York: Dutton, 1961).

8. C. NARANJO and R. E. ORNSTEIN, *On the Psychology of Meditation* (New York: Viking, 1971).

9. See W. SCHUTZ, *Here Comes Everybody: Bodymind and Encounter Culture* (New York: Harper & Row, 1971) for an exposition of what growth centers can offer. See also JANE HOWARD, *Please Touch* (New York: McGraw-Hill, 1970).

*Healthy
Personality:
An Approach
from the
Viewpoint of
Humanistic
Psychology*

14

RELIGIOUS ORIENTATIONS
AND HEALTHY PERSONALITY

INTRODUCTION

Man is a freak within nature. Animals simply live their lives until it is no longer possible. They do not wonder whether it is worth it. Man needs reasons for living, and if there are none, he begins to die. Man not only needs reasons for living; he also needs, more than animals, to learn how to live, how to survive and prevail in the world where he is born.

For millennia, religion provided man with reasons for continuing to live when living became difficult, and knowledge to master the hostile forces of untamed nature. These functions of religion are more evident among primitive people than they are in modern, industrialized societies, although the Old and New Testaments of the Judeo-Christian Bible explicitly tell man that he must live["I call heaven and earth to witness against you this day, that I have set before thee life and death, the blessing and the curse; therefore, choose life, that thou mayest live, thou and thy seed" (Deuteronomy, 30,19), Jahveh is quoted as telling the Hebrews, through Moses], and how to live. The decalogue, the ex-

tended accounts of laws, ordinances, and prohibitions contained in Deuteronomy, have been likened to divinely presented instruction to man in agriculture, ecology, intergroup relationships, family counseling, dietetics, and morale-building. The Sermon on the Mount is an explicit lesson on how to live with one's fellows.

In primitive religions the myths tell of how the world began and how the gods showed the way to hunt, fish, till the soil, live with one another, and make tools and weapons. At sacred times of each year, primitive peoples retell the account of their beginnings and celebrate their good fortune at having been blessed with ancestors who chose to start the world and show them how to live in it. The ways of living in primitive societies are sacred; there is no aspect of life which does not require the blessing of the gods for its success and which is not regulated by strict taboos. Indeed, in such societies, to fail to observe the taboos is to threaten the existence of the group, and so violation is punished by expulsion or death.[1] There is no need for Eskimos to execute someone who does not hunt in the way revealed by their gods. If he does not hunt seals in the way of his people, he will not kill any, and he will die. Eskimos would kill only those who violated taboos about ways to live harmoniously with one another, because these would create group dissension. In the brutish conditions of the polar Arctic, Eskimos had to cooperate in hunting and to share their food, their spouses, and their tools or life would have been impossible.

Modern man has "desacralized" most of his life. For man, religion has become less a living reality and more a ritual which gives people something to do on sabbath Saturday or Sunday. Few people pray to get their automobiles started or to insure success in a sales campaign—they call the mechanic or the salesmanship consultant. Yet religion lurks beneath the surface of the consciousness of even the most outspoken atheists and agnostics, for whom no formal religious symbols are experienced as sacred. Man is incurably religious. What varies among men is what they are religious about.

What Is Religion?

Beyond all else, religion is an *experience*, the experience of being addressed by a divine presence, of being called.

Healthy
Personality:
An Approach
from the
Viewpoint of
Humanistic
Psychology

William James' [2] classic *The Varieties of Religious Experience* gives many accounts of persons who felt their egos dissolve and experienced union with all life, indeed all the universe. The lives of the Christian saints and Hebrew prophets also offer first-person accounts of what it feels like to be spoken to by God, or to believe oneself to be Jahveh's spokesman.

Religion is also the experience of the sacred and holy. The symbols and representatives of God inspire an attitude of awe and reverence among the faithful adherents to any formal religion. The experience of the sacred involves fear of the power of God, and sometimes an attitude of loving surrender, entrusting one's life to the good will of the deity.[3]

The great religions also function as *ethical systems* for their followers, providing them with instructions in living that are deemed to be of divine origin. The assumption is that if people will live with one another in the ways described in their scriptures or in the oral traditions, then life will be long, fruitful, and peaceful.

Religion provides man with the definition of *ultimate concern* and value.[4] "God's will" is held to be the highest purpose of living in the Judeo-Christian and Mohammedan faiths. Some aspects of God's will are explicitly stated in the scriptures of those religions, whereas others are left unclear, calling for guidance from priests, rabbis, and holy men. Whatever a person takes to be the highest value in life can be regarded as his god, the focus and purpose of his time and life. Thus, a person may devote his life to the accumulation of wealth or the acquisition of political power. He may live for eating, for indulging in sex, or for keeping the love of his parents at all costs. Whatever a person spends his time and effort for, even to the point of endangering his health and his life, can be seen as his equivalent to God, the ultimate concern of concerns. The Old Testament regards such uses and aims of one's life as the gravest sin of all, the sin of *idolatry*. It was punished by death, because any deviation from living in the ways prescribed by Jahveh, through Moses, was a serious threat to the Hebrew people's lives and to their group solidarity.[5]

Religious Orientations and Healthy Personality

Many students raised in some orthodox religious tradition abandon it when they attain the capacity for independent thought and criticism. After taking courses in psychology, sociology, and comparative religion, they find that what their parents or clergymen presented as absolute truth was not. Indeed, some students find that the Bible has been used to justify outright tyranny, as in the case of white exploitation of black peoples and the anti-Semitic attitudes of bigoted Christians. After reading and discussion, many students come to see the faith of their childhood and of their parents as superstition and as an obstacle to life itself. Yet religion of some form is part of the human condition. One does not have the choice between being religious or not. One only chooses what one will be religious about, and the ways in which one will be religious.

Religion is thus a *way of being*. To act religiously means that one will not let anything interfere with the action in question. The primitive person would never consider living in any way other than the way of his people, which he believes was taught by the founding gods. Even to think about some other way of relating to parents than the prescribed way would inspire dread. The experience of dread is the anticipation of some unspeakable punishment and death for violating a taboo. Many supposedly nonreligious students do things religiously, such as take exercise, study their textbooks, or pursue popularity, motivated by vague feelings of dread. They do these things as if their lives depended on it. Religion, in this sense, appears to resemble rigidity and compulsion, like the ritual obsessions and compulsions found in some neurotically disturbed persons.

Everyone begins his life indoctrinated with the religion of his family and community. The family religion is part of the "facticity" which each person has to do something with, as he must do something with all other aspects of his situation. He can acquiesce and follow in his religious tradition, ignore it, change it, rebel against it—but as in all other existential situations, he is free to take a stand. His personal religious orientation, like his conscience, becomes his responsibility. We can speak, then, of personal religious orientation as an achievement and a challenge. Further, we can evaluate whether a person's religious orientation is conducive to growth and to satisfaction in living, or whether it is an impediment to healthy personality. Some students may prefer to use the term *philosophy of life* rather than religion, because the latter term may signify a belief in a

Healthy Personality: An Approach from the Viewpoint of Humanistic Psychology

supreme being, and they prefer to be atheistic or agnostic. For our purposes, it does not matter, because we are using the term *religion* in a way which reconciles any contradiction between belief in a God as such and a philosophy of living which a person follows religiously, as his view of the good life.

A religious orientation is healthy if it enhances life and fosters growth of one's powers as a human being, including the power to love, to be productive and creative. Thus, no matter whether a person be Christian, Jew, Moslem, Hindu, or Buddhist, the criterion of whether his religion is healthy is provided not by the piety and scrupulosity of his ritual observances, but by its effect upon life. Is he a vital, loving, strong, growing person who does not diminish others? Or is his piety accompanied by prudery, inability to love others, and lack of joy in living. I have often served as a psychotherapist to clergymen and members of their families. I found that much of the suffering was a direct outcome of their need to *appear* pious before themselves and others. The action essential to make their lives more livable was initially experienced by them as sinful. Actually, their religion, the object of their ultimate concern, was not God so much as a "respectable" appearance, in the name of which they were sacrificing the joy and vitality of their lives. Some clergymen felt they could only begin to live religious lives, that is, lives which served their God (life itself, not a church, or a church organization) if they left the organized church. And so they did.

Idolatry: Unhealthy Personal Religions

In the times portrayed in the Old Testament, idolatry was taken to be the ultimate sin.[6] Idolatry meant worshiping and living for the products of man's hands, or natural objects—in any case, gods which are less than the "one and true God" (Jehovah, or Jahveh). In an effort to demystify some aspects of the Judaic and Christian faiths, I have tried, as an hypothesis, to replace the word *God* with the word *Life,* or Life itself. Thus, where the Old Testament might say, "God spoke to Moses," I would restate it as, "Life 'spoke' to Moses." This is another way of saying that Moses, in a moment of keen insight and ultimate concern, "saw" the connection between some way of living and the flowering or destruction of life itself. "Idolatry" would mean equating some part of life with *all* of life. Thus, no animal, stone, place, or person could merit "worship"—living in ways to enhance the "god"—without peril to the worshiper. If idolatry was a "sin," then a sin must mean action which destroys life, if not at once, then ultimately. Indeed, the word *sin* means "off the mark," as in archery when the bowman is aiming and shooting inaccurately. A more contemporary interpretation of sin would be "off the beam"—as an airplane straying off the radar track.

True devotion to God would mean "living in a life-giving way." Sentences like "God loves a repentant sinner" would mean that, if a person had been living in a sickening, even lethal way, then to repent would mean to "turn," to stop living in a destructive way. Such cessation of devitalizing ways of life would instantly start a healing process—which may account in part for "miracle" cures and faith-healing. If the sinner then lived in a more vitalizing way, he would enjoy abundant health and a more richly livable existence. In this way, I can see a connection between the religious teachings of the Jewish and Christian bibles and the secular principles of healthy personality.

The secular problem, of course, is akin to the formal religious problem of how to discern what God, or Life itself, demands of a person if "God's will is to be done," or if life itself is to be enhanced. Authoritarian answers, learned by rote from some scriptural source, or from some clergyman, are not viable guides to action, nor do they foster growth in the persons dependent upon such authority for guidance. Clearly, to live in the way demanded by life itself calls for continuous independent study and learning, for growth of the abilities to perceive, think, reason, and see connections between one's condition and ways of living. Thus, a person whose life is blocked or vexed by disease, failure, stagnation, or other decrements of vitality must enlarge his perspective to see vitalizing ways out of the dilemma. Authentic prayer to God works for persons who are formally religious. When they say they prayed, and God "showed them the way out," what happened was that the act of "surrender" involved in dialogue with the deity enabled a person to suspend his present perspective and experience a larger view (see Chap-

Healthy Personality: An Approach from the Viewpoint of Humanistic Psychology

ter 2). A less formally theistic person would consult "life itself" as a guide to experimental action. The experience of enlivenment would provide him with proof that new paths of experiencing and action were the right ones for him.

It would be elegant if the experience of vitality functioned as a steady beam in the background of a person's awareness, so that he could swiftly notice when his experience and action were sapping his life. He could then change something in his situation before he sickened. Reich believed that persons had the capacity to "tune in" to their vital energy so as to avoid devitalizing relationships and roles. The re-embodying techniques mentioned in Chapter 6 can serve this function by enhancing sensitivity to the body.

SOME COMMON IDOLATRIES

Grades. Idolatry of grades or of popularity has produced suffering among many students. They pursue these goals at the expense of their health and of close, loving relationships with others. I have served as therapist to students who failed to develop a single close friendship during several years at college, so obsessed were they with the necessity to maintain a straight "A" average.

Breeding. Worship of a large family, or at least regarding restriction of the number of births as some kind of sin, is now an idolatrous form of religious practice. Excessive breeding produces overcrowding, pollution, and the incipient pressure to war and revolution that one finds in all overpopulated areas, such as parts of New York, Bombay, San Juan, Djakarta, and China.

Love Affairs. A love affair becomes idolatrous, ceasing to engender and enhance life for the lovers and others when its pursuit results in the neglect of true interests on the part of one or the other of the lovers. A true interest is any activity, relationship, or object which is essential to life, and the neglect of which diminishes life. Thus, a student might enter an affair which at first lends zest to the existence of the lovers. When continuation results in neglect of work, when jealousy and possessiveness endanger health, then to continue the affair is to neglect true interests. The affair has become idolatrous, destructive of life.

Thus, *life itself* becomes the criterion for judging whether or not those activities, relationships, institutions, and life

Religious Orientations and Healthy Personality

styles which one pursues religiously are compatible with healthy personality. If a religious way of life is vital and meaningful and if the conditions for life objectively are being met, then it is a healthy religion. Otherwise, it is not. It is in this light, for example, that the Catholic prohibitions against divorce, birth control, and celibacy among priests and nuns are undergoing very careful, indeed agonizing, appraisal among intelligent Catholics and within the higher ranks of the Catholic hierarchy.

Family Structure. The present form of family life held to be ideal and perhaps divinely inspired in the Western world is likewise being challenged as idolatrous (nonlife-giving) by many younger people. The experimental search for alternative life styles, communal marriages, "open marriage," polygyny and polygamy, marriages contracted on an annual basis, with options for renewal—all these attest to the realization among more educated people that a form of life, once sanctioned by the churches as holy, must be changed when it is discovered to diminish and destroy, rather than enhance, life. Formal religion frequently becomes the spokesman for traditions which have lost meaning and which diminish life among the traditional observers.

Suicide and Bases for Existence

Suicide is illegal in our society, and it is regarded as contrary to the teachings of the Judeo-Christian religions. There are times when to give up one's life or to take it can be seen as the most meaningful and loving action a person can undertake, as an expression of the affirmation of life. Thus, in times of war a person may give up his life to save many others. It is not that such a hero detests his life; rather he sees that he can fulfill the meaning of his life best in that situation by giving it up so that others may live. Some suicides can also be seen as expressions of the affirmation of life, as when an elderly person chooses to die from an overdose of drugs or a self-inflicted wound rather than face years of invalidism, pain, and solitude.

A person may come to equate his present identity with the only basis that he has for the possibility of living at all. It is as if he is saying to himself, "The only way in which I know that I can exist, and that I deserve to exist, is if I have the love of my parents, or if I get the highest grades, or if

Healthy Personality: An Approach from the Viewpoint of Humanistic Psychology

312

I am loved by that girl." The problem with such flimsy bases for identity as warrants for existence is that when the parental love is taken away, the affair breaks up, or a course is failed, the person becomes convinced that he can no longer live at all. He may then attempt suicide. When someone has been seen by the community as an honest person and he is proven to have stolen sums of money that have been entrusted to him, he may commit suicide rather than acknowledge to the world that he has been living under false pretenses.

The wish to be dead thus can function as a test of the life-giving power of one's personal religion or philosophy. If it is a healthy religion, a person will be able to find new possibilities in life even when he has lost that which had previously given life its zest.

Healthy Religion and Humanistic Conscience

Steady contact with one's sense of vitality and enlivenment functions as the basis of humanistic conscience.[7] It will be recalled that humanistic conscience functions as a "call," or a summons, to desist from some way of living which was "sinful" ("disobedient" to the laws of life), or off the beam, and a moral command to "come round right." If authoritarian sources of conscience have truly been replaced by a humanistic conscience, a person can then entrust his experience of guilt to guide him in ways of living that insure healthy personality. Authoritarian conscience refers to moral precepts that have been taken uncritically from parents and clergy; conforming with these precepts engenders diminished life. Thus, to a person still afflicted beyond childhood with an authoritarian conscience, sin would be defined as violation of taboos, and virtue as obedience (to authority, not to life), without reasonable consideration of whether the taboos have any relevance or contribution to the quality of life. The person who has achieved a health-engendering humanistic conscience has a different sense of sin and guilt. Guilt is engendered when he diminishes life in himself and others, not when he violates some rule imposed upon him by his parents, through the medium of an authoritarian conscience. The latter represents another kind of "idol," obedience to which diminishes life.

The words to a hymn attributed to the Shakers (a now-defunct Christian sect which flourished in the late nineteenth century in the United States) express the concept of sin and of humanistic conscience in a beautiful way. The irony is that the Shakers died out because they did not believe in sexual intercourse; the articles of their religious faith were authoritarian and nonlife-giving, despite the hymn:

Simple Gifts

'Tis a gift to be simple, 'tis a gift to be free
'Tis a gift to come down, where we ought to be
And when we find ourselves in the place just right
We will be in the valley of love and delight.
When true simplicity is gained
To bow and to bend we will not be ashamed
To turn, turn, will be our delight
'Til by turning, turning, we come round right. [my italics]

Religion, Attitude Toward Death, and Healthy Personality

Only man, among all living creatures, can know he will die. A person may experience death as an abstract concept which has no connection with his life and no influence upon the way that he lives. He may live his life routinely, giving no thought to the way in which he spends his days. Existential philosophers designate such automatic, unreflective lives as inauthentic. According to these philosophers, *authentic* existence begins when one's own death becomes a reality, when a person encounters death in some inescapable way such that after the realization, he knows his years are finite. It often takes serious illness or a nearly fatal accident to give vivid meaning to death. Such experiences confront a person with the challenge to *choose,* to decide how he will spend his life, where he will live it, with whom he will live, and how he will make his living. Death forces a person to question the meaning of life in general, and of his own life in particular. Many people make radical changes in their lives following the encounter with death, such as marrying or divorcing, changing jobs, spending more time with children or in nature, than they had hitherto.

Death is so inexplicable and so terrifying for many that they repress all awareness of it; they refuse to think about the death of parents or friends, and they may believe vigorously in a life after death, so that death will "lose its sting." Although hopes for an afterlife in some version of Heaven may give comfort to people whose actual lives are dismal, such hopes make people resign themselves to miserable conditions which could conceivably be ameliorated.

One of my students, Sharon Graham, did an experiment to explore the relationship between attitude toward death and styles of interpersonal relationship. She found that college students who believed in some form of afterlife did not enter relationships in ways as intense and mutually self-revealing as did students who accepted the reality and finality of their personal deaths. It was as if, because they had acknowledged that they would die, they could not waste time in trivial or superficial personal relationships.[8]

One's personal religion, if it functions to foster and maintain healthy personality, can be expected to help a person live authentically with the fact of his death. A healthy religious philosophy should encourage him to live decisively, intensely, and in growth-promoting ways. There is life-giving value in a religion which provides comfort and meaning to life when suffering and death must be experienced; however, it is an unhealthy religion, indeed, which functions only as a tranquilizer and does not encourage a person to live fully and with growing awareness in the time he has.

The reality of death is even denied in hospitals, where physicians and nurses frequently conceal the imminence of death from patients with terminal conditions. Thus, the patient is denied the opportunity to encounter death while he is still conscious and able to give structure and meaning to the life behind him. Elizabeth Kubler-Ross,[9] a Chicago psychiatrist, pioneered a seminar on dying, in an effort to help clergymen, doctors, and nurses to handle their own fears of death, so that they, in turn, could help dying patients face death in noninfantile fashion.

Religion, Culture Change, and Healthy Personality

Religious Orientations and Healthy Personality

Every person learns from his predecessors how to relate to others in "the right way," the way that is sacred; he learns, not just how to till the soil, hunt, fish, wear clothes, raise children, but how to do these things *in the way of his family, or his people.* These ways are deemed sacred, not to be ques-

315

tioned, much less altered, because in being sacred they are held to be ways commanded by God or the gods, and hence essential to life itself. This is the authoritarian religion of which Erich Fromm wrote. So long as a group lives in a stable physical environment, with unchanging technology and resources, the traditional, religiously lived ways may be compatible with survival of the group and a rich, meaningful life for individuals. But when society changes, crises arise for the society as a whole and for individual members. The traditional way of life which gave meaning and direction to individual existence becomes an obstacle to survival in the changed circumstances facing the group. Tradition then becomes idolatrous rather than life-enhancing. Traditional ways and values interfere with new learning essential for adaptation to the changed times. But the new ways may be deemed sinful from the perspective of the traditional religion. Thus, immigrants to America often found themselves scandalized at their children's "immorality" as they became acculturated.

In developing countries facing industrialization and overpopulation as in India, or Indonesia, the young people are addressed by the challenge and temptations of a way of life made possible by modern technology, but the clutch of tradition and traditional religion produces powerful conflict. In contemporary America, children born after World War II have lived in a world of increased affluence and technological magic, so that television, space travel, and world travel by cheap jet transportation are a normal part of their existence. The possibilities for living in ways that differ from their parents' have increased radically. And so young people, especially of the age of high school and college students, face conflicts between tradition, in the form of parental expectations, and the realities of their present situation. Traditional religions in the West have not been helpful in the solution of the problem of how to live; indeed, in America, growing numbers of clergymen of all denominations have been leaving their established churches to live secular lives which they find more viable than efforts to live as clergymen.

Healthy personality calls for a sense of values and meaning in life that give existence a purpose. Rapid cultural change challenges institutionalized authoritarian religions. Many young people in America have begun to explore na-

Healthy Personality: An Approach from the Viewpoint of Humanistic Psychology

tive American Indian religions, such as the Peyote cults, and Eastern religions, such as Hinduism, Yoga, and Buddhism, for guidance in their lives. Others are exploring mystical branches of traditional faiths, such as Hasidism within Judaism, Sufism—a mystical branch of Islamic faith, astrology, the I Ching, tarot. Others become "reborn Christians" and dedicate themselves fervently to following in the ways of Jesus Christ. All these current explorations of guides to existence can be seen as expressions of a sense of uncertainty about how to live in the midst of changing times, when old guidelines provided by parents, churches, or tradition no longer sustain life.

MYSTICISM AND HEALTHY PERSONALITY

People turn to mysticism when traditional ways of life are no longer possible because of catastrophe, conquest by another people, or the effects of technology. Mystical religions and practices can function as sources of creativity and inventive ways to live. They also can encourage a kind of anti-intellectual attitude, a distrust of reason which ultimately proves disastrous. There is mystery in life, and rational thinking is not always a reliable way to solve riddles of existence. Mystical practices may indeed enable a person to tap sources of creativity buried within him, so that problems of existence can be solved as if by inspiration. If mystical practices eventuate in more creative ways to live, then they are compatible with healthy personality. If they serve as evasions of responsibility for the search for viable ways, so that a person depends upon his horoscope or some equally impersonal guide to choice, then he is replacing one rigid religion with another. His health and personal growth are not likely to be fostered through such dependency. There is no alternative to a personal search for meaning and direction when traditional guides to existence have been outdated by changing times. Although the search is seldom easy, no one can do it for another person anymore than someone else can do one's own dying.

Religious Orientations and Healthy Personality

Religion and Healing

Sick people do not always respond to conventional medical treatment and some turn in desperate hope to religious systems of healing, or to healers who work from the standpoint of a different theory of illness and its treatment. The Catholic shrine at Lourdes, in France, attracts millions who make the pilgrimage there in search of a medical miracle. Many regain their health, or at least arrest the lethal development of the symptoms which brought them to their quest. Clergymen are consulted by the gravely ill, to pray with and for them, that they may overcome their diseases and gain new hope and life. From time to time, new healers with extraordinary powers appear and gain a following. For example, a Brazilian cab driver, Lourival de Freitas, performed many operations with an unsterilized pen knife, apparently opening abdomens to remove tumors and puncturing eyes without harm to his patients. In the Philippines, the Reverend Tony Agpao and his assistant appear to part flesh and bone with their bare hands. He functions as a nonmedical "surgeon" to Philippine and American patients who seek his services. I viewed a color film made by one patient who had been operated on by Mr. Agpao's assistant— I saw his bare hands kneading the area to be opened, and then it seemed to open, with blood spilling from the wound. What looked like blood clots, tendons, and bits of flesh were snipped off, and then the sides of the wounds were pressed together. In a twinkling, it "healed" without seam or scar. The entire "operation" took less than five minutes. There was no pain. In the same film I saw Mr. Agpao's hand apparently open the abdomens of several gravely ill patients, three of whom were in the room with me watching the film. He tells his patients to change their lives after they have been healed.

Mr. Naidu, a Kali healer in Guiana, South America, has an impressive record of healing psychosis, kidney disease, cancer, and other illnesses. His system is deceptively simple —he prays with his patient, tries to discover how the patient is "living wrong," and urges him to "live right." He does not accept his fee unless the patient gets well. If the patient does not respond to the initial consultation, Mr. Naidu prays and fasts for several days. If there is yet no response, he prays, fasts, and walks on coals. In the last instance, the patient almost without exception gets well.

Evangelizing clergymen often carry out healing ceremonies characterized by prayer and the laying on of hands. Laymen abound who discover that they can heal by a touch, or a massage, and that they see an "aura" of diverse color emanating from the body which changes magnitude and hue with changes in health.

I have never seen an aura, which does not mean it does not exist. I retain an open mind about the more (to me) astonishing aspects of healing through faith, but I hold to a theory of illness which helps me to make sense out of confirmed instances of healing through prayer, ritual, and the healer's charisma.

According to this view, people sicken because they do not "live right," as Mr. Naidu puts it. When ill, they are frightened, and frequently without hope. The initiation of an attitude of hope is itself healing, or it initiates the healing reflexes. Anything which arouses hope and faith will arrest a progressive disease and permit healing to begin. If the sick person will then change his life from the style which engendered his disease to one that is more life-giving, then he will not only regain his health, but he will keep it. Both Mr. Naidu and Mr. Agpao insist that their patients must change their lives if they are to stay healthy.

This rationale appears to underlie the Christian Science system of healing. The emphasis upon understanding how one has become sickened, the mobilization of hope, and the changing of style of life from one that sickened to one that heals appears to be a common denominator in the non-medical healing approaches. Probably in those cases where such treatment is both effective and harmless, it accounts for healing brought on by conventional medical intervention too.

I believe that as more research is done, medical approaches to healing will be altered in the direction of the religious ways, so that pharmaceutical and surgical methods will increasingly be replaced by rest, meditation, and alteration of life style to one that engenders and maintains health.[10]

Religion and a Good Society

A person's religious orientation, if it is to foster healthy personality, must be re-examined at various stages in his life. The child begins life with an authoritarian religious orientation. If he is a growing person, he will eventually come to doubt and challenge the arbitrariness of the taboos and commandments which comprise this faith. As a person learns about life, it is to be expected that he will modify his

Religious Orientations and Healthy Personality

religious views in the light of reason. Many people simply replace one orthodoxy with another, when their faith in the first has been shaken. Thus, an authoritarian Baptist may become converted to Judaism or Catholicism and be more strict in ritual observance than persons reared in those faiths. Some students abandon their family religious tradition and pursue astrology, psychology, transcendental meditation, or Yoga with the same fanaticism and lack of critical perspective they showed toward the family faith. If one's religious orientation is health- and growth-engendering, then it will prove itself by its consequences. The test of one's religion is in the quality of existence that it evokes, in the meaning it gives to life, and in the life-enhancing effect it has in the midst of life itself. Religion, in its truest sense, is a relentless *search* for life. Organized religion—the churches—frequently provide *answers,* and interfere with, even prevent, the search.

History is a record of oppressive social and political systems in which masses of men were exploited in cruel, dehumanizing ways. History likewise provides accounts of the way in which organized religion did nothing to encourage exploited people to act courageously and intelligently to improve their lot. The history of the Christian and Islamic faiths yields at least some evidence to show that their official leadership often colluded with the political leadership to maintain the political and economic status quo. The orthodox church of czarist Russia did little to reduce the aristocrats' exploitation of workers and peasants, and in World War II persons of the same faith slaughtered each other, presumably in the conviction that God was on their side.

Healthy personality calls for enlightened perspectives upon the society within which one lives, and it calls for active engagement in providing social conditions suitable for humans to live and to develop their potentialities. If one's personal religion does not encourage him to grow in understanding of his society, and to protest unjust policies, then it is no more than a tranquilizer; it is then the "opium of the masses," as Marx saw it, or culturally shared compulsion neurosis, which Freud maintained it was.

One of the functions of organized religion should be to produce heaven on earth. In less ornate language, this means striving to find ways to govern and to organize society in ways that are just. Justice, in this sense, means that everyone has the opportunity to realize his possibilities as a human being, no matter what his class, religious or ethnic origins, or sex. In a sense, religion is a quest for, and offers a vision of, a utopia.

UTOPIAS, CHURCHES, AND HEALTHY PERSONALITY

There have been many efforts to describe utopian societies, for example, Samuel Butler's *Erewhon,* Plato's *Republic,* Aldous Huxley's nightmare utopia *The Brave New World,* and George Orwell's chilling vision of life in *1984.* Even Hitler's view of society, as described in *Mein Kampf,* was a kind of utopia for Germans, but not, of course, for the victims of the Nazi regime he organized. Canaan, the promised land, was to be utopia for the ancient Hebrews. B. F. Skinner described a utopian society in *Walden Two* organized along lines suggested by his theories of human conditioning. James Brown has described how the world might be in 2070 A.D. in his novel *The Troika Incident.* The student is encouraged to read as much of the utopian literature as he can find, because everyone is a utopian thinker, implicitly or explicitly; everyone affirms some view of the good life in a good society, and one should be informed about the way some good thinkers have portrayed these.

The trouble with utopias is that one person's heaven is another person's hell. A way to organize society, distributing resources and wealth so as to enrich the life of one group, produces tyranny, mystification, and exploitation for another. A male-dominated society may be utopian for men in our culture, but it hardly pleases those women who have become aware of limitations imposed on them because of their sex. South Africa produced a near-utopian society for white native-born Afrikaaners, but the more than 15 million blacks hardly see the policy of *apartheid* as utopian for them.

The challenge for organized religion and churches is to examine whether their preaching has contributed to economic and political regimes that are just and utopian for *all* sectors of the population. Throughout history, churches have taken sides with the ruling elite, in opposition to larger sectors of the population which have felt themselves unjustly exploited. There is no record of protest from church officials at the annihilation of Aztec, Inca, Mayan, or North American Indian cultures and religions. The Christian

Religious Orientations and Healthy Personality

321

utopian view was not utopian for the "natives." A religious denomination and its church is compatible with healthy personality if it champions and works for the establishment of a just society in which none feels exploited, because none is, and where the means to foster healthy personality and the fullest personal growth are available to all.

Those who attend churches and synagogues can work toward the "de-dogmatizing" of official church positions on contemporary affairs. There was hardly a ripple of comment when a news item issued by a Protestant church economic council appeared showing that the organized Protestant churches in the United States had investments of over $300 million in prime war industries—at a time when the United States was involved in the Vietnam War.

The so-called Protestant ethic, which affirms the virtue of hard work, postponement of pleasure, and accumulation of capital, is itself under challenge by growing numbers of people. The character structure which made the development of the capitalist economy possible is incompatible with living in the affluent society which that "driven" character type produced. The antisensuality of the Protestant ethic is the special target of several authors who were reared in that world view, for example, Thomas Hanna (*Bodies in Revolt*), Sam Keen (*To a Dancing God*), Norman O. Brown (*Loves Body*), and Michael D. Lowman (*The Phoenix*). The religiosity with which human energy and natural resources were dedicated to the expansion of capital destroys the quality of life for many, and so Protestantism itself is under serious re-examination, in order to undo the apparent collusion between political and economic systems and church doctrine.[11]

So long as there is poverty, exploitation of people, and destruction of the environmental conditions for life, there is ample challenge to everyone's religion to seek to make the world and its myriad societies a place where healthy personality is possible for everyone.

Some Existential Suggestions

Institutionalized religion readily becomes more institutionalized than life-giving to the persons it is supposed to serve. It is enlightening for a person to learn about religions

Healthy Personality: An Approach from the Viewpoint of Humanistic Psychology

322

other than the one in which he has been reared. If he has prejudices and misinformation about other faiths, he will be serving the interests of healthy personality if he corrects his misconceptions and outgrows his prejudices.

It is especially good to learn about Eastern religions, as their influence spreads from the East to this hemisphere. It is rewarding to reread the Old and New Testaments as a grown person, struggling to identify with the perspectives of Moses, Jesus, and the various prophets, as an exercise in historical and sociological imagination.

SUMMARY

Religion provides men with reasons for living, with a system of ethics, with the experience of the sacred, with a focus for ultimate concern. A religious orientation contributes to healthy personality if it enhances life and fosters growth of one's capacities to love and grow.

Idolatry, in contemporary life, means living for something less than life itself, for example, for success, wealth, or one's family. One's religion is idolatrous if it does not provide daily existence with life-giving challenge and meaning. A healthy religion enables a person to live decisively and to face death with courage. It preserves human values during times of culture change. There is healing power in profound religious fatih. A healthy religion does not collude with the ruling elite of a nation, but instead helps men struggle to achieve a just society.

NOTES AND REFERENCES

1. See M. ELIADE, *The Sacred and the Profane: The Nature of Religion* (New York: Harper & Row, 1961). This book was an eye opener for me and taught me much about religion as experience of the sacred.

2. W. JAMES, *The Varieties of Religious Experience* (New York: Macmillan, 1961). (Originally published in 1902.)

3. ELIADE, op. cit.; R. OTTO, *The Experience of the Holy* (Oxford: Oxford University Press, 1958).

4. P. TILLICH, *Systematic Theology,* 3 volumes (Chicago: University of Chicago Press, 1963).

5. E. FROMM, *You Shall Be as Gods: A Radical Interpretation of the Old Testament and Its Tradition* (New York: Holt,

Religious Orientations and Healthy Personality

1966), pp. 44 ff. See also his *Psychoanalysis and Religion* (New Haven: Yale University Press, 1950).

6. My debt to Fromm, in this discussion, is obvious. See FROMM, op. cit. I have also been influenced by Martin Buber's writings. See M. BUBER, *Eclipse of God: Studies in the Relation Between Religion and Philosophy* (New York: Harper & Row, 1957); *Two Types of Faith: A Study of the Interpenetration of Judaism and Christianity* (New York: Harper & Row, 1961).

7. FROMM, *Psychoanalysis and Religion,* op. cit.; *Man for Himself* (New York: Holt, 1947).

8. SHARON GRAHAM, quoted in S. M. JOURARD, *Self-disclosure: An Experimental Analysis of the Transparent Self* (New York: Wiley-Interscience, 1971), Chapter 21.

9. E. KÜBLER-ROSS, *On Death and Dying* (New York: Macmillan, 1970); A. STRAUSS and B. G. GLASER, *Awareness of Dying* (Chicago: Aldine, 1965).

10. Christian Science, of course, is the best-known non-medical system of healing in the United States, where it was founded by Mary Baker Eddy. A review of current shamanistic healing practices around the world is given in A. KIEV (ED.), *Magic, Faith, and Healing: Studies in Primitive Psychiatry Today* (New York: The Free Press, 1964). I think the "psychic surgeons," like Tony Agpao, are authentic healers, but their "surgery" is sleight of hand. I don't know about de Freitas' ability to stick a knife into someone's body, apparently doing surgery without sanitary precautions. See the personal account by ANNE DOOLEY, "Psychic Surgery in Brazil," *Psychic,* 1973, Vol. 4, pp. 22–38.

11. S. BUTLER, *Erewhon* (New York: Fernhill, 1965); F. M. Cornford (Trans.), *The Republic of Plato* (London: Oxford University Press, 1941); A. HUXLEY, *Brave New World* (New York: Harper & Row, 1958); G. ORWELL, *1984* (New York: Harcourt Brace Jovanovich, 1971); A. HITLER, *Mein Kampf* (Boston: Houghton Mifflin, 1943); B. F. SKINNER, *Walden Two* (New York: Macmillan, 1948); J. C. BROWN, *The Troika Incident* (Garden City, N.Y.: Doubleday, 1970); T. HANNA, *Bodies in Revolt* (New York: Holt, 1970); S. KEEN, *To a Dancing God* (New York: Harper & Row, 1970); N. O. BROWN, *Loves Body* (New York: Random House, 1966); M. D. LOWMAN, *The Phoenix: An Existential and Conceptual Account of Personal Growth* (Boulder, Colo.: Shields, 1974).

15

PSYCHOTHERAPY AND
HEALTHY PERSONALITY

INTRODUCTION

When a person's life is bogged down in painful impasses so that he cannot work, play, or enjoy satisfying relationships with others, it is time for him to seek help. The professional psychotherapist or personal counselor can help him understand how he has behaved his way into a devitalizing trap, and how to grope his way out. Many people keep going so long as they have contact with someone who is serving a psychotherapeutic function for them. They sicken as soon as this contact is broken. There are millions of "therapeutic people" in society. These "social therapists" are increasingly being sought to serve as volunteers at crisis centers and mental health clinics. Gerald Goodman [1] trained college students to serve as nonprofessional therapists for delinquent children, and laymen answer telephones at suicide prevention centers. People who have conquered some affliction such as blindness, loss of limbs, drug addiction, or alcoholism will often devote part of their time to helping others transcend their difficulties. *The professional psychotherapist seeks to understand the theory of personal disintegration and growth, in order to comprehend the fullest variety of difficulties in living.*

A professional psychotherapist may be a psychiatrist, a clinical psychologist, a counseling psychologist, a social worker, or a clergyman who has undertaken training as a personal counselor. A psychotherapist must pass qualifying and licensing examinations before he can ethically notify the public of his availability. This is necessary to insure minimum standards of competence and of ethical responsibility. Marriage counselors and family therapists have also developed standards of professional competence that must be met before a person can work privately or for some hospital, clinic, or agency.

A distinction is often drawn between personality counseling and psychotherapy. In counseling, some specific life problem is the chief focus of the therapist's and patient's attention. The aim is to release the person's problem-solving powers so that he will be able to resolve the problem by himself, without giving up his autonomy. With therapy, the aim is to achieve more basic changes in a person's way of experiencing and acting in his world.

Some Theories of Psychological Suffering

Mental Disease. For some centuries psychological suffering and deviant behavior were held to be evidence of mental disease. The medical specialty of psychiatry was developed to understand, prevent, and cure these diseases. In the history of psychiatry, the "treatments" proposed for the so-called mental diseases were often more destructive of life than the suffering itself. For example, for several decades people diagnosed as "schizophrenic" were treated by electrical shocks applied to the brain and by a form of surgery called prefrontal lobotomy.

Largely through the influence of R. D. Laing in England and T. Szasz in the United States, the view that deviant behavior and difficulties in living are evidence of a "mental disease" is being reconsidered. As Szasz states,[2]

The concept of insanity, or mental illness . . . enables the "sane" members of society to deal as they see fit with those of their fellows whom they can categorize as "insane." But having divested the madman of his right to judge what is in his own best interests, the people—especially psychiatrists and judges, their medical and legal experts on madness—have divested themselves of the corrective restraints of dialogue. In vain does the alleged madman insist that he is not sick; his inability to "recognize" that he is, is regarded as a hallmark of his illness. In vain does he reject treatment and hospitalization as forms of torture and imprisonment; his refusal to submit to psychiatric authority is regarded as a further sign of his illness. In this medical rejection of the Other as a madman, we recognize, in up-to-date semantic and technical garb, but underneath it remarkably unchanged, his former religious rejection as a heretic [p. xvi].

Growth Impasses and Fostering Growth. In more recent years, psychological suffering has come to be regarded by many psychotherapists as evidence of an *impasse in personal growth.* Such therapists conceive of man as an organism with a fundamental tendency to grow toward health and fuller functioning, who may need help in identifying the factors which block his growth. This "growth model" has gained increased acceptance as the medical model is being abandoned.[3]

Inhibition of Learning; Fostering New Learning. "Behavior therapists" see psychological suffering as a by-product of inhibitions and distortions of the learning process.[4] According to this view, "maladjusted" persons persist with interpersonal and emotional habits which no longer meet their needs. Humans have incredible learning capacity, and when environments change, they have it in their power to learn new modes of conduct. Neurotic and psychotic persons are viewed as people who have not "extinguished" inefficient habits in order to learn more adaptive modes of behavior. Psychotherapy is viewed as a learning process, with the therapist functioning as a "behavior modification" specialist.

Inauthenticity. Therapists with an existentialist orientation view psychological suffering as the outcome of inauthenticity. The sufferer is seen as alienated from his real

Psycho-therapy and Healthy Personality

self, from his fellow man, and from his natural environment. The task for the therapist is to reactivate "authentic being" in his patients. This means helping patients to recognize, to be, and to disclose their real selves and to dispense with contrivance and phoniness in dealing with others.[5]

Duality and Promotion of Nonduality. Still another view of psychological suffering has been introduced into the thinking of American and some European therapists from the Eastern philosophies of Taoism and Buddhism, and the integration of these ideologies, as in Zen Buddhism.[6] This is the view that man suffers in consequence of a "dualistic" view of the world. According to this frame of reference, man has gotten into difficulty with himself, his fellow man, and the natural world by identifying his entire being with just a part of it—the ego which controls behavior. In so doing, he has made a fallacy comparable to identifying or equating an entire heating system with the thermostat which regulates it. The thermostat simply is *not* the entire heating system; it is only part of the whole. When a man sees himself as an ego or a self which is in control of his body, his behavior, or his personality, then he experiences himself as separate from, or different from, his body, his nature, and his fellow man. This separation is most graphically illustrated by the phenomenon of self-consciousness—a close synonym for the more difficult term *dual mode of being*. When we are self-aware during transactions with people or when we perform some task, such as playing the piano, our behavior is effortful, exhausting, and likely to be ineffective. Self-consciousness presumes that we are suppressing our spontaneous response tendencies. We suppress spontaneity because we distrust our organisms. The therapist influenced by Zen Buddhism seeks to "trick" or to invite his patient to produce spontaneous, unpremeditated behavior, and to learn thereby that nothing dreadful will happen when he is thus unself-conscious. This mode of behaving is described as *nondual*. It corresponds with the experience of the swimmer who, when he is first learning the strokes, is very much aware of the placement of his arms and the rhythm with which he kicks his legs. At some point, however, the novice swimmer "lets go," "loses himself," and "lets swimming happen." If his training has been adequate, his stroke will be smooth, rhythmic, and effortless.

Healthy Personality: An Approach from the Viewpoint of Humanistic Psychology

328

Summary. The preceding overview of causes and proposed cures of psychological suffering will give the student some idea of the ferment which continues to go on in the psychological healing professions. All of the interpretations that were cited have some truth to them, but no single one of them explains all cases of suffering or all cases of successful treatment of suffering.

Who Is a Psychotherapist?

Psychotherapy is a profession which calls for extensive training. Although psychotherapy was long seen as a medical specialty (literally, treating diseases of the body and mind by psychological means), it is now legally practiced by members of other professions, notably, psychology, social work, the ministry, and teachers and educators. Despite differences in terminology, theory, and institutional affiliations, effective psychotherapists share many personal characteristics, and their training inculcates similar ways of being with their clientele.

What Effective Psychotherapists Do

Therapists Listen. The activity therapists engage in most is listening. They provide an understanding audience for a troubled person, often the first such audience the patient has ever had. The patient discloses himself to his therapist more than he has to any other person. Even with the reassurance of professional confidence, however, many patients are reluctant to trust the therapist; it is at the point where patients resist further disclosure that the tact and professional skill of the therapist are called upon.

The Therapist Respects His Patient. The relationship with the therapist is often the first time in the patient's life that he has been respected as a unique human being by anyone. The therapist reveals the respect by not manipulating the patient or putting conditions on his attention and interest.

Therapists Enlighten and Demystify. Frequently, a patient is suffering because he does not know what is going on in his family, his place of work, or, for that matter, in the world. He may believe that his parents love and confirm

*Psycho-
therapy
and
Healthy
Personality*

329

him when in fact they are doing all in their power to interfere with his growth and his confidence in himself. He may not be aware that his spouse has been "playing games," pretending to be weak and helpless so that he would neglect his career in order to pay attention to her. If the therapist learns how these relationships affect his patient's experience and action, he strives to impart his understanding to his patient.

Therapists Are Attentive to Dreams and "Body Language." Therapists have learned that patients repress many possibilities of experiencing, and they seek to provide an atmosphere within which such repression is released. They encourage a patient to pay attention to his dreams, in order to discern hints about possibilities of growing, and perceptions too painful, initially, to be acknowledged, but which appear more or less disguised in dreams.

Therapists will also be attentive to their patient's bodies— not only facial expressions and "kinesics" (meaningful gestures), but also the very way the person looks. They inquire into excessive obesity, flabbiness, physical tension, muscular rigidity, and other manifestations that all is not well with the person.

Therapists Invite Patients to Greater Immediacy. It was Fritz Perls' great insight that patients, indeed most average people, spend much of their waking time *out of sensory touch with the here and now.* Rather, they worry compulsively about the future, or pick over their memories for recollections of failures and past pleasures. This reduces their sense of vitality, of being intensely alive. Perls' Gestalt therapy teaches patients to pay attention to what is going on in their bodies and their immediate surroundings, right now, to feel the excitement of living with the joy and pain of the present, rather than escaping into pale intellectuality or wistful remembrance of things past.

Therapists also are attentive, however, to a defensive flight into the present. If someone evades remembering the past, because of past pain, or refuses to think about a problematic future, the therapist may invite the patient to give each time dimension of his life its due consideration.

Therapists View People as Embodiments of Fantastic Possibilities. By the time a patient has come to seek professional help, his view of himself has come to be that of a person with little strength and little personal worth. Indeed, significant people in his life have encouraged him to regard himself as useless, weak, of little moral worth, and so on. They may have told him, repeatedly, that he will never be any different, that he is fated to failure. Therapists know that descriptions of people are actually subtle invitations to become or remain as described. They know, as well, that a person can be in any way that anyone imagines, and in any way that has meaning to him. When a patient believes he cannot cope with his difficulties, that he has no reserves of strength, no hidden possibilities of growing in new dimensions, then he will act so as to confirm those views of himself. The patient views himself as weak; the therapist relentlessly attributes to him strength and untapped potential for growth. Each tries to persuade the other he is correct. If the patient wins the argument, he loses his chances to transcend his difficulties. If he loses the argument with his therapist, he changes his view of himself and his world and comes to act in new, more growth-fostering ways. Why is the therapist so relentless in attributing the capacity to transcend difficulties to his patients? Because a psychotherapist, perhaps more than anyone, knows from personal experience and from the experience of others of man's great possibilities of growing and overcoming impasses in life; he will not be shaken in this belief, which he holds "religiously" because it is scientifically founded. The patient who does not experience his own possibilities of overcoming difficulty is simply out of touch with reality.

Therapists Inspire Faith and Hope in Patients. A therapist is a professional person, and he is consulted in his office. The very setting as well as the decision to go to this setting seem to inspire in the patient a certain confidence that help will be received, that there may be hope for a better life. These attitudes and expectancies are factors in recovery. One of the puzzles that continues to vex health researchers is the manner in which an attitude of hopelessness seems to foster illness, whereas the inspiration of hope and expectation of help seems to stimulate wellness. Patients frequently get well no matter what a therapist says or does. Researchers have likened psychotherapy to the "placebo effect," which has long been observed in the field of medicine. Physicians sometimes prescribe medicines that

Psycho-therapy and Healthy Personality

come in large, colorful capsules, or that taste vile, but are actually inert—sugar or colored, flavored water. Patients report that following the ingestion of these placebos, their symptoms are relieved. My hypothesis is that healing is a reflex process which goes on by itself unless the person's attitude and beliefs interfere with it. If a sick person will simply relax and let healing go on, it will proceed at its natural pace. If he believes he will die or has no reason to go on living, these attitudes, mediated by certain brain functions, can impede the healing process. The placebo, seen by the patient as "powerful medicine," convinces him that he is in good hands. He then relaxes and permits healing to proceed by itself.

In psychotherapy, the hopeless patient is confronted by a professional person who inspires confidence, and who offers informed hope that the patient can transcend his difficulties and get on with more effective living. This hope, if communicated, changes the patient's way of experiencing his situation. He will then keep trying new approaches to his dilemmas until he discovers a mode of behavior that yields health instead of chronic misery.[7]

Therapists Function as Exemplars.   There is a sense in which a therapist is a leader of his patients, guiding them to ways of acting which generate health and growth. As in all forms of leadership, the direction to be taken is most convincingly demonstrated by example. The effective military commander does not say "forward," he frequently says "follow me." The effective teacher is the one who is himself an exemplar of the joy afforded by dedication to study. One would hardly place much faith in a therapist who emphasized the importance of authenticity when he was himself phony, self-concealing, and manipulative. Indeed, recent research has shown that "modeling"—serving as an example—is the most powerful way one person can influence another, especially if the exemplar is seen as a person with desirable characteristics. In a later section, we shall see how many of the self-help therapeutic groups are effective because they are led by persons who provide living proof that an infirmity which incapacitates others can be conquered.[8]

Therapists Are Not Just Competent: They Are Good Human Beings.   Anybody, whether a professional psychotherapist or not, who displays the preceding qualities in his

Healthy Personality: An Approach from the Viewpoint of Humanistic Psychology

life with others, is a good human being. I don't know anybody who is this way all the time, but I know that psychotherapists strive to be this way as steadily as they can. Fundamentally, a person committed to these ways is a man with
enlightened goodwill toward his fellows. A layman can cultivate the same qualities and skills to be helpful to others,
and to enrich the quality of his personal relationships (see
Chapter 10).

PSYCHOTHERAPY AS A KIND OF PERSUASION

It seems clear that professional and nonprofessional therapists are helpful because they persuade a suffering person
to change his behavior in some way. I find terms such as
persuasion, invitation, and *leading by example* more valid
metaphors for describing the process of helping others than
medical or behavioristic terms (*treatment, shaping, reinforcing*). Therapists are effective only when they succeed
in presenting an invitation or challenge which seems worthwhile and feasible to the sufferer. Psychotherapists are most
convincing and effective at helping persons overcome the
difficulties which they have been able to transcend in their
own lives. As exemplars, they can persuade a sufferer to try
making changes, where someone else might not be effective
at such persuasion. A sufferer needs to be convinced that
there is some chance, some hope of overcoming the barriers
to a better life. A hypnotist tries to convince a patient that
he has the power to transcend by direct suggestion. A good
psychotherapist persuades, sometimes directly ("You can
do it, go ahead and try") and sometimes by attribution of
strength to the patient, taking it for granted that he can
conquer the circumstances which hitherto overpowered
him.[9]

PSYCHOTHERAPISTS AS SECULAR PROPHETS

There is a sense in which psychotherapists have moved
into the domain formerly under the aegis of formal religion.
Over the centuries, men relied on prophets, priests, witch
doctors, and shamans for guidance in ways to live. When
they encountered disease and failure, they would return to
the priest for his healing rituals and oracular pronounce-
ments of the wishes of God (or the gods). A contemporary
psychotherapist espouses a set of beliefs about life-enhanc-

ing ways to act. This set of beliefs is scientific in origin, but it is possible to reconcile the highest ethical precepts of Judaism, Christianity, Islam, Hinduism, and Buddhism with scientifically informed knowledge about the enlivening and devitalizing consequences of ways to live. At a later point in this chapter we shall explore more fully the similarity between contemporary psychotherapists and the teachings of biblical prophets.

Settings for Therapy and Promotion of Growth

THE CONSULTING ROOM OF THE PSYCHOTHERAPIST

In Western society, physicians and priests have traditionally been consulted when life became unlivable through disease and personal conflict. In more recent times, psychiatrists and clinical psychologists have been the specialists of choice for sufferers in the middle and upper classes. These specialists have been consulted in privacy, and they have traditionally charged substantial fees, so that their services are unavailable to the bulk of the general population. Many clergymen and social workers have received training in personal counseling and psychotherapy, and the profession of "counselor" has emerged in the past decade, under the aegis of colleges of education; this increase in counseling personnel has made individual psychotherapy increasingly available and less costly but, of course, the availability of growth-fostering professional people is still insufficient to meet the psychotherapeutic needs of the public. Poorer and less-educated people generally are treated in clinics, and the treatment is more often with drugs, electroshock, and hospitalization than lengthy psychotherapeutic sessions.

In recent years, the "medical model" for comprehending psychological suffering has come under attack from workers in the field of healthy personality; depression, anxiety, and neurotic and psychotic symptoms are coming to be seen not as signs of "mental disease," but as the outcome of *not growing*, of persisting in ways of living past the time they were life-enhancing.

The replacement of the medical model by a growth model makes it possible for therapeutic help to be provided for people in many settings besides the private consulting room of the private practitioner in a one-to-one relationship.

Healthy Personality: An Approach from the Viewpoint of Humanistic Psychology

Several psychiatrists, psychologists, and laymen in London organized a group they called the Philadelphia Association. It was to be devoted to exploring different ways to treat the so-called mental diseases, especially schizophrenia. Ronald D. Laing and Aaron Esterson were among the founders of this association, the idea for which came out of some research into schizophrenia on which they had collaborated. It was their hypothesis that "schizophrenic" behavior and experience was not evidence of a disease process, but a natural and desirable process of personal growth and self-healing. Their work with the families of people diagnosed as schizophrenic convinced them that the patient was not so much sick as reacting to attitudes of rejection and to the familial mystification and disconfirmation to which they were subjected. Although the patients did indeed display "delusions," hallucinations, and altered perceptions of reality, Laing and Esterson showed that these symptoms were intelligible in light of the way the patient's family interacted. For example, if a patient complained her parents were always discussing her behind her back, the parents denied this to her face, and then talked about her as soon as she was out of earshot.

Laing and Esterson believed that conventional psychiatric treatment for schizophrenia was damaging rather than helpful to the sufferer; drugs, electroshock, and prefrontal lobotomy were viewed more as violence than as enlightened efforts at healing. As an alternative, the members of the Philadelphia Association acquired an old building in east London, called Kingsley Hall; Mahatma Gandhi stayed in a small room at this place in the 1930's. The building was to serve as an experimental community, where people designated schizophrenic could come to stay, and rather than be treated, they would be encouraged to explore the personal meaning of their confusion and suffering. There would be psychiatrists living there, as well as students, artists, and nurses, but within Kingsley Hall there would be no distinctions among people based on profession or status. The theory was that the schizophrenic was in the process of struggling to find or create a viable identity for himself when the old identity could no longer be lived. The stay at Kingsley Hall was to

Psycho-therapy and Healthy Personality

335

be viewed as a time to carry out a voyage of self-discovery, without being distracted by psychiatric intervention and treatment.

Out of the Kingsley Hall experiment, which ended after a couple of years, there emerged an informal organization of "check-out" and "blow-out" places, private homes or residences for communal living where people who were "losing their minds" could go, not to be treated—since the places were not hospitals—but to check out of their past life, go crazy if they needed to, and do this in the company of people who had been through similar experiences themselves.

Laing and his associates are professional psychotherapists who wished to "deprofessionalize" their profession—to show how people can learn to help one another without the necessity of medical or psychiatric intervention.

CRISIS CENTERS AND PSYCHOTHERAPY BY TELEPHONE

In the past ten years or so, "crisis centers" have been inaugurated in many cities around the United States, where persons with any kind of human difficulty can obtain immediate psychotherapeutic help and guidance from professional people about whom the troubled person might not have known. In some cities, these centers are listed in the telephone directories and the classified advertisements as "suicide prevention centers," whereas in others, they are called "hot-lines," or crisis centers. Typically, they are staffed by volunteer workers who have received some training in the arts of listening and responding helpfully to troubled individuals. Workers at suicide prevention centers seek, in addition to being helpful over the telephone, to locate the suicidal person, so that direct personal contact might be made with him.

Nonprofessional Self-help Groups

Alcoholics Anonymous (AA). Alcoholics Anonymous is perhaps the best-known self-help group, and has been in existence longer than any other such association. Chapters of AA exist in nearly every city and town in the United States, as well as in Canada. The members are persons who have been addicted to alcohol, who had learned that they can avoid drinking by regular association with alcoholics who are struggling to remain "dry." A member tempted to take a drink may call upon another member who will sit with him, perhaps just to provide company or encouragement to overcome the urge to drink to the point of stupor.

Integrity Groups. Integrity groups were begun under the leadership of Hobert Mowrer,[10] as ways for people to help one another stay honest. They are groups of eight or ten people who meet regularly at one another's homes and engage in absolutely honest talk with one another about the ways in which they have been conducting their lives outside the group meetings, and how they relate to one another within the meetings. Mowrer began experimenting with, and participating in, these groups when he discovered that conventional psychoanalytic therapy was ineffective in helping him overcome a tendency to profound depression. What ultimately proved of greatest avail to him in his struggle with depression was avoidance of inauthenticity in his dealings with others. Lying was, in a sense, an addiction comparable to alcohol or drug addiction; truth-telling, while frequently painful, was seen as the only path to a livable life for sufferers from intense guilt or depression.

Synanon. Synanon is a group organized by drug addicts to help one another fight the intense urge to ingest narcotic drugs, such as heroin or barbiturates.[11] The addicts who founded Synanon discovered that the most effective way to "kick" the habit was to associate with fellow addicts, who engaged in brutal honesty with one another. Addicts are experts at rationalizing, at deceiving themselves and others in order to maintain their addiction. Direct confrontation between addicts, pointing out instances of evasion and lying, was found to be effective in helping the addict stay "clean." Synanon members also engage in honest work, making a contribution to community life.

Other Groups. Many other kinds of nonprofessionally led therapeutic groups and associations have come into being because the participants discovered such association to be less costly and usually more effective than conventional psychotherapy. For example, *Weight Watchers,* though a profit-making association, has proven that groups of overweight people can control their food intake and slim down through regular association with one another, sharing experiences of sadness and suffering associated with obesity and encouraging one another to adhere to their dietetic regimens. As with the other groups, the participants feel they understand one another's problems better than any outsider can, even if the outsider has medical or psychological training. Comparable associations have been started by tobacco smokers who wish to stop smoking and parents of mentally retarded children who wish to avoid the experience of guilt and shame frequently occurring in such parents. In fact, associations of people with common problems or impediments to a full life provide a hopeful and valid path to healthier personality without resort to costly professional help.

SOME COMMON THERAPEUTIC FACTORS IN SELF-HELP GROUPS

Self-help groups are effective because a participant encounters others struggling to transcend self-defeating ways of living. Those who have struggled longest, and most successfully, serve as leaders by example. The senior "struggler" knows the many ways to give up and the importance of relentless struggle. He shares his experience with his fellows. The novice members can see living examples of the possibility of avoiding intoxication with alcohol or narcotics, of overcoming self-defeating habits and of transcending handicaps of all kinds (see pp. 136–138). In all the self-help groups, radical honesty with oneself and others is encouraged by the simple act of engaging in it. Participants are encouraged to come to know one another, to disclose themselves honestly, and to invite honest confrontation between themselves and others. Moreover, they are challenged to keep struggling with the difficulties rather than yield to them. This is the way some professional psychotherapists function, even sharing with their patients their own personal experience with neurotic or psychotic disturbances.[12]

"Behavior Therapy" and Behavior Modification

Some mental hospitals have instituted behavior modification programs in order to eliminate the patients' symptoms. "Good" behavior is "reinforced" with better rooms, access to TV sets, better food, and eventual release from hospital, whereas "bad" behavior—symptoms—goes unreinforced. There is evidence that such regimes are effective at shaping socially acceptable behavior, even in long-term patients.

An individual therapy based on behavioristic principles is simply called *behavior therapy* (as opposed to psychotherapy). Joseph Wolpe, a psychiatrist from South Africa, is one of the better-known practitioners and writers about the procedure. People suffering from discrete symptoms, such as phobias, inhibitions, or compulsive acts, are put through "extinction" procedures, desensitization, aversive training, and programs of positive reinforcement for desirable behavior. The claim is made that such behavior therapy is more effective than conventional personality therapies based on interviewing procedures.[13]

A related procedure is what its practitioners call precision teaching or behavior management. Ogden Lindsley and Henry Pennypacker show people who wish to change some aspect of their behavior that this can begin by first counting the frequency with which the behavior appears and recording it on special charts. Once a rate has been established, the behavior "manager"—who might be a teacher, a therapist, a friend, or the person himself—then commences a search for ways to reduce the frequency with which the behavior appears. Frequently, the very act of counting makes the person more aware of what he is doing, and he reduces the frequency without further ado merely by deciding to do so. In other cases, as in reducing food intake, smoking, or drinking, aversive conditioning and other methods for altering contingencies of reinforcement may be introduced.

I tried to stop smoking by following the method suggested by the work of Pennypacker—that is, counting pipe-lights and charting them so as to establish a "base rate." Then I lost faith in that procedure. I came upon a method that inspired more confidence in me. I began taking a deep "yoga" breath every time I felt the urge to light my pipe, reasoning that if an inhalation of tobacco smoke is a breath of death, the appropriate response to an urge is not to count it, but *to oppose it,* with a "breath of life." In five days I lost all urge to smoke tobacco—after twenty-five years of addiction. (I did gain about 20 pounds in five months after stopping). I estimated the frequency of yoga breathing episodes from the time I began, to the time I stopped five days later. (I did not become addicted to yoga breathing.) An episode was defined as the time I started the yogic deep breathing until I lost the urge to smoke. A "yoga breath" entailed slow inhalation while counting to eight, holding the breath for eight seconds, and then releasing the breath to the count of eight. I performed about sixty such episodes in the first twenty-four-hour period, and on each succeeding day, the need for them was halved—thirty, sixteen, nine, five, and then, every day or so, I experienced a mild urge to smoke which was easily eliminated by a breath.

My behavioristic colleagues tell me I simply "extinguished" smoking behavior because my breathing episodes showed a typical extinction curve. I wondered why I was not learning to become as chronic a yoga breather as I had been a chronic smoker.

ENCOUNTER GROUPS FOR PERSONAL GROWTH

Growth centers, schools, universities, and churches offer the opportunity for growth-seekers to participate in "encounter groups." There are many philosophies of encounter group practice, and diverse techniques by which the leaders and the participants seek to increase the depth of self-disclosure and the immediacy of interpersonal contact. In some groups, the leader (who usually is trained as a psychotherapist as well as a group leader) may invite the participants to start a meeting with diverse physical-contact procedures, such as holding hands in a circle, to get the feel of the others present. In an encounter group, the participants are then encouraged to talk about their immediate feelings and perceptions of themselves and the other participants, with the emphasis upon the here and now. Usually they identify themselves only by their first names, so that social, familial, and occupational roles are unknown—the participants are there simply as human beings trying to help one another to be more open, to find new possibilities for growth within themselves.

The leader may function as a technician, as one who limits his participation to facilitation of communication within the group; he may function as a group therapist, trying to interpret what is going on in ways that will foster insight; or he may combine a number of roles, and participate in the group as an exemplar of openness and the courage to encounter others in a spirit of honesty and loving concern.

Healthy Personality: An Approach from the Viewpoint of Humanistic Psychology

Many people find the experience of an encounter group exhilarating, as a time for self-discovery and self-expression in a confirming atmosphere. For many it serves as the beginning of a project of self-renewal. This is most likely to be the case if the group has been led by a qualified leader. Other participants go only once, finding the meetings too threatening, the encounters with others too aggressive. This outcome is most probable when the leadership has been inept.

However, I believe that the encounter group movement has encouraged freer communication among people and has helped foster healthier personality in numerous settings, for example, in schools and universities, in marriage, and in communities.

As with the self-help groups mentioned earlier, some groups organize themselves without benefit of a leader and meet regularly for purposes of honest self-disclosure because they find the experience rewarding. Indeed, it is now possible to obtain tape-recorded and written instructions as to the best ways for a group of people or a couple to get helpful interaction started.[14]

Places for Personal Growth

For centuries India provided its educated people with places to which they could retreat for meditation and renewal of their lives. These *ashrams* were places sheltered from the bustle of everyday practical life, frequently in the countryside, but sometimes in the center of a large city like New Delhi. A *guru* (a teacher of spiritual truth) is the head of each establishment, and he or she provides the guidance to the people who come to live there or who seek an audience. The pace and style of life at an ashram is radically slowed down. The pupils, or seekers (it is difficult to find an appropriate Western term to describe them), are encouraged to spend much time in solitude for meditation and to carry out a program of Hatha Yoga postures. Diet is simplified, meals are usually communal and vegetarian, and each person lives in a small private room or cell. People stay for a day, week, months, or years. Or they may continue their customary life, but go to the ashram as one might go to church or temple, for spiritual guidance.

The Western world has not had an exact equivalent of

*Psycho-
therapy
and
Healthy
Personality*

ashrams available for persons who have wanted to get away for self-renewal. In 1963 Michael Murphy, a Californian graduate of Stanford University, inaugurated a Western equivalent of the Sri Aurobindo ashram at Pondicherry, where he had spent eighteen months in retreat and meditation several years earlier. He utilized a piece of land with natural hot springs in Big Sur, California, as a place to invite scholars and therapists for weekends, were they could conduct informal seminars on the current status of their work. The first such seminar was conducted by A. H. Maslow in 1962. As the years went by, the center, now called Esalen Institute (the Esalens were a tribe of Indians who used to live in the region), came to be called a "growth center" where people could come for weekends or longer periods of time to participate in encounter groups, to experience various body-awakening disciplines (see Chapter 6), or to take part in Gestalt therapy workshops conducted by Fritz Perls. Residential programs were inaugurated, where the students could spend up to a year participating in all the seminars and workshops concerned with the enlargement of their awareness and stimulation of growth, and perhaps become qualified to conduct workshops and seminars themselves.

Since Esalen Institute first came into being, the idea of a center devoted to personal growth has become widespread, and there are several hundred in existence around the Western world. Although growth centers are not identical with Indian ashrams, there is a similarity in that there is the commitment to self-exploration, to reinvention of one's life, and to radical honesty in one's relationships with others. The people who operate Esalen Institute, bake the bread, cook the meals, conduct encounter groups and offer Rolfing sessions and massage. They live a kind of communal life and serve as exemplars of ways to be "in one's body," and ways to be with one another, which are believed to be most life-giving and conducive to personal growth.[15]

The Role of Prophet in Psychotherapy

In Chapter 14 I discussed formal religion from the standpoint of the consequences for healthy personality of living in accord with formal religious teachings. I will conclude this chapter with some excerpts from two lectures I gave to professional psychotherapists, which develop this parallel between the social functions of the ancient prophets and contemporary psychotherapy.[16]

Over the years I have been examining and re-examining psychotherapies and psychotherapists from the standpoint of different models and metaphors. The one model most compelling for me over the past ten years is that of exemplar, or role model of authentic existence. Now the very term *authentic existence* means more than simply living in truth and choosing one's existence. It also implies increasing enlightenment, so that one can make choices compatible with life, growth, and self-actualization. Psychotherapists in increasing numbers have been taking their own lives and growth seriously, seeking to authenticate their professional contacts by being exemplars themselves of the quest for growth, truth, and self-fulfillment. And they are seeking, some of them, to share their visions and knowledge with masses of others; to function, in short, as prophets outside the consulting room.

The psychotherapist, according to this view, embodies part of the way of a prophet, that of being an exemplar of the way of life he wishes to invite others to follow for their own good, and, by implication, for the good of the community. And he is a prophet when he points out the truth about destructive behavior. Old Testament prophets were desirous that the polyglot aggregation of Hebrew tribes might overcome their limited and autistic perspectives and become a people, a community called Israel, united under one God, living in exemplary ways as a beacon and example to all mankind. An extraordinarily modest ambition.

According to Abraham Heschel,[17] a prophet is extraordinarily sensitive to evil; he feels it keenly, and refuses to excuse or ignore it. He shrieks of what he sees. He pays attention to what others regard as trivialities, too obvious to note, but which signify a person or a people hellbent on destruction of self and the very conditions that make life possible. A prophet is, without compromise, committed to the highest good of which man is capable, and he mourns, castigates, and incites in order that medi-

*Psycho-
therapy
and
Healthy
Personality*

343

ocre men might rise to those heights. Like the outsiders of whom Colin Wilson wrote, the prophet sees too much, hears the groans of pain to which others are deaf. Yet the prophets have a compassion for mankind and they seek to invite all men to take responsibility for the fate of man and life in this place and time. The prophets feel the blast from heaven; they inveigh against callousness, indifference, and yet take no pleasure in the lot to which they have been called. Prophets are seditious, cranky threats to the status quo.

This is the way Heschel answers the question, "What manner of man is the prophet?" I see adumbrations here, as I said, with Colin Wilson's outsiders—the raw nerve-endings of our time: Lawrence of Arabia, Nijinsky, and other characters who never could be swallowed up by the hypocrisies and false values of their times, but who, as Wilson points out, were destroyed because they lacked insight and didn't know what was going on.

What psychotherapist measures up to the stature of a prophet rather than a mere outsider? Which is a true and which is a false prophet? Wilhelm Reich,[18] I feel, was a prophet as well as a genius who had magnificent revelations to share; I cited his work in many places throughout this book. He died in prison in Lewisburg, after a fight with the government over some aspects of his work, which he lost. Many thought Reich had become psychotic. Perhaps he had. This does not minimize his prophetic functions. Brock Chrisholm,[19] a Canadian psychiatrist, became a prophet after World War II, at risk of his reputation. He preached against the teaching of certain myths to children, such as the Santa Claus story, so they would be less vulnerable to incitements to war as adults. Israel Charney, a psychotherapist, has written of the viciousness that prevails in marriage, in families; Auschwitz can be foreseen in the German family structure. Ronald Laing and Aaron Esterson, both psychotherapists, are prophets in their writings, pointing out how the family serves as a place within which some members are sacrificed to the mental hospital rather than allow the cosmetic image of a happy family to be besmirched.[20] Thomas Szasz is serving a prophetic function in his writings on "The Myth of Mental Illness" and the "Manufacture of Machines." [21]

The psychotherapists whom we consider great, I have argued, are great not because of their theories, which are efforts to scientize existential courage and enlightenment, but because their lives were threatened by some aspect of facticity and they learned how to transcend it, and could teach others how to be free and upright in the face of doting, destructive parents, addiction to heroin, or lack of awareness of others' destructive games.

Sigmund Freud mastered some forces which could have prevented him from becoming the man who invented psychoanalysis. He suffered *Portnoy's Complaint,* as millions of people in the West have: a seductive, doting mother and a father who was both strong and weak, loved and feared. The result of struggling with such conflicting parental demands has been neurosis and diminished self-actualization for man. Freud's courage lay in facing his recollections and fantasies, his sexuality, his anger, and discovering that one's past need not preclude fuller functioning, whether genital, intellectual, or physical, in adult years. I believe he was most effective as a therapist with persons whose suffering grew out of anti-growth forces comparable to those which he tamed. The therapeutic technique he taught others has not been notorious for its effectiveness. Freud showed *in his very person* that it is possible to marry, make love, raise children, and defy all kinds of social pressures in one's time and place in spite of having been raised as a middle-class minority group member, with parents whose demands and expectations were not always compatible with free flowering of individuality. He might have helped his patients more swiftly if he were not so shy, so reluctant to share his experience with his patients.

Carl Rogers was reared in the American version of the Protestant ethic. Such upbringing produces a strict conscience, one which keeps people "at it" when there is a frontier to conquer, a fortune to be made, duty to be fulfilled. This is the way of the "inner-directed" character so well described by Riesman. This conscience makes for conditional self-regard; it obstructs empathy and makes it difficult for a person to be "congruent" in his dealings with others. I would propose that Rogers' greatness and greatest effectiveness lie not in his invention of the client-centered techniques, nor in opening psychotherapy to scientific research, nor in his theories, but rather *in his conquest of the upbringing that would limit his growth.* He is a model of a way to be, a way which, when adopted, makes for more mutally confirming and authentic relations with others and which averts sickness.[22]

The fact that seems obvious to me about life in the time of the Old Testament prophets is that no one knew how to live in a way that would sustain life for self and others; and no one knew how to live in a way that would foster growth of more than a brutish few of man's infinite possibilities. The statutes, commandments, ordinances that Moses received "from God" may be regarded as the inventions of a highly imaginative and intelligent and compassionate man. Perhaps God spoke through him. Moses fascinates me—how did he (or they) arrive at a statement of ways to live in that time? Perhaps being reared in a civilized culture (Egypt) without being of it was a factor. Moses' writings and teachings were the equivalent of the writings of Dr. Spock, Ralph Nader, Rachel Carson, Adelle Davis, Mohandas Ghandi, and other contemporaries who have tried to help people live in viable ways. Failure to live in a viable way is to court disease, stultification, and death. This is as true today as it was in Biblical times.

Today's psychotherapists treat people whose growth is stultified, who are not living right for themselves and possibly not right for others. The therapist is prophetic insofar as he has learned, and authenticated in his very being and presence, viable ways to live—what the ancients may have called "righteousness." If they invite others to change their ways and threaten them with dire consequences if they do not, they are being as much prophet as the times admit. The prophets tried to make men realize their freedom to choose and to choose to change from "sin" to righteousness. A psychotherapist who is not as sensitive to self-destructive behavior and who is not committed to learning and living and leading in viable ways is neither prophet nor therapist.

One of the defining characteristics of the Old Testament prophets was the idea that the one true God spoke through them. This, I believe, is the metaphor signifying that the prophet was able to achieve a perspective on his

Healthy Personality: An Approach from the Viewpoint of Humanistic Psychology

culture which enabled him to see what those more acculturated could not see. The psychotherapist in modern days must be capable of achieving such an outsider's perspective, of attaining what Buber calls distance, but he must also have the capacity to "enter into relation," in order to have his vision and message heard. In modern terminology, an effective psychotherapist, like an effective prophet, can detach himself from prior ways of being and then return into community with one other, or many others, and share his vision. But I hold the hypothesis that the prophetic psychotherapist and the psychotherapeutic prophets are effective to the extent to which they embody, in their very being, the ways to live that are most compatible with life together in this time and place. It is not possible, I argue, for a true prophet to preach one way and live another. This may require that the psychotherapist in his prophetic function (which is not incompatible with healing) may be, for the moment, a very irritating, infuriating person who discloses truth that hurts, that fosters guilt, anxiety, and intense suffering. But, like the prophets, he does not confront for the joy of inflicting pain, but out of profound concern. If the therapist, like the prophet, is angry, it is because there is something to be angry at. We can view Carl Rogers' wrath at certain dehumanizing aspects of graduate and undergraduate education and his promulgation of encountering as "a Way," as a case of a therapist "gone prophet." [23]

Frank Shaw,[24] my late friend whose ideas are not widely enough appreciated, viewed talent in phenomenological–behavioristic terms: talent was a matter of a specialized fascination with something in the world that one could not resist tinkering with in order to make it "right." We might look afresh at prophets and psychotherapists in order to discern whether they might resemble one another in terms of talent, thus defined. It is clear that the therapist and the prophet are fascinated by "sin"—life-destroying behavior—and by suffering: they cannot neglect it in self or in others. It is as if they are receiving sets tuned in permanently on the wave length most interesting to them. But the fascination is not a passive one. No psychotherapist I know of, and no prophet who is recorded, could resist responding to the sufferer (the

347

prophets felt God's suffering), in spite of the fact that many therapists claim that indifference to whether one is helping the other is, paradoxically, the best way to be helpful. Prophet and therapist alike will not rest until they are doing what they deem best to remedy the situation.

Some Existential Suggestions

Everyone can function as a psychotherapist, to some extent, with other people in his life. Truly to listen to the other person, and to share with him one's own experience with difficulties comparable to those he is undergoing, is a very psychotherapeutic thing to do. Advice to people with difficulties is seldom the most helpful thing to offer, unless it is requested. Even then, to offer advice to someone with difficulties in living may earn for the advice giver a new dependent.

Human sharing of ways of coping with, or even stoically enduring, difficulties, is a valuable gift for people to give one another. Of course, challenge and attributing strength to people who see themselves as weak and helpless will seldom do harm.

As for seeking professional help for oneself, psychotherapy from a qualified person is usually expensive. If one is bogged down with impasses in life, the expense is worth it. Where possible, shop around for a psychotherapist with whom you feel some human rapport, one who will answer your questions gladly.

SUMMARY

Psychotherapists are trained to help people explore new ways of being when their customary ways have led them into impasses or sickness. They come from a variety of professional backgrounds—psychiatry, clinical psychology, social work, the ministry, and school counseling; and they espouse diverse theories which account for the causes of psychological suffering. The "medical model," which views deviant behavior as mental illness, is gradually being replaced by other perspectives. One of these regards psychological suffering as a by-product of impasses in personal growth; the psycho-

Healthy
Personality:
An Approach
from the
Viewpoint of
Humanistic
Psychology

348

therapist is seen as an expert at fostering further growth. Another view holds that suffering stems from inefficient habits; the psychotherapist then functions as an expert in learning. Yet another view holds that people suffer from the results of inauthentic being. The therapist who holds this view then functions as a guide and exemplar of authenticity. Some psychotherapists are influenced by Zen Buddhism, and they see psychological suffering as an outcome of a dualistic, self-conscious state of being. The therapist then functions as a kind of guru who unifies the sufferer's experience.

Psychotherapists provide a beneficial influence for their patients by being good human beings. They listen keenly to what their patients have to say, they respect their patients, and strive to make sense of their condition. They regard each person as the embodiment of fantastic possibilities, and they inspire them with hope and the courage to struggle further with the difficulties which have temporarily overcome them.

Although many psychotherapists continue to conduct their practice in a private consulting room, a movement has begun to provide "check-out places," where people can go to change themselves, without professional intervention. Many nonprofessional self-help groups provide psychotherapy for fellow sufferers; for example, Alcoholics Anonymous and Synanon are lay organizations where alcoholics and drug addicts who wish to control their addictions can seek help from fellow addicts who already have begun to live without drink or drugs.

A recent development in psychotherapy is an adaptation of learning theory called behavior modification. Principles of conditioning are applied to the control of behavior, both in mental hospitals and in private practice.

Encounter groups and growth centers have proliferated in recent years, as yet another resource for people who seek to pursue personal growth beyond their present levels of functioning.

Psycho-
therapy
and
Healthy
Personality

NOTES AND REFERENCES

1. G. GOODMAN, *Companionship Therapy: Studies in Structured Intimacy* (San Francisco: Jossey-Bass, 1972). A good introduction to what psychotherapy is all about is E. KRAMER,

Beginning Manual for Psychotherapists (New York: Grune and Stratton, 1970). Also K. A. COLBY, *Primer for Psychotherapists* (New York: Ronald, 1950).

2. T. S. SZASZ, *The Manufacture of Madness: A Comparative Study of the Inquisition and the Mental Health Movement* (New York: Harper and Row, 1970); R. D. LAING, *The Politics of Experience* (New York: Pantheon, 1967).

3. See F. PERLS, *Gestalt Therapy Verbatim* (Lafayette, Calif.: Real People Press, 1969); also his posthumous volume, *The Gestalt Approach and Eye Witness to Therapy* (Ben Lomond, Calif.: Science and Behavior Books, 1973); C. R. ROGERS, *Client-Centered Therapy* (Boston: Houghton Mifflin, 1951); C. A. WHITAKER, and T. P. MALONE, *The Roots of Psychotherapy* (New York: Blakiston, 1953); J. DOLLARD and N. E. MILLER, *Personality and Psychotherapy: An Analysis in Terms of Learning, Thinking and Culture* (New York: McGraw-Hill, 1950).

4. J. WOLPE, *The Practice of Behavior Therapy* (New York: Pergamon, 1969); L. P. ULLMAN and L. KRASNER, *Case Studies in Behavior Modification* (New York: Holt, 1965); also their book *Behavior Influence and Personality: The Social Matrix of Human Action* (New York: Holt, 1973), Chapters 10 and 11.

5. J. F. T. BUGENTAL, *The Search for Authenticity: An Existential Analytic Approach to Psychotherapy* (New York: Holt, 1965); S. M. JOURARD, *The Transparent Self* (New York: Van Nostrand Reinhold, 1971), Chapters 16, 17, 18; S. M. JOURARD, *Disclosing Man to Himself* (New York: Van Nostrand Reinhold, 1968), Chapters 7, 8, 9.

6. A. W. WATTS, *Psychotherapy East and West* (New York: Pantheon, 1961).

7. J. D. FRANK, *Persuasion and Healing: A Comparative Study of Psychotherapy,* 2nd ed. (Baltimore: Johns Hopkins Press, 1973).

8. JOURARD, *The Transparent Self,* op. cit., Chapter 18, "The Psychotherapist as Exemplar."

9. FRANK, op. cit.

10. O. H. MOWRER, *The New Group Therapy* (New York: Van Nostrand Reinhold, 1964).

11. L. YABLONSKY, *Tunnel Back: Synanon* (New York: Macmillan, 1965).

12. JOURARD, *The Transparent Self,* op. cit., Chapter 19, "Self-disclosure and the Encounter Group Leader."

13. WOLPE, op. cit.; KRASNER and ULLMAN, op. cit.

Healthy Personality: An Approach from the Viewpoint of Humanistic Psychology

14. See L. Blank, Gloria B. Gottsegen, and M. G. Gottsegen (Eds.), *Confrontation: Encounters in Self and Interpersonal Awareness* (New York: Macmillan, 1971); G. Egan, *Encounter Group Processes for Personal Growth* (Belmont, Calif.: Brooks Cole, 1970).

15. W. Schutz, *Here Comes Everybody: Bodymind and Encounter Culture* (New York: Harper & Row, 1971) offers a perspective on growth centers.

16. S. M. Jourard, "Prophets as Psychotherapists, and Psychotherapists as Prophets," *Voices: The Art and Science of Psychotherapy,* 1971, Vol. 7, pp. 11–16; "The Transcending Psychotherapist," ibid., 1972, Vol. 8, pp. 66–69. See also S. Kopp, *Guru: Metaphors from a Psychotherapist* (Palo Alto, Calif.: Science and Behavior Books, 1971), for analogies between psychotherapy and other human endeavors.

17. A. Heschel, *The Prophets* (New York: Harper & Row, 1969).

18. The magnificent as well as the sad aspects of Reich's life are given in accounts written by his son, and by a former wife. See Ilse O. Reich, *Wilhelm Reich, a Personal Biography* (New York: St. Martin's Press, 1969), and P. Reich, *A Book of Dreams* (New York: Harper & Row, 1973).

19. B. Chisholm, Can People Learn to Learn? (New York: Harper & Row, 1958).

20. R. D. Laing and E. Esterson, *Sanity, Madness and the Family* (London: Tavistock, 1964); E. Esterson, *The Leaves of Spring: A Study in the Dialectics of Madness* (London: Tavistock, 1970). See also I. Charney, *Marital Love and Hate* (New York: Macmillan, 1972).

21. T. S. Szasz, *The Myth of Mental Illness: Foundations of a Theory of Personal Conduct* (New York: Harper & Row, 1961); T. S. Szasz, *The Manufacture of Madness: A Comparative Study of the Inquisition and the Mental Health Movement* (New York: Harper & Row, 1970).

22. Rogers discusses the development of his work in C. R. Rogers, "My Philosophy of Interpersonal Relationships and How It Grew," *Journal of Humanistic Psychology,* 1973, 13, 3–16.

23. C. R. Rogers, *Freedom to Learn* (Columbus, Ohio: Merrill, 1969).

24. F. J. Shaw, *Reconciliation, a Theory of Man Transcending,* S. Jourard and D. Overlade (Eds.) (New York: Van Nostrand Reinhold, 1966).

16

THE HUMANISTIC APPROACH
TO PSYCHOLOGY

INTRODUCTION

Sartre described a scene in which a voyeur peeps through the keyhole into a bedroom.[1] *Suddenly he is discovered by another, and becomes, thereby, an* object *for the other, and for himself. His experience of his freedom oozes away, and he feels himself transmuted from a subject into a thing. Whenever a person is caught in the act, when someone hitherto concealed is seen, then the viewer turns the one looked at into stone. Psychologists have been inviting the subjects of their research to become as natural objects, like stones. The surprising thing is that the subjects have co-operated. I cannot fathom why, because I do not know of any good that has accrued to the subject as the consequence of being a subject, that is, an* object. *This is a strong statement; yet I do not believe that the quality of personal life has improved as a result of eighty years of scientific investigation of human consciousness and action. In fact, there is more basis for me to believe the knowledge of men we have acquired has been used to control and limit him rather than to enlarge his awareness, his dignity, or his freedom.*

Psychology as a "Natural" Science

In research, as most psychologists have practiced it, subjects are recruited and asked to make themselves available to the psychologist for observation, interviewing, and testing. He records their speech, actions, and reactions with various kinds of equipment. He analyzes his findings and publicizes them. Typically, the psychologist defines psychology as a scientific discipline which seeks to understand the behavior of man and other organisms. Proof of understanding is evident when the psychologist can *predict* the action or reactions under study, by pointing to predictive signs, or by bringing them under some kind of deliberate *control*. Great pains are taken to insure that the observer does not influence the behavior he is studying, so that the persons or animals under study will show themselves as they really are. Ideally the subjects of study would not know that they were being watched because the experience of being observed affects action.[2]

It is clear from this description that scientific psychology has been patterned, since its inception by Wundt, after the natural sciences. Although we now draw distinctions among natural, social, and behavioral sciences, in each of these, similar assumptions are held by the respective scientists, for example, that determinism prevails and that the laws which govern the phenomena under study can be discovered if the right questions are asked of the subject matter in the right way.

Science, so understood, embodies two ambitions which enchanted me as a youngster. One was the wish to read the mind of others. It was fascinating to try to discern what was going on behind my friend's or some stranger's opaque exterior. Did they like me? Were they going to harm me? If I could see into or through them I would have fair warning about their intentions, and I could govern myself accordingly. In fact, if I could read minds in this way, it would give me a certain power over others.

Such power over others was the second childhood wish. I imagined what it would be like to be able to get other

The Humanistic Approach to Psychology

353

people, and animals, to do exactly what I wanted them to do. Snake charmers and hypnotists provided a model of the type of control I sought, in entertaining these fantasies. To this day, I am intrigued by trainers who can get animals to perform intricate tricks.

Let us look at psychology, as a natural science, in the light of these childhood quests for omniscience and omnipotence. It seems fair to say that psychologists aim to read their subjects' minds, and to gain increments of power over their experience and action.

In the dawn of history, man was probably victimized by nature; animals, plants, seas, and soil all acted with "minds" of their own, indifferent to his needs and wishes. When nature was seen animistically, early men could seek some measure of prediction and control by talking to the souls, spirits, and gods which moved natural happenings. They would try to propitiate or bribe those animated beings, in order to get them to tell their intentions; this would help a man get power over hostile nature, and over untrustworthy, unpredictable strangers. Presumably, those men who could best foretell the future and influence the outcome of events were seen by their fellows as having either more powerful gods or a closer relationship with the gods. In any case, nature was seen as capricious and hostile; man could improve his lot if he could read her mind (predict what was going to happen) and get her to act in ways that would serve his needs and interests. Natural science was developed to tame and demystify hostile nature.

The modern scientific psychologist faces his subjects and his subject matter in a posture similar to that of the natural scientist. The other man's action is not always friendly to someone's interests. Someone can gain if a man's action can be predicted (i.e., if his mind can be read, if his face becomes a transparent mask through which his stream of consciousness can be read), and if he can be induced to act in ways that serve someone's interests. The subjects of research in scientific psychology are deliberately seen as Other, as one of Them, as *a part of nature different from the scientist and those other persons whom the scientist designates as Us.*

Yet we must remember that a psychologist is a human being, living in a time and place, in a society with a class structure, a power structure; and he has economic interests.

Healthy Personality: An Approach from the Viewpoint of Humanistic Psychology

Typically, he is salaried and the costs of his research are borne by private or public agencies. We have to assume that these agencies will not willingly countenance research which will undermine their power over people. A pharmaceutical firm is unlikely to spend millions of dollars in the study of placebos, so that drug use in medicine will be diminished. It does not seem far-fetched to me to regard the most rigorous, truth-seeking psychologist as a servant, witting or unwitting, of the agencies which pay him and his costs. The agencies that believe it worthwhile financing research into human behavior typically believe that their interests will be furthered if man's behavior becomes more predictable. They want men to be transparent to them (while they remain opaque to the others), and they want to learn how to make men's action more amenable to control. Men who can be controlled can serve the controller's interests without knowing it—in which case we would say that they are mystified. If a psychologist studies men and makes their action predictable and their experience transparent to some elite—but not to the persons he has studied—then he is indeed a functionary, even though he may be a passionate seeker of truth. He may share the class interests of the elite, and he may serve those interests by viewing the subjects of his research as "Them," creatures not unlike natural phenomena—floods, earthquakes, animals—which must be understood in order that they can be tamed.

My hypothesis is that unless the behavior scientist explores the broader social, political, and economic implications of his work, he is a functionary indeed; worse, if he does not realize it, then he is being mystified by those who employ him.

The psychological testing movement, likewise, can be seen in this light, as a quest to read people's minds and to fathom their talents, strengths and weaknesses, to serve someone's ends, not necessarily the ends of the person being tested. Beginning with Binet's contribution, up to and including that of Rorschach, the ability of one person, the tester, to discover something about the testee is not necessarily good for the latter. I can remember the excitement I felt, as an undergraduate, when I first heard about tests of intelligence, and of personality, by means of which one person could literally make another transparent. But now the

*The
Humanistic
Approach
to
Psychology*

355

blacks and other so-called culturally deprived people are less than sanguine in their appreciation of what psychometrics are good for. In fact, quite properly, many blacks see the testing movement as one of several means by which their subordinate status in the education establishment, and hence the professional world, is maintained. And as we come to take a fresh look at psychiatry, for which profession the projective and many objective (like the MMPI) tests of personality were developed, we see that psychiatric classification is less an analogue of differential medical diagnosis, and more a subtle way to invalidate a human being.[3] Projective techniques can be seen as violations of the Fifth Amendment of the Constitution—sneaky means of finding out about a person. "Unobtrusive measures," which have come to be seen as an answer to uncooperative research subjects, or to experimenter bias, likewise are ways to get a person to reveal himself unwittingly, thereby giving information which may not help him.[4]

Am I saying any more than that knowledge of man, like knowledge of nature, gives power, and power corrupts? Perhaps not, but to say that is still to say something which we in psychology must take into account. Are we seeking the truth about man that sets all men free? Or are the truths we discover only making some men more free and powerful, while others become more vulnerable to manipulation?

It seems clear to me that the image of man assumed by a psychologist will affect his research strategies, his theories, and his ways and areas of consulting. If he views man as a natural object, rather than as a being like himself, his science and its applications will be as I have described.

I will now look at the fields of psychotherapy and counseling, as well as at the behavior-modification movement.

Once again, economics rears its head. Psychological practitioners who apply scientific knowledge of man artfully, do not sell their services cheaply. If they are in private practice, they charge substantial fees to the individuals and agencies which engage their services. Otherwise, they are retained or salaried by government or private agencies, to utilize their know-how in order that the agency might fulfill its aims more fully. For example, psychologists are employed by advertising agencies and business concerns of many kinds in order that the public being "served" will more readily

Healthy Personality: An Approach from the Viewpoint of Humanistic Psychology

buy the company's products or in order that workers will produce more, and more cheaply. Sometimes the service sold by the psychologist is knowledge about how masses of people will respond to symbols; sometimes, he trains people in the art of seeming sincere, friendly, and authentic.

The arts of counseling and psychotherapy, seen from the perspective of a natural science of psychology, become arenas for the practice of techniques, ways to influence the experience and hence the action of the client or patient. Psychoanalysts, behavior-modification experts, even client-centered counseling technicians are all encouraged to believe that if they master a repertoire of laboratory- or clinic-tested techniques, they will "get the patient to change." Of course, the techniques of behavior modification by environmental control, as in token economies in mental hospitals, represent a subtle exercise of power. Hypnosis, shaping, and aversive conditioning all represent ways to alter someone's action. The person who employs these techniques can remain invisible behind a professional manner. If he practices his techniques well, he will earn a fine salary from a grateful agency, or high fees from those rich enough to afford his services. Those individuals who are rich enough to afford his services are seldom spokesmen for liberal change in the political and economic system within which they earn the money to pay for their "treatments." Moreover, as some of the more radical psychiatrists are beginning to assert, psychiatric intervention, of whatever sort, is a kind of social control aiming to invalidate, and perhaps avert, dissent.

If the basic and applied behavior science we have developed thus far has primarily been a quest for knowledge which makes men predictable and controllable, then clearly what is called for is a complementary science, one which uses scientific discipline and knowledge to liberate a man from being the victim not only of the forces of nature, but *also of the concealed efforts of other men to influence him for weal or woe.*

The Humanistic Approach to Psychology

Man's action and experience are indeed affected by mass media, by leaders, by genes, by his past experience, by reinforcement contingencies, by his biology and physiology, and by the social and interpersonal setting within which he lives his life. Any way of discerning how these realms affect experience and action is of some use to the person himself, and to others. I think that we psychologists have not served that person. Perhaps this is what humanistic psychology, or psychology as a *human* science, can do.[5]

Psychology as a "Human" Science

In 1957 I began to study self-disclosure. This was before I ever heard of anything called humanistic psychology. I was trained in experimental as well as clinical psychology, and a program of research has always been part of my view of the practice of my profession. I chose self-disclosure as a subject for scientific study because I began to wonder what we knew about the conditions under which people would reveal personal information to others. Freud pointed out that psychoanalysis entailed overcoming a patient's reluctance to let his analyst know him, and psychotherapeutic practice called for being an encourager and listener to another's intimate disclosure. And so, using what I regarded (and still do) as appropriate techniques for research, I began collecting self-report data from thousands of people about their past disclosure to parents, friends, and other target persons. I wanted a scientific understanding of self-disclosure in order to predict and control this kind of behavior. Certainly that is what my scientific training in Toronto and Buffalo encouraged me to do and think. Ironically, I soon discovered that *one of the most powerful correlates, if not determiners, of one person's self-disclosure was self-disclosure from the other person in the dyad.* Several questionnaire studies pointed to this hypothesis, and we confirmed it in numerous experimental interviews conducted under laboratory conditions. We found that we could maximize a person's disclosure of personal data by offering such disclosure first, as a kind of invitation, or as an example of what action was appropriate to the situation. My students and I, in conducting these experiments, did not *pretend* to disclose personal subject matter. We *really did,* and it was sometimes risky and embarrassing; but we functioned in the spirit of adventurous inquiry, and found the outcomes we have mentioned.[6]

I had begun to experiment with my ways of being a psychotherapist, beginning soon after I discovered that my training did not prepare me to be helpful to Southerners

Healthy Personality: An Approach from the Viewpoint of Humanistic Psychology

358

with difficulties in living. I had begun as far back as 1952 to break my professional anonymity, by sharing with a client any experience of mine with problems comparable to those he was exploring with me. I found that such authentic sharing, within bounds of relevance and common sense, encouraged my patients to explore and reveal their experience more fully and freely than was hitherto the case for me. It was as if I had bungled onto a new kind of technique but one which entailed some risk, indeed, some inclusion of my patient into the world of Us, rather than seeing him as one of Them—the neurotics, the psychotics, and so on. This experience in conducting psychotherapy appeared to support my survey and laboratory findings in the study of self-disclosure. But my experience as a psychotherapist influenced my view of research more profoundly.

I was motivated to be helpful to the person who sought my professional help, and I found, increasingly, that one way to be helpful was to demystify the patient insofar as it was possible. The patient suffered from difficulties in living because he did not know what was going on. People lied to him, and he to them. Some patients were mystified by nature, others by social structures. It was difficult to know oneself, others, and the world. Our therapy sessions could be seen as an effort at authentic communication between two persons, so both of us would know what was going on. I found myself sharing *my* understanding of how people not only mystified one another, but invited others to be diminished creatures. I would show and role-play the way people attributed imaginary traits to one another, which they would then embody and act out—like Gênet becoming the thief he was defined to be early in life. Gradually, my understanding of what a psychologist's task might be underwent a change. I came to see that, if hitherto, research and practice grew out of a view of man as a natural phenomenon, to be studied by an elite in order that he might be better mind-read and controlled, it would be elegant to strive to do psychology *for* man. This, I came to see, must be what a humanistic psychology would be and be for.

The Humanistic Approach to Psychology

Humanistic psychology could be defined, I saw, as an effort to disclose man and his situation *to himself,* to make him more aware by any and all means, of what forces were influencing his experience and hence his action. I could see that human subjects would not really disclose themselves, would not really let themselves be known to researchers or anyone else whom they had reason to distrust, and so we commenced a program of research within which the researcher was as much to be interviewed by the subject as vice versa. Though we made only a beginning at this, the results confirm that different perspectives on man will emerge when more research is done.

If various institutions aim to control man's action and experience in order to serve the institution's aims, then a task for a humanistic psychology could be to study the means by which the propaganda, rules, and environment produced conformity, so that a person could better choose to conform or not to conform. I discovered in the process of this inquiry that for one person to lie to another is an effort to control his experience and action, so that he will be mystified. This is exactly equivalent to the situation of man facing a hostile nature that he does not understand. Not to understand is to be vulnerable to prediction and control— victimization, whether by mystifying nature, or by one's lying and self-concealing fellow man. To be understood, and not to understand the one who understands you, is indeed to be vulnerable—to be a transcendence transcended, as Sartre puts it.

George Miller, a past president of the American Psychological Association, urged his colleagues to "give psychology away." As natural-science psychologists learn about "determiners" of man's experience and action, humanistic psychologists (who can be natural-science psychologists too) can make apparent to all, the ways in which their freedom is being eroded by hostile nature or hostile people.

Psychological research, from this perspective, becomes an enterprise wherein the subject becomes privy to the aims of the researcher, where he is free to learn about the researcher as the researcher learns about him.

Counseling and psychotherapy, from the standpoint of humanistic psychology, become enterprises where patient and therapist share relevant experience so that the former can become more enlightened, more liberated from influences that constrain his growth and self-actualization. Indeed, I find myself using the word *therapy* less and less, seeking some metaphor more aptly descriptive of what goes

Healthy Personality: An Approach from the Viewpoint of Humanistic Psychology

360

on in such helping transactions. Terms like *teacher, guide, guru, liberator* all suggest themselves, though all sound fairly pretentious. But in all these cases, one thinks not of a person manipulating another, reading his mind in order to gain power over him, but of a dialogue between I and You.

Some Existential Suggestions

Try this exercise of imagination: imagine that your closest friend or the person whom you love best has suddenly been transformed into a rat, or into a robot controlled by a computer program. How would you relate to him? Clearly, it would be a case of you having to control the rat, or choose a program for the robot. Certainly your relationship with that person would change from the way it was when you attributed freedom, dignity, and responsibility to him. Now imagine that the person is a person once more. When he was a rat or robot, how would you go about studying him, to understand how his behavior worked? How would you learn about him when you attributed personhood to him?

If you intend to pursue psychology as a research career, or as a profession for helping persons live more fully, which perspective on man will you select? Man as an object, or man as a person, or both? There *may* be times when human welfare and knowledge of man are furthered by assuming man, as a topic of study, is a natural object totally subject to natural law. I am not certain that such times exist.

SUMMARY

When psychology is pursued as a "natural" science, man, the subject of study, is dehumanized. Frequently he is studied in order to help other people control and predict his behavior, and not necessarily for his well-being. An alternative way to study man is described—where the investigator encourages the persons whom he is studying to interview him as thoroughly as they wish, in order to test his trustworthiness. I discuss my own research briefly, which shows that when a psychological researcher, diagnostician, and psychotherapist make themselves accessible to their subjects and patients, the latter behave differently from when the professional person preserves his impersonal anonymity.

The
Humanistic
Approach
to
Psychology

[This chapter also appears as an article: S. M. JOURARD, "Psychology: Control or Liberation," *Interpersonal Development*, Vol. 2 (1971–72) pp. 65–72.]

1. Research psychologists would do well to read Sartre's sensitive account of the experience of being looked at. See J.-P. SARTRE, *Being and Nothingness* (London: Methuen, 1956), p. 259.

2. Rosenthal produced much evidence to show that the experimenter is an important influence on the behavior and experience of subjects in psychological research. See R. ROSENTHAL, *Experimenter Effects in Behavioral Research* (New York: Appleton-Century-Crofts, 1966). Efforts to make allowance for the "experimenter-effect" are discussed in A. G. MILLER (ED.), *The Social Psychology of Psychological Research* (New York: Free Press, 1972).

3. See T. SZASZ, *Ideology and Insanity: Essays on the Psychiatric Dehumanization of Man* (Garden City, N.Y.: Doubleday, 1970).

4. For a review of methods to study man without his awareness, see E. J. WEBB, D. T. CAMPBELL, R. D. SCHWARTZ, and L. SECHREST, *Unobtrusive Measures: Non-reactive Research in the Social Sciences* (Chicago: Rand McNally, 1967). See also A. WESTIN, *Privacy and Freedom* (New York: Atheneum, 1967).

5. An introduction to psychology as a human, rather than a natural, science, is A. GIORGI, *Psychology as a Human Science* (New York: Harper & Row, 1971).

6. My research in self-disclosure is presented in S. M. JOURARD, *Self-disclosure: An Experimental Analysis of the Transparent Self* (New York: Wiley-Interscience, 1971). The implications of this research for theory, and for human life, are given in my other books: *The Transparent Self* (New York: Van Nostrand Reinhold, 1964; 2nd ed., 1971), and *Disclosing Man to Himself* (New York: Van Nostrand Reinhold, 1968).

Healthy Personality: An Approach from the Viewpoint of Humanistic Psychology

NAME INDEX

Adler, A., 5, 13, 29, 30
Adorno, T. W., 171
Agpao, T., 318, 319, 324
Alexander, F., 119
Allport, G. W., 71, 94, 119
Alper, Thelma, 202
Ansbacher, H., 30
Ansbacher, Rowena, 30
Ardrey, R., 93
Aresteh, A. R., 31
Arieti, S., 243
Arnold, Magda B., 119
Assagioli, R., 21–23, 29, 31
Aurobindo, Sri, 342

Bach, G., 101, 118
Bakan, D., 94
Bales, R. F., 218, 219, 264
Barber, T. X., 57, 149
Barlow, J., 57
Barnes, Mary, 59, 219
Barron, F., 93, 103, 119
Behanan, K., 149
Bell, N. W., 243
Berdyaev, N., 56
Berke, J., 59, 219
Berne, E., 13, 29, 30, 149
Bettelheim, B., 202, 228, 243
Binet, A., 355
Birdwhistell, R., 122, 148
Blake, W., 50
Blank, L., 350
Blatz, W. E., 16–18, 29, 30, 91, 92, 289, 303, 304
Bowlby, J., 92, 119
Briggs-Myers, Isabel, 30
Brill, A. A., 119
Brown, J. C., 304, 321, 324

Brown, N. O., 322, 324
Brown, R., 71, 170, 218
Bruch, Hilda, 149
Btflsk, J., 231
Buber, M., 13, 14, 29, 30, 56, 119, 167, 174–175, 193, 202, 233, 241, 242, 243, 264, 324, 347
Buddha, 53
Bugental, J. F. T., 29, 350
Butler, S., 321, 324

Caesar, J., 138
Cameron, N., 202
Campbell, D. T., 362
Camus, A., 50
Cantril, H., 70
Capp, A., 231
Carkhuff, R. P., 243
Carnegie, D., 240
Carroll, J. B., 71
Carson, Rachel, 346
Cason, H., 118
Castañeda, C., 40, 54, 57, 59
Charney, I., 101, 118, 265, 344
Chichester, F., 296
Chisholm, G. B., 344, 351
Cleveland, S., 44, 58, 122, 123, 148
Colby, K. A., 350
Comfort, A., 284
Cooper, D., 210, 219

Dabrowski, K., 203
Dalal, A. S., 149
Darwin, C., 301
Davis, Adelle, 346
Davis, J. F., 94
De Ropp, R. S., 59

363

Name
Index

Name Index

*Name
Index*

SUBJECT INDEX

Subject Index

Subject Index

Religion, and attitude toward death, 314–315; and culture change, 315–317; and a good society, 319–322; and healing, 317–319; and healthy personality, 305–322; meanings of, 306–309

Remembering, 42

Repression, 87–88, 178–181; of emotion, 113–115; of sex, 278–279; of somatic perception, 121

Role, authenticity, 214–215; versatility, 207–208

Roles, age, 213–214; and emotion, 115; family, 209–210; learning of, 208–209; sex, 211–213; sick, 206–207; and sickness, 215–217; and the social system, 205–207

Rolfing, 140–141

Security, and body-experience, 126–127; independent, 16–18, 289–291

Self, and body, 126–129

Self-actualization, 23–26, 89

Self-alienation, 164–166

Self-concept, 151–156; and identity, 155–156; social influences on, 153–154

Self-consciousness, 36–38

Self-disclosure, 163–164, 223–224, 358–359; and authenticity, 168–169; and love, 260; and personal growth, 231

Self-esteem, 75; and body, 127–128

Self-ideal, 151

Self-realization, 10, 21–22

Self-reliance, 13

Sensory deprivation, 79

Sex, and healthy personality, 267–283; and love, 247, 281–282

Sexual arousal, 272–273

Sexual development, 268–270

Sexual intercourse, 276–277

Sexual motives, 270–272

Sexual problems, 282–283

Sexual repression, 278–279

Sexual revolution, 267–268

Sickness, and growth, 189–190; and need-privation, 83–84; and roles, 215–217; and unembodiment, 144

Skills, 18

Social control, 205–206

Social interest, 5

Socialization, agents of, 205; and emotion, 109; and roles, 205–207

Solitude, 50–51

Somatic despecialization, 145

Somatic perception, 121, 124–125

Somatic specialization, 143–145

Sports, 298–299

Sufis, 38

Suicide, 312–313

Suppression, of emotion, 110–112; of sex, 277, 279

Symbolization, 10

Synanon, 337

Therapy, nonprofessional, 336–338; for sex problems, 282–283

Thinking, 42–43

Threat, 174–176; and defense mechanisms, 176–188

Touching, 138–140

Unconscious, 21–22, 84–88; healthy features of, 88–89

Unembodiment, 121–125

Unhealthy religion, 309–312

Unhealthy sexuality, 271–272, 277–279

Utopias, 321–322

Values, 14–15

Vegetotherapy, 10

Vocational change, 293–296

Vocational choice, 286–291

Warming up, 145

Weeping, 101–102

Will, 5–6

Women's liberation, 216

Work, choice of, 286–291; meanings of, 292–293; and sabbatical leave, 296

Yoga, 37–38, 141–142, 339–340, 341; and personal growth, 192–193

Zen, 12, 37–38, 328

Subject Index